TOUCHED BY THE ~~~~~~ IES

THE
SHADOW
PROPHECY

INTERNATIONAL BESTSELLING AUTHOR
JESSICA LYNCH

Copyright © 2020 by Jessica Lynch

All rights reserved.

No part of this book may be reproduced in any form or by any electronic or mechanical means, including information storage and retrieval systems, without written permission from the author, except for the use of brief quotations in a book review.

Cover by Jessica Lynch

She's destined to stay
More than a Lover,
    a Consort, a Friend
When Dark mates Shadow
The reign of the Damned
    Shall come to an End

*fall in love
with the
shadow man...*

TOUCHED BY THE FAE   *PREQUEL*

FAVOR

INTERNATIONAL BESTSELLING AUTHOR
JESSICA LYNCH

Copyright © 2019 by Jessica Lynch

All rights reserved.

No part of this book may be reproduced in any form or by any electronic or mechanical means, including information storage and retrieval systems, without written permission from the author, except for the use of brief quotations in a book review.

Cover by Jessica Lynch

FOREWORD

The **Touched by the Fae** series is a set of three books (plus an extended epilogue and this prequel) featuring Riley Thorne, a twenty-one-year-old woman with a tragic past. The death of her foster sister might be the inciting factor that lands her in the asylum, but it was only her most recent loss.

Her first, and the one that sets her on her path?Being abandoned by her mother as an infant.

In this short story, I'm introducing the readers to baby Riley; Nine, the Dark Fae who is fated to love her; and the mother & father who sacrificed everything to save their child.

This series will be all about the Shadow Prophecy and the relationship between Riley and Nine. To understand how it all began, *Favor* is a glimpse into the past. *Asylum*, the first book in the series, will begin twenty years after the events of this short and will be heavily impacted by what happens. I like to think of this as an extended prologue that also works as a follow-up to Ash & Callie's duet, **Rejected by the Fae** (which shows how they meet, fall in love, and have their baby... all while fearing the cruel Fae Queen, Melisandre), starting with *Glamour Eyes*.

As you'll see in this short story, Nine might have agreed to watch over Riley because of, well, a favor, but there's so much more to it than that. Make sure to check out the complete **Touched by the Fae** series to read all about it.

Until then, enjoy!

xoxo,
Jessica

PROLOGUE

The soldiers came at dawn.

Aislinn wasn't surprised. Despite her glamour saying otherwise, he knew for a fact that Melisandre was a Dark Fae. But, as the longstanding queen of Faerie, she insisted on being surrounded by a court full of Blessed Ones.

The Seelie.

The Light Fae.

Ash's kind, and the ones who turned their backs on him when he took a human woman for his mate.

Their apartment was warded. Ash made sure of it. It was supposed to be safe. Tucked in the middle of a human city, as far from Faerie as he could get, Ash made his home with his human mate, hoping and praying that it would be enough to shield them from his former queen.

The iron that kept his family hidden left him drained, his golden skin faded to a sickly yellow. His sun-colored eyes lost their spark when they lost their magic; only when he set his gaze on his lover and their child did they seem to glow like they once did. No one would have ever expected one of the Fae Queen's favored to have fallen so far so fast.

He wouldn't change it for anything. Finding his true mate, even spending a few short human years with his Callie... it was worth everything he sacrificed when he chose to forsake Faerie, coming to live with his human in her world.

They should've had forever. Turned out, forever wasn't very long at all.

Melisandre was coming for them.

No. She was coming for his *daughter*.

Ash would die before he let any of the Light Fae get their hands on his child. The reason was simple, too. Because of the blasted Shadow Prophecy, if Melisandre managed to touch the baby, she'd kill her. No doubt. In a bid to keep her reign over Faerie as all-encompassing as it had been for centuries, the Fae Queen would slaughter an innocent child without even blinking.

Except his baby wasn't an innocent child. She was a halfling: half-human and half-fae. A *nothing* in the eyes of his people. With her mixed blood, she never should've even caught the queen's attention. If it wasn't for the baby's unique gift, she never would have.

But she did.

And now the soldiers had found them at last.

Though he long hoped that this would never be necessary, Ash was prepared. It might not be the best of plans. At least it *was* one.

He reached into his pocket. Ever since it became more and more obvious that—whether it was true or not—Melisandre believed Ash's child was the one spoken of in the Shadow Prophecy, Ash had taken to carry the tiny pebble with him. If it was between giving his child up to one Dark Fae or the other, he knew exactly which one he chose.

He placed the pebble into Callie's hand, then grabbed her wrist, yanking her close enough that he could slant his mouth over hers. One quick kiss. One last kiss. He had to make it count.

Her big blue eyes were frightened, her panicked pants short. He breathed in her scent, savoring her essence, wishing there was enough time for just one other taste of his exquisite human.

But there wasn't. He could sense the soldiers preparing to invade the building. If there was any hope that she could escape, Callie had to leave *now*. She had to take their child and flee while he stayed behind.

"Grab the baby," he ordered. As much as they tried to deny this could happen, he'd prepared Callie as best as he could over the last year. She'd listen to him. She knew what was at stake. She'd listen to him, even if it killed them both a little to be apart. "Get in the elevator and go. That should save you."

It was another reason why he chose this building. Their apartment was on the second to last floor and it was a long climb up. A fae fresh out of Faerie was drenched in too much magic to even try to take the elevator. It would short out immediately, trapping them in the metal box. Ash knew that from experience. If Callie hid with their daughter inside of the elevator, she'd be safe for a while.

That's all he could ask for.

"But what about you?"

I'll be fine.

The words burned his tongue, the back of his throat, before he could even open his mouth to utter them.

Lie.

"Don't worry about me," Ash said instead. "Focus on our daughter. You have to get her to safety."

Truth.

Callie threw a glance back at the closed bedroom door. Warring instincts played out on her pretty face: love and dedication to her mate mixed with the maternal need to care for their child.

Ash reached out, folded her fingers over the pebble in her hand. Once he was sure it was safe—once he had her attention again—he said, "You know what to do."

It wasn't a question. As soon as it became clear that their daughter might fit the Shadow Prophecy, Ash did everything he could to prepare his mate for the inevitable. Since he couldn't hide her entirely on his own, Ash knew that Melisandre would make a move for the baby before long. Over the last year, he'd come up with this emergency plan, telling Callie everything he could about his former life, his queen, his life at Court. He spilled ancient secrets. He made her understand.

And he impressed upon her the power of the touch, and the power of the debt.

Callie nodded. It was shaky, but it was a nod.

"The pebble will be enough to get him to help you. The debt he owes me now belongs to you, Callie Brooks. If he wants to free himself of it, he'll do what you ask." Ash leaned in, rubbing his nose against the edge of her cheek. "We'll meet each other again. I promise you that."

A slight burn. In his heart, he hoped he was telling the truth. In his head, he knew that the likelihood of that wasn't high.

Still, he would try. He had his family to fight for. To *live* for.

Callie grabbed his arms, fingers digging into his biceps as she hugged him close.

"I love you, Ash."

"I love you more than the sun and the moon put together," Ash murmured. "Never doubt that."

"I won't."

He kissed the top of Callie's white-blonde head. "Get the baby. No one can ever get their hands on her. Promise me, Callie."

"I promise."

Humans could lie. But, as her pale blue eyes went dark in determination, Ash felt the power deep in her soul.

Callie would protect their child, or die trying.

Just like he would.

CHAPTER 1

The speed limit for the winding Mulberry Bend was twenty-five miles per hour. Twisty as a viper and just as dangerous, the Black Pine Town Council fought to make the half-mile stretch a safe fifteen.

They lost, of course, and eventually settled on tucking a police car at either end whenever they could. Locals knew it was a speed trap and made sure to avoid it whenever *they* could.

Callie Brooks wasn't a local. If she'd been asked, she would've said Black Pine was just a dead tree, not a small town in the middle of nowhere. Oblivious to the speed limit and the threat of cops, she kept her foot jammed down on the pedal, urging the speedometer past sixty, seventy, even eighty.

The old car rattled. Her heart in her throat, her hands gripping the steering wheel tight, she prayed the rusted, busted engine held out.

"Come on, come on," she muttered, giving the car a little more gas. It sputtered and she gritted her teeth. "Just a bit longer."

Ash's instructions ran endlessly through her mind like a song on repeat. She couldn't forget them. As soon as it became clear that his people weren't going to leave them the hell alone, he'd drilled them into her head.

First, she had to get a car. Buy one, borrow one, steal one, she had to get a car and then head west. It didn't matter where she was going, so long as it was away from the apartment. The iron crowbar they kept hidden in their bedroom would help and he made sure she took it with her when she grabbed the emergency diaper bag and their baby before escaping the soldiers.

She had to do what he said. Because, if she was following his instructions, that meant they had been separated.

If she was following his instructions, that meant that Ash had sacrificed himself to buy her some time.

Callie wouldn't waste the head start. She couldn't. Not when their daughter's life was on the line. So get a car and go—and keep on going. She couldn't stop for anyone or anything. Not until she saw the shadow. Callie hadn't asked what shadow. She already knew. It would be the darkest shadow she had ever seen and she'd just… she'd *know* it when she found it. With her sight, Ash was betting everything on the fact that she would.

Then, only then, was she to use the name.

Despite the terror coursing through her veins, she navigated the curves recklessly as she continued her frantic search. Wind whipped in through the broken window, stinging her eyes. It hurt, but she kept them open. She had to. Hours into this drive, hours of worrying about Ash—where was he, how was he, was he okay?—had worn her down, but Callie was running on a dangerous cocktail of fear, determination, and the fierce nature of an angered mama bear.

It was closing in on the evening, the sun getting ready to set for the night. Callie wasn't fooled. Just because the sun and moon were preparing to trade shifts, that didn't mean that she was safe. With the Dark Fae and the Light both chasing after her, searching for her—searching for her child—Callie couldn't let her guard down. The dark wouldn't allow her any relief. The Blessed Ones might not be able to chase her once night had fallen, but the Cursed Ones would be free to take over.

Unless she sold her soul for protection first.

She would. She absolutely would. There wasn't a single thing that Callie wouldn't do to keep her daughter safe. Especially now that Ash was... he was—

He'll be fine, Callie told herself. Ash was strong and he was quick and, even if he lost most of his power when he chose to stay in the mortal world with her, she didn't doubt that he couldn't hold his own against the soldiers the Fae Queen sent after him.

He could do it all—except continue to shield their daughter. Which was why Callie was speeding a stolen Buick down a twisted road, more than five hours away from the home she'd built with Ash these last few years. Their union, while not the first of its kind, was still pretty rare. To produce a child? Almost unheard of. No one knew what to expect from a child that was half-fae living in the mortal world. That she was immune to her father's touch wasn't a surprise, even if it did make things difficult once whispers of her birth reached the Seelie Court.

And all because of that damned prophecy...

As she came out on the other side of the Mulberry Bend, the trees dispersed and the road opened up. The last vestiges of the day's sunlight reflected off of her rearview mirror, nearly blinding her. Callie gulped, shielding her tired eyes with one hand while the other continued to grip the steering wheel tightly. She searched for shadows and, despite the late afternoon hour, she found them. Shadows were everywhere she looked—just not *that* type of shadow.

Her heart heavy, her stomach tight, she wished fervently that Ash had been able to run away with her. Logically, she knew why he hadn't. He was needed at the apartment, holding their home against the queen's soldiers, doing everything he could to buy her some time to get out with the baby. Callie didn't care about *logic*. She wanted her lover, her husband, her mate to be with her instead of sacrificing himself to his former brothers-in-arm.

The car started to whine, bucking as she pushed it harder. How long had it been since she stopped for gas? The gauge was on empty but it had been stuck like that since the first time she refueled. That's what she got for stealing a car so old that it didn't have an alarm. The last thing she needed was to run out of gas now. That wasn't in the plan. If she couldn't find the shadow tonight, Ash told her to find a place up high to hide from the Dark Fae who were sure to join the hunt as soon as they were able. How, without a working car?

Callie spared one anxious peek out of the broken window. She knew she was racing the sun and, so far, she was winning. There was maybe another hour before she'd have to give up for the night. If she was lucky, maybe she would find a way to contact Ash, make sure he was okay, even if he hadn't answered any of her summons yet.

But she couldn't do that if she ran out of gas in the middle of nowhere.

She discovered it almost by accident. Torn between worrying about Ash and the soldiers and praying she'd stumble on a gas station before it was too late, she spied the gas pumps in the distance a split second before her eyes slid over to the shadow.

It was an old-fashioned gas station, empty and alone. Tired, anxious, and afraid, Callie couldn't decide if that was a good thing or not. She didn't see any other cars. No people, either. Standing opposite of a closed bank and an abandoned diner, the station had three rusted pumps, a dingy shop with a faded sign proclaiming it to be the "Snack Shack", and a lean-to shed about a hundred feet away from the furthest pump.

The shed was built on an angle, its shadow trapped beneath a slanted roof. So focused on the promise of fuel, Callie glanced at the shed once, turned to aim for the nearest gas pump, then, with a jolt low in her stomach, she slammed on the brakes before staring at the shadow again.

The Buick rattled and jerked to a sudden stop right as her heart started to pound like a jackhammer inside of her chest. Because it wasn't *just* a shadow. It was a patch of black, a shadow so dark that it was a piece of night in the middle of the afternoon.

Exactly as Ash described it.

She did it. She *found* it.

With a whine of protest, the old car bucked as she hit the gas. Callie pulled right into the gas station, narrowly missing the curb as she headed straight for the shed instead of the pumps.

Gas could wait.

She didn't bother to kill the engine, flinging open the driver's side door as soon as the brakes stopped squealing again. Knowing she didn't have far to go, she left the baby in the car seat as she jumped out, tripping her way to the edge of the shadow.

"Ninetroir," she gasped out. "Please. I need you to help me."

It was supposed to be instantaneous.

Nothing happened.

No. No, no, no. No way. It was supposed to—

Wait.

Her heart was thudding so wildly, the beat nearly drowned out Ash's instructions. Callie struggled to keep the tears back. Her eyes burned, both from frustration and how she strained them, searching the depths of the unnaturally dark shadow for some sign that he was answering her. She curled her fingers. Forced herself to swallow.

No one was there.

What did she do wrong? There had to be something. Ash was so careful to prepare her, and he was sure she could do this. She *could* do this. For her mate, for her daughter, for—

And then it hit her. Her mistake. She'd made a big mistake. Because the name might be everything during a first summoning, but it wasn't the *only* thing.

She swallowed a second time, desperate to get this right, then tried again.

"Ninetroir." Her voice was shaky yet sure. Her world was crumbling around her, but she knew better than to give any of the fae power—or ammunition—over her. Squeezing her trembling hands into tight fists, the tangle of her white-blonde hair settling over her shoulders, Callie repeated Ash's exact wording: "I command you to appear. *Now.*"

A figure materialized at the far end of the shadow, blinking into existence as if he'd been there all along. Tall and slender, he moved forward with a purposeful, regal stride. It didn't seem possible, but he took more steps than the space should have allowed and didn't appear to get any closer. At first. And then, suddenly, there he was.

It worked. It actually *worked*.

Callie's knees went weak with relief even though she knew that the summoning was child's play compared to actually getting him to agree to hear her out. One step at a time. She could convince him. She *would*.

No other choice.

Because of who he was—because of *what* he was—the fae didn't leave the sanctuary of the shadow. Still, enough light fell on him so that Callie could finally come face to face with Ash's old comrade in the Fae Queen's guard.

Ninetroir.

At first glance, he was absolutely beautiful. Of course he was, though Callie had been expecting that. Big silver eyes gleamed from inside the dark shadow, a beacon searching for whoever had been foolish enough to call him by his true name.

She felt her breath catch. If she allowed it to, his glamour would charm her to do his will and then she'd never get the chance to beg him for his help. She had to concentrate. Looking closer, Callie used her skill to see what was really there. He was beautiful, yes, but it was all wrong. His features were unnaturally perfect, his neck was too long, his body stretched too thin. His flawless skin? It was so pale, he seemed like he was glowing. The faint shine reminded Callie of the moon which made sense. Ash told her once that, unlike his kind, Ninetroir was a creature of the night.

A Dark Fae.

His hair was a contrast to his fair skin, surprisingly darker than the shadow that contained him. Midnight black, short but wild, she could see the points of his ears poking out through the soft curls.

Purple bruises underlined his strange silver eyes. They had remained unchanged as she looked through his glamour. Ninetroir's eyes were the windows to his madness, to his tempered fury, to his cold and calculating nature—and the only thing that his magic could never truly hide.

The bright silver darkened to a stormy grey as he narrowed gaze on her. Thin lips pulled down into an expression of outright dislike. Callie got the impression that he wanted nothing more than to squash her like a bug.

That wasn't anything new. Most of his kind looked at her like that.

"Where did you get that name?"

His voice was lovely, soft and alluring. But it was harsh, too, and Callie hoped it was worth the risk to involve such a volatile and capricious creature.

Part of her wanted to run back to the car and speed away. Except Ash trusted Ninetroir and she trusted Ash so, despite her instincts, she stayed.

"Ash gave it to me," she told him. She was surprised to hear how steady and calm her own voice sounded. Considering how fast her heart was racing, it was nothing short of a miracle. "I mean, Aislinn did."

"So you have his name as well," he observed coldly. His lips curled. "You're brave to invoke them so carelessly."

"Not brave," she admitted. "Just desperate."

"Yes. Desperation. You absolutely reek of it." Ninetroir's perfect nose wrinkled. "And fear."

Callie shook off his condescension. A faint surge of annoyance cut through the terror long enough for her to say, "You don't seem surprised."

"Why should I? Humans are fragile. Weak. You should always be afraid." He cocked his head slightly, watching her reaction. For a brief moment, he almost seemed interested in her before he straightened up, glowering. "You waste my time. It would be a favor if I simply ended your pitiful existence here and now. Tell me why I shouldn't."

The fae don't do favors. Ever. It was one major point that Ash wouldn't let her forget. If a fae was offering a favor, it was a trick.

Or a death sentence.

She drew back, the fear growing exponentially as the Dark Fae scrutinized her. "Because... because you *can't*."

Ninetroir's eyes flashed. "Can't?"

"Ash—*Aislinn* told me you wouldn't."

"Who are you?" demanded Ninetroir. "Who are you that dares to use his name so familiarly? I—" He stopped, then frowned. "You're her. You're his?"

She nodded.

"Oh. You *dare*."

Ninetroir huffed. His form started to flicker, the outline of his body fading in and out.

Callie felt her drumming heart leap into her throat. She threw her hand out toward him as if that would keep him in place. As if she could even touch him. "Ninetroir, no!"

"He was a fool to give his own name away so freely." Despite his disinterested expression and mocking frown, there was fire in his eyes and a bite to his clipped words. "I would have thought he'd guard mine better. He should have known that even *that* wasn't enough to get me to talk to you."

"Ash is gone," she rushed out, terrified that Ninetroir would disappear before she could tell him why she summoned him in the first place. "For hours, all morning... all afternoon now... I called him and I called him, but he didn't come. That's why he gave me your name, why I had to use it. I had no choice. He wanted me to do this."

"Because Aislinn is gone," he agreed. For the first time that she noticed, Ninetroir shuttered his eyes slowly before resuming his unnatural stare. "He has gone where your words won't reach him again. Even if I wanted to, I can't change that."

That stung. It really friggin' hurt. Callie felt like he had reached out of the shadow and slapped her, it hurt that much.

He couldn't lie. That's one of the first things she learned about his kind. As much as she wished otherwise, he was telling the truth. And, okay, she'd kind of suspected it ever since Ash went silent, but she dared to hope—

Except it didn't matter now *what* she hoped.

No. She refused to believe that. Ash might be gone, but nothing was forever. Callie learned that four years ago. Nothing was forever, not when the fae were involved, the immortal, mythical, ethereal race. And not when she had a little girl, one part human, one part fae, to protect.

This was what her mate wanted. He wasn't truly gone so long as she had something to fight for—something to live for. That's what he told her before he kissed her goodbye one last time.

Swallowing back the lump in her throat, Callie pushed on. For her child. For *Ash's* child. "If he… if he really is *gone*," she said, allowing her voice to break on that terrible word, "then it's even more crucial that you help us."

"Help?" The word sounded foreign, almost alien in his lyrical voice. "We don't help. I *won't* help, especially not a human. Now, if ever I'm in a generous mood, I might strike a deal, only you'd be an even bigger fool to accept it. Aislinn would have known that, too, so I guess it's lucky for you that I'm not feeling the least bit generous."

"Please, Nine—"

"If you're smart, you'll forget that name. And you'll forget you ever saw me." He took a step away from her, staring unblinkingly at Callie as he commanded her, "Go. Close your eyes to us. Forget Faerie." It was another order. "Run far. Run fast. Escape the queen while you still can."

"Don't leave me." She couldn't follow him into the shadow.

If he vanished, she'd lose everything she had left. "It has to be you."

There wasn't any wind. At least, not in Black Pine there wasn't. But as Ninetroir moved toward her, looming on the edge of the shadow, his curls ruffled in the wind, his long black coat flapping behind him. An air of menace suddenly surrounded him.

"Me? Why does it have to be me, human?"

Callie bristled at his cold, dismissive attitude, hating the reminder that she was human and he wasn't. That Ash wasn't. That her daughter wasn't—not totally.

It never bothered Ash, and Callie didn't give a shit, but she was lying if she said she wasn't aware of what his kind thought of hers and any union between the two. To the fae, to any of the ruling races in Faerie, humans were toys, simple playthings to be used and abused and discarded when through. Ninetroir's scorn and barely masked disgust said it all: Ash and Callie weren't supposed to fall in love.

A human with the gift of sight fated to meet—then mate—a Light Fae, one of the Fae Queen's guards?

It wasn't supposed to happen.

The fae believed in true mates. Fated mates. soulmates. Most spent their very long, very lonely lives waiting to find their other half. It wasn't supposed to be a human. Even Ash was surprised at first, almost unwilling to believe that Callie could be his.

She was, though. The two were meant to be together forever.

Only now Ash was gone. And, if she didn't get Ninetroir to help her, who knows how much longer before his people got their hands on their daughter?

While she fretted, Ninetroir was waiting for her answer. He already proved he wouldn't wait for long.

Why me?

How to explain?

Callie had to be careful. A fae couldn't lie, but they were experts at twisting the truth to suit their purposes. Even compared to her Ash—who did it more out of habit, then always apologized profusely—Callie was a novice. Lying to family and friends about her fae lover... that was nothing compared to this.

She couldn't lie. He'd know in an instant. She couldn't twist her words, either, or he'd melt back into the shadows.

But telling him that Ash was convinced the Dark Fae would help because he was so much younger than his brethren... bad idea. Reminding him that he'd once been the closest thing to a friend that Ash had had? Nope. Questioning his loyalty to their queen? It wouldn't work.

And then she remembered the pebble.

"Because of this," she said, slipping her hand into her pocket. She plucked out the pebble, letting it fall and nestle in the crook of her palm. Holding it in front of her, she made sure Ninetroir could see it.

About the size of a nickel and three times as thick, there wasn't anything remarkable about the pebble. Even so, when Ninetroir realized what she held, he inhaled sharply.

"He *wouldn't*."

"He had to."

"I should have expected this of Aislinn. He was always too soft for his own good." Ninetroir's silver eyes gleamed as he demanded, "Give it to me."

She wasn't quick enough. When she was prepared, Callie could use her built-in defenses to fight back against the fae's glamour and compulsion spells. But that was when she was prepared.

Tired and worried and warring with grief, she wasn't quick enough. Ninetroir called her to him.

She couldn't refuse.

Because of the sun, Callie had no choice but to move toward him. She wished she had thought to bring the iron crowbar she used to break into the Buick with her for protection but that was still in the car. Hoping Ash had been right to trust in this Dark Fae, she shivered and held out her hand.

Except, just as she was about to offer the pebble to him, Ninetroir disappeared.

CHAPTER 2

Swallowing her frustration, shaking off the cobwebs of magic that settled over her, Callie opened her mouth to call for him when she heard the plodding steps coming from behind and suddenly understood why Ninetroir was gone.

"Um—miss?" He sounded young. Confused and hesitant. "You need any help?"

Her reaction to the unexpected interruption was instant. Callie closed her fingers around Ash's pebble, pressing her fist against her back to hide it just as she spun to face the stranger.

It was a guy, just like she thought from the curious voice. From his outfit, it was obvious that he worked for the gas station. An attendant or maybe a mechanic. He had on a pair of washed-out overalls with a stained rag hanging off of a belt loop. His hands were grubby, the undersides of his nails black. Approaching her, he brought the greasy smell of grime and oil with him. Fair hair stuck out from underneath his cap. The faded logo stitched on the front matched the sign that hung crookedly in front of the Snack Shack in the distance.

His cap was pulled down so low, Callie couldn't make out much of his face except for a pair of thin, weather-chapped lips. She thought about his young-sounding voice and noticed a small amount of pale peach fuzz sticking to his chin. He was probably only a couple of years younger than she was.

Still, she thought in relief: *just a kid.*

He cleared his throat. "Miss?"

"Wha—no, no. I'm sorry. I'm fine."

"You sure 'bout that?"

Callie nodded quickly. This was her fault. So consumed with summoning Ninetroir when she spied the shadow, she forgot all about the gas station—and its staff. No wonder he was acting so concerned about her. She could only imagine how strange it seemed. Frantic and disheveled, Callie was speaking to an empty shadow while her Buick idled and her daughter slept. She must look like she was fresh out of an asylum or something.

She had to brush him off, get him to leave. Time was too precious to waste, especially when she was on the cusp of getting Ash's old acquaintance to agree to help her.

The attendant cleared his throat. His head lifted and, beneath the brim of his hat, his shadowed expression showed concern. "Because I can always—"

"No!"

Her refusal came out much sharper than she intended it to. The one word exploded out of Callie, echoing in the still summer air. That was the nerves. As silence followed, she took a deep breath, fighting for control.

Then, giving the attendant the most charming smile she could considering the circumstances, she said, "I mean, no thank you. It's been a long drive and I'm not quite there yet, and I had to get out to stretch my legs before I went to the pumps. I'll probably need you in a minute, but I'm okay right now."

Callie might not be all that vain, but she wasn't oblivious, either. She knew she was pretty. She also knew how to make that work for her. She tucked a strand of her long white-blonde hair behind her ear, letting her fake smile almost reach her wide blue eyes.

It might have been her sight that caught Ash's attention in the first place, but she knew that wasn't what had attracted the powerful fae. Or why he had stayed with her before he accepted that she was his true mate.

The attendant, it seemed, didn't want to leave, either.

Because of his cap, she still couldn't see the whole of his face. But she could see his lips and the way they quirked as his head bobbed slowly up and down. Up and down. Up and down. He was looking her over. *Appraising* her.

"That so? If you don't mind me askin', where you goin', miss? My shift's nearly over." His voice was a little stronger now. Almost brazen. "If it's local, maybe I can show ya the way myself."

Callie's smile froze on her face. "Uh, well... look, thanks for the offer, but I've still got a way to go."

"How far?"

"Excuse me?"

"How far?" he pushed. "'Cause I'm off tomorrow, too."

Callie's breath hitched and she gulped. The fair hairs on her arms stood at attention as a shiver coursed down her spine. She didn't know why, couldn't really understand her reaction, but that didn't make it any less visceral. Something about this guy had her danger alarm clanging loudly.

That was the difference between humans and the fae to her. At least, when it came to the magical race, she could see through their glamour. With humans, she never knew what lurked beneath a friendly facade until it was too late.

Just a kid? Yeah, right.

Covering up her unease with a forced laugh, Callie stepped away from him. Without her consciously realizing it, the attendant had slipped closer until only a few feet separated them. "That's sweet and all, but I think I'm okay. I'm still gonna be needing that gas, though, so, if it's okay, I'll move my car over to the pump in just a sec."

"That's fine by me," he answered with a shrug.

But he didn't move.

Callie wanted to scream in frustration. Why couldn't this guy get the hint?

Another smile, more strained this time. "Just want to finish stretching, get some fresh air. Only take another couple of minutes."

"Sure."

She couldn't tell if he understood what she was implying or if he was ignoring it on purpose. While she itched to shove him back toward the Snack Shack, the attendant inched even closer.

That's when he paused. His head cocked, as if he heard something, then turned slightly so that he was glancing at the car. He gave a visible start.

Callie didn't know if he could see into the back of the car where her daughter was peacefully sleeping. Something told her yes because, all of a sudden, his attitude did a total one-eighty. He shrank back, stepping away from her, as if he no longer had any desire to get near.

He even went so far as to hold his grubby hands up high as if warding her off.

"Let me know when you're ready for that gas, ma'am," he said quickly, backing away. Not miss, she noticed. Ma'am. Fine with her. "I'll, uh, I'll be inside if you need me."

He didn't even wait for the relieved *thanks* that rested on the tip of her tongue. As if anxious to get away from the mother and her child, he touched the brim of his cap before disappearing inside the dingy shop.

Callie waited until she was sure she was alone again before she spun back toward the shadow, the ends of her hair twisting around her arms with the force of her motion. She hoped and prayed that Ninetroir had enough interest in Ash's pebble to have lingered nearby.

"Nine—"

"I'm here." And he was. Ninetroir wore the shadow like a second skin, gone and back again in the blink of an eye. "Tell me. Where's the child?"

Callie's heart stopped. For a single moment, she was frozen, her thoughts spinning even though her body had stopped moving. The attendant might have been able to spy the sleeping baby, but Ninetroir's unnerving eyes hadn't traveled beyond her.

So how did he know about her daughter?

Then she remembered. Her entire family was in danger because the Fae Queen had her suspicions that Callie and Ash's daughter was the half-fae child spoken of in the Shadow Prophecy. It didn't matter that Ash tried to convince Callie that the odds of their daughter being the one destined to overthrow the Fae Queen were minuscule at best. The queen believed it and that was all that counted.

Of course Ninetroir knew. All of Faerie knew.

With a tremble in her words, Callie admitted, "She's in the car."

"Bring her to me."

That's what she'd been afraid of all along. Everyone wanted their little girl. Why would this Dark Fae be any different?

Still, she had to try. Now that Ash was gone, Callie refused to let his sacrifice be in vain. She would protect their child, or die trying.

"You... you won't touch her, will you?"

A flash of fury rippled across his inhumanly beautiful face. He regained his composure in an instant, but she knew what she saw.

"I won't repeat myself, human."

Get the baby... Only Ash's absolute certainty that Ninetroir was their last—and only—hope had Callie heading back to the Buick. If her mate thought he could be trusted, if he believed that Ninetroir respected the pebble as much as he thought he would, then Callie would, too.

She just hoped she wasn't making a monumental mistake.

Somewhere in the back of her mind, she noticed that the Buick's engine had finally given out in the time since she summoned Ninetroir. It didn't even faze her anymore; she had lost track of how many appliances she'd thrown away because Ash's appearance in the apartment had short-circuited them. The longer he stayed in the human world, the more his magic faded, but she hadn't forgotten those early days when she had to replace her phone twice and her precious Keurig three times before she caught on that Ash was responsible for them shorting out.

She turned the car off anyway, leaving the key in the ignition before opening the door to the back seat. Her daughter was awake now. Dark blue eyes blinked sleepily, her chubby little fist nudging at her cheek. Torn between leaving the child where she sat and doing what the Dark Fae commanded her to, Callie made the decision. With a soft coo and a heavy heart, she unbuckled the straps and scooped her daughter out of the car seat.

Callie kept the baby nuzzled against her breast, tucking her face in so that the shock of white-blonde hair on her head and a sliver of her rosy cheek were all that was visible to the Dark Fae.

"Put her down. Let her come to me."

"She's barely one—"

His eyebrow quirked. "You're not going to refuse me, are you?"

No. Callie couldn't and Ninetroir knew it.

The dirt that surrounded the lean-to shed was dusty, dotted with rocks and the spare patch of grass. She placed the baby down gently, laying her on her belly. Now alert, the baby pulled herself up so that she was in the position to crawl.

Her dark blue eyes stared right at the patch of black that shimmered beneath the shed's slanted roof. Callie didn't know what kind of sight her daughter had—whether she had the same gift that Callie did, or one of her own—but she was absolutely sure that the baby saw the fae hidden in the shadow. A little laugh bubbled out of her, one of joy and glee and pure innocence, and she moved toward the darkness.

This was it.

When she crawled to the edge of the shadow, her daughter reached her hand out, then looked up at Callie as if needing reassurance.

Though it was the last thing she wanted to do—no way did she want to show any sort of evidence that the Shadow Prophecy might be true—Callie nodded encouragingly. "Go on, sweetie. It's okay."

The little girl crawled closer. Her fingers touched the shadow.

Only it wasn't truly a shadow. It was a portal to Faerie, the only place a Dark Fae could manifest in the human world when the sun was still out. Only a Dark Fae could dwell in a pocket like that—a Dark Fae or a shade-walker.

There should've been a barrier. A paper-thin barrier that could be breached by the Cursed One for a few seconds before the sun took its toll. A human shouldn't be able to cross the barrier.

The baby crawled right through it as if it didn't exist at all.

The little display was all Ninetroir needed. Callie lunged for her daughter before she could be swallowed up entirely by the shadow, snagging her by the heel of her bare foot. The baby didn't struggle, recognizing her mother's touch, and she let Callie pull her back into the human world without so much as a flailing fist or a frustrated kick.

Once she had her child back, Callie picked her up, tucking her under her chin. Her breath came out in a rush, ruffling the fair strands of hair on her daughter's head. Her heart beat triple-time, realizing how close she came to losing her.

One look at Ninetroir's expressionless face and Callie knew —she *knew*—that, if her daughter had made it all the way inside the portal, she would've lost her then and there.

"She's the one."

It was a flat tone. No surprise. No curiosity. Just fact.

If he only suspected before, Callie provided him with proof. No denying that.

No need to beat around the bush anymore, either.

"They're after her. I think I know who. You probably do, too. We've got to finish this before they find me."

He didn't say anything. At the spark of recognition that flared in his eyes, though, she felt her heart sink. He *did* know, didn't he?

And then he murmured under his breath, so softly that she wasn't even sure she heard him right, "How do you know they're not already here?"

Callie ignored his comment. She couldn't think like that. Not now. He had to be someone she could trust because Ash believed he was. She couldn't do this on her own. Her mate swore she wouldn't have to.

Shifting her daughter so that she was supporting her with one arm, Callie offered out the other. She unfurled her fingers from her tightly clenched fist, revealing the pebble she still clasped in her hand.

"Ash told me you owed him a favor. No," she said hurriedly, remembering his instructions, "not favor. A debt. Now, look, I don't pretend to understand any of this or why this stupid, little rock is so important. I'm only doing what he told me to. For me. For our daughter."

Ninetroir twitched and his lips thinned in obvious disgust. She didn't need that. Callie already knew exactly what he thought about her child.

"Ash said that this pebble is your debt. He gave it to me which means that you owe me now. You want to wipe the slate clean? Fine. Do one thing for me and you can toss it away for all I care."

Callie knew she was pushing her luck. She was alone, she had no one else to turn to, and she had just given Ninetroir everything he needed to run back to his queen and tell her that Callie's daughter was a half-fae shade-walker. He owed her no loyalty, and she was beginning to suspect that the Dark Fae didn't feel like he owed Ash any, either.

But then Ninetroir nodded.

"What would you have me do?"

"If I didn't have to ask you for this, I wouldn't. Trust me. I'm *desperate*."

Pressing up against the edge of the shadow, Ninetroir held out his hand. "I want to see the stone."

She couldn't hesitate. Even in the few seconds it took for her to approach him, she could already see the tips of his pale fingers starting to burn at the edges. Hoping she wasn't making another mistake, Callie tipped it into his waiting palm.

A pebble fell, but it landed like a boulder. He lost his composure for the smallest of moments, a mere heartbeat. His shoulders slumped, weighed down by the obligation inherent in the tiny rock. Ninetroir flexed his fingers as if he couldn't believe the power in the geis, then he drew his hand back into the safety of the shadow, leaving a faint trail of smoke and the lingering scent of scorched flesh.

He curled his injured fingers around the pebble, causing it to vanish from sight. When he opened his hand again, it was gone.

Another nod. Whatever had just happened, one thing was clear: he was going to do whatever he had to to repay the debt he owed to Ash. Not for the first time, Callie wondered why the Dark Fae owed her mate, but she kept quiet. This definitely wasn't the time to ask.

"Whatever you want me to do, it'll be done," announced Ninetroir. "Anything to be free of a debt to a human."

"Take my daughter with you. Bring her with you wherever you go. Protect her when I can't."

She could tell that her plea was the last thing that he had expected her to ask of him.

"Bring... bring a *halfling* with me to Court?" Ninetroir was visibly horrified. Apart from the earlier loathing and disgust, it was the first true expression to cross his beautiful face. "You dare to ask me for such a thing?"

She didn't relent. "You owe me your debt. I charge you with her life."

"It would be a mistake." Ninetroir shook his head. "No. Pick something else."

"I can't."

"You will. You don't know what you're asking of me. I refuse."

She couldn't let him.

"I could force you to," Callie threatened desperately. "With the right command, I could make you do it."

"I would hate you for it."

"That's fine, if I knew she was safe."

"But what if I hate the girl?" asked Ninetroir. "Who would then protect her from *me*?"

Callie knew in that second that she'd gone too far. In her haste and her fear and her worry, she'd forgotten that Ninetroir wasn't Ash. He had no reason to humor her. He might be anxious to repay an old debt. Still, he would never forget her slight if she didn't appease him now.

And she wouldn't be the one who paid for the insult. Her daughter would.

"I take it back," she blurted out. "I want to change my bargain, pass this… this debt onto my girl. Watch over her. Keep her safe until the threat passes and she can finally take care of herself."

Ninetroir shook his head. "You still presume too much, human."

He started to melt back into the shadows.

She couldn't let him leave.

"Wait! I'll let you touch her!"

Callie never even saw him move. Though he stood on the edge of the shadow, he seemed to loom; barely a foot separated them now. A sudden hunger—feral and lurking in the depths of his eyes—was at odds with the guarded expression he wore. Only someone with sight as keen as Callie's would've spotted it.

"A touch?" he murmured. Ninetroir's tongue darted out, moistening the corner of his lips. "You'd allow it?"

Her stomach writhed with guilt at just the thought of it.

"Yes."

"And you know what that would mean?"

She nodded.

"Deal. I accept your bargain. Bring the girl to me."

"One touch," she reminded him. "I'll let you have *one* touch. Anything else she'll have to give you—but only after you explain its risks to her. She has to understand. It's the only way."

"Yes, yes." His impatience was clear. He held out his hand. "Give her to me."

Callie moved her daughter out of Ninetroir's reach, purposely keeping her in the last of the direct sunlight so that he couldn't get to her just yet. "You have to make her understand first. Promise me."

His silver eyes flashed angrily. She could tell that he had a retort, though he kept it to himself. From everything she learned from Ash about the power of the touch, she knew he wouldn't let this chance pass him by. He probably would have agreed to anything to be able to steal some of her daughter's strength.

She shouldn't do this.

She had no choice.

"Promise me," she said again.

He nodded. "You have my promise that I won't touch her again without her permission. And, now, we have an accord."

Coming from a fae, that was as unbreakable of a bond as she could hope for. He couldn't lie, and he couldn't cheat. He might trick her to get what he wanted. That was a given—after all, he *was* from Faerie. Callie just hoped that she'd be around to warn her daughter herself.

If not...

Callie cut that thought off mid-stream. No time for what-if's and maybe's. She had no choice, right? Nodding to herself, trying to convince herself that she was doing the right thing, she moved her daughter up to the shadow. Her hand brushed up against the barrier; she couldn't push past it. But the baby slipped easily from this world to the next, her head, her face, her throat inches away from where Ninetroir watched her.

His strange eyes sparkled. A hint of color filled his pale cheeks, a faded pink flush. He licked his lips and reached for the baby.

He had hands like a pianist, long and thin fingers that were as pale as the rest of him. Ninetroir paused when he was almost there. Callie saw his fingers tremble just enough to make her wonder if there was another way. Then his expression darkened and she changed her mind entirely.

She tried to move her child back into the sunlight. Too late. She was too late. Or Ninetroir was too quick. Either way, he managed to rest his fingertips—healed, they were already healed—against the side of the little girl's face.

He took a deep breath, closing his eyes as the feeling closed in over him.

"It is done," he whispered, leaving Callie to wonder what *she* had done. "For as long as she needs me, this child is under my protection."

When he opened them again, his gleaming eyes weren't just silver. They shone like a freshly polished piece of jewelry, sparkling and vibrant in their brilliance.

Callie got one blinding look into their unending depths before they suddenly winked out. Just like that, Ninetroir was gone for the second time.

CHAPTER 3

The terror and worry that she'd been fighting against since that morning crashed into her like a wave the moment he disappeared. Clutching her baby tightly, she had the sinking suspicion that, despite her best efforts, she had fallen under his charm. That he had used his glamour to put her more at ease during their negotiations, lulling her into something close to security while she was too worked up to notice it.

Why else would she have agreed so readily to such a tether for her child?

Now that he was gone, she felt it all come back. Frantically, she wondered how Ninetroir's bargain could be broken, where he might have built in some sort of loophole for him to escape while she forfeited his debt to Ash.

At least, her daughter was safe. For now, she was safe.

A giddy laugh bubbled up from within her.

Safe.

Callie loved the way that word sounded inside her mind.

"Ma'am, you still doin' okay over here?"

She heard the voice and knew right away why Ninetroir had disappeared the way that he had. Turning slowly, she found herself face to face with the same young man as before. He was still wearing the dusty baseball cap with the Snack Shack logo on it. Just like earlier, the most she could see under the wide brim was his chin.

"What? Oh… yes." The wave of relief she felt now that she had Ninetroir's promise made her feel light. Free. Let the queen's soldiers catch up with her now. At least her baby would be safe. "Yes, you wouldn't believe how much better I'm doing."

"That's good, I guess. Just makin' sure you don't need nothin'."

Callie suddenly remembered the car's dead engine. "Actually, I might be having a little engine trouble now. I guess, if you're not busy, I could use some help after all. Do you think you could…"

"Take a look? No problem." The attendant already had his back to her as he loped easily over to the quiet Buick. A moment later, the hood was up and he was fiddling with the engine inside. "I think I see what happened here. It might take me a couple of minutes, though. You want to go on inside, see if you want a snack? I should have you up and runnin' again in a few."

A snack sounded heavenly. When was the last time she ate? When was the last time she fed the baby?

Baby first. While he fiddled around with the engine, she strapped her daughter back into the car seat. The diaper bag was tossed onto the back seat next to her. Callie grabbed it, pulling out one of the two bottles remaining.

Her daughter let out a gurgle of excitement when she saw the bottle. Callie felt her heart ache. Not only was her baby as good as gold, not crying once since the moment the soldiers tracked them down in their apartment that morning, but she seemed content to wait until her mother was ready to provide supper. As if she knew just how important this all was.

After giving her baby a quick kiss, Callie offered her the bottle of milk. The baby took it, holding it herself as she curled up around the baby blanket that Callie had kept stowed in the emergency diaper bag.

Now that the baby was settled in the back of the Buick, Callie kissed the idea of a snack goodbye. She could wait. As soon as the attendant got the car up and running again, she could put a couple of towns between her and Black Pine, then worry about food for herself.

And that's when she realized that, while she could wait to eat, there was something that she couldn't wait to do.

"I, jeez, do you have a bathroom?"

"Sure do." He pointed behind his back. "There's a door on the right side of the shack. Single stall. You can't miss it."

"Thanks."

Ducking into the back seat again, Callie tried to figure out how she was going to bring her daughter with her into the bathroom. Now that she knew she needed to go, waiting wasn't an option. At the same time, the baby was already starting to doze between taking pulls off of her bottle. Callie didn't have the heart to disturb her.

"You can leave her there," the attendant offered, guessing what she was worrying over. "I'll watch her for you."

If she could trust him, that would make her life so much easier.

If she could trust him.

"I don't know. Maybe I shouldn't—"

"Honest. It's no trouble."

Callie paused, then decided it would be ridiculous to disturb her daughter just to haul her into the stall with her. She didn't seem to need her diaper changed, either, so she couldn't even justify her worry with using that as an excuse. Besides, Ninetroir was just as responsible for her now. If the gas station attendant even so much as looked at her daughter the wrong way, his contract would hold the Dark Fae to helping her.

That made her mind up for her. Callie closed the back door gently, watching her innocent daughter eat. The rise and fall of her chest, the way her lids seemed to droop as she struggled between resting and eating her supper... it calmed Callie enough to step away from her for a few minutes.

She'd be back before she knew it.

"Be a good girl, Zella, sweetie. Mommy will be right back for you," she promised, blowing her child a love-filled kiss before walking away.

Callie had no idea that that would be the last time she ever saw her baby.

Rys of the Seelie Court, and one of the Fae Queen's current favorites, sensed it when the human woman gave in to his compulsion. It had been subtle, a mere suggestion, and he barely used any of his waning power to trick her into agreeing. Night was drawing nearer and he'd have to return to Faerie soon. Between pushing against the power of the Dark Fae that the human summoned and trying to compel her to leave with him before the sun ran out, Rys was desperate to leave the human world with his prize.

The soldiers thought that brute force would've been enough to get to the Shadow. The queen might have put on a front like she agreed with her generals, but she knew that a fae like Rys would be better suited to get the job done.

No way he would ever let his queen down. Even if he *did* have quite a few ulterior motives of his own.

He watched the exchange of the pebble—the touch—and Rys's plan shifted in that moment. He'd do enough to satisfy his queen, knowing that he'd get what he wanted in the end, too.

It would all be worth it. Stalking the human mate, tracking her on her frantic flight, following her to the empty gas station, even pretending to be a… a human mechanic. Right when he thought he finally had her, Rys kept his head bowed while pretending he knew what in Oberon's name he was doing with her useless vehicle. As soon as Aislinn's human finally listened to him and moved far enough away from the halfling child, he gave up the pretense, straightening again.

Rys had been warned about how well she could see through glamour and, while the disguise was too simple and crude for his liking, it served its purpose. She never expected a thing. Lifting the brim of his cap, shadows fell across his face. Because he was a Light Fae, they weren't anywhere near dark enough to hide the vivid gleam of his golden, sun-filled eyes.

Nothing excited him more than a good hunt. And this one? It was only the beginning.

For now, though, it was cutting it too close. It was time to snag his current prey before the sun went down and the Dark Fae regained the power to stop him.

Well, *try* to stop him.

Ha. Rys grinned. As if the youngling fae could do anything to stop *him*.

He took the cap from his head, shaking loose his long mane of golden hair. It fell past his shoulders, swaying in the late summer breeze. Because he knew better than to leave any proof of his existence behind at this ramshackle, rundown, former gas station, he tucked the cap into the pocket of his atrocious overalls. Then, with a silent promise toward the child, he stalked toward the bathroom.

Prophecy or no prophecy, you'll be mine someday.

WHILE HER MOTHER WAS GONE, THE LITTLE GIRL SNUGGLED INTO her car seat. She finished the last of the milk, letting the plastic bottle slip from her pudgy fingers, falling with a soft *thump* against the stained floor below her. Within minutes, she was fast asleep. She slumbered peacefully, unaware that everything she'd known in her short life was in the middle of changing forever.

Night soon fell. The moon rose high in the velvety black sky, shedding some light on the abandoned vehicle. Without waking, she turned towards the shadow that slipped and slithered and crawled across the cracked leather interior.

She reached for it, then smiled.

From his side of the shadow, looking down at the power and the promise in the infant's content smile, Nine knew then and there that he was as lost as her poor, unfortunate parents were.

The Light Fae might have gone for Aislinn and his human. He didn't like it, but there was nothing he could do for them. But the child? She belonged to one Dark Fae in particular.

She belonged to *him*.

Or, he amended, remembering the Shadow Prophecy and the pebble in his pocket, it would be more truthful to say that he existed to be hers.

Forever.

And there wasn't a damned thing he could do to change that.

fall in love with the shadow man...

TOUCHED BY THE FAE   BOOK ONE

ASYLUM

INTERNATIONAL BESTSELLING AUTHOR
JESSICA LYNCH

Copyright © 2019 by Jessica Lynch

All rights reserved.

No part of this book may be reproduced in any form or by any electronic or mechanical means, including information storage and retrieval systems, without written permission from the author, except for the use of brief quotations in a book review.

Cover by Jessica Lynch

FOREWORD

Asylum is the first in a series that will tell the story of a young woman named Riley Thorne. While it's clearly a supernatural series, full of magic, mayhem, adventure, prophecies, and romance, it also features some real world issues, too.

Because of the way the Black Pine facility is designed—it's a home for "wayward juveniles"—nearly every in-patient grapples with their own issues. So, please, consider this a content warning for mental health, doctors, eating disorders, and more. Riley's official diagnosis is schizotypal personality disorder because of her insistence that the fae are real—and that they're after her. No one believes her, and her struggles color this whole first book.

As you read the series, though, you learn that that *is* true. The fae *are* after her, but that doesn't diminish her last six years of recovery inside of the asylum. Or the phobias she's developed along the way.

I want to give readers the opportunity to make an informed

decision about whether or not this is the type of book for them. If you choose to continue, I hope you enjoy the first part of Riley's journey!

xoxo,
Jessica

PROLOGUE

It always seems to be raining whenever I visit the cemetery.

Just my luck. Within minutes, I'm already soaked. I wish my shirt had a hood, something, anything to cover my head. No dice. Despite the year-round air conditioning in my room, I always sleep in a basic tee; it's the only time I can let the bare skin of my arms go uncovered. My favorite hoodie is probably right where I left it: tossed on top of my dresser. If it wasn't for the chilly rain, I wouldn't need it.

I know every inch of this place. I mean, I've spent more than enough time here. I head toward the closest mausoleum. The name on the outside says Richardson, and it's got the widest overhang on this side of the cemetery. I duck beneath it, shrinking against the marble in a fruitless attempt to avoid the raindrops. They're falling hard and fast, plopping against the flattened grass, spraying dots of mud against the hem of my pajama pants.

A light bobs in the distance. Up. Down. Up. Down. I follow the white splotch as it moves further out. It's the caretaker, making his last rounds of the night. The glowing blob of light? His lantern going on the journey with him.

I know the old guy's routine almost as well as he does. First, he'll check to make sure no one is stupid enough to be caught on the grounds this late at night—especially during another summer storm—then he'll head back inside, lock up his office, close the gates, and go home.

My eyes trained on the moving light, I keep to the shadows where I know he won't find me. The shadows have always protected me. I'm safe here.

Not that I can explain *how* I got here. Hell, I don't even know how I'm going to make my way back. Acorn Falls is about a half an hour away from Black Pine by car—and I never learned to drive. On foot? Hours, easy.

That's okay. The cemetery tonight? This is where I'm supposed to be. It's where I belong.

Closing my eyes, I listen to the pitter-patter of the raindrops hitting the graves around me. The wind screams and howls and I stay tensed, waiting for the clap of thunder or the crash of lightning. A storm's brewing all right. When I open my eyes again, there's hardly any difference. It's too dark to make out anything now that the lantern is so far away.

It's only growing colder out, too. I hug myself, pulling my thin t-shirt close, shivering when the clammy tips of my leather gloves cut right through the soaked material. The rain has washed the rest of the day's warmth right away. A few strokes shy of midnight, I'm almost freezing. It doesn't help that the marble of the mausoleum leeches any body heat I've got left.

Still, I refuse to leave.

Not yet.

The storm is my friend. Eager to get out of the rain, the cemetery caretaker half-asses his job. His luck is a tiny bit better than mine and he manages to shine his light back in my direction without even meaning to before glancing away. Like every other time I've inexplicably found myself at this cemetery, he doesn't know I'm here.

Phew. I'm just glad that the mausoleum shields me while the shadows hide me. It was a close call. When he shifts again, I let out a sigh of relief between chattering teeth.

His lantern is nothing but a pinprick in the distance as he moves further and further away. Suddenly, the light is gone.

I wait a few minutes more. My teeth won't stop chattering and I'm damn lucky that I don't slice off a piece of my tongue when it slips between my molars. Inside my gloves, I can feel my fingers becoming prunes; the water always finds a way to seep in. I find myself wishing I had a napkin or a towel. For too long I had to be careful to keep my brand new hands dry. All these years later, it's a reflex. I guess it's just too hard of a habit to break.

When I hear the roar, I think the thunder has arrived. That's before twin lights turn on and break up the gloom. Headlights. The caretaker has started his beater of a truck. I duck down, making myself even smaller as I press my back up against the mausoleum. My skin is white, my pale blonde hair a few shades lighter. Even though my t-shirt is black—my gloves, too—if he peeks this way again and I'm not hiding, no way he'll miss me.

The marble is so cold that it feels like I've been stabbed. I hiss through my teeth, but I don't move away from the wall until I see the truck lurch toward the front gate. Mud sucks at the tires. The car whines as he surges forward, stopping when he reaches the opposite side of the entrance.

The caretaker keeps his truck running while he jumps out and yanks the gate closed. He locks it, trapping me in the cemetery with my demons and my ghosts.

I let out another soft sigh of relief. To be honest, I much prefer it that way.

Madelaine's grave is located on the west end of the cemetery, not too far from the Richardsons' mausoleum. Balling my hands into fists inside the squishy gloves, I push off of the mausoleum's outer wall and step lightly onto the flooded grass. It's slick and slippery. I come close to falling a couple of times. Once, I nearly lose my slipper in a deceiving puddle. I grit my teeth and keep on going. I don't know how I got here, but I know why I've come.

It's little more than a drizzle when I find the right resting place.

The Everetts marked her grave with a giant stone angel. It's hard to miss, but I run my gloved fingers along each wing, recognizing the carved lines and the chip on the right side. Almost six years later, through the rain and sleet and the snow, and that chip is still the same size.

I hardly pay any attention to the rain, the damp ground, even the chill as I kneel in front of her grave. Moving my hand lower, I trace each letter in her name until I'm satisfied that I'm with my sister again. I turn so that I'm sitting on the marble base, resting my back against her headstone.

There are no words. I sit in silence, my head bowed into my chest.

It's only when the rain quits at last and the sky starts to lighten that I wonder if anyone from the asylum has noticed that I'm gone.

CHAPTER 1

The first thing I see when I open my eyes again is my window. Six bars stretch vertically across the lengths of the glass plane. And it hits me.

I'm not at the cemetery. I'm back at Black Pine again.

The *asylum*.

Breathing in deep, I can't get the smell of wet graveyard soil out of my nose. My bangs are plastered down to my forehead, but it has to be sweat. I mean, there's no way that I actually could have left my room.

I haven't been on the outside in close to six years.

I shove my bangs back. They squelch against my leather gloves. I can't stop my shudder. Getting my gloves wet is even worse than when I'm forced to bare my hands in front of an audience. My stomach was already queasy from a poor night's sleep full of vivid dreams and bad memories. The damp leather gloves make it so much worse.

Might as well get up. There's no chance in hell I can even think about going back to sleep now.

That's nothing new. Not for me. I always wake up before seven. I can't remember the last time I was jerked from my sleep by the facility's wake-up calls. Not since I stopped taking my sleeping medication regularly, I bet. More often than not, I'm up and dressed before the morning tech knocks on my door and tells me it's time to get going. Most days I even have my bed made.

After all this time, I know the routine.

Amy is peppy, a real morning person. Today she chatters about her most recent attempt at potty-training her son while she checks my vitals. Blood pressure, pulse, temperature... she seamlessly goes from one test to the next, marking the results down on my chart. Once she pronounces me fit as a fiddle, she sends me off for my morning meds and my shower.

A blonde technician I don't recognize is standing in front of the chalkboard at the nursing station. She writes the morning message quickly before hurrying off, wiping the chalk dust from her hands onto her scrubs. A faint white ghost hand leaves a trail down the side of her light blue pants.

I turn to look at the board. It says the same sort of thing it usually does, for those who can't remember:

Today is Sunday. You are at Black Pine Facility for Wayward Juveniles. This is the residential ward for the 19-21 age group. It is raining outside. All windows must remain shut.

I feel better knowing that it's raining out. That explains part of my dream, even if I still can't figure out why my hair was so damp. Leaving it at sweat, I snort at that last line.

This technician must be new to Black Pine if she thinks we can open any of the windows here. Despite its stupid name, we all know that the asylum—sorry, Facility for Wayward Juveniles—is really more of an old-fashioned, obsolete psych hospital.

Come on. We're on the fifth floor. They're not going to risk us jumping. None of these windows open.

It's sad, in a way. Last night's dream makes me remember how much I miss the fresh air. If I breathe in deep, I can still smell the damp earth and the rain on the marble gravestones.

Shit.

I've got to remember not to tell any of my doctors about that. If they think my hallucinations are stretching to different senses, who knows what they'll prescribe for me next. All I *do* know is that I'm pretty sure I can't stomach any more medication.

Speaking of medication—

Three other patients are already lined up at the nursing station, waiting for their morning meds. Since Amy started at our end of the floor, it's all girls. Our crew will be the first in the showers, too. Sometimes I suspect that Amy does it on purpose, waking the girls up first so that we get that extra half an hour to use the showers before the boys do, but she's never said. Then again, I've never asked.

I learned a long time ago not to bother asking any questions. People lie. It's what they do. And, hell if I know why, but I've always been able to tell. It gets depressing after a while. I've gotten used to tuning it out, even if I can't turn it off entirely.

Carolina brings up the rear, her long dark hair a curtain as she nibbles on her thumbnail. I get in line right behind her, trying not to notice just how loosely her Black Pine tee hangs off her bony frame. She's the most recent chick to join our floor. New meat, too, not one of the kids on the fourth floor who aged out to ours. She's quiet, seems sweet, and even if she didn't open up during group therapy, I'd still have a pretty good idea why her parents tossed her inside with the rest of us.

When she senses me lingering a couple of steps behind her, she shoves her sheet of hair over her shoulder, her eyes friendly as she grins over at me. Nope. I immediately drop my gaze to the tiles. They're a pristine white speckled with grey, and though I've seen them every day for the last two years, they're suddenly the most fascinating tiles in the world.

I mean, look at that speckle over there. With the shadow and the shape, it reminds me of a dolphin. And that one—

Carolina lets out a soft sigh, then shuffles so that she's facing the front of the nurse's station again.

I want to tell her that I can't help it. That it's not just her, either.

I don't.

I can't.

Besides, if she's locked up in here with me long enough, she'll learn. Unable to form personal relationships, abandonment issues, a deep-seated fear that everyone I've ever known or loved will eventually leave me... that's why I'm at Black Pine.

Well, those are *some* of the reasons why I'm committed here.

The line moves quickly. Our morning nurses are quick and efficient. It's their job, them and the techs, to make sure that us juveniles have a strict routine and that we stick to it.

Before we're even up, the medicines have already been doled out into individual dixie cups with our names scribbled on the side in black marker. When it's my turn, I step up to the nursing station. Already looking past me to the next in line, the nurse hands me the cup that says **R. Thorne**.

I peek inside, giving the cup a shake. Four pills roll around the bottom, just like every morning. Since there's no point arguing with the nurse, I toss them back before moving aside and making room for Meg. I chase my meds with one of the apple juice cups left out on a tray. The bitter taste still lingers on my tongue. Ugh. No matter how long I've been doing this, I've always hated this part.

Too bad there's nothing I can do about it.

In other facilities, patients are allowed to refuse their meds. Not me, and not most of us at Black Pine. It's one thing if you voluntarily stick yourself inside, but nearly everyone I've met in my six years here has been tossed in by someone else. A mother. A grandfather. Maybe an aunt, uncle, or a second cousin twice removed, I don't know. Because we come here when we're minors, it's usually the adults that make the call.

In my case, the state has control of me. It was either here or prison, and even if *I* don't think I'm crazy, I would have to be if I picked prison over the asylum. When I turn twenty-one in two weeks, I'm finally free of this place.

That means I only had to do six years. If I chose prison, the sentence for manslaughter is almost fifteen.

AFTER I SHOWER AND CHANGE INTO FRESH CLOTHES, I HEAD OFF TO breakfast.

There are two tables in the dining area: one for the girls, another for the guys. I must have taken longer to wash up than usual because I'm the last chick to take her assigned seat. The guys start to trickle in about ten minutes later, filling up their table. When it seems like we're missing someone, I do a quick headcount. Twelve. Someone's not here.

It takes me a second before I realize it's Jason, a tall, light-skinned black boy who always had an optimistic outlook. He's still not here when the morning techs announce that it's time to eat. I vaguely wonder what happened to him. I'm the oldest in our ward, so close to twenty-one that I can almost taste it, so he hasn't moved on before me.

Maybe he's been released. Maybe he's in trouble and they're

keeping him confined to his room. I give it another few seconds of thought, then let it slip away.

In-patients change. Techs change. Doctors change. All that matters is that I'm still here.

For two weeks, three days, and a couple of hours longer, I'm stuck inside.

I can not *wait* to get out.

At least it's Sunday. Sundays are way easier than most other days. Because it's the weekend, our schedule is a bit more lenient. Yeah, we still have to get up ass early, but we get an hour for breakfast, then another hour to just kind of unwind before sessions start.

I won't see any of my doctors today—not until Monday—but there's Lorraine, my social worker, who I see once a week because the courts say I have to, my mandatory daily check-in, plus group therapy. It's usually art on Sundays. Actually, it's art therapy most rainy days. Or whenever the facility staff runs out of ideas for us.

Whatever.

On the plus side, Sunday is pancake day. It's a treat. Something to look forward to.

Of course, not everyone is happy. In her high-pitched whine, Whitney complains that she's allergic to chocolate and all of the pancakes are contaminated. She insists that Amy throw the whole tray out, pouting when Amy whips out her clipboard with her notes on it and reminds her that Whitney's only allergens on file are cat dander and pollen. Because she's used to Whitney's complaints—she pulls this same stunt every Sunday—Amy offers Whitney a blueberry pancake instead, but Whitney scowls and jerks her plate closer to her.

Chocolate it is.

I drop two blueberry pancakes on my own plate. After I

cover them in butter—no syrup for me, the pancakes are sweet enough—I start to chow down. I'm not big on interacting with the others, for obvious reasons, but I guess you could say I'm a people-watcher. As I eat, I look around the room.

Carolina has the seat across from me. She isn't eating, I notice. She just rips her pancake up into smaller pieces before pushing the pieces around her plate. If you weren't watching her, it would seem as if she'd eaten some of it. If you weren't watching, or if you didn't know any better.

I'm not the only one who sees that. Standing back, clipboard up as she keeps an eye on our breakfast table, Amy frowns. Grabbing a pen from her pocket, she makes a note on the clipboard. That sucks for Carolina. She probably just lost another point for that and, since she's a new case, that might mean another day committed.

Poor kid.

Slap.

Everyone looks over at the boy's table, including me. Vinnie, an excitable white guy with spiky black hair, is standing up, his hand outstretched. Considering Tai is sitting across from Vinnie, syrup glistening on his cheek, half of a pancake stuck to the side of his throat, it doesn't take a super genius to figure out what happened.

That's when Whitney lets out a shrill shout.

"Food fight!"

It doesn't get any further than that. Amy tosses her clipboard onto the dining cart, Louis already rushing forward to settle down the guys. I roll my eyes at their antics. Once you make it to this floor, we're supposed to be adults. No one here is younger than eighteen, but I get why we're still considered *wayward juveniles.* A food fight? Seriously?

That's a waste of good pancakes.

While Amy and Louis work on separating Vinnie from a furious Tai, I peek over at Carolina. Both tables are too involved in what's going on over on the boys' side to notice the way that she's staring wistfully at the food on her plate. It's like she wants to eat, only she can't bring herself to.

I think of Amy's clipboard and the note she left on Carolina's chart. Before anyone can catch me, I reach out and snatch one of the largest chunks of pancakes from her plate. Her dark brown eyes light up in relief when she realizes what I've done—and why I've done it.

She gives me a grateful smile.

I want to smile back. I really do. She's new, but Carolina seems nice, and it's not as if I've got too many friends already that I don't have time for any more. If there's one thing I learned, though, it's that people come and people go.

I *want* to smile. I can't. I don't. Instead, I shove the whole piece of pancake in my mouth. Oops. Can't be friendly if I'm too busy chewing on a pancake. Sorry.

Once I finish that piece, I focus on my plate. The butter is a melty, delicious mess. Sure, it drips a little, leaving a shiny, oily streak on my right glove that's barely discernible among the other scratches and marks. That's what happens when you wear leather gloves around the clock. I've already stained them with everything under the sun. What's one more streak?

Today's pancakes are delicious. I put my two away before I feel a little full and decide against a third. Amy nods encouragingly as she gives me the okay to get rid of my garbage.

I've given up trying to explain that, unlike Carolina and some of the asylum's other "guests", food has never been a problem for me. My appearance, either. That surprises some of my doctors. With all of the problems they insist I have, poor body image isn't one of them. So many of the kids here hate the way they look.

Not me. I never have.

Well, except for my hands. But that makes sense to the professionals. There's a reason behind that—and it doesn't have anything to do with the things I used to see, or the voices I heard when I was a kid.

CHAPTER 2

Of us all, Dean is the grumpiest after breakfast. Definitely not a morning person. If the techs let him, he'd easily sleep until noon. Of course, the techs never let him. It would go against our routine and, oh boy, that's just not going to happen. But Louis does have to resort to threatening Dean's television privileges to get him up and ready before we eat.

Whether it's spite or his grumpy nature, Dean retaliates by taking forever to finish his meal. He's usually the last one to come slinking into the day room, the common area where we all kind of gather together when we're not in session or confined to our rooms.

Today's the same as every other day. Routine, right? By the time Dean joins us, most of the chairs are already occupied, especially the ones closest to the screen. I've staked out my perch on one of the sofas, leaning into the far side, careful to keep enough space between Kim and me so that we don't accidentally bump into each other.

The television is tuned to some kiddy channel. It always is on the weekend. It doesn't matter that most of our group grew out of Spongebob and My Little Pony years ago. This is a juvenile facility, the kids inside ranging from six to twenty-one. I'm used to it, and I barely pay attention to the laughter coming from the screen.

Now that we're enjoying our free time, I think about this morning. About the scent of graveyard soil in my nose, and the way my bangs lay plastered to my sweaty forehead.

My dreams—when I have them—are weird. That wasn't the first time I fell asleep and dreamed of returning to a place that I should be staying far away from. I wish I could blame my nighttime meds, but I know it's not them; my sleeping pills make it so that I can't dream. Still, it's super weird. I mean, who *wants* to spend their nights in an empty cemetery?

Well, except for me, I guess. When I'm sleeping, at least.

But when I'm awake?

I... I don't know what I would do.

I'm gonna find out soon, though.

Two weeks, three days, and a couple of hours until freedom. That's all I'm looking forward to. Two weeks, three days, and a couple of hours until Lorraine signs off on my file and I start the next phase of my life. I'm not sure what's next, but I know one thing: it's better than sitting around in Black Pine. Lately, I can't help but think of this place as a hellish kind of limbo. I think I've learned everything I'm going to, I haven't had an episode in years, and if I dream about leaving the asylum after hours, at least I know it's just a result of my overactive imagination.

I mean, there are *bars* on my window. How could I sneak out —or come back without anyone realizing it?

Dean shuffles into the day room, muttering to himself as he does. It never makes any sense—not to anyone but Dean, anyway—and I zone him out, too, until he plops his wide body in the gap left between me and Kim.

Suddenly, I'm paying super close attention.

It seems to happen in slow motion. The couch gives a small bounce at his weight, my body jolting just enough to shift sideways. His Black Pine t-shirt clips the side of my left hand. I sense the faint brush of fabric against the edge of my glove. My reaction is as immediate as it is over the top: my whole body stiffens for a heartbeat before I jerk and leap away, desperate to put some space between us.

One problem with that. I must have been sitting on the edge of the seat or something because, when I jump, I end up in a pile on the floor. Like, my ass slides right off before hitting the carpet with a muffled *thump*.

Pain shoots up my spine. I ignore it. All I can think about is how close Dean came to brushing his arm against mine.

Just like I'm used to the other kids' quirks, they've all seen me at my worst. A couple of months ago, I was banned from the day room for seven straight days because I swung a remote at Jeffrey all because he thought it would be funny to stand in front of me, his hand extended, mockingly repeating, "I'm not touching you, I'm not touching you," over and over again. I missed, since I didn't want to get too close, but I lost a couple of points for that fight.

It was worth it.

Dean didn't do it on purpose. I know he didn't.

Now if only I could convince myself that.

Because they're used to me reacting like this, none of the other patients do anything to help me. It would only make things worse. The last thing I need right now? A panic attack. I don't get as many now that my meds are regulated, but when I *do* get them, they come fast and terrible.

I can already tell my heart is racing. My breath is short, my body tight. I feel like I just missed getting hit by a car.

That's what Dean's touch feels like to me. Like a car accident.

I try to take a deep breath and choke on the air. My head is spinning. I can't get up off of the floor.

It's the new technician with the long blonde ponytail that tries to help me. She had poked her head in the day room, checking up on us, gasping when she sees that I'm sprawled on the floor. She's a blur of pale blue scrubs as she hurries into the common area, hiking her pants up as she squats by my side.

She holds out her hand.

Her pale, unscarred hand.

I flinch.

To me, it's like she's shoving a poisonous snake in my face. Her skin is that dangerous.

"What are you doing down there? I know the floor can't be that comfortable. Come now, take my hand. I'll help you up."

No.

No.

The words won't come. I shake my head frantically, pulling away from her.

Her hand follows me.

No!

"No... no touching," I wheeze. The words are garbled, harsher than I mean, almost like I spit them out at her. I can't help it. "Back off."

"I'm not trying to hurt you. I just want to help."

She just wants to touch me.

"I said back off!"

This new tech slowly pulls her hand back. Her lips quirk into some semblance of a professional smile—designed to soothe me, though hell if that's gonna work right now—but it's not enough to hide the worry in her hazel eyes.

She's too new to Black Pine. She doesn't know me, though I'd bet a stack of Oreos that she's heard all about me.

That worry? It's because she has no clue what I'm about to do. With my reputation, she's got a pretty good reason to worry.

Today, I'm good. Nothing out of the ordinary. I do what I *always* do.

I sit on my hands.

One of the other girls snickers. Whitney? Wouldn't doubt it. A high-pitched voice fills the sudden quiet next. *Zehn. Neun. Acht. Sieben...* Someone's counting backward from ten in German. That would be Allison. When she's uncomfortable, she slips into German.

It could be worse. It could be French. Allison likes to speak French when she finds something funny.

I'm so not laughing.

Dean gets up. My vision is hazy, my heart *thump-thump-thump*ing away in my chest, but I make out the big guy as he gets back to his feet and lumbers away from the couch. He squeezes himself between Martin and Casey on the other sofa.

I make sure to dodge just enough to avoid his knee bumping into my shoulder before focusing on the tech. She seems to have gotten closer to me in the last few seconds.

I don't like it.

"Riley," she says softly. So she *does* know who I am. I figured. "Listen to me. I'm sure you know that the rule's only to make sure that you guys don't touch each other. I have to touch you if I'm going to help you off the floor."

She's telling the truth. I can tell.

It doesn't matter.

"No touching," I insist.

Okay. So maybe I sound like I'm panicking a little. I *am* panicking.

No touching. It's the only rule I live by. I learned early on that bad things happen to me whenever I let someone touch me without my permission. And I'm not talking about people messing with my personal space or groping me without my consent.

I'm talking about *control*.

If you let one of the fae touch you, they can make you do things you never would—and you can't stop them. And the worst part is that it's almost impossible to tell if someone is human or not. The monsters have the power to make themselves look like anyone they want, wearing a glamour that hides who they truly are.

The fae are tricky like that. They treat humans like toys, playing with us, twisting the truth, crossing all boundaries to get permission for a touch that steals half of who you are.

Six years ago, I was blamed for the fire that killed my sister. I didn't set it—I *know* I didn't—but that didn't mean a damn thing when I finally broke down and admitted the truth about the fae. That they've followed me all my life, waiting for me to trip and offer them my hand.

Just like this tech wants me to do right now.

I made that mistake once. The golden-haired, golden-eyed fae male who convinced me that I could trust him minutes before he started the fire. Even though I knew better—I'd been coached, I'd been taught, I'd been trained better—he came so close to stealing more than a touch.

At the last second, I found the courage to tell him no, that I wouldn't follow him wherever he led. He punished me for my refusal. Me and Madelaine. I said no, she didn't, and the world as I knew it went up in flames.

My doctors spent years convincing me that the fae don't exist. Logically, I know they can't. Mythical, ethereal creatures from another world who are interested in me, a twenty-year-old orphan in the middle of nowhere? Logically, I know I created my imaginary friend, the fantastical world of Faerie, and a set of intricate rules to follow as a way to work through the abandonment issues I've dealt with since my mom disappeared when I was a baby.

The meds are supposed to help. The sessions with my therapists, my case manager, the doctors... they're supposed to help. They usually do. I can go months without feeling like I'm being watched, or worrying that the golden-eyed fae male will find me again.

And then someone tries to touch me and it all comes crashing down.

I'm not crazy. I'm not broken. I just believe in beautiful monsters who are willing to do anything they can to get their hands on me—even burn down a house with me and my sister inside of it.

The tech reaches for me.

Hell *no*.

My skin crawls as I scoot away, my back slamming into the side of the couch. I might have gloves to protect my hands, but what about my neck, my throat, my chin? Nope. I don't know her.

I won't let her touch me.

I *can't*.

The tech hovers, hand outstretched, visibly confused. She doesn't know what to do. I almost snap at her to leave me alone, though I manage to keep my mouth shut when I see Amy step into the day room.

She's carrying a tray of drinks. Water, iced tea, juice. Some mid-morning refreshments for our downtime. Her eyebrows lift when she reads the scene. Without losing any of her usual charm, she calls out, "Is everything alright in here, Diana?"

The blonde technician rises from her crouch. "Just checking on one of the patients."

Amy's soft brown eyes land on me. Understanding dawns in an instant and she nods. While she places the tray of drinks down on an empty table, she says, "Riley, let's get up off of the floor, okay? You'll stretch your gloves out if you lay on them like that."

My gloves. Amy knows exactly what to say. I value my gloves more than anything else I own. Every Christmas Mrs. Everett buys me a new pair of gloves to cover my hands. I work so hard to soften the leather, molding them to my fingers like they're a second skin.

It's only June. Who knows if I'll get a new pair in December? I have to make these last.

Besides, I know Amy. Amy, she's safe. She gestures for Diana to back off—*finally*—giving me enough space to awkwardly climb back to my feet. It takes a few seconds for the dizziness to pass. When it does, I exhale roughly.

I feel better now.

After I wipe the palms of my dusty gloves against my pants, I slip back onto my spot on the sofa. With Dean gone, there are at least three feet separating me from Kim.

"Better?" asks Amy.

I nod.

And that's it. It's over. A peek out of the corner of my eye reveals that Diana is still looking at me curiously. Since I don't want to face her right now, I turn so that I can watch Amy take a spot next to the table where she set down the drinks. Her trusty clipboard is tucked under her arm. She pulls it out, flips the page, then clears her throat.

"In a few minutes, I'm going to let you guys come up and get some refreshments. It's Sunday, so we'll be doing some group therapy in the day room in a bit, but first I've got a quick announcement so listen up, okay? We all know that Dr. Waylon left, right?"

A couple of people vocalize their answers. I just nod. I liked Dr. Waylon. She didn't push. I was sad to see her go, though I long ago lost track of which number psychologist she was. Ninth? Tenth? Something like that.

"Good. Well, I'm happy to announce that her replacement is finally ready to take over. And, even though it's Sunday, he's decided he wants to get a jump on meeting with you guys. As the oldest group, this ward is up first."

There's a chorus of groans, me included. It's never fun when we get a new doctor because they always insist on opening up old wounds, then digging around inside of them. Even though they're all given our case files when they start at Black Pine, the doctors want to hear it straight from us. And, well, there just comes a point when I'm sick and tired of telling them that, despite all evidence otherwise, I really don't belong in here.

If they understood that the fae were real, they'd realize that everything that has ever happened to me—everything that I've ever done—is a direct reaction to *them*.

Too bad every single doctor, therapist, psychologist, whatever I've met with since I've been locked inside the asylum is convinced that my belief in the fae is one of the biggest clues that I *do* belong at Black Pine.

After a while, I just gave in and agreed with them. The fae aren't real, I've got no one to blame but myself for Madelaine's death, and my insistence that no one can touch me is an irrational phobia, not the result of being taught otherwise since I was a little girl.

Two weeks, three days, and a couple of hours.

I can do this.

As the groans die down, Amy purses her lips. She looks genuinely sorry for us. "I know, I know. But let's all be on our best behaviors, okay?" When no one answers, she sighs. "*Okay, guys?*"

I'm feeling a little grateful for the way she helped me a few minutes ago. "Right."

A couple of others half-heartedly agree with me.

Amy smiles. "That's better. Now, for those the new doctor wants to meet..."

Glancing down, she consults her clipboard. I wait for what I know is coming. I give her three names before she says mine.

"Martin."

The pyro. Makes sense.

"Whitney, you're after Martin."

Whitney might have a flair for the dramatic and a tendency to whine, but she's also been on suicide watch three separate times since she switched wards last summer. The techs keep a close eye on her. So do the doctors.

"Allison."

I hope the new doc is multilingual or good luck getting anything out of Allison. On her good days, she might humor you by speaking in English, but having her answer in French or German or even Japanese is almost as likely. I think it's really cool how she knows so many languages, too. We're only a couple of months apart in age and we've moved through the asylum together. She's not my friend, not really, but she did teach me how to say *fuck off* in like six different languages by now.

"And… Tai. The rest of you will meet with him on Monday or Tuesday."

Tai? That's… that's a surprise. Not that she calls out Tai. I mean, his anger issues are some of the worst I've seen since I've been inside. It's just that I was almost positive she was going to call on—

"Oops. Hang on a sec. Looks like I almost forgot one."

A post-it note is stuck to the top of her page, the bright yellow square noticeable against the printed sheet. She plucks it off, bringing it closer so that she can make out the scrawl. I gulp, already resigned.

Here it comes—

"Sorry, Riley. Dr. Gillespie wants to see you first, right after we finish up here."

Yeah. Of course he does.

CHAPTER 3

In the asylum, we get a different professional every couple of weeks. Someone's always leaving or switching floors—even me. I'm used to it by now.

And, no matter what floor I'm on, every single newbie finds their way to my ward sooner or later. I absolutely hate it, but I guess I'm used to that, too. They all want to stop and gawk, probably since I've gotta be the most infamous in-patient here.

And not only because of the fatal fire.

My first memory is of the footage from the day my mother abandoned me. I never knew her, don't remember my dad, so the ten minutes of grainy, black and white video from a bank's security camera is the closest I'll ever get to the family that didn't want me.

Each second is ingrained deep in my brain. The erratic driving as she pulls into view of the camera. How she throws open her door before hopping out of an older model car. She rushes forward, talking to a patch of empty air toward the edge of the screen. It seems as if she's having an intense discussion with nobody; the camera didn't have sound so I'll never know what she said. A few minutes into it, a gas attendant appears, then leaves her alone.

It gets a little... a little *weird* after that. The footage captures her running back to the idling car, taking an infant—one-year-old Riley—from the back seat, before letting her crawl around for a few seconds in the dirt. She scoops the baby back up, gestures wildly at nobody again, then returns the baby to the car in time for the attendant to re-approach her.

I don't think she had any idea that the camera was there. Or maybe she did. Either way, she keeps her back to it most of the time as if hiding her face. Watching the footage, there are a few different angles that help me create an image of her in my mind. She was an average height, slim, with a sheet of pale hair cascading down her back. She kinda looks like me, though that might just be wishful thinking on my part. No one knows for sure that that woman was really my mom—how could they when neither one of us was ever identified?—but the older I got, the more I saw the resemblance.

Plus, the Shadow Man told me it was. Imaginary friend or not, I believed him—until he abandoned me, too.

I don't know her name. I don't know where she came from. Cops don't, either. The footage wasn't clear enough for them to figure out who she was. And no one ever came forward to report either of us missing.

The car she left behind? It had been stolen on the same day she disappeared. The only things she kept inside were me in my car seat, a half-packed diaper bag, and an iron crowbar. When I got older—when I learned the truth about the fae—I wondered if the iron was a clue that they were involved. The Shadow Man assured me that my mother was a human and, because of that, the fae weren't interested in her. But then he would never tell me why they were after me...

Still, that sucked to hear. I liked the idea that my mother had no choice but abandon me in an old, run-down gas station. I didn't want to think that she *chose* to leave me.

She did, though. Leave me, I mean. It's right there in black and white. She heads out of one frame, appearing in another as she walks away from the car. There was a side door that led to a bathroom. She goes inside. A few minutes later, the gas attendant marches over there and follows her in.

Neither one of them appears in the footage again. When the bank manager found me the next morning on her way to open up, there was no sign of my mother anywhere. The gas attendant, either.

No doubt in my mind that *he* knew about the cameras. He was extremely careful to keep his face hidden, even going so far as to wear a cap to cover it up. He was just as much a mystery, especially when the cops discovered he didn't even work there.

He *couldn't*.

The gas station closed down the year before I was born.

So whether he meant to hurt my mother or they planned it together, the undeniable truth was that two people went into that bathroom, no one left—at least, not according to the footage—and I was left to fend for myself outside of a gas station when I was barely a year old.

The papers caught wind of the story. Back then, they called me Baby Jane Doe and my picture was everywhere. Didn't help. No one came forward with any information about me. They didn't seem to know who I was, where I came from, or how two people could enter a single bathroom and disappear without a trace. I had no family, no name, no record. Neither did the woman.

I was the biggest news story in Black Pine for the rest of that summer.

Hundreds of people called in, wanting to adopt the poor, abandoned, mystery baby. The news ran nightly segments at first, then weekly, all trying to make sense out of something so damn senseless.

They never did, and eventually I became yesterday's news.

I'm what happens when the cameras turn off and the cops run out of leads. Baby Jane was a nuisance, her mother an escape artist who didn't want her kid. In the end, I got tossed into the system. I only managed to break out of it when I got put in the asylum.

It's always amazed me that my story started in that backward little town and, fifteen years later, this is where I ended up again.

My first foster family gave me a name—Riley Thorne—and a birthdate—the day I came to live with them. They were a nice couple and they tried their best to shield me from the truth of it all. I don't blame them for trying. Or giving me up five years later when it became clear that I wasn't like other little girls.

Name stuck, though. That's something, at least.

I've always liked Riley better than Jane, anyway.

DOCTOR GILLESPIE IS NOT WHAT I'M EXPECTING.

He's younger than I thought he'd be, for one thing. Thirty, maybe thirty-five. A babyface. White guy with pasty skin. His short hair is a brassy red that clashes with the green and gold plaid button-down shirt he's got on. Bright blue eyes shine from behind a pair of gold-rimmed glasses. He even has a small goatee covering a pretty weak-looking chin.

He stands up and comes around his desk to meet me, holding out his hand.

I don't take it.

"Ah... that's right." His voice is nasal, like he has a cold or something. "I remember that from your file. The haphephobia."

My hands clench inside of my gloves. I *hate* that word.

"I don't like to be touched," I tell him, not bothering to hide my scowl. "That doesn't mean I'm afraid of it."

"Let's call it a poor choice of words on my part then, shall we?" Getting the hint, Dr. Gillespie pulls his arm back, folds his fingers into a fist, absently rubs the side of his pressed khakis, then gestures for me to step into his office. "Come on in, Riley. Take a seat."

I have half a mind to pretend that I'm not Riley. Something else I hate? How all of the doctors and the techs act like they know everything about me when they wouldn't even be able to pick me out of a line-up unless someone else pointed out who I was beforehand. Just because I'm the first patient Amy sent to see him, that doesn't automatically make me Riley Thorne.

And that's when I remember the whole haphephobia exchange. Yeah, I totally gave my identity away when I refused to shake his hand. Plus, the leather gloves stretching past my wrists are probably a pretty big clue, too.

He's got me.

Annoyed, I ask, "Where?"

"Excuse me?"

I wave at the three seats haphazardly positioned in front of his cluttered desk. Every flat surface in the room is completely covered: mountains of books, folders, reams of paper, half-packed moving boxes. It looks like a bomb went off in here.

This used to be Dr. Waylon's office. Before that, Dr. Froud. Dr. Calvin, too. Dr. McNeil. None of the real big doctors—the ones who have convinced themselves they can fix… no *rehabilitate* us wayward juveniles—seem to stick around Black Pine for long. I swear, it's like every time I'm finally getting used to one, it's time for them to leave. And then the next shrink wonders why my abandonment issues never get any better.

I've lost track of how many people have occupied this corner office. Each one left their stamp while they used it, but it was always clear it belonged to a medical professional. This disaster? You could've fooled me. This is definitely the messiest it's ever been. Boxes are stacked everywhere, all in different stages of being unpacked. One of his diplomas is hanging crookedly behind the crowded desk. The desktop is covered with manila patient files.

Dr. Gillespie's cheeks turn the same color as his hair. Mumbling an apology under his breath, he swoops down and clears the seat closest to me. His arms full, he turns in a circle before moving his pile next to the filing cabinet by the window.

"Don't mind the mess," he says with an awkward laugh. "The facility director thought I was going to start tomorrow, but I wanted to do an informal session with a few of you juveniles since I arrived a couple of days early. I had hoped to be moved in before they started but I guess we'll both have to make do."

Once his arms are free again, he motions for me to take my seat. I do, perching my gloved hands royally on the arms of the chairs as soon as Dr. Gillespie slumps into his seat behind his desk. My back is straight, my gaze locked on the nervous doctor. I don't break eye contact, purposely watching him the way a cat would watch a mouse.

I think I'm making him uncomfortable. His face is now the color of a firetruck.

Good.

He's the one who wanted this session. He wanted to see

what Riley Thorne was made of. And, except for how vulnerable I get during my panic attacks, I'm made of stronger stuff than any of my doctors ever expect.

Okay, then.

Let's go.

Clearing his throat, squirming a bit under my direct stare, Dr. Gillespie attempts to regain control of our meeting. He flips open a notepad and picks up a pen, tip to the paper, ready to write down anything he finds interesting.

Not if I can help it.

"Now, Riley," he says, "how are you feeling today?"

Standard question. I have to answer it at least five times a day from five different people.

I give him my standard response. "Feel fine."

"How's your mood?"

I shrug. "Okay, I guess."

"That's good."

I don't have any idea how he can make sense of his mess, but he does. Picking one manila folder out from a stack of ten, he opens it up and begins to rifle through all of the papers inside. The stack is at least half an inch thick.

I can only imagine what my other doctors have written about me on those sheets.

Dr. Gillespie grabs his pen, scribbles something on a middle page, then closes the whole folder. He rests his hands on top of it. "I'll be honest. I'm sure you know that I've already gone over your file. Still, I'd rather hear it from you. Tell me, Riley. Why are you at Black Pine?"

My jaw goes tight.

Why am I at Black Pine? It's bad enough that I'm forced to admit the reasons why I'm here every morning during community group. Why does he need me to say it? He has the answer at his fingertips.

My first instinct is to snap that I'm a wayward juvenile. Black Pine's full name is a bit of a joke inside, especially among the older crowd. What the hell is that supposed to mean? Wayward juvenile? I guess it's better than saying it's a psych ward for kiddies, right?

And they wonder why we all just call it the asylum.

I don't say that, though. Instead, I fiddle with the edge of my glove, pulling on it, stretching out the leather. Under my breath, I mutter, "I'll give you a hint. It's not haphephobia."

He hears me.

"Fair enough."

Okay. His easy comment catches me off-guard. With Dr. Froud, a flippant comment like that would have earned me a ten-minute lecture on respect. Respecting him, respecting me, respecting the facility, respecting my diagnosis.

He was a bore, let me tell you. I was glad when Dr. Waylon finally replaced him.

Dr. Gillespie's glasses slide down his narrow nose as he looks over at me. He shoves them up, but not before I can see the earnest look in his eyes. Oh, man. He's one of *those*. The type of doctor who thinks we can be friends, who thinks that he'll finally be the one to make me all better.

Wonderful.

"I'm curious about the gloves, though," he says. "You want to tell me the story behind them?"

Do I want to?

No.

Do I know better than to push my luck with a new doctor?

Yup.

For one second, I think about taking my gloves off to make a bigger impact, then decide against it. I can barely stomach the blotches, the scars, the ruined skin myself—and they're *my* hands. I really don't like anyone else to see them. Dr. Gillespie is no exception.

Glancing down, I move my hands into my lap, running one hand over the other, grateful for the leather that protects them and hides them at the same time.

"I got burned really bad a couple of years ago," I explain. He's read my file. He knows exactly how I got burned, too. "I had to have skin grafts. When my hands finally healed, the doctors said I could keep gloves on if they felt too sensitive."

"That was in the accident," he guesses. "When your foster sister died."

That's how everyone here refers to it. The *accident*. It's better than what the courts called it.

The murder.

"Yeah," I admit, finally looking away from him. My last glimpse is of his impish face and the satisfied smile he wears.

It isn't a game, even if I treat my stay in Black Pine like that half the time. It makes the endless routine—the tiring monotony—more manageable when I do. But it isn't a game. Not really.

Even so, at that moment, we both know that Dr. Gillespie has won this round.

CHAPTER 4

I didn't do it.

You'd think after all these years that I wouldn't have to remind myself of the truth. As I step aside to let Martin enter Dr. Gillespie's office, my heart is thudding, my stomach tight. I didn't do it, but it's super hard to convince anyone of your innocence when you're an in-patient in a facility like Black Pine.

After a while, you give up on trying. Either the doctors believe you or they don't. Whatever. The only important thing is that *you* don't forget.

I didn't kill Madelaine. I couldn't. We might not have been blood, but we were still sisters. I never would've hurt her. My hands are destroyed because I tried to *save* her.

Despite what the papers first reported, the courts didn't really think I had anything to do with her death. If I did? It wasn't on purpose. During the autopsy, the medical examiner discovered that Madelaine had a broken neck. At fifteen, I was barely one-ten. I couldn't even open a pickle jar without Mr.

Everett's help. No way I could have done that to her on my own.

But the fire...

The fire is what made the cops, then the courts look at me like a suspect. And that's because I told them that it was a beautiful man—no, a beautiful *fae*—with long gold-colored hair and glowing golden eyes who started the fire *and* killed my sister.

He was the one who tricked Madelaine, charming her toward him, enticing her to give him her neck only for him to snap it easily. He's the one who built a circle around her body and set it on fire. The one who dared me to come and get her, who laughed as my hands burned.

He did it all. And then, my hands blistered, my throat raw from screaming, he vanished and I was left to take all the blame.

Kindly at first, then more firmly, everybody told me that I made him up. That he couldn't possibly exist—that the fae didn't exist—and I used this fantasy to explain the fire. The official statement was that I had a breakdown when I found that Madelaine had died in such a tragic accident. In my grief, I lit a fire as if I was trying to make it all go away.

Of course, then I went ahead and told them about Nine. I spoke about my Shadow Man in such great detail that they decided that my troubles started long before I was fifteen. I just didn't get a diagnosis until then.

Schizophrenia at first, until they settled on schizotypal personality disorder once I told them that, while I see and talk to the fae, I understand they're not *real*.

Anxiety with near-catatonic panic attacks.

And, no matter what I told Dr. Gillespie, just a touch of haphephobia.

That is why I'm here.

It's been a long six years. I learned early on that no one else believes in the fae so I started to pretend that I didn't, either. After a while, I wasn't pretending. So long as I take my morning meds, I'm fine. Sure, I lose it when I think someone might touch me, but that's just self-preservation. Better safe than sorry, right? Nine warned me not to let anyone touch me. So what if there's no Nine? That means the warning came from my own mind and, if there's one person in this world I can rely on, it's me.

I'm the only one who has never let me down.

As I head back toward the day room, my hands folded, gloved palm pressing against gloved palm, I let my thoughts return to Dr. Gillespie. Young guy, eager to prove himself.

I give him six weeks.

Art therapy is underway by the time I rejoin my group.

Because we need more space to get creative, we don't have art therapy in any of the smaller group rooms. We take over the day room, spreading out on the sofas and the chairs, using plastic tray tables and the kind of art supplies you see in pre-schools.

I'm gonna be twenty-one, and I still spend my weekends drawing with crayon.

Lucky, lucky me.

When I was younger, back when I was grouped in on some of the other floors, it was a little different. Black Pine has a program that works with the true juveniles, putting them through school, helping us prepare for real life when we're finally released. I got my GED by the time I was seventeen, and I went through all the prep courses. I know how to balance a checkbook, use a program to fill out my taxes, and I've even done mock interviews to prepare me for getting a job. When they let me out, I should be fine on my own.

There are more prep courses when you get moved to the final ward. Our group—nineteen through twenty-one—is all about getting prepared for release. One way or another, you age out of Black Pine at twenty-one. With a good report, they put you into a halfway house, help you transition on the outside. A bad one means moving on to another facility.

Yeah. No, thanks.

Like sessions and meetings with our counselors and social workers, those courses are scheduled on weekdays only. Weekends are considered downtime. Art therapy is a definite, just like extra television time if our ward's been good.

Because it's technically considered a group session, the television is off. With everyone hard at work, all I can hear is the muffled rubbing of crayons against paper, Dean's occasional muttering, and the therapist's constant stream of half-hearted encouragement.

After what happened this morning, I make sure to take one of the few open seats by the closed window. Water streams down the frosted glass; it's still raining hard out there. The therapist—a slender Asian man with short black hair and a kind smile—brings me a tray table, a few sheets of paper, and a handful of crayons.

He's been here before and he knows better. Instead of handing the supplies to me, he places them on an empty seat not too far from where I'm sitting.

"Thanks."

"We just started, Riley. Today's session is an easy one. I want you to draw something that's been on your mind lately. Turn your paper over when you're done, then we'll discuss your feelings at the close of today's session." He nods when I reach out, grabbing the tray table, slapping my hand on top of the crayons so that they don't roll right off. "Any questions before you begin?"

I shake my head. This is pretty common for art therapy. I know what to do.

Same rules as normal. Nothing morbid or gory. Nothing violent. Nothing that gives away the truth that some of us are kinda disturbed. Art therapy is supposed to be productive, yet positive.

We save our demons for the psychologists.

My drawing is a repeat, too. Choosing a grey crayon over white paper, I begin to draw the stone angel that watches over Madelaine's grave. She's never too far from my thoughts but, since my dream last night, she's been constantly on my mind. The meeting with Dr. Gillespie didn't help me even a little.

I don't plan on doing the whole end-of-session sharing time, though. No point. Most of the other patients have seen this same drawing before. Even if I refuse to talk about my sister, they all know what the stone angel means.

Oh, well. I gave up trying to convince them of the truth, too. Either they think I'm responsible for her death or they simply don't give a crap. It's not like it's their business, anyway.

I'm just adding the small chip that marks the stone angel's right wing when the quiet is broken up by the sound of someone crying. And not just *cry*, with sniffles and whimpers and barely-there tears. Nope. These are *sobs*. Big, wet, wracking sobs that start as a groan and end with a choking gasp for air.

My crayon slips from my hand. Like everyone else in the room, my head shoots up, searching for the sobber. I feel a twinge deep in my gut. I recognize it. It sounds like someone is in the middle of a panic attack—except, for once, it isn't me.

It's Carolina, the girl from the meds line this morning.

She's not too far from me, sitting on one of the sofas. Her tray table was perched on her lap. As I watch her sob, her body shakes and the table somehow falls. I could almost swear I saw her shove it away from her the instant before it dropped but, honestly, I'm not even thinking about that since the tray table bounces and her artwork flutters and lands a few inches away from my feet.

Not gonna lie. Since it's Carolina, I'm expecting to see like a mirror or a supermodel or something like that drawn on her paper. I remember, last time the therapist told us to draw up something that we wished for, she drew a plate of food.

I'm not wrong. In the center of the page, Carolina used the black crayon to draw a very tall, very skinny figure with long hair. Two dots—grey—must be her eyes. A red blob is attached to the figure's hand. An apple? Maybe. It does have a thin brown line drawn on the top, almost like a stem.

I don't know why the drawing would set her off. It seems innocent enough to me. But the rest of the paper is blank and Carolina is still crying.

The therapist rushes over, swooping the paper off of the floor as if he also figures this drawing is the reason behind her outburst. Folding it into quarters, he hides it from sight before settling next to Carolina, talking softly, trying to calm her down.

Good luck.

It's pointless. The entire group gives up on their drawings, watching as Carolina dissolves further into inconsolable sobs; I know I'm not alone in being glad it's not me who's lost it this time. I'll give the therapist credit, too. He tries his best to get her to explain her reaction but, in the end, he gestures for one of the techs to take over.

Louis retrieves Carolina, ushering her out of the day room and down the hall. We all listen as her sobs die down, not because she's gotten over it, but because she's gone far enough away to keep being an interruption.

Too late for that.

By the time she's gone and the art therapist has regained control over our group, the hour is up. I'm kinda glad.

Even though I'm not quite done with my picture yet, I turn the paper over so that I don't have to look at Madelaine's angel.

WE'RE SUPPOSED TO GET OUR NIGHTTIME MEDS FROM THE NURSING station. Not me. I've always been one of the only exceptions.

That night, after dinner, I don't go back to the day room with the other kids. Back when I first came to live at Black Pine, I used to have this really weird habit of sitting in the corner and talking to the shadows that played out on the wall before they got my meds regulated. Now, just in case, I get more quiet time than most.

I blame Dr. McNeil. Smartass. He's the one who decided it would be better if I went straight to my room at night where, if I start to talk to the walls again, at least I don't rile up the other kids.

Amy's my morning tech; her shift is over at six. The earliest I go back to my room is seven so that means I have to deal with a nighttime tech. Of course, they don't trust a tech to bring the meds to our rooms. Duncan, my regular nighttime tech, makes sure to accompany whichever nurse is on duty. She brings the meds, while the big goon stands guard, making sure that I behave and take my pills.

Tonight's nurse is Nurse Stanley.

Nurse Stanley is a sour-faced woman in her early fifties who is nearly as thin as Carolina. She has a perpetual frown and hands that look like claws. Her bleached-blonde hair is pulled back so tight that her eyes seem to bulge out of her head. She reminds me of a frog that's been starved for too long.

She even sounds like she's croaking when she says it's time for my meds. I can smell the smoke that clings to her uniform. At least that explains the croaking—though I still like my version better.

Duncan looms in my doorway, his back to the hall, massive arms slapped across his wide chest. He's so tall and bulky, he barely fits. I resist the urge to roll my eyes. The way he stares me down is overkill. I'm probably the least likely escape risk in the entire ward, yet he always insists on watching me like I am.

Nurse Stanley carries a small plastic tray with two dixie cups on it, just like normal. She holds out one of the cups, pinching the bottom with two fingers, and says, "Three pills tonight, Thorne. Two white and a pink. Dr. Gillespie put the order in himself."

Nurse Stanley is used to my haphephobia. There's no chance of an accidental touch when she leaves the top of the cup free for me to grab.

Taking the cup from her, I peek inside. She's right. I poke the little pink one with the tip of my glove. It's new—and that's different. I haven't had a med change since they took my blue pill away.

That one wasn't so bad. Whenever I saved a couple to take at once, they made me feel like I was floating on a cloud.

I wonder what the pink pill will do before realizing it doesn't matter. I don't plan on taking it tonight.

Before Nurse Stanley starts to get impatient, I toss the contents of the cup in my mouth. Practice makes it easy to stick the two white pills behind my upper molars. The pink pill is so small I nearly swallow it. I manage to slip it underneath my tongue just in time.

I drink the water from the second cup carefully. As the tablets melt, the taste is really awful, but I don't give it away on my face. Once I've drunken enough, I make sure to open my mouth and show Nurse Stanley that my meds are gone.

She grunts and takes my water cup back. "Lights out at ten, Thorne."

I give her a tight-lipped smile and wait for her to leave. I've suspected for a while that she knows I don't always take my nighttime meds—too bad she can't prove it. Honestly, I'm not so sure that she'd give a crap either way. And it's not like I do it all the time. Only when it's Nurse Stanley, and even then so occasionally that she hasn't had the chance to catch me at it yet.

It's just... I can't stand how my sleeping pills make me feel. I don't dream when I'm doped up, and they leave me feeling hazy, lost, and stupid when I wake up the next morning. So what if I miss a dose or two? At least I take my morning meds religiously.

I'm not so stupid that I spit the pills out right away. Sometimes Nurse Stanley comes back or she might send Duncan in to see if I need anything before they lock me in for the night. I count to fifty before I figure the coast is clear.

I pluck the three pills from their hiding places and stash them in the toe of my slipper with the rest of my supply.

And if the bottom of the slipper is crusted with dried, caked-on mud? I pretend not to notice before tucking my slipper under my bed again.

CHAPTER 5

I'm just falling asleep when I hear it. My name. Whispered as softly as a breeze drifting through the night's sky, I swear I hear someone say my name.

"Riley."

My door is locked. I have no phone. No radio. No television. The walls are so thick, there's not even an echo whenever Emma screams at night and, on her bad days, she has some awful dreams.

I shouldn't be able to hear a damn thing—

"Riley."

—and then I hear it again.

I almost stop breathing. It catches in my throat, my heart starting to race so fast—beat so loud—that it almost drowns out the inexplicable whisper. Inside my gloves, my hands grow clammy, slick with a sudden sweat. There's no way I should have heard that, I'd only be proving everyone in Black Pine right if I admit that I did, but I can't... I can't *deny* it.

That voice? The one I shouldn't be hearing?

It's eerily familiar, a voice I know all too well.

Even if I haven't heard him call my name in almost forever.

"*Riley...*"

It's a mistake to open my eyes. The room is dark; I can barely make out anything. A weak stream of light fills the gap between my door and the floor. Between that and the faint, hazy moonlight breaking through the almost purple cloud cover, inky, black shadows bounce off of the end of my bed. Anyone could be hiding in my room and hell if I'd know. I'm as good as blind and, suddenly, I wish I hadn't realized that.

I squint. "Hello?"

My voice comes out strangled. Unsure. A second later, I'm not positive I said a word at all.

Nobody answers. *He* certainly doesn't.

I pull my thin blanket up, kissing my chin while keeping my eyes narrowed at the darkness. My attention is yanked toward the far corner of my room. Where the two walls meet, the shadows are deeper than they should be. It's not just dark there —it's pitch black.

And that's when I see it.

Call it my overactive imagination, wishful thinking, or a trick of the shadows. Whatever it is, I'm still staring when I catch a flash of silver from the dark depths. Silver—

The Shadow Man had eyes of silver.

That's it. I'm not going through this shit again. Gulping, I close my eyes so tightly that I create bright sparks dancing across the inside of my eyelids. My heart skips a beat, my fingers trembling as I slip my left hand over the edge of the bed. I lean over, searching the floor.

Where is it? Where— *there.*

My slipper is right where I left it.

Desperate times call for desperate measures. I don't even

care which ones I grab. Scooping a couple of pills from my stash, I fumble in my self-imposed darkness, managing to toss them into my mouth after a few false starts.

With the memory of that silver flash fresh in my mind, I swallow the pills dry.

Anything to go to sleep right now.

"Tell me about Madeline, Riley."

At Dr. Gillespie's opening comment, I stiffen.

He's just going straight for it, isn't he?

Normally, I would brush him off. Every single one of my doctors, my psychiatrists, my counselors, and my psychologists learn before long that there are two topics that guarantee I'm gonna clam up: my mom and Madelaine.

Thing is, I'm still kinda shaky from last night, from the voice I shouldn't have heard and the wave of fear that hasn't quite subsided yet, so when Dr. Gillespie mentions Madelaine so easily, all I can mutter is, "You're saying it wrong. Her name was Madelaine. And there's nothing more to tell."

Dr. Gillespie nods, then makes a note on the upgraded journal lying flat on his desktop.

It's Monday. I have a session with Dr. Waylon first thing on Mondays and, now that she's gone, I get to spend the hour with Dr. Gillespie instead. My routine at Black Pine is simple enough: three sessions a week with my psychologist, and daily check-ins with any of the available psychotherapists. As annoying as it was, yesterday's meeting with Dr. Gillespie counted as a check-in.

This is my first real session. He wasted no time at all before asking about Madelaine. That's better than talking about my diagnosis, I guess. Considering my dreamless sleep and my sinking suspicion that my auditory hallucinations might have started up again, it's safer to keep the discussion centered on Madelaine.

Of course, I'm not about to offer up any information myself. Everything he needs to know about my sister or me is in my file. If he wants more, he's going to have to drag it out of me.

Something's different about the doctor today. Despite how heavy my head feels, how the whole world seems fuzzy and hazy to me, I immediately picked up on the change. Maybe it's because of his office. It's in a much better state. The desk is orderly, clean and organized, and the few boxes that aren't unpacked yet are stacked neatly in one corner.

Dr. Gillespie's definitely more prepared this session. Glancing at something written in his portfolio, he peers at me through his glasses while wearing a determined expression. "Let's start at the beginning. How long did you know her? She was the Everetts' first adopted daughter. Isn't that right?"

"Yup."

"And you were there for three years?"

"Two."

"So you knew Madeline—Mad*elaine*, sorry... you knew her for two years?"

I nod. No harm in admitting that. "Sounds about right."

"And you got along well with her?"

"Best of friends."

Dr. Gillespie raises his eyebrows, obviously intrigued by—or concerned with—my flippant attitude. I'm too tired to care. Plus, I've got way too much running through my mind to worry about pissing off the new guy. Jutting my chin at him, I dare him to keep asking me questions that I have no intention of really answering.

He purses his lips. "It's been six years since the accident. Do you miss her?"

Every single day. "Yes."

"Mmm. Are you sad that she's gone?"

"Of course I am."

He nods, picks up his pen. "Do you wish it was you instead? The one who died in the accident... do you wish it was you?"

Wow. He really went there, didn't he? With a snort, I turn my head. I'm not even gonna try to give him a half-assed answer to *that* one. It's a trick question. I say no and I have no remorse. I say yes and they put me on a watch. No, thanks.

But then he tosses out a question that has my head jerking so quickly, I nearly give myself whiplash—

"Why did you let her die?"

It's the *let* that cuts me to the bone.

It's one thing to accuse me of doing any of it. Setting the fire, making her fall—because that's how they explain away her broken neck. She was found in the basement of the empty house so, obviously, she fell and snapped her own neck. The accusations are nothing but background noise to me by now because I *know* I didn't do it.

That doesn't mean I'm not responsible. I am. If I hadn't let the fae male touch my hand, Madelaine would still be alive and there's nothing I can do to change that now.

And somehow this doctor I've known for like five minutes has picked up on it.

I'm on my feet before I realize how much his pointed question affected me. I thought I could do this. Meeting with another psychologist fresh to Black Pine... I thought I could do this like I've done a dozen times before. Nope. And maybe he's better than I thought. Maybe he did it on purpose, a shot in the dark that managed to hit home. I don't know.

But this is why I refuse to talk about my sister if I can get away with it.

My fingers flex. I need to feel leather wrapping my fingers, my palms, my wrists… I need the reassurance it gives me as my hands start to tremble and shake. I slap my palms against my sides, my gloves muffling the sound of the hit as I try to hide my reaction.

Yeah. That's easier said than done.

Dr. Gillespie's lips curve just enough to show how pleased he is at my reaction. Torn between anger, regret, and shame, I glare over at him. His eyes shine behind his glasses.

I want to smack that smug expression off of his face.

"What kind of question is that?" I snap back. "What kind of doctor would even *ask* something like that?"

In an instant, I know I've gone too far. Dr. Gillespie might be new, and he might be young, but he's a professional employed by the facility that runs my life. He's the one with the power.

And he knows it.

His whole face closes off as he points at my vacant seat. "Sit down, Riley."

I don't move.

The doctor raps his pen lightly against the top of his desk. "There's still plenty of today's session to go. Don't make me tell you to take your seat again."

His nasal voice goes sharp, straight to the point. There's a threat in there that he doesn't bother to hide, slowly reaching his hand out toward the old-fashioned handset phone perched on the right corner of his desk. With the press of one button, he could alert anyone in the asylum that I'm acting out.

I know exactly what will happen if I refuse to sit and he hits that button.

I have to listen. Last time I openly disobeyed one of the head doctors, they confined me to my room for three days with only my own distorted memories to distract me. They messed with my meds then, too. I got maybe six hours of sleep the entire time. I was a mess by the end of that suspension, though I can say I definitely learned my lesson.

So did my doctors. I got my blue pills back for that entire summer.

I sit down, though I'm not happy about it. Crossing my arms over my chest, I clamp down on my teeth so hard that it sends a shock of pain along my jaw. I fight to hide my wince. Dr. Gillespie sees it anyway.

Behind his gold-rimmed glasses, he sees everything.

To my surprise, his voice gentles as he says, "You made your point. You don't want to focus on Madelaine today? That's fine. I understand that. We have plenty of sessions ahead of us. We can table her for another time. Would you like that?"

So maybe he's being a little condescending. Whatever.

"Yeah." I force myself to relax, to let it go before the anger overwhelms me and my emotions take over. I'm still not over yesterday's panic attack, either, and that's clear. I shudder on a breath, making myself small as I lean back into my chair. I'll regroup in a second, ready myself for round two in a bit. Just... just not yet. I shake my head. "Yeah, I would."

"Okay. We can do that. I want you to know that I'm just here to help you, Riley."

Ugh. Now he sounds earnest.

Was I overreacting?

Possibly.

With a shrug, I tell him, "I know."

"Your sister is a delicate subject."

Yeah, that's putting it mildly. "Mm-hmm."

"What about Nine?"

And, just like that, any gratitude I worked up because he was willing to drop Madelaine vanishes at that one syllable. Because Nine? It's not just a number. Not to me.

It's a man.

The *Shadow Man*.

I blink, try to come up with a way to change the subject, then decide my best bet is to play dumb.

"Nine what?"

"Not what," corrects the doctor. "Who."

"I don't know what you're talking about."

"That was his name, wasn't it? Your... childhood friend?"

Is he serious? Good god. He's trying to be *delicate*.

I guess there's no point in pretending now. "Oh. Are you asking me about my first documented hallucination, Dr. Gillespie?"

Hallucination. That's how all of the adults in charge refer to him now. When I was a kid, my foster parents called Nine my imaginary friend. When I was old enough to know better, he became a hallucination.

To me, Nine was always just the Shadow Man.

My earliest memories involve Nine. Without a family of my own, he became the one constant in my life. He followed me from foster home to foster home, almost as if he could track me anywhere. He didn't always come to see me, though. Nine had his own life, his own responsibilities, and he could go weeks at a time between his sporadic visits. But when he did appear? It was as if no time had passed at all.

I don't know why I loved him so much. He was cold and he was distant. Firm. He had no patience for my tantrums, and he threatened to not come back whenever I begged for him to stay. That was just Nine, though. In his own way, he showed me how dedicated he was to me. Only visiting at night when the shadows came, vanishing long before the sun rose the next morning, he spent years teaching me, coaching me, taking care of me in the guarded way he had.

No mom. No dad. Nine was the only one I could count on until I made it to the Everetts and I bonded with Madelaine.

I don't want to talk about my sister. But Nine?

I can talk about Nine.

Before Black Pine, that would've been impossible. I mean it. Before I came to the asylum, I was so twisted up inside. I was convinced that the Shadow Man who visited me my entire childhood had to be kept a secret. Nine insisted on it. He warned me that, if I told anyone about him, there would be consequences.

I was a kid. What did I know?

So I blabbed, and he disappeared. I haven't seen him since I got tossed inside of Black Pine.

The doctors told me it was because they finally got my medications regulated. For the longest time, I was convinced it was because I spilled all of Nine's secrets at my hearing. Then I eventually accepted that he was just a figment of my imagination and I was glad that I banished him from my brain.

At least, I *thought* that he was gone for good. For the last six years, I worked with my psychotherapists, my techs, my mental health counselors, and my social worker to accept that Nine was nothing more than a figure in my mind.

So why did I hear his voice again last night?

No. Not going there.

Didn't hear a voice.

Nope.

Okay. Dr. Gillespie wants to talk about Nine? Sure. Fine. I'll talk about him. Maybe that will send the Shadow Man away again.

Two weeks, two days now, and a couple of hours before I'm

out of the asylum. This is not the time to imagine that Nine's back.

I rub my forehead, pushing my bangs out of my face. "What do you want to know about him?"

"Everything you can tell me. From the beginning. How far back can you remember him being around? What's your first memory of him?"

That's... that's an unusual approach. Most of my doctors feel like they have to convince me over and over again that Nine was never real. After a while, it sunk in—rational thinking tells me that there's no such thing as magic and the fae and an otherworld called Faerie where anything can happen.

Still, even all these years later, sometimes I ask myself: *what if*? What if it was all real? Nine and his shadows, and the golden-eyed fae with the power to control fire?

Is Dr. Gillespie doing the same thing? Seems like it. Who knows? Maybe this is some new form of therapy, humoring the patient, actually believing that their hallucinations and their delusions are true.

I decide to go for it.

"I was very tiny, three or four, or maybe even younger. I'm not sure—it's like he's always been there. He always came and sat with me in the nursery at the Thorne's house, singing strange songs to help me fall asleep." I don't mention that the songs weren't in any language I've heard since then, or that I would stay up and listen because having him near made me feel safe. "He didn't come every night. Didn't expect him to. Busy guy, but he always said someone sent him to watch over me."

I almost add that, when I was little, I used to think he meant my mom. I don't anymore. Like forgetting the threat of the fae, I long ago accepted that my mom never wanted me.

"Really?" He sounds surprised. "Three or four? That soon? And you remember it?"

And... we're back to my diagnosis again.

None of the professionals can believe that my symptoms manifested so early—or that it took until I was fifteen and Madelaine was dead before anyone took them seriously.

I clench my fists so tightly that my fingers are straining against my gloves, pulling the leather taut. "You'd be surprised at how far back my memory goes."

"What did he look like? Did he change his appearance over time or look the same?"

That's a pretty standard question. And a safe one.

"They can make themselves look however they want." Dr. Gillespie wags his pen at me, gesturing for me to elaborate. I shrug. "Black hair. He used to wear it short, then let it grow out some. Crazy silver eyes, like dimes or something shining out of his face. He was super pale, too." He was also the prettiest man I've ever seen in my life, but I don't tell the doctor that. Instead, grasping for something else to say, I add, "He looks exactly the opposite of the golden fae."

I regret the words almost as soon as they're out.

His hand twitches. The pen he was clutching slips from between his suddenly lax fingers. "Fae?"

Oops. My throat goes dry, the memory of that fae trying to push it's way through. I'll talk about Nine. But the monster? "I... I don't want to talk about that. Forget I said anything."

Dr. Gillespie is wearing that same knowing look from before. He's read my file. There's no way he doesn't know about the golden fae, a creature of fire and laughter and the power to make others do whatever he wants them to. Like how he lured Madelaine to him, or how he caused me to wear these gloves forever.

Nine is safe. I'm not afraid of him.

But the golden fae who promised to come after me?

I visibly shake.

Dr. Gillespie sees that, too. Aware that I'm so close to the edge, he backs off. "Then tell me more about Nine." When I don't argue, he pushes. "So your first memory is from very early on. What about your last? How often did he appear to you? What would he say?"

As someone who was initially diagnosed as schizophrenic before my personality disorder was pinpointed, these are the sorts of questions that I'm used to. I'm so relieved that he's letting the golden fae go without pressing me for answers, I willingly continue to discuss Nine.

Besides, I know what he's expecting from me. He wants crazy? I'll give him bonkers.

For the next twenty minutes I ramble on, telling the doctor everything I remember about Nine: from how he rarely strayed from the shadows, to the very clear warnings he gave about never letting anyone touch me. I probably just confirmed my haphephobia to Dr. Gillespie. That's fine. Like I told him before, I'm not afraid to be touched—not exactly. It's more like I was brainwashed from a very early age that if you let anyone with Faerie blood touch you, you give them power over you. A touch of your hand is like giving the fae permission to reach inside of you and steal part of your soul. For the magical race, that power is everything.

Madelaine's murderer proved that six years ago.

Logically, I know the fae can't exist. Deep down, I accept that they do—and that no one else will ever believe me. So I might as well keep on pretending.

It's a good thing it doesn't bother me when I lie—to the

doctors, the techs, or even myself—or my stomach would always be tied up in knots.

There's a strange look on Dr. Gillespie's face as I speak. His pen is still where he dropped it. I don't think he took a single note. He's peering at me closely, as if trying to figure out if I really believe any of what I just told him.

This is new to me, too. For once, I told one of my doctors the absolute truth, even if I stopped short of admitting that I heard Nine's voice for the first time in years last night. Let him think I'm lying. It's freeing to realize that I honestly don't give a crap what this man thinks of me.

I'm out in two weeks, two days, and a couple of hours. My release is already in motion. Unless I do something really terrible, I'm out in half a month.

When I'm done—when there's nothing left I want to share about the Shadow Man—Dr. Gillespie takes a deep breath. I don't think he knows what to make of any of that. We both gotta know that my file says I'm not a big talker mainly 'cause I have a hard time connecting to other people.

But that wasn't for Dr. Gillespie. That was all for me.

He waits another few seconds before he chuckles weakly. "Quite… quite an imaginative child."

"Yeah." I shouldn't feel this triumphant. "That's what each of my first four foster families said, too."

And the point goes to Riley this time around.

CHAPTER 6

I didn't always have to hide Nine. For most of my life, though, I did.

When I was little, barely a toddler, my first foster family —the Thornes—thought it was cute. Nine was the opposite of a bogeyman, someone who came to protect me instead of scaring the shit out of me. He told me stories, but he made a mistake in trusting that I would keep them to myself. Five-year-olds don't know how to keep secrets. And the Thornes didn't know what to do with a child who preferred the company of shadows.

I moved in with the Baxters next. He was... he was careful. When he found me—and he always found me—Nine made sure to come late at night, long after my new foster parents were asleep. I was so happy to see him again that I was willing to promise him anything. I kept him a secret for two years while he spent countless nights telling me about his home—about Faerie —and the race of people who lived there.

The Blessed Ones and the Cursed Ones. Despite the names, he warned me that neither of the fae were good—or to be trusted. And, most important of all, I should never, ever give one of them permission to touch me.

I was a kid. I didn't know better. Nine was my whole world. He told me how the fae could use glamour, one of their special magic tricks, and make it so they looked like a regular human. How was I supposed to know a real person from the bogeymen he put in my head?

I didn't.

I had my first full-blown panic attack in first grade when the gym teacher grabbed my arm and I wasn't expecting it. Shit hit the fan back then. In the end, the teacher was suspended, the Baxters couldn't handle my new condition, and they put me back in the system.

So then I got shipped off to the Morrisons.

They were a married couple of fiction writers. A little bit hippie-dippy, they both encouraged my imagination and even understood my pre-teen need for space.

Well, in the beginning they did.

I trusted them. I hoped they would be able to protect me from the fae during the day the same way that Nine did at night. Yeah, *no*. Not really. When I admitted there was a Shadow Man who visited me while they slept, telling me stories of Faerie and the fae, my foster parents thought I was a creative just like them.

When they found me hiding under my bed, looking for comfort in the shadows there, all because I swore that the neighbor's dog had eyes of fire and I was terrified it might be a fae in disguise, they started to get a little worried.

When I screamed bloody murder one night after Mr. Morrison tried to tuck me in, they decided I might just have too vivid of an imagination for them.

Nine followed me to the Wilsons, too. I was about twelve then. Older. More wary. I started to ask him questions—mostly about why he kept visiting me, but I tried to learn more about my mom, too—and never really got any answers from him. My hero worship was starting to wear off at that point. I remember telling him that he should leave me alone if he wasn't going to give me the answers that might help me protect myself. We had arguments—okay, *I* argued with *him*—but Nine wouldn't budge. All he would say was that it was his job to protect me.

He promised me that my keeping him a secret would help with that. He reminded me again that, if I told anyone about him, he might not be able to come back. And I was mad, so, so mad at him, but he was my lifeline. I didn't really want him to go. So I kept my mouth shut.

That is, I kept my mouth shut until the Wilsons heard me talking to myself the nights that Nine visited me. They knew my story, knew that I had some issues, and they were just waiting for something like this to happen. They threatened me with therapy if I didn't explain myself.

So I did. They sent me to therapy anyway. When the first doctor mentioned the dreaded "s" word—*schizophrenia*—the Wilsons sent me away so fast, I never even got to pack my room up.

Dicks.

It worked out for me, though. For a little while, at least. Because up next? The Everetts.

They were experienced foster parents. They'd already adopted a girl they had fostered—Madelaine—and Mrs. Everett was an ER nurse. The Everetts thought they might be the home I'd been looking for my entire life. My history didn't frighten them. They swore they would get me any help I needed. I believed them.

And that's why I purposely didn't tell them about Nine when he eventually found me in Acorn Falls.

I was a contrary teenager with abandonment issues. I know that's no excuse, and I probably should have confided in them the first time I heard Nine whisper my name from the shadows. But he'd been there for so long, my loyalty was to the Shadow Man before anyone else.

He warned me again that my silence was imperative. As I grew older, I was only becoming more and more vulnerable. For some reason, the fae were still hunting me; in answer to my incessant questions, he said I'd know why in time, just not yet.

Still, it was important for me to remember the power of the touch. If any of them got their hands on me, they'd charm me and possess me and that would be the end of my life as I know it.

Turns out, Nine wasn't wrong.

Not even a little.

I don't spend much time with the other patients. At first, it was because the doctors thought I would hurt them. Now? They're more concerned that I'll hurt myself.

I do get to spend breakfast with the others in my age group, and I have to participate in most of the group therapies: community group, which I hate, and recreational therapy, which is usually the best part of the day.

Today we're watching an old movie. It's in black & white and it has something to do with someone's missing bird. There's this hardass detective and some two-faced lady that even I can tell is bad news. I didn't think I would like it, even though Amy insists it's a classic, but it's pretty good.

It was actually getting kind of interesting when Amy angles the remote at the television, pausing the movie.

"Okay, guys. It's just about four o'clock. If you're expecting any visitors today, they're waiting for you in the meeting room. If you're not, then that's alright. You can stay with me and we'll watch the rest of the movie."

Ugh. My stomach drops. Visiting hour.

My least favorite hour of the whole day.

We have visiting hour daily, from four to five regular. It never changes. And since the facility's staff doesn't trust us to let any friends and family we might still have left into our ward, they designate an open room on the first floor for visiting hour. There are plenty of small tables and chairs set up down there so there's at least some semblance of privacy.

Not that it means anything to me.

Louis waits in the doorway. Nearly everyone in the group gets up and forms a line in front of him. Whether they know for sure that they're getting a visitor or they're just hoping, the others file out of the day room.

I don't. No point. I know there's no one out there for me.

Not anymore.

When I first got tossed into Black Pine, the Everetts would come to visit me from time to time. They moved away from Acorn Falls after the accident and now live in a city that's about six hours away by car. They couldn't visit me every day, but they tried to make it once a week to show me that they weren't giving up on me. With Madelaine gone, I was all they had left.

Of course, it didn't last long. Once a week turned into once a month until I noticed that Mr. and Mrs. Everett started to take the trip separately. About two years into my stay, I found out they had gotten divorced. The strain of Madelaine's death, plus my institutionalization, was just too much for them.

Before long, Mr. Everett stopped coming at all. The last time Mrs. Everett visited me, three Christmases ago, I pleaded with her to stop. It's bad enough I'm the reason they lost their child. It kills me that I'm to blame that they lost each other, too.

Mrs. Everett is a saint. I still get an occasional letter, not to mention gifts for my birthday and Christmas, and I'm good with that.

It's way more than I deserve.

Only two out of the twelve of us stay behind: me and Meg. That's not so new. Meg had visitors for a while, but a few months ago she stopped going down with the techs. I don't know why. I've never asked.

Amy waits until they're all gone to pick up the remote again. "You ladies want to finish the movie?"

I want to know who killed who. "Yeah."

Meg doesn't say anything. Since she doesn't shake her head no, Amy takes it as a yes. She turns the movie back on.

Out of the corner of my eye, I peek over at Meg. I don't know her story too well. Everybody inside has their quirks and their issues. Meg? She's mute. Everything I've learned about her is from the gossip that spreads from group to group, ward to ward. I heard that she was in a real bad accident with her brother and sister. She was the only survivor, but it messed her up. Physically, she's fine. That's why she's here with us instead of a regular hospital. She *could* speak, she just doesn't want to.

I get that.

It used to be me and Meg and Jason who stayed behind in the day room during visiting hour. He's still not around. I vaguely wonder for the second time what's happened to him.

But then the movie starts to get interesting again and I forget all about everything else.

Knock, knock.

I glance up from the book I'm reading. I know I heard that knock, but I wasn't expecting it. I had only just climbed into bed after hurrying through dinner. I thought reading a book might distract me enough that, even if I start hallucinating again, I can ignore it. Besides, I've read this one before. It's pretty good.

I set it down. My door's not locked—we don't get that luxury—but we do get to pretend that we have some choice when we're in our individual rooms.

"Yeah?"

"We're coming in, Thorne. Time for your nighttime meds."

Ugh. I recognize that rasp of a voice. Duncan.

He's early, too. Sure, it's June, and I know that days are longer in the summer, but a quick glance past the bars on my window shows that the sun's still out. Weird. The nurses don't usually do the nighttime rounds until at least seven.

Oh, well. Could be that, since I turned in early, they decided to bring me my pills so they could get it out of the way. That's fine. I'm gonna take them, too.

I sure as hell don't want to dream tonight.

"Sure. Gimme a sec." After all these years, I know the drill. After I pull on my hoodie, tugging on my sleeves so that every bare inch of my arm is covered, I get up and move across the room. "Okay. Ready."

The door opens. Duncan peeks his head in, verifying that I'm not about to jump past him and make a break for it or something. Only once he decides that I'm not a risk will he step aside and let the nurse in while he watches over him or her.

At least, that's how he usually does it. Not tonight. For the first time ever, he goes against his normal routine. Instead of guarding the door like a bouncer, he strolls right into my room. He's not alone, either.

Long, blonde ponytail. Pale blue scrubs.

It's the tech from Sunday. Diana.

What's she doing here?

It doesn't make any sense. She's just a tech. Besides, it's Tuesday. Knowing my schedule and sticking to it is one of the things that keeps me sane inside of Black Pine. Just like how I know that Amy is off on Wednesdays and Saturdays so that Penelope is my main morning tech, I know which nurse to expect on Tuesday nights.

"Where's Nurse Stanley?"

"She's busy," answers Duncan. "We have the okay to give you your medications today."

My gut goes tight. It feels like someone twisted it up in a knot, grabbed both ends, and pulled. I *hate* this feeling. Even worse? I know exactly what caused it.

Duncan just lied to me.

"Are you sure about that?"

He nods. I'm watching him closely now, and I notice that something... something's really not right. His dark eyes are glazed over and he's wearing this crooked smile that doesn't seem normal. And maybe it's because I don't think I've ever seen Duncan smile before... I don't know. It's creepy, though, and I know he just lied to me again.

Diana approaches Duncan. She taps him on the shoulder and he crouches enough to allow her to whisper something to him. The big man nods. A second later, he disappears, leaving me alone with the blonde tech.

That's worse. I'm not sure why, but it seems worse. And there's nothing I can do about it.

I'm still not comfortable around her. She makes my fingers itch. I want to back up further, duck into the shadowy corner. I keep getting this feeling like she's about to reach out and grab me or something. She won't have my permission, but I don't think that would stop her.

I sidle along the wall at my back, watching her as she turns to smile over at me.

Just like my nighttime nurses always do, she's carrying a tray with two cups. She picks one up, her smile never wavering. If she notices how I'm slowly moving away from her, she doesn't give any sign of it. She just holds the cup out toward me.

I take it. I have no choice. I snatch the cup out of her hand, careful not even to brush her skin with the edge of my glove. Then, once I've put space between us again, I look inside.

There's only one pill in the cup.

I blink. Nope. Still just one.

"Where the rest?" I ask.

I look down at the pill again. Yikes. I've never seen anything like it before. It's a horse pill, as big as a nickel, with a yellow center that looks wrong. The rest of the pill is white and speckled with green. It kind of reminds me of this mint Madelaine used to love. It definitely doesn't look like any sort of medication I've ever seen before.

I shake my head and offer it back. "Yeah, no. I'm not taking this."

"Oh? Is that so?" Diana's laugh is sickly sweet. "You'll take anything I tell you to."

I gasp—and it has nothing to do with what she just said to me.

Her eyes are hazel. I remember from Sunday. When I was on the floor of the day room, when she was trying to help me stand, I looked her in the eyes. They were hazel.

They're not anymore.

Now? They're a vivid, shining shade of gold.

There's no time for me to ease into one of my panic attacks. What happens next? This is full-blown hysteria.

I can't stop myself. As if I'm thrown back to the horrible afternoon when Madelaine died, I lash out. Totally out of control. I toss the cup, jamming the heel of my slipper against the pill. When it doesn't even break, I lunge forward, slapping the tray out of her hand.

Then, because I'm not even thinking a little bit, I back up, irrationally seeking the corner on the far side of my room. Once my back slams against one side, I wedge myself into the corner. In the back of my mind, I realize that all I did was trap myself even more—and Diana is watching me with those eerily familiar golden eyes.

I have to get out. I start banging on the wall.

I'm screaming, too. Don't know if I'm making sense or if it's just noise. The only thing I'm worrying about is how I'm going to get the hell away from Diana and her gold-colored eyes. The leather slaps against the wall, my right slipper flying off my foot as I flail. I need her to get back. I need her to stay away from me.

I crack the back of my head against the wall. The screams turn into screeches.

Duncan comes running in. He's certainly not smiling now. Head bowed, his body like a running back's, he leads with his shoulder, picking me up as easily as if I was a rag doll. Hell, I'm probably more of a rag doll than a living, breathing woman. I'm useless. I can't do anything except scream my lungs out, begging someone, anyone to save me from her.

It only gets worse when I realize that *Duncan is touching me.*

He tries to restrain me on my bed. I flop like a fish. He outweighs me by a good hundred pounds, but I'm fighting mad. He throws his weight around, pinning me down by my arms. I'm wild, but he has the leverage. I'm not going anywhere now.

I want to calm down. I really do. Except all I'm thinking about now is that he doesn't have my permission to touch me. He's making it all so much worse. Diana melts into the background as more and more people come pouring into my room.

Her eyes are still flashing gold.

I'm still screaming like a fucking banshee.

Over my shrieks, I can sort of make out Duncan's warnings. If I don't stop, he's going to get the straps. A white woman with wispy brown hair joins Duncan. That's the head nurse—Nurse Callahan—and she's trying in her no-nonsense way to organize the facility's staff. I'm still thrashing, trying to buck Duncan's weight off of me. When I feel another set of strong arms on my bare legs, I kick out with all of my strength.

I connect. I hear a sickening *crunch* when I hit someone. I don't know who. I'm in no state to give a shit.

The last thing I remember is the prick of the needle that one of the nurses plunges into my exposed calf. Even as I'm being sedated, the hysteria won't subside. All I want to do is calm down enough to warn the staff that the monster that killed Madelaine is in the room with us all—but I can't.

As the medicine courses through me, I can't do anything at all.

CHAPTER 7

"*Riley.*"

I hear my name. I know it's mine, even if there's a... a disconnect. Like, I know *I'm* Riley—but that's about *all* I know.

Where am I? It's dark and my head feels heavy. My body, too. It's almost like my arms and legs have been weighed down by something.

"*Wake up.*"

Am I sleeping? Makes sense. It would explain this woozy, weird feeling. Why fight it? I'll just lay here and sleep it off. Then, when I'm up again, I can forget the voice that's so clear and so close, it's like he's inside of my head.

"*Listen to me.*"

Is he still talking? I want to tell him no, that I don't want to listen to him, that I want him to go away, but I can't. My tongue is too thick in my mouth. I can't even screw open my jaw.

"*Open your eyes.*"

No. That's impossible, too. My eyes feel like they're glued shut. I could probably pry my lids open if I wanted to.

I don't want to.

"Riley..."

Stop saying my name.

"I've missed you." The voice turns soft. Cajoling. It's a beautiful voice, lilting, like a lullaby. Despite not wanting to listen to him, I can't help it. Peace settles over me as most of my worries, anxieties, and discomfort simply melt away. *"It's been far too long."*

Who is he? Why does he sound like he knows me? It's been far too long... Though it feels like I should know who he is, I don't know his voice. It's so pretty, though. Anyone who sounds like that can't be all bad.

Right?

Wrong.

So, so wrong.

I blink my eyes open. The first thing I notice is that I'm not in my room. I'm lying in a bed—but it's not my bed, either. The blanket is softer, thicker than the one I have at Black Pine, and the sheets beneath my back feel like silk. The walls are painted a soft yellow—not industrial white—and the window to my right is missing its bars.

The second thing I notice?

I'm not alone.

As my eyes slide over to find the owner of that lovely voice, fear comes rushing back, seizing control. I nearly choke.

Because there he is. The golden-eyed fae who killed my sister.

He's tall and unnaturally slender, just like I remember. From his side of the empty room, he looms over me, his shadow stretching out to cover the edge of this unfamiliar bed. His face… damn it, his every feature is breathtaking. Bronze skin, long golden hair, a body that would make an Olympic sprinter weep in shame.

He's beautiful, so angelically beautiful that I almost want to cry myself. In my mind, I always think of the golden fae as a monster. He doesn't look like one, though. He never has. It's his callous nature, his cold and capricious ways… it's how easily he killed Madelaine because I refused him… *that's* what makes him a monster.

Then there are his unnatural eyes—

His eyes are gold. Pure gold. They shine out from his face, his most mesmerizing feature of all. They're like two miniature suns burning bright as his lips curl in delight.

At first, I'm beyond terror. I'm so scared to see him standing there that I can't even scream. I'm paralyzed. Then I remember Diana had the same eyes as the ones set deep in his face.

The hysteria.

The sedation.

It's a dream.

No—a *nightmare*.

I shudder out a breath. Whatever he's doing here—no matter why I conjured him up during my drugged sleep—he can't hurt me and I *know* that.

Still, my voice shaky, I whisper, "It's you."

He holds out his hand. "Come to me."

Hell no. Not even in my dreams.

And it has to be a dream right now. I'm in an unfamiliar room with the monster from my memories and, while I know better than to get any closer to him, I'm not freaking out. Not really. I'm angry, sure, but also kinda calm. I've *got* to be dreaming. I mean, I have this hazy, vague feeling that I should be running, should be screaming, should be trying to escape—but I'm not. I'm just glaring over at this creature.

He's as terrifying as he is beautiful.

And then he shakes his head. His perfect lips tug into a frown.

He holds out his hand again.

"Zella. *Come.*"

I don't know what it is that he said. Not the part where he orders me to come to him like I'm a dog or something—that part I've got. But that first word? It seems familiar, almost like I should know it, the way it sings in my ears and settles in my soul. I grasp at it, trying to capture it, but it disappears before I get the chance.

Besides, I'm a little bit preoccupied with my body's strange reaction to his command.

I actually *obey* the fae.

I don't have any control over my actions. Like a puppet being manipulated by its strings, I rise from my lying position, my arms jerking wildly, my legs weak and wobbly. I swipe the blanket aside, then get to my feet. Once I'm standing, I try to dig in my heels. Doesn't work. Something is pulling me toward the golden fae—magic, charm, a compulsion—and it's too hard for me to fight against it.

I finally manage to break the spell when a precious few feet separate us. I shake my head, scrabbling backward so that he can't reach out and touch me. It won't stop him from striding closer, but I don't care about that right now.

I only care about the power he just showed me he has.

Though I can't tell you how he did it, I know his little display was on purpose. A calculated move to remind me that *he*'s in charge. That, despite every bone in my body refusing to willingly move toward him, he has the magic and the strength to command me to go to him—and I *did*.

That scares me more than knowing I'm in the same room as him.

I swallow back my frightened gasp. "What did you just do to me?"

"You made me do it." He can't deny it—we both know he was responsible for dragging me from my bed—but I'm not surprised to hear him blame me. Of course it's my fault. The fae are never wrong. "I need you to understand this. There's too much at stake here. I don't want to have to compel you to listen to me, but I will if you force my hand. Time is short and I've come for you as I promised."

He did. Six years ago, when he sacrificed Madelaine because I told him to leave us the hell alone, he promised that he would return. That he would come back for me.

In the safety of my dreams, I let myself think back. He might have control here—but he can't hurt me while I sleep. It's not how it works. It's not how any of this works. He can talk to me, he can show off his magic tricks, he can remind me of promises —of *threats*—that I've long since buried… and that's all.

The golden fae is the reason I allowed myself to accept that the fae were nothing more than an elaborate hallucination because I was mentally unwell. If I made them up, then I didn't have to worry about them chasing after me for the rest of my life. I wouldn't have to spend years looking over my shoulders.

I'd be able to forget his sworn promise that he'd come for me again one day.

And now he's here and, instead of panicking or closing my eyes to shut him out, I'm watching him closely, absolutely sure that he is as real as anyone else I've ever known.

I shake my head. "This can't be happening. You're not supposed to be *real*."

"And you're not supposed to resist me."

That's all thanks to Nine. If he hadn't warned me what the fae were capable of back when I was a kid, I would've been lost the first time I met this monster. I saved myself then—it was Madelaine who paid the price for the fae's interest in me.

And now he's back.

"Why? Why me? What do you *want* from me?"

"I've waited long enough. It's time that you become my *ffrindau*."

His *what*? It's another unfamiliar word in a strange, harsh accent that is at odds with his lyrical voice. I don't think it's English, but if it is? There's only one word that sounds like that that I know.

"Friends? You want me to be your *friend*? You've got to be fucking kidding me!"

His golden eyes flash. His lips curve as he peers down at me. The fae is wearing a... a hungry look that has me stepping away from him again.

That doesn't stop him. Honestly, I'm not sure if there's anything I could do to him that would.

He glides toward me. Everything about him is graceful, peaceful, lovely—but I know better. I'm staring up at a man-eater who doesn't know whether he wants to toy with me first, or go straight for the kill.

"Stay away from me." I throw my hands up in warning. "Back off— *whoa*."

As if I needed another clue that this has to be a dream, I get one when I see my hands.

My *bare* hands.

I'm not wearing my gloves. I *always* wear my gloves.

It's bright where we are. The light shines on my mottled skin. I marvel at the blotches, the scars, the fine lines, and the raw pink patches that mingle with the once-damaged flesh. Looking at my reconstructed hands is even worse than coming face to face with the golden fae.

At least, when I wake up in the morning, he'll be gone. I'll have these hands forever.

I remember a time when my hands were my own, not these monstrosities. Back before me and Madelaine decided we should skip school that Monday morning and hang out in the basement of an abandoned house down the street from the Everetts. Back before the golden fae appeared out of thin air and convinced Madelaine to dance with him, no matter how much I begged her not to. Back before the fire and the pain and the realization that Nine hadn't lied, that the fae and all of Faerie was real.

The fae don't live by the same rules that we do. They can hurt you—and they *will*.

I made a mistake. Staring at my ruined palm, letting the memories distract me from what the hell is going on right now, I made a huge mistake. I sense movement, a rustle of the wind, and when my head jerks up, he's right there.

He holds up his hand. His perfect, bronze-colored hand. Fingers pointed up, palm facing out.

"Dance with me, Riley."

I almost hurl.

Dance with me, Riley.

He knew my name then, too. He commanded me to dance, then he commanded me to leave with him, and I refused. Just like now, my refusal surprised him that day in the basement. I tried to warn Madelaine, I tried to tell her that he was beautiful, but he was fae, and that made him more dangerous than anything she'd ever known before.

Sometimes, on my worse days, I remember the look of betrayal in her big brown eyes the instant before he took her hand, then snapped her neck.

"Never."

"Zella. *Dance.*"

There's that word again. I hear it and I'm helpless to do anything except obey.

Under the sway of his power, I lift my hand and press my palm against his. I don't know what's worse: the spark, the sizzle when our bare skin touches, or how his long, lean perfect fingers make mine look like they belong on Frankenstein. My stomach twists. My mouth clamps shut, choking on a silent scream. I try to yank my hand back and I can't. I just *can't*.

His other hand is a brand on my hip. I feel the heat through my Black Pine tee. When he pulls me closer, lining my front along his lean, muscular body, it's like I'm burning up inside. He's full of fire and temptation, burning bright as the sun, and his golden eyes flash as he tilts his head, gobbling me up with his gaze.

"Zella," he murmurs again. "Stay with me."

I give in. I can't fight it. Knowing it's a dream, praying that this doesn't mean a thing, I recognize that some part of me doesn't want to pull away from him. For years, I used to hate Madelaine for giving up so easily, falling prey to this monster's charm before he snapped, but I can't help myself. Everything from his soft voice to his mesmerizing eyes is hypnotic. If he killed me right now, I don't think I would do a single thing to stop it.

I don't like the idea of dying. I want to live. In two weeks... two weeks and a couple of days... I'll be released from the asylum. Not free, though. His hand against mine, his body against mine, his soft voice echoing around me as he starts to sing… I figure out something that will be devastating when this dream is over.

Now that the golden fae has found me again? I'll *never* be free.

Music starts to play. A soft hum, it tickles my ears, makes me forget that I'm playing with fire. Literally. I've seen the golden fae create enchanted fire with the snap of his fingers. It's how I burned my hands, after all. After throwing Madelaine's broken body on the floor, he surrounded her in a circle of fire, daring me to save my sister.

I couldn't save Madelaine then. Something tells me that there's no saving me now, either.

So I dance.

It's easy to lose myself in the sensation. With his help, I move so lightly that it's as if I'm drifting up off of the floor. He laughs softly in time to the music, a mix of a chuckle and a sigh.

I keep my eyes closed so that I don't have to look at his.

I don't know how long we're dancing for when he speaks again. I hear him clearly, his mouth right next to my cheek as he whispers, "You know what I am."

I've always known. "Yes."

"But you don't know *who* I am."

I know enough. He's the golden fae. A monster. The creature who killed Madelaine.

The creature who's trying to seduce me right now.

I'm not innocent. I'm not all that naive, either. I wasn't always in a good foster home; I spent the long months in between in the system, bouncing from group homes to institutions. I lost my virginity at thirteen with an older boy before I went to live with the Everetts, before my haphephobia got so bad. When I could give permission, I actually *liked* being touched. It's just... when you start to see monsters everywhere, it's hard to know who to trust.

I know better than to trust him. A dance is just a dance, even if the way he's moving right now reminds me of so much more.

But not with him. Never with him.

He presses closer.

"Do you want to know who I am?" he whispers.

Hell no.

I shake my head again, so frantically that his lips kiss my ear. It burns and I try to pull away.

He holds me tighter.

"So be it," he concedes. "But know this: I will always come for you."

I don't know if he means that as a promise or a threat. Some of the fog lifts. The words... I've heard them before. From him? I'm... I'm not sure.

The music grows louder, as if trying to drown out my thoughts. My heart is beating in time to it. I try to focus. The magic is fading, my senses returning. What the fuck am I doing? I push with my free hand, yanking with the other. His grip is so strong, I begin to suspect that he'll never let me go.

We're spinning now. When I finally find the strength to open my eyes, everything is a blur of gold and white. I don't know how far I fell under his spell. Pretty damn far and I'm still trying to crawl out from under it as we go faster and faster. He slips his fingers between mine. Another touch.

"Don't fight it—don't fight *me*. You're safe now. I'll never hurt you."

A shiver courses through me. Or maybe it's him. I'm trembling as he saps all of my strength. Not only do I stop fighting, I actually lean into his embrace. I'm not sure I can support myself without holding onto him.

I wait for the twist in my belly that tells me that he's lying to me. The fae can't lie, but how can I believe him after he killed Madelaine?

I can't—but my stomach stays settled.

He means every damn thing he says to me.

I DON'T KNOW HOW LONG I'M SLEEPING FOR BUT, WHEN I FINALLY come out of my sedation, I wake up to the sound of music in my head. It takes me a second before my dream rushes to the front of my mind.

When it does, I pop up in my bed like a panicked jack-in-the-box. I lift my hands high, putting them in front of my face, flipping them back and forth until I'm sure that they're both covered all of the way with my leather gloves.

Because it *was* a dream. Just a dream brought on by the sedatives.

There was no golden fae. No dance. It was a terrible, strange nightmare that I forced my broken brain to live through after the way I hallucinated that the blonde tech had eyes just like the golden fae. I imagined her hazel eyes were gold, and paid for it by being sedated by the nursing staff.

At least I didn't wake up strapped down. That's a plus. And there's weak light streaming in past the six bars on my window. It's morning.

But *which* morning?

I get my answer shortly. It's Amy who comes in and does my vitals. Just seeing her is a big clue that I lost more time than I thought. If she's here, then it's Thursday at the earliest. I lost all of Wednesday.

She confirms it as she rattles on, going a mile a minute as if she's trying to make up for the time I was out. Not once does she mention my sedation, though she swiftly checks the bruising where they jabbed me with the needle before she covers the purple lump with a fresh bandage.

I wait until she takes a breath before I ask her the only thing I care about.

"Where's the other tech? Where's Diana?"

Especially on the heels of my strange dream, I know I never want to go near her again. The dream put things into perspective for me; with a clear head, it's a relief to realize I had been seeing things. The flash of gold I saw in her eyes? It must have been a trick of the setting sun since it *was* early when Diana and Duncan came to bring me my medicine.

Still, just the thought of coming face to face with her again— just the chance that maybe I'll see that flash again—has my breath picking up. It's a little more labored than it was before.

Amy looks touched, almost like she mistook my worry for concern or something. I wonder if she got my motives wrong.

Yeah. She totally did.

"Oh, Riley." She goes to pat my hand, remembers in an instant which patient I am, then pats the edge of my bed instead. "It's so sweet of you to worry about Diana."

Sweet? Nope. More like covering my own ass. I can't have another attack like that. I'm so close to getting out of the asylum. I'm not about to let anything jeopardize that. I could just see it now. The nursing staff and the techs tell the doctors that I'm a threat and, look at that, my release gets put on hold. Instead of going to the transition house, I get referred to an adult facility.

I can't let that happen.

"Where is she?" I ask again.

Amy frowns, like she has bad news and doesn't want to share it. My pulse picks up, settling only after she tells me, "Well, the truth is that she was transferred out of your age group yesterday. Now, don't blame yourself, okay? Things happen. It's not your fault."

From the tiniest twinge at the bottom of my stomach, I know Amy is lying. It's a kindness, though. She's actually trying to make me feel better.

Because Diana getting tossed off our floor?

We both know that it *is* my fault.

CHAPTER 8

No rain today.

I peeked out of my window before I shimmied off my hoodie, tossed it onto my dresser, and followed Amy into the hall. I know it's not raining, and the morning message says some motivational bullshit about sunshine in our lives so I know it's another gorgeous sunny day that I'm missing out on.

The morning passes me by in a haze. I'm jumpy, the last of the sedatives working their way out of my system. It makes me feel off, and it's only worse when I notice a couple of the other patients watching me closely.

It makes me antsy. *I'm* supposed to be the people-watcher.

Their stares have me hunching my shoulders, ducking as I walk, anxiously tugging on my gloves as I pretend not to see them gaping in open interest at me.

My daily check-in is a lecture. I'm not looking forward to my meeting with Lorraine the next time I see her. No doubt that Black Pine informed her about my meltdown as soon as they sedated me. I'm starting to get worried that what happened the other night's gonna affect my chances of getting released on time. I spend most of lunch toying with my meal, trying to come up with a good excuse for how I reacted when Diana tried to bring me my meds.

One thing for sure? I'm not about to admit that, for a second there, I thought she was the golden fae in disguise. Especially since I can still feel the heat of his hand against mine from the dance we shared while I was under.

I don't know what kind of group therapy I was expecting that afternoon. It's not raining, but a cheery therapist named Tonya claps her hand and insists we try some more creative therapy. She's too new to realize that it's a real bad idea to treat our age group like we're some kind of democracy. When she offers to let us vote, most of the therapy session is wasted when half the group wants music therapy and the rest decide on art.

Now, I'm not a big fan of art therapy. I've always thought it was a waste of time, especially for our group. But if it's art therapy or music? I'm going art. Just the idea of a music therapy session is a trigger for me after last night.

Nope. If I never hear another note again, I'm good.

The vote is a joke. We're split down the middle, six to six. I blame Whitney for that. She kept quiet at first, only making her vote when she figured out it would create a tie. I'm not surprised. That's Whitney for you. She gets a kick out of watching our group argue like children, a real shit-starter.

I'm so not in the mood.

"I don't care about the rest of the group," I announce to the room, "but I won't do music therapy. Get a tech. Take one of my points. I don't care. I won't do it."

Tonya is new to Black Pine, but she's an experienced therapist. I might not test that way, but my refusal today is a clear example of ODD. Oppositional Defiant Disorder. No matter what she says, she can't make me.

Her voice immediately adjusts. Instead of happy and go-lucky, she's suddenly calm. As if her soothing tone will get me to change my mind.

"Riley, we're going to decide as a group. Whatever the group decides, that's what we're going to do. I hope you understand."

I huff. That's not going to work. Sorry.

"Umm… excuse me?" Carolina raises her hand. "I'd like to change my vote. Can I do that? I… I don't mind art therapy."

Lie.

That's a lie.

And I don't even need the twinge that hits my stomach to know that. Everyone in our group was there the last time we had art therapy. Carolina's sobbing fit was the talk of the ward the whole rest of that night. Why would she switch her vote?

I glance over at her. Though she was talking to Tonya, her dark eyes are locked on me. Carolina is watching me.

And I know exactly why she switched her vote.

"Thank you, Carolina. Now it's seven-six—and, no, Whitney, that's it for changed votes. Art therapy it is. Ready? Let's go."

Along with her idea of democracy, Tonya gives instructions that are supposed to be liberating—but they're just kinda vague. She tells us to grab some paper, some crayons, then draw whatever our hearts tell us to.

Jeez.

Another rookie mistake with a group like ours.

I can already imagine what some of the other patients are gonna draw. She didn't even reiterate our normal rules about keeping it clean and violence-free.

I didn't mean to be such a pain before, and I know I'm already walking on thin ice. I'm not about to push any of the staff by drawing something inappropriate. She wants me to let my creativity flow? Okay. I can try.

Today, I grab a sheet of black construction paper. I grab a couple of crayons, then choose the yellow crayon first. Putting the tip to the dark paper, I start to doodle aimlessly. No real direction or anything. In fact, I'm barely even paying attention as the half-hearted, absent strokes start to develop into something very familiar.

Yellow skin, yellow hair, yellow eyes. Without even meaning to, I've drawn a caricature of the golden fae from my dream.

When I catch on to what I've done, I tear the paper into six equal strips, then start ripping each strip into five pieces. Within seconds, there's nothing left but thirty black squares, some with an indistinguishable yellow squiggle running through it.

If only I could erase the monster from my mind as easily as that.

At the end of the session, Tonya is disappointed that I have nothing to share. Turns out she doesn't think that making confetti is constructive or creative so, after Carolina switched just to help me out, I still lose credit for the hour's session. Amy makes a note on my chart. I'm sure Lorraine or my case manager will ask me about that, too.

Great.

Fucking great.

THAT NIGHT, DINNER IS BROUGHT TO MY ROOM. I DON'T EVEN GET the chance to eat with the rest of the group.

I expected it. They think they're punishing me for my outburst on Tuesday night, but I prefer it—even if it means Nurse Stanley is the one who keeps me company while I eat.

She leaves when I'm finished, taking my tray with her. She isn't gone long, though. About an hour later, she comes back to do my nighttime vitals, bringing my meds with her. No Duncan tonight, though. Frankie follows her in the room, paying me close attention as if he's waiting for me to flip out any second now.

Whatever. It's been a long day and I'm exhausted. When Nurse Stanley places my cups on the dresser, I peek inside just long enough to make sure they're my regular meds before tossing them back.

Of course, when I *want* them to, the damn things don't work.

I lose track of how long I lay awake in my bed, unable to fall asleep. I don't have a clock in my room. I've never needed one. With the techs acting as my alarm clock on the rare occasion that I don't wake up on my own, it seemed like a waste.

Apart from my dresser with my hoodie folded on top, my bed, and my nightstand, my room is empty. I didn't bring a book with me tonight and, besides, it's 'lights out'. The moon is full, hanging high in the sky. It's bright, but it's not bright enough to allow me to read.

Instead, I lay flat on my back, blanket pulled up to my chin, and watch the moon through my barred windows. Dark clouds roll across the sky like liquid ink. Hours pass. I'm still not tired.

I'm beginning to wonder if we'll be in for another storm tomorrow when I hear the faintest rustle and freeze.

No, I tell myself. It *can't* be.

"*Riley.*"

I immediately close my eyes. A second later, I lift my hands out from under my blanket and clamp them over my ears.

No, no, no.

Not again.

It should have worked. The leather gloves, plus how tightly

I'm pressing my palms to my ears... it should have worked. No way I should be able to hear anything other than the frantic drumming of my frightened heart.

But then I hear, almost as if he's annoyed—

"Don't be ridiculous. I know you're still awake."

Of course I am. Who knows how long he was watching me before he made a move? That's the thing about Nine. He was always so quiet. He could've been here for as long as the moon's been out, I don't know. I remember that about him. He never let me know he was there until *he* was ready to announce his presence.

Like the way he whispered my name.

If he'd been watching me, he would've seen me with my eyes open, staring out of my window. He would've seen my reaction, watched me as I covered my ears and shut my eyes.

It's a good thing that only a few seconds have passed. When I open my eyes again, they're still adjusted to the dark and the gloom. I pull myself up into a sitting position, resting on my forearms, searching for the owner of the voice I know all too well.

The other day, I refused to acknowledge him. I swallowed my pills and went to sleep and pretended that Nine hadn't come to see me for the first time in six years. But that was the other day. After what happened the last time I slept—well, was sedated—I think part of me was waiting for Nine to return.

The golden fae found me. Maybe it was only a matter of time before I conjured up my Shadow Man again.

I know every inch of this room. If he's here, I know exactly where to find Nine. My eyes are drawn to the deepest, darkest shadows where two of the walls meet in a corner.

And there he is.

I've never forgotten what Nine looked like. I know all about glamour, of course, the fae's ability to appear however they want to, but Nine has always appeared the same. He was tall, slender, an ageless beauty. His skin was pale, almost ghostly so, a stark contrast to his midnight hair. He had a sculpted face, all harsh angles with an unforgiving mouth.

Nine never smiled.

He's not smiling now, either. His silver eyes flash and gleam, a pair of headlights beaming through the darkness of my room. He's staring at me. He doesn't seem to blink at all. I get the crazy idea that he's too busy watching me to close his eyes for even a second.

That's okay. I'm not blinking, either.

This… this isn't how I remember Nine.

It's him. No doubt about that. Still tall, slender, his body cloaked in a long, black coat that swishes in the shadows as he dares to take a few steps closer. A sliver of moonlight falls on his face.

I gasp.

He's stunning. Like, I'm sitting in my bed, staring at him, *stunned* stunning. Holy shit. I don't know if I've ever seen anyone who looks as good as he does. And, okay, I always harbored a crush on him. Why wouldn't I? He was the only guy I knew who actually seemed to care about me when I was younger, but his perfection was a little off-putting. Plus there was the whole age difference and power dynamic. I was a kid. Nine was a Shadow Man.

Now he's one hell of a man.

Whoa.

His hair is different, too. The last time I saw him, he'd grown it out to his chin. Now it falls a few inches past his shoulders. It looks so soft. I just want to run my fingers through its length.

But that would be touching. And Nine was very clear on his no touching rule.

Wait—*no*. I can't let myself fall into this obvious trap. I managed to make it through six years without him. I worked hard to put him behind me, to pretend that the Faerie realm with its magic and its threats were stories I made up during a lonely, unstable childhood.

I've been pretending so long, I don't even know what's real anymore.

My panic attacks? They're real.

The anxiety and terror when it comes to someone grabbing me without my permission? That's real, too.

The Shadow Man might be just as real as my diagnoses—he certainly looks real to me right now—but I can't act like I believe that. That's a one-way ticket straight to Black Pine's adult facility.

Nope.

It can't be Nine.

He disappeared when Madelaine died and all of Acorn Falls heard me blame the fae.

I don't know where he went. Don't know why he's back, or why he's trying to talk to me again right after I dreamed of the golden fae.

I sure as hell don't like it, though.

Squinting in the gloom, I meet his unblinking gaze. Besides being stunned by his radiant beauty, I'm so scared by what his sudden appearance could mean. I'm angry, too. I'm not panicking yet, but that's probably because I'm actually kinda shocked that he's visiting me for the first time in years, plus I have this urge to throw myself into his arms.

No. No touching.

I slide my gloved hands under my ass. If I'm sitting on them, he can't touch me—and I can't reach for him.

Then, swallowing back the ball of emotions that are lodged in my throat, I snap, "What are you staring at?"

Because he *is* staring. And, okay, there are probably a hundred other things I could have said to acknowledge him—something like, "Who the hell are you, stranger in my bedroom," since I'm not about to admit I remember him—but his stare is bothering me.

"It's been a long time," he says in answer. Long time? No shit. "You look different."

I do? Well, so does he.

"What are you doing here?" I demand.

"Don't tell me you've forgotten about me."

Nine's voice is soft, lyrical, alluring. Just like the golden fae. But it's harsh too, like it used to be. It always made me think he was mad at me. Whenever it softened, I felt like I won a prize.

The harsh edge grates against the last of my nerves. "How can I forget you?" I demand. "There's no *you* to forget. Anyway, I made you up when I was a kid. You shouldn't be here!"

I can't believe what I'm seeing. For years, I believed in him —trusted him, *loved* him—and then he was gone. For years, I've been lectured, coached, medicated, and convinced that he never existed. And, yet, here he is. My imaginary friend, almost exactly as he was back then, standing a few feet away from me.

I wonder, if I yell loud enough, will the sound carry through the wall? Probably not. I could bang on the door, hope that one of the overnight nurses is passing by. Would they help me? Or only sedate me again?

I don't scream. Just in case. I *don't* scream.

But I whisper. "No. *No.* You... know what? You're not real.

You're not. You're a hallucination, that's all. You shouldn't be here. I took my pills."

"I assure you, I'm as real as you are." He hesitates before extending his arm. His skin is so pale, it seems to glow in the moonlight. "Touch me and prove it to yourself."

A hysterical laugh bubbles up and out of my throat. "Ha! If you really were Nine, you'd tell me not to touch you at all."

He smiles. The simple quirk of his lush lips has my stomach tied up in knots. Nine's grin is even worse than Dr. Gillespie's— but for totally different reasons.

"Ah," he says softly, "so you *do* remember."

Suddenly, I'm twelve again, smiling adoringly up at Nine, preening because his voice has gentled. No, no. *No*. I'm older now and, if not wiser, then definitely wary. I've only got two weeks until I'm twenty-one and I can put this all behind me.

I push away, scoot back, slamming my head, my neck, my back against the wall behind me. I slip my hands out from under my ass, clutching the hem of my blanket, yanking it so that it covers me to my belly button. I'm wearing my Black Pine tee to sleep like I always do and the bared skin on my arms has me wishing I had the will to get up and get my hoodie.

I can't, though. I'm still stunned, frozen in my bed.

Nine is waiting for me to say something.

So I do.

"What are you doing here?"

The smile fades. His expression goes stony, his silver eyes dimming noticeably. "You were supposed to be safe. No one should have been able to track you here, but... it's time, Shadow. They found you. She knows where you are."

They.

The fae.

I've spent almost twenty years waiting for them to find me.

Last night, the golden fae male followed me into my dream.

At least, I *thought* it was a dream.

Wasn't it?

Shadow... god, I haven't heard that name in so long. I missed it. I didn't even realize how much I did until Nine threw it out there like that, another way to remind me that—whether or not I've made him up—we have a history together. Shadow. Because he only came at night, because he stayed to the shadows himself, it made me feel so precious that he cared enough to give me a name that reminded me of him.

Even though I've been Riley Thorne since my first foster family, I used to love being Nine's Shadow.

Right now, though? I would gladly never hear that name again if it meant that he hadn't just said that the fae have found me. My whole life, the fae have always been my very own personal bogeymen. For reasons I've never been told—because Nine always insisted I was too young to learn them—the fae have been hunting me for years. At least, that's what I let myself believe.

Because, you know, this isn't real.

I cling to that certainty. What else can I do?

Nine has an answer for that. "Come on. Get up. We have to go. You have to leave with me."

Leave? Doesn't he see the bars on my window? "What? No. I can't."

"But you can." His silver eyes flash hypnotically. "I'll show you. Now give me your hand."

I almost do, too. There's something about the way he said that, so simple, so insistent... I have my right glove halfway off before I realize what I am about to do.

I shake my head, clearing it. Angrily, I yank my glove back on. "Don't do that!"

"Do what?" he asks.

"You know what! You're trying to trick me."

"I'm trying to *save* you. It's all I've ever done. It's all I can do."

He's not real, he's not real...

The chanting inside my head doesn't help. Nine's still standing there.

"Let me prove it. Don't you want to know why I've come back now? I've just learned that this place isn't safe for you anymore."

Um. Does he really not see the bars on the window? My door's locked. No one can get to me—

Before I can point that out, he says, "They've already made themselves known to you, haven't they? I'm not the first from Faerie that's come to see you. Am I right?"

He's not real, he's not r—

"How did you know that?"

He blinks. I think it might've been the first time since he stepped out of the shadows that he shutters his eyes before opening them wide again. The silver shines, illuminating the dark expression on his beautiful face.

"I didn't know," he says roughly. "But I feared it. Rys got to you first."

"Reese?" The single syllable sends a shiver down my spine. "Who's Reese?"

Nine shakes his head, long hair rippling down the back of his coat. "There's no time. When it comes to you, I can't even trust my kind not to interfere. A Seelie? Impossible. You've got to come with me. We'll talk later."

Yeah. No. "I'm locked in an asylum, having an argument with one of my hallucinations. I think I can decide if there's enough time or not."

Nine scowls. It doesn't do a damn thing to make him look any less gorgeous. "You know very well that I'm not a hallucination."

I ignore that. He's right, of course. My meds are supposed to keep them away, yet here he is, even after I took my complete dose. I reach over and pinch my arm. It *hurts*. There goes the hope that I fell asleep without realizing it and this is all another crazy dream.

"Either tell me what you're talking about or go. Who the hell is Rys and why should I care that he's after me?"

"Not after you. He already knows where you are. He can take you away whenever he wants to. That's why you have to come with me now. You can't let him get his hands on you. He'll do anything for a touch."

Anything? Like, I don't know, use magic to step into my dream, make my gloves disappear, and compel me to dance with him while pressing his palm against mine?

Uh-oh.

I think back to last night, the terrible dream with the golden fae. How he asked me if I knew what he was, then who he was. I didn't.

I guess I do now.

"Rys... is that the name of the monster who killed my sister?"

Nine frowns. "He's not a monster. Rys is a fae—"

Obviously. I already figured out that part. "Yeah? Tell me something I don't know."

"—like me."

My jaw drops.

Okay, then.

I definitely didn't know *that*.

CHAPTER 9

Nine isn't a fae. He *can't* be.

If anything, he's my Shadow Man: part bogeyman, part guardian angel. The one who spent my whole childhood warning me about the fae. Not once, in all those years, did he ever admit he was part of the race he was protecting me from.

"What? No... *no*. That's not right."

"Sorry to disappoint you. I thought you knew. I never hid what I was—"

"I would've remembered if you told me you were one of them!"

Nine doesn't say anything. He just bows his head, shielding his strange silver eyes, letting his long, wavy black hair fall forward like a shield.

He's gorgeous, no denying that. Just like the golden fae, Nine is absolute perfection. But they look nothing alike. They're total opposites, even if they do have total disdain for humans in common.

That's something I *do* remember. As my hands burned, my throat raw from screaming, I remember the puzzled look on the golden fae's face—on Rys's face—as he said, "She was just a human."

As if that made her life worth less than his. As if that made *my* life worth less because I'm a human.

My whole childhood, Nine didn't hide the fact that he was purposely looking past me being a human in order to help me. I thought it was because he was something totally different than what he was warning me about. A Shadow Man, a creature tied to Faerie who had his own motives, his own magic.

I never thought he was part of the ruling race. Or that he was teaching me to protect myself from his kind.

"How can you be a fae, too? You don't look anything like the other one."

"There's no time for this—"

I need to understand. "Make time or get the hell out of my room. You're the one who told me to stay away from the fae."

"Except for me. Listen, I can explain in detail when I've gotten you somewhere safe."

Bullshit. "I'm safe right here."

"Riley—"

I can't do this right now. I *can't*. "Know what? Forget it. I don't want to hear anything else from you. You abandoned me six years ago and I did just fine without you. I don't know why you decided to come back now, but you wasted both of our time. Just go."

"*Riley—*"

"I'll scream," I threaten.

"You have to forget this nonsense and come with me. You don't have any idea how much trouble you're in right now."

"Yeah? And why's that? Because you won't tell me. You've

never told me anything except to keep my hands to myself and guess what, Nine?" I show him my gloves. "That didn't work out so great, did it?"

"Very well." Nine glances over his shoulder, peering into the inky blackness of the shadow as if he's searching for something. He nods. "You're not wrong. Dawn isn't for a few hours yet in the human world. There's some time. Ask your questions. I vow to answer them if I can if that's the proof you need to trust me on this."

Trust Nine when I just discovered the truth about him? Yeah, he's got a snowball's chance in hell of that happening.

But I also recognize that I've backed him into a corner. For some reason, he's desperate to get me to agree to leave with him. He thinks answering my questions will make me trust him again?

Sure. Let's go with that.

Hey. The fae can't lie, but humans sure can.

"How are you both fae?"

"Don't you remember how I told you there were two kinds of fae?"

Now that he mentions it, I kinda do. "The Cursed and the Blessed."

He nods. "That's right. The Cursed Ones are the Unseelie, the Blessed Ones the Seelie. Two different races make up the same people, all of us lorded over by the Fae Queen."

"So you're saying there's good and bad types. Blessed and cursed." My heart skips a beat. "Which one are you?"

"It's not as simple as that. Good and bad… no. I've told you this before, Riley. Those are human concepts. In Faerie, it comes down to Light and Dark. One rules during the time of the sun, the other when the moon is out. It's when we are at our strongest, that's all it means."

I don't have to ask which one he is again.

Dark Fae. Nine's skin is ghostly white, his eyes that freakish silver, but his hair is midnight black and he wears the shadows like a second skin. Plus, he always made sure I knew that he could only come to the human world at night.

And now I finally know what the beautiful monster is.

A Light Fae. Golden eyes, golden hair, golden skin. He lit the house on fire during the afternoon—in the sunlight.

Rys must be part of the Seelie class then, the Blessed Ones.

Okay, Nine totally just made his point. No way would anyone ever consider Madelaine's killer a good guy. And Nine, as dark as he might be, has only ever been kind to me.

I'm just about to ask him *why* when he continues and I don't get the chance.

"Just because he's a Light Fae, a Seelie, don't make the mistake in thinking he's not dangerous. He's still a fae, and one who will stop at nothing to get what he desires."

Has Nine forgotten about everything Rys has cost me so far? Madelaine, my poor hands, and the last six years in the asylum?

I'll never forget for a second how dangerous he is.

I show Nine my gloves again. "Yeah. I know."

"Do you really? He was just playing then. You were a child, nothing more. Last night, he hunted you down, stole another touch. It only made him stronger. It'll get worse when you hit your twenty-first birthday."

Because they're letting me out of Black Pine, I guess, and Rys will have an easier time looking for me. But how the hell does *Nine* know that?

Pretending like I'm not suddenly spooked by the idea of Rys forever searching for me, I shrug. "I still have more than two weeks until then to worry about my birthday."

A strange expression flashes across his face, there and gone again. For a second, it looks like he's about to argue with me before he changes his mind.

Shaking his head, long hair spilling down the back of his strange coat, Nine says, "Rys is even more dangerous now. A fae who has set his eyes on a lover is often ruthless and the laws say—"

A too-loud chuckle bursts out of me. "A lover? Oh, come on."

"You must take this seriously, Riley. He's convinced himself that he wants you."

Dance with me.

Stay with me.

I'll always come for you.

He said those words to me when I was fifteen. He said them again last night, and so much more. The way he pressed his body against mine, the way his lips brushed my ears, how he moved like he was trying to claim me while I was too enchanted to pull away from him.

Suddenly, I'm not laughing any longer.

Because it wasn't a dream. It was a seduction, and I don't know how far I let him take it.

From the look on Nine's face, I'm thinking way, way too far.

"No. You've got that all wrong. He... he's sorry about Madelaine. That's all it is. He just wants to be my friend."

The air whistles as Nine draws in a short breath. His cheekbones are so sharp, they could slice through paper. Eyes flashing, he demands, "Rys said that to you?"

Didn't he? "Well, yeah."

"Friend. He said *friend*?"

"Something like that."

Nine looms over me, his expression darker than it has been. "This is important. What did the Light Fae tell you?"

"I don't know. Hang on. It was—" Come on. What was that weird word he used again? It sounded so much like 'friend', but foreign. Too bad Allison is down the hall. She'd be able to help me figure it out. It was almost German... I shrug. "Friend-ow. Maybe."

Nine pales. Seriously. I mean, the guy's already super white. Now, though? He loses any color he has left.

"*Ffrindau?*"

That's it. "Yeah. Why? I get that it's bad—no way I want to be friends with a psycho fae killer, but at least he's not chasing after me like all you other monsters."

His scowl returns with a vengeance. I'm not sure if it's because I made a point to lump him in with the other fae—he's fae, I still can't believe that my Shadow Man is one of *them*—or because I'm not letting the golden fae bother me as much as I used to. In my dream, he promised me he'd never hurt me and, one thing I know for sure, it's that the fae can't lie.

Which is why I'm stunned at what Nine says next. Because, as much as I wish it wasn't the truth, I know it must be.

"*Ffrindau* doesn't mean friend. It's an ancient term from a dead Faerie language that still lives on today. If Rys thinks of you as his *ffrindau*, you're in even more trouble than if he was hoping to capture you on behalf of the Fae Queen."

My heart just about stops beating. "Really? Why? What does... what does that word mean?"

"It means mate. soulmate, to be precise."

"Soul *what?*"

Nine clenches his jaw so tightly, I can see a muscle tic. "Mate. He doesn't want to be your friend. He wants you to be his bonded mate for all eternity, whether you're meant to be his or not."

There's something in the way he says that. When I was a kid,

I always understood that Nine knew tons more than the little bit he told me. He had all the power then—if he wanted to guard his secrets, there wasn't a damn thing I could do about it.

It's different now. I'm older, tougher, and I'm teetering on the edge of a massive breakdown. I spent six years convincing myself that the fae weren't real. Now, when I'm so close to being free, to putting my nightmares behind me—as if I really *could*—now I have to deal with this?

The fae can't lie. Nine's finally confessed that he's one of the Faerie folk, so he can't lie, either. He can twist the truth any which way he wants to. In the end, no matter what, it'll be the truth.

I'm at my breaking point. He knows more than he's telling. Good chance he'll ignore my next question, though he promised to answer me before. Still, I have to try.

"Am I?"

"Are you what?"

I swallow roughly. "Meant to be his?"

To my surprise, the answer comes quick. "No."

"How do you know? How can you be so sure?" A sinking suspicion hits me. "Am I meant to be with one of your kind? Is that why the Fae Queen is sending you people after me?"

Nine keeps his mouth clamped shut. He inhales through his nose, then exhales sharply. The word sounds like it's been dragged out of him when he finally whispers, "Yes."

And I know, because I've always been able to tell when someone's lying to me, that that *is* the truth.

Oh, boy.

I think I liked it a lot better when he didn't answer my questions.

I don't sleep at all that night.

Even after Nine slips back into the shadows, vanishing from sight right before the sun comes up, I stay huddled in my bed. I'm too afraid to close my eyes now. What if I do and I'm transported back to the empty room where I danced with Rys?

I wait until my wake-up call that morning to throw open the door and plead with Amy to get me in to see whatever doctor is free.

Nine isn't real. Rys isn't real. I can't let them be. My life's so much easier when there's no such thing as the fae, and I spent the last few hours reminding myself of that. There has to be a reason why, after all this time, I've had three separate episodes back-to-back. Sometime this morning, after the sun came up and I was still searching shadows for a figment of my imagination, I finally remembered my nighttime meds.

This all started on Sunday night, when I first could have sworn that I heard Nine's voice calling my name. Know what else happened on Sunday? I met Dr. Gillespie and he put in an order for a new medication.

That pink pill. Whatever the hell that thing is, it's not working.

I need a med check.

Just my luck, though. The first available doctor? Dr. Gillespie.

Because of course.

I almost have to laugh. Running on no sleep, as anxious as I am, I would rather talk to anybody else in Black Pine before Dr. Gillespie. And, sure, it's been a few days since our disastrous last session on Monday, but hell if I've forgotten how I told him all about Nine. The last thing I want to do right now is admit that I imagined a full-blown conversation with Nine for the first time in years.

I can hear the doctor now. He'll either say that I'm relapsing—again, tell me something I don't know—or that this is a breakthrough. Knowing how these psychologists all work, most likely he'll decide that it's because I opened up to him about Nine.

I hope not. I don't think I could sit there and look at the satisfied, smug expression on his impish face if he decides he's been here less than a week and he's already "fixed" me. Then again, if my verbal diarrhea our last session is what brought on these recent episodes, maybe he'll be the one who gets in trouble for it.

Here's hoping. All I know is that it's Friday, I won't have another check-in with Lorraine until Monday, and any of the other doctors for our ward are all booked up until this afternoon at the earliest.

It has to be Dr. Gillespie.

"Riley, it's good to see you again. How are you today?"

"I'm tired." So, so tired.

Dr. Gillespie nods knowingly. "Well, yes, that happens sometimes as the sedation wears off. Your body is rested, but it takes a couple of days for the serum to dissipate and the grogginess to fade away."

I sink deep in my seat. "You heard about that?"

Of course he has. And look, I wasn't even a little wrong when I thought I'd be forced to see him with a smug grin.

Damn it.

The doctor opens his portfolio, picks up his pen. "Why don't you tell me why you're here? It's not your day to see me for a session, and I don't have you down for a check-in. I squeezed you in, so I only have a few minutes before my next patient. If it's okay with you, let's get right to it."

Okay. Right to it. I can do that.

"I need a new med check."

"Why would you say that?"

Why not? "I don't think my pills are working anymore."

"Which ones? Because I'll be honest with you, Riley. They don't work if you don't take them like you're supposed to. Every dose, every day. It's the only way you're going to see improvement."

Is he serious? Great. Looks like Nurse Stanley might've stopped by, had a chat with the new doctor. I don't care. Keeping my features neutral, I refuse to give away the truth on my face. I'm not kidding. And I didn't come to his office because I wanted a lecture.

I need *help*.

"I take all of my pills," I lie. At least, I have been the last few nights. "Every day, at the nursing station in the morning, then when a nurse and a tech bring me my pills at night. I don't want to see these hallucinations, you know."

"Mm-hmm."

Jeez, I would *love* to slap that stupid, smarmy grin right off his face. At this moment, if the asylum staff could assure me that I'd actually *be* alone, the solitary confinement to my room would so be worth it.

"Look, I'm telling you the truth. They don't work anymore." I grit my teeth and clench my fists, my leather gloves groaning in protest. I have to make him understand. "I don't know what else to say. You order a new pill for my nighttime cup and, ever since then, Nine's been back. I want him to go away."

That's all I had to say.

"You've seen him again?" Shoving the portfolio away from

him, Dr. Gillespie leans forward in his seat, palms flush against the desktop. His big, blue eyes widen in abject surprise. "When? Where did you see him? Did he say anything to you?"

I'm taken aback by his reaction. I shimmy in my seat, climbing up so that I'm sitting straight. If he keeps acting weird, I'm ready to bolt out of here.

"Why do you care?" I ask him suspiciously. Then, because I can't help myself, I add, "You probably don't even believe me."

The doctor clears his throat. He leans back, a different kind of smile stretching his thin lips. "I'm your psychologist, Riley. I *have* to believe you." Dr. Gillespie pushes his glasses up his nose before pulling his portfolio—and my file—back toward him. He picks his pen up again. "Now," he says, "some questions about your... your friend. Did you hear him speak to you at all?"

"A little," I tell him. "But I... I don't remember what he said."

Because there's no way that I heard him tell me that Madelaine's killer thinks he's in love with me. Right?

Right.

"What about your vision? Did you actually see him?"

I shrug. "I don't know. I might have. The room was dark."

And Nine is a Dark Fae.

Shit.

"This didn't happen until I started taking that little pink pill the other day. It's not working. Please." I'll beg if I have to. Anything's better than going back to the old, familiar paranoia, expecting the fae to find me at any given moment. "You've got to do something to help me."

Dr. Gillespie opens my file, gesturing at something on the top page. "This says your medication has been changed multiple times over the last year. Something to do with a dependence on—"

"My blue pill."

"Right. According to Dr. Waylon's report, though, it seems to be the only prescription that ever helped you." He's quiet for a moment before he starts scribbling away on a page in his portfolio. "I'll keep your current dose as it is, but I'll add your old medicine to the order. We'll track your progress over the next couple of days and then we'll go from there. How does that sound?"

"Anything that'll work," I say honestly. I can hear the relief in my voice and don't even bother to disguise it. "Thank you so much."

"I want you to promise me something, Riley."

Right now I'm so glad that Dr. Gillespie is willing to do something to help me—whether he's humoring me or not—that I'd promise him my firstborn kid. Whatever he wants, he can have it.

"Anything."

"If you see Nine again, listen to everything he says. Remember it. Write it down if you have to. I'll get you some paper to keep by your bed, make sure the techs know it's approved. You're getting close, Riley, and you're running out of time. It's important that we get this straightened out. Keep notes and then come see me as soon as you can. I'll help you make sense of it all."

I nod. That's something I can do. I just hope that, once I start taking my blue pill again, I won't have to.

CHAPTER 10

I decide to chance eating dinner with the rest of the group tonight. If I get stuck with another nurse watching me like a hawk while I choke down dried-out chicken and watery jello for another night, they might actually have to restrain me this time.

I think Amy feels sorry for me. She hangs out past six when her shift is over, talking with Kelsey, one of the nighttime techs who takes over for the girls when Amy and Penelope are off. I don't know what she says, but I'm not rushed to my room when they lead us to the common room to eat, so that's something.

Dinner is beef stew with biscuits on the side. Comfort food. It tastes even better knowing that I'm eating it out in the open instead of in my room.

And it's not like I missed spending time with the other guys in my group. I didn't. Most of them are still watching me closely, waiting for me to pull a trick out of my gloves or something. I'll be the talk of the ward until someone else is more interesting than me.

Lovely.

It's better than going back to my room early, though. A lump forms in my throat every time I think of being locked inside, with its corner and the too-dark shadows that linger there.

Dr. Gillespie promised he'd fix my dose. I have to believe that it's going to work because, if I don't, it's way too easy to fall into old habits. Part of me wants to believe that Nine's back—even if he's returned with dire warnings that I'm willfully ignoring—while the rest of me just wants the fae to go away for once and for all.

Could I give up Nine to be sure that I never have to deal with the golden fae again?

In a heartbeat.

My reaction to his sudden reappearance last night was too weird. It's one thing to have an affection for the Shadow Man who helped me through my lost and lonely childhood. And, sure, you could say that I felt some sort of affection for him when I saw him again. Affection and a super strong attraction that scares me almost more than the idea that Rys is real, he's gunning for me, and I can't escape.

Dance with me.

Stay with me.

I'll always come for you.

I cough, choking on a lump of carrot that goes down wrong. Tears well in my eyes as I swallow roughly before taking in great, big gulps of air.

Yeah. *Almost.*

I see Kelsey start toward me, then pause when I get myself under control. No one tries to slap me on my back or make sure that I'm okay. Smart. Who knows how I'd react if they touched me, even if they're trying to stop me from choking?

My throat burns. I take a couple of sips of water. It helps.

I know I'm dragging my heels, taking forever to eat my meal. I have this feeling deep inside that I shouldn't go back to my room. Something's coming. Something's going to happen. It's a hunch. A twisted premonition.

Jeez, I really hope my blue pill does what it's supposed to tonight.

The table begins to empty around me. I wonder if I could ask one of the techs if there are any extra biscuits. For the first time today, my stomach is settled. I've been feeling queasy ever since I woke up following the sedation. The comfort food is helping. I'd eat more if I could.

As if she can sense my hunger, Carolina rises from her seat. She picks up her bowl of stew, her biscuit—both obviously untouched—and moves around the table. That catches my attention. The garbage is on the other side of the room. Why is she coming this way?

She's wearing this crooked, hopeful little half smile on her too-thin face. Her dark eyes seem more sunken in than they usually do, purple bruises underlining them. She glances at me, then her gaze darts away. Like she's looking for someone—or she's desperate to avoid being caught doing something she's not supposed to.

Carolina's twitchy, too. Nibbling on a bottom lip that's so dry and cracked, it's gotta hurt like hell, she stops when she's about a foot away from me. She jumps in place when I look up at her. Her stew sloshes against the side of her bowl, splashing on the table, my arm, and the side of my glove.

"Oh, no! I'm sorry... I didn't mean to—"

"It's fine," I tell her.

"Let me clean it up."

With shaky hands, she sets the bowl down, the biscuit right next to it; the biscuit is partially wrapped in a napkin. Carolina grabs another napkin, eager to clean up her mess.

I move my hand out of her reach before she could dab at the spill on my glove. "I said, it's *fine*."

"Oh. Sure." Carolina gulps, then gives one last swipe with her napkin. "I... I really am sorry."

"Accidents happen. Don't worry about it."

"Here." She pushes her biscuit toward me. "You looked like you enjoyed yours. I thought you might want mine."

We'll both get in trouble if any of the techs notice that she's giving me her food—and that I'm taking it. Better get rid of the evidence. Mumbling a quiet thank you, I snatch the biscuit and take a huge bite before Kelsey or Frankie see me at it. Chew. Swallow. I do it again.

And that's when I notice the black smudge where the biscuit sat on Carolina's napkin. The biscuit is buttery, and it left a ring-shaped grease stain that caused the ink to run and turn blurry. Because, when I squint and look closer, I realize that's what the black smudge is.

It's writing.

Someone wrote four tiny lines on the napkin and covered it with a biscuit.

Setting the half-eaten biscuit on my plate, I pick up the napkin and squint to make out the words:

> *Find me after dinner.*
> *We have to talk.*
> *Tell no one else.*
> *She has eyes everywhere.*

I read it twice. It's not so blurry that I'm reading it wrong. But what the hell does *that* mean?

Lifting my head up, I start to ask Carolina. She's gone, though. While I was reading her note, she picked up her bowl and scurried away from the table. I watch as she dodges Kelsey, waiting until the techs are busy to get rid of her dinner.

Once she does, she turns back to look at our empty table. I'm the only one still sitting here so even if I could pretend she didn't mean for me to find this note, that disappears when our eyes meet.

I recognize that look. Carolina is lost, she's confused, and she's reaching out. I've got no fucking clue why she picked *me* of all people, but I've been where she is. She needs help.

Too bad I can't even help myself half of the time.

With Carolina's napkin crumpled up and hidden in my fist, I go to my room after dinner because that's what I'm supposed to do. It's routine. Besides, it's not like I don't know that the techs and the nurses are keeping a closer eye on me than usual these last couple of days.

Part of me wonders if Dr. Gillespie put them up to it, or maybe Lorraine—my social worker is trying to do everything she can to make sure I'm released on time and, as much as I hate to admit, my breakdown the other night didn't do me any favors. Could be that they're all still on guard because they're expecting a repeat performance.

Regardless, I decide to wait until after I take my nighttime meds to see if I can sneak out to see Carolina. Lockdown isn't for another two hours. It might not be something I usually do—or, well, have *ever* done—but I can go visit another patient in my ward until lights out.

Ignoring Carolina's note isn't even an option. I have to know what she's talking about. Normally, I wouldn't give a shit. We all have our issues. There are countless professionals inside of Black Pine who are qualified to help her. Me? What can I do?

Nothing, that's what. Doesn't matter, though. It's the last line that got to me. *She has eyes everywhere...* She? Who the hell is *she*? It's bad enough that I've got Nine's warning about Rys and the other fae running around in my head. Am I supposed to be worrying about a *she* now?

Only one way to find out.

It's Friday night which means—thank God—no Nurse Stanley. No Duncan, either. He's been out since the night I lost my shit with Diana. A rumor has been circulating on our floor that the *crunch* I heard that night was the sound of my kick breaking Duncan's nose. Oops.

Whatever the reason, it's Frankie who comes with Nurse Pritchard tonight. I actually like this nurse. She's the oldest nurse in the ward, with thick, white curly hair that looks like there's a baby sheep sitting on her head. I don't see her very often, only when Nurse Stanley is having a night off, but she always smiles as if she's glad to see me.

She wears glasses that are half an inch thick and still squints through them. I used to practice fake-taking my meds with Nurse Pritchard before I was confident I would fool Nurse Stanley.

I'm not gonna need those skills tonight.

Her hands are shaky as she holds out my dixie cup. Careful to avoid her fingers, I grab the cup before she spills the pills onto the floor. I don't really want to take meds that hit the ground but, desperate as I am right about now, not gonna lie—I'd take them if they landed in a toilet.

Four pills line the bottom: my recent dose, plus my blue pill. I send a silent thank you to Dr. Gillespie as I toss the pills back. The water helps them go down easy.

Like Nurse Stanley, Nurse Pritchard expects me to open my mouth and show her that it's empty inside. Unlike Nurse Stanley, Nurse Pritchard seems satisfied that my pills are gone.

She should. Considering what happened last night, no way I'm missing this dose.

Frankie is built like Duncan, big and bulky, but that's the only similarity I can see. For one thing, Frankie is olive-toned, straight Italian, and Duncan is black. Duncan's bald head gleams like an eight-ball while Frankie has this thick, greasy black hair that he wears slicked back. Duncan always glowers. Frankie is a chatterbox. Now that I'm acting like a model patient, he chitchats while Nurse Pritchard takes my vitals and administers my medication.

I'm half listening to him. I give one-word answers when he pauses to take a breath. I guess it's enough. It's not like the techs expect that much from me anyway.

When they're done, Frankie helps Nurse Pritchard leave my room. He closes the door behind them, but it's not locked. Not yet. I can go track down Carolina as soon as I'm ready to.

Even though I'm anxious to see her, to find out what her cryptic note means, I'm not in a rush to leave. I decide to stick it out in my room for a few minutes, give Frankie and Nurse Pritchard some time to move on to the next patient. I know Emma next door gets her meds brought to her room, too, as well as Tai in the guys' section of our floor.

The last thing I need is to draw attention from the facility staff because I'm acting out of the ordinary. I haven't spent the evenings outside of my bedroom since my first year inside of Black Pine and Dr. McNeil discovered I was talking to the shadows in the common room. As soon as I think it's emptied out a bit, I'll go see Carolina.

It's probably not the best idea, but I go and lay down on my bed. I'm not ready to go to sleep yet. I'm still wearing my hoodie —I'll take that off after I get back—and I traded my sneakers for my slippers; since I've given up on hiding my pills, I'm back to wearing my slippers before I go to bed. If anyone asks what I'm doing out of my room, I'm sure I can come up with something later.

I'm exhausted, though. Thanks to last night's hallucination, I haven't slept in more than twenty-four hours. My body is rundown. I feel achy and drained. Add that to my heavy dinner, and it's already a struggle for me to keep my eyes open. My mouth stretches wide as I try to fight a yawn.

I really want to see what's going on with Carolina. I *do*. But maybe I'll be able to make more sense out of this strange situation if I just rest my eyes for a couple of seconds.

I FALL ASLEEP BECAUSE OF COURSE I DO.

I'm only human.

It's not for long, though. An hour? If that. It's barely a refresher and, honestly, I feel worse for my short catnap. I've got this terrible taste in my mouth and I wish I'd left some of my water from my dixie cup to rinse it out. Ugh.

Something woke me up. I didn't mean to fall asleep in the first place, but as soon as I resurface, I realize exactly what cut into my rest.

The hum starts out low before it turns into an insistent buzz.

I crack my eyes open in time for me to notice that one of the fluorescent light bulbs over my bed is starting to go bad. It flickers on and off, the hum growing even louder whenever it turns dark. Since it's still on, I know it's not past lights out time yet, and I'm wondering if I should go see if I can find Carolina now.

And that's when I hear his voice.

"*Riley.*"

Oh, come *on*. I took my blue pill. It's why I went to see Dr. Gillespie this morning and begged for a med check. My pride was worth it. I didn't want to have to deal with Nine coming to see me again. I would've done anything to make it all go away.

Obviously, Nine didn't get the memo.

It's weird. I'm not used to seeing him unless it's super late and super dark. The flickering light doesn't do much to hide how hot he is.

Damn it. You'd think I would've toned down his ridiculous good looks the next time I conjured him since I'm so desperate to get rid of him. Seriously? Why does he have to be so gorgeous?

Though, as I get a better look at him in the dying light, I notice that he's a little bit different after all. I didn't think it was possible, but his skin has gotten even paler. His silver eyes seem duller than they did, the dark circles underneath a blemish on his otherwise perfect face. He's still wearing the same, strange, coat—it's like a leather duster but... but *not*—and it's not sitting right. It's kinda askew, one shoulder dipped lower than the other, his wavy hair trapped beneath it as if he threw it on in a hurry.

Still, no denying he's Nine. And he's in my room.

Again.

I sigh. Really? It's the only thing I can do right now. Anger and denial didn't do shit last night. I guess I'm up to barely masked frustration.

"You've got to be kidding me. What part of *you're not real, leave me alone* didn't you get?"

The Nine I knew from my childhood would've threatened to leave if I was so disrespectful. Not this Nine. Not the new, updated version of the Shadow Man.

This one just lets out a soft exhale. "You're still here."

Why does he sound so relieved? Where does he think I could've gone? "Well, yeah. But I'm supposed to be here." Then, in case he's forgotten, I add, "You're not. Why did you come back?"

"I wasn't sure if I'd be able to make it in time. I had to wait for the shadows to return to get to you and I thought, by then, I would've just missed you."

I can't help myself. I wave at the window. "Hello? Bars." I turn so that I can wiggle my fingers at the closed door. "Fully staffed facility. I've been locked in here for years. I'm not getting out for a couple of weeks. I'm not going anywhere."

"It might not be your choice."

His harsh words send a shiver up and down my spine. I don't like the way he said that. "What's that supposed to mean?"

"Did you forget everything I told you last night?" Nine clicks his tongue in annoyance. "I expect more from you than that."

Hallucination or not... figment of my imagination or a real-life fucking fae, I don't really care. At that moment, all I can think about is the Shadow Man I used to know and how I spent most of my life constantly searching for his approval. One kind word from Nine would have me floating with happiness for days.

A flippant or, worse, callous comment? It was like being slapped in the face.

I used to cry whenever I disappointed Nine. I used to pout whenever he treated me so coldly.

Now?

I'm just *angry*.

"Don't talk to me like that," I snap, sitting up so that I can glare over at him. "Don't know if you've figured it out yet or not, but I'm not a little girl anymore."

His silver eyes flash, reflecting the fluorescent light as it continues to whine and flicker. "Believe me, Shadow. I certainly noticed that."

Another shiver. The way he looks at me right now? I don't need my weird talent at being a human lie detector to know that he's telling the truth.

And I like it. I like the spark of interest way more than I should. Harboring this strange attraction to Nine is wrong in so many ways. I thought I was over my crush when he abandoned me shortly after Madelaine's death. I almost believed that I'd be happy if I never saw him again.

Having him so close, having him within arm's reach should I absolutely lose the rest of my sanity and actually *touch* him... I realize that I've been fooling myself all along. I might change my mind come morning, but now? Just like I couldn't accept that the golden fae was a hallucination even as I was dancing with him in my dreams, I know that Nine is real.

He's always been real.

Which means—

Panic begins to creep in. Blood drums in my ear, my breath picking up as I try to get air in quicker than I need to. The room starts to spin and I twist so that I'm about to climb out of my bed, slippers flat to the floor as I grip the edge of my mattress with gloved fingers. Okay. *Okay.* I just need my meds to kick in. The blue pill will work. It's always worked before. It will work and then I'll be drifting away, leaving Nine behind as another nightmare.

Maybe if I keep on pretending, it'll finally come true.

"You're not real. You're *not.* You're a hallucination, Nine. I see you. I hear you. But you're not real."

"Ah, Shadow…" Nine leans forward. He doesn't leave the shadows in the corner, but I can tell from the dark expression that flitters across his face that he… he wants to. "I know this is a lot. You spent too long inside this place. It served its purpose, it kept you safe, but it went too far. I wanted you to be hidden from those who long to hurt you. I never expected you to forget all about them." He pauses. "About me."

"I've never forgotten," I say truthfully. "How can I? When, every morning, I have to confront that I'm here because I told the world that a fae killed my sister? I can't forget, but that doesn't mean this is really happening."

Nine spits out a word. Another one of those foreign words.

I try to echo it. "Ash-lynn? What?"

"He agreed that this was the only option I had. The asylum. It might have kept you alive, but at what cost?"

So this Ash-lynn person is a guy. It's not the golden fae—Nine called him Rys—which means there's another one out there who knows about me.

Great. Just great.

"Who the hell is Ash-lynn?"

"I can't explain. Not yet. Not now." Nine shakes his head when I start to argue. "Later, Riley. I swear it. But not now. Now, we have to go." He holds out his hand. "Come with me."

And… we're back to that again.

"I can't leave the asylum. I'm not like you. I can't just disappear."

"That's what you think."

"Nine—"

"You can leave this place any time you want to," he tells me.

And then he drops the bomb:

"How else are you visiting the cemetery?"

CHAPTER 11

How does he know that? *Nobody* knows that. Apart from drawing her stone angel during art therapy, I never share my sister with anyone in here unless I'm forced to during sessions.

Hell, even I've spent the last few years believing that my nighttime visits to Madelaine's graves are just really, really vivid dreams. Rain-soaked bangs? Sweat. Mud on my slipper? I must have stepped in something in the common room. I made excuses for it all because I *had* to. Anything else was impossible.

"How do you know that?" I demand.

Nine arches one midnight black eyebrow. It's a dark slash in his pale face as he says, "Do you deny it?"

"They're just dreams."

"For some, perhaps. But not for a shade-walker."

"A *what*?"

"It's a gift. A fae blessing. A shade-walker has the power to travel through shadows," Nine explains. "You can go wherever you want, whenever you want."

"I'm not a shade-walker."

"You are."

He's telling the truth. But this is... this is *insane*. And that's saying something, coming from someone like me.

"Really? I've wanted out of here for close to six years now," I scoff. "I'm still here."

"Oh? That's probably because you've never tried before."

He's got me there. I can honestly say that I've never seen a shadow and thought, *Hey, I can travel through that.*

Nine is serious. I can tell. He's wearing the same expression he always used to wear whenever he told me stories about Faerie. Like he's teaching me something that I need to know and —oh, shit, I'm not supposed to be buying into any of this.

"Shade-walking is easier to do when you're sleeping. Your conscious mind will fight against what it deems impossible but, unconscious, there are no limitations to what you can do. Explains your graveside visits. With a little practice, you can control the shadows. It's a Dark Fae gift. I can teach you how to use it."

"Wait— *wait.* I'm not saying I believe any of this, but if I do? How do I have this gift?" A horrible suspicion hits me. "I'm... I'm not a Dark Fae or something, am I?"

Nine scowls at the same time as I realize that my horrified expression probably just insulted him. "No, you're not. It's a Dark Fae gift, but some are just born with it. In your case, you were—it's what drew you to the Fae Queen's attention. No changing it now. It's time for you to use that. If anything happens to me, it might be the only thing that can save you."

I ignore that part. The fae have been chasing me for more than twenty years according to Nine. They can wait five more minutes while I wrap my head around this whole shade-walking thing.

And it's not like I *want* to believe him—I don't—but there have been too many mornings where I woke up exhausted with dirty slippers and the smell of graveyard soil in my nose.

"Okay," I admit. "Fine. So I visit the cemetery in my dreams. But I always wake up here. I'm not really going anywhere."

"Yes, Riley, you are. You have to understand. You come back to this place because it was safe. This asylum took over as your protector while I kept you shielded. But that time is over with. I'm here to take my job back." Nine extends his arm. "Come to me. Give me your hand."

It's the one thing I can't do. Not even for Nine. Too many years being taught that I should never, ever willingly touch a fae makes me refuse. Now that I know he's one of them, it's not even a question.

"I can't."

"You can," argues Nine with a frustrated sigh, "but you won't."

I shrug. "Call it what you want. I'm not gonna let you anywhere near me. Sorry."

"Very well. Then I'll just have to do it myself."

What? *No.* "You're not allowed. You need my permission. You can't—"

The creak of my doorknob turning cuts through the room, interrupting my frantic shouts. I clench my jaw shut, clamping my teeth together because, if I don't, I'll start screaming. I know I will. And the last thing I need is to be sedated again.

Frankie peeks his head inside of my room. The fluorescent light bulb continues to flicker, the light bouncing off of his oily hair. I only realize how loud the hum has gotten when Frankie glances up at it in confusion.

I use those two seconds to steal a look at the corner.

As sudden as he arrived, Nine is gone. Good. I don't know

what would have been worse: explaining Nine to Frankie if the big tech saw him, or dealing with reality when it turned out that Frankie couldn't.

He points up at the dying bulb. "This just go out?"

I can't speak yet. My heart is lodged in my throat, thumping away like mad. Okay. I was wrong. The absolute *last* thing I needed right now is to deal with one of the techs walking in on me while I'm having a full-blown freak-out at Nine.

Who cares that the Shadow Man is gone? It actually makes it *worse*.

Gulping, trying to force back the lump inside my throat, I simply nod.

"I was coming to tell you that it's lights out. Gonna lock the doors in a few. You okay in here, Thorne?"

My mouth is dry. That was a direct question. I'm not so sure I can get away with nodding again. My voice is weak, a little shaky, as I try to come up with a reason why I look like I'm about to lose it. Frankie's not dumb. I see the furrow in his brow as he peers closely at me. He knows something is up.

I point at the light. "Just trying to figure out how to get it to stop doing that. It's kinda freaking me out, the way it keeps flickering like that. You don't think it's gonna blow, do you?"

He glances up at it in concern, as if the idea has occurred to him, too. "Better safe than sorry," he decides. "I'll go get maintenance."

"Oh. Really? Thanks."

"Hang tight. I'll be right back."

Frankie closes the door behind him when he leaves. There's not much time. I immediately scramble out of my bed, tiptoeing toward the door. There's a small, square window in the center. I peek out into the corridor.

Nurse Pritchard is standing near the nursing station, filing a chart. Kelsey is putting her coat on, ready to end her shift. Frankie is nowhere in sight.

"I don't like the way he was looking at you. He watched you too long."

At the sound of the lyrical voice with a harsh edge, I whirl around just as the fluorescent light finally gives out. It pops, the light dimming as the annoying humming whines to a stop. All I can hear now is my frightened breathing.

Nine moves like a cat. I mean it. I never see him come or go. He's just *there*. Where did he disappear to?

Even worse, why do I insist on bringing him back?

Squinting in the sudden darkness, I pick him out from the rest of the shadows. "I thought you were gone."

"I'm not going anywhere without you, especially now that I'm sure the asylum has been compromised. Someone has to protect you, Shadow. I gave my word. I must do this."

There's a threat in there that's impossible for me to ignore. I back up against the closed door, prepared to bang on it if he even so much as looks at me funny. "Stay back. You can't touch me. I won't let you."

"That's fine," Nine says solemnly. Then, for the first time tonight, he steps out of the pitch-dark shadows in the corner. The air shifts and I know—I just... I just *know*—that Nine is actually here with me. Not in the same room, not tucked in the shadows, but within touching reach. He's really, really here. And then he tells me, "I don't have to have your permission for this."

"For what? I don't understand—"

"There's no time. He'll be back."

"Nine, what are you— *no!*"

He grabs my arm in a grip so tight that I can already imagine the bruise that will be there in the morning. I try to jerk out of his grip, but it's impossible. He yanks my arm and, suddenly, the room starts spinning like I've gotten tossed inside of a tornado.

I open my mouth to scream but the sound gets lost in the rush of air. My hair starts whipping around me, the white-blonde strands mingling with Nine's raven-colored waves. Dark mixed with light. Black and white.

Ha. As if it was that simple.

Everything blurs. Wind whooshes through me, an angry breeze that slaps me with the ends of my hair, my cheeks rippling at the force of it. It's a chilly burst of air that freezes the tips of my ears. They've always been super sensitive and it's been so damn long since I felt the wind on my skin like that.

It doesn't last long and by the time my teeth are chattering from the chill, a suppressing heat slams into me. I choke, then gag. That's probably not because of the temperature change. The spinning is making my already queasy stomach violent.

I used to get car sick when I was a kid. This is ten times worse.

I clamp my eyes closed, screwing my jaw shut so that I don't throw up my beef stew all over Nine's shadowy coat. He might deserve it for what he's doing right now, but I'd only regret it in the end.

My whole body jerks, like when you're riding on a train and it stops short. If Nine wasn't gripping my arm so tight, I would've gone flying when the world seems to just… stop.

Once I'm standing still, once I'm sure the world has stopped spinning, I crack my eyelids open—and immediately wish that I *didn't*.

My first thought is that I probably should've paid closer attention to what the nurse stuck in my dixie cup because one of those pills has got to be wrong. I'm tripping pretty hard on something. That's the only way I can explain what I'm seeing.

The sky is this freaky pink. Not a soft pale color, either, but a dark magenta mixed with large swirls of a deep, burnished gold. I don't see any sun or stars or even clouds. Just a purply-pink sky.

The trees are even worse. I mean, they're beautiful—but they look like they're made of crystals. If it wasn't for the heat here, or the fact that it's still June, I'd think they were bare trees with a silver bark, empty branches dripping with icicles. I don't know how else to explain their sparkle and shine.

The air is thin here, or maybe I've forgotten how to breathe. I bend over with my gloves on my knees and look at what *should* be the grass. It looks like spun sugar or dental floss or, well, anything but grass. Because in the real world? Grass isn't this shade of a pretty light blue.

Hunched over, torn between running my fingers through the weirdo grass and flipping out because it's starting to hit me that I'm not in the real world anymore, I finally notice that Nine isn't holding onto my arm.

For one horrible second, I think that I lost him in the whipping wind, but then I turn around and he's looming behind me. From the look on his gorgeous face, I'm betting he didn't expect to be in this strange place anymore than I do.

He catches my eye. Without a word, he puts one long, pale finger to his lips. There's a shiny patch of raw skin along the side of his finger and most of his hand.

I've seen marks like those before. Nine has a freshly healed burn.

"Where are we?" I whisper. And then, because indignation can only protect me so much and I'm two seconds away from shaking in my slippers, I hiss, "So I know I haven't been on the outside in a while, but I think I would've remembered if the sky was *pink*."

Nine ignores my question. "Just stay close to me. We went a few portals too far. We shouldn't be here. I'll give you a couple of seconds to recover, then we'll try again."

Is that a threat? Now that I'm standing straight again, freaking out has won out and I'm way too busy to notice much of anything else. I force myself to pay attention to Nine. He's a fae, right? A Dark Fae who just proved we can both walk through shadows together. He knows what he's doing, right?

A couple of seconds, then we're getting the hell out of here. Okay. That calms me a little.

I still don't know exactly what this place is. I start turning in circles, marveling at its strange, undeniable beauty when, suddenly, I glimpse someone in the distance, halfway hidden behind one of the trees. I jump back. From his whisper, it's obvious Nine doesn't want anyone else to know we've popped in. Crap. That's definitely a person over there.

I blink. Wait a second. That's... that's a *person*. Not a fae. His skin is a light brown shade—not bronzed, not moonlight pale—and, even from where I am, I can tell that he's shorter than Nine. He's still tall, though. And there's something about him that's... that's *familiar*. Squinting, I look closer.

No fucking way.

Nine is hanging back. The Shadow Man's gotta be proud of himself. He got what he wanted. I'm here, wherever here is, and I'm not screaming my head off.

Yeah. That's about to change.

Before he can stop me, I bolt. I have to be sure that I'm right. I don't know how it's possible, but I have this absolutely awful suspicion about the guy tucked behind that weirdo tree over there. Who knows? Maybe I'm deflecting. I don't want to deal with Nine so why not run off into this unknown place?

"Riley," he hisses after me. "No!"

I ignore Nine. He's bigger than me, and probably faster, but I want it more. I pull up to the tree seconds before I sense Nine closing in on me from behind. That's more than enough time for me to prove that I wasn't seeing things.

It's Jason. And he isn't moving.

Still as a statue, his big, black eyes wide but unseeing, he has one hand held out in front of him as if he was begging before he was frozen in place. The wispy, floaty candy floss that's supposed to be grass is creeping up his legs, wrapping around his knees. He's trapped.

I've got to get the hell out of here before that happens to me next.

I back into Nine, hitting his chest with my shoulder in a frantic attempt to escape the terrible truth in front of me. I bounce off of him, my hoodie and his jacket protecting me from another touch. He reaches for me. I dodge him easily, my gloved fingers trembling as I press them to my lips.

Jason. The goofy, smiling, optimistic guy from Black Pine. He always seemed nice, and he spent countless sessions detailing the big plans he had for what his life was going to be like when they finally let him back out.

He's been gone from the asylum the last few days. I remember missing him at breakfast... what day was that? Sunday. Pancakes. He wasn't there. He was missing.

No.

Not missing.

He's in Faerie. With a certainty that I can't explain, I know that's where he is.

And, now, so I am.

CHAPTER 12

"What happened to him?" The words slip out through the gaps between my fingers. I'm shaking. "What happened to Jason?"

Nine makes a rough sound in the back of his throat. Not a scoff, or a huff. It's frustration mixed with fury and, despite my shock at seeing Jason like that, I can tell Nine's not mad at me.

But hell if he isn't angry.

"You know that human?" he asks.

I nod.

"Then he's a warning to you."

What? "I don't—*what*? What do you mean, a warning?"

"The Fae Queen. These are her gardens. She would've left him here for you to find him if you came to Faerie before she had you brought to her." Nine's silver eyes don't seem so out of place in this otherworld. They shine in his face, a perfect match to the bark on the tree that shadows Jason. "He was in the asylum."

It's not a question. I nod anyway.

"How long?"

I swallow roughly. "I don't know. A year maybe? Two. I didn't really pay attention. He was nice, though. He doesn't deserve this."

"If he's here, then you can be sure the human deserves a fate far worse than this," Nine says coldly.

The iciness in his voice stings me. I flinch, then step away from him, balling my hand into a fist and dropping it at my side. "How can you be so heartless?"

"I'm not. My loyalty is to only one who has human blood." Me. He's talking about me. "Besides, he was as good as dead the first time he let Melisandre touch his soul. He belonged to the queen. To leave him in her garden as a statue is a kindness compared to what I would have done to the mortal if I discovered he was working against you."

"Jason?" I turn to look at the statue again, trembling noticeably when it's pretty damn obvious that he really *is* a statue. He hasn't moved an inch. "He wasn't working against me. I barely knew the guy. He was just another patient inside—"

"No. He wasn't." Nine glides easily around me, blocking Jason from my sight. "Don't you understand? I needed you safe. I needed to put you somewhere protected before the Fae Queen sent her soldiers after you. But she did anyway. Not fae—you would've sensed them in your domain the second they crossed into the human world. But another human? You'd never guess they were on the side of the queen."

"I don't get it. Why would he work for her?"

"Not just that human," Nine admits. "As soon as I discovered that they knew where to find you, I took the first portal to the asylum. It wasn't just the male. I could sense more than a few touched humans inside that place. It's why I knew I had to get you out of there before any of your enemies got to you first."

I immediately think of Diana, the blonde tech whose eyes flashed golden the other night. Of how uncomfortable she made me. What about Dr. Gillespie? He was always way too interested in Nine. How many times did I think it was super weird how my psychologist was humoring me by acting like my hallucinations were real?

Too many, but it made sense if *he* knew that they weren't hallucinations at all.

He's telling the truth. As painful as it is—as incredibly unbelievable as it is—Nine is telling the truth.

"Why?" I forget in the heat of the moment that Nine wanted me to be quiet. The word bursts out of me with all the subtlety of a bomb going off. I'm an almost twenty-one-year-old orphan. I'm not supposed to have *enemies*. "What the hell does she want with me?"

"It's because you're the Shadow."

I'm not a statue, but I go still like one.

I know that voice. Lilting and lyric, it's deep enough to belong to a man, and rich enough to make me want to turn around and see him—even though I know better.

When I manage to break my sudden spell of paralysis, I search for him.

There he is. Rys. The golden fae—the Light Fae—who killed my sister has joined us in the gardens.

In this strange place, he is absolutely brilliant. His lovely, bronze-colored skin is nearly a match for the swirls in the sky, his golden eyes flashing and reflecting the silver trees. He moves purposefully but easily, like he doesn't have a care in the world. Long, tawny hair drifts behind his lean body as he glides toward me.

His lips part. A whisper on the still breeze.

I have an irresistible urge to go to him—

"Riley," snaps Nine. "Stay strong. Fight it."

But I don't *want* to—

"Shadow," Nine says, more feeling in his harsh voice. "Stop moving!"

I jam the heels of my slipper into the fluffy, wispy, flossy grass. My shins strain as I fight the pull toward Rys. And it's not just because Nine told me to stop.

I want to stop.

I do. When about ten feet still separate me from him, I finally manage to put on the brakes. I'm panting at how much of my strength it took to fight the compulsion to go to him, but I stop.

"You've taken too many liberties, Rys." Nine moves so that he's standing beside me. He points at the Light fae. "I could sense your brand on her skin the second I returned to her. You touched her."

"And you've told her about the Shadow Prophecy before she came of age," Rys counters. "Seems we both did a little trickery."

"I did no such thing. I kept to the terms of my bargain."

"You called her Shadow."

"It's just another name for her. That's all."

"Ah, that's right. Because you don't know her true name." Rys turns to me, his eyes sparkling in delight. "We've shared more than a touch, you and I. Isn't that right?"

Whether I'm doing it to myself or he is, suddenly the song from the night I danced with him in my dreams is filtering in through my ears, beating against the back of my skull. I grit my teeth, desperate to ignore it.

I can't. Not only that, but my hands grow even hotter inside of my gloves. I can't forget how I let him touch me, the sizzle I felt when our bare skin connected, or how weak and drained I was as he sapped me of all my energy.

He touched me. And I *let* him.

I wrap my arms around me, hugging myself. Nine moves forward, shielding me with his body as he steps between Rys and me.

"You interfered," he accuses the other fae.

"You say interfere, I say that I'm just doing what I must to claim what's mine. I'm not like Melisandre. The prophecy doesn't faze me, Nine. Riley's got enough blood in her to be a proper *ffrindau* for me. I want her. I've waited long enough to take her. Leave her with me and your debt is repaid. You can go."

Nine reaches into his pocket. Of all things, he pulls out a rock. Seriously. A rock. About the size of a nickel, he holds it up, then lets it nestle in his palm. He cradles it like its heavier than it appears. "You don't have the power to clear it."

Rys holds out his hand. "Then pass it to me. I'll gladly take it."

What are they talking about? I thought I was confused because I was still shaking off the woozy feeling that hits me every time Rys pulls that command shit on me. Nope. When Nine looks at the rock in his palm, before vanishing it into the depths of his coat again, I can honestly say I have no clue what the fuck is going on.

"A rock?" I blurt out. "What's so special about a *rock*?"

Rys grins. "It's a token of Nine's favor for a human."

Nine's entire expression closes off. "It was no favor, Rys. You know that. It was a command."

"From a human," Rys says again. His grin widens, turning almost predatory. "A mother's last command to protect her infant daughter." He traces his jaw with his slender, bronzed, pointer finger. "Though, I've often wondered, shouldn't her fate free you of any debt you feel obligated to repay? Yet still you linger about my mate, like an unwanted shadow."

His words are like an arrow to my chest. My whole body jolts as I realize with a sudden start that I'm the infant daughter Rys is talking about. The human? That's got to be my mother.

They're talking about my *mom*.

I whirl on Nine. "My mother asked you to protect me?"

"Commanded," corrects Rys cheekily.

I can't even look at him. Mate? That's gonna be a nope. Maybe if I hope real hard, he can join Jason in being a statue in this freaky garden.

Besides, my attention is super locked in on Nine. He knows it, too. His silver eyes have dimmed, the razor-sharp edge of his cheekbones jutting out as he sucks in a breath.

"My mother commanded you to protect me?" I ask him a second time. I wave behind me, gesturing where I think Rys is still standing. My hands are shaking. "What does he mean by debt? And her fate? What happened to my mom?"

"Yes, Nine. Answer her," Rys calls out. "You were at the gas station that day. You know."

I'm sure Nine can see the hope in my expression as I gaze up at him. Apart from the grainy, black and white footage from twenty years ago, this is the only thing I've ever heard about the woman who left me behind.

I long ago accepted that she'd done it on purpose.

Could it be that she had no choice?

"Do you?" I ask him. "Do you know what happened to her? To *me*?"

Nine glares past me. If looks could kill, the Light Fae would be six feet under this candy floss grass in a heartbeat. "I left her alone after the contract was made. I have no idea what happened to Callie after I returned to Faerie. Riley's my concern, not her human mother. And I've done everything to protect her, like I said I would."

I'm used to Nine's cold and callous attitude when it comes to humans. I've known for a long time that I'm the only exception when it comes to his outright disdain for anybody in the human world. I was so happy to have him care about me—even if it was in his stilted, limited way—that I never second-guessed him when he said he was sent to watch over me.

I had no fucking clue that he'd been *commanded* to.

This is a double gut punch. I learned two things just now. One? My mom's name is Callie. I tuck that deep inside, that small nugget of information that brings me closer to the woman I lost. And two? Nine only ever looked after me because someone forced him to.

I don't have my mom. I guess I never really had my Shadow Man, either.

"Is that why you visited me as a kid?" I ask him. "A… a debt?"

The fae can't lie, but I'm betting that Nine's wishing that he could because it takes him a few pointed seconds before he finally nods.

"Yes."

"She made you do it."

"Yes, but, Riley—"

Nope. That's all I needed to hear.

"I want to go back to the asylum," I say, interrupting him. "Take me back. Now."

"I can't." He says *can't*. I know from his demeanor that he means *won't*. Now I know where I got it from. "It's not the place for you any longer. You can't go back."

I whirl around, facing Rys. "You."

Rys arches one of his perfect eyebrows. His smile is playful. I hate him for that. "Yes, my *ffrindau*?"

Ffrindau. I know what Nine said that meant. soulmate. Yeah, right. That's never gonna happen, but I'm not above using this fae to get what I want. "Can you bring me back to the asylum?"

"I'll do anything you ask of me."

"She doesn't need you, Rys. She has me." Nine bristles, visibly annoyed. That's... that's new. He never used to let me see such an emotional reaction. Rys has obviously gotten to him.

"We can't go back to the asylum, Riley, but we don't have to stay here."

Nine's whole demeanor changes as he turns to me. It almost sounds like he's pleading—but why would a fae plead with a nobody human like me?

Then he says, "I'll take you somewhere else to keep you protected," and I remember.

That's right. Because of his debt.

Huh. No thanks.

Right now, I don't want either one of them. My shock's fading. Blood is rushing past my ears as my heart beats out of control. My vision is dimming; black spots are closing in on the corners. I'm on the verge of a monstrous panic attack. I take a couple of deep breaths in an attempt to calm myself. It's useless. It feels like something inside of me is clawing its way out. I gasp and pull on the collar of my hoodie, trying to get more out of this weak air before I lose it entirely and I can't go home at all.

Neither Nine nor Rys has noticed that I'm teetering on the edge. Nine is staring at the Light Fae. Rys is wearing a smirk that shouldn't be half as attractive as it is.

"If you take her, I'll just chase after her."

"You can't follow her in the shadows."

"No," Rys agrees. "But plenty of Melisandre's soldiers can."

I don't know who this Melisandre person they keep bringing up is, but I've got a pretty good guess. Who seems to have a reason to come after me *and* has access to soldiers? She's got to be the Fae Queen.

And we're currently in her gardens. While Nine and Rys bicker like children, I'm a sitting duck. Nine wanted me to be quiet? Yeah, that ship sailed a while ago.

I don't want to turn into a statue like Jason.

"Nine," I say, because if the choice is between my Shadow Man and the golden fae, I know who I'm sticking with, "let's just go. I don't care where. I can't stay here. It's too hard for me to breathe."

In an instant, Rys loses the last of his playful nature. He grows deadly serious and, in his golden eyes, I get a glimpse of the dangerous, capricious creature who snapped Madelaine's neck because he wanted to prove a point.

I choke on another gasp, throwing my hands up as I stumble back. Nine is slender, but he's tall. If I crouch a little, I can hide behind him.

The way Rys is looking at me all of a sudden, I *have* to.

"You will stay with me," he says in a booming voice at odds with its normally smooth and cajoling tone. It's an obvious command. I shiver and start to stand up straight, though there's nothing about his words that make me feel like I must.

I hesitate, keeping Nine between us.

Rys glowers. Hate fills his gaze as he glances at Nine before he turns to me. A mixture of lust and desire twists his expression until I know that there's no way I'm getting out of this without him trying to call me to him again.

I'm right.

"Come to me. Come, Zel—"

He never finishes his command.

Nine stiffens. I'm not so sure why—and his back is to me so I can't see his face—but I sense a change in him as soon as Rys starts to say that weird *Zella* word again. Before Rys can utter the second syllable, Nine's pale skin begins to glow.

He spares one glance at me, a quick peek to make sure I haven't moved, then he zeroes in on the Light Fae.

If Rys's shine is brilliant in this strange place, Nine's vibrant silver glow makes him absolutely terrifying. The fierce expression on his face isn't helping me, either. Holy shit. I've never been afraid of Nine before, but I guess there's a first time for everything because I'm about to flip the fuck out.

I gasp for another breath, certain that I'm about to just pass out already. Only the fact that I'm in Faerie—I'm in the Fae Queen's gardens—keeps me standing. I'm already super vulnerable. Fainting here?

Might as well just walk up to her castle and say hi while I'm at it.

While I struggle to hold it together, Nine lifts his hand again. After muttering something in that harsh, foreign language of his, he makes a gesture I don't understand. I can't really see it. Blackness is creeping up on the edge of my sight, though I wince and squint when he stretches his fingers. It's like he's turned a flashlight on. A bright silver beam shoots out at Rys, breaking up some of the fog that's clouding my vision.

It pushes the Light Fae back a few feet. The grin slides from Rys's face as he lifts one delicate hand to shield his gaze.

"You shouldn't have done that, Nine."

"Leave us," he orders. "You don't believe in the Shadow Prophecy. I've dedicated too many years to it. The Shadow belongs to the Dark Fae. Accept it."

"Aislinn was a Light Fae," Rys counters. "My claim is stronger."

"Fate will win."

"Or perhaps the queen will."

No, I think as I allow myself to give in to the panic scrabbling against the last of my consciousness. It's been there since I first saw the magenta sky mixed with gold, the crystalline trees, Jason the statue. I'm light-headed and weak, the anxiety crashing into me like a wave. I don't fight it anymore.

At the moment, I decide that *Riley* will win.

I remember what Nine told me. When I'm conscious, I can't accept that I can do that shade-walking shit. But what if I'm *not* conscious?

There's no sun here—but there are shadows everywhere. Lurking behind the unnatural, fantastical trees, like the one that's nearly hiding Jason, I see the shadows and, despite my cloudy, fuzzy head, I have to wonder.

It's worth a shot.

I start to fall, my eyes rolling into the back of my head. Every part of me locks up, my arms shrinking against my torso as I let myself go, aiming for the patch of hazy black that stretches across the ground.

I lock my jaw as I collapse. I refuse to give either of them permission to catch me before I hit the ground.

I only hope the weird grass is as soft as it looks.

CHAPTER 13

When I come to again, the first thing I look for is my window with its six bars across it.

Nope. No window. No bars. All I see is the night sky above my head and it hits me: I'm not at Black Pine anymore.

I'm not even *inside*.

A handful of stars twinkle in the distance, a few bright spots in the blackness above me. It takes a second before I understand that I'm lying on my back on the cold ground. Grass cushions me. I can feel it scratching me through my hoodie.

With a grunt, I roll onto my side. I blink a few times, trying to get my sight back, then use the dim moonlight to peer at the grass surrounding me.

It's pointy. Kinda brittle and dry, flat where my body pressed it into the dirt.

And, thank God, it's *green*.

I don't know where I am. Not quite yet. At least I can be sure of one thing, though: I'm not in the Fae Queen's gardens anymore.

"Riley. You're finally awake."

I'm not alone, either.

Nine is crouched beside me, his body low, the tail of his long jacket flaring out behind him. It flaps in the cool wind. It's not so warm here, not so humid, and when I tilt my head back so that I can look at the sky again, it's a relief to see that I'm back in the human world.

Lowering my gaze, I pull myself into a sitting position. I can feel the weight of his open stare and purposely avoid his eyes, his words, and his presence. I'm so stinking pissed at him, I want to knock him over. It would definitely be worth having to touch him.

I put my petty revenge on the back-burner when it finally clicks. I recognize the scene around me with a sudden jolt. Okay. Hold on. I know *exactly* where I am.

There's the gate, unlocked for the moment, though I know the caretaker's habits. At ten minutes to midnight, he'll start his final rounds before he locks up for the night. A couple of rows away from where I am, I see the Richardsons' mausoleum, the stone behemoth that shielded me from the rain the last time I was here.

And there, somewhere on the west side of the cemetery, I'll find the concrete angel that stands guard over Madelaine's grave.

It's like what Nine said. I could run through shadows while I'm awake and nothing would ever happen because, after six years of therapy and denials, it's too hard for me to believe in the impossible. When I let myself faint, though? I must've hit that shadow and my body brought me back where I belong.

Nine got in my head. I should've landed in my bed at Black Pine—it's where I've traveled every other time I, well, I sleepwalked through the shadows. All of his arguments about the asylum being compromised got to me. Self-preservation must've kicked in. I'm not in Black Pine.

I'm in Acorn Falls.

I don't know how much time has passed. It's late, the chilly temperature washing away the last of the evening's heat. Besides the fact that it's pitch-dark around me, Nine's presence is a pretty big clue that it's still night out. As soon as the sun's up again, he'll be gone.

I… I don't know how I feel about that yet.

I'm so used to ducking and hiding when I find myself suddenly in the cemetery. Especially now that I know I'm really *here*, I don't want the grizzled old caretaker to find me sitting on a plot, hanging out with a fae who can shoot laser beams out of his palm.

That totally happened. It all happened. Escaping the asylum, visiting the Fae Queen's gardens, finding Jason… confronting Rys. It all happened.

I wait for the panic to crash over me. It doesn't. I think I've been pushed way past my limit at this point. Like, I'm so spent, I'm looking at the impossible series of events from tonight and just shrugging them off. I mean, it can't get much worse, can it?

I'm glad I made it here. Just knowing that I'm hiding out in the Acorn Falls cemetery gives me a tiny bit of peace. Doesn't matter how I got here. It's night. Nine might be here, but Rys isn't. The Fae Queen isn't.

It's something.

I lean against the nearest gravestone. *Robin Maitland, 1912-1989.* She had a good, long life. *Treasured wife and mother.* She sounded nice. I don't think she'd mind me using her final resting place to take a breather.

The chill of the marble stone cuts right through the material of my hoodie.

Eh. It's not so bad. It could be raining.

The grass rustles, the swish of Nine's duster whispering in the wind as he gets to his feet. He moves so that he's standing in front of me. Without a word, he offers his bare hand out.

"I know you're kidding." I sound tired. So very tired. These small catnaps aren't doing enough for me to recharge. Slumping back on the grass, I lean against Robin Maitland's headstone. It's as much for support as it is to cover me from the caretaker's lantern. "Get back down. You don't want to get us caught."

He doesn't move. "I'm not worried about what a human can do to me."

No. Of course not.

"Yeah. Well, maybe I'm worried about what you'll do to a human. It's not the caretaker's fault we crashed here."

Nine blinks. His outstretched hand falls to slap the side of his thigh. "You'd want me to spare him? He's obviously a threat to you."

So I was right. Dark Fae or Light Fae, it doesn't matter. Just like Rys killed Madelaine as almost an afterthought, Nine wouldn't even think twice about offing the cemetery caretaker.

The fae might be beautiful, but they're also terrible.

"He's not a threat. He's an old man who takes care of the graves at night. I don't want any trouble."

Even as I say the words, I know it's pointless. Trouble? I'm already in it up to my ears.

"As you say, Shadow."

Shadow. I wince, closing my eyes. Did he really have to go there?

"Don't call me that."

"It's your name."

"*My* name is *Riley*."

"That's what your first human family called you. That's not your name."

My stomach drops to my slippers.

That's right. Not only has he hidden this prophecy thing from me but, holy shit, he actually *knew* my mother.

"So my mom named me Shadow?" I say warily. I wish I had more energy. I want to get up and pace, maybe even rant and scream and demand Nine tell me *everything*, but I'm too tired. I haven't gotten more than an hour or two of sleep in almost two days. Plus, my panic attacks always take every inch of my strength. I push on, though, because I have to. "Or do you call me that because of that stupid prophecy the other monster mentioned?"

"He's not a monster."

"Po-ta-to, po-tah-to. He's a killer."

Nine smartly stays quiet.

I grab a handful of the grass that covers Robin Maitland's grave. I won't touch him, but I'm frustrated enough to throw the blades at Nine. They flutter in the wind, covering the tip of his shiny boot.

He frowns. "Was that necessary?"

Yes. "Tell me about the Shadow Prophecy."

"What if the human finds you here?"

"You just said you'd spare him if I wanted you to. I want you to. It'll be fine. Now, stop stalling. I went with you to that weirdo place. I left Black Pine. Now it's your turn. What was he talking about? What's this prophecy and what the hell does it have to do with me?"

Throwing his coat behind him, Nine crouches down so that he's right beside me. His silver eyes beam in the darkness, brighter than the lantern the caretaker uses. He isn't blinking, watching every tired line on my face as I wait for him to answer.

I want to go to sleep, but I'm still shaken up from the scene with Rys. What if I do and he follows me into my dreams again? I can't risk it. Not yet.

"Tell me about the prophecy, Nine. Please."

Maybe it's the *please* that gets to him. I'll never know. After nodding a few times, Nine begins to explain.

"There's an ancient prophecy in Faerie. Melisandre has been queen for almost two centuries and she has no plans on abdicating anytime soon. She's ruthless, Riley, and she's gone further than most to secure her crown. The lesser citizens call it the Reign of the Damned, though she takes tongues from those who say it."

I swallow reflexively. She cuts out tongues? Oh, shit. "Okay, well, she sounds like a peach. But what does this queen have to do with me?"

"It's the Shadow Prophecy. It's been said that a shade-walker —the Shadow—will have the power to defeat the Fae Queen. With Melisandre's death, the Reign of the Damned will come to an end. You can imagine that she's desperate to keep her head."

Tongues and heads. Good thing I still haven't eaten—my stomach lurches at the images he's sticking in my mind.

And that's not even the worst of it.

It takes me a minute to process what he just told me. I don't know what I was expecting him to say—but you can bet it wasn't that. I'm not like Rys. I'm not a murderer. I don't care what this stupid prophecy says. I'm not about to kill anyone— especially not the Fae Queen.

I'm just a broken human. How would someone like me go up against an all-powerful faerie queen in the first place?

"So what? I'm supposed to be this Shadow person because I can walk through shadows? You can do it, too. You said it was a Dark Fae gift."

"It is. The Shadow has human blood, though. It can't be a fae."

Oh. *Wonderful.* "Is it true?" I demand. "Am I the Shadow?"

"She believes you are," Nine mutters. "That's all that matters. She'll end your life before you get the chance to end hers. When you were a child, she wasn't so concerned. But now that you're coming of age…"

Coming of age. How much do I want to bet that, to the fae, that means twenty-one?

You've got to be kidding me. All of Nine's mentions of a villainous *she* start to pop up in my memories. After the golden fae—after Rys—asked me to dance that first time and he killed Madelaine when I refused to leave the Everetts with him, I forgot all about the *she* who was after me. I had a real monster, a male monster, that I spent years obsessing over.

I never knew that it was the Fae Queen who was really after me.

Gulping, I ask him, "And there's nothing I can do about it?"

"Not right now."

That's not a no. I know better than to push him, though. When I was a kid, Nine hated it when I asked him questions. He'd rather I sit and listen because, eventually, he would tell me everything he thought I needed to know. To have him answering my questions, treating me like an equal… I shouldn't be so impressed, but I am. So the bar hasn't been set all that high for me. I get it. He made me a promise because he wanted something I didn't want to give him. Now that I'm out of the asylum, he could decide that that bargain has been met.

I have to get more answers out of him before he shuts the conversation down. He'll do it. I've seen him.

Besides, there's nothing I can do about the queen right now. So she thinks she has to kill me because I want to kill her? I'll leave her alone if she doesn't bother me. That seems fair.

So what if I "come of age" in two weeks? As far as I'm concerned, being twenty-one means two things: I'm out of Black Pine and I can finally buy booze legally.

Committing regicide? Yeah. I'm good.

At least now I know why my mom would've turned to another fae to protect me. I still don't know how she is involved—how she knew Nine, or that the fae were real to begin with—but it makes sense. Nine is a cold bastard. If there was anyone I'd choose to be a protector, it would be him.

"You knew my mom."

Nine's expression goes blank. It wasn't a question, but he treats it like one. "We've met."

"That's what he said. I didn't want to believe him."

"Who? Rys?"

I can't bring myself to say his name. "Yeah. The Light Fae. He said she commanded you to watch over me. How? She's a human."

His eyes dim. "Do you believe him?"

That's not an answer. Is my Dark Fae trying to be tricky?

"Hey, if you can interpret that any other way, be my damn guest. But I think that he was being pretty clear with what he said. No double meanings that I can figure out."

Nine turns away from me. His strong profile beneath the moonlight has me wondering why I'm trying to pick a fight with him. He sighs and, for a moment, when the cloud cover passes right over the moon, I think he's fading back into the shadows.

Then the clouds roll swiftly by and Nine is still there, avoiding my earnest gaze.

"Fine," he admits. "When you were very young, I struck a bargain with a human woman to repay an old debt of mine. Your mother. I gave her my word that I would watch over you if anything ever happened to her. I have only done what I promised to do."

It's a good thing I'm sitting on the ground. I feel like I've been sucker-punched. A sense of betrayal weighs my gut down like rocks. I'm suddenly aware that I never pushed for the reasons why he constantly visited me when I was little. I took it for granted that he wanted to—not that he was forced to.

Or that, all along, he only acted on orders from a mother who wanted to keep me protected.

"And you never thought that you should tell me that?"

Nine has the nerve to look surprised, like he doesn't quite understand why I'm so upset. "Why would I?"

"She was my mother!" I explode. "You let me spend my whole life thinking she didn't want me!"

"Yes," he says softly. His calm tone just makes me angrier. "But what would knowing that have done? It won't bring Callie back."

That's it. That's the last straw. You can only take too much until you crack and, deep down, I've been a fragile mess for most of my life. I've got this tough facade, hardened over the years, but it's only that—a facade. I've been splintering for a while now.

Of everything he's said, the casual way he uses her name is it. It's enough to make me shatter.

I push up off of the ground. Pure fury burns through my fatigue. My cheeks feel like they're on fire. My hands, too. I want to push him. To shove him. To hit him and hit him and hit him until Nine knows what it feels like to hurt the way that I'm hurting now.

His betrayal cuts like a knife. Tears spring to my eyes, almost like blood on the floor.

I don't want him to see. Wiping angrily at my face, the leather burning against my skin, I storm away from him.

"Riley... Riley! Stop. Where do you think you're going?"

Without turning around, I snap back. Let the caretaker hear me. I don't give a shit.

"Me? I'm going as far away from you as I can. Look." The moon's shining high over my head. It leaves a sliver on the dirt path, shadows wafting on the borders. "Shadows. Maybe I can jump in one and I'll be back at Black Pine." I leap, landing unsteadily, one of my slippers slipping out from under me. I angrily jam my foot back inside. "Oh, well. Guess not."

Nine takes two purposeful steps closer. His entire form is tensed. He's ready to come after me if I don't listen to him.

Yeah. Let him try.

I stomp off again.

His voice follows me. "Riley. You must stay with me. Rys has his own motives, but the queen could send any of my kind after you while it's still dark."

Wow, Nine. That was absolutely the worst thing to say to me right now.

I whirl on him, shoving my hair over my shoulder so that I can focus all of my unadulterated rage on him. "And?" I shoot back. "Maybe I should stick it out and wait for him. The Light Fae told me more about what's going on in my life tonight than you did in *fifteen years*."

"Don't say that. You don't know what he's capable of. He killed your friend just to get to you."

That's a slap in the face. I recoil from his harsh words.

As if I had forgotten *that*.

It takes a second for me to recover enough to retort. "Oh, yeah. Thanks for that, by the way. I know you left me behind, but at least you could've warned me about him before he snapped my sister's neck."

"I was trying to protect you."

I clap. The leather muffles the sound. "You did an amazing job. Six years in the asylum, haphephobia, and the ugliest hands you'll ever see. Plus, Madelaine's dead. She was my sister. Why couldn't someone protect *her*?"

"There's more to it than that." Nine gentles his voice. He's trying to placate me, to keep me from flipping out entirely, saying or doing something I'll regret. It's like pouring gasoline on the raging fire of my emotions. "If you would just calm down and let me explain—"

I shake my head. No. *No*. It's too little, too late. I don't want to hear anything else he has to say. No more worthless 'explanations'. Humming out loud, I cover my ears in a bid to drown his sensible voice out. I don't care if I look crazy. After all this time, I've gotten used to it.

And then Nine does something that I'm not expecting. Moving so fast, as if he teleported from his spot to right in front of mine, he lashes his hand out, wrapping his deceptively strong fingers around my wrist.

My sleeve rides up enough for his fingertips to find a patch of my skin. It sends a shock through my entire system, making me let out one hell of a primal scream. Nine tears one hand from my ear before he yanks his arm back.

As soon as he lets go of me, I clamp my mouth shut. I throw

myself backward, ducking to the grass when I see the lights in the caretaker office come blazing to life.

The door creaks open, followed by a shout.

"Who's out there? The cemetery's closed. Don't make me call the cops!"

My pulse thuds. Huddled in the grass, I shove my sleeve up, rubbing his aggressive touch from my skin. I can still feel it lingering there. I wipe at the patch, trying to erase it. Not because it's Nine or because he's a fae, but because that wasn't my choice.

The caretaker stands on the porch for a few seconds that seem like a lifetime. I can't tell if Nine slipped into the shadows and disappeared or not. I don't see him, but I'm also super focused on the open door. I shouldn't have screamed. I didn't want to involve the old man. And, sure, the cops might be able to help me—but not if I get busted for trespassing.

As soon as the caretaker decides he scared some no-good screamer off his property and heads back inside, Nine is suddenly there again.

He's cradling his right hand. Unless I'm seeing things—and my night vision is actually kinda amazing—there are these faint wisps of pale grey smoke coming from his palm. He flexes his fingers, careful to keep his hand turned toward his chest.

I'm immediately distracted from my anger. What's up with that?

I jerk my chin at him. "Aren't you going to give me a hand up?"

Nine holds out his left hand to me.

Yeah, that didn't work the way I wanted it to.

I shake my head. I definitely don't take his hand. "Forget it. What's up with the other hand, Nine?" An eerily familiar scent drifts on the breeze. My stomach turns. I know it too well—it took months before I got it out of my nose after the fire. "Why does it smell like burning flesh?"

He doesn't say anything. Instead, his lips pulled into a thin line, Nine shows me his hand. Each finger is burned raw, red blisters on every inch of his palm.

I stare in horror.

His pale skin is utterly destroyed.

CHAPTER 14

"What the *hell*—"

Nine blinks, stretching his fingers as if he's trying to slough off the ruined skin. I want to tell him to stop. His face is completely stoic. Except for the constant stretch, he doesn't give any indication that his hand's gotta be killing him.

"And now you see why I must have your permission."

Because he touched me. Without my permission, he can't leech any power from a touch. I didn't know that it burned the shit out of *him*, though.

I think back to the recently healed skin I saw on his hand earlier. It was when we landed in Faerie, right after he grabbed me without permission in my room. I know fae have crazy fast healing abilities—it's part of their magic—but I never put two and two together before. He must've been burned then, too.

So why did he do it? Why was it so important to him that I leave the asylum? Or listen to him try to explain? He had to have known what would happen if he grabbed me when I wouldn't let him.

I'm grateful when he tucks his burnt palm back into his chest. It reminds me too much of what my hands looked like after I reached through the enchanted flames to get to Madelaine. I didn't know she was dead. I had hope, and I would've walked through fire to save my sister. She was my best friend—except for Nine—and she was normal. Even better, she treated me like *I* was normal. She didn't deserve to die.

Rys dared me to save her. I tried. I really did. I managed to push my hands through the fire that circled Madelaine's body. It was so hot. So fucking hot. It burned the skin right off my hands, the white-hot agony making it impossible for me to go any further.

I blocked out a lot of what happened next. Dealing with my grief following Madelaine's death was almost as difficult as what I went through to save my hands. The burns were so bad that I needed multiple surgeries just to get to the point where I could finally have an autograft done. Seeing Nine's injury now, my fingers start to throb in sympathy pain.

I drop my face into my hands. The leather against my skin is familiar and reassuring. I breathe in deep. It helps.

Until Nine starts to speak again.

"Listen to me." I peek at him through the slivers of space between my fingers. "You must—"

Okay. That's it.

I drop my hands.

"I'm done."

"Shadow—"

Gritting my teeth, I tell him, "Don't call me that."

"We have to get you somewhere else. A building with iron in

it would work. Either up high or down below. It'll throw the soldiers off your scent and then we—"

I cut him off right there. "There is no we. I told you, Nine. I'm done. Go. Leave me the hell alone. You don't have to keep on pretending that you care what happens to me."

Nine blinks. "I'm not pretending."

He only cares because he feels like he's repaying the woman I never got the chance to meet.

"My mom told you to protect me, right?" That's what Rys said. "You said the Light Fae didn't have the power to wipe the debt clear. Do I?"

"You don't know what you're saying."

Maybe I don't. "Yes or no?"

"I'm supposed to help you. I've accepted my duty. It took me years to understand, but this is what I'm supposed to be doing. Don't do this. Not now, Shadow. Not when I know the soldiers are after you."

So that's a yes, then. Okay. "Nine, consider your debt paid in full."

His silver eyes flash. I can't tell if it's in annoyance, anger, or relief, but a dark shadow passes across his face as his glowing eyes light up his beautiful features. He dips his right hand into the pocket of his jacket, pulling out the same rock he showed Rys. When he opens his hand, I see the rock—and I notice that his hand is almost completely healed.

"I'll go because you've asked me to, not because I consider the debt closed. I'm still clinging to the bargain, Shadow. I won't return this yet."

His rock? What the hell do I want with his rock?

"Whatever. Just go."

He nods. "If you need me, call me. I'll return to you as soon as I can."

I turn my back on him. It's tough, seeing Nine so defeated. My whole life, he was my knight in the shadows. My guardian. My protector. If this is the last time I see him, it's a shitty way to go out.

But I can't do this. I wasn't kidding when I said I'm done.

"Yeah, well, don't hold your breath."

There's no answer from behind me.

I glance over my shoulder.

Nine's already gone.

I SPEND MY FIRST NIGHT ON THE OUTSIDE *INSIDE* OF A MAUSOLEUM.

I've got nowhere else to go. My first instinct was to find a way back to Black Pine and I figure out way too late that I let my trip home slip through my fingers when I forced Nine to leave.

And, sure, he might think I have this skill to shade-walk, but I'm just starting to fully accept the powers of the fae after six years of pretending they don't exist. Even though I obviously moved out of my room at the asylum, it's going to take me a minute to figure out how *that* happened.

Madelaine is buried here in Acorn Falls, a well-to-do little nook of a town about a city or two over from Black Pine. This is where the Everetts used to live before they moved more than six hours away. I lived here with them for close to two years, before the accident and the hearings and the decision that I should be kept inside of the residential ward at Black Pine until I was twenty-one.

I should know where I am and how to get back. I don't. Besides, it's the middle of the night. What can I do? I'm not gonna be able to stay here long-term, but there's no harm in staying over until morning. If I start wandering in the dark, I'll end up even more lost.

At least, that's what I convince myself as I start looking for a place to hide.

My instincts lead me to the old mausoleum that shielded me from the rain the last time I was here. The Richardsons' mausoleum is big and wide. Not too long after I sent Nine away, the caretaker left. It's just me here now. Maybe I can hide on the backside of the big mausoleum and get some sleep. I'm already exhausted. I'll never make it 'til tomorrow if I don't get some real shut-eye now.

For once, luck's on my side. After I stumble over mounds of earth and silent graves, I see that the door is cracked open, almost as if someone has been expecting me. A thick piece of wood is wedged between the stone wall and the door, leaving just enough space for a slim person to slip inside.

I'm no Carolina, but I make it inside by holding my breathing and squeezing my way in.

The mausoleum has a strange smell, musty and chemical; considering what else is in this crypt, it could be worse. There is one questionable puddle along the far wall. I just make sure to stay on the other side, about three feet away from the wall full of caskets.

I keep my head down, figuring that, so long as I stare at the concrete floor instead of the ornate shelves, I can forget that there are dead bodies in here with me.

It's fine. I'm not afraid of the dead. The dead can't touch me.

They can't do anything to hurt me at all.

I sit cross-legged on the stone floor, running the edge of my gloves along the side of my slipper. I'm tired, sure, but I think I've gotten to the point that I'm *over*-tired. I feel like I drank two espressos, then chased it with an energy booster or something.

I'm buzzing, super focused. I use the sense of touch to ground myself. Without being able to touch another person, I've gotten used to touching *me*. I run my fingers along my slipper, my calf, my knee, my arm. I'm here. I'm in one piece.

For now.

I peer at my slippers. They're damp, but still clean for the most part; flecks of dried mud cover the side and are stuck in the treads. Because I had planned on visiting Carolina, I'm not in my robe or my pajamas. I've got on my hoodie, but at least I'm also wearing an old pair of faded jeans. That'll help me out tomorrow.

For now, I'm grateful for the freezing air conditioning the Black Pine staff keeps running all year long. Even though the summer days are warm, the summer nights are chilly, so I'm kind of used to this weather. It's really cold inside of the mausoleum, though. Without my hoodie, I don't think I could have made it through the night.

Eventually, I crash. It had to happen. Even though I keep thinking I hear someone coming—Nine, Rys, the caretaker, I don't even know anymore—I drift off to sleep, curled up on the stone floor of the mausoleum.

I don't know how long I'm sleeping. It feels like it's only been a few minutes when I'm blinking myself awake again, but the air is different than it was. Thicker. Heavier.

The inside of the mausoleum isn't as gloomy, either. Light filters in through the crack in the door. I'm so happy to see it. One, because the light tells me that it's daytime. I made it through the night. And two, no one closed the mausoleum behind me. I'm not trapped in here with the dead.

No, I'm just an escapee from a glorified psych hospital. 'Cause that's so much better.

Slowly, I pull myself up into a sitting position, stretching my stiff arms and my achy legs. Apart from that, I don't really move. Moving means accepting that I have to come up with a plan to get back to Black Pine.

I never thought I'd feel homesick for the asylum. I totally do. I'd do anything to be back there right now. I'm too worried, too scared, too apprehensive to feel hungry, but that's not gonna last. I'm gonna need to eat soon.

And what about my pills? My morning meds? I can't say for sure if they actually did anything. Still, I know withdrawals are no joke. I can't just stop taking my medication and assume that everything's gonna be okay.

How long will it take before my body realizes it's missing them? I've heard horror stories about withdrawals. I'm not looking forward to it.

My head is heavy on my shoulders and I give it a few experimental rolls on my neck. My hair feels knotted and tangled as it hangs down my back. I wish I had a hair-tie or a rubber band or something to get it out of my face. I twist it and tuck it beneath my hoodie for now. Wiping my dirty gloves on my even dirtier jeans, I start to stand. I was thinking I should wait to break out again until it's a little later, maybe while the caretaker is at lunch. I don't want to risk getting caught leaving the mausoleum, but I can't sit here any longer.

I stay on the dark side of the crypt, pacing back and forth, anything to get rid of this nervous energy. My slippers pad almost noiselessly against the stone floor. When I turn, they shuffle; apart from that, there's no sound. At least I'm used to the quiet. It's one thing that has never bothered me. I enjoy it. It's helpful, too, because when I hear the rustle coming from nearby outside, I'm not caught entirely unaware.

Not that I can do anything about it. By the time they get close enough that I realize they're heading for the open mausoleum, there's no way for me to get out first.

I freeze. Is it the caretaker? Did he finally pick up on the fact that the mausoleum is partially unsealed and he's coming to check it out? Or, worse, was the door propped open because they're getting ready to put another casket inside?

Oh, no, no, no...

A ray of golden light falls at my feet as a very tall, very beautiful fae slips gracefully inside of the crypt. Even in the dark, dank gloom, Rys seems to shine.

So, uh, not the caretaker then.

At that moment, I don't think I've ever wished to have a weapon on me more than I do now. A baseball bat, a lead pipe, anything. He's paused in the entryway, but I know that's his way of making a grand entrance.

I don't want to let him get any closer and I resort to holding up my hands to ward him off.

"Stay back," I tell him. "Don't come any closer."

Rys's gleeful laughter sends chills up and down my spine. He places one hand to his chest. "Is that how you greet your mate?"

Not this garbage again. Seriously, I think this guy belongs in the asylum. It's as clear a case of obsessive delusions as I've ever seen. Then there's the fact that I know he can go into violent, murderous rages in one second, before laughing and smiling charmingly in the next.

I back away. One of the casket handles on this side of the crypt jams into my back, the one above it barely missing the bottom of my head. I let out a grunt of pain, though I don't take my eyes off of Rys.

"What are you doing here? How did you find me?"

"Now that you're finally coming into your power, your soul

is reaching out for its mate." Rys advances on me. My breath catches in my throat. "I have the power to follow you wherever you go. You gave me that, Riley."

"I didn't give you shit!"

"Oh? Is that so?"

"Yes! You're not supposed to be here. I don't want you anywhere near me, you freak."

Rys stops on the edge of the light. The corners of his mouth turn up slightly, revealing gleaming white teeth. I can't help but notice that his canines are longer than the rest. They look like fangs.

"Unlike my kind, humans can tell an untruth. I suggest you get better at it if you want me to give up on our mating, my *ffrindau*."

"Wait— you think I *want* you chasing after me?"

He does. I don't need to use my talent as a gauge to know that he does. This fae actually thinks that I like his attention.

What the hell?

It's like the day with Diana and her gold-colored eyes all over again. My breathing starts to quicken now, shallow breaths as I struggle to take in more and more oxygen. If I'm not careful, this could turn into one of those debilitating attacks that leaves me on the floor, sitting on my hands. I can't have that. I've gotta keep calm.

I've gotta get out of here.

Though I told myself—and him—that I didn't want his help, I find myself blurting out: "Nine!"

Rys shakes his head, long, fair hair swaying hypnotically as he paces along the line that separates the light from my dark side. He purses his lips, visibly annoyed that I've said Nine's name.

"Don't waste your breath," he says, pouting. "Nine won't come."

I hope he's wrong. I need Nine. He's the only one I can get to help me keep Rys away from me.

I try again, "Nine, I'm sorry. Please come back!"

"He can't. There are rules, Riley."

My body shivers whenever he says my name. I thought it was fear the first time I shook. Now I'm not so sure. He makes *Riley* sound so beautiful. I should hate it—and I don't.

This can't be happening.

I focus on what he just said. Because, despite Nine telling me that he would come if I call for him, he isn't here.

I glare over at the Light Fae. I'm sure that he won't hurt me—other humans are fair game but, for the moment, as long as he wants me to, like, marry him, he's not gonna kill me or anything. I push past my terror and my conflicting emotions when it comes to Madelaine's murderer. He's the only one who seems to want me to know what's going on.

Let's go.

"What do you mean, rules?" I demand.

Rys laughs lightly. It's such a sweet, gentle laugh, and I think that's what scares me most. He's dangerous, a menace, and yet I feel myself being drawn to him. I don't understand it and I have to stop myself from leaning in toward him.

He knows what he's doing. It's why I'm pressed up against the wall of caskets. I'm stuck among the dead people in this mausoleum all because part of me kinda likes the idea of walking up to the Light Fae.

"First of all, it's daylight. The Dark Fae are crippled during the time of the sun. He can't whip up a portal and come running without his precious shadows. And even if you're lucky enough to find one, calling him Nine isn't enough. He doesn't have to respond to it—it's not his true name. It doesn't have the power."

"True name? What's that mean? Nine's not his name?"

"Not his true name. It's like how you want to be called Riley and I'm Rys. Nine chooses to be called Nine, but it's not the name that you can use to command him." He pauses. "I don't know his, but I can give you mine. I wouldn't mind being under your command."

"That's okay. I'm gonna pass."

His grin widens. "Would you like me to tell you yours?"

CHAPTER 15

That... that was the last thing I expected him to say. In my experience, Rys doesn't take rejection too well. The creepy grin is bad enough. But to offer to tell me *my* true name?

"What? No. I don't have a true name. I'm not... I'm not like you. I'm human."

"Mm." Rys makes a non-committal noise in the back of his throat. His golden eyes shine. "Are you so sure about that, my mate—"

"Not your mate."

He ignores me. "—that you don't have a true name? Think it over. There isn't a single name I can use that will have you doing my bidding?"

Come, Zella.

My whole body goes icy cold. That word. How many times did he use it and, suddenly, I was doing something I never would have in a million years?

"Come to me. Stay with me," purrs Rys. I notice he doesn't

say *Zella* now. Why not? He holds out his hand. "Take my hand. Just one touch. One dance. I swear, you'll be glad you chose me. The Shadow Prophecy will ruin you, Riley. Come with me. I'll save you from the Fae Queen. If you're with me, she'll forget all about you. If you choose Nine... well, he's a Dark Fae. She'll never believe you're not the Shadow."

Choose Nine? That's the part that sticks out at me the most. Who said it was a contest between the two fae? One's a monster, the other my former protector.

"Why does that matter? That Nine's a Dark Fae and you're not?"

He beckons me toward him.

I stay where I am.

"Just one more dance," wheedles Rys. "I need the touch, and then I'll tell you everything you've ever wanted to know about Nine."

That's very tempting. For years, Nine told me everything about Faerie and the fae—but he didn't tell me a damn thing about himself. Not even his name apparently. Rys obviously has more answers that he can provide... but I can't touch him.

I can't.

It's about possession. He's making it clear that, for some reason, he wants me. That's how the fae live. They want what they want when they want it. Nine warned me of that a long time ago. When it comes to humans especially, the fae love to possess them. To take them, to charm them, to turn them into mindless slaves, to leave them, to destroy them, to forget all about them.

And it all begins with the touch.

"Dance with me. One dance," he whispers, "and we'll both have everything we've ever wanted."

I know what he's doing. He's done it before, when I was

sedated and I allowed myself to believe that it was a dream. Just one dance—it's nothing but an excuse to steal another touch, to take another part of my soul.

"You killed Madelaine," I accuse him. I have to remember that. No matter what, he can't take that back. But, and I'm ashamed to admit this, my protest is half-hearted.

"I did," he agrees. "She was a means to an end. If I knew then that she actually meant something to you, I might've done things differently. You must remember, though, she was just a human."

"*I'm* a human."

"Mm. So you keep saying."

There's that noise again. He doesn't agree with me.

Okay. That's it. I'm done talking to him. If I keep on listening to what the Light Fae has to say, it won't be long before he talks me into doing whatever he wants me to. His glamour is way too strong, my defenses are weak, and I need to get my head on straight.

Something's wrong. I should be way more frightened than I am. I *should* be afraid. I'm stuck in a mausoleum with a mythical creature who murdered my sister—and now he wants me to willingly give him everything I have. Only a few days ago, seeing his eyes shining out of Diana's face put me into hysterics. I should be losing it right now.

He didn't use that *Zella* word. I don't think he needs to. I mean, he drew Madelaine to him with his beautiful smile and his lilting voice. Maybe that's exactly what he's doing to me now. He's charming me, using his glamour and his fae magic to compel me to go to him.

Once again, Rys holds out his hand expectantly. From the look on his face, I can tell that he thinks he's got me.

If that's all he wants, then that's the one thing I'm gonna make sure he doesn't get.

All I have on my side is the element of surprise. Now that I'm paying attention to it, I can almost feel his charm pulling me further toward him as another second passes. I already stepped away from the wall of caskets behind me, my slippers shuffling as I edge toward him. If I don't fight back now, I'm screwed.

I'll only have one chance. It'll be risky, but it's the only choice I have.

He waits for me in the weak stream of light. I keep thinking about how the Light Fae are powerful during the day, with the Dark Fae coming out at night. Unless I'm imagining it, Rys is purposely avoiding the shadows on this side of the mausoleum.

Guess we're gonna find out.

I move closer to him. When I'm standing on my side of the invisible line that's separating us, Rys reaches one long finger out toward my cheek. He stops when he's a few inches away. It's like there's a barrier that he can't break through.

Know what? There probably is.

It has everything to do with these rules the fae live by. I know all about this one. I haven't given him permission to touch me, and he's not willing to get burned when he's so confident that I'll give in to him.

Giving him a meaningless smile, I sidle around him, draping my arm around his slender waist as if I'm getting in position to give him the dance he's been hoping for. Rys shivers at my purposeful touch. My stomach revolts, my skin crawling as I make contact, but I don't pull away from him until I've moved behind him.

Then, with all of the strength I have in me, I place my gloved hands on the small of his back and shove.

He wasn't expecting me to attack him. I know that. If I didn't let him think he won, didn't give him a little taste of me with the seductive stroke across his side, Rys never would've been caught off-guard like that.

I hated every second of it, but it was worth it. He never expected it and I manage to push him into the dark depths of the shadows before he even has the chance to retaliate.

I wasn't wrong when I realized he was avoiding the shadows on purpose. The second he crosses the line, Rys lets out an unholy scream of terror. The shadows streak his bronze skin, turning the deep, rich color an inky black. His eyes light up like they're on fire.

The last time I saw him do that, he let loose a stream of flames that surrounded Madelaine.

I've gotta get the hell out of here before he does it again. I race toward the slim opening of the mausoleum and, sucking in my frightened breath, I pop out on the other side.

The heavy stone door is held open by a block of wood that's been wedged underneath. I kick at it wildly, willing it to come loose. My slipper goes flying. I don't give a shit. I almost break the big toe on my right foot as I slam it into the wood on the second kick.

It works, though. Three good, strong kicks and the wood pops free. The slab slams shut with a bang that causes my ears to ache. It echoes, or maybe that's the dying whine of Rys's furious scream when he realizes that I truly have refused him.

Again.

I don't wait around to see if Rys was able to escape the tomb before the door sealed him inside. I don't even stop to see if any of the visitors to the cemetery witnessed me bursting out of the mausoleum and closing the door behind me.

With one slipper and half a prayer, I book it the hell out of there.

DON'T STOP RUNNING.

Don't look back.

Rys could be behind me. I'm not about to look. I don't want to be some horror movie cliché, getting caught by the bad guy because I was too stupid to take off when I had the chance.

The fae are a magical race. The Dark Fae can shade-walk. I saw that firsthand when Nine broke me out of the asylum. The Light Fae? If Rys's abilities are any clue, I know they can control fire. Good chance he can find a way to escape the Richardsons' mausoleum.

I'll take any lead I can get.

I haven't sprinted like this since my middle school days, and even then I half-assed running the mile. A cocktail of fear and adrenaline erases the last of his commands. I shake it off and keep running, tearing a path through the neatly tended graves. I know this cemetery. I know exactly where I am—where I have to go.

The gate isn't too far from the Richardsons' mausoleum. I'm so focused on heading right toward it, I don't even notice that I'm running right by the caretaker's office until I hear his grizzled shout behind me.

"Hey, you! Watchu doin'? You can't run in the cemetery!"

Like hell I can't.

He chases after me, but I'm already too far ahead. Still, I hear him shout, "Get back here!"

Yeah. That's gonna be a nope. I'm still kinda disoriented. I shook off the cobwebs of Rys's compulsion magic, but the lost feeling I woke up with earlier hasn't faded yet. I'm in Acorn Falls—the cemetery proves that—but that doesn't do a thing to help me figure out how I'm going to get back to Black Pine. It's only about half an hour away by car. On foot? I don't know. Definitely a lot longer than that.

I'll figure that out later. Right now? I dash right through the open gate, heading straight because it's in front of me and that means I'm widening the gap between me and the mausoleum where I trapped Rys.

The gravel road that leads to the cemetery is uneven and rough. The sharp edges of the rocks and pebbles bite into my poor, tender bare foot. I push past the pain. Getting out of here before Rys can come after me is the only thing I'm thinking about.

I'm not a fae. I'm not like him. I don't have a true name. I *don't*. But when he says that word, when he calls me Zella, I lose my head. He's proven it enough times already. No matter the reason behind it, he can use it to command me to do whatever he wants me to. I can't let that happen.

He wants me to do the fae equivalent of 'til death do you part with him. Not gonna happen. I'd rather spend the rest of my life inside of a facility just like Black Pine than willingly tie myself to Rys.

That's the thing, though. He has the power to compel me to be his... his *ffrindau* thing. I have to get away from him until I can come up with a plan B. Sticking around, hoping Nine will take pity on me after my temper tantrum isn't gonna work, either.

Keeping pushing forward.

Don't look back.

I can't run anymore. It's pure luck I managed to hang on to this slipper. It protects my left foot as I half-hop, half-jog over the gravel path. I curl my toes against the matted fluff to keep from losing this one, too. Once I make it to the main road, I take it off and tuck it inside of my hoodie pocket. I figure, better to have no shoes on than have people wonder why I'm wearing only one slipper.

Not like I'm not gonna get a couple of odd looks already. It's the end of June, the sun shining down on me. Definitely not hoodie weather. My jeans should be fine, though they're rumpled and stained. I probably look like I just rolled out of bed or something.

Great. There goes any hope of staying under the radar.

What if someone's out searching for me? I mean, they have to be, right? Technically, I'm an escaped mental patient. They won't know how I got out—and I know they won't believe me when I try to tell them—but as soon as Penelope came to wake me up this morning, the whole asylum must've gone on high alert when they realized I was missing.

I'd like to think that the Black Pine staff would keep my disappearance in-house to save face. Too bad I know better. During my first year at the facility, one of the patients managed to slip out during visiting hour. It was madness. Absolute chaos. The staff locked down the rest of the asylum until they found her, hours later, munching on a donut at a nearby coffee shop.

She walked out because she had a craving for a jelly donut and the whole place went nuts. I've been gone for almost a whole day by now. They must be losing their minds.

I only hope that, when I make it back there, they don't hold my escape against me. It wasn't my fault—and who am I kidding? Nine's stunt has just caused me to kiss any chance of a timely release from the asylum goodbye.

Whatever. Right now? I don't care. Black Pine's kept me safe from the fae for six years. For my sanity's sake, I have to believe that Nine is being too careful. That it's still my only hope. I've gotta go back. Then they can lock me up. Throw away the key.

I don't care.

Anything to get away from Rys.

Acorn Falls is just as I remember it.

It's a small, close-knit town full of rich people. The Everetts were comfortable enough to make their home here for a while; if Madelaine had survived, I'm sure they never would've left. It's... I guess *quaint* is the best word for it. It has an honest-to-god main street called Oak Tree Road that cuts through the town, lined with a variety of shops. Most of them are local businesses: antique shops, bakeries, delis, pet stores, collectibles, and memorabilia. Stuff like that. You won't catch a McDonald's anywhere near here, though I lose count of the Starbucks after I pass my third one.

Considering it's Saturday, the streets are nowhere near as crowded as I thought they'd be. After I've been walking for almost an hour, I run into a group of rich, teenage white boys. They're loitering on a corner, sharing a single cigarette while they glower in their starched polo shirts and hundred dollar haircuts.

Typical Acorn Falls boys. When I first came to the Everetts, I had my fun with a couple of them before they began to bore the crap out of me. I was a good time to them, and they were nothing to brag about it.

I don't recognize any of the group. Doesn't matter. They're all the same. Today, when they think they're big enough to catcall at me, I stare at each of them as I stroll by, my bare feet slapping against the hot, summer sidewalk.

When I can feel the weight of their leers, I smile. Lifting my hand, I wave at them, making sure they all get a good, long glimpse at my leather glove.

I'm tired. I'm scared. My feet are killing me. I've got no shoes, a stained hoodie, ratty hair, and mud splattered all over my legs. I'm still a chick with a pretty face out on her own. There are four of them and one of me. The streets are empty. I must look like easy pickings.

My smile widens.

I've got nothing to lose.

Not one of those boys holds my gaze for more than a split second. When I've made it past them, the tallest of them stamps out the cigarette and gestures for his friends to follow after him as he leads them back the way I came.

I keep going forward.

I still haven't figured out where I'm going. I'll have to do that soon. Without any money or a phone, though, it's not gonna be easy. I tilt my head back, looking over the rooftops of the buildings that surround me on both sides. The sun's starting to set. I let out a huge sigh of relief. Once the sun's gone, that's a good ten hours or so before I'll have to worry about Rys again.

He can't come out at night.

Nine can.

He didn't answer me before, but that was because it was during the day. Right?

I'm hanging all of my hopes on it. Nine owes me. He pulled me through the shadows and left me all alone. And, sure, I did send him away. But you know what? He should've known better than to go.

Ugh.

Stupid Dark Fae.

Stupid prophecy.

Stupid queen.

Why the hell did they have to decide that I was the stupid Shadow?

I don't want any part of it. They can't make me be what they want. Besides, it's a fae thing and, whoops, I'm not a fae. Sorry.

Pick someone else. Anyone else.

Just… not me.

It's bad enough that there's no going back from this. They can start tossing blue pills down my throat and that would never be enough for me to go back to pretending that the mythical race doesn't exist. Too much has happened. For the first time in years, my eyes are fully open to the magic around me.

Even though there's been no sign of Rys since I booked it from the cemetery, I'm on high alert. I try not to make it too obvious, though. Every couple of steps, I turn my head one way, then the next, constantly aware of my surroundings. I use the shiny, reflective glass of the storefront windows to look all around me—

—and that's exactly how I find out I'm the lead story on the five o'clock news.

I was daring a quick peek inside the window of tiny, no-name, indie electronics store when I glance at the televisions propped up on display and nearly have a heart attack.

My face is staring back at me from like five different high def screens. It's an old picture, taken straight from the papers. A shot of me leaving my juvenile court hearing weeks after Madelaine's death—right before they shipped me off to Black Pine.

Six years have passed. I haven't changed that much; on the outside, at least. I gape at the image filling the screens. I remember when I was that fifteen-year-old girl. I wore my hair shorter in those days. I was tanner, too—my skin was always sun-kissed back then—and a couple of pounds heavier.

I look resigned in that picture.

I recognize the expression intimately. It's the same one I've seen in the mirror every morning since then.

I'm so consumed by the image from a lifetime ago, it takes me a second before I realize there are words plastered on the screen directly beneath the picture.

My jaws drops when I read them.

Black Pine Patient: Missing One Week

CHAPTER 16

In the glass, I see my open mouth reflected back at me. I gulp. Stare. Then, a heartbeat later, my lips move.

"A *week*?"

It comes out like a squeal. I gasp, then cover my mouth with my gloved fingers.

A perky brunette appears on the screen as my picture is minimized to a square in the upper right corner. No sound—or maybe I can't hear it through the glass, I don't know—but there are no captions, either, so I can't figure out what she's saying about me.

I only know it can't be anything good.

One week missing?

Are you kidding me?

How?

No. Seriously.

How?

I only left *yesterday*.

I don't get it. It's not… it's not possible. And I know that this is only one more impossible thing to lump in with the rest, but time is time. Seconds. Minutes. Hours. I was at Black Pine only last night and, while I slept for a little while, it wasn't like I fainted and stayed knocked out for *six whole days.*

According to the news, though, I did just that.

I don't get it. However, before I can even attempt to wrap my head around it, my senses start to ping. I catch a flash of black and white cruising toward me out of the corner of my eye. The ping turns into clamoring warning bells.

Ah, crap.

Black and white cars mean only one thing.

Ten minutes ago, I would've been relieved to see a cop car pulling up along the curb behind me. Flag it down, explain who I am, see if the cop would be willing to give me a lift back to the asylum.

I can't. Not now. If I go back, they'll want to know where I've spent the last week and I won't be able to answer them. Not can't—*won't*. And what will happen to me then?

Well, my worst suspicions were confirmed with the news report. Whether it's been one day or one week, the Black Pine staff has told everyone that I'm out here.

And, not only is Acorn Falls close enough to the asylum, but it's where I lived last. How much do I want to bet that this is one of the first places they looked?

I have to find Nine. He got me into this mess. He can get me out of it.

He *has* to.

The cop idles at the curb. I shift so that I can get a better look at him in the reflection of the glass. He's a big guy, thinning hair on top, a travel mug in his hand as he watches me through the passenger side window.

Uh-oh. Even without the shopfront acting like a mirror, I

know what I look like: matted hair from the stone floor; rumpled clothes that are more suited to the cranked-up air conditioning of the facility than a summer afternoon; bare feet. And, I think with a sinking stomach, my gloves.

I shake the sleeves of my hoodie so that they cover most of my hands.

Did he see?

Tucking a strand of hair behind my ear, I move so that I'm facing away from the window. I glimpse over at the car. Not good. He traded his mug for some walkie-talkie-looking radio thing. His lips are moving while his beady eyes stay locked on me.

Shit.

Time to go.

I'm no actress, but I try. With a shocked expression and a little jerk as I shake the sleeves of my hoodie down to cover even more of my gloves, I pretend like I just remembered something super important. Then I frown, like I'm annoyed at myself. Shoving my renewed fear aside, resisting the urge to run again, I slowly walk away.

Staying calm is hard. With every casual step, my knees shake with the need to just take off. Sure, I might get away from this cop, but what if there are more?

Don't make it suspicious, Riley. You can do this.

After I put a block between us, I give in a little. My walk turns into a speedwalk. Then, as my momentum carries me, it becomes more of a jog.

When I've made it another full block, I chance a peek over my shoulder. That's a mistake. He's still watching me and, in those few seconds, I give him a full look right at my face.

The lights flash, the air torn apart by the keening sounds of the siren as he flips it on.

I take off like a shot.

If it were any other street in Acorn Falls, he'd have had me. We're still on the main street, Oak Tree Road, so the advantage is mine. It's how it's set up. This part of the town is like a little village inside of a bigger city. Shops are built on top of shops, the wide glass windows open and inviting. Very few side streets veer off of Oak Tree, just little breaks in the road to allow people to access the back.

People, not cars.

What are my odds? I didn't get that great of a peek at the cop, but he seemed like a big guy. His hair was thinning and I'm pretty sure I saw some grey; he's older.

Come on, Riley. Think!

Would he be willing to get out of his car and chase me on foot?

I'm gonna find out.

I dart down the first opening I find, letting out a frustrated grunt when I come face to face with a five-foot-high, chainlink fence complete with a thick, metal padlock. I know why it's here. It's supposed to keep cars from trying to squeeze in between the shops to get to the alleyway behind it.

I can't let it stop *me*.

Jeez. I haven't done anything like this since I was fifteen. Sticking my battered, bruised, and bleeding bare foot into one of the holes in the fence, I grimace as the twisted iron bites into my instep before doing the same thing with the other one. I grit my teeth and climb.

Once I get to the top, I toss my body over the side. In my panic, I don't shimmy down the fence the same way I went up it. Forgetting that I'm high up in the air, I hop the fence and land *hard* on the asphalt below me.

I don't hear a snap or a crack when I hit, but my right ankles gives, then both of my knees buckle. I don't collapse in a heap or anything, but I barely stay standing. A sharp, shooting pain screams up and down my right leg before it immediately turns dull.

I hope like hell I haven't broken anything. It'll definitely make my reckless running away a bit more difficult if I have.

Shuddering out a breath, my brain whirs with a hundred different possibilities. What am I supposed to do?

I hear the sirens whine. They're getting closer. I might've been able to outrun him at first—and I was right, he didn't get out of his cop car—but this is his beat. He knows this town way better than I do. I haven't been back since I was fifteen and, even then, I only lived here for two years.

It doesn't matter if he stays on the other side of the fence. The air echoes with the sound of another siren. The alley I'm trapped in is open on this side. For all I know, he's sent out a call for help and he's got his buddy from the radio coming for me.

This alley is wider than the narrow path that led to the fence. It's designed for delivery trucks to reach the back doors of the businesses that line up along Oak Tree Road. If another cop car spots me, it'll have no problem reaching me.

But not if I'm not here for them to find.

There's a manhole a couple of feet away from the shadow of the fence. Luckily for me, the lid's not sitting where it should. Maybe the town was doing work recently on this side street and they forget to reset it. Doesn't matter. It's my only hope.

I hobble toward it, sizing up the gap. There's probably enough space for me to slip inside of it if I really try. And it's not like the cop chasing me will ever expect me to do that.

No one in their right mind would choose to go into a sewer.

Despite my stay at Black Pine, I'm not crazy. I'm not broken, either.

What I am is *desperate*.

The Fae Queen wants me dead. Rys wants me for his mate.

Nine wants to repay his stupid debt.

What do I want?

I don't know, but getting picked up by the Acorn Falls PD isn't high up there on my list. So down the manhole I go.

It's a tight fit. Tighter than when I forced my way inside of the Richardsons' mausoleum. But I want this more, and my leg hurts even worse than my tender feet. I can't run. My only choice is to hide.

I make it work.

There's a rusted ladder right inside of the entrance to the manhole. Going backward, I feel blindly with my left foot until I find it. It's slimy and cold, and I hate the idea of putting my foot on the pitted piece of metal.

I do it anyway.

Unlike the mausoleum, the sewer smells exactly the way I thought it would. Once I'm all the way inside of the dark, dank hole, I hang onto the ladder with one arm so I can pull my hoodie up and over my nose. It doesn't help. I swallow roughly, fighting back a gag. It's a good thing I haven't had a thing to eat since last night's stew. I feel like I'm about to hurl.

Or maybe that's because I'm so damn afraid that the cop is going to find me. I don't even know for sure that he recognized me as Riley Thorne, the missing girl from the news. He might've gotten a good look at me and figured rightly that I was in deep shit.

Of course, now he's got to know that I'm not innocent.

Innocent people don't run from the cops.

My queasy stomach lurches when I hear the sirens approaching. They grow louder and louder, then suddenly die. The hum of an engine not too far away replaces it. The slam of a car door.

Jingling keys, and the heavy steps of an overweight police officer.

A loud huff.

I close my eyes and will my heart to slow down. It's racing so fast, beating so loud, I almost expect him to follow the thud and the thump to my hiding place. My fingers sting from clutching the ladder rung in front of me so tightly. I'm pressed up against the structure, leaning on my good leg.

This is it. Any second now he's going to realize that there's nowhere else I could go...

The crackle of his police radio cuts through the tension. I just about stop breathing. My pulse pounds. I can't understand the muttering and hiss that follows the crackle. It's too indistinct to make out from inside of the manhole.

The officer has no problem. He responds with a low growl that carries. "No. No sign of her on this side." A sound like ringing bells. I think he just kicked the fence. "She had to have run out on your end."

Some more static.

"Yeah. No shoes on, like I said. Black sweatshirt. Jeans. Leather gloves, too. Looks just like the picture they sent over last week."

The other cop says something else. I wish I could hear it.

"Look, I'll meet you over on Elm. She's fled Oak Tree on foot so that's our best chance. We can fan out, hit downtown again." Another burst of static, then, "Yeah. Copy that. I'm on my way."

His keys jingle a little faster as he moves away. The cop pounds the pavement back, his steps fading the further he gets from the fence. A minute later, the sudden roar of the engine causes the ladder to tremble. I don't pry my gloves from my tight hold until the only thing I can hear is the soft tinkling of the water trickling far beneath me.

Gritting my teeth, I start to climb down. I've got no choice. If the cops are up here looking for me, then I'm going down until I can get my head on straight and figure out just what I should do next.

The ladder goes all the way to the bottom. There's a ledge down here, overlooking a groove in the sewer. It looks like it was built to hold a small river or something but, thank God, there's nothing more than a trickle of a foul-smelling liquid.

Great. Looks like I found the source of the stink.

I don't get too close, moving as far away from it as I can until my back is against the slimy brick wall. Then, because there's nowhere else to go—and I'm beginning to ache all over—I sit on the edge of a puddle of something thick and oily. When the sliver of light from up above hits it, I see a rainbow. It's a spot of something beautiful in this terrible place.

I almost have to laugh.

At least I'm safe. For now, I might be alone, but I'm safe.

I don't plan on staying down here long. Just long enough to catch my breath, maybe, and to give my sore leg some rest. Sooner or later, I'm going to have to think about food—my anxiety makes me lose my appetite, but I'm already feeling weaker than I usually do. And I'm not about to sleep in a sewer.

I have to draw the line somewhere.

I keep my eyes squinted until I get used to the darkness surrounding me. I can't see much more than what's in front of me. The sliver of light is enough for me to be sure that I'm alone. No rats. No alligators. No—

The light sparks. It goes from a weak stream to a blinding flash. I shriek and throw my hands up as if that's going to save my poor retinas.

Out of nowhere, I hear a thunk and a slapping noise from right next to me. The splash of that dirty, oily water as it sprays up and cuts right through my jeans is chilly and uncomfortable. My eyes sting, but they fly open anyway. I blink rapidly, trying to get my sight back, then swallow my terrified squeal when I see what it was that caused the splash.

There, lying on its side in the puddle as if it's been tossed at me, is the slipper I lost in the mausoleum.

*fall in love
with the
shadow man...*

TOUCHED BY THE FAE   BOOK TWO

SHADOW

INTERNATIONAL BESTSELLING AUTHOR
JESSICA LYNCH

Copyright © 2019 by Jessica Lynch

All rights reserved.

No part of this book may be reproduced in any form or by any electronic or mechanical means, including information storage and retrieval systems, without written permission from the author, except for the use of brief quotations in a book review.

Cover by Jessica Lynch

FOREWORD

Shadow is the second book in the **Touched by the Fae** series. It takes place directly following the end of *Asylum*, the first book. Events of that book are referenced as Riley's story continues, and while you can jump right in, it's not a stand-alone. To get the entire story, all three parts—*Asylum, Shadow*, and *Touch*—should be read in order.

I hope you enjoy part two! Like *Asylum*, because it's the second book of a longer story, *Shadow* ends with a cliffhanger. I'm being totally upfront about that—the conclusion to Riley's story will finish with the third book.

Still, I really want readers to enjoy the ride as we see all the ups and downs of what it's like to be hunted by the Fae Queen!

xoxo,
Jessica

CHAPTER 1

The slipper mocks me.

It's lying on its side in an oily puddle that shimmers in the single sliver of sunlight, the once-white material dotted in mud, streaked with grime. The last I saw it, I'd left it behind me when I was running out of the cemetery, right after I trapped the fae chasing me inside of a mausoleum.

That was hours ago. Since then, I discovered that I lost a week of my life and, oh yeah, I'm considered a *fugitive* from the asylum I spent the last six years locked inside. And, since I *am* a fugitive, instead of asking the police officer in his cruiser for help, I ran away from him, using my memory of Acorn Falls' back streets to escape.

It might've cost me a busted ankle when I hopped a fence and landed hard on the concrete, but I managed to dodge the cop in time. That was a plus. The downside? He had a partner or something waiting on the other end of the alley. I had to hide—and the only place I could find was beneath a half-open manhole cover.

You heard that right. Because I had no other choice, I shimmied past the small gap left from where the manhole cover sat crookedly on the ground, then climbed all the way down into the smelly, dank sewer.

I thought I was safe. I thought that the cops would never think to follow me down here, and that I was out of reach of the fae chasing me.

Yeah. Right.

Now I'm huddled in the bottom of a damp, dark—did I mention smelly?—sewer, my ankle throbbing, my heart racing.

And he's found me. Rys, the golden fae—the Light Fae—the brilliant, beautiful monster who killed my sister... who works as a soldier for the Fae Queen who wants me dead... who offered to protect me if I chose to *mate* him... he's found me.

I can't pretend otherwise. After he tracked me down to the Acorn Falls cemetery where Madelaine is buried, I let him think that I would allow him to touch me. For any of the fae, there's power in a touch. All he had to do was brush my cheek—with my permission—and he could take a part of me. My life, my strength, my soul... Rys could feed on a single touch, making him even more powerful than a Seelie already is.

Of course, I was bluffing. My whole life, I've been told over and over again never to let the fae touch me. My guardian and mentor, a Shadow Man who called himself Nine, brainwashed me into keeping my hands to myself. Sure, I might have ended up a bit haphephobic—fear of touch, though it's not so much fear as just the idea of touching someone else can bring on the mother of all panic attacks if I'm not prepared for it—but at least I'm still alive.

Madelaine... isn't.

It's my fault, too. One of the only times I forgot how dangerous and ruthless the fae are, my sister paid the price. I burned my hands trying to save her, but I was too late. Madelaine was gone, I blamed the fae, and I found myself being committed to the Black Pine Facility for Wayward Juveniles.

The fae couldn't follow me there. For six years, I took my meds, attended my sessions, listened to a revolving door of psychologists and shrinks tell me that Faerie isn't real.

Somehow, I believed them.

Bad idea. Seriously. Without the threat of the fae forever chasing after me, I let down my guard. A couple of days ago—or more, I don't know where my missing week went—I slipped up and pressed my ruined palm against Rys's bronzed, perfect hand as we danced. I thought I was dreaming.

I wasn't then.

I'm not now.

When I kicked the piece of wood that kept the mausoleum door open, it slammed shut, trapping Rys inside. He's fae, so I didn't doubt that he'd find a way out eventually, but I thought I had a little more time.

The slipper tells me otherwise.

He's responsible for it. I know he is. I might have been able to shut him in there, but I lost my slipper in the process. It flew off my foot, landing inside the mausoleum a split second before the stone door echoed its slam. I eventually jammed the spare slipper in my hoodie pocket and, as I throw myself back, hiding in the deepest, darkest shadows as my head goes in a hundred different directions at once, I can feel the weight of the slipper's twin against my queasy belly.

The sliver of sunlight is the only illumination in the whole sewer. It's weak, barely enough to let me see more than a foot in front of me, but I don't need that to be sure that Rys is hiding somewhere.

I don't see him. The slipper is here, but he isn't. At least, not where I can find him.

I'm too tired for this crap. Tired and, well, I'm just plain over it.

"Where are you?" I call out.

"Wherever you want me to be."

I jump. My back scrapes against the rocky wall, something cold and wet dripping down my neck as I hit it. I spit out a curse, my hand flying up to wipe the slick of moisture from my skin at the same time as I climb forward on my knees.

Where is he? Where—

There.

Tall, slender, lithe body. Bronze-colored skin, long tawny hair, and a pair of golden eyes that shine like miniature suns in his shockingly angelic face.

To my surprise, he's looking down at me with an indulgent expression. I'd been expecting fury. I still remember his howl of outrage as I shoved him inside the mausoleum and closed him in. If I ever saw Rys again, I thought he'd want to throttle me for what I did.

From the heated look he's giving me, I can tell that he's got all kinds of plans for the two of us—and throttling me ain't one of them.

He *tsks*, then grins. "Oh, Riley. Do take care of yourself."

I glare over at him. It's hard, since he's so bright and the sewer is so dark, and I can barely make out the self-satisfied smile tugging on his pouty lips, but I refuse to let him think I'm happy to see him.

"How did you do that?" I demand.

"Do what, my love?"

The denial is immediate. "I'm not your love."

"Mmm. Yet, perhaps." His golden eyes glow so vividly, I

have to squint to keep from being further blinded myself. "What did you mean by that anyway? Do what?"

I wave my hands, gesturing at the space in front of him before shielding my gaze again. "You weren't here. You *weren't*. And then, all of a sudden, you were right next to me. How the hell did you do that?"

"I could tell you, even teach you the same skill, but…"

"Yeah?"

Rys shrugs. "It would cost you."

It would. And I can't afford his price. "No, thanks."

"A trade, then?" His voice gentles, like it's an off-handed suggestion. His expression gives him away, though. At this moment, I could ask for anything and he would give it to me. That kind of power is heady, even if I don't want anything to do with the Light Fae. "I know I'll have to earn another touch. I understand the game. But what about a barter?"

That's probably worse. A fae can't lie, I know that much, but the Faerie races are so tricky, he could be telling me the absolute truth—and still be manipulating me.

Like now. Even though I like to think I know better, I can't stop myself from saying, "I don't have anything you want. And a touch is off the table. No way am I letting you get any closer to me."

"Fair enough. As for your end, why don't you let me decide whether you have something that suits me. So, is it a deal? Do we have an agreement?"

He's gotta be kidding, right? "No."

Rys laughs.

The sound sends shivers coursing through me.

"Do you know?" he says cheerfully. "You're the first soul in more than a century who has said no to me—and now you've done it repeatedly. It's so... so *refreshing*. Ah, Riley. And you wonder why I desire you as my *ffrindau*."

Forget shivers. My blood runs *cold*. He can't possibly think I've forgotten what that fancy foreign word means. soulmate. Madelaine's killer is still insisting that I'm supposed to be his bride or something like that.

That's why he keeps running after me. Chasing behind me. Not because the Fae Queen is making him, but because he's convinced that *me*—a human orphan on the run from the asylum—and *him*—an ageless, mythical creature with powers I can't understand—are somehow meant to be.

Yeah, no.

Not. Gonna. Happen.

I pull myself up off the nasty sewer floor, backing into the dark shadows so that I'm almost hidden. Rys sees me. The way his unearthly beautiful face follows my every move, it's impossible to really hide, but I feel better being cloaked in the darkness.

And, okay, maybe knowing the ladder is right by my hand is a bonus, even if it's really wishful thinking. I've got no shot at beating him up the ladder. I learned long ago that the golden fae is as fast as he is vicious and cruel.

I have to remember that.

My hand closes on the rung nearest to me. "How did you know where to find me?"

"It was obvious. You're the Shadow."

I'm so sick and tired of the two fae telling me that. I don't *want* to be this Shadow person, and I'm still not too sure exactly what they expect of me except that I'm "destined" to off the Fae Queen.

Somehow, I don't think that that's what Rys is talking about right now.

"What do you mean?"

"The mausoleum. This"—he wrinkles his perfect, perfect nose—"sewer. The pockets call to you. You instinctively search them out. It was only a matter of following them to you. And here I am."

I still don't get it. "What's a pocket?"

He waves his hand past me, toward the darker side of the sewer. I mean, the whole thing's pretty dark. It's a pit down here. But as he gestures a little further to my right, I suddenly see… something.

It's a patch that seems impossibly black, like a spot of starless night that no light can reach.

That's just at a quick glance, though. The longer I stare at the patch, the more it seems to change. It sparkles. Shimmers. Gleams.

Invites.

I edge closer to it. I don't even realize that I've moved until my glove slips off of the rung when I get too far away from the ladder.

"That's right," Rys says approvingly. "Good sight, my love. I wonder what else those pretty blue eyes can see."

Not enough. I can pick him out of the gloom—he gives off enough light just by being Seelie, he's like a flashlight—but he's the only thing I can see down here.

No hope.

No escape.

Except for the shadow. For some weirdo reason, it calls to me. I can't think of a reason not to listen.

Especially since Rys hasn't made a move to follow me.

I know I'm right when he says, "I'm sure you won't mind if I stay over here. The pockets belong to the Cursed Ones." He turns sharply, spitting behind him, then swivels back before I can take another step. "They make shadow travel between the worlds possible for the Dark Fae, so they belong to the moon and her ilk. For one of my kind, they're almost as bad as iron."

That... actually makes sense to me.

During those nights when I was little, when Nine was still the Shadow Man who spent hours telling me about Faerie and why I should never, ever let the fae touch me, he went to great lengths to impress how powerful the fae are. With their glamour and their charm, they could look like anyone, convince anyone to do just about anything.

However, from Nine's lessons, I also learned that the fae do have a weakness. Two of them actually—now three, if I count how carefully Rys stays away from the darkness.

One is that they can't lie. Tricky and manipulative, Nine warned that any fae worth his pointy ears could find a way around having to always tell the truth. So it was a weakness, but not a fatal one.

The other, though? Iron. And there isn't anything they could do about that.

I guess, for the Light Fae, the dark shadows leech their power and their strength just like iron does to any of the faerie kind. But if the Dark Fae use the shadows to their advantage, what about the Light Fae? What makes them stronger?

As if he can read my mind, Rys finally moves forward. No. Not *move*. He... he glides, almost as if he's floating. Unlike Nine, he doesn't wear a long coat that hides most of his body. Rys—going with the whole Light Fae, Blessed Ones thing—is all decked out in white, a stark contrast against his darker skin. His shirt is tight around his torso, long sleeves billowing as he steps gracefully toward me.

He pauses when only a few feet exist between us. I let out the breath I didn't even realize I'd been holding since he started to move in my direction. Even though he just told me that the portal is harmful to a Light Fae, he can't stay away.

Part of me wishes he would—but a secret desire has me hoping he'd come a little closer.

What's wrong with me?

Honestly, I'm so freaking tired of being *alone*. He's proven that he's willing to do whatever he has to to get whatever he wants—*me*—and I haven't forgotten that. I haven't.

But he's here. And, for the moment at least, I'm okay with that.

He smiles. It's a gorgeous grin, his pouty lips split just enough that I can see his blindingly white teeth peeking through the gap.

As he lifts his hand, I flinch away from him.

Only he isn't reaching for *me*.

"The Dark Fae love their shadows." Rys sticks his hand into the weak light streaming down from up above. His whole form goes from a pale golden color to a vivid, glowing bronze. "As you can see, my people are drawn to the light."

"What… what did you just do?" I whisper.

"I'm a Light Fae. Seelie. I can walk in the sun, take strength from its warmth and its shine. I can't move in the darkness, but so long as there's a hint of light, I can travel anywhere between the human world and Faerie."

So that's how he did it. How he found me in the sewer, and how he followed me into the mausoleum.

That sucks. I mean, seriously.

If all it takes is sunlight for him to come after me, I won't be safe unless I resign myself to absolute darkness. Otherwise, I'll never truly be able to escape any of the Seelie—including Rys.

The shadows are keeping him at bay. For how long, though? Back in the mausoleum, he wasn't about to cross the line between the sunlight and the way-too-dark depths of the musty building if it meant he'd risk being weakened or burned. Eventually, he would have. I'm absolutely sure of that—it's why I had to fight back and run before he gave in to the urge.

Just like he's doing right now.

Rys holds out his hand. He looms in front of me, close enough that he's all I see, with just enough distance that I know I'm safe from his touch.

For now.

I gulp.

I'll never make it up the ladder in time. Still, I think I've got to try when my body bows back, desperate to avoid the slightest graze of his fingertip.

His smile is one part invitation, one part threat, as he purrs, "Come with me, Riley."

I'm so distracted by his nearness, by the way his golden eyes seem to burn their way straight to my soul, it takes me a second to understand what he said.

Come with me.

"What?" I'm so surprised he'd try that again, I don't even tell him no straight off. When will he finally get it? I'm lonely, but I'm not suicidal. "Go with you? *Where?*"

"To Faerie, of course. You belong with the fae. You belong with me."

Oh, no, no.

I most definitely *don't*.

"Let me take you away from this place," Rys murmurs enticingly. His voice is low, yet it seems to echo in the darkness. "No more bars on your windows. No more looking over your shoulder. You'll be free with me."

He's got to be kidding.

If I give myself over to the Light Fae, I'll be more trapped than if I stayed committed to the asylum for the rest of my life. At least, at Black Pine, I'd *have* one.

I swallow roughly, bracing my back against the slimy sewer wall, ready for him to lash out, then say bluntly, "Hard pass. I'd rather live down here in this sewer forever than go anywhere with you."

CHAPTER 2

He blinks. For a split second, shadows play across the sculpted features of his face, as if he isn't sure how to react to my answer.

I hold my breath again.

Like the slipper he tossed into the sewer to signal his arrival, I'm still waiting for the other shoe to drop. He doesn't like being told no. And after the way our little chat in the mausoleum ended… he's not really going to let me off the hook so easily for that, right?

I… I might be wrong.

With a wounded expression that is as posed as it is manipulative—and, damn it, it actually *works*—Rys shifts so that his full splendor is on display in front of me. He holds out his hand imploringly. "What do I have to do to prove that my feelings are real?"

"*You* are not real," I counter.

It's a reflex—and, after everything that's happened to me

lately, a half-hearted one. The more I insist that the fae are not real, the more I'm beginning to question what *real* even is.

Once upon a time a Shadow Man who kept me company at night was real. Art therapy and morning med lines at the nursing station used to be real. Right now, real means hiding out in a smelly sewer and having a conversation with a mystical stalker who murdered my best friend.

What will be real tomorrow?

I'm not sure. With Rys's next comment, it seems as if I'm going to find out.

"It's very nearly the time of the shadows," he announces with a sultry pout. "I must leave you soon, but I won't be gone for long, my love. As soon as the sun rises again, I'll return for you."

"Don't. And I told you. I'm not your love, asshole."

Rys throws back his head. The laughter he lets loose is even more joyous than before. "*Asshole,*" he repeats. He makes the curse sound like poetry. "It's *perfect.*"

Oh, yeah? I have half a mind to call him some other choice names—but I don't. I know how capricious the fae can be, Rys more than most. Sure, he finds my attitude funny… now. Two seconds ago, he was pouting at me. How quick before he turns on me again?

Better not push my luck.

I can't explain why I'm almost… almost disappointed at his announcement that he has to leave. Some part of me doesn't want him to go. The part that doesn't want to let him touch me, but isn't succumbing to another panic attack at the thought of it is surprisingly okay with having him down here—as long as he stays away from me, that is.

Climbing into the sewer to escape the cop changed things.

On the outside, I can't take care of myself. I want to—but how? I don't have anything except for the clothes on my back. I'm still super stinking pissed at Nine, and Rys is a monster with an angel's face, but at least they both have a reason to keep me safe from the Fae Queen.

And, okay, I'm not so sure what those reasons *are*... doesn't matter. I'll take what I can get.

Truth is, down here in the sewer, I can admit that I never should've forced Nine to leave me alone in the cemetery. I've been by myself for so long that it was nice to have company. Nice to have someone who seemed to care about *me*.

Even if Nine didn't actually mean it, it was still nice to pretend.

It's tougher with Rys. There's something about him. I guess you could say he's almost intoxicating. Actually, that's about right. It's how I feel around him: I'm drunk, just one sip past the last of my good decisions. I slap my cheeks and swallow heavily. I've got to sober up before I make a big mistake.

Like accepting his hand and begging him to take me from this place like he offered.

No. *No.* That's his glamour talking.

Of course he's gorgeous. Their astonishing good looks make the fae the most dangerous of predators to their chosen prey: humans.

I can't let myself forget that for even a second. He's a murderer who killed one of the only people I cared about when I told him no six years ago. Rys might seem like he's enjoying himself right now—but what happens when I say no again and he catches on that I actually mean it?

He followed me to Black Pine. He followed me to Faerie after Nine helped me escape the asylum. He followed me to the cemetery, then used a sliver of sunlight to join me in a freaking sewer.

And now I have to look forward to him chasing me down tomorrow? When will it stop?

"Why? Why do you insist on coming after me? Why won't you leave me alone?" He's not like Nine, he has no reason to answer me, but I can't stop the demands for answers from slipping out. "Look, if the queen sent you, and you really give a shit about me, just tell her I'm missing. I don't want anything to do with this."

Rys runs his tongue along his bottom lip, tucking the tip in the corner for a moment as he regards me. I'm wearing filthy jeans, a dusty hoodie, leather gloves that cover my hands, yet that one look makes me feel like he's stripping me on the spot.

He smiles. "So it seems my rival has finally told you about the prophecy."

Rival? Oh, jeez. I think I liked it better when he was the bogeyman in my nightmares, the golden fae killer who threatened and mocked and scared the absolute crap out of me. This lovesick male who's convinced himself that we're meant to be together is terrifying in a whole other way because he *just won't let this go.*

I ignore him. As angry as I am with Nine for intentionally hiding the truth about my mom from me all these years... as confused and lost and just plain defeated as I am, I know who I'm siding with all the way—and it's not the Light Fae watching me like he'd like to gobble me up.

He's gorgeous, but he's not Nine.

Rys wants to own me. He told me that once, back when I was fifteen and he was trying to lure me away from my foster family. After he followed Madelaine and me to an empty house at the end of the Everetts' street, he appeared suddenly in the basement, popping into existence near a window that let in a stream of early afternoon light.

I had never seen anything as glorious as he was. In my mind, I called him the golden angel because, after all of the stories Nine told me that painted the fae out to be monsters, I never thought anyone who looked so beautiful could be so terrible.

I was wrong.

Dead wrong.

For an entire year after I watched Rys kill my sister before burning the house down around us, I re-lived her death constantly.

From the moment the golden fae with the angel's face appeared in the basement where my sister and I were hanging out after cutting school, to his pronouncement that he came to take me away with him, to how he turned his golden gaze on Madelaine

The music. The dance. The snapping of her neck, and the fire that circled her after she fell. How I reached for her, how I screamed my voice hoarse, how Rys laughed and laughed and laughed before he vanished and I had no choice but to flee the hungry flames.

Therapy helped me process it, and my psychologists helped me understand that it wasn't my fault. With the right meds and a little distance—plus my nighttime visits to the cemetery where I poured my heart out to the stone angel that marked her grave —I was able to go days, then weeks, and finally months at a time without watching her die.

With Rys looming in front of me, the depths of the sewer

trapping me like a rat in a cage, there's nothing left for me to do but remember.

"You belong to me."

"Come to me."

"You're mine."

I said no.

I tried to walk away.

And he charmed Madelaine to come to him, compelled her with his fae magic to offer her hand for a dance, then snapped her neck as punishment for my defying him.

With the image of Madelaine's broken body seared into my mind, the pain of seeing her dead mingling with the agony of being burned by Rys's conjured fire, I start to tremble.

The doctors were full of it. And I might just be insane for not screaming the sewer down around me as I face off against this heartless creature.

Love?

Rys doesn't know what love is.

I'm the reason Madelaine is gone. For that reason alone, I'll never give in to him.

From across the sewer, Rys's golden eyes gleam with the secret knowledge that, no matter how I deny him, in the end he'll win.

He's fae. They don't know how to lose.

I can't do this right now. I've run out of adrenaline at this point, and my stomach has twisted itself into one giant knot. I'm two seconds away from hurling the empty contents of my angry stomach. If the bile splashes and stains his pristine white pants, that's all the better.

He'd deserve it.

Six years. It's been six years and I remember that terrible afternoon like it was yesterday. For six years, I worked to forget it—to try to believe the alternative events that the courts and my doctors tried to convince me were real—and now that I'm face to face with Rys again, I know what's really real.

And I know that I'll do whatever it takes to make it all go away.

Even tell the Light Fae the truth.

"Nine told me about the stupid prophecy, okay? About how... how the Shadow is destined to take out the queen. How she's got this crazy idea that I'm the Shadow—"

"Melisandre doesn't think so," Rys interrupts. "She's sure of it."

Great. That doesn't make this any better. "Well, you can tell her from me that she's got nothing to worry about. I'm not killing anyone." In a burst of anger, I jab my gloved finger in his direction. "There's only one murderer here and it sure as hell ain't me."

It takes him a second to get it. His lips tug downward. If he was a regular guy, his brow would be furrowed. He's part of the fae, though, and not a single wrinkle mars his perfect expression.

"Are you still mad about the human girl?" he asks, like he's surprised by my reaction.

"She wasn't just some girl," I snap in indignation. "She was my *sister*!"

Rys has the nerve to wave me off. "She was human, and, I'm sorry, but she was far more fragile than I realized. If it makes you feel better, I wouldn't have broken her beyond repair if I actually thought you cared about her."

Wow. I mean... *wow.*

"You never should've been there in the first place," I spit out. "If you would've left me alone, Madelaine would still be alive."

"Maybe. Maybe not. Time will tell, my *ffrindau*." Rys angles his head, frowning when he notices that his precious sliver of light is little more than a thin line disappearing into the darkness. "Alas, for now, time also grows short. I wish I could stay and play with you. But, you see, my kind, the Seelie, the Blessed Ones... we're not suited to the dark. I'll leave that to your accursed prince of shadows. Me? I need a little more... mmm... *illumination.*"

His lyrical tone when he brings Nine up again—because who else could he mean?—is so mocking, I have this sudden urge to pick up my dirty slipper and fling it at him. First, he casually mentions how carelessly he murdered my sister, then he puts down Nine, the only person who—for whatever reason—has always been there for me. Who the hell does he think he is?

I'm already screwed and he's made me so stinking furious. So what if I piss him off? It would only go to prove that I'm not wrong when I think of the Light Fae as an actual monster.

Before I can grab the slipper or flinch or, I don't know, try to hobble up the sewer's pitted ladder just to get away from him, Rys reaches out into the dark space in front of him. He uses one of his long, slender fingers to draw an imaginary line in the air. Three more follow, a perfect square. It looks like he's playing some weird game of charades, or maybe practicing his pantomime.

And then he presses the flat of his palm against the square he's drawn. There's some give to it. Rys pushes gently and—

I gasp.

His hand is gone. Seriously. His whole hand disappears, and most of his wrist, too, like a giant eraser has rubbed them right off. Just... just *gone*. From the middle of his forearm up, I can see every inch of him despite the dark because of his sudden shine. His golden glow has gone from dim to full blast again. It only makes it more obvious that a part of him has vanished into thin air.

"Maybe," Rys says, giving his arm a jerk, "with this, you'll start to things a little more clearly."

His hand reappears as he backs away from the square—and it isn't empty. I can't really see what he's holding. Whatever it is, it's black and narrow. After swooping low, Rys sets it gingerly at his feet before aiming the same finger at it.

There's a spark, followed by the tang of metal in the air.

I'm immediately blinded.

I clamp my eyes shut. Too late. The night vision I've gained since hiding out in the sewer is all but gone. I can't see a damn thing except for the fiery flash.

Keeping my eyes closed isn't an option. Not with Rys looming nearby. To think of being so vulnerable, standing with him with my eyes closed... No. *No.* I absolutely refuse to let the Light Fae have any advantage.

My breath is shaky, my head spinning, my heart racing. Despite the orange glow that washes over the inside of my eyelids, I crack my eyes open, peeking out through barely open slits. The flash is still there, but at least it's contained now.

Blinking a couple of times, I get enough of my night vision back to see what it was that he made appear.

It's... it's a lantern. And Rys is using the same fire that burned my hands to fill it.

I choke on a gasp. My face goes hot, my chest tight, and I can feel the phantom pain of the burns that ruined my poor hands when he dared me to reach through the flames to save my sister.

I couldn't save Madelaine, just like I can't take my eyes off of the fire.

I'm mesmerized by the light and all I keep thinking of is how hot the flames are. I should know. My whole body shivers; the heat makes me see how cold I am. I haven't lost the chill from the mausoleum and the sewer is even worse. My teeth start to chatter.

Still, I finally manage to say, ""Keep that away from me."

"Why? Surely you're not afraid of the light."

"No," I tell him honestly. "Just the flames."

The answer pleases him. Rys shines nearly as bright as his fire.

He bows low, the ends of his long, tawny hair kissing the sewer floor as he bends. "I hope my gift serves you well." He straightens, his lips a sly curve in his eerily perfect face. "Think of it as a reminder that, as reckless and as dangerous as fire can be, it's nearly indispensable when embraced by something equally as strong."

Huh?

I shake my head. "I don't want it. Take it back."

Just like that, just like I was afraid of, Rys's good humor fades. A dark look shadows his expression, his brilliant shine suddenly dim. In that instant, I remember with a start just why I have good reason to be so afraid of this fae.

His voice changes, going from warm and flirty to absolutely icy. "Where I come from," he says coldly, "it's considered a slight to refuse such a generous gift."

Crud.

"*Please* take it back."

"No," he pouts. "But because I *am* so generous, I will choose to look past your insult. And, as a token of my desire for you, I'm even willing to give you another gift."

"That's okay—"

"*Zella.*"

My mouth clamps shut.

Rys's smile returns slowly. "Much better."

He moves closer, walking toward me, almost dancing on the tips of his toes. I can't do anything to get away from him. Once again, he says that strange Zella word and I'm too stunned to do anything but stand there like an idiot. I notice that he's careful to avoid the pocket he pointed out, but he walks right through the shadows surrounding me as if they don't bother him at all.

When only a few inches separate us, he raises his left hand so that it's right in front of me, then folds his fist. He squeezes it tight, concentrating, and when he opens it back up again, there's a small pile of golden glitter sitting in his palm.

I'm still frozen in place, but whether it's from his compulsion or because I'm too terrified to move, I'm not sure. Either way, as Rys presses his lips together and lets out a breath of air that sends that glitter shooting straight at me, there's not a single thing I can do to avoid it.

It hits me full in the face. My spell of paralysis is immediately broken. Letting go of the ladder rung again, I try to wipe it off my cheeks, off my lips, out of my eyes, but it sinks right in. I try to blink it away. That doesn't do anything, either.

Whatever it is that Rys blows at me, it's powerful stuff. Within seconds, I'm already feeling drowsy. Dizzy, too.

Rys watches me closely as I drop down to my knees. The stone floor of the sewer is cold and damp and hard. A jolt of pain shoots through both legs as my knees hit the ground; between my throbbing ankle and the impact to my knees, I don't think I'm moving anywhere for a minute.

Not that I could. I'm too weak to even pull myself back up to my feet.

Now the slimy, dark walls of the sewer seem to be spinning around me. The ground moves sideways, or maybe that's me.

What was that stuff? What has he *done* to me?

I sprawl out on my belly. I'm too disoriented to even care

that I'm lying in the smelly, oily muck in this sewer. It's not that I don't know how nasty this is. I do. But I just can't *do* anything about it.

My eyes are already shuttering.

"Sleep well, Zella," Rys purrs somewhere above me. He shifts, lowering down to my side, nearly brushing my cheek with his hand. Half asleep and almost unaware that I'm doing it, I lean into his touch. "Dream of me."

CHAPTER 3

I don't dream.

I rarely do. It's a side effect of my meds. Some of my nighttime pills make it so that I can't fall asleep deep enough to dream. As I come to slowly, aware that I was asleep and now I'm kind of not, I realize that I didn't dream—and, for some strange reason, I'm not only relieved, I feel like I won something.

Waking up is a fight, though. That *is* unusual for me. Ever since I was forced into the asylum, I'm always up before the rest of my floor. Not today. Not now. It's almost like I'm drifting under the waves, floating along, no intention of breaking the surface.

I don't think I'm going to get the choice to stay under much longer. It's a gradual process, but my restful state is slipping away like grains of sand in a timer. I try to hold onto it. A warning beats against my hazy brain, telling me that I don't want to wake up. I'm warm, though my face, my ears, my nose are a little cold, and I'm safe while I'm asleep.

Right?

I... I'm not so sure.

For some strange reason, I ache all over. My bed isn't the softest, sure, but it feels like I'm sleeping on the floor. My back is super stiff. While I keep my eyes screwed shut, a weak attempt at tricking myself into thinking I'm still asleep, I curl up into a ball, trying to twist my body into a better position.

It doesn't work. My side is screaming and I roll over, flopping on my back, my arm flung outward as I stretch.

My fingers brush against something fuzzy. Images of rats and caterpillars and, I don't know, mutant spiders go running through my mind. My eyes spring open.

Suddenly, I'm wide awake.

One second. That's all it takes. One second where I gasp in terror, unable to keep from imagining a big, fuzzy, mutant spider running across my hand, then I react. I throw my blanket off, then try to jump out of the bed.

Impossible.

I'm already flat on the ground. There's nowhere else to go but up.

Scrambling into a sitting position, I push off of the hard ground, desperate to get away from the monster spider I've imagined.

I'm disoriented. It's strangely dark where I am, with a heavy, dank, musty chill hanging in the air. I'm halfway to my feet when my bare foot slides on something slick, something sleek, and I stumble forward, throwing my hands out in front of me to break my fall.

I land on my hands and knees, the same material I slipped on cushioning me enough so that I don't shatter my kneecaps. Like I thought before, the floor is hard—and it *is* the floor. It's hard as marble and just as cold; the shock of the temperature cuts through my leather gloves. My fingers scrabble to find purchase against the slippery swath of thin fabric beneath me. Once I'm resting against my heels, I blink, trying to figure out where I am and what the hell is going on.

Okay. So, it's not my room, and not only because I'm missing the six vertical bars stretched across my window. Can't have any bars—there's no window where I am. No bed, either. Just the encompassing dark and, as I blink rapidly, trying to get my sight back, a pale light illuminating the gloomy space surrounding me.

I blink again, focusing.

I'm not seeing things. A faint orange glow stretches out, touching everything around me. It's not enough to help me make any sense of my strange surroundings, but the eerie gleam makes me nervous. That's... that's weird. I should be glad that there's any kind of light here—

Light.

Light Fae.

I remember. Suddenly, I remember where I am and why.

I'm in the sewer, and I'm hiding.

Or, I *was*. I didn't do such a great job since he found me.

Rys.

My head jerks toward the source of the faint orange light. Facing it head-on, the fire inside is so bright that I have to shield my poor, stinging eyes with the shadow of my glove.

The lantern. How the hell could I have forgotten for even a minute? The fierce flames flicker, licking at the glass enclosure. It's an unmistakable leftover from the Light Fae before he left me and I—tired and afraid and alone—fell asleep in the confines of the empty, chilly sewer.

No. *No.* It's all coming back to me now. The smug expression on his sculpted face, the promise—the threat—in his bright gold eyes, the way his perfect lips pouted before he conjured up his weirdo dust and blew it right in my face.

That's right. I didn't just fall asleep.

I was *put* to sleep.

Dick.

Lifting my hand to my face, I rub my eyes, my cheeks, my lips. Now that I've remembered, I can actually feel the dried remains of his stupid powder on my skin. I wipe angrily with my gloved fingers. When that doesn't do anything, I yank my hoodie's sleeve until it's pulled over my thumb, then scrub.

Better.

At least, my face is. I knock the dust off, my nose wrinkling when I catch a whiff of something nasty. Phew. A terrible stink is coming off of my sweatshirt. Even worse? I can't tell if it's coming from me or if it's something I might've touched down here in the disgusting sewer.

I blow air through my nose, trying to get the stink out. Then, because I don't want to accidentally sniff that crap again, I roll my sleeve up and, still on my knees, I scoot away from Rys's lantern.

I remember that fire, too. My hands hurt just looking at it. Rys might have pretended he was leaving it behind with me because he cared. Yeah. Right. It was just another way for him to remind me that, no matter what, as a human squaring off against a fae, I'm forever at his mercy.

I can't stay down here. Glancing up, I don't see anything. I'm not exactly sure what that means. Did the manhole cover get shifted, settling in place so that I'm trapped down here? Or is it dark up there? The stream of sunlight that eked its way down earlier is gone.

So is Rys.

How long was I sleeping? No way to tell. At least I feel rested, like I've slept for a while.

Not gonna lie. That scares me a little bit. I don't know what he hit me with or what it did to me except for knocking me out. Where did he go? Why did he leave me here?

Considering I lost a week after my pitstop in Faerie with Nine, I'm terrified to discover that I've been sleeping down in the sewer for a couple of years, like I'm Rip Van Riley or something. After everything that's been happening to me lately, I don't even think that would surprise me.

I gotta do something. Stand? Standing sounds like a plan.

My knees are okay. That's good. I felt a jolt all the way from my knees up to my thighs when I slammed into the stone floor, but no permanent damage.

I didn't experience any discomfort when I got to my feet, either. I give my ankle an experimental turn. No pain. Maybe getting some sleep wasn't so bad after all.

Shifting a little, I put my full weight on my bad ankle. The only thing I feel is that same silky, sleek material under my bare foot. I had forgotten all about it once I saw the glow and remembered Rys's lantern, but it's the same unfamiliar blanket I'd been sleeping under—and that I slipped on when, still half-asleep, I convinced myself that I'd brushed up against something fuzzy.

One question, though. All I have are the clothes on my back, my gloves, my sweatshirt, and that's it. Where did I get a blanket from?

I'd never tell him so, but Rys's lantern comes in handy. Squatting down, I move to the side, allowing the bright flames to illuminate the crumpled fabric that's sprawled on the ground from where I kicked and slid on it. I can see the outline of a large, thin blanket that, when I pick up the corner and run it between my fingers, is way heavier than it looks. It's made of a glittering black material that looks like satin but feels like flannel.

It's a strange shade of black, dark yet almost reflective of the Light Fae's fire. And while I have no freaking clue what this is or where it came from, I... I've *seen* material like this before. I'm almost positive. Unless I'm wrong, the long, duster-looking coat that Nine always wears is made of this stuff.

That's so weird.

What is it doing here? I doubt Rys blew that crap in my face, then conjured a blanket out of thin air to tuck me in. Something tells me that, even if he did, he'd never use anything that would remind me of his "rival".

This blanket? It totally screams Nine.

Too bad it couldn't be from him. I mean, Rys did say that he had to leave since it was... what did he call it? The time of shadows. Nighttime. As a Dark Fae, Nine could cross back over from Faerie—but how could he find me? I'm hiding in a sewer. Despite how easy it was for Rys to track me down, this has got to be the last place on earth anyone would ever expect me to be hiding.

And that's if he was even looking for me in the first place.

No chance. Not after the scene in the Acorn Falls cemetery. I told Nine that I never wanted to see him again and, even after he told me that he'd come if I wanted him to, I promised that I would never change my mind. So what if Rys seemed convinced that Nine would come for me?

He wasn't there when I sent the Dark Fae away. He doesn't know that, at that moment, I meant it. Just like I meant it when I told Rys that I'd rather live in the sewer than go anywhere with him.

I glance back up at the ceiling again. I really, really don't like how I can't tell if the manhole cover has been replaced or not.

Now that I've learned that Rys's kind of fae needs a ray of light to appear the same way that Nine travels through shadows, maybe it's a good thing that I *don't* know. No light means I'm safe from Rys either way.

For now.

A shiver courses down my spine. My body trembles. I can't tell if it's from residual fear or because it's freezing down here since, well, it is. My sweatshirt isn't doing enough for me in the sewer.

The black blanket looks thin, but it kept me warm. I want to wrap myself up in it. Tugging on the hem twisted between my fingers, I pull the blanket toward me.

Something moves with it.

What the—

I yank the blanket roughly, watching it slither across the stone floor, almost folding in on itself as I reveal more and more of the pock-marked stones and cobbled path. The tail dips into the oily puddle inches away from my bare feet, leaving a trail until it's close enough that I just toss it to the side.

The orange glow lights up something small, round, and a sort of pale-ish color. It's a little bigger than a golf ball, smooth all the way around, with a darker, rosy patch on the side closest to me.

Well, that explains the fuzzy. It wasn't a mutant spider after all that I brushed against when I rolled over. It was a peach that had been nestled by my hand, hidden beneath the blanket.

Okay, then.

So… *is* it a gift from Nine? Like the shadow blanket, I'm thinking the piece of fruit might be an offering from the Dark Fae. Who else would've known my weakness for a perfectly ripe peach? When I was little, I went through a phase where the only thing I would eat was sliced peaches swimming in the sugary syrup of a fruit cup. Even now, as an adult, peaches are my favorite.

It's sitting on the dirty ground. When I pulled on the blanket, the peach moved so that I can't even pretend that the thin fabric is protecting it from the grimy stone floor. Know what? I don't care. I really don't give a shit.

I'm *starving*.

Rys put me to sleep hours ago. The beef stew I ate last seems like a lifetime has passed since then. I mean, depending on how I look at it, it's either been more than a day or a whole week since my last meal and I feel it in the pit of my stomach. Just the sight of the peach, sitting between two cobbled together pieces of stone, has me salivating.

Before I think better of what I'm about to do, I squat down and scoop it up. Maybe I shouldn't eat this gifted peach. After rubbing the rosy side on the least filthy patch of my hoodie, I decide that I just don't care what I *should* do.

I take a bite. It's simply sumptuous. Sticky juice trickles down my chin; I wipe it away with the back of my glove. The peach is so tender, so flavorful, that it nearly melts in my mouth.

And then I swallow.

I know right away that something is wrong. As soon as the peach is down, my mouth fills with the most rancid, sour taste. Once, when the Everetts went out for the evening, me and Madelaine snuck into their liquor cabinet and shared an entire bottle of peach-flavored vodka. We got so sick off of it that we spent the entire night throwing up in our shared bathroom.

That's what my mouth tastes like now. The acid backwash of artificial peach vomit. It's freaking nasty.

What's worse? I immediately sink my teeth back into the peach.

The same thing happens.

Over and over again—I can't help myself. No matter how bad I know it's gonna be when I swallow, I can't stop myself from taking another bite.

Another.

And another.

I only stop when my teeth clamp down on something hard. I lift it up to my face, squinting in the harsh glow of Rys's lantern. I've already eaten down to the pit. There's about half the peach left on the other side, but before I rotate it, I see something wiggle.

What the—

It's green and small and it's... it's *wriggling*. I'm immediately reminded of an inchworm. You know. Those tiny creepy crawlies that have a reputation for popping out of apples.

Only this is a peach and, holy crap, I almost *ate* it.

I shriek, then toss the peach across the sewer. It lands in a puddle with a soft splash, spraying the nasty muck outward. One drop manages to get inside the lantern. It hits the flame with a sizzle.

My stomach rebels. Just the idea that I was seconds away from swallowing that little squirmy, wormy-thing has me gagging. The sour taste in my mouth doesn't help; I kind of think that has more to do with my sudden nausea than seeing the worm inching its way across the peach's pit. I swallow roughly, breathing shallowly through my nose, trying to control it.

I heave. Gritting my teeth together doesn't do a damn thing. I wrap my arm around my belly, chanting *don't puke, don't puke* over and over again as if that's going to help.

Spoiler alert: it doesn't.

I've got to be one of the worst sick people ever.

Throwing up has always made me super miserable, I tend to get whiny and complain when I feel weak, and I get kind of testy at the slightest headache. Luckily, I've got a pretty strong immune system. I haven't gotten a cold in years, I can count the stomach flu's I've had in my life on one hand, and I rarely get headaches.

I've definitely got one now.

This? This is the mother of all migraines, too. It's like a rock band is playing their second encore at the base of my skull. My eyes are screwed shut because even a glimpse of the lantern's light has my stomach turning.

There's nothing left in there. I've thrown up everything in my stomach and then some. I've got to be dehydrated, too, which isn't doing the pounding in my head any favors. The sewer had its own nasty smell when I first came down here to hide. Now, the stringent, acrid stink of vomit mixed with the cloying scent of that awful peach is all around me.

Any time I breathe through my nose, the rancid stench has my weak stomach twitching. What makes it so much worse is that I'm not sure if I want to hurl again, or fish the half-eaten peach out of the dirty water and take another bite.

I'm not even hungry. Right now, even though it's been hours since I first bit that peach, I feel so crappy that I don't know if I ever want to eat again. It's like there's this... I don't know... *compulsion* almost. I don't want to do it. Just thinking about it makes me feel ten times worse, but I'd be lying if I said that I wasn't tempted.

I lose track of time. Wrapping that strange blanket around my shoulders, wiping my mouth with one of the corners, I curl up into the fetal position and promise myself that, as soon as I regain enough strength to climb out of the sewer, I'm begging someone—anyone—for help.

I'm sick. I'm filthy. I'd just about kill for some water to wash out my mouth and rinse my face.

And that's when I hear a sudden gasp, followed by a soft growl, and I decide that when I thought that I'd beg anyone for help, I was tempting fate.

"Oh, Shadow." The familiar voice with its alluring lilt and undeniably harsh edge makes my heart race and my stomach twist. "You should've called me."

Nine is lucky that I'm too weak to do anything but lie here otherwise I'd flip him the bird.

Call him? How the hell was I supposed to *call* him?

When I sent him away from the cemetery, I didn't know if I would ever see Nine again. I told him I wouldn't want to—because, contrary to the fae, I can totally lie—and then, when Rys tracked me down the next morning, he basically confirmed that I was SOL. Without knowing Nine's true name, his Faerie name, I would never be able to summon him for help.

Know what, though? He's here now. He found me again.

The least he could do is help me after how much his peach has made me suffer.

"Water."

"Did you say something?"

I tried. My lips are cracked, my throat way too dry. My head throbs so bad that I squint and wait for a beat between the pulses to spit out that word again: "Water."

I'm so desperate for a drink that I'm seconds away from crawling on my belly and lapping at the puddle where my slipper still sits, mud and oil and all.

Luckily, I don't have to do that. Nine murmurs for me to stay where I am—like I'm really in any shape to move—and disappears. I can tell. Just like when he appeared in my room at the asylum, once I sense him near me, it's easy to pick up on how different the air feels when he's gone. Like… like it's lighter somehow.

Or maybe a bad case of food poisoning and severe dehydration has me cracking up more than usual.

Yeah.

It's probably that last one.

CHAPTER 4

Nine isn't gone for long. The air grows heavy again a second before I hear his voice. As if he can tell that I'm suffering, he keeps it low.

"Riley. I have your water."

"Don't touch me," I whisper. I want that water so bad, but not enough to give him permission.

The air shifts around me. I can sense him at my back for a heartbeat, and then he's gone again.

"The vial is behind you." He pauses, then offers, "I can put it in your hand if that helps."

"I got it."

My arm feels like it weighs a hundred pounds. My eyes still closed, I reach out blindly, a cold sweat breaking out on my brow as I search for Nine's vial. He murmurs directions that filter in like white noise. I tune him out. When the back of my hand knocks into something that feels like glass against my leather glove, I fumble around until I've got it in my grasp.

There's no lid. I try not to spill any of the precious water as I drag it to my lips and tip the contents back. A tiny stream dribbles out of the corner of my mouth where I missed. At least I get some.

It's the cleanest, most crisp water that I've ever tasted—and I'm not just saying that because I feel like garbage. It's a mouthful, if that, but it's enough. It rinses the horrible taste away from my mouth, moistening my dry tongue, and getting rid of the pointy, pinchy pain at the back of my throat.

The pounding in my head subsides a little, too. The headache is still there, my stomach still angry and empty, but at least I can finally open my eyes—barely.

It isn't much, but I try my best to glare up at him. "Damn it, Nine. Why did you do this to me?"

His eyebrow rises as his lips thin. "What exactly is it that you've think I've done?"

Pulling myself into a sitting position, cracking my eyes open a little wider in time to watch Nine as he pointedly shifts to avoid Rys's lantern, I point across the narrow sewer.

"Don't pretend you don't know. It was your stupid peach that made me puke up my guts," I say accusingly. "Were you trying to poison me, or was that just a lucky side effect?"

"Peach?" echoes Nine. "I didn't give you any peach."

"Someone did. It was under the blanket you left behind."

"I left nothing. It wasn't possible for me to. The shadows have kept you hidden and, after the cemetery, I thought I should give you your space. It took me until just now to find you."

Oh, no. Oh, no, no, *no*. It had to be Nine. Because, if it wasn't, where the hell did that demon peach come from? As sick as it made me, I decided it had to be a terrible coincidence because Nine would never knowingly hurt me. But if he didn't leave it—

"Where is the peach?" he asks roughly.

"It's over there," I tell him. I try to push myself up off the ground and fail miserably. My legs are wobbly, my arms too weak, and I collapse in a heap before I've climbed a few inches off of the ground. I gesture at the flickering flames in the lantern. "Take that if you need help."

Nine throws a dark look at the lantern. "I recognize the fire. Let me guess. It's another gift from Rys?" A muscle tics along the edge of his smooth alabaster jaw as he clenches his teeth. "He found you first."

Yeah, well, that much is obvious.

A second later, I pick up on what Nine said and I have to swallow again to keep the bile from rising up in my raw and aching throat.

"*Another*?" I say. The word comes out like a croak. I swallow one more time, pushing back the taste of spoiled fruit that returned with a vengeance. "Do you think he's the one who left the peach for me? Why would he want to poison me?"

Nine doesn't answer me right away. Neither does he grab the lantern or take it with him as he starts to search along the black edge of the sewer wall. He doesn't need it. After a few seconds, he bends down. When he straightens, I see the half-eaten peach grasped loosely between his long, slender fingers.

He holds it up, his silver eyes dimming to a fierce gun-metal gray as he glares at it. "I'm not so sure he did."

I don't like the way he said that. "What's that supposed to mean?"

"That he—" Nine stops there, shakes his head, then starts again. "It's a very old faerie trick. Think of Hades and Persephone, the story of the pomegranate. Feeding a human faerie food is a sure way to force them into Faerie."

My stomach—already so messed up—drops. "What?"

"If a human tastes faerie food, they won't be able to survive without it. Human food won't satisfy you ever again. If you want to keep from starving, you'll have to go to Faerie and stay there."

"What?"

I can feel the niggle of panic as it begins to come to life. One positive to being this freaking sick is that I don't have the strength to fall into another attack. It still sucks. All around me, the air grows heavy. It's hard to breathe.

I want to scream.

And I thought it was bad when I saw the wriggly little worm and had a freak-out that I almost ate it. Now he's saying I'm gonna have to go to Faerie because I was too hungry to resist the gift of the peach?

Oh, *hell* no.

I'm shaking. It takes the last of my strength to finally get off of the ground. Pulling myself to my knees, I peer up at Nine imploringly.

"Help me, please. Make this stop. Make it go away. You can do it. I know you can."

"Riley—"

"You want me to beg? I'll beg. I'll do anything you want me to. I won't go back there, Nine. I don't belong in Faerie."

Nine's expression closes off. His silver eyes gleam, the points of his ears peeking out through the inky strands of pitch-black hair as he looks down on me. His nostrils flare and, drawing back, he points down at me.

"Don't beg," he orders. "I don't ever want to hear you beg me for a thing. That's even worse than you trying to thank me. Trust me, Shadow. You don't ever want to be in my debt."

Thank you... know what? I actually remember that.

It's from one of Nine's earliest lessons back when I was a kid. The fae don't like to be thanked. You can nod your head, even offer a curtsy instead, but never, ever say thanks. Either you're doing what Nine just warned me of—putting yourself into the fae's debt—or you're offering mere words in exchange for whatever it was the fae went to the trouble of doing.

At least, that's how they see it.

Come *on*. I can't plead with him to help me, and even if I got him to agree, a 'thank you' would be a major slap in the face.

What the hell am I supposed to do?

I stick my finger down my throat, hoping that that will help get rid of the poison; it won't, but no one's accusing me of thinking rationally right now. I've already thrown up everything in there and then some so while it triggers my gag reflex, nothing comes out.

I lay out on the sewer floor, my hands wrapped around my middle. My sides ache from the uncontrollable heaves. Now my mouth tastes like rancid peach, acrid vomit, and dirty leather.

So that didn't help. Not even a little bit.

Did I really think it would?

I moan. Can't help it. I'm so miserable, and so freaking upset, it's all I *can* do. And now my only hope is staring down at me as if this is all my fault.

I blame Rys. And the peach. And the Shadow Prophecy for good measure.

I'm not going to Faerie. As I return to my fetal position, I figure this is as good a spot to die as any. Right now, I don't doubt that that's what's gonna happen.

From somewhere above me, Nine lets out a sigh.

"I'll do it. For you, Riley, I'll do anything. But you won't like it."

I perk up just enough to prop myself on my elbow. "I don't care if I'll like it. Fix me."

"First, there are a few things you need to understand."

No, I don't. "If it will make this feeling go away, do it. If it will keep me from having to go back to Faerie, I don't care what you have to do."

"Be careful, Riley. It's not in a fae's nature to explain the terms before entering into a contract. I'm doing you a kindness. You want me to tell you what will happen if you agree to let me help you my way."

Not really. Maybe it's the panic attack, or the threat of what eating the peach means, but I'm feeling even weaker as another second passes. I want it gone. I want it gone *now*.

"There's no time."

"There's plenty. If I had found you after another moonrise, I don't think it would take. I had to search countless portals until I found Rys's trace and here you are. There's still time enough. The charm from the faerie food... it's still fresh."

"Trace?" I echo, letting out a groan as my head begins to pound against my skull again. It's so hard to think, but that sounded way important—and like Nine was trying to slip it by me by bringing up the demon peach. "Rys's trace? What... what does that have to do with me being poisoned?"

He hesitates. I brace myself.

It's never good news for Riley when Nine has to think about what he's saying.

He takes a deep breath—I'm amazed he doesn't gag on the stench—then, as he exhales, he says, "You still wear his brand. You never gave me permission to touch you, so my mark never settled on your skin."

Okay. Maybe I'm too out of it to really function, but that makes even *less* sense to me. And I'm over it.

"What, unh... jeez, Nine, I'm freaking dying here. If you're gonna fix me, do it. Otherwise, just let me die in peace."

"You won't die. I won't allow it."

Another moan. His magic water must've worn off. My

stomach hurts so bad now, I want to cut my gut open, rip it out, and throw it into the depths of the sewer. Anything to make the pain stop.

"Honestly," I grit through clenched teeth, "the way I'm feeling right now, I don't think that's gonna stop me. Quit stalling. Do it."

"I won't take another touch without you understanding why I must."

Whoa.

Hang on.

Touch?

Who said anything about a *touch*?

I'm okay with removing my stomach to get rid of the pain. But to willingly accept his touch… suddenly, his insistence that I take a second to listen to him makes a ton more sense. Even as sick as I feel, my instinct is to crawl away from him.

"Touch?" I want to hurl again. It's a miracle that I keep from sitting up and folding over. "Why would you even say that?"

Nine crouches down low, close enough that I can see his fancy black boots, the silk of his pants, the tail of his shadowy duster—but far enough away that I can dodge his touch if he reaches for me.

He gentles his voice as he begins to explain.

"There are two ways to erase what his peach has done. I can touch you, give you some of my strength while leeching the poison from you. Or, if you'd prefer, I can burn the poison and Rys's brand from your skin. It's extreme, I know it is, but you shouldn't risk the Light Fae being able to track you by following his mark. Touch magic or fire, it's your choice. Either way, I'll fight the peach's charm and make it so that Rys won't be able to follow you unless you call for him. That's the best that I can do."

I dare a glance up at Nine's face just as his pale gaze flickers over to the flames dancing inside of Rys's lantern. My stomach clenches and, this time, I can't stop myself from lurching up, finally folding over, and gagging.

By the time this newest wave of unspeakable agony washes over me, I want to cry. And that's nothing compared to how it feels to know that Rys marked me in a way that his touch is like a fancy fae GPS tracker or something.

How? Maybe it really is the peach getting to my head, but I don't get it. The fae can't lie, and Rys told me...

"That's not how he found me," I argue. "He... he told me he knew to follow the pockets—"

"That was true. What he didn't add was that, from the moment you let him touch your skin, he could follow you across time itself. It's part of a fae's magic. Those touched by the fae can never escape the brand."

Great. Just freaking great. Nine tells me this *now*?

Okay. *Okay.* He's not really leaving me any choice. I guess I should be glad that he's explaining this all to me so that I'm going into this with my eyes open. He didn't have to do that— and it wouldn't change anything anyway.

I'm not going to Faerie.

Nope.

"Let me just... okay. I let you touch me, I'm finally free of the Light Fae... but then you'll know how to find me. Right?"

"Yes. Until the fire burns off my brand, or you give another precious touch away."

"You keep saying, unh, fire." I wipe my mouth with the back of my glove, then lean on my elbow again so that I can marvel at the leather that covers the ruined flesh. "Is that why..."

I can't say it. Maybe I'm being ridiculous, maybe I'm too sick to even entertain my wild train of thought, but I can't say it.

Nine understands. "Yes. It's part of the Seelie's light magic.

When you refused Rys, he wouldn't leave knowing that, after all that time, you still had my touch on your skin. He found a way to remove it."

That's not all his damn fire did.

"It wasn't so easy for me to find you after that," Nine adds, "but rumors led me right to Rys. He wants you. You know that, Riley. He's always felt like he had a claim to you, from the moment the Fae Queen assigned him to find your mother and bring you to Faerie. He didn't. Obviously, he didn't, and he's the only one who knows why. I told you that the asylum was a safe place to keep you out of Melisandre's reach. What I neglected to add was that Rys helped me arrange it. It was a compromise. We'd work together to keep you protected until you came of age. After that, it was every fae for himself. He charmed you into giving him your touch. He'll always have power over you until it's gone. And that's not even counting the peach.

"I told you. You have the choice. You can burn the brand away, using the fire he left behind. Rys won't be able to come after you then and it should be enough to counter the food from Faerie."

"Should," I echo weakly. "What if it doesn't?"

"Then it was all for nothing. When the Shadow comes of age, she's also supposed to come into her powers. Melisandre's spies warned her where you've been hiding. As soon as you were the right age, she planned on having you brought to Faerie to face her."

To face her. Right. What was it Nine said in the graveyard? That the Fae Queen has no problem killing me just so that I don't kill her first. Doesn't matter that I'm not the murderess type. She's fond of her throne, her power, *and* her head. What was one pesky human, especially when she had no problem turning us into decorations for her garden?

If I let the faerie food take hold, I'm done. I'll never be able to eat anything else again. And where do you find faerie food?

Ding! Ding! Ding!

Faerie.

That's right.

Well played, Rys. The bastard fae used my hunger against me. I didn't want to follow him to Faerie—whether he wanted me to stay with him, or he would sacrifice me to get on the good side of his queen when it finally sunk in that I'd never be his *ffrindau* thing—so he found another way to get me to go.

Nine already told me, and I can't deny it: if I can't fix this and *now*, I won't have a choice unless I want to starve to death.

And I would. I totally would. Before I gave in and let Rys win, I would totally do it.

Not now, though. With Nine here, and my stomach killing me, I have one last chance. It goes against everything I was ever taught, everything Nine ever told me, but self-preservation is the only thing I'm thinking about at this second.

I don't really want to die. Not if I can save myself.

Or let Nine save me.

"I accept."

"Riley—"

"Better the devil I know, right? If it's you or Rys who can track me down, it's no contest. Touch me, Nine. Do whatever the hell you have to do. Don't care. You have to save me."

For the second time, he hesitates.

My eyes are slits in my face as I grit my teeth through another wave of debilitating agony. He's not moving any closer.

What is he waiting for?

His gaze flickers back to the lantern. "The fire will hurt, but you'll have your freedom. The Shadow deserves her freedom."

"In real life, shadows are stuck to the bottom of a person's shoe. There's no such thing as freedom, Nine, not really."

"Riley—"

A whimper escapes my throat. I can't keep it back. Another wave of nausea shudders through me, but even that pales in comparison to the terror that jolts my senses at just the thought of going anywhere near an open flame.

For my whole life, I've been conditioned to hate being touched. All it took was one fucking awful afternoon to make me throw away all that brainwashing. I hate the idea of giving him permission to lay his hands on me—but there's absolutely no way that I'll ever willingly let fire lick at my skin again.

How can I make him understand?

My brain is fuzzy. So much of my focus is on keeping my stomach from lurching into my throat, but I clench my fists and *think*.

Nine's my Shadow Man—but he's also a Dark Fae. And I know exactly what I have to do to get him to do what *I* want.

"I'm giving you permission to touch me, Nine. You get to take the power in the touch while I get to hide from Rys and forget that stupid freaking peach. Sounds good to me. So, do we have a bargain?"

"No." He pauses, then adds, "The terms are not fair."

Since when does a fae give a shit what's fair or not? Unless he thinks I'm trying to pull one over on him. Is the touch not enough? What else can I offer him?

There's only one thing I can think of. "I'll throw in my true name. If you don't already have it, I'll give it to you. Is that better?"

"You misunderstood me. When I said the bargain wasn't fair, I meant it's heavily weighted in my favor. For anyone else, I'd agree—but not you, Shadow. Remember that. This touch will be different than any you've felt before. Deeper, so much deeper, there's a risk that there might be other... effects."

Effects? What's that supposed to mean? And why is he telling me this *now*?

I don't get the chance to ask. Before I do, Nine edges closer.

His silver eyes are blazing. I don't know what the hell is going on, but his eyes are shining so brightly that they seem to glow. No—they *are* glowing. Between that and Rys's lantern, the dark gloom of the sewer isn't so bad.

I'm so used to Nine's detached personality. Most of my memories of him are as an emotionless Shadow Man who acted like a babysitter, a teacher, and an unwilling guardian at the same time, until I was fifteen-years-old and he simply disappeared.

From as far back as I can remember, he always looked the same way as he does at this very second. He never aged and, except for growing his hair out, he never changed. Though I often wondered, I never once asked him how old he was. He looks like he's maybe twenty-five—but he's looked that way since I was a kid.

I know I've grown up. I've definitely changed. I'm not the same little girl I was when Nine started to tell me stories of magic, of another realm, and a race of superior beings who could steal my soul if I let them touch me even once.

Right now? My pleading face is reflected in his wide, glowing eyes. He's still not blinking. It's like he's trying to drink in my image, as if he's desperate not to forget this moment. I recognize the hunger there, and the absolute despair etched into every feature on his beautiful face.

Nine's expression is wretched. I've never seen him wear such a look like that one before. And, okay, I'll be the first to admit that I've made very few personal relationships in my life. But

I've known Nine since I was a toddler. He doesn't let his guard down very often and, when he does, it's the most intimate, revealing experience ever.

My heart thumps wildly, beating against my ribcage. And this time? It has nothing to do with a panic attack.

Whoa.

"I won't take your name," Nine says in that lyrical voice of his. The harsh edge has been softened, but the way he watches me unblinkingly? The steel is there. "After this is done, it's important that you keep something for yourself. It's fair that way. So, if you'll accept it, I'll gladly offer my name instead."

I blink.

Seriously?

For a fae, giving up his true name is the ultimate sacrifice. It's making himself vulnerable in a way that I could never really understand. With his true name, he's returning some of the power he's going to take back to me.

I shake my head. It messes with the constant headache, but I don't care. I've seen first hand what it's like to have someone else control your true name. The loss of control every time Rys calls me Zella…

"Nine, you don't have to—"

"My name is Ninetroir."

It slams into me, knocking me back, sending me to my ass. I just manage to break my fall as I land on my gloves, but I'm still stunned.

He did it.

He totally did it.

I don't even have to repeat it, either. Just hearing the way he murmurs his own name, the three syllables wrap around me next, warming me up in the chill of the dank sewer. It settles into my skin, reverberating in my throbbing head, burrowing into my heart.

I'm sick as a dog, plus worried that I'm coming out of this mess even more screwed up than before, and still I know that I'll never forget how to echo his name.

It's mine and, at that moment, I know that I'll never give it back.

I exhale. As a reflex, I almost thank him; at the last second, I remember myself. He's fae. *Ninetroir*. There's only one thing to say.

"Do we have a deal now?"

"Yes."

And, when he moves toward me, I only flinch a little. But I don't inch away from him.

I'm breathing heavy, and that doesn't have anything to do with my anxiety or fear or the damn charmed peach, either. Right when his fingertip is mere centimeters away from me, it hits me that I'm actually waiting for his touch instead of actively avoiding it.

Crap.

It was the look on his face that did this to me. I know it was —and I can't do anything about it anyway. Besides, he wants this so badly. And I've already agreed.

I gulp. Nine's pale finger lands against my cheek. It's chilly.

Then he strokes my skin.

It's the most gentle caress I've ever experienced in my life.

The next heartbeat, I totally get what he means by *effects*.

Pleasure almost immediately replaces the pain. My stomach is still queasy, my throat raw, but a toe-curling pleasure starts low in my gut, a tightening coil that has my back arching as the heat spreads outward, filling me up entirely. It feels good.

Amazing.

When a husky moan escapes my lips, it has nothing to do with how shitty the peach made me feel.

It has everything to do with how bad I want to climb Nine like he's a tree.

I'm delirious. Dehydrated, too. Scared out of my freaking mind.

And super, super horny.

It's been so, so long since someone touched me like they wanted me to enjoy it. And I do. I really, really do.

"There." Nine's whisper echoes all the way to my soul. I don't feel like any of it's missing, though there's a rich, throaty note to his tone that tells me that he was just as affected by his touch as I was. "I think I got it all. Now, lay down, Riley. Sleep it off. Come tomorrow you'll be yourself again."

No, I think. I won't.

I'll be *his*.

Like I haven't been my whole life already.

"Lay with me," I mumble. Punch-drunk and weak as a newborn kitten, I can't stay upright. I sprawl on my belly, patting the stone floor next to me. "Stay with me."

"I'll stay," he says. "But over here. It's better that way."

He's wrong, but I'm too tired to argue. "Okay. Don't go, though. I want you here with me."

"I'll stay until I can't."

Spoken like a true fae. "Night, Nine. Love you."

"Don't say that. You'll only regret it later on."

I might. Doesn't mean it's not the truth. And, still coasting on the pleasure his touch gave me, I find that I just don't have it in me to lie right now.

From the time when I was a kid and all I had to look forward to were my nighttime visits with the Shadow Man, I've always loved Nine. I just could never tell him so.

It feels so freeing to finally get that off my chest.

On a peaceful sigh, after tucking my elbow under my head, I close my eyes.

I don't even notice when he finally does leave me. One minute he's there, leaning against the ladder because he's keeping his distance—and he's not about to sit down in the sewer.

Not that I blame him.

The next time I find the strength to open my eyes again, I'm all alone. Did he whisper his goodbyes? Possibly. I kind of remember his face, his whisper, his promise. Feeling dizzy and hazy, plus a little loopy, he's gone and I'm alone.

On the plus side, no Rys.

I'll take what I can get.

CHAPTER 5

"**Y**ou're looking better."

He's full of shit. We both know it. I don't need a mirror to see how much of a disaster I am.

At least I'm feeling better. I can sit up on my own now, too. I've moved further down the sewer, away from the manhole cover and the ladder that leads up above. It's darker, colder, and the smell of vomit still lingers.

I've gotten used to it. That, and the layer of grime on my skin.

I stretch, wincing when it seems like everything aches. I guess I should've been expecting that. How long did I sleep anyway? I wipe my eyes with the back of my glove, then shove my tangled hair out of my face. It's dark in the sewer—well, darker—so I know I must've slept for a while.

Plus, that's Nine. Not Rys. If my Shadow Man's here, that's a pretty big clue that I made it through another sunset.

"You're back. Where did you go? I woke up earlier and you were gone."

"If I want to stay at full-strength, I have to leave when the shadows are gone. I can appear in a portal if necessary, or if commanded to, but the sun steals too much of my power in your realm."

I knew that. Nine told me that a long time ago, when he was in one of his rare talkative moods. I kept asking him why he couldn't stay with me all the time—and he finally gave me the answer. Though he never confessed back then that he was fae, he didn't hide that he belonged in Faerie and I belonged here.

Or, I *did*.

"Anyway, I've brought you something."

Nine has a bundle tucked inside of his long coat. When he takes it out, it almost seems as if he's removed part of his coat with it. It's the same shade, the same strange material, the same shimmering texture. It's an oblong shape, his pale fingers standing out against the pitch dark color of whatever he's holding.

Then he lays his palm flat, the material falls away, and I see what looks like a… a roll, maybe?

I breathe in deep. Over the muted stink of old vomit and dirty sewer, I catch a hint of freshly baked bread on the thick air.

I wait for my stomach to rebel. When it doesn't, I decide I'm ready to chance eating again.

Question is: *should I?*

"What is that?" I ask suspiciously. "Where did you get it from?"

"It's safe. Human food. I won't let you starve down here. And, unlike the precious Blessed Ones, I won't resort to tricking you with food from Faerie."

That's good enough for me. "Set it on the ground."

Once I have the bread in my glove, I try to give Nine back the black wrapper thing.

Nine shakes his head. "That's for you, too. Consider it a gift from me. Freely given, I want nothing in return for it."

A gift? For me?

Really?

I take a better look at it. Just like I thought, it's silky, a real shiny, deep black color, and it reminds me of the blanket that I woke up with right before I ate the peach. It's smaller, though. Like a scarf, only I have no idea what it is—or why Nine's giving it to me.

"Am I supposed to know what this is?"

"Yes."

"Well, I don't."

"You will."

Oh, great. More riddles. "What's it for?"

"Whatever you want it to be for."

Whatever. Right now I want it to be a bread holder, I guess. Works for me.

The bread is freaking delicious. I take the first bite hesitantly, waiting for it to turn against me the same way that the peach did. When it doesn't, I gobble up half of the roll before realizing that I probably should make it last.

It's light, it's fluffy, and it's still warm. The only thing that would make this better is—

"Water?"

He holds out a vial.

How did he guess?

Mouth still full, I nod.

This time, though, I don't tell him to set it down. When he begins to crouch down, I actually stop him. Well, after I quickly swallow my mouthful of breath, I do.

"It's okay. You just surprised me with the bread. You can hand me that. I… I didn't mind it when you touched me before."

Nine slowly rises. But, first, he sets the vial of water down on the floor. "You don't mean that."

I kind of do.

I kind of liked the way it felt when he touched me—the pleasure that drowned out the agony—and now that I'm feeling more like myself, it's a shock to realize that I want to experience that again.

The even bigger shock? That I was bold enough... reckless enough... to admit that out loud.

I don't know for sure what Nine did to me yesterday. I would've thought, before the whole peach thing, that I'd rather die than let another fae touch me again. That's how strong my, well, my brainwashing was. He spent my whole childhood warning me against the power of a fae's touch magic. Especially after I saw what it did to Madelaine, I hated the idea of letting one of those monsters get their hands on me.

Then I ate the peach and I actually knew what it was like to think I was dying. My whole thought process switched in an instant. I would've let Nine do anything—and I mean *anything*—to me if it meant he saved my life.

The question I'm struggling with now is would I have felt the same way if it was another fae offering to heal me? Rys?

I don't think I would.

Nine's caress changed something. There was affection in the gesture, and an unholy heat in his eyes that I know I didn't imagine. He wanted to touch me. And I wanted him to.

Not just because I was cursed. Not because I didn't have a choice.

But because it's Nine.

My Shadow Man.

His touch might have erased the effects of the peach, but it did more than that. It allowed me to look past my hatred and fear of the fae and see the truth right in front of me. That the love and affection I had for my only friend has blossomed and bloomed into something way different now that I'm older and he... he's different.

The Nine I used to know would never have let me see that look in his eye. Just like how I can pick up on Rys's overt lust, I know what I saw when Nine thought I was too sick to notice.

He's into me.

And, the two of us alone in this sewer, he's trying to hide it.

Sure, a dirty, smelly sewer isn't my first choice of a romantic setting, either, but now that I'm feeling even better than before—Nine's bread was a huge help—I want to talk to him about how he seems even more irresistible than he ever did before.

I don't get the chance, though. Before I can say a word, my expression gives me away.

"Riley. Please. Don't look at me like that."

I decide to play dumb. Because this conversation? It's gonna happen whether Nine wants it to or not. He owes me that much at least.

"Like what?"

He shakes his head. "If I pursue this, then that means that I accept the Shadow Prophecy. All of it. Don't ask me to do that. Not now. Not when you're in so much danger."

I don't know what that has to do with anything. I didn't bring up the prophecy. Hell, I'd be happy to never mention it again—especially the way he tacks the word *danger* on at the end like that.

"But you feel this, too, right?" I blurt out. "I mean... I'm not crazy. Nine, I need you to tell me that I'm not crazy."

"You're not crazy. You never were. The asylum... you were there too long. It affected you too much. But you're perfectly sane."

"Don't sidestep my question. You know that's not what I meant."

He keeps quiet.

He does.

I can't.

"I thought it was crazy, just how drawn to you I am. Then I thought it was because you were the only stable thing in my life since I was a kid. But these feelings I've been having… shit, ever since you first appeared to me back at the asylum… they're not the sort of feelings a kid has. I… I—"

I think I might get what he meant when he said the touch might have some other effects. This is bad. It's like his touch was some kind of truth serum or something like that.

I can't lie. I *want* to. Spilling my guts like this a problem. A huge one. I want to lie.

I can't do that, either.

"—I think I love you. And not in the way I should love a guardian-type figure. Love you like in the way that, if you asked me to be your *ffrindau*-thing right now, I'd probably say yes."

Is it possible to die of embarrassment? The peach didn't do the job, but the pained expression that flashes across Nine's features followed by the almost sad look he wears now might just be the nail in my coffin.

Shit, that's pity, isn't it? I spilled my guts, said things I never should've said in a million years, and the Dark Fae *pities* me.

"It's the touch making you feel this way," he says after an awkward silence, his voice harsh and low but still achingly beautiful—just like Nine. "It's part of the magic. If it didn't make the human have good feelings toward the fae giving the touch, it would make it harder to compel them into doing it again. Give it a few days. It'll go away."

Part of me wants to believe that. But the part of me that used to doodle *Riley + Nine 4ever* when I was like twelve... she's not so sure.

I decide it's time to change the subject before I embarrass myself any further. If the effects of his touch mean that I've got a wicked case of verbal diarrhea, it'll be better if I switch the conversation around so that Nine's doing most of the talking.

Besides, I still need a shit ton of freaking answers.

"Um, okay. But, in the meantime, can you do something for me?"

He bows his head. A quick, decisive jerk upward. A nod.

Okay.

"Tell me more about the prophecy."

"I've told you all you need to know."

Not really. Sure, I guilted him into explaining it while the two of us were hiding out in the cemetery, but after my visit from the Light Fae, I'm beginning to think I got the cliff's notes version. There's more to it, I know there is, and Nine gets so defensive whenever it's mentioned, I'm convinced he's the best one to tell me.

"Ninetroir. Please."

I don't add any kind of order. It wouldn't be right. After everything that Rys has done to me, most of it because he controlled me with a word of his own, I absolutely refuse to *make* Nine do something.

"You've said my name."

I nod.

"But no command."

"You're my friend." Whatever he is—whatever my wayward psyche wants him to be—he's probably the only friend I have right now. "It wouldn't be right to make you do something. Trust me. I freaking know."

It's a reminder that, no matter what, I'm still at the mercy of

Rys knowing my true name. Nine wouldn't let me tell him last night, but that doesn't change the reality that, if the Light Fae *does* find me again, he could eventually use *Zella* against me.

Nine doesn't react to that reminder. Nope. He totally latches onto something else I said.

Interesting.

"I've never had a friend before. In Faerie, there are those working with you, and those working against you. Friends are for the weak."

"For the humans?"

"Yes," he says honestly.

"Well, I'm a human. So you can be my friend."

His lips thin. I'm not so surprised.

My manipulation tactic works, though. I might've meant what I said. Still had an ulterior motive—and it works.

"I've told you of the prophecy before," Nine begins, sounding resigned. "In Faerie, there are plenty of ancient tales that get passed down. Because my people are long-lived and practically immortal, there are the elders who keep the scrolls from the days of the Tuatha Dé Danann. The first of us. The Shadow Prophecy… is one of the earliest prophecies, but it's only become important since Melisandre stole the throne from Oberon. The Reign of the Damned. For the last two hundred years, the promise of the Shadow coming to end her is all that's kept hope alive for some of the less powerful races in Faerie."

Two hundred years…

Long-lived and practically immortal…

So, yeah, that explanation opens up a whole new can of worms. I can't help but remember the casual way that Rys mentioned centuries. He's at least that old.

What about Nine?

I have to know. I have to ask.

"How old are you?"

"Does it matter?"

"That's so not an answer."

He shrugs. "Old enough."

"Neither is that. Come on, Nine. Why won't you tell me?"

"Time works differently between both worlds. A Seelie comes of age during their twenty-first summer. My kind mature a little slower. The Unseelie come of age during their twenty-fifth winter. After that, time flows, but we don't measure it the way that humans do."

I cross my arms over my chest. "That still doesn't answer my question. How old are you Nine?"

He closes his mouth, firming his jaw.

He's not going to tell me, is he?

"I don't care. If that's what's weirding you out. Unless you're like a thousand or something." I wince when Nine doesn't even blink. "You're not that old, are you?"

He shakes his head.

Well, that's something.

I start to ask another question, to bring the discussion back to how exactly this ridiculous prophecy says I'm supposed to, I don't know, *end* the Fae Queen's reign, when Nine cocks his head to the side, his long wavy hair falling forward like a waterfall of black ink.

"Time grows short. I have to be leaving you now. I'll return as soon as I can."

My heart leaps into my throat. "What? Already? It seems like you just got here."

"It's later than you think. And you still need your rest."

No. What I need is to finally escape this sewer and start figuring out my next step. It was Nine's genius plan to break me out of Black Pine in the first place. He seems to know what the hell's really going on.

I need to stick with him.

"I want to go, too."

"To Faerie? No. That's impossible."

His quick denial is like a slap in my face. "What? You won't take me with you?"

"I can't. Don't ask that of me. The risk... Melisandre is untouchable in her realm. You're coming into your power now that you know it exists, but you're not ready yet."

"Fine. Then you stay here. With me. I don't want to be alone anymore."

"It isn't so simple as that."

Seems pretty simple to me. "Tell me this: is it possible for a Dark Fae to stay in the human world if they wanted to?"

"I told you. I would lose nearly all my power. Even a touch wouldn't replace most of it."

"So... what you're saying is... I'm not worth it. Cool. Got it."

"Riley, you know that's not it at all. If you need my protection—"

"Didn't say I needed anyone's protection."

He ignores me. Good call. I'm being bitchy. Childish, too. I can hear it, but I can't stop myself. Rejection has always been my weakness. I pretend like it doesn't matter because, hell, over the years, I should've gotten used to it.

Abandoned by my mom no matter what her reasons were. Going through five foster homes in less than fifteen years. Mr. Everett turning his back on me before I finally told Mrs. Everett to stop bothering with me... No one ever wants me. I'm always being shoved aside, sent back, hidden away.

I should've gotten used to it. Part of me did. It seemed to

hurt less and less as the years went on, but the sting was always there.

Hearing Nine try to explain why he has every intention of leaving me to rot in a dark, dank sewer in Acorn Falls is just about killing me. Excuse me for lashing out.

I'm not so good at expressing my feelings.

Nine, either.

He presses his lips together as he watches me with his eerie stare. Breathes in through his nose, then exhales on a harsh sigh.

"Riley," he begins.

Nope. I've heard enough of it.

"Go away. You have to leave? Leave. I don't want to talk to you anymore."

"This again?"

Yup. This again. Just like when I got pissed off at Nine while we were facing off in the cemetery, I'm pushing him away.

It's all I know how to do.

No. Now that he's trusted me with his true name, I know how to push him even *harder*.

"Ninetroir—"

His eyes flash in an open warning. "You said there wouldn't be a command."

I did say that.

"And you said that we weren't friends," I say coldly. Then, before he can say a word, I cross my hands over my chest. "Ninetroir, I command you to go."

He immediately winks out of the sewer.

I gulp and, slinking down to the hard ground, tears making it even harder to see in the orange glow of Rys's lantern, I lift Nine's scrap of silk up to my face and rub roughly at the corners of my eyes. It erases the tears, blocking out the light at the same time. Embracing the darkness, I move the silk so that's in front of my mouth, my nose.

My breath is shaky. One lungful of air in, though, and all I get is a whiff of Nine. The silk carries his scent. I twist it between my gloved fingers, pressing it against my face.

You know what else it's good for?

Muffling my sobs as I realize that, once again, I sent away the only friend I had.

This *sucks*.

CHAPTER 6

So, Nine was right.

I regret it all the next morning after I cry myself to sleep. And I mean *all* of it. From the way I told him how I felt while riding high from his touch magic, to my bratty reaction when he couldn't give me what I want... I don't know what the hell I was thinking.

The answer to that is easy, I guess. I'm not too sure I *was* thinking.

Crap.

I'm so freaking embarrassed. I can't believe I threw myself at him like that. What's wrong with me? What made me think that, despite the crush I've harbored for way too many years, Nine would actually be interested in me? Shoot, half the time I'm not even sure he *likes* me.

My Shadow Man, he's... I don't know, like an otherworldly creature with powers I can't even begin to understand. And I'm Riley Thorne, a human who's only involved with the fae and Faerie because of a prophecy that I can't escape from.

I'm the Shadow.

Whatever the hell *that* means.

Oh, Rys told me. Nine did, too. This prophesied chick who's supposed to act like a savior for the fae. Don't know why they think that should be me but, as both of the fae admitted, it doesn't really matter what *I* think. So long as the Fae Queen believes I'm out for her head, she won't leave me alone.

Isn't that peachy?

Peach...

Ugh. I'm never gonna eat another peach again so long as I live. Which, if the Fae Queen has her way, won't be long at all.

Wonderful.

Because of the threat she poses to me, Nine won't risk bringing me to Faerie with him. Rys will, but only if I agree to mate with him. Yeah, that's gonna be a no. Marrying my enemy to save my skin? Even I'm not that desperate.

That leaves me one choice.

I've spent years accepting that the only person I can rely on is *me*. I might not have gotten myself into this mess. Still, I guess it's gonna be up to me to get out of it.

A small shadow forms on the opposite wall, a distorted shape that seems to grow as it moves. My eyes are drawn to it, my hands curling into fists, ready to push up off of the ground if I have to.

It's a rat. That's totally a rat over there. It skitters along the far side of the narrow sewer, its long, bald tail slithering behind it as it dashes past Rys's lantern.

A couple of days ago, I jumped and freaked because I imagined that my hand brushed up against a fuzzy spider. Not now. My first instinct is to reach out and grab the silk thing that Nine gave me. Still feeling bitter, frustrated, and sad, I ball it up and throw it at the rat. Poor thing's claws clatter against the stony ground as it squeaks and scrambles to escape.

I feel bad for it. Just... not as bad as I feel about my situation. Ugh.

Thinking is *hard*. Focusing, too. My brain is pounding like a drum against my skull, pulsing angrily as I try to come up with some kind of plan.

I'm not having much luck.

This is definitely the worst hangover I've ever had. I wish I had some more of that water Nine brought back for me. I'm so thirsty that, for a second or two, I start thinking about drinking from that nasty puddle again. When I actually agree that it would be worth it to get rid of this godawful dry mouth, I realize I'm in trouble.

Yeah. If dirty sewer water starts to sound tempting, I've gotta do something about that.

There's only one thing I *can* do.

Tilting my head back, I look up at the ceiling way above me. That small sliver of light in the distance gives me some hope. So long as the manhole cover isn't flush against the road, I can still pry my fingers in the gap and leverage my shoulder against it to get it to move.

Of course, that's easier said than done. After I fish my slipper out of the puddle where I left it, I jam it on my foot, then yank the other one from my hoodie pocket. I take a second to fluff it, to bend it back into shape, then slip it on. My body is as stiff as the material on the side of the stained slipper. My knees creak as I pull myself up, my back screaming at me.

Jesus. I'm almost twenty-one and, after the last couple of nights I've had on the hard sewer floor, my poor *everything* aches like I'm eighty. It's nothing a couple of aspirins and a nice hot shower won't fix, but since it's not likely I'll get either one of those things anytime soon, I suck it up and start climbing the ladder.

Halfway up, I realize that my ankle feels fine. Maybe it's because the rest of me hurts like hell, but I don't even feel the slightest twinge as I go from narrow rung to narrow rung. That's one good thing. How far was I really gonna get if my ankle was still banged up from when I ran from that cop?

Just when I get to the top, I remember the silk scrap that I tossed at the rat. I purposely left behind Rys's lantern—because I just couldn't willingly get any closer to that enchanted fire—but I know I'll regret it if I don't go back for Nine's gift. I might be hurting from the way he rejected me last night, but I'll get over it. I always do. And, whether I like it or not, Nine's the only one I can turn to. The silk scarf thing is the first thing he's given me in years.

I want it back.

I glance down, picking out the orange haze and the pinprick of light that marks the lantern. The fact that it's so small makes me realize how far up I've climbed.

I really, really don't want to go down there again.

So I don't. I hesitate on the last rung for a few seconds, waffling between giving up on it—the rat probably ran off with it out of spite for all I know—and going back to get it. I finally found the strength and the balls to leave the sewer. I've got to keep going.

That lid is freaking heavy. It takes every last bit of energy I have to knock it aside enough to climb back out. My hoodie almost gets snagged as I struggle to push my way out, and it takes holding my breath to fit, but I do it.

It's early. Like, the sun has just risen *early* early. I'm so stinking happy to see that it's daylight that I let out a huge sigh of relief as I crawl out of the sewer. I draw the line at kissing the asphalt beneath my hands and knees, but it's close. I don't even care if there's a cop waiting up here for me. The second I'm out, I collapse on my belly and just breathe in the fresh air.

Once I've settled myself enough to focus on my next step, I jerk up my head. Because it's early, the alleyway is empty. No cops. No delivery trucks, either. And, I realize after a second, no Light Fae lurking nearby to say *gotcha*.

I was almost expecting to find him up here. Now that I haven't, I can admit that to myself. Nine told me that he managed to erase Rys's mark on me when he did… whatever it is that he did to me. I wanted to believe him.

Maybe I can.

Okay. No cops. No Seelie. That's good. I didn't want to hide any longer so, even though I thought I could be caught the second I poked my head aboveground again, I left the sewer.

The bad part?

Because I really did think I'd be caught, my brilliant plan never got any further than getting out of the sewer again.

What am I supposed to do now?

First things first. I get off the ground, wiping the gravel and the grime on my gloves off and onto the thighs of my dirty jeans. In the sunlight, I can see all the crap I've got on me—dirt and mud and oil and who knows what. I reach around, wiping my palms on my ass.

There.

Better.

A stray wind blows, sending my hair into my face. It stinks. Like *really* stinks. Oof.

The wind bites against my cheek, the strands of hair tickling my nose before I slap them away. It's… it's a little bit chilly out. That's weird. It's June. It must be even earlier than I thought for it to be so cool out in June.

At least my hoodie won't stand out. My rat's nest hair might, and the questionable stains that cover my poor jeans... not to mention my muddy, dirty slippers... but at least my clothes are weather appropriate and my gloves are hidden from view.

I'll take it.

Besides, it's not like I plan on sticking around here for people to start wondering what I'm doing lurking behind the back of the downtown shops. I might not have anywhere I can go just yet. Doesn't mean I can stay here.

What to do? What to *do*?

I don't have any family. My mom's gone. I never knew my dad. My sister's dead, and I totally pushed my last foster parents away after her death. Besides, even if I wanted to go to the Everetts for help, they moved to a city more than six hours away by car—and that was before they split up.

All I have is Nine. And, after how big of an ass I made of myself, I'm not about to call him for help. I might have his true name now. After the way I commanded him to leave, I can't bring myself to call him back, especially since it's daytime now.

You know what sucks? It hits me that I didn't stay in the freaking sewer so long because it was convenient. I stayed because I honestly didn't have anywhere else to go.

I can only imagine how frustrating the search for me has got to be—and that's if the hospital staff is still looking instead of writing me off as a bad bet. The sad truth is that, based on my history, I've never been able to call any place home. Apart from my time in Black Pine, I spent more time in Acorn Falls than anywhere else. No wonder they had the cops patrolling the streets in the quaint little town, almost as if they expected this would be where I ran off to.

I guess they were right.

Might as well go visit the last home I knew.

CHAPTER 7

I had this crazy, reckless idea that I should head back toward the edge of town. It's where the Everetts used to live, and the part of Acorn Falls that I remember the best.

With my hood up and my head down, I take the back streets, careful to avoid anyone who might get antsy and call the cops on me. Once I got away from the more crowded downtown, odds of being singled out get lower. I don't loiter outside of any street in particular, keeping my walk slow and steady as if I'm just getting fresh air instead of being on the run.

My stomach starts to grumble a couple of hours into my trek across town. Eventually, I'm gonna have to figure out what to do about that. Bitching and moaning and wishing I hadn't eaten the last of Nine's bread isn't gonna help me right now.

I keep walking.

After I hear the whispers of the few people passing me by, I stick to the trees. It seemed like a good idea. My hoodie is a more purple-y shade of maroon, my jeans a dark denim, and I don't stand out among the trees that line the road. The shadows linger here, and it's so much cooler in the shade, but it's better than prancing out in the open in my slippers.

The trees are... odd, though. Not green. Not totally. Some of them are capped with leaves that are red, orange, even yellow. Dead leaves, scattered leaves, cover the dry ground. They crackle so loudly under my steps, I start to dance from brown patch to brown patch of dirt to avoid them in case someone else can hear me.

Then, when I finally duck out of the woods, cross three streets, and find the Everetts' old house, I begin to think I've made a wrong turn somewhere.

It's been six years. I know that. The Everetts haven't lived here in ages. I guess I just thought that it would still be standing here, some tiny bit of the before time that could help ground me while I got my crap together.

The address is the same. The same **134** painted on the side of the mailbox posted by the curb. The same size house.

Everything else is different. From the row of flowers planted in front of the porch to the child's tricycle parked near the sidewalk, this isn't the house I lived in for two years. Glancing up, I search for the window that led to my old room. My curtains had been black.

These are pink.

The driveway is empty. The lights are off.

No one's home.

I'm glad. Standing at the curb, staring up at the house—wondering *what if*... I need a few minutes to myself. The last thing I need is the new owners wondering what some freaky girl is doing watching their house.

The Everetts' old house isn't the only thing that looks different than it used to.

When I'm finally done grieving the life I lost when Madelaine lost hers, I start to shuffle away from the Everetts', accepting that I came all this way because I needed to say goodbye one last time. Something catches my attention out of the corner of my eye and, well, I can't help it.

Can't stop myself, either.

On a shaky breath, my gaze slides over so that I'm peeking at the house at the far end of the street, tucked behind a shield of trees that keep it almost completely hidden from sight.

Six years ago, it was an abandoned two-story house with boarded-up windows. The paint was a paler shade of grey, the shutters peeling, the grass overgrown. They called it the Wilkes House for reasons no one could ever tell me. No one lived there then, or had in recent memory.

I remember it as if it was yesterday.

When it came to Madelaine Everett, I've got to admit that I was the bad influence between the two of us. I was thirteen when I came to live with the Everetts, and though Madelaine was almost fifteen, my years in the system had given me a crap ton of experiences—some good, most not—that she'd never had. The Everetts had adopted her when she was three. Unlike me, they were the only family she'd ever had.

Even though we had looked enough alike that we could pass for being blood-related—same blonde hair, though mine was so much lighter, and the same deep blue eyes—our personalities were opposite. I was always the half-empty type, a wary and independent teen who kept expecting to be sent back to the group home because I was too much trouble. Madelaine was sweet. Kind. She did everything to make me feel welcome and, because of that, she became so much more than just my friend.

She was my sister. And she treated me like one, too.

I trusted her. More than I trusted anyone besides Nine, I trusted my new sister.

Six months into my stay with the Everetts, I told her about the fae.

Madelaine, who was older than me yet so much more naive, laughed at my fears. Trying to soothe my worries away, she claimed they were just fairy tales.

Faerie something, all right.

She didn't believe me. Up until the moment Rys pulled her close for their dance, then snapped her neck because he believed that she was the only thing keeping me from leaving with him, I don't think Madelaine ever thought the angelic-looking creatures were a threat.

She paid for her ignorance with her life. And I've carried the guilt that I couldn't save her ever since.

This house is a reminder of that terrible night. There's only one problem, though: it shouldn't be standing. The last time I saw it, the entire basement was engulfed in flames. It should be a hollow shell, a burned-out husk, or a pile of rubble.

It's not. It's a whole freaking house.

I'm stunned by it. If I didn't know better, I'd think that I imagined the whole fire.

I have to get a better look. I have to make sure what I'm seeing is *real*. Leaving the Everetts' old place behind me, I head straight for the house at the end. The paint job is fresh. The grass is still kind of tall, though it's been tended to recently. The windows are new. So are the shutters.

Once I'm standing right in front of it, I notice something I missed before. There, planted by one of the wild bushes forming a border around the front and side of the narrow house, is a wide yellow sign. In black letters, it announces that the Wilkes House is **FOR SALE**.

Okay, then.

Someone must have rebuilt the house since it burned down, and now they're selling it.

Just like six years ago.

Throwing a glance over my shoulder, checking to make sure that no one on the quiet street has noticed me skulking closer and closer to the empty house, I quickly dart to the right. The tall trees towering around me are the perfect cover. Once I go around the back, no one can see me.

I know that for a fact. These trees are exactly the same as they used to be and I'd never been caught sneaking in before.

A rush of nostalgia slams into me as I face the back porch—the porch and the same red door that shone like a beacon for a couple of reckless kids once upon a time.

I couldn't tell you how often me and Madelaine snuck inside of the Wilkes House to hang out because it was always vacant. For as long as I lived in Acorn Falls, this house was for sale without a single taker.

And that was before the tragedy that took place in the basement.

Something tells me that, despite the work someone obviously put into this house, it's gonna be on the market for quite some time.

Hmm. That gives me an idea.

I wonder…

Biting down on my bottom lip, I force myself to head toward the porch. For some reason, ever since the first time we had the brilliant idea to sneak inside, the back door was always open. It was kind of like the house was waiting for us.

I climb up the stairs, my heart thumping nervously as I reach for the knob. I can feel the solid metal through the thin leather of my worn glove. I take a deep breath and twist.

The knob turns easily under my hand.

It's open.

I could push the door in and step inside and the only thing that's stopping me is the smell of burning flesh in my nose and the cracking snap of Madelaine's broken neck.

It echoes in my ears. That's not all, either. At that second, I swear I hear the tinkling music that played when I danced with Rys, followed by a haunted scream.

My throat burns with the urge to join in. I nearly lost my voice that day. Between yelling at the golden fae and screaming for Madelaine to be okay before howling in agony as I burned my hands with Rys's enchanted fire, I wasn't able to speak for days after the tragedy.

Then, when I did, I told everyone who would listen about the fae and ended up in Black Pine as a result.

Nope.

Can't do it.

I scurry down the stairs, nearly losing my left slipper in my hurry to flee. I've got to get out of here. I've got to get away. This was a bad idea. A stupid fucking idea. I would've been better off going back to the cemetery. At least there I could be with Madelaine and not just her ghost.

Trapped in the past with my memories and bad decisions, I make a worse one. I totally forget that the real world exists until I emerge from around the back and hear someone call out to me.

"Riley? Oh my god! Riley? Is that you?"

They know my name.

Wait—

I know that *voice*.

Against my better judgment, I don't run. Oh, I'm ready to. Make no mistake, my default state is to book it if she gives me even the slightest sign that I've got to go, but I stay standing near the corner of the house, giving her a chance to call out again before I take off.

She's standing on the sidewalk in front of the Wilkes House, body turned as if she was walking past it when she saw me appearing from the back. She moves slowly, careful not to spook me, and I get a full look at her face.

I was right. I *did* recognize that voice.

The first thing I notice is the dark brown hair that she's wearing loose around her shoulders. Next? The oversized burgundy coat that does nothing to conceal her too-small frame; it kind of highlights it instead. Jeans that are way cleaner than mine, plus a pair of expensive fur boots that are way out of season but probably cost an arm and a leg.

I've never seen her wearing such nice clothes before. When we were both inside of Black Pine, the patients wore simple sneakers, plain jeans, and a Black Pine tee.

When we were both inside of Black Pine—

Well, we're not now.

"Carolina?" The name slips out. "What are you doing here?"

"My God, Riley. It *is* you!"

While I stand here, frozen and still, Carolina surges forward. It's only when she's crossed the yard, her arms open as she dashes toward me, that I realize her intention. I take a few hurried steps back, throwing my hands up to block her. She might not be fae, but that doesn't mean anything to me.

Old habits die hard.

She immediately stops dead in her tracks. Her dark eyes go wide, her mouth opening to form a perfect '*o*' before she lets her arms fall to her side.

"I'm sorry. I... I forgot. It won't happen again." She claps her hands together, a silent promise to keep them to herself and not touch me. So she remembers my quirk. Good. That's something. "I'm just so glad to see you."

Glad? Really?

Why?

Up close, she looks as tired as I feel. I can see that she's wearing a heavy layer of caramel-colored powder to hide how deathly pale she's become. She might have tried to cover up the dark circles that shadow her eyes, but that doesn't work, either. Still, there's a spark in their depths that's undeniable, plus an honest grin splitting her chapped lips.

I don't know why, but she really is happy to see me.

"Riley, thank goodness. I can't believe I finally found you after all this time. Everybody's been so worried about you. Ever since you disappeared from Black Pine, I couldn't help but think that— oh. *Oh*." The winds shifts suddenly and I can tell what caused Carolina's soft *oh* by the way her nose wrinkles. "You, uh… where have you been? You kinda smell like you've been hiding out in a dirty bathroom or something."

The words pop out before I can hold them back. "Sewer, actually."

"*What*?"

Oops. "Forget it," I say, shaking my head. "What are you doing here? Shouldn't you be back at the asylum?"

It was a simple motion. Shaking my head, I mean. I don't think anything of it—until Carolina's hand flies to her mouth, her eyes suddenly wide as she stares at me.

She doesn't say a word. Not to answer me, not to point out that I'm still wearing my slippers, not to ask me more questions about where I've been. She just… *stares*.

I'm immediately self-conscious. Yeah, I know what I must look like. I guess once she got past my stink, she's finally noticing that I'm a walking disaster.

"You okay?"

"Your ears," she breathes out.

What's that supposed to mean? My ears? What's the matter with my ears?

I reach up, my glove probing gingerly along the lobe, then the rim. Feels fine. Nothing wrong, and if it feels more sensitive than usual, at least there's no pain. I continue exploring, moving my fingers along the top of my ear—

Whoa.

Hang on.

Gentle exploration turns into freak-out mode in a heartbeat.

"What's wrong with it?" I demand, tugging the top of my ear.

"They're, um..." Carolina gulps. "They're kinda pointy."

Ah, *hell* no.

I have to see. I have to know for sure.

There's a car parked in the next driveway over. Leaving Carolina gawking in the middle of the lawn, I race over to it, shoving my long hair over my shoulder so that I can get a perfect view of my ear as I duck down. I angle my head, getting a peek at my ear in the side view mirror.

That's not my damn ear.

Holy shit. Carolina wasn't kidding.

What the—

Last time I looked in a mirror—and who knows how long that's been?—the top of my ear was rounded. Just like hers. Just like a regular human's.

Now, though?

The top of my ear extends about a half-inch higher than it used to, with the absolute tip coming to a point.

I push away from the car door, hissing out an angry breath right before I straighten up. My hand reaches for my ear again, as if it's changed shape in the last few seconds. Nope. Same size. Same shape. No doubt about it, either.

I have fae ears.

Why the fuck do I have fae ears?

The panic is swift and terrible.

Unlike the other times I've had attacks, this doesn't have anything to do with a touch. It's worse, though. So much worse.

My chest hurts. I feel like I'm being squeezed, the whole world collapsing in on me as a girl I barely know watches me with horror on her face. I can't get enough air into my lungs. I choke as I gasp, my head spinning, my heart racing.

What happened to my ears? They look just like Nine's. Just like Rys's. They're fae ears.

But what are they doing attached to my head?

How did this happen to me?

I walk away from the car, as if by leaving the mirror behind me, I'm somehow making my ears normal again.

How?

I just… *how*?

It hits me like a brick to the back of my skull when I'm halfway back to where I left Carolina. I stagger, then suck in another breath that does little to help me calm down.

And I curse. "It was the fucking peach."

She hears me. Her head jerks in my direction, a strange expression crossing her face in a flash. "Peach? Did you just say peach? Riley, what did you do?"

The way her voice goes high-pitched like that, the worry in her tone… she sounds as scared and worried as I am—except I'm all that plus super freaking pissed.

Effects… I thought the way I all but threw myself at Nine was what he was talking about when he said there might be effects from the peach. I remember the feel of the point beneath the thin leather.

Effects? Yeah. That's an understatement.

Carolina is watching me closely. I can't tell if she's waiting for me to answer her, or she's just hoping for another glimpse of my new weirdo ears.

Okay. First things first. If I don't want her to ask any other questions—if I don't want her to wonder if I need a return trip to Black Pine—I need to get myself under control.

It's difficult. Really difficult. I keep remembering the way my ears looked in the mirror and it takes everything I have not to start to spiral again.

"It's nothing. I just… I ate a peach I shouldn't have, alright?" I stomp my foot against the pavement. It sends a jolt all the way up past my knee, my slipper doing nothing to cushion the blow. Panic gives way to absolute anger when I think of Rys's demon peach again. "I can't believe this shit. The stomachache was bad enough. Now I've got these weirdo ears? Oh, *come on*."

"They're fae ears," murmurs Carolina. "You… you have fae ears."

I immediately freeze.

Whoa.

It's one thing for me to think that. But Carolina… how the hell does she know that?

How does she know?

How does some random patient from Black Pine *know*?

CHAPTER 8

"Fae ears?" I repeat, right back on the edge of losing it again. I reach for the points of my ears, my stomach lurching when I feel how unnatural they are. I have this sudden urge to hide them. I shake my head again, knocking my hair over my shoulder, covering them up. And then I play dumb. "What's that supposed to mean? Fae? Why would you say that?"

"Because that's what they are."

She says that in such a way, it leaves me wondering how she can be so sure.

Then she goes on to ask, "Are you twenty-one?," and I'm too stunned to do anything but demand to know what that has to do with anything.

"It's important," she adds. "I know you were getting close to aging out of Black Pine. Almost twenty-one. Did you hit your birthday yet?"

I... I have no idea. My immediate reaction is to tell her no. I still had two weeks to go until my birthday when Nine pulled me out of the asylum. I lost a week somehow after my trip to Faerie. Who knows how much time I lost after Rys pulled his stunt with the knock-out powder and the peach?

"Depends. What's today's date?"

I don't know what's worse: the look of pity she gives me when it hits her that I'm serious, that I really don't have any clue what the date is—or the way my legs feel like they've been knocked out from beneath me when she tells me that we're halfway through October.

"No fucking way," I breath out. "It was just June."

"Um, it wasn't. Riley, June was four months ago." A look of understanding dawns in her dark eyes. "You've been to Faerie."

I'm too rattled by everything else she's said that she catches me off guard. Instead of denying it, like I'd normally do, all I can say is, "How did you know that? How did you know any of this?"

"Time works differently in Faerie. Depending on how you travel there and where you go, moments on the other side could pass like days or even longer here."

That answers one question. It always bothered me about how I lost that one week after taking a pit stop inside of the Fae Queen's garden. Nine told me once that time doesn't work the same and Carolina just confirmed it.

Again, I have to wonder: how does *she* know that?

As if she can read my mind, Carolina tells me.

"I've been to Faerie myself a few times. I always had to explain it as I was taking a trip out of town. I'm human, so losing time is the worst thing that happens to me. If you were on the other side when you came of age… well, it might have brought your fae side out then, too. It would, uh"—she gestures nervously to my pointy ears—"it would explain what happened to your ears."

I blink, my hands falling to my side as I pick up on what she's saying without actually saying it.

No way.

No freaking way.

It's… I can't process that statement. Impossible. It was bad enough when I found out that Nine was a Dark Fae. Now this chick I barely know from the psych ward where we met is saying that I'm fae, too.

Oh, hell no.

"Wait. Hold up. Are you telling me that you think I'm fae?"

"Not fully," she says quickly. "Half, at most. If you were a full-blood, I'd know. Over the last year, I've developed a keen eye when it comes to the fae. Not much help now, but I can tell the difference if I pay close enough attention. And you might not have seen me, but that just made it easy for me to watch you. You definitely are part-human."

My jaw drops.

Carolina frowns. "What's wrong?"

What's wrong? Did she really just ask me that?

"You know all about the fae." It's not a question. Not this time. Why would it be? She's made her knowledge of Faerie totally clear.

Even so, she nods.

Am I in bizarro world or something? Sorry. I thought I was in Acorn Falls—but this can't be happening.

"You know about the fae and you knew I was one of them? You were *watching* me? And you never said shit to me about any of this before?"

Did I raise my voice? Probably. My hands clench into fists at my side. Carolina's gaze darts toward them and she throws her own hands up in a placating gesture as she backs away.

"I… I might have guessed. The ears were a surprise because I wasn't... I didn't know for sure. That's okay. I'm just glad to see you again. Now that I know I'm right, it's even more important that I talk to you. Is there anywhere you'd like to go so that we can sit down and, um, maybe chat?"

"Are you serious?"

She takes a deep breath, then nods again. I'm visibly scaring her—and, considering my history, that's not a surprise—though she's just as noticeably standing her ground.

"You have no idea how serious I am," she tells me. "I've been looking for you for ages. I... I almost can't believe you're here. This is perfect."

"For you maybe. To me? This is fucking *nuts*."

"Riley, no—"

She doesn't get it. Right now, I'm not too sure I really am grasping what the hell's going on, but we're definitely not on the same page.

Let me fix that.

"Look, if I believe what you're saying, that means that, all this time, you were right down the hall. Someone who could assure me that I wasn't as crazy as they all thought I was. Someone who knew that the fae and Faerie actually exist. But you didn't. I never knew. I don't get it. In community group, when we had to talk about why we were there—"

"I couldn't tell anyone why I was committed," Carolina cut in. "They never would have let me out again if they knew the truth. Besides, except for you, I knew they wouldn't believe me."

"So why didn't you tell *me*?"

"I tried."

"Yeah, right."

"I did," she insists.

I huff. Before I try to fight back, I think about what she's saying. I haven't known Carolina all that long, and I did my best to ignore her like I did everyone else at the asylum, but she's kind of got a point. I remember the little things. The glances in the meds line, the tentative smiles. That time during group when she chose art therapy over music therapy because I did. The biscuit she offered me at dinner.

The note scrawled on the greasy napkin underneath it.

Okay. Fair enough. Maybe she actually did.

"You left me that note," I admit.

"The day you disappeared from Black Pine. I remember."

"You wanted me to come see you."

Carolina nods eagerly. A strand of long, dark hair falls into her face. She tucks it absently behind her—not even a little bit pointed—ear.

"You wanted me to come visit you. To talk to you then, too."

"I couldn't stay quiet any longer. You needed to know. Something happened the night they sedated you. Two techs were gone by the next morning. I don't know what happened to the woman, but I saw them escort the big, bald tech out past the window in my room. I've seen that look in his eyes before. He was touched."

"Touched?"

"Touched by the fae. Just like you are."

I don't want to believe that she's right. She is, though. Deep down, I know it. Duncan was acting so weird that night, and I sensed something wasn't right about Diana the first time she tried to touch my hand. The way her eyes flashed gold right before I flipped out and the nursing staff had to sedate me… all I could think about was the fae.

I finally left the sewer because I made a decision to put the fae behind me. Carolina's appearance in Acorn Falls was a surprise, the reveal that my ears have changed one hell of a shock. I don't want to think I have anything to do with the fae. I definitely can't handle being told that, all along, I've been right—it was everyone else around me who let me think that I was broken.

I'm out. I'm never going back. And, you know what?

I'm done.

She can tell that I've been touched. Did I need the reminder that I gave part of me to Nine only to have him throw it back in my face? Sure, he offered me his name instead, but that touch made me believe I wanted something he couldn't give me.

Nine is gone. Rys can't find me.

I'm tired. I'm hungry. And, for the first time in a while, I'm wishing this is all just some horrible hallucination.

Yeah.

I'm *done*.

Without another word, I turn away from Carolina. Barely ten minutes ago, I was standing in front of the back door of the Wilkes House, trying to find the balls to go inside. I couldn't. The déjà vu was too damn strong.

Now? Now I don't have any other choice.

At least I know the door's not locked.

I don't head straight to the back. Just in case, I've got to cover my ass. With the way my luck's been going lately, somebody will see the for sale sign out front and decide that they want to take a peek inside. Even if it's just for the night, I'm not taking any chances.

The metal pole holding up this side of the wide sign is cool to the touch. I can feel the chill through my thin gloves, a reminder that it really is October now. Forget losing one week before. Somehow I lost more than *four freaking months*.

Even worse? With every other bomb that Carolina has dropped on me, the idea that its October instead of June is barely a blip on my radar. My head's still spinning at the idea that I'm either turning into one of the fae—or that I've always been one. And then there's how Carolina seems to know even more about the Faerie races than I do...

With a grunt, I jerk the pole, lifting the left half of the for sale sign out of the packed dirt. I immediately reach for the second pole.

"Riley?" Carolina's soft voice floats after me. "What are you doing?"

Isn't it obvious?

I finish pulling the sign out, then carry it around the back. I tuck it behind a bush on the side, laying it flat against the dried mulch. Good chance someone's going to notice it's missing soon. That's fine. I know I can't stay here long but, for now, it's better than the sewer.

"Riley?"

Carolina has followed me. I notice that she keeps looking nervously behind her as if she's expecting someone to come out and scold us for hanging around the empty house.

Yeah, so she's definitely not from Acorn Falls. One thing I remember from my years at the Everetts is that the well-to-do community always had a very "mind your own business" policy. So long as you don't draw attention to yourself, the friendly neighbors are more than willing to leave you the hell alone.

How else could Madelaine and me sneak in and out of this very house all those times without getting caught once? If Rys hadn't tried to convince me to leave with him that terrible day six years ago, no one would have ever learned about the way my sister and I turned the empty basement into our home away from home.

I don't know what's going on. My memories of this house

are twisted with the trauma of the day Madelaine died. I remember the fire. There *was* a fire. My hands are proof of it.

But the house is still standing. Looking almost exactly as it had the morning before Rys set his blaze, the abandoned Wilkes House is here, it's empty, and it's open.

And there isn't a soul in either world—the human world or Faerie—who would believe that I'd willingly turn this house teeming with the horrors from my past into a sanctuary for my troubled present.

The way Carolina is watching me as I wipe the dirt from the palms of my gloves is another vote in the *Riley has finally snapped* column. She doesn't even know the truth behind this particular spot—she's only here because the Everetts' old house is down the street—and she obviously thinks I've lost it.

Maybe I have. Who knows? Sleeping inside the house where Madelaine died isn't what I really want to do, either.

But it's not the sewer. And, right about now, that's good enough for me.

I bound up the porch steps before I lose my nerve. The second my glove closes on the doorknob, I hear Carolina again.

"Riley?" Her voice wavers on my name. "You can't go in there."

That's where she's wrong.

Because yes.

Yes, I can.

Human Riley couldn't. The Riley who's just discovered that she has fae ears?

There isn't a damn thing that she can't do.

Without letting go of the doorknob, I turn toward Carolina.

"Look, I'm tired. I haven't eaten in a while and that was after I threw up my guts for the last two days. Now you want me to believe that after years—*years*—of hiding from the fae and their existence, I actually *am* one? All because my ears look like someone put them through the pencil sharpener? I just spent who knows how long in a dirty, smelly sewer. I'm going in this empty house, finding a corner to hide out in, and going to sleep. Maybe, in the morning, this will all be some really terrible dream or something, I don't know. It's worth a shot."

"There's so much more I need to talk to you about. Why don't you come home with me? My house isn't too far from here. Come with me, Riley."

Come with me.

The last time someone tried to get me to leave this house with them didn't work out so well for anyone involved. And if a fae couldn't glamour and compel me into giving up my independence, this chick will never be able to pull it off.

She figures that out as soon as I start to enter the house. It's dark in there, but it's also growing even darker outside. Hey, at least it should be a little warmer inside.

"Okay," Carolina calls after me. "That's okay. We can talk here. Would you be mad if I come in, too?"

"Can I stop you?"

"No. Not really."

That's what I figured. "Whatever. My abandoned nightmare house is your abandoned nightmare house."

You think that would've given her a second's pause. It doesn't. Before I'm even a few steps into the house, Carolina is moving quickly, slipping inside at my heels.

Was that a mistake? I hope not. Another of one of Nine's lessons—funny how they're all coming back to me now—was to be careful not to invite the wrong sort of creatures into your home.

But Carolina isn't fae. I might be struggling with what *I* am at the moment—she's still human. No denying that. So, after she closes the door behind us, I don't give the invitation another thought.

I think the dark bothers her. Not me. I actually feel a little more at peace once the door closes behind her and we're hidden among the shadows of a bare kitchen.

Carolina, on the other hand, searches the walls until she finds a light switch. She flicks it once, twice, then a third time. The *click-click-click* sounds like shots in the dark.

Because, yeah, it's still super dark in here.

"There's no electricity in here," Carolina announces needlessly.

I shrug, zeroing in on the sink. After whispering a fervent prayer under my breath, crossing my fingers against my thigh, I reach with my left hand and twist the tap. The metal twists, the pipes groan, and rusty-colored water spits out of the faucet. Within seconds, the water clears.

Yes!

I gesture at the sink so that Carolina can see. Then, before I can stick my head under the stream, I turn it off. That can wait until I'm alone again.

"Hey," I tell her, "it's got running water. That's way more than I've been used to lately. I'll take it."

"Right. You said something about the sewer before. Did you... you weren't serious about that, were you? Where have you been, Riley?"

"It doesn't matter. You said you wanted to talk. That's fine. But I think it's my turn to ask the questions now. Like this biggie: what are you doing here anyway? How did you even get out of the asylum?"

"You mean the Black Pine facility?"

I nod.

"There was no point in staying there after you left. I checked myself out."

I blink, surprised. "You could do that?"

"Sure. It was part of the deal I made when I checked myself in."

That's right. While most of the juveniles on our floor were put into the asylum when we were minors and we had no choice, there were a few exceptions. Carolina joined the nineteen-to-twenty-one age group last year so she's definitely older than eighteen. I guess she'd have some say when it came to how long she was inside.

I'd say *lucky*, but I know better.

"What about you? You weren't released when you disappeared. I know because the whole place went on high alert when the techs realized you were gone. How did you do it? I have to ask. Breaking out of the facility is supposed to be impossible."

Supposed to be. Just like I'm supposed to be human and Carolina is supposed to be just another patient who forgot about me once I was gone—

—like I forgot about Jason until me and Nine chanced up my former groupmate-turned-statue in the Fae Queen's garden.

I shake my head. I made a conscious decision to pretend that that never happened. I had to. Not only was the threat of the Fae Queen made real in that very moment, but Nine said that Jason—a human working for the fae inside of Black Pine—must have been plotting against me before he met his fate.

Now that Carolina is here, now that she's admitted to knowing something about the Faerie races, I keep getting flashes of Jason's dark face, his terrible expression, and the way he was positioned in the garden, his body language screaming in fear before he was frozen.

I have to kill this conversation.

"I had help, okay? So I left a couple of days early. Big deal. Besides, it's still my turn to ask the questions. Why did you check into the asylum in the first place if you left as soon as I did?"

"Help," she echoes, ignoring my last question entirely. She nibbles on her bottom lip, then asks softly, "Was it the fae?"

Crap. Did she really have to go there again?

"You keep bringing up the fae. I don't want to talk about them. Okay?"

"We both know that won't make them go away."

As much as I'd rather pretend otherwise, I do. I do know that.

To my continued surprise, so does she.

CHAPTER 9

I'm torn between wanting to make her tell me everything she knows about the fae and trying to sell the act that I have no idea what she's talking about. After six years in the asylum, I've gotten pretty good at convincing others that the fae aren't real.

Will it work with Carolina? I'm thinking no. I might have had a shot earlier, but once she saw my ears? Once she saw me freak out because, yeah, I definitely had no clue that that happened to me? Yeah. The time for hiding the truth is way behind us.

Doesn't mean that I need to tell her all the dirty, smelly details about what's happened to me since the fae came back into my life.

That's not all, either. Something warns me against giving her any information about me, Nine, or what I've been dealing with. Then there's my shade-walking. Shadow travel. Nine said it was a gift. I decide my weirdo talent should also be a secret.

You know what would be good right now? A distraction. Her

brow furrowed, her nose wrinkled, Carolina is watching me so closely, I feel like she can see everything I'm hiding. Letting her inside the house was a mistake. Choosing to enter it myself was probably pretty stupid, too.

Oh, well. Nothing I can do about that now. Except, maybe, kick her the hell out.

Right before I do, my stomach grumbles. Loudly. So loud, the snarling growl rumbles like thunder in the quiet of the empty room.

Hey. I wanted a distraction, didn't I?

"Sorry. It's been"—Jesus, *months*, right? Except for the bread Nine gave me, the last thing I ate was the beef stew and the biscuit Carolina used to cover up her note and that was back in June—"...a bit since I've had something to eat. You don't... you don't have like a snack or something on you? In your car? Your bag? I'll even take some tic-tacs at this point. Anything."

Oh, man. The second the words are out, I realize exactly who I'm talking to. Carolina tries to hide her reaction, I'll give her credit for doing whatever she could to cover it up, but I see her wince and I feel like a complete ass.

"If you don't," I say hurriedly, "that's fine, too. I was just asking. I guess I kinda forgot..."

I can't even finish my sentence, letting the words trail off right there. Eesh. How could I have forgotten why Carolina was at Black Pine in the first place? The fae might have been a big part of it—at least, that's what she made it seem like—but there's no faking her other condition.

"If you need food, I can take you to get some."

She still wants me to leave with her. That's... odd.

"Don't worry about it. I'll find something somewhere eventually."

"Let me do it. You don't have to come with me. Just open the door for me when I come back and I can bring you whatever you want."

Okay. That's it. I've always been paranoid, looking out for myself, always expecting that anyone helping me is doing it because they want something from me. It's a hard-earned lesson, thanks to years spent in the foster system—not to mention Nine's lessons throughout my childhood—and it's only gotten worse since I got committed to Black Pine.

I'd brushed off every mention of Carolina looking for me because I didn't want to know why she was. I just wanted her to go, especially once she started bringing up the fae.

This, though? This is really weird.

"Why?" I ask. "Why do you want to help me so bad? You don't even know me."

My eyes have adapted to the dark. I don't miss the pleading look that flashes across her face, or the way she folds her hands in front of her chest. "It's because you're my only hope."

"Me? Why would you say that?"

Carolina shudders out a breath. "Whether you want to tell me or not, I know you're being chased by the fae. You've been touched by them." She pauses for a heartbeat, sure that I'm not going to argue before she drops another bomb: "Me, too. I've been claimed by a Dark Fae who will only let me free if I find the Shadow. That's you, Riley. You can save me."

I just about stop breathing. The way she says that, so earnest, so sure... I swear, I can hear the way she capitalizes the 's' in Shadow. She isn't just pulling that name out of thin air.

She doesn't just know about the fae. She knows about *me*.

And, for some absolutely insane reason, she thinks that I can help her.

Play it cool, Riley. Don't give it away.
Deny everything.

"The what?"

"The Shadow. From the Shadow Prophecy. It's why I've been searching for you for so long, why I wanted to talk to you inside of the facility. If you were who I hoped you were, my mistress promised me freedom if you do your part."

"My part?" I parrot back. Nine told me that my part in the prophecy boils down to offing the terrible Fae Queen. Since that's never gonna happen, I continue to play dumb. "You sure you shouldn't check back into the asylum, Carolina? Because you're sure talking crazy right about now."

It's a low blow. I mean, we met in a psych hospital. Throwing around the c-word… that's fucked up. I know it is. But I also know that it'll be impossible for me to escape the burden of this stupid prophecy if I've got someone else putting the weight of it on my shoulders.

I just want the fae to leave me alone. Why doesn't anyone get that?

"You don't believe in the prophecy, do you?" Carolina's face falls. She shakes her head, wrapping her arms around her middle. "You don't believe you're the Shadow they're talking about. Either that, or you don't know."

She's not entirely wrong. I don't know all the details—because no one will tell me, and I've blocked a lot of what Nine did explain—and I definitely I don't *want* to believe that I have anything to do with the Shadow that both Nine and Rys keep bringing up. That's not important, though.

First the fae, then the prophecy.

How does she *know*?

I try to scoff, act like I think she's making it all up. At the same time, my fingers start to tremble inside my leather gloves.

"You're right. I don't know what the hell you're talking about. And, honestly? I don't really care. You can go now, alright? I told you I was tired. Unless you're gonna call the cops or, shit, the doctors on me, just leave me alone. I can't help you. I can't even help myself."

"But you can. Don't you understand? You're the Shadow, Riley. I wasn't sure, but the way the darkness is drawn to you—"

"What? Why would you say that?"

"Look." She points toward the floor.

I gasp. It's dark in the kitchen. I know that. Without electricity, the empty room seems darker than even outside. But, from my knees down, there's a patch of darkness willowing around my jeans, almost vanishing the bottom of my legs in the inky black smoke.

"What the *fuck*?" I kick out one of my legs, the wisps clinging to it dissipating like cotton candy hitting your tongue. It's like they melt away from my body. As soon as my slipper is back on the floor, another strand wraps immediately around my ankle. "What's happening? Who's doing that?"

"You are. I told you. You're the Shadow. You're the halfling—half-human, half-fae," she adds, raising her hand, gesturing to her ear. "You're the one they talk about in the prophecy."

"The prophecy," I snap. I'm hopping in place, trying to get rid of the shadows that are undeniably following every move I make. I don't like it and I can't get rid of it, and the way she just puts it out there—just calls me a halfling—makes my stomach sink as if I swallowed a bellyful of rocks. "I don't know anything about a damn prophecy."

At the anger in my voice, Carolina backs up. She doesn't go too far, though. "Would you... would you like to?"

I stop hopping. The shadows are, well, not forgotten, but suddenly not as important. "What are you saying now?"

"Okay. Hang on. I got something for you—for the Shadow.

I've been holding onto this for a while, hoping that I could show it to you. I almost memorized it, but I don't want to get it wrong. Are you... you gonna stay here?"

"You sat through community group with me. You knew about Acorn Falls. Black Pine is out," I add uselessly. "Where else do you think I can go?"

Carolina is kind enough not to point out that I'm right. Instead, she gestures for me to stay where I am before turning toward the door.

"Where are you going?"

"It's in my car. I'll be right back."

Car, huh? I guess that's just another difference between Carolina and me. I spent the last six years inside the asylum. Now that Nine admitted that it was as much as a "safe" place to stick me to keep me off the Fae Queen's radar as it was a psych hospital—sorry, facility for wayward juveniles—to convince me that the fae aren't a threat, I'm even more jealous of the experiences I missed.

Driving? Nope. I was fifteen when I got tossed inside. No learner's permit, even if I might have taken a joyride or two. A license? Forget it. It's why walking all over Acorn Falls almost seems natural to me. It's not like I could do anything else.

I don't have a phone. No ID. No money.

No food.

And Carolina has it all. The expensive clothes. The freedom to come and go from the asylum as she pleases. Now a car?

Damn it. I should hate her.

She knows more about the fae than I do, too. Now she knows that, thanks to my weird ears, I have something to do with them. And, for whatever reason, she's actually willing to help me understand what's going on. She actually seems desperate.

I should hate her.

I can't.

That's not hate that twists my gut when I look at her bony frame, her sunken-in cheeks, and the haunted look in her eyes. That's *pity*.

"Fine." I nod. "I'll be waiting."

Girl's fast. I don't know exactly where she left her car, but she's gone and back in a couple of minutes. She knocks on the back door, obviously expecting that I might have locked it behind her, then slinks back in slightly out of breath.

A hesitant yet almost triumphant grin stretches her lips as she holds out a folded piece of paper.

"Here you go. The Shadow Prophecy."

My pulse picks up at those three words. Can't help it. It seems to happen every time I hear them.

Shadow Prophecy.

Freak out.

Shadow Prophecy.

Panic.

I try to shove it aside, focusing on what's in Carolina's outstretched hand. I glance at the paper, but I don't take it. Instead, I jerk my chin over at it. "What's that?"

"You said you don't know what it is. Here. It's not much, but it's something." As if she's just remembered that I don't like getting too close to others, she sets the folded piece of paper onto the counter. "It's handwritten. You might need to use the moonlight to read what it says."

"My eyes are good in the dark," I mumble, already reaching for the paper. I need to know what it says.

I recognize the handwriting. It's the same as the scribble on the greasy napkin Carolina slipped to me that last dinner at Black Pine. It must be hers.

The kitchen is gloomy, the only light streaming in from the

window overhanging the sink. I don't need it, though. Like I told Carolina, my eyes have adjusted to the darkness and it only takes a small amount of squinting to read what's scrawled on the page:

> *...with the Iron she's destined to stay*
> *more than an adviser,*
> *a confidante, a friend*
> *when Dark meets Shadow*
> *the Reign of the Damned*
> *shall end...*

Even though it's only a couple of lines, I read them again and again, trying to make sense of them, then turn the paper around to see if I'm missing anything. "Is this all?"

"It's all I have," Carolina answers. "There's supposed to be more to the prophecy, but you don't want to know what I went through just to get this part. Since I was supposed to find out if you were the Shadow, my mistress gave me just enough to know what was at stake." Her brown eyes light up. "She wants to see you end the Fae Queen's reign. If you do, I'm free."

The Reign of the Damned. That's what Nine said they called Melisandre's reign—right before he added that part about the queen cutting out the tongues of the poor creatures who called it that.

I gulp. The action is reflexive.

So is my lie.

"I don't know what any of this means."

"You don't?"

"Nope." I hold the note back out to her. "Sorry."

She's looking at me as if she's hung all of her hope on me. I'm thrown back to my last night at Black Pine. When Carolina nervously approached me at the empty dinner table, offering up her biscuit while wearing an expression eerily like the one crossing her too-thin face right now.

She presses her lips together, shuddering on an inhale through her nose, then a rough exhale. For a second, I have this sinking suspicion that she's gonna start sobbing—like I saw her do a couple of times inside the asylum—before she turns so that the paper is facing me again.

She points to the top line. "This part? Iron? That means here. The human world. Iron is harmful to fae and you won't find barely any in Faerie. Then this." Her finger moves down the page. "The adviser and confidante part? It's talking about the Dark Fae who's supposed to partner with the Shadow and help her face the Fae Queen."

You know what? I remember Rys saying something like that to me when we were in the sewer. That the prophecy mentioned a Dark Fae who was supposed to help me end the Fae Queen's reign somehow. He seemed to think it meant Nine and, not gonna lie, I'm kind of thinking the same thing, too.

I'm still stuck on the whole *end the Reign of the Damned* line, though. Nine's convinced that means I'm supposed to freaking *kill* the Fae Queen. Me. Riley Thorne, who can't even get close to another person without wanting to scream out a warning.

"Is any of this making it clearer for you?"

Yes, actually. But Carolina doesn't need to know that.

"Not really."

"It will. It has to." After carefully folding the note again, she slips it into her jeans pocket. "Besides, it doesn't matter now. It's not important. We're both in the human world together. The Fae Queen never leaves Faerie so, as long as we stay on this side, we can figure this out. The only thing is that the Shadow... that *you* have to defeat Melisandre. And I'll do whatever you want me to do to help."

Wait a second. Hold on. Who said anything about me signing up to kill the Fae Queen? I can barely fight off a Light Fae who's going easy on me because he's sure we're supposed to be bonded or something like that. How am I supposed to be able to defeat their *queen*?

I don't care what the prophecy says. Not gonna happen.

"What if I don't want your help?" I shoot back. "Who says I even want to see the Fae Queen? I definitely don't want to kill her. Let her stay queen. She's not hurting me."

"Now."

"What?"

"She's not hurting you now," Carolina whispers. "And that's only because a human girl is beneath her notice unless she decides to play with you. And, trust me, you won't like her games. But you're not a human anymore, are you?"

My hand lifts up to my new fae ear, the leather smoothing down the pointed tip.

Shit.

I've been hoping that, if I forgot about them, they might've gotten better.

Nope.

"Carolina—"

"Please." Her voice drops even lower. I can barely hear the single word as she looks up at me, meeting my gaze straight-on. Tears well in her big, dark eyes, shining in the moonlight. "As long as Melisandre is queen, I'm trapped. Maybe not inside of Black Pine, but I'm still trapped. You're my only hope."

Ah, hell. I feel like I've kicked a defenseless puppy.

I know what's it like to be trapped, too. In my foster homes, the kids' homes, the asylum… this is the first time in my life that

I'm on my own, and even now I'm still looking over my shoulder, running from the fae—and my past.

Maybe coming back to this house—actually sneaking inside like I used to do when I was a kid—is messing me up more than I thought it would. Normally, I wouldn't even bat my eyes at that puppy dog awful look she's giving me.

Now, though?

Part of me wants to throw open the door and tell her to go. The other part? It wonders if maybe I've been looking at this all wrong. You can only run for so long before someone eventually catches up. But if being the Shadow and accepting that the stupid Shadow Prophecy is something bigger than I am means that I can maybe do something to free Carolina, who knows? Maybe I can free myself at the same time.

I failed Madelaine. Carolina thinks that I can help her.

Sure, I can't even help myself half the time, but I might as well try.

"Okay. Fine. Whatever. I'm not about to start planning how to kill the Fae Queen or nothing, but if you think I can do something to help you with your fae problem, I'll try. No promises—"

Carolina starts toward me. I go stiff and, sensing my discomfort, she holds up her hands. "I won't hug you, Riley. I really, really want to, but you'd hate it, and I'm not about to push my luck."

"Thanks." I let out a huge sigh of relief. "Appreciate it."

CHAPTER 10

All I want to do is go to sleep. After promising her that we could talk more in the morning, I realize that she's too hyped up to want to leave me alone just yet. Too bad. I either need food or sleep, and since Carolina is, well, Carolina, sleep is my only option.

When she immediately tries to convince me that I need to leave the empty house, trade it for someplace safer, I start to regret being such a soft touch.

I mean, her arguments make total sense. Not gonna deny that. I'm technically squatting, and what'll happen if the realtor comes by or a neighbor notices that the for sale sign is gone? Since I'm still hiding the fact that, no matter how long it's been, I'm a fugitive from the asylum, I'm really pushing my luck, hoping that the cops don't find me hiding out here.

She offers to take me anywhere I want to go. She's got the car, right? I could get out of Acorn Falls—but I don't want to. Not yet. Not while my biggest threat can follow me anywhere and won't rest until I'm back in Faerie.

Like I said, no one will ever think to look for me here.

Eventually, she backs down. Either that, or she finally gets that she's not going to get me to change my mind. I'm stubborn like that. And Carolina? She wasn't kidding when she said she wants to help me, even appearing to be unwilling to push me to the point where I tell her to go away and leave me alone. Dropping the subject for the second, she instead offers to go back to the sewer and get the gifts I purposely left behind when I ran.

I sure as hell don't want them, but she points out that, in an empty house with no electricity, a magic-fueled lantern full of Faerie fire will come in handy. The blanket, too. And, with a knowing look in her dark eyes, she repeats the very same warning Rys gave me the last time I saw him.

It's a mistake to turn down a gift from a fae. You never know who you're offending—or how they will repay the "slight".

We sneak out after it gets dark. Carolina kept her expensive-looking, shiny car parked a few streets away from the Everetts' place. My jaw drops when she points out which one is hers, and it hangs open for the whole ten-minute drive across Acorn Falls, heading back into the heart of the small town toward the alley I'd been hiding out in.

The girl drives like the devil himself is behind her. The devil, or maybe one of the fae.

It's a possibility. I can't help but stare in the rearview mirror, expecting to see someone on our ass. Add that fear to my tendency to get car sick and, by the time I'm shuffling toward the familiar manhole cover from this morning, my stomach is so queasy that I'm glad Carolina didn't have any food on her.

I refuse to let her climb down into the sewer. Her clothes are too nice and, well, I don't really want her to see where I was hiding out for so long. I won't say I'm embarrassed or ashamed, because I'm not, but Carolina has her own demons. She doesn't need to share mine any more than she already is.

Plus, I'm not sure what I would do if Nine decided to pop his head in right about now.

The climb into the sewer is a lot easier after Carolina offers to swap her sneakers for my slippers. She engages the flashlight on her fancy phone, giving me a little light to work with as I climb down the rusted, pitted rungs again.

Oof. It stinks worse than I remember.

The lantern is right where I left it. The fire hasn't died one bit since he conjured it, the flames dancing willfully against the confines of the lantern. I hate it. After opening the wound of Madelaine's murder by returning to the old house, seeing the magic fire is like pouring salt right in there and rubbing it for good measure.

I grab the stupid thing, my fingers aching with the memory of what it felt to burn. Gritting my teeth, I do a quick sweep. No blanket, I notice. The silk scarf Nine gave me is gone, too.

On a second sweep, I see the remains of the demon peach that nearly poisoned me. When I notice there's a shadowy lump next to it, I move the lantern closer, strangling my scream when I recognize what the lump is: a dead rat.

How much do I want to bet that it's the same rat I threw my scarf at this morning—or that the peach worked way faster on its little furry body than it did on me?

That's it. Time to go.

Once I've climbed up the ladder again, I hand the lantern off to Carolina. She doesn't seem bothered by it. I don't realize how close I am to buckling under another panic attack until she's holding onto the lantern and I can get away from the destructive fire.

She tucks it securely in the back seat of her car, far from me in the front, and we're off again.

The trip back takes nearly three times longer than the one out. At first, I suspect that Carolina is driving out of Acorn Falls because she's decided to, I don't know, kidnap me or something ridiculously as crazy. I'm wondering just how much it's gonna hurt if I throw open the door and jump out of the car while it's moving when I figure out what she's doing.

Acorn Falls is a small town with small businesses. While Black Pine is only a town or two away on one side, the northern border of Acorn Falls touches the edge of an urban city. It's late, well past midnight, but Carolina finds me a fast food restaurant. We hit the drive-thru, my mouth watering before she even pulls up to the speaker.

"It's on me," she says. "Get whatever you want."

I'm not about to say no. And I don't. I order close to twenty dollars worth of food—Carolina hands over a credit card without a word—and I have just enough restraint to stop at one burger so that my stomach stops rumbling. I'll eat the rest once we get back.

When we pull up in front of the house, Carolina insists on parking a couple of spots away before walking me inside. During the drive, while I was shoving that burger in my face, she mentioned she lives in a suburb not too far from Black Pine and, because she was so close, she took the ride into Acorn Falls once a week in the hopes that she might run into me.

Because she thinks I can help her.

Can't forget that part.

Whatever. I grab the bags of food and my drink, leaving Carolina to grab the lantern from the back seat. She tries to shield it with her slender body, bowing over the flame. It's so freaking bright, you could probably see it from down the block.

I just hope no one's looking.

Once we've snuck through the back again, I plop my butt on the floor and start to tear into the bags. The first burger was only a snack. I'll probably regret it in the morning, but I'm *starving*. I can't wait another minute to eat the rest of this food.

Carolina places the lantern on the kitchen counter. Good spot. It's behind me, so I don't have to see it, and it's far enough away that I'm not so put off by it being in the room with us. Plus, the height gives it strength, splashing light over the floor where I'm sitting.

Careful to keep some distance between us, Carolina joins me on the floor. She's not looking at me, though. Her eyes are narrowed on the food I've set out on napkins in front of me.

She's frowning at it, but there's no denying how wistful she looks.

In the car, at the drive-thru, I asked Carolina if she wanted anything. I didn't think she would, and I wasn't surprised when she shook her head and didn't order a damn thing for herself.

Now I feel like an ass. I gesture at the food.

"You want some? I've got more than enough. We can share."

She shakes her head. "No, thanks."

"I don't want to push you to do something you don't want to. I mean that. And I get it. You've got this thing about food. I'm not gonna judge. But it's here if you want it."

I grab one of the wrapped burgers and slide it closer to her.

Her eyes watch it as the plastic wrapper crinkles against the wood floor. I can see the way her hand twitches, almost like she's itching to reach for it.

And then she sighs and turns so that it's not tempting her. "Can I ask you a question?"

"Sure."

"I know why you were at the facility. I'm local. Even before I first heard of the fae, I remember the story of the Everett girls and the fire."

I stiffen. Of all the things I'd thought she might say, that's probably at the bottom of the list. "My name is Thorne," I say, correcting her. Can't help it, either. "Only Madelaine was an Everett. She was adopted. Not me. I was just a foster."

"Right. Sorry. Anyway, I knew you ended up at Black Pine. When my mistress told me that I could find the Shadow inside the same place, I wondered if there was more to the fire than was on the five o'clock news."

It's bad enough that I'm back in this house. Six years later, without a single sign that this place nearly burned down to the ground, I'm here again, hiding out again. So dinner put me in a much better mood. That doesn't mean I want to sit here and be reminded of what happened to me the last time I snuck inside the Wilkes House.

I pop a fry into my mouth. Chew. "Is there a question in there somewhere?"

"Kind of," admits Carolina. "I know why you were in Black Pine. Why did you think I was there?"

Good thing I had already swallowed. If not, I might have choked.

She's... she's kidding, right?

"I don't know. I mean, I know what you talked about in group. It's 'cause you... your..." I can't bring myself to say the word out loud. Thinking back on it, Carolina never did, either. Instead, I wave at her skeletal frame. "You know."

Her expression turns sad. She looks down at her hands in her lap. They're more bone than flesh. "Yeah. I do. Good excuse, huh? What I talked about in group... it's how I got my parents to agree to a voluntary check-in. They wanted to help me. But it's not what you think... it's not what any of them think."

Call it a premonition or something, but a horrible feeling starts to prickle my stomach. Almost like fear mixed with a terrible sense of déjà vu. Uh oh. "Then what is it?"

"It's not that I don't eat because I don't want to. I can't, Riley. I... I physically can't. That fry would turn to ash the second it hit my tongue."

"You didn't." Tell me she didn't. "You didn't eat food from Faerie."

She nods miserably, careful not to meet my horrified face. "Last year. I didn't know better, and my mistress told me it was a treat. She offered me an apple—"

"That's okay," I cut in. "I had a peach, but then Nine came and he fixed me. I'm not cursed anymore. He can fix you, too. I'll call him for you."

"No!"

"What? Why not? He can help."

"My mistress offered me an apple," Carolina repeats, "but then it was a pear, some grapes... a peach. It didn't matter how sick I got, I couldn't stop. No one told me what would happen if I didn't. Now it's too late. Unless my mistress feeds me from her hand, I can't eat. No one can help me, especially not another fae."

"But—"

"I didn't tell you that because I want you to feel sorry for me. Honest. I've almost gotten used to the hunger and she's fair enough that, so long as I do what she says, she doesn't let me starve. You, though... I'm kinda worried about you. A fae fixed you, right? How? How did he do that?"

I don't want to admit what I let Nine do to me. "He just did. He felt bad for me. He was being kind. That's all."

Carolina shifts. She goes from sitting on her ass to rising up on her knees, almost hovering. "No. Oh, no, no, no... you have to listen to me, Riley. The fae who fixed you... however he did it, whatever ulterior motives he had, he wasn't doing it to be kind. The fae don't know how to be kind."

"Nine's different," I argue. "He's not like the Light Fae I know, the one who killed my sister—"

"Light or Dark, they're all terrible. If you let your Dark Fae get too close, even if he's the one in the prophecy, he'll take everything you have and leave you for dead." She sounds so certain. So bitter. "Like my mistress. She uses faerie food to get me to do what she wants. I behave, I get to eat. If I don't, she punishes me with hunger. I'll do anything to break free from her control before..."

Carolina doesn't finish her sentence. She doesn't have to.

...before she gets left for dead.

That's it. I've lost the last of my appetite. Shoving the pile of half-eaten fast food away from me, I say, "That's why you want me to be the Shadow so bad."

"It's part of the bargain. I help you end Melisandre, I don't have to rely on the mercy of my mistress to eat." Her lips thin, her cheeks even more noticeably sunken in than before. "I won't beg like a dog looking for scraps. I *won't*."

Rys is a Light Fae. A Blessed One. The first time we met, he killed my sister because he thought she was a nothing human who was an obstacle to get to me.

Carolina said the fae female who touched her was a Dark Fae like Nine. A Cursed One. If tricking the human girl into eating faerie food to turn her into her trained pet was considered a treat, I'd hate to find out what she did when Carolina pissed her off.

Or what she would do if she ever discovered that Carolina was plotting against her.

"The fae are big on their bargains, aren't they?" I muse, more to myself than to Carolina.

"That's something else I learned too late. They're tied to their contracts, but don't ever forget that it's about following the letter of the law, not the spirit. If they can cheat you, they absolutely will, and they'll do it as they're forced to only tell the truth."

Carolina picks up the wrapped burger that's still sitting untouched between the two of us. She squeezes it, then rears her hand back and lets it fly. The burger hits the wall on the far side of the kitchen with a wet slap, then lands in a pile of mangled patty, scattered lettuce, and splattered ketchup that, in the dancing light of Rys's lantern, looks way too much like blood.

"You can't ever trust them," she says in a voice so soft that you'd never guess she just chucked a burger across the kitchen. "You can't trust *anyone*."

Whoa. And I thought *I* had trust issues.

Carolina hates the fae for her own reasons. I respect that.

Don't blame her, either. And, sure, she definitely wants to use me so that she can break free of the Dark Fae who controls her.

I'm surprisingly okay with that.

Way I see it, it would've been worse if she tried to sell me that she wanted to "help" me because she felt bad for me. Knowing she has her own motives—hearing her put them out there like that—actually makes me trust her more.

We both want to escape the fae. Carolina wants to be free of her tie to the Dark Fae female who controls her food. Me? If I keep my head down, keep myself hidden from the Fae Queen, I'm good.

I decide to keep that to myself. I'm not a moron. Carolina's offer of help is very much conditional. She believes wholeheartedly that the Shadow will give her her freedom. And, since she also believes that I'm the Shadow, she's going all in on me.

If I tell her that I have no intention of going to Faerie or meeting the Fae Queen—let alone *killing* her—I know that Carolina's generosity will shrivel up. For now, I'm gonna take what I can get for as long as I can.

Whether I'm way tired or just relieved to finally have someone on my side, I let down my guard enough to invite Carolina to stay that first night. She can't, though. As late as it is, she has to drive home so that her parents can make sure that she's okay. Since I haven't had an adult care about me since the Everetts when I was fifteen, I don't really get it, but she insists.

Then she promises that she'll come back in the morning if she can get away.

Honestly, I don't hold my breath. As soon as Carolina leaves and I lock the back door behind her, I try to find a soft patch of floor in the depths of the dark shadows inside the empty living room.

It doesn't seem right to go upstairs. For a few seconds, I wonder if I should hide in the basement—but I can't even bring myself to step onto the landing.

Living room it is.

No dreams. With a full belly and eyes that just can't seem to stay open any longer, I fall asleep easily—and I don't dream.

Thank freaking God.

Halfway through the night, I start to shiver. The temperature dips at night during October, especially in Acorn Falls, and no electricity means no heat. I pull the sleeves of my hoodie off of my arms, tucking them against my middle, trying desperately to warm myself up. It must work because I fall asleep in a curled-up fetal position, too tired to even care about the chill.

I'm up with the sun. The way it angles in through the bare window, the bright rays seem to slap me awake. I squint and groan and pull myself up so that I'm sitting instead of lying sprawled out on the hardwood floor.

Something whispers as I shift. Glancing down, I see the same black, silky blanket pooling around my waist, rustling beneath my filthy jeans as I move to get a better look at it. I blink, peering down at it, not quite sure what I'm looking at.

In the morning light, it seems to glimmer. Sparkle. Shine. A dark, rich cocoa color that ebbs and flows through the pitch-black material. It's so much prettier in the daylight. And, just like when I was in the sewer, it did an amazing job keeping me comfortable and warm.

One question, though: how did it get *here*?

I left the blanket in the sewer. I had no choice. When I went back for it, it was missing. Nine's scarf, too.

Did it... did it follow me here?

Or was it another gift?

Nine? No. He wouldn't have. I'd sooner believe it was a blanket fairy or something ridiculous like that than think Nine left it after the way we left things between us.

I don't know where it came from. Can't explain it, either. And, honestly, having a weirdo blanket following me around like a puppy dog is the least of my worries right now.

It's so strange, too, and not only the material it's made of. It's so warm when I have it on, but it doesn't seem to weigh anything at all. Seriously. When I pick it up, folding it loosely so that I can stick it in the corner before I trip on it, it feels like air.

It's so, so weird.

Once I toss it in the corner of the empty living room, I lift my hands to my head, running my gloves through the tangled snarls that used to be my long, white-blonde hair. It's all one big knot now, no thanks to another hard night sleeping on the hard floor, and I try to finger-comb some of the more mild tangles out.

Of course, that stops the first time my fingertip accidentally brushes against the sensitive tip of my newly pointed ear.

My stomach sinks.

How the hell could I have forgotten about that?

Easy. After being told my entire life that the fae are dangerous, mythical creatures, it's a shock to even *think* I could be one.

So I choose not to.

Denial's worked for me so far. Might as well keep it up.

Hey, right now, it's the only plan I've got.

CHAPTER 11

My hands fall to my side, settling against my thighs. Even through the leather gloves, I can feel how stiff my jeans are. They're so covered in dirt and grime and who knows what else, I wouldn't be surprised if they stood up on their own when I finally took them off again.

Thinking of that makes me realize that I've got to pee. I know there's a bathroom on this floor—I used it last night after Carolina left—and I'm hoping there's at least one other with a shower or a tub in it. With the daylight streaming in through the windows, this is the perfect time to check out the upstairs.

Before I can head to the stairs, though, I hear a tentative knocking coming from the back of the house. My heart stops beating for a second, I'm so suddenly convinced that I've been found out, before I realize that only one person would be tapping so politely, yet insistently, on the kitchen door.

When I unlock the door and yank it open, I'm right.

It's Carolina. She's come back, just like she said she might—and she didn't come empty-handed, either.

"Holy crap," I breathe out. "What's all that?"

"I don't know how long you'll want to stay here," she answers, stepping carefully into the house so that she doesn't overbalance and fall over. Between the bundle made up of a comforter and a pillow nestled in her arms, the overstuffed backpack strapped on her back, and a huge plastic shopping bag hanging in the crook of her elbow, it's a possibility. "I wanted to be prepared. Where should I put this?"

"Um. The living area, I guess. That's where I slept last night. It didn't feel right going in the basement."

I don't explain. I don't have to.

She doesn't pry. As soon as I add that part, Carolina stays silent, carrying her load into the living room.

At least, she stays silent until she notices the billowy blanket that I haphazardly tossed into the corner and promptly forgot about.

She gasps. Her reaction isn't as bad as when she saw my new fae ears last night. It's close, though, as she marvels and stares. And then she grins.

"Shadows," she says softly. There's triumph in the way she almost murmurs it. "See. I knew I was right."

Huh?

"You talking about that?" I jerk my thumb over at it. "It's just a blanket."

"Sure it is. Now. With the way you can manipulate the shadows, they can be whatever you want them to be. That's so cool."

I blink. "Are you telling me that my blanket is made of shadows?"

"Well, yeah." Carolina frowns. "Wait... didn't you weave the shadows into a blanket on purpose?"

I would've had to know that it was possible in the first place to do it on purpose.

Whoa.

Is it?

I mean, this isn't the first time I found myself wrapped in a patch of darkness lately. It's not even the first time I woke up with a black blanket that I couldn't explain. The scarf might have been a gift from Nine, but he never claimed the blanket I slept with in the sewer.

Is it really possible? Did I do that?

I just... I don't get it. When I woke up this morning, the blanket was thin, silk-like, but it's definitely solid. Sturdy. As light as it was, I couldn't rip it. The shadow—if that's even what it was—that wrapped around my legs last night reminded me of thick smoke that disappeared as soon as I kicked it away.

I glance over at Carolina. The look on her face is so disappointed, I don't have the heart to tell her that I honestly found it easier to believe that there's a blanket fairy dropping off blankets than that I've whipped one up out of the shadows myself.

So I lie. Again. "Oh, uh. Yeah. I totally did. I was just teasing."

Her frown wavers for a beat, then turns into a hesitant grin. She sets the bundle in her hand down, lets the plastic bag hanging off her wrist land on the floor with a muffled thump, then shimmies the backpack off of her back. "You look better. Did you sleep well?"

"Didn't dream, so that's something."

"Any... any visitors?"

"Nope."

I'm kind of annoyed about that, too. Nine assured me that he erased Rys's brand so that he wouldn't be able to track me down anymore. But Nine... I'd be lying if I said that I didn't hope he'd at least pop in after the sun went down to check on me.

He didn't. I would've known. He didn't, and I don't want to think about how disappointed that makes me.

So I don't.

Instead, I jerk my chin over at Carolina. She might think that I look better after a night's rest. I wish I could say the same for her. The circles under her eyes are puffy, a dark purple, almost like a pair of black eyes. Did she get any sleep?

I'm not so sure.

"How about you?" I ask. "Sleep okay?"

"I was too busy to sleep," she tells me, stifling a yawn behind her bony hand. "I've brought you some things. In case you needed it, I grabbed you a pillow and a blanket," she adds, pointing at the bundle by her feet, "and I thought you might like a change of clothes. I figure we're about the same size—"

I'm not really a big girl, but I'm definitely bigger than Carolina. "Uh..."

She winces as she bends low, snagging the backpack by the top handle. "Before I got hooked on faerie food, I mean. These are all from last year. It should fit you."

I'll make it work. Anything to get out of the clothes I've been wearing for way, way too long. "Thanks. I... I don't know what to say."

"You don't have to say anything, Riley. I told you I'm going to help you. This is helping. Here."

Setting the backpack between us, Carolina unzips the top and starts pulling stuff out of it. A toothbrush and toothpaste kit. A hairbrush. Deodorant. A bar of soap. Body spray. I try not to take it too personally—I know I smell ripe, and I'm dying for any kind of bath. At first chance, I'm checking to see if there's a shower. If not, I'll bathe in the sink if I have to.

She's brought me three shirts. A pair of jeans and—my feet want to rejoice—some plain white sneakers. And, tucked at the bottom of the backpack, a box of granola bars and two bottles of water.

Then, after it's empty, she picks up the plastic shopping bag. It's pretty full.

"There's underwear in here. It's new. I stopped on the way back and got you fresh panties and socks. I didn't know what kind of bra to get, so I got a sports bra. I hope that's okay."

It's more than okay. It's so freaking thoughtful, I don't know what to say. So, to keep from saying anything at all, I reach out and grab the box of bars. Tearing open the top, I grab one at random, rip the wrapper off, then start chewing.

Oops. Can't blubber like an idiot if my mouth is full of a granola bar. Sorry, Carolina.

While her hunger is obvious from the way she watches me chow down, she doesn't say a damn word about it. She just smiles.

And I know that I'm stuck with her until the prophecy comes true—or I can find somewhere else to hide out at.

Over the next couple of days, I begin to think that neither one of those things is coming true any time soon.

Every night, Carolina leaves as soon as it gets dark, returning early the next morning with her backpack filled with more things that she thinks I can use. By the third morning, I've got enough food to last me a couple of weeks, and five changes of clothes. Because she could tell it was bothering me, she took my old clothes with her that second night, washing my hoodie, my slippers, and my jeans.

They feel so much better on my skin once they're clean.

And even though the water is cold and stinks like rotten eggs as it spits out of the shower head, it's fucking *heaven* to wash up in the upstairs bathroom. Carolina carries Rys's lantern in there so that there's light for whenever we have to do our business.

I leave it there. Out of sight, out of mind.

Kind of like Rys, too.

You know what's even better? The freedom to do whatever the hell I want, *when* I want. I've never been able to do that. When I was at Black Pine, everything was routine. Sessions with the psychologists, community group, meetings with my social workers, therapy... every bit of my stay in the asylum was regulated, from light's out to the food.

Especially the food.

We got three square meals, sure, but, with a few exceptions, it was always hospital food. You don't like it—you just get used to it. What makes my stay at the Wilkes House with Carolina's daily visits so great is that, though she brings me things like apples and cheese, she also sneaks in a snack or two.

Like chips.

Jeez, I missed chips.

I pick up the crinkly bag, my mouth drooling at the promise of crunchy, salty goodness inside. "Is this for me?"

Stupid question. Who else would it be for?

Carolina nods. "I thought you might like them."

I actually do. I don't know if it was luck or what, but this brand is one of my favorites. I used to pig out on these chips all the time when I lived with the Everetts.

"I'll save these for later. Thanks."

"You don't have to do that. It's okay. Go on. Have a couple."

Right. Let me just stuff my face with chips while Carolina watches.

I set the bag aside. "I'm fine."

That girl is stubborn. Before I can even move them out of her reach, Carolina purses her lips, grabs the bag, and pops the chips open. Then she puts the bag on the floor again and nudges them toward me, careful not to get too close.

"Just because I made a mistake, it doesn't mean you have to go hungry. Please."

What's worse? Turning away her gift because it makes me uncomfortable or stuffing my face in front of her knowing that it's impossible for Carolina to snack on a chip? In the end, I eat a couple to make her feel better, then I do the same thing I've done since that second morning.

I talk. And I talk. And, hell, I don't shut up at all.

I know. It surprises me, too.

It's been three days since I've been hiding out in the Wilkes House. I've done most of the talking, which is tough since Carolina doesn't really want to hear about my past experiences with the fae—she just wants to focus on how I'm going to fulfill my role in the prophecy.

I can't help it, though. Being back in Acorn Falls, squatting in this house... it's like I'm dealing with Madelaine's death and my first real brush with the fae all over again. I spent six years talking to my doctors, stubbornly refusing to discuss the mother who abandoned me and the sister I saw die.

There's something about Carolina. She doesn't talk much at all, and she gets it. Really gets it. It's such a relief to be able to tell someone about the shit I've seen and actually have them *believe* it.

But I also want to know more about my new... I don't know... partner in crime, I guess. I want to know Carolina's story. About the Dark Fae who tricked her into eating faerie food and how she found out that the fae were real in the first place.

She, uh, doesn't want to share any of that with me.

I quickly pick up on her reluctance. I can't tell why exactly, but every time I try to change the conversation around to her instead of me, Carolina becomes wary and kind of apprehensive. She tends to fiddle with her fingers in her lap, staring down at the floor, gulping nervously as if the words burn. She rubs her throat a lot, the haunted look in her dark eyes even more noticeable on the rare occasions that she lifts her gaze to watch me looking at her curiously.

We spend a lot of our time together rehashing the few lines of the Shadow Prophecy scrawled on the piece of paper that Carolina keeps in her pocket. We talk about Black Pine, too, and some of the doctors and patients that we both knew. I almost want to ask her about Jason, especially since Carolina told me how she's got this strange sense of knowing when someone has been touched by the fae, but I wimp out before I do.

Bringing up the Fae Queen? That's okay. Carolina wants to know what my plan is, how I'm going to use my newfound Shadow powers to take on Melisandre. It's a good thing that I've regained my ability to lie because, yeah, none of that's gonna happen.

I wait for her to ask me about Nine or, hell, even Rys. She doesn't. Just like how she can't bring herself to discuss her mistress—the Dark Fae who tricked Carolina into doing her bidding—she doesn't want to know anything about the two fae males that I'm hiding out from.

Instead, at my urging—okay, my *nagging*—Carolina eventually tells me how she drew the attention of her mistress. Last year, when she was on the edge of turning twenty, she started to notice that some people she ran into had a weird hazy glow around them. If she looked closer, she explained, it was almost like she could see a whole other person.

Glamour. Carolina can see through glamour.

Not all that well, though. Like any skill, she's gotten better over time. She might not have recognized that the pretty woman who offered her an apple was a Dark Fae back then, but she admits that it only took a couple of days before she suspected that the blonde tech, Diana, was wearing a glamour.

So she was from Faerie. I freaking *knew* it.

Some of the other stuff Carolina tells me is stuff that I already know. The fae's inability to lie is one, how they rely on glamour and charms and compulsions is another. Plus just how much power the fae can steal with a single touch once permission is granted.

Which, you know, is usually a given when a gorgeous fae chooses to charm a human. According to Carolina, it's close to impossible to refuse a fae once they've set their mind on you.

That makes me think of Rys. Of how Madelaine couldn't, and how I might not have been able to if it wasn't for Nine's lessons. Of course, then I think of Nine, and how even now there isn't much I wouldn't do for him.

So, yeah, she's got a point.

She also tells me things I didn't know, like she's running a fae school for a single student: me. Like glamour. Despite the way I can slip through shadows when I'm unconscious, or how I can twist them and pull them and turn them into blankets without realizing it, I'm a sucker for glamour. Apart from picking up on notably fae traits—pointy ears, bright eyes, super good looks—I can't see through the glamour.

That worries me, so I choose not to focus on it.

Oh, and then there's faerie food. That's a biggie. Nine was right. It seems like food from Faerie is the epitome of forbidden fruit. It can give you energy and strength when you're inches away from passing out, heal nearly any wound, extend a human's life so that they're almost immortal—but, from the second you take a bite, you're cursed... unless you have a Dark

Fae guardian willing to suck the poison out before it takes hold.

Once it does? Part of the curse is that you can only eat faerie food for the rest of your very long life. Nothing else will ever satisfy you again. Without the magicked fruit, your body will just give out.

I'm watching Carolina's body give out right in front of me.

It's been three weeks since she had anything to eat. When she told me that, I was torn between being horrified and being pissed, and I snapped.

"Are you kidding me? You've got to eat. Ask for more fruit or something. Anything. You're gonna *starve*."

Okay, so I went months without food—but that's only because I lost time somehow thanks to fae magic. In reality, it was at most a day and a half, and I was super hungry between meals.

Three weeks?

I'd be dead.

With the sun's rays highlighting her sunken-in cheeks and the black circles beneath her eyes, poor Carolina looks like she's halfway there.

I don't get it. I really don't. Sure, I understand that relying on faerie food to survive means that she'll never be completely free of the magical, mythical race, but that's got to be better than wasting away to nothingness.

Not for her.

"It's not about asking," Carolina says softly. "I would have to *beg* for more. And I'm so very tired of begging. I'd rather starve."

Not on my watch. "You don't have to beg. Look, I can call Nine. He's a good guy. If you need some faerie food, I'm sure he'll get some for you if I ask him to."

Her head jerks up suddenly. A flash of panic flitters across her face. Her voice drops to a whisper. "Riley, you can't."

"Sure, I can. It'll suck, 'cause I did tell him that I never want to see him again, but it is what it is. You need help. And, hey, it's not like I don't tell Nine to leave me alone all the time anyway. He knows I don't mean it."

Because that's the truth right there. No matter how mad he makes me, no matter how much it hurt to have him reject me like that when I was so vulnerable, I never mean it when I lash out at him.

I *can't*.

Whether I want to or not, I love him. Can't really deny it since I let it slip while under the influence of his touch. I'm gonna have to own up to my twisted feelings sooner or later. If it means that I can stop Carolina from dying right in front of me, I'll use Nine's name.

But she won't let me.

Surging up on her knees, she throws her hands out. "You don't understand," she bursts out, her hand inches away from closing around my wrist. She freezes before she does, then shakes her head wildly. "You can't, Riley. She wouldn't like that. She'd never allow one of her kind to interfere. It's better if you leave your fae out of it. It will only make it worse for me. Please."

"Okay."

"Promise me. Promise me that you won't call him here."

"I promise."

She sinks back on the ground. A soft sigh of relief escapes her. "When you get rid of Melisandre, I'll be free of my mistress. That's the bargain. We don't need to involve anybody else."

"Carolina, what if—"

"I believe in you. You're the Shadow. You can do anything."

A crooked grin tugs on her chapped lips. "I'm hungry, but I'm used to it. I'll survive. I've made it this long."

"Let me go get you some water at least." It won't do anything to satiate her hunger, but water is the only thing on this side that she can get down without throwing it back up. "Can I do that?"

She nods, folding her skeletal body in on herself, knees to her chest, arms wrapped around her legs so that there's no chance of her brushing up against me as I climb to my feet and move past her toward the kitchen.

It's only after I've left the living room that I notice something.

My pulse is steady. I didn't flinch, or jerk out of her reach. My hands are clenched at my side, but that's not because I was trying to brace myself for an unwelcome touch. They're clenched because I have half a mind to pop into Faerie, find the Dark Fae responsible for this, and punch the Unseelie female dead in the nose. I'm not a killer, but a sucker punch would totally be worth however much time I lose crossing over.

Huh. Look at that. Absolute fury trumps panic. I'm so stinking pissed at her reaction, at what Carolina's faceless mistress has reduced her to, that I actually would have let her touch me without even the smallest niggle of fear if it made her feel better.

Somehow, over the last couple of days, I've grown used to having her around.

Even worse? I've started to care about her.

When Carolina leaves me at night, I have to battle with my guilt over leading her on. She thinks I'm working on this great plan to confront the Fae Queen when, in reality, half my time is spent on wondering where Nine is. The other half? I'm trying to figure out my next step.

I can't stay in the Wilkes House forever. Despite her repeated offers, it doesn't feel right to drop in on Carolina's parents. I have this sinking suspicion that they'd take one look at me and have me on my way back to Black Pine within the hour.

No, thanks.

As the days go by, I can't stop obsessing over Nine, either. Since the first time he visited me in my room at the asylum, this is the longest I've gone without him crossing over to see me. I don't like it. I'm not ready to swallow my pride and invite him back, but I wouldn't send him away if he showed up.

He... doesn't.

At first, I wonder if he expected me to linger in that nasty sewer. I mention it to Carolina my third morning after I spent two sleepless, dreamless nights worrying where Nine went. Almost apologetically, she reminds me about the touch—and how the brand it left behind on my skin means he can follow me anywhere. He's just *not* because I told him to stay away.

Good going, Riley.

Seriously.

Carolina says that I should've expected it. To the fae, humans like us—even part humans, I guess—are looked at as toys, basically. They play with us when they have nothing better to do. Once they're occupied, or they no longer have any use for us, we're discarded.

Thrown away.

Forgotten.

Trash.

It's not really a surprise to me that, without Nine to keep me company—or even Rys to argue with—I rely more and more on Carolina. It's easier now that I'm out of the asylum. It almost feels like how it used to be with Madelaine. And it's not just the food and the clothes and the bonding over how much the fae have ruined our lives, though that's definitely up there.

It's the way she makes me feel like a normal twenty-one-year-old woman and not some kind of crazy, broken chick. Sure, she looks at me like she expects me to solve all of her problems, but I'm kind of doing the same thing.

Together, we can put the asylum behind us. We can pretend that there's nothing wrong with us.

In the abandoned Wilkes House, we can be as free as two fae-touched humans can be.

CHAPTER 12

At the end of our fourth day together, when Carolina is getting ready to head out for the night, she starts to apologize.

I barely pay attention to it. Honestly, that's nothing new. She has a tendency to "sorry" everything to death. I've gotten used to it.

I let it roll off my back, brushing the crumbs of my dinner from my lap before I stand up. I always walk her to the back door so that I can lock it behind her, then make myself a nest of the blanket and pillow she brought for me.

I don't mind the alone time. It's almost like light's out at the asylum all over again. No television. No books. Just me and the shadows.

Nowadays, though, when I say shadows, I mean that.

Literally.

I haven't told Carolina because I don't want her getting her hopes up, but I've been practicing with pulling the shadows toward me. I haven't gotten the nerve to try shade-walking again—and, thank God, I haven't made any nighttime trips while I was sleeping—and I still don't know how to consciously conjure a shadow thick enough for it to pass as a blanket.

I'm making some progress, though.

Hey. I'm the Shadow. I might as well figure out what that means since, apart from the limited lines scrawled on Carolina's paper, no one has been able to tell me what I'm supposed to do about it.

Seems as if I'm gonna have more time to sit around and practice by myself when Carolina nervously clears her throat and makes an announcement.

"So, um, I should probably tell you. I'm not going to be able to come back for a couple of days."

Okay. Now that's different.

If Carolina thought she could get away with it, I'm sure she'd find a way to spend every waking second with me, pushing me toward coming up with a plan to defeat the Fae Queen. Between me losing my shit if she tried and her parents calling her every night to make sure she was on her way home, she can't, but she makes up for it by spending all day here with me inside the Wilkes House.

"My parents are taking me out to our family's lake house for a long weekend to see if it helps to get out of the city," she adds, overcompensating by over-explaining. Like usual. "My dad's worried about all the time I've been spending out of the house and my mom is convinced that, with the right remedy, they can fix me. I tried to tell them no, but they weren't having it. I've got to go."

"That's okay."

"I'd rather stay here." I'm sure she would. She nibbles on her bottom lip, ducking her chin. "I don't like leaving you here alone."

"Hey, I promise, it's gonna be okay. Don't look so sad, Lina. I'm a big girl," I tell her, trying to say it with a teasing tone so that she doesn't think I'm being ungrateful. "I don't need a babysitter. I'll be fine for a couple of days."

"I know you will. Just in case, though, I got a couple of things for you that I thought might come in handy."

She disappears into the kitchen, returning a few seconds later with a shopping bag. "Here."

There's a baseball cap tucked inside. I can use that to cover my ears. Smart. Two boxes of dye. And a pair of oversized sunglasses.

Look at her. She's given me a DIY disguise kit.

"In case you want to leave the house," she says, confirming my guess. "It's been a while since they've posted any updates about you on the news, but my mom keeps in touch with my psychologists at the facility. They haven't given up on you yet. I wasn't sure if you'd want to color your hair—I got brown and red 'cause both will cover up the white-blonde pretty easy. The hat will cover it up, too, if you don't want to go that far."

I was thinking the same thing. "Thanks. This is a big help."

I mean it, too. I'm so over sitting inside of the abandoned house. Even if it's just walking around Acorn Falls, it's better than hiding in the dark.

Carolina reaches into her back pocket, pulling out a clear plastic sandwich baggie full of money. "This is for you, too. I'm not sure how long I'll be gone for and you might have to get some stuff while I'm out."

"I can't take that from you."

"It's the least I can do, Riley. Trust me. Don't spend it if you don't want to, but I'll feel better knowing you have it."

"Okay. Sure." I hold out my hand. She drops the baggie into the cup of my palm. After the close call that first night, there hasn't been a single accidental touch over the last few days. I disappear it into the front pocket of my hoodie. "For emergencies."

She hesitates. I can tell there's more on her mind than just her upcoming trip. I'm proven right a second later when she adds, "You know… you don't *have* to stay here by yourself. You can come with me. My parents won't care. The lake house is nice. You'll be hidden and safe there."

Not this again. I have to say no. She knows it, too. Doesn't stop her from asking.

And, okay, it's a nice gesture—it's just a totally empty one. We've never talked about it explicitly 'cause of the whole 'Carolina doesn't talk about herself' thing, but it's obvious that her family is pretty well-off. I mean, they've got a freaking lake house. Of course they have money.

They're also super overprotective of her. How much do I want to bet they'll flip out if they learn that Carolina isn't going to out-patient therapy during the day? That she's spending all of her free time squatting inside the Wilkes House with Riley Thorne, Black Pine escapee?

I can't pretend they don't have a television or read the news. My face was plastered on every news channel, paper, and website. The second they figured out who I was, I'd be on my way back to Black Pine and hell if I'm ever stepping foot in there now that I know that it's a place where the fae stick humans to forget about them.

Then there's Carolina's fae. The Dark Fae female has absolute control over her, and she's holding Lina's freedom over her head like a carrot on a stick. I know that's why my new friend is so eager to keep me happy. Her fae wants to see the Shadow

Prophecy play out and, so long as I'm the halfling Shadow they're focusing on, Carolina will do anything she can to get me to face off against the Fae Queen.

Once Melisandre is gone, Carolina doesn't have to rely on her fae for faerie food; the geas she's under disappears under the contract she made. She won't ever be able to eat real stuff again, but she also won't have to beg her fae for a bite to stay alive.

Until then, she might want to stay on my good side. She has no choice except to do what her fae requires her to.

It's something else I've been thinking about when I'm by myself. I like Carolina, she's been good to me, and I've even gotten into the habit of calling her Lina. We get along, both of us bonded by the shitty hand life dealt us when we got involved with the fae.

Even so, I'm not that naive. Sure, she might mean it when she insists she wants to be my right hand man—and she does, because my lie detector tingle hasn't gone off once these last few days—but if her fae changes her mind and asks for something else, she'll do it. I accept that. Carolina could hand me over in a heartbeat if her fae decides I'm taking too damn long.

It's better that I stay here.

I shake my head.

She sighs. "That's what I figured."

"Sorry."

Oof. The shocker there is that I actually kind of mean that. I'm wary of my new friend. Still, I don't like to disappoint her, especially since she's suffering way more than I am.

Her lips twitch, like she's trying to force a half-hearted grin. "Don't be. It was a longshot, but I had to ask. Since I'm gonna leave you by yourself, I've got something else for you."

This baggie comes from her front pocket. It's way smaller than the one filled with cash, too. Carolina tips it over, letting something drop in her open palm. Once she has it, she slips her finger through the loop, lifting her hand high so that I can see what she has.

It's a necklace.

A weirdo necklace, too. The chain is made of some kind of dark brown rope, thin, like leather sinew or something like that. Hanging at the bottom of the string, there's something metallic that's been wrapped in knots, creating a strange-looking charm.

I peer closer. It's gun-metal gray, long and pointy.

What the—

"Is that a nail?"

She twists her wrist, sending the necklace twirling. My sight is good enough to pick up the stray moonlight filtering in through the window dancing softly against the dark metal. Yeah. I'm pretty sure that it's a nail. Good thing that the point on the end looks like someone blunted it.

I could just see myself poking out my eye with it by accident.

"Wear this, okay?" Carolina says, holding the necklace out. She waits for me to offer her my palm again before she lets it land against the leather of my glove.

So, uh, the necklace weighs more than I expected. My hand dips and I feel my stomach tighten.

Not a normal nail then, is it?

I slip it on over my head because she's expecting me to—and because I can't come up with a good reason not to. The weight of the necklace is a little bit uncomfortable. Instead of leaving it on the outside of my hoodie, I tuck it under the material, letting it settle between my boobs.

Better.

"It's an iron nail. Pure iron."

Well, that explains it. Iron is one of the fae's only weaknesses. Because I'm only part fae—the ear part, at least—it makes me feel a little off. That's it, though. Just like I can lie when I'm not under the influence of Nine's magic, I can handle iron without any problem.

"In case one of the Cursed Ones comes after you, the iron nail might buy you some time to get away. The more iron, the better, I'm sure you know that already. I mean, with enough iron, you can really hurt them—maybe even kill them."

The chain seems to hang even heavier. "Are you saying I could use this nail to kill Nine?"

She says Cursed One, I think of Nine. It's a knee-jerk reaction. So is my horrified expression at just the idea of hurting him.

The rest of the fae can go scratch themselves. Not Nine, though.

Never my Shadow Man.

Carolina frowns. "Not kill, no. It would hurt him. He might not even heal properly. It would take a lot more iron than that to finish him. I didn't know you were going after him, Riley. Isn't the Shadow supposed to kill the Fae Queen?"

Like I need the reminder. Because of the stupid Shadow Prophecy, the Fae Queen has made it clear to her Court, her guard, and her soldiers that it's either her head or mine. Both Rys and Nine admitted that to me.

That's why I asked her. She's the one who first said *kill*, not me. I swear, it's like everyone is homicidal. I don't care what any of them say. The prophecy Carolina showed me doesn't mention anything about having to off anyone.

The Shadow ends the Fae Queen's rule. It doesn't say how.

I cling to that.

I'm not a killer.

I'm *not*.

And I won't let them make me one.

But I am a liar. "Yeah. I just wanted to make sure that I don't accidentally hurt someone else along the way. I hate the fae"—well, except for one—"but that doesn't mean I want them to drop dead at my feet."

Carolina's brow furrowed. "A scrap of iron isn't powerful enough for that. You'd need a Brinkburn for that. And good luck finding one of those."

"A *what*?" I've never heard that word before.

"It's nothing. A rumor I heard one of the times I was in Faerie. I'm not even sure it's real which is why I never brought it up before. Anyway, that's not the point of the nail."

Carolina reaches beneath her blouse, pulling out a nail on a string just like mine. Her nail has red stains along the sides. My first thought—*is that blood?*—is quickly squashed when I realize it's got to be rust.

Whoa. How long has she been wearing hers?

She shows it to me, then tucks it back under her shirt. "It something, right? The iron won't keep the fae off your trail forever. It does make them have to work a little harder to find you. And, like I said, it might hold them off for a bit if you get to use it."

She's sold me. I'll wear the nail. She's right—at least it's something.

"Thanks. You didn't have to do that."

"Promise me you'll wear the necklace. That you won't take it off no matter what."

Again with the promises. Hey, if it makes her feel better...

"Yeah." I place my hand over the lump in my hoodie. You

know what? I actually feel comforted by the scrap of iron. "I will."

I miss Nine like an ache deep in my gut. Without Carolina as a distraction, it only gets worse.

So it's not just the power of the iron that makes my stomach feel funny. Truth is, I haven't felt right in days. I thought it would get better as time went by.

Nope.

I dream of him.

And I don't normally dream.

Jeez, I sound like a lovesick idiot for allowing him to affect me that deeply, but it's true. I don't go anywhere while I'm sleeping, probably because I've purposely avoided the whole idea of shade-walking since I decided to keep that little gift a secret from Carolina. I fall asleep in my nest of blankets and shadows as soon as I'm sure I'm alone, then wake up in the same spot shortly before Carolina's knocking softly at the back door.

My head is full of visions of Nine. While I sleep, I see him doing all sorts of mundane things. For some reason, he always seems to be out in the fantastical Faerie realm on his own. I get the feeling that he's searching for something. But what?

No idea.

There's no sound in my dreams. Only pictures. That's all I need really. Nine is so stinking gorgeous, from his sharp cheekbones to his shoulder-length hair and the shadowy duster that hugs his slender body. He moves with purpose, an obvious air of determination following behind him as he keeps on going, oblivious that some part of me is there.

It takes until the third night of me having the same sort of dream before I realize what's so different about this Nine. My whole life, the Shadow Man was a haughty, emotionless specter who haunted my nights and served as both my mentor and my only family. He was the only one who never abandoned me—well, until I was fifteen and Rys's fire burned away the tie the existed between Nine and me. Still, he was the only constant in my life.

He was always the same.

Until he finally found me at the Black Pine facility. Everything changed then, Nine most of all.

Sure, his hair was longer than it had been when I was a kid, and he seemed to carry a weight on his shoulders that never existed before; back then, Nine was absolutely untouchable. He was also this impassive, detached person who was more of a teacher than a friend.

The Nine who appeared in my room at Black Pine and helped me shade-walk right out of the asylum seemed to wear his heart on his sleeve. He might have started to watch over me because he entered into a bargain with my mom over twenty years ago. Now that I've come of age, I don't think that's the reason why he's still watching me.

He's attracted to me. It might've been a while since I had a guy looking at me the way he does, but Nine is into me—but he's stubborn enough not to want to act on it.

I get it. I *do*. There's the whole power imbalance to think about. Nine is an immortal Dark Fae who hasn't aged a day in the twenty years I've known him. He's known me since I was just out of diapers. He's watched me grow, teaching me and shaping me into the person I've become.

Who taught me the fae weren't to be trusted?

Who pounded the refrain into my skull about touch magic so deeply that I developed anxiety and haphephobia over it?

Who was always there for me? Praising me when I did well, and showing his disappointment when I failed him?

Who was the only one who cared for me? Who did it all because I needed to know the truth about the fae if, as the Shadow, I had any chance of surviving until I came of age?

I might have ended up a damaged, wary halfling in the human world who has massive panic attacks when anyone tries to touch me, but I'm still freaking alive.

And I owe it all to Nine.

Is it any wonder why I spent my whole childhood and awkward teenage years crushing on him? He was my Shadow Man, my knight in a long, dark coat, the only person who was there for me. I always loved him, even when I hated him for leaving me after Madelaine died, and those same complicated emotions returned almost immediately after Nine reappeared in my life for the first time in six years.

After that night in the sewer, when I let him touch me and then I all but begged him to do it again, those feelings have only gotten more twisted and confusing.

I love him. I want to see him again.

I want him to touch me.

And, most of all, I wish I *didn't*.

It's like an addiction. Once I got past Nine actually physically touching me, all I remember is how good it felt. Instead of making me feel like I'm out of control, that I have no choice, his magic calmed me, soothed me, made me feel special.

It made me feel loved.

That's pretty heady to someone who's been abandoned, left behind, and tossed around her entire life. When I was a kid,

Nine was the only one I could count on. The only one who was always there for me.

Now?

Now I want more from him. I want more than he's willing to give me and that... *that* is the main reason why I force myself to keep from calling for him. When I promised Carolina that first night that I wouldn't invite Nine in, I knew right away that it was a lie. I couldn't go that long without seeing him.

I just needed the sting of his rejection to fade a little before I went back for seconds. His touch will wipe away the soul-crushing loneliness, the pressure of not knowing what my next move is gonna be, and the cocktail of fear and paranoia that, the moment I walk out of the Wilkes House again, the Fae Queen will appear and try to murder me before I get the chance to end her.

I miss Nine. I miss the way he calls me *Shadow*, and how he turns every conversation into a lecture because he's convinced my ignorance when it comes to Faerie is going to get me killed. My Shadow Man, my first and best teacher... I don't even think he realizes he's doing it, but he does—and I miss it.

I miss the way his brilliant silver eyes light up when he sees me. How he looks at me like I matter. How, now that I'm coming into my own power as the Shadow, now that I'm older, the power dynamic has shifted enough that—whether he meant to or not—he allowed me to pick up on our mutual attraction.

I made the mistake of telling Carolina about that once. *Once.* She was quick to remind me that the touch of a fae can do a lot to a human, depending on what the fae was after when they got their taste.

If I'm addicted to the way his touch made me feel, the fae *crave* it. Touch magic is like a drug. It makes the Faerie races believe they're invincible—which, considering they only have a couple of weaknesses, that's saying something. To get me to agree to let him touch me again, any fae could've used their magic to make me think that there's something between us. If I thought Nine might be into me—and I let myself believe I still loved him, and in a totally different way than I did when I was a kid—then I'd be willing to give him permission to touch me as much as he wanted.

And maybe that's true. Could be. I sure acted like a moron every time Rys came around after he branded me.

But this is different. I know it is. And for one important reason, too.

Rys touched me. He told me he's in love with me. The Light Fae did whatever he wanted to show me that he wants the two of us to be mated.

I don't love him, though. Even after he touched me, I never once felt a spark toward him. Sure, I wasn't as afraid of him as I was right after he charmed Madelaine right to her death. I know that meant he charmed me, too, especially when he kept calling me *Zella* and compelling me to do things I never would've, but I don't love him.

I love Nine.

I'm too fucked up to know what kind of love it is. We've got too much history, and I sure as hell have too much baggage. Romantic love? Platonic love? Brotherly? Something. I can't put a label on it when I'm not even sure I'm going to see twenty-two at this point.

But, still, I definitely miss my Shadow Man. Carolina's been a treasure trove of information these last few days, plus a huge help. No denying she has an ulterior motive, though. She's eager for me to plot how I'm going to rise up against the Fae Queen.

Nine has more answers. I know he does.

He knew my mother. I'm willing to bet, if I confront him with my new pointy ears, that he knew I was also half-fae.

What else is he keeping from me?

I don't know. I won't know until I get over my stubbornness and call for him to see me again.

It's been four days in the human realm. Did enough time pass that I can use Nine's name without having to eat crow first?

Guess I'm going to find out.

CHAPTER 13

In the living room of the Wilkes House, there's a corner tucked near the stairs that I avoid.

It's not like the basement. It doesn't take a genius—or a shrink—to figure out why I won't go down there. I can go near this corner without feeling like all of the air has been sucked out of the room—I just *don't*.

Ever since that first night here, I noticed that the corner was darker than it should be considering the way the moonlight shines through the open window. It's like there's a boundary surrounding it. At a certain point, the light stops, like it ran into a brick wall.

The corner of my room at the asylum had a strange shadow just like that. A patch of darkness that seems eerily out of place.

I know instinctively what it is.

I made my bed on the other side. It's where I sleep, far from the bathroom where Rys's lantern is kept, and opposite of the dark corner. Carolina thinks it's because I'm careful to stay tucked out of sight in case someone decides to peek in the front window. She keeps suggesting that I should at least find a bedroom upstairs where no one would ever see me.

I can't. I don't tell her why, but I have to stay in this room.

I have to keep an eye on the portal.

Who knows what might come popping out if I'm not watching it?

I've given up on arguing that I'm the Shadow. After she pointed out the blankets and explained that I manipulated the shadows into something that I could actually touch, I decided it was kind of ridiculous to keep denying it. Either I have this weirdo skill because of the prophecy, or because it's something a fae can do—and since I don't want to focus on the fact that I'm half-fae, the Shadow it is.

And, if I'm the Shadow, that means that the Fae Queen's not going to just let me go. Rys can't find me, and Nine obviously won't come for me unless I ask him to, but this is the freaking queen of Faerie we're talking about. Eventually, someone's coming for me.

It's been twenty years that I've had that threat hanging over my head. I know time doesn't work the same in Faerie, but it's running out. If she was waiting for me to come of age, that deadline's already gone.

She could come for me at any time. Right now, there's nothing I can do except wait, and practice, and hope like hell that I can figure out a plan on the fly.

It's only been a couple of days since I had to accept that I really am the Shadow and, thanks to Carolina smuggling that scrap of paper out of Faerie, there really is a prophecy. I'll come up with a plan sooner or later.

For now, I've only got one thing on my mind.

Sitting in the dark house has done wonders for my night vision. I've always been able to see better than I probably should have—perk of being half-fae, maybe—and now I'm almost like a freaking cat, it's that good. Propping my back up against the wall, I tuck my shadow blanket around my hips and focus on the portal across from me.

"Ninetroir."

My voice cuts through the dark room.

It's instant. One second, I'm alone. The next?

I'm not.

I knew it was a portal. I freaking knew it. The patch of impossibly black space is suddenly full. He blinked into existence within a heartbeat, the pale, slender figure coming closer and closer as he strides forward.

Just in case I opened the portal and some other Dark Fae has crossed over, I take a deep breath, reach inside of me, and tug. The shadows at my waist thicken, then start to waft higher and higher, providing me with a thin shield—and some cover—as the fae moves into my sight.

The air shifts. It grows heavy, with an electrical charge that seems to carry on the currents. The little hairs on the back of my neck stand at attention as I grit my teeth, fighting against a shiver.

He's so beautiful, I want to shake loose my shadowy cocoon and throw myself right into his arms.

Whoa.

Down, girl.

Between the way his skin has an unearthly pale glow and his bright silver eyes shimmer and shine, I see everything through the thin gauze of my shadows. The impatience, the flash of fear, the worry.

He can't see me, can he?

"Shadow," he calls out. His voice has that harsh edge to it

that was a major clue when I was younger that I pushed my emotionless Shadow Man way too far. "Where are you?"

I drop the shadows, letting them pool around my waist. "Here."

His eyebrows rise sky-high. Relief dances across his face before his lips curve just enough to cause my heart to pound in my chest.

Is it just me or does he actually look impressed?

"You learned how to pull the shadows toward you."

I've been working on it for three nights now. Every hour I spent cursing and thinking I was even more nuts for continuing to try is worth it just to see that look on his face.

I don't want him to know that, though. I shrug. No big deal, right? "Once I realized I could do it at all, it was actually kind of easy."

"And shadow travel? How's that coming along?"

I want to smile and just manage to hang on to the urge. Same old Nine. He's slipped right into his role as my teacher, just like usual.

I don't want to disappoint him so, instead, I lie. "I'm still trying to figure it out."

There's something about shade-walking that doesn't sit right with me. It made me nauseous the only time I shade-walked while conscious, like motion sickness on steroids, and that doesn't even count how I landed in the Fae Queen's garden. If there's a risk of that happening again, I'm good. I'll stick to playing with the shadows instead of walking through them.

I nod up at Nine. "So. You came."

"You called."

"I thought you said the name wasn't enough. That I needed to add a command."

"For any other human, yes. For you? A command… it isn't

necessary. I just needed for you to say my name, to know that you were ready to face me again."

Any other human… only I'm not a human. Not entirely.

With his answer, Nine's just given me the perfect opening to ask him about my half-fae status. Except, now that I have the opportunity, my tongue feels like it's glued to the roof of my mouth. I can't get the words out.

I… I don't want to know.

Doesn't matter. Before I can find the balls to spit it out, Nine moves toward me. Something flashes in his eyes. Something I can't describe or explain. I just know I don't like it.

"You're hazy." His lips thin. "Riley, what have you done?"

I lift my hand up so that it's resting on the bulge in the front of my hoodie. Carolina's gift. I fold my gloved hand around the lump, covering the nail.

"Me? Nothing," I lie. "Maybe it's the fence outside. I think it's iron. You guys don't like that, right?"

Nine narrows his brilliant stare on me, focusing on the way I'm basically feeling up one of my boobs.

I drop my hand.

"Perhaps," he agrees. Stepping away from the portal, Nine crosses the room in a few powerful steps. I stay where I am on the floor, mainly because I just don't have the energy to get up. He pulls something out of his pocket when he's in front of me, crouching down to hold it out. "Here. You forgot this."

I recognize it immediately. The silky fabric piece that Nine gave me, but that I left behind in the sewer after I tossed it at a rat.

"I didn't mean to," I tell him honestly. I reach out with grasping fingers, closing my leather glove around the tail end of it as Nine offers it to me. "When I went back for it, it was gone."

Once I have it, I rub it against my cheek. It's even softer than I remember and, to my delight, it still smells like Nine.

It reminds me of my shadows, too, only way stronger and way thicker. This has definitely gotta be silk or some other real material.

I glance over at him. "You know, I haven't figured out what it's supposed to be yet."

"Yours." And that's all he says about that before he glances around the room. I know he can pick up every detail. The Shadow Man from my childhood had always amazed me with how well he could see in the dark. "Is this where you ran off to after you sent me away?"

I shrug, tucking Nine's scarf thing against my side so it's next to me. "Yes."

"Alone?"

I might have fudged my promise to Lina that I would stay away from Nine, but she had to have known that the lure of the fae is almost impossible to resist. That doesn't mean I'm going to break another promise. Because she probably did know that Nine's *my* weakness, she got me to swear not to tell the Dark Fae about her.

"Yeah. Who else would have come with me?"

He doesn't have an answer for that. Doesn't stop him from trying to scold me in that way he has.

"You shouldn't be here," Nine says with a scowl. "I can sense traces of Rys's power inside. There's not enough iron to shield you if he comes looking for you."

"I thought you told me he couldn't. Wasn't that the whole reason why you had to touch me? To get rid of Rys and his awful peach?"

"He won't need his brand to track you down here," Nine says pointedly. "I know what this place is. Once he realizes that you were foolish enough to return, he'll find you without any help."

Was it foolish to come here? Oh, yeah. I've thought the same thing a hundred times since I first snuck inside of the abandoned house. Didn't stop me, though.

I never figured Rys would care enough to track me down at this place. Foolish? Nah. That was just *stupid*.

I should've known better. Rys is fae. Seelie. He might've left me alone all those years between the first time he asked me to dance, and then when I actually fell for it when I thought I was dreaming, but something's changed since then.

He wants me to be his *ffrindau*. His soulmate. I don't honestly think he's going to give me up as easily as that, even if I'd deluded myself into thinking he would.

"I'm afraid," I whisper into the dark room, hugging myself. It feels so good to be able to admit that to anyone, even if it's to Nine. Carolina has this idea that the Shadow is fearless—but Riley definitely isn't. "Of Rys. For years, just thinking about him made me want to puke, I was so scared. But now... I'm afraid because, when he's there, I'm *not* scared anymore. It probably doesn't even make sense. I'm so damn tired and... I don't know—"

"It's the glamour," Nine murmurs softly.

I glance up at him. He's moved away from me, going just beyond the open window. The moonlight streaming in bathes him in an otherworldly glow that makes him even more beautiful.

Damn it.

This was a bad idea. A really fucking awful one.

He's a distraction I don't need. So gorgeous it hurts, and a temptation that makes me want to do all the wrong things.

It would be worth it, too.

Wait. He said something. I confessed how conflicted I've been over Rys these last few days, and then—

"I'm sorry." My hand creeps up to my head. Tucking a stray lock of hair behind my ear, I ask, "What was that?"

"The glamour," Nine says again. "Some humans are immune to it. Your mother was. It's one of the reasons she caught your father's attention in the first place."

Callie. My mother. The woman who, for reasons I still don't know, met with Nine at an abandoned gas station, begged him to watch over me, then left me behind while she just… disappeared.

The human woman who created a child with a fae, only to leave her at the mercy of the Fae Queen.

Me.

"So it's true then. My father… he was like you."

Nine doesn't react. If he's surprised that I came to that conclusion based on his comment, he doesn't show it.

Or maybe he saw my pointed ear when I tucked my hair out of my face.

I hope so. I did it on purpose.

The only thing he does is shake his head. "Not like me, Riley. He was Seelie. A Light Fae. Like—"

"Like Rys," I supply. Why am I not surprised? "So that makes me…"

"Half-Seelie, half-human. It's not common, but it's not unheard of, either. Their mating should have created a halfling. Someone who could resist iron and tell a lie, but who was particularly vulnerable to being touched by a fae."

I think of the iron nail nestled in between my boobs. Except for the weight, it doesn't bother me at all. Then there's the way I'm lying to Nine right now. He believes that I've been bunking here alone because Carolina's always gone before night falls. He's got a point. No fae can do that.

But I've also got these weirdo gifts.

I run his solemn words through my head again.

...should have created a halfling...

"I'm not just a halfling, am I?"

Nine shakes his head. "A Light Fae, whether full-blooded or half, will always shy away from the shadows. Even as an infant, you were drawn to the darkness. The first time you shade-walked, Aislinn knew that you were different. And he knew, should Melisandre discover your secrets, she'd destroy you."

"Ash-lynn," I murmur. "I remember... you mentioned him before."

"Aislinn," Nine repeats, correcting the way I said the name. "Your father."

A fae who fell in love with a human. Who married a human, and had a child with a human. Who gave up Faerie for a human—

If he could, and it's possible, then that means—

Maybe my Shadow Man can, too.

CHAPTER 14

I push that thought far, far away. I can't. I just... I *can't*.

"What about you?" I say hurriedly, forging on with the conversation because the alternative is getting stuck in my own thoughts—and my own fantasies. "I've never been afraid of you." A horrible thought pops in my head. "Are you charming me right now?"

"No."

Doesn't matter that he can't lie. Once the suspicion hits me, it's not so easy to shake it. It would make sense. How could I go from wanting nothing to do with him while I was still in Black Pine to, well, confessing my feelings for him in such a short period of time?

Carolina says it's the touch. Maybe she's right—or maybe it's something else entirely.

Please let it be something else.

"How do you know?" I demand. "You're fae. Maybe you're doing it and it's not on purpose. It's just who you are."

"Riley. No."

"But—"

"My glamour has never worked on you. I tried when you were a child. You were too young to understand my kind. I wanted to appear as a friendly creature, knowing a mortal child would never accept one of the Unseelie. Imagine my surprise when you saw me for exactly who I am." He lets out a huff. Like always with Nine, I can't tell if he's pleased with me or annoyed. "You called me the Shadow Man. It was as good a name as any, as well as an apt choice. But, trust me, the form I tried to present looks nothing like the darkness that I am."

I was so little when he first followed me to the Thornes. I always thought he called himself the Shadow Man. When I recently learned that he was fae, I thought he had tricked me.

But I was the one who gave him the name?

Even worse, if this is Nine's true appearance, I'm *screwed*.

He was right. Even as a kid, I had never really been all that afraid of the dark. An unwanted touch, definitely, but the dark? Nope. I guess, if I had to fall for a fae, at least it's a Dark Fae.

"Why?" I ask him. "What makes you so special?"

Nine's eyes shutter. I'm pretty sure it's the first time I see him blink. He closes his eyes, the lid closing over the glow for a heartbeat before it comes back, like a flashlight flickering on and off.

"It could be that you're the Shadow."

Oof, Nine. Wrong answer.

The words explode out of me. "I'm not the Shadow!"

He nods. "Yes. You are."

Okay. Fine. "Well, I don't *want* to be the Shadow. That better?"

"There's no escaping it. Whether you're the child of the Shadow Prophecy or not, Melisandre believes you are. You became the Shadow the day she first sent her soldiers after you."

I've spent days trying to pretend that I'm not even a blip on the powerful Fae Queen's radar. I mean, really? Just because I can do some cool parlor tricks with shadows, that doesn't mean that I'm gunning for her or anything. She's got to know that.

Of course, then Nine has to go and mention freaking *soldiers*.

I scoff. I have to, because if I don't, I might just puke. Soldiers? Hell, no.

"You told me when I was a kid to watch out for the fae because they'll be coming for me one day. I think I would've noticed it if I had soldiers after me."

Nine is silent. He's quiet for so long, in fact, that I start to let myself think that maybe—just maybe—I found a hole in his logic. Maybe he was wrong. Apart from Nine and Rys, I've never encountered another fae. And, okay, Carolina seems to be all aboard the "Fae Queen is after Riley" train, but maybe she's wrong, too, right?

And that's when Nine hikes his pants up, then lowers himself so that we're eye to eye. The tail end of his shadowy duster pools around him, wafting in the slight breeze from the partly open window.

"You were barely a year old," he begins, his voice developing a rasp that I've never heard from Nine before. It's still got that inherently fae-like enchanting quality, but more emotion than my Shadow Man has ever let slip into his tone. My breath catches in my throat as he continues. "She has spies everywhere, in the human world and in Faerie. After he mated his human, Aislinn left the Seelie Court. He forsook his people—and his queen—to live on the other side, despite what it did to his power and his strength. Melisandre kept watch over her favored guard, hoping to sway him back to her side. And then you were born.

"She discovered your ability to shade-walk. I don't know

how. Aislinn would've hidden it with everything he had, but she found out and she sent her soldiers after you. A dead halfling would be no threat to her reign... only the guard that eventually found you chose to spare you. Your mother wasn't so fortunate."

To hear him mention my mother's death so callously freaking *stings*. I mean, she's been gone for twenty years now, and it does something for me to know my parents' last act was to sacrifice themselves for my safety, but it doesn't seem to bother Nine at all.

He's fae, I remind myself. No matter what, I can't change that fact. He's fae, just like Rys, and the death of some human is as inconsequential to him as me swatting a fly that's pissing me off with its buzz.

Despite his cold facade, he obviously mourns my dad. My mom? She was just a human.

And I'm a halfling.

Why do I matter?

I want to ask him that. I don't, though. I'm too afraid of what his answer will be.

Instead, I wave my hand, scattering the shadows that cling to me. The more upset I am, the thicker they become, which isn't helping me in the denial department. I scowl. "I don't want to talk about my mom, alright?"

Nine's eyebrows wing up. He's seeing the shadows respond to me, too, isn't he? "Then we won't discuss her."

"Good."

"That doesn't change the situation, Riley. Now that you're free from the asylum, you've lost the last of your protection. I can't bring you to Faerie. We got lucky that Melisandre didn't sense your presence that day in the garden, and since she left that statue out for you, I'm certain she'd been expecting you.

Next time, it won't be a frozen human. It'll be one of her guards."

"Good to know. So I'm not going to Faerie anytime soon. That's fine."

Nine lets out a frustrated exhale. Running his pale hands through his long, dark hair, he shoves it out of his face, revealing a pointy ear that looks just like mine.

"For how long, though? There's no wards. Barely any iron and almost no protection. Rys never should've forced my hand. We both agreed that the asylum would've been a safe place for you. Hiding you under Melisandre's nose, as it were. He was supposed to wait until they released you before we found another place to keep you away from the queen."

"I thought I imagined you telling me that," I confess. "The peach made me so sick, I thought it was something I made up. No way did I think you'd *ever* work with Rys... are you—" I shake my head. This is too much. "So, let me get this straight. You really are the reason I was in Black Pine all that time?"

Nine stiffens. His hands fall to his side. With a shake of his head, his hair settles in place again, hiding his ears. Suddenly on guard, he nods. "More or less."

"And you worked with Rys to put me in there—and that's *after* he killed my sister? Are you *kidding* me?"

"We had a bargain. Though we're"—Nine pauses, as if searching for the right word, and, in my mind, I hear Rys whisper *rival*—"from opposite factions, we both had one thing in common. Both of us had our reasons for protecting the Shadow. We each agreed to place you somewhere you'd be safe until you came of age. As soon as you started to come into your power, our contract was met and we were both free to return to you."

I'm not so interested in that. I know what happened after Rys appeared in my dreams, and how I thought I heard Nine call for me before I actually saw him a few days later.

No. I'm still trying to figure out why these two powerful creatures put aside their differences to take care of *me*.

"Okay. Now, you went to all that trouble because you and my mom had a bargain, too, right? You were supposed to watch over me."

Nine slips his hand into the pocket of his jacket, pulling out the same pebble I've seen him carrying before. He lets it fall in his palm, almost as if he has to assure himself that he still has it, then closes his fingers over it. When he opens his hand again, the pebble is gone.

And he nods. "Yes."

"So what was his reason? Rys. Why would he want to keep me safe?"

Nine's gorgeous face closes off. He doesn't give off a single hint of what he's thinking as he says, "If you really want to know why a Blessed One does anything, you're asking the wrong fae. I know what Rys says his reasons are. He believes them to be true. Is there more to it? Of course. But you'd have to go to him for answers."

Is this a test?

It feels like a test.

Either way, I shake my head. "Yeah. I'd rather not."

"That's smart, Riley," Nine says, and I hate that his approval helps make this terrible situation not so bad. "Rys, for all his years, has always been impulsive. He should've waited and, now, here we are. He's playing for your heart while I'm hoping to save your life."

Well, of course Nine doesn't have to play for my heart. I handed that to him ages ago and, whether it's because of the touch or not, I realize he never gave it back.

Wrapping my arms around my knees, I peer over at him. I just... I just let myself look at him.

Nine is like a magnet. Even from my spot across the room, I can still feel the strength of his pull.

When I'm spending time with Carolina and our conversations inevitably turn to the fae again, it's so easy to be mad at him, to hate him, to wish he would stay away and maybe all of my trouble—and Carolina's heavy expectations—would go away, too. But then I see him again. All of that anger, confusion, and certainty is a long forgotten memory. It doesn't seem real.

At this moment, Nine is the most real thing to me.

"I hope you do," I say at last. When Nine cocks his head to the side, curious, in that almost alien way that he has, I add, "Save my life, I mean."

"I will do anything I can to keep you safe. You have my word, Riley."

A contract.

Nine just entered into a contract with me.

Does he know what he's done?

His eyes flash, a brilliant silver that brightens up the gloom in the dark living room. He takes a deep breath, his nostrils flaring, his cheekbones jutting from his sculpted face as he punctuates his vow with a look that dares me to refuse him.

Oh yeah. He knows. He absolutely knows. That was no slip of his tongue. Like any other fae with his magic, Nine made me a promise without even trying to get something out of me in return.

If it was anyone else, I'd consider it a rookie mistake. With Nine, though? I don't even want to begin to wonder what that's about.

I honestly don't know how I'm supposed to feel, either. I should be terrified of him and his strength. Hell, I should hate him for the way he was the puppet master pulling my strings my entire life. I should totally command him to stay away.

But I can't.

Maybe I let him touch me too many times and his hold is strong. Or maybe it's our bond. Ever since I was a little girl, Nine was always there for me. Even when I was convinced that he abandoned me like everyone else I've ever known, he was only doing it because it helped me survive the Fae Queen. Nine might have disappeared from my life these last six years, but I got to *live* because he worked with Rys to shield me.

He worked with the Light Fae who was responsible for my sister's death—and who thinks that I should date him anyway.

Jesus Christ, my life is screwed up.

When Nine's with me, though, it doesn't seem so bad. I should want him to go, to leave me alone. But, touch or no touch, I really want him to stay.

He does. I don't send him away, and he stays until just before the sun comes up.

And that's when I do something I'm not so proud of.

Right before *he* enters the portal, I call out after him.

"Why do you always have to leave?" I demand. I'm whining, but I just don't care. "If you're supposed to keep me safe, why can't you stay? Find a way."

"That's just the touch talking. You don't really want me here." He believes that. He honestly does. And the worst part? There's a good chance he's right. "The sun will be here soon. I have to go back."

"Then take me with you."

Nine frowns. "You know I can't do that. I might as well hand you over to Melisandre myself."

I cross my arms over my chest. "You know what? I don't think you want to. Faerie's huge. I remember you telling me it's unmappable, but it's freaking huge. You could hide me there. I know you could."

"I won't risk it. Now, stay here. I'll be back for you as soon as the shadows fall." He hesitates a second before he adds, "If you need me before then, find the darkest shadow you can and call my name. I'll come."

I'm so mad, I snap without thinking.

"I *won't* need you."

He doesn't react.

Instead, he says softly, "Even so, I'll return tonight. If you insist on staying here until we find you somewhere safe, I'll bring you some rowan. For now, turn your clothes inside out. It's a small help, but it might be enough until I come back."

Because it's an old habit, I tuck Nine's instructions in the back of my head, then mutter under my breath. "I'd rather go with you."

He heard me. I figured he would.

"No," Nine says forcefully. "You wouldn't."

And, before I can counter with another childish retort, he slips into the portal and disappears.

I wait to see if he'll come back. Don't know why he would—he never did, no matter how many times I pleaded with him as a kid—but I guess, despite growing up, I still have that innocent hope when it comes to Nine.

But he doesn't and, feeling lost, alone, and rejected, the quiet Wilkes House seems almost oppressively so in Nine's absence. The air shifts as soon as he's gone. The fact that my first instinct is to command him to come back after it's clear he won't on his own is a huge problem.

And I don't even have Carolina coming over shortly to serve as the distraction I so desperately need.

I can't stay here. Maybe I really am nuts, but I swear I can still taste the way his scent, his magic lingers in the cool air. No matter how many shadows I wrap myself up in, it doesn't help. I can't follow him, either, and it frightens me that I... I think I would if I could.

Yeah, no. I can't stay here.

Even though I still haven't gone to sleep yet, I scoop up the baseball cap and the sunglasses Carolina brought for me, then slip out the backdoor just as the sun is coming up.

CHAPTER 15

So, I go to the movies.

Hey. It seemed like a good idea at the time.

I'd forgotten all about the indie movie theatre tucked on the border of Acorn Falls. It's not so far from the Wilkes House. I'm maybe walking for about an hour when I stumble upon it and see that they're running a special.

Four movies for the price of one. If I buy a ticket, I can sit inside and watch a movie marathon. It sounded perfect. I don't blow through much of Lina's cash, I've finally got the chance to get out of the house I've been hiding in these last few days, and what's the chance of anyone recognizing me in the darkness?

One problem, though.

I've been up since yesterday morning, my disappointment over Nine leaving me has switched over to embarrassment when I think of the way I acted, and I'm super exhausted after walking around this morning. The second the house lights go down and I'm snuggled down in my seat in the last row of the theatre, I can already feel my eyes grow heavier and heavier until they're closed.

The next thing I know, I'm not in the theater anymore.

I don't have a freaking clue where I am. No idea. Then again, the room is so hazy, it's like it's full of fog or something. No matter how hard I wave my hand, it does nothing to clear the space.

I can pick out a couple of details. I'm indoors. That much is obvious. There's this thick, lush rug under my feet; my sneakers sink deeper and deeper into the shag with every step. The walls are white. High windows arching over my head let in a light so bright, it reflects off the hazy mist.

To my left, I see stairs. An ornately carved banister wraps around the spiral set. When I see it twinkle, I realize that it's not any kind of wood or metal—it's glass. Weird. It looks sturdy, though, and I might've reached for it if I didn't notice the large, heavy door set in the wall off to my right.

The fog is thinner near the door. It's big. Huge. I can put another of me on my shoulders and still not hit my head on the door jamb. It's painted the same pristine white as the wall. If it weren't for the lines that marked its shape and the expensive-looking doorknob, I don't even know if I would recognize it for what it is.

The knob twinkles like the banister. It's a pale gold, pulled in a shape like a massive diamond. I... I think it's crystal.

This weirdo place has a crystal doorknob.

Okay, then.

Yeah.

I've *definitely* never been here before.

I drift toward the door. I've got this idea that I should open it up. It might lead to another room, or even outdoors. Either way, it's information I won't have if I linger in this eerily quiet space.

Everything around me seems so expensive, I'm almost afraid to breathe in case I break something.

I can't bring myself to grab the fancy doorknob. Up close, it doesn't look so sturdy. What if the crystal shatters against my leather glove? My hand's outstretched, inches away from the curve of the knob, and I just can't do it.

Come on, Riley. What if freedom's out there? Or, better yet, some answers?

Yeah. I'm gonna turn the knob.

Suddenly, a voice comes through the door. I draw my hand back. I don't know if it's freedom out there, but there's definitely something—or someone—on the other side. Once I recognize the familiar voice whispering through the door, it hits me that I might be trapped in this strange room, but answers… I might just get some of those.

She doesn't sound muffled. How thick is that door? Though her voice is quiet and low, it comes through clearly.

My stomach drops.

You've got to be kidding me.

"I can't stay long," Carolina murmurs. There's a deferential note that I've never heard from her before. I don't like it. "She's expecting me back in a few days of human time."

She… How much do I want to bet I know who she means?

"You'll stay as long as I require you to. Find a way around the truth if you must, but if you have to keep up the pretense that you're on the Shadow's side, you will. You've done an admirable job so far, Carolina. If I didn't know you were completely human, I'd wonder if you shared some faerie blood."

Carolina… even if I didn't recognize the first voice, the way the rich, haughty second speaker uses her name seals the deal for me.

I figured she wasn't alone. She had to be talking to someone, right? The way she says human, though, it's probably not her parents.

But she's supposed to be with her parents.

Ah, *crap*.

I really freaking hope this is a dream. That the stress from being on the run, coupled with the way I left things with Nine before I snuck out again, has messed up my head. I was tired, so it makes sense that I would fall asleep.

But I usually don't dream.

I pinch myself. The leather rubs against me as I squeeze, leaving a red patch on the pale skin peeking out between the end of my glove and my sleeve. It, uh, it kind of hurt, too. Isn't that the universal test? Pinch yourself and if it hurts you're not dreaming.

Well, that can't be good. Because if I'm not dreaming, then that means I might have shadow traveled here by accident just in time to overhear a conversation between Carolina and her mistress.

"I need an update. The Shadow has already come of age and, yet, she still hasn't come to Faerie. What is she doing in the Iron? Gathering weapons? Is she still in contact with the traitors?"

"No, mistress. I've told you before. Her experiences with the fae have left her wounded. She wants nothing to do with the Seelie or the Unseelie. She still believes she's mostly human, even after I pointed out that she wasn't. She has no desire to come to Faerie. She doesn't want to face the queen."

A laugh follows. A throaty, terrible laugh.

A *cruel* laugh.

"She doesn't have to *want* to do anything, silly girl. It's been foretold. She will come to Faerie if you have to convince her to open a portal and push her through yourself. Or would you rather I find another human to take your place? You failed me when you couldn't get to her inside of the asylum. She's handed to you on a silver platter and still she hides. When will the Shadow play her part? I grow weary of waiting."

"I'm sorry. Her time inside has made it difficult for her to believe that Faerie is a real place. She definitely doesn't think she's responsible for following the prophecy. I've tried. I made her understand that she's my only hope—"

"Ah. That is quite clever. She won't risk leaving her nest to save her enemies. But if you are her friend…"

"I'm not just her friend," Carolina corrects. "I'm human. The Shadow doesn't realize that, sometimes, we can be as dangerous as the fae."

She's not wrong. Before I was in a position to eavesdrop on her, I never would've thought Lina was a threat. She's so small, I could break her in half if I had to, and my newfound skills with the shadows—and, okay, shade-walking—make me even more of a threat.

But there's something else I have that Lina doesn't: a sense of loyalty. Once I dropped my guard enough to let her in, she was one of my people. Sure, I didn't really have any intentions of, you know, *killing* the *Fae Queen* or anything like she wanted me to. I still would've figured out some way to help Lina. Even if I had to swallow my pride and ask Nine to bring us food from Faerie, I would've done it.

What's worse? Even hearing her plotting with the Dark Fae who holds all of the power over her, I still would. She might be betraying me right now—might have been betraying me all along—but I actually get it. I do. When it comes to doing whatever you can to save your life, you have to make concessions.

And, after all, who am I really but some chick from Black Pine?

I want to leave. Last thing I need is to get caught at the door, listening to their conversation. I can't, though. When the Dark Fae speaks again, I stay.

I have to listen.

"Tell me about the fruit. Having my guard leave it for her in the dark of her shadows stole half of his power. I hope it was worth it. Did she eat the peach?"

"I... She did."

"And?"

A pause, then Carolina admits, "It didn't work."

"Why not? It works on all humans. It certainly worked on you."

"Yes. But the Shadow is half-fae. That's what the prophecy says, and I've seen her pointed ears myself. She's definitely a halfling. So maybe that's why it didn't work."

Lie. Even in this hazy, strange space, I feel the discomfort tugging at my gut and I'm sure of it. Lina just told her mistress a lie.

Of course, she did. When I first discovered the truth behind why she never ate, I wasn't thinking straight. I immediately told her about the peach and how Nine was able to save me from the curse. I offered to get him to help her. So she knows that the peach made me sick and that Nine's touch healed me.

She didn't tell the Dark Fae female that, though.

Why?

And even more importantly, who the hell left me the peach? I was convinced it was Rys. Is he working with this nameless, faceless power? Or was it some other fae who tried to poison me?

"Perhaps she needs to eat more. Did you give her the other fruit I provided?"

"She wouldn't take it. She told me the peach made her sick, that she'd rather stick to the cheese and bread I brought for her."

She trusts me more than she did in the beginning, and I'm still working toward leading her to you. I think, after I return from this trip, she'll be so glad that she's not alone anymore, she might just leave the house again."

"Do what you must. The iron gate surrounding the house makes it difficult for my guards to cross the boundaries, even in daylight. I'd send Unseelie after her, but she controls the shadows in her domain far better than a halfling who's just come of age. Unless she opens the portal and invites them in herself, she's impossible to reach in the Iron. I need her in Faerie. I need you to do this for me."

Guards again.

Why does she keep mentioning guards?

A niggle of suspicion starts to form in the back of my mind. I'll be the first to admit that I've purposely forgotten a ton of what Nine taught me about Faerie. When countless social workers, therapists, and psychologists repeat over and over again that the fae aren't real, the fairy tales told to you by your imaginary friend are some of the first things to go.

When it comes to guards, though? Who else would have guards except for the woman in control of all of Faerie?

No. That can't be true. As my queasy stomach just proved, I can still sense the difference between the truth and a lie. Over the last few days, I would've known if Carolina was really working with the Fae Queen instead of a random Unseelie who wanted to see the queen fall.

Right?

I freaking hope so.

Unfortunately, there's no time for me to run through every conversation I had with Carolina, every mention of the fae she was compelled to serve. Not when she says with absolute agreement, "I will."

"You did well, pet. I think you've earned a reward. For your loyalty, I think I can spare an apple from one of the trees in my garden. As I recall, they're your favorite."

"Yes, mistress."

Carolina sounds so strange. It's like hope mingled with defeat as she bends to the will of the Dark Fae female. It's the promise of the apple that does it, I figure. She didn't have to beg for a bite—she just had to sell me out to get one.

Or did she?

"However..."

"Mistress?"

"Tut, tut, Carolina. I thought I instructed you to come alone."

A gasp, followed by a shaky response, "I... I did. I told my parents I was going outside to sit in the sun like you said for me to. I followed your guide to the garden. No one else was there."

"Is that so? I sense darkness contaminating my light. There, on the other side of that door. Prove it to me. Prove that you're still loyal to your mistress and, perhaps, I'll spare you this time."

Oh, *shit*.

There's not enough time for me to move.

The door swings open. I'm blinded by a flash even brighter than the white room I'm in. I turn to run, but my legs don't seem to be working right. The shag carpet has turned to tendrils around my feet, keeping me in place. Panic rushes through me. I yank, desperate to get away from the truth of what's on the other side of that door.

And that's when I feel myself begin to fall.

"Excuse me... Miss? Um. Hello?"

My eyes fly open.

A scream's halfway to my lips when I recognize the round-faced boy who took my ticket at the door. He has one hand outstretched as if he was about to shake me awake. There's still enough space between us that my phobia isn't triggered.

If he had touched me, no way I could have kept that scream back.

His other hand clutches a flashlight that's angled down on the tacky, multi-colored carpet. Faint, dark spots dance in front of my vision. He must have shone it on my face right before I came out of that strange dream.

At least that explains the flash.

Now if only I could come up with a rational reason behind the strange conversation I created between Carolina and her mistress…

The usher's face is young and worried. He clears his throat when I still haven't made any move to get out of my seat. "I'm so sorry, miss. I didn't mean to startle you, but the last movie has ended. It's time to close up the theater."

"What?"

I swivel in the chair, looking over at the massive screen in front of me. The house lights are on; it's just a big, white rectangle waiting for its next projection. No movie. I glance around. There's nobody left in the theater except for me and the usher. "Oh, jeez. I didn't realize I was sleeping for so long. Shit. I'm sorry."

"It's okay." He hesitates, and then, since I'm still sitting with my ass firmly planted in the seat, he adds, "Do you need me to show you the way out?"

I shake my head. I can't explain my weirdo behavior, though I should probably apologize for it again. It's not his fault that I'm so freaking out of it.

I woke up so suddenly, it seems like part of me is still back in that strange place. I remember everything about where I was: the ornately carved banister, the plush rug, the crystalline doorknobs. It takes more energy than I have to pull myself back.

How much time did I lose? I remember when the first movie began, but not much more than that. Since I'm still inside of the movie theater, I don't think I actually went anywhere. Then again, how many times did I shade-walk to the cemetery while I was at the asylum only to go back as soon as the sun came up?

Nine said it was because I felt safe, that even as I was sleeping, my body knew where to take me. Is that what happened here?

I don't know. Considering what I overheard, I don't think I want to stick around and figure it out.

The usher is hovering near me. With a half-smile I don't mean, I push up out of the movie seat and slip past him, careful not to brush against him as he turns to follow me out of the theater.

The manager is waiting at the front entrance to let me out before they lock up for the night. I offer her a mumbled apology, keeping my head down as I hurry out through the glass doors.

I can't believe I did that. Sure, I didn't get any sleep last night after Nine left, but that was just reckless. Drifting off like that? Crap. The whole point of ducking into the movie theater was so that I got out of the Wilkes House while still staying inconspicuous.

Yeah. Fail.

No way that manager or the usher is going to forget the strange chick in the baseball cap and the gloves who kept them from closing up. Wonderful. All I need now is for the news to run an update on my story and have one of them put two and two together.

Tugging my baseball cap low, I tuck my sunglasses in my

hoodie pocket—wearing them this late at night is a dead giveaway that I'm up to no good—and start to book it down the empty street.

It's late. Cold, too. My poor hoodie and t-shirt aren't nearly enough to shield me from the way the temperature has dropped while I was inside the theater. I rub my arms, grit my teeth, and suck it up because, hey, it's not like it's going to be much warmer when I get back to my hide-out.

I go back to the Wilkes House because it's late and I haven't come up with a better plan. As soon as I sneak around the side of the house, checking that the for sale sign is still hidden among the bushes, I wonder if maybe I'm better off finding a secluded alley to sleep in.

The back door is open.

I don't mean just unlocked. Without a key, I couldn't lock it behind me when I slipped out this morning. But I know for damn sure that I closed it. And now? As I climb the porch, I'm stunned to find the door thrown inward.

That's... that's not good.

You know what's also pretty bad? How, without even hesitating, I march right up the porch stairs.

Once I get to the top, I tiptoe into the kitchen, careful not to make any noise at all. Just in case.

The kitchen is clear. The bathroom, too. Taking a deep breath, wishing I had a weapon and realizing too late that I don't, I creep into the living room, my attention immediately zeroing in on the figure lying sprawled out on the floor.

I squint, then scowl.

It's Carolina.

She's lying on her side, sleeping on the floor, her long dark hair acting like a pillow instead of the one tossed in the far corner. I don't know what she's doing here. She told me last night that she wouldn't be back for a couple of days.

Then again, she also told me that she was on my side.

Some human lie detector I am. I've got no doubt she went to the lake house otherwise my Riley senses would've been going off like crazy. She probably even expected to be gone that long.

Guess plotting with a Dark Fae really changes your vacation plans.

I'm feeling bitter at how she played me, coupled with annoyance at how frightened I was when I saw the back door open. Carolina should've known better than to leave it thrown open wide like that.

Was she trying to get us caught?

She doesn't stir as I stomp into the room, purposely walking with a heavier step just to be petty. She continues to lie there on the floor, sleeping peacefully, as if she wasn't recently plotting on how to trick me into eating more faerie food.

The moonlight streaming in through the window highlights a scrap of white on the floor. I pause, looking down at it. What...?

Huh.

A piece of paper lies a few inches away from her outstretched hand. Without bothering to stop and read it, I reach down, pick it up, and shove it in my pocket. It's not important; if it's hers, I'm glad it's mine now. I can look at it later after I wake Lina up and rip her a new one for working with the Unseelie against me.

Her betrayal sucks. I would've liked to pretend that everything I heard was some kind of vivid dream, but after dealing with the fae lately, I know better.

And I can't *wait* to hear how she's going to explain it.

"Carolina? Hey. It's me. Wake up."

She doesn't answer.

I crouch down next to her, grabbing her by her arm so that I can shake her awake.

I know in an instant that something's wrong. She's too cold. Too stiff.

She isn't sleeping.

I swallow the bubble of terror in my throat. One more shake, and another whisper. "Lina?"

Why the hell am I whispering? She can't hear me.

At that realization, it feels like someone with a giant hand reached in through the window, picked me up like a toy, and *squeezed*. My breaths are a rattle, short and shaky. I can't swallow. My eyes are moving rapidly, dancing all over the gloomy room, desperate to land on something, anything except for my dead friend.

Because she's dead.

Carolina is dead.

Deaddead*dead*.

No matter what I try, I can't look away. I'm drawn to her body like a moth to a flame.

And I whimper.

This isn't panic. This is so many times worse than the irrational fears I've lived with for so long. This is something else entirely. I've only known it once before, when the firemen cleared the remains of this old house and I finally understood—without any doubt or alternate explanations—that Madelaine was really, truly dead.

This is what happens when the shock starts to subside.

This is grief.

And, as I stare down at Carolina, I have to wonder why it's hitting me so hard like this.

It's because I let my guard down. Because I let someone in. I only knew Carolina—or *thought* I knew her—for a handful of days. How much of it was a lie? Based on what I overheard earlier, it could be most of it. It could be all of it.

She was going to betray me. She was going to sell me out to the Fae Queen if it meant she could have back her freedom.

I can't even blame her. If it came down to it, if throwing Carolina to the fae meant I'd never have to deal with any part of Faerie again, I might have done the same.

And now she's dead.

Oh my god.

She's *dead*.

CHAPTER 16

I sense Nine the second he comes up behind me.

I don't have any idea how long he's been here, if he stumbled on Carolina before me, or if he just so happened to slip in through the portal some time before I returned to the Wilkes House, or if it's just bad luck on his part that he's returned to find me mourning my friend.

He said he would come back. I see the black bag he's clutching in his slender fingers. The rowan he promised? I've got the t-shirt under my hoodie turned inside out like he told me to, but with my friend lying on the floor in front of me, it all seems a little too little too late.

He reaches inside of his duster, disappearing the bag in an instant. He probably realizes it, too.

"You know this human girl?"

I can't find my voice. I nod.

"Did you know that she was touched by a very strong Dark Fae?"

Another nod.

Nine crouches low. His dark coat fans out behind him as he bows his head. His raven-black hair covers him like a curtain, hiding his face and Carolina's peaceful expression. The way his head is angled, it almost looks like he's giving her a kiss.

A sob bubbles up from my throat. Or maybe it's a laugh.

The world's most twisted version of Snow White. That's what this is. Only Carolina was poisoned from her first bite of apple; it just took almost a year for her to finally succumb to it. And Nine? He might have been my Prince Charming once, but what can he do for Lina now?

Unless—

"Touch her," I tell him. My voice is thick. I swallow roughly, then try again. "Nine, please."

He doesn't say no. Instead, he asks softly, "She's eaten food from Faerie, hasn't she?"

He slowly straightens. Since that's the opposite of what I want him to do, I can't handle it. I start to beg. Anything to save Carolina. "It's okay, right? You saved me when I did. All it took was a touch. Touch her. She won't care if it fixes her."

"I'd do anything you asked of me. But this is beyond even my type of magic." He backs away. "Say your goodbyes, Riley. I'll take care of her after you do."

"Take care of her now! She's not dead... she *can't* be. She was just fine. She was supposed to have another apple. Her mistress promised her another apple." Carolina's stubborn expression, the way she told me fiercely that she would never beg for a bite. Is that what happened? "Damn it, Lina, why didn't you eat the fucking apple?"

"It was too late. Even if she did, and she might have, it would've only prolonged the inevitable," he murmurs. "The brand's too deep. She was charmed for too long."

"She wasn't charmed. She was cursed." I whirl on Nine. I

want to lash out, to hit him, to make him hurt like I'm hurting. I don't. I can't. I'm right back where I began. Just the idea of touching anyone else—even Nine—has me ready to crawl out of my skin. Instead, I point a leather finger at him. "You could have touched her. You could have saved her."

"It wouldn't have helped. You know that, Riley. When the shock fades, when you get past your grief, you'll accept that."

"She was my friend," I whisper. I don't care what she did or what she planned, she was still my friend. "She didn't deserve this."

"I'm sorry. I am. But we're fae. It's part of our nature."

I goggle up at him. I'm not as furious as I was. More… stunned.

"Are you justifying what that other Dark Fae did?"

"Shadow—"

My voice is nasally. Dull. I swallow my tears, then croak out a warning. "Don't call me that."

"Riley. Listen to me. Sometimes this happens. The girl made her choice when she made her bargain. No one eats faerie food by accident."

"I did."

"No. You didn't," Nine argues. "You were tricked. You'd been to the garden where that peach grew, your fae side recognized it for what it was, and you ate it. If you were human, you never would've been so tempted—and I never would've been able to reverse the curse. I'm sorry. This human was as good as dead from the minute she took her first bite. It's why my kind risk coming to the world of iron. Humans are susceptible to magic because it doesn't exist in this world. Not really. A touch, a bite… the rush of power is worth every risk. Unfortunately, the fae think of humans as playthings. Nothing more. And, sometimes, some of us can be a little… rough."

Rough. Right.

Rough, like snapping the brittle neck of a sixteen-year-old girl like it was a twig.

Rough, like using food to control a twenty-year-old woman, and allowing her to waste away to nothing.

Rough, like sending soldiers after a young mother and her fae mate because a prophecy had your panties in a twist.

Nine might be cold, he might be guarded, but at least he'd never been rough. That caress across my cheek that night in the sewer was as loving a touch as I've ever had. And he's fae.

Is that *his* nature?

Thinking about how his touch made me feel as he drew the peach's poison out is so much better than focusing on what happened to Carolina. What if—

I shove up my sleeve and hold my arm out. "Touch me."

"You don't know what you're saying—"

Oh, yes. Yes, I do. "I won't command you, but I'm asking you to. Do it. Touch me. I don't care how you do it, just take the pain away. Glamour doesn't work, okay, but what about compelling me? If you're all I care about, then it won't matter that someone else I cared about is dead."

My mom.

Madelaine.

Carolina.

They're all gone. And I'm still standing here.

Nine's not. Not anymore. As if he expects me to lunge toward him and grab his hand in mine, he backs away until a couple of feet separate us.

And then he tells me no.

"If I could, I would. I'd do anything for you, but I can't do that. Don't ask it of me."

"Why not?"

He doesn't say a word. And it's not because he doesn't know the answer, either. He can't lie and, if he replies, he'd have to tell me the truth.

"Seriously? You want me to suffer? I thought you cared about me."

"More than you know," he says, then adds in a harsh aside, "and more than I should."

I don't believe that. "If you won't do it, I could try calling for Rys."

He knows my true name. If I told him he could touch me, glamour me, compel me, the Light Fae would jump at the offer in a heartbeat. Too bad I'm bluffing. I'll give permission to Nine, or I'll give it no one.

But my Shadow Man doesn't know that.

"You don't have his name."

"Do you?"

Again, Nine clenches his jaw, keeping his mouth shut.

I'll take that as a yes.

"Use it. Call him for me. Arrange for him to come in the morning, I don't care. I just need someone who will make this all go away."

"So instead of letting me help you in the ways that I can, you'd ask me to give you up to Rys? After all these years of paying my debt, of protecting the Shadow, of waiting for my—" He cuts off his words with a furious shake of his head. His hair whips around a face that is suddenly beautiful and terrible. "I think you want *me* to suffer."

"Hey! Don't throw my words back at me."

"What do you want from me, Riley? What else do you expect me to do?"

"Honestly? I just want you to go back to Faerie, if that's where you came from. A Dark Fae is responsible for this, no matter how you choose to look at it, Nine. It might not have been you, but that doesn't really change anything about how I feel right now. I... I don't want you near me. Please go."

Nine reacts as if I've swung at him. He recoils just enough that I notice, his lips pursed with such force, his cheekbones jut from his face. It's the most emotion I've seen from him tonight.

You know what? *Good*. I want him to hurt, too.

It's gone in an instant as the powerful fae regains control. Just like he used to when I was a child and he wanted to slap back at me, he pulls himself to his daunting height, staring down his nose at me.

Right now, with Carolina's body a few feet away from me, I just don't give a shit.

He looms in front of me. "What? No command this time?"

I shake my head.

"So you'd leave me the choice, then, eh, Shadow? You just expect me to leave you alone when you're like this? I think that's worse than involving the Blessed One."

That's exactly what I expect. "What does it matter anyway? That's never stopped you before."

I hear a whistle. Only after it dies away do I get that that was Nine sucking in a sharp, furious breath.

Did I offend him?

Too damn bad.

He's fae. Isn't that what he just said? It's in their nature not to be bothered by what happened to some pesky human. So I've got some Seelie blood in me. As far as I'm concerned, it means I've got pointy ears. That's it. And being this close to death—finding my friend like this—is too much for me.

Nine was right. This *is* shock. The numb feeling that's overtaken how angry and upset and scared I was right after I found Carolina? The absolute disbelief that this can't be happening?

It's not going to last. It didn't with Madelaine, though that's probably because I had to deal with the third-degree burns on my hands at the same time. I don't want Nine to be watching me when the shock disappears and it hits me—really hits me—that Carolina is gone.

"Just go," I say wearily. "Leave me alone. Leave me and Lina alone."

His silver eyes flash a warning. "I won't always do what you tell me to. You've commanded me once before. Will you be able to again?"

Don't know. But, if he doesn't get the hell out of here now, we're gonna find out.

"You don't know what you're asking of me."

He throws that in my face so often. It's true, too. I don't know, and that's because, no matter what, *he won't freaking tell me*. You think he'd be jumping at the chance to slip away after the way I treated him last night. Sure, it's a total one-eighty, and maybe he really was right and his touch finally wore off.

Suddenly, I'm glad that he refused to touch me again. If I fall even deeper under his spell, I might forget how dangerous the fae really are.

"I'm asking you to give me space. Can you do that?"

"I'll go, on one condition. Fair enough?"

My laugh is hollow. "Are you trying to bargain with me, Nine?"

"If you like. It isn't much I require. Do you still have my gift?"

Is he serious? "The scarf or whatever it is?" When he nods, I jerk one shoulder. "Yeah. Somewhere."

"Keep it close. If you leave this house, bring it with you. Let me believe that, even if I can't be with you, something that I've given you is. Will you do that for me, Shadow?"

"Fine. Sure. I'll do it."

The words are barely out of my mouth when I feel a whoosh of wind blow the hair away from my face.

He's gone.

I HAVE TO VISIT MADELAINE.

It's almost a compulsion. Since there's no way in hell I could stay at the house with Carolina's body still in it, I had no choice but to get out. I don't bother with the backpack because I don't want it to slow me down. Stuffing Carolina's cash in one pocket, Nine's silky scarf-thing in the other, I make sure I'm still wearing my necklace. Then, as I'm careful to avoid looking at the shadows that are creeping in, covering every inch of the place, hiding Carolina as I finish packing, I dash through the house and run out of the back door.

I leave the front door wide open. It's all I can do. Burning down the house like Rys did... not gonna lie, the thought did run through my mind. It would be so easy, too. Just knock the lantern in the bathroom over and let the enchanted fire take care of this mess for me.

I couldn't do it, though. I... I *couldn't*. Carolina might have been working against me all along, she might've been ready to betray me before her fae betrayed *her*, but she didn't deserve what happened to her.

She didn't deserve to die.

Instead, I jerk both windows up as high as they go, then fling the front door open. There. I won't leave Carolina in the dark, abandoned house forever. Someone will find her—I just need them to find her *after* I'm gone.

As soon as I've gone a few blocks over, I tug my hands. I'm

not sure if the shadows lingered after I left. If they did, I just erased them. As soon as someone goes to check out the open door and cracked windows, they'll find Carolina and, hopefully, get her back to her parents.

It's the best I could do for her.

After that, I run. I'm not even trying to act natural. I've got to get far away from that house and I just don't care how I do it. If anyone figures out that I was the one hanging around Carolina recently, I know what that will mean.

I go from being Riley Thorne, escaped Black Pine patient, to Riley Thorne, murder suspect.

Not again.

I can't go through that again.

I almost got manslaughter after Rys killed Madelaine. I only managed to avoid that because the courts decided I needed to be put in a mental health facility. This time?

Can't risk it.

I'm out of shape. Have I ever been in shape? Probably not. I push myself, though, despite the way each breath is a struggle, the stitch in my side so sharp, it's like someone is stabbing me repeatedly. I stick to the back roads, the woods, any place that provides cover under the weak moonlight. The ground is uneven. I run into a shadowed bush, the sharp branch tearing through my sock, leaving a trickle of warm blood running down my ankle, staining the once-white fabric.

It's all worth it, though, when I make it back to the Acorn Falls cemetery. I bitterly regret not taking the time to learn how to shade-walk since I could've arrived in seconds instead of hours, but I let it go when I force my trembling body through the tiny gap left between the locked gates.

It scrapes the crap out of my belly, my upper arms, and my thighs, but I squeeze through. I'm actually kind of glad to see that the cemetery is locked up. That means, for the rest of the night at least, I won't have to worry about the groundskeeper.

Rubbing at the pain in my side, I hobble to the west side of the cemetery, only feeling like I've outrun Carolina's ghost when I see Madelaine's stone angel looming in front of me.

Up close, the grave looks slightly disturbed. New flowers line the front of the stone angel that marks my sister's final resting place. I recognize them. They're daisies. Definitely out of season for this time of year, but they'd been Madelaine's favorites.

I don't know what the date is. When I met Carolina outside of the Wilkes House—which was less than a week ago, not counting any time I might have lost since then shade-walking to Faerie—she told me it was October.

As I move closer, getting a better look, I almost trip over something long and skinny that's been left in the grass that borders the edge of my sister's plot. It's... it's a shovel. Not a huge one, maybe about two feet long with a metal spade attached at the bottom, I'm betting someone brought it to plant Madelaine's flowers and accidentally left it behind.

Just in case, I leave it where it is. I've got no use for it.

Instead, yanking my sleeves over my gloves, trying to preserve any warmth I worked up during my frantic flight, I curl up at the base of Madelaine's stone angel and let loose the tears I've been holding back.

I couldn't save Madelaine.

Couldn't save Carolina, either.

According to the Shadow Prophecy, the Shadow is supposed to save Faerie from the cruel Fae Queen.

What kind of fucking terrible savior am I if I can't even save the people that matter?

CHAPTER 17

When I wake up to someone talking to me, my first thought is that it's the groundskeeper.

Then I hear my name.

Whispered in such a lyrical, musical voice, the male voice calls my name and, though I'd give anything I have to fall back into blissful unconsciousness, I warily open my eyes.

The sun slaps me awake. Holy crap, it's *bright*. It's the first thing I notice. I didn't mean to fall asleep, though I guess between my shock, my grief, and my exhaustion… it was inevitable.

So, I have to admit, is this.

Rys.

He's leaning against the right wing of Madelaine's stone angel, his hip cocked, his lips parted just enough to reveal his blindingly white teeth. Gotta give the Light Fae credit. It's a perfect pose, highlighting his gloriousness—and I'm willing to bet all the cash in my pocket that he's done it on purpose.

Even the bright sun breaking through from behind him pales in comparison to his golden glow.

Where are my sunglasses? I had them when I sat beside Madelaine's grave. They must have fallen off when I slumped over. Where— ah. Without taking my squinted gaze off of the threat in front of me, I pat the grass with my palm until I find them.

I slip the shades on. They don't do a damn thing to dull his shine.

"Ah, Riley. I've been wondering how long before you came back here. That's something else I adore about you. You're so... *predictable*."

Predictable. I think about yanking my shoe off and throwing it at him. I never did get the chance to whack him with my slipper the last time we met, and I'm sure he'd change his tune about me being predictable after that.

No. It's not worth it.

"What do you want?" I push up off the ground, backing up so that he's not so close to me. "What are you doing here?"

"Clever girl. You finally figured out a way to erase the trace I left with my brand. I suppose my rival did it for you."

Rival? Oh, hell, no.

He called Nine that once before, too. It bothered me then because I couldn't even imagine wanting anything to do with either fae; I was still angry with Nine, and I'd rather dive head-first into Faerie and take my chances with the Fae Queen than let Rys touch me again.

It bothers me now because, even after the way I left Nine— again—my feelings for him haven't changed. And because the only reason I don't turn and run away screaming whenever Rys pops in for one of these chats is because he's using glamour to charm me into believing he's harmless.

Glamour... Nine warned me about this. I swore when he confessed the truth about the glamour that I wouldn't allow it to affect me. Sure, the last time Nine warned me against his race's magic, I developed a phobia of letting anyone touch me.

This is different.

Pushing the sunglasses to the top of my head, I squint over at Rys.

He's obviously not expecting that reaction and, unsurprisingly, he's immediately suspicious.

His playful grin vanishes. "What are you doing?"

My mom could see through glamour. Carolina taught herself to do it, too.

If they could, so can I.

It's tough to look at him so directly. No wonder I let myself be charmed for so long—it hurts too much to stare at his brightness, as if I'm staring at the sun. The shades might be able to help, but I don't want anything to come between me and finally looking past the layer of magic that Rys has cloaked himself in.

It works.

Holy shit.

It *works*.

It's like I've been looking at him through a glass of water. Suddenly, the glass shifts, the water moves, and I can see him clear as day.

I gasp.

At first glance, he's still the same Rys. Bronze skin, golden hair, and vivid eyes.

There's more to it, though.

Oh my—

Yeah, so I don't know how I ever thought he was angelically beautiful. The strength of the glamour, I guess, because, in the light of day, he looks as alien as I always knew he was. His slender, lithe body looks stretched; it's way too thin and I begin to wonder how it's supporting his oversized head. His shine has dimmed, his long hair looking lanky and pale—more like straw than spun gold—as he watches me suspiciously.

His eyes are the same. Burning bright with a frightening intensity, Rys's attention is focused unblinkingly on me. He leans forward, almost like he's prepared to lunge toward me.

His casual air? Gone. The charm that seemed to ooze off of him? Nope. With the haze of the glamour dampened, it's like I can finally see what's been in front of me all along.

I couldn't understand why, whenever Rys popped up, I wasn't as afraid as I should've been. Carolina blamed it on the fae's magic, and even Nine admitted the fae's glamour could lull me into a false sense of security if I let it.

Panic starts to rise up in me. I choke on a breath, desperately trying to force the discomfort and fear back. I cling to the belief that, so long as Rys is still convinced that he loves me, he won't hurt me.

I must make sure I don't give him any excuse to.

Step one: force the panic back. It's easy enough because I keep telling myself that Rys won't touch me. I won't give him permission, and he's already proved that he won't cause himself pain while he's sure that I'll come around eventually.

I promise myself a monster freakout once I get away from Rys.

Now I just have to get away.

He knows. He knows something's up and, without any remorse, the Light Fae plays the only card he has.

"Zella, listen to me."

I listen. I can't do anything else. Can't run, can't flinch, can't scream. He's powerful enough that his plea is a command.

So I listen.

"Nine can't save you," he tells me. "The Cursed Ones have earned their title. Come with me. I'm not the monster you think I am. All I've ever wanted was to love you. Forget the prophecy. Forget Nine. He'll only be your downfall. But I? I'll be your savior. And all it will cost you is—"

He takes a pause for dramatic effect. In that second, he stops talking so I can stop listening.

Angry and scared, I grit out the word through clenched teeth for him:

"Everything."

My stomach tightens and, in a flash, I remember how it's possible he tried to lure me to Faerie with the use of the enchanted fruit. Nine can't save me? If he hadn't used his touch magic to get rid of the curse, I might have ended up just like Carolina.

And that makes me *furious*.

"Love me? Is that what you call trying to trick me into eating the cursed peach so that I'd have to go to Faerie and rely on you to survive? That's not love. That's manipulation."

"Peach?" echoes Rys, a curious inflection in his lilting voice. "I never offered you a peach."

He's not lying, but that doesn't mean he's telling the truth. He can twist it, tweak it, mold it into something new—but I refuse to buy into it.

"You didn't have to. Leaving it in the sewer after you put me to sleep... you had to know I'd eat it."

I don't know what it is that I said, whether my accusation stings, or he's just pissed that he got caught. Rys stares across the grave at me, his golden eyes unblinking as he drinks me in. Something's different. Something changes.

He frowns, then says, "I gave you no peach."

I hate that I can feel the ring of truth in his words.

"Stop it—"

He raises his hand. "I swear it to Oberon. I'd never hurt you, Riley. I've told you that before. But the trickery… that changes things."

No. It doesn't.

"Zel—" he begins.

"Don't call me that," I snap back. It just bursts out of me. I don't even know what he was going to say next, but I don't want to hear it. I don't want to be forced to listen, either. Blood pounds in my ears. With that racket, I'm not even sure I *could*. "If you care about me so much, stop using that word against me."

"It's not a word, my love. It's your name."

So what? I figured that out ages ago. After everything Nine told me when it came to him giving me his name, it made too much sense. Considering the way that Rys was able to command and compel me by calling me Zella, it had to be my name.

Well, my fae name. My true name.

It's not my *name*.

"I'm Riley. Not Zella. Not Shadow. *Riley*. Use it."

Rys regards me for a moment, a sly grin forming on his pouty lips again. Whatever passed between us before over the peach, it's gone. As his eyes grow impossibly brighter, I know I made a mistake somewhere.

But where?

He waves his hand downward, a slash through the air. "Done."

I sag as he lifts the compulsion.

That was way too easy, I think. I'm still waiting for him to point out where I went wrong; if there's one thing I know, it's that the fae love to gloat.

And then Rys starts talking again. I'm not compelled to listen, though I can't block out what he says next.

"But, since I've done something for you, you must do something for me. It's only fair."

More alarm bells go off. Fair? Just like I've learned that the fae don't do favors, there's no such thing as fair. If Rys is throwing that word around, trying to tempt me into a devil's bargain, I'm screwed.

He's holding off on commanding me with my name because he wants me to give in on my own. The fae like to know that they have the power—they like to *win*.

It's not going to last. I know it won't.

I have to get out of here.

I back away quickly, going so fast that I nearly land on my ass when I stumble over something in the grass. I throw out my hand, managing to regain my balance before Rys has even risen from his pose against Madelaine's gravestone.

"I don't want much. Just a trifle, really."

"Yeah? What do you want from me?"

"I'd tell you forever, but that would only send you running back to my rival. For now, how about a dance?"

Dance with me.

Stay with me.

I'll always come for you.

He's not letting this go. He's not letting *me* go.

"Give me what I desire and I'll never have need to command you. One touch, Riley." His perfect nose wrinkles. "It doesn't have the same ring as your true name, but if it pleases you, my love, I'll use it. Now, come to me. I've waited long enough."

His hand twists. His hands, with those too-long bronze-colored fingers, they're twitching as if he wants nothing more than to reach out and grab my throat. Gulping, I force myself to meet his stare again.

My stomach drops to the dirt.

I know that look. That expression. How many guys looked at me just the same way when I was younger? The older boys in the group homes while I was still in the system, and the rich kids at Acorn Falls who thought I might be a good time when I first moved to the Everetts.

That's lust splayed across his face, a desire to get his hands on me, to take everything I have to offer—and then some.

He wants a touch. He wants my strength. My power. My soul.

My life.

He wants me to be his mate.

And he won't take no for an answer.

He hasn't mentioned how far he's willing to go to get me to agree to being with him. Not this time, at least. The Light Fae doesn't have to. Without his glamour tricking me into thinking that this mythical, ruthless killer is charming and kind, I remember who exactly Rys is.

The golden fae—the *monster* I've spent so long running from—who killed my sister because she was in his way and, well, because he could. However he's tried to make amends for something that would never have seemed important to a fae, it doesn't really matter.

Not to me.

Rys is no better than the Dark Fae that let Carolina die.

I shudder. Can't help it. Thinking about Lina hurts too damn much. It's too fresh. I can't stop remembering the way she was crumpled on the floor, her dark hair fanned out over her face like a mockery of a shroud. Even the way her necklace spilled on top of a chest that was horribly still.

Her nail—

Iron.

Hope slams into me as an idea begins to form. Before he can move away from the grave marker, I reach inside of my sweatshirt, yanking out the nail knotted on the middle of the leather string around my neck.

Rys laughs. Instead of that light, lyrical laugh that floats on the air, this one grates on my nerves like fingernails down a chalkboard. I wince, but I refuse to drop the string. Instead, as if it's a crucifix and Rys a demon, I wield it in front of me, warning him back.

The laugh should have been my first clue that it wasn't working like I hoped.

Rys narrows his brilliant gaze at me. A feral grin splits his lips. "Oh, how quaint. So someone has clued you in to the power of iron?" Laughing to himself, he takes another step toward me. "Pity that small trinket isn't strong enough to stop me from taking what's mine. I grow tired of playing nice. I won't command you. But it's time for us to go."

He reaches out for me.

I almost lose my damn mind.

"You can't touch me," I say, the sudden wave of panic slamming into me, making my voice low and rough. I forget all about the iron nail as I fold my fists, drawing them up inside the sleeves of my hoodie. "You'll burn your hands if you do."

"And won't that be fair? After all, I did do the same to you once. It was necessary to erase Nine's mark. Once I claimed you as mine, I couldn't let my *ffrindau* wear a Cursed One's brand. I never thought it would damage you as much as it did, though. That would be your human side, I suppose. Anyway, all that to say that I've thought it over. I caused you to burn once and didn't even claim my mate. This time, if it means you're mine,

Riley, I'll gladly feel the fire." His lips curve, the points of his teeth almost as bad as the points on his ears. "I'll heal, but the pain will be worth it for all the pleasure we'll share, my love."

He's serious. He means it.

He's going to touch me.

"Don't do that," I plead. It's barely a whisper. I hate how close I am to begging, but Rys is advancing and it's too late to run, and his fingers are too, too close. "I'll hate you forever. Just… go away. Leave me alone. You love me? Prove it. Don't steal a touch."

"You've left me no choice. Don't fret, though. It will be fine and, in enough time, I know you'll forgive me. After all, a long life shared with me is far better than the alternative."

I gulp, my mind racing, trying to come up with some way to get away from him before I *can't*. Carolina's nail was a joke. He's still gliding closer and it's like my sneakers are rooted to the grave soil.

"What's the alternative?"

"Oh, Riley. If the queen stops toying with you, you won't even have a life at all."

Why did I ask him that? I had to know what his answer would be.

And now I have to add that delightful thought to the mess that's my poor brain right now.

Focus, Riley. You're only gonna get one shot at this.

This time, when I stumble, it's completely on purpose. I fall forward, cushioning my knees by landing on one and bending the other, my hands grabbing for the grass as I topple over.

My heart is thumping wildly. There's a lump in my throat that I can't get past. I want to hurl, but I'm already committed to this reckless, stupid plan. Closing my fingers around the handle, I ready myself.

Rys is leaning down, his hand outstretched. It looks like he's just trying to offer to help me up.

No, thanks.

"I think," I begin, tightening my grasp, ready to spring up. "I think I'll take my chances."

Know what? The Light Fae has never given me enough credit. Because of my human side, Rys has always underestimated me. That was his mistake. Just like the time in the mausoleum, I have to use whatever advantage I can get.

Right now, this heavy shovel is all I've got.

He's not expecting me to lunge toward him. As I spring upward, dragging the shovel with me before swinging the metal blade up at his head, I pray to any god that can hear me that the blade is made of iron.

I'm not really aiming. A heady mixture of panic, fear, anger, and sadness guide my swing. At that second, Rys is the golden fae who killed Madelaine, the Dark Fae who tricked Carolina into starving to death, the faceless Fae Queen whose paranoia about a ridiculous prophecy ruined my fucking life.

Okay. So I'm not so strong and the shovel is way heavier than I thought it would be. Except for the way the very edge slices right across the height of his left cheek, I barely make contact at all.

From the howl Rys lets out, you would've thought I bashed his head in.

His hands fly to his face. I've never heard such a terrible scream in my life, not even the high-pitched shriek of terror I let out the second Madelaine's neck snapped and her body dropped to the floor. Rys's howl... it's unearthly and ear-splitting and it stuns me right to my center.

I drop to the ground. The shovel clatters by my side as I raise my hands, clamping my gloves over my ears.

It doesn't help.

It's at that moment that I know I'm dead. Believing that Rys would never retaliate against me might have been *my* mistake.

A fatal one, too.

Because Rys sure isn't and, despite the way he professed his love for me, he's still an unpredictable fae male and I seriously doubt he's going to let me live after that attack.

Nothing happens right away. As quickly as it started, Rys's unholy screams stop. Or maybe that's the leather muffling my hearing. I'm not about to drop my hands and check, though I do jerk my head up. I'm scared—absolutely terrified—but I'm also stubborn as hell.

He wants to kill me? He's going to have to look me in the eye as he does it.

Only something's not right. I... I can't see his face. I can't see much of anything at all.

Rys usually has a golden shine. He's a Light Fae. I've gotten used to it. This, though? Something totally different. In the middle of Madelaine's plot, he's burning up like the sun, bright and blinding. As I stare up in shock, a blazing heat blasts from him, shooting out in all directions.

Flames lick at the grass, the dirt, the graves surrounding us. The source of the fire? Rys.

Oh, man.

Rys has transformed himself into a *fireball*.

Yup. I was right.

I'm toast.

Beads of sweat erupt all over my body. The stink of burning hair fills the air. My mouth dries up, my eyes stinging from the heat. It's like I've climbed into an oven. I start to choke, to gag, and I just manage to yank the collar of my hoodie up so that I can breathe a few seconds longer.

This is it, I realize. This is the end. Rys is going to burn me to death using his enchanted fire. No quick death for me.

Sucks, but I probably didn't deserve one.

Closing my eyes, I wait for the all-consuming pain.

It, uh, it never comes.

Just when I expected my skin to start blistering or for me to pass out from holding my breath, a brisk wind blows past. Or maybe it's not a wind that's pushing through the fire, but the sudden absence of the hot air that makes it seem so much cooler.

What the—

Wiping my eyes with the back of my sleeve, I wait until they're not stinging any longer before I crack them open slowly, afraid of what I'm going to see.

The heat is gone because the *fire* is gone.

Rys, too.

Not gonna question it. No more Light Fae looming over me, a murderous glare twisting his once-perfect features? Yeah. That's my cue to get the hell out of here while I still can.

I stand up. My legs are shaky as I rise. Too bad. I have to get out of here. It's too much to hope that I imagined the way Rys dissolved into flames like that. And, now that he's left me here on my own, I've got no one else to blame for the scorched grass and piles of ash.

So, yeah. Definitely didn't imagine it.

Adrenaline starts pumping through my veins; it's overwhelming, but it's not panic, so I'll take it. The fight or flight reflex is in charge right now. My limbs feel free and light, instead of every step being a chore. Okay. I can do this. If I'm careful, I can get the hell out of the cemetery before anyone figures out that I've been to visit Madelaine.

I don't know what makes me look back one last time before I

book it— but I do, and then I stare. I can't believe what I'm seeing.

No—

I don't *want* to believe it.

There's at least a ten foot radius of damaged ground: flowers reduced to ash, charred grass, black dirt. It's all dead except for one perfect circle of untouched green grass that survived the flames. I see the remains of the shovel: the handle unscathed on the inside of the circle, the blade a fiery shade of red.

And I realize that the exact spot where I huddled on the ground is the only spot that is still alive.

Because I'm alive.

Because, despite being a murderous fae who had his face slashed with the sharp edge of a shovel, Rys kept his word and didn't hurt me.

Whoa.

CHAPTER 18

I hate myself for it, and I would never admit what I did to anyone else, but before I left the Wilkes House for the final time, I checked Carolina's pockets. I found some extra money that I shoved in my pocket with the scrap of paper she left behind, but no keys.

Probably a good thing, too, since I don't know how to drive. I would've figured it out, though.

Anything to get away from there as soon as possible.

That same disappointment coupled with the frantic need to escape is rushing through me as I sneak out of the back of the cemetery. Rys's fire had to have attracted someone's attention. Sure, maybe the old caretaker is off duty since it's the middle of the afternoon. This was prime visiting time. Someone had to have seen that.

A chain link fence surrounds the back half of the place. I have much better luck with this one. After landing with a solid *oof*, I start to run. It doesn't matter where to. I just have to get *away*.

As I put Madelaine's grave in my rearview, I realize that there's a reason why I don't know where I'm going. Just like when I finally left the sewer, it's not because I'm lost. I literally don't have anywhere to run to.

I can't go back to the Wilkes House.

The Acorn Falls Cemetery? Not a chance.

Black Pine? Only if I want to be sedated into a stupor. That would leave me easy pickings for the Fae Queen and whatever touched human she might still have placed inside of the asylum.

I've got to finally say goodbye to Acorn Falls. It's been months since my break-out and, while I doubt they're looking as intently for me, it would be super risky to stick around when someone might recognize me. With the chilly weather, my gloves and my hoodie are as much of a disguise as Carolina's baseball cap and sunglasses. It's still not worth the risk.

Before I go, I make a decision. It might be a stupid one, but I don't have much choice. I'm not going to get too far without something to eat and a shit ton of caffeine to keep me moving. I don't want to risk booking a hotel in town—and it's not like I have ID or a credit card, either, just a big wad of cash—so I resign myself to another restless night hiding out somewhere safe.

First, I'm going to head into the downtown area, pray no one places my face or my gloves, and try to get something to hold me over for a bit.

There are plenty of delis and cafes on the crowded main street. I have my pick of them, and decide that the one sandwiched between a make-your-own pottery place and the brick corner seems like a good spot. Shoving my hands in my hoodie pocket, I duck my head and dash across the open alleyway that separates one block from the next.

I'm forever on alert. Sure, it's been months and I doubt

anyone expects that I've been hiding out in Acorn Falls all this time. Even if I wasn't on the look-out for the cops, I'd still be glancing over my shoulder. I was taught from childhood that the fae could be anyone—or anywhere.

It wasn't so bad when I pretended they weren't real. Now that I've lost any hope that I can go back to being ignored by the fae, I'm just waiting for one of the Fae Queen's soldiers or guards to find me like they did to my poor parents.

Right as I'm passing the alley, I see a shadowy lump leaning up against the corner's edge. It looks like it might be a pile of garbage, especially because of the tattered rags and stained blanket that covers most of the mound. I give the pile a second look, though, because I've learned that you can't be too careful.

And that's when I see the eyes peering out of a dirty, soot-covered face.

It's a man. At least twenty years older than I am, with weathered skin, a tangled beard, and a long, crooked nose, he's huddled underneath a torn blanket, his chin tucked into his chest as he stares at the brick wall across from his spot.

His head swivels as I start to pass him by. I hope that he doesn't ask me for any money. I don't have much and, until I figure out my next step, the bundle I got from Carolina has to last.

I lower my gaze, feeling like a piece of trash myself as I pretend not to notice him. I don't even know what he's doing here. Acorn Falls is too well-off for the townspeople to allow bums and beggars hanging around their downtown—especially their idyllic main street. It gives me another reason to want to dash past him. I wouldn't be surprised if the cops haven't already been dispatched to move the guy along.

Just as I'm going past him, I hear something that has me stopping dead in my tracks.

"I wouldn't go in there if I were you."

If I had thought to wonder what his voice would sound like, I'd have expected a harsh growl. It's not. Kind of like the opposite actually. It's light and lyrical and, unsurprisingly, I'm immediately on guard.

It was also a whisper. I'm not really sure if he was talking to me or himself and, despite my instinct warning me to get out of there, I edge a few steps closer to him.

Once he knows he has my attention, his head turns, staring straight ahead again.

A sickly sweet smell clings to his tattered clothes. I recognize it. It might be the middle of the afternoon, but this guy has already had a few. I breathe through my nose, trying to get the scent of booze and sweat out of my nostrils as I lock eyes with the man.

He wasn't slurring. His eyes? Not only do they seem intelligent and clear, they're also an electric blue. No red in sight—or, I admit, because I'm suspicious and paranoid as hell, *gold*.

Not that that matters. That's glamour for you. It's not just a charm. It's the greatest disguise, the perfect camouflage for a dangerous predator. Unless you have the ability to see through it—like my mother—or develop the skill like Carolina had, glamour is another way for the fae to make humans into their playthings.

It can't be Nine. He already told me straight that, for some strange reason, I'm immune to his glamour.

Could this still be a setup, though?

Oh, yeah.

I mean, Rys dressed up as a homeless squatter in the middle of Acorn Falls? Why not? After what just happened in the cemetery, I wouldn't put it past him to regroup once he recovered, then do whatever he had to to make me pay for it.

And it's not like he's the only one I have to worry about coming after me, either.

"I'm sorry." I keep my tone even. Calm. Conversational. *No, I don't suspect that you're a Light Fae trying to trick me, why do you ask?* I cock my head and squint, trying in vain to find some sign that he's wearing a glamour like I did with Rys. "Did you say something to me?"

"That I did." He jerks his thumb behind him. It's unmistakably in the direction of the cafe I was heading for. "Wouldn't go in there if I were you. Try Charlie's on the corner of Main and Honeysuckle. Coffee's better. Clientele, too."

The fae are tricky. I've learned that the hard way.

Me?

I'm over it.

I lower my voice and, as bluntly as possible, I ask, "Rys? Is that you?"

"Reese? Am I supposed to be?"

I squint, peering closer myself. Either the way I saw through Rys's glamour earlier was a fluke or this guy is exactly what he appears to be: a dirty, dingy drunk slumped in the alleyway.

Huh. Guess not.

I shake my head. "Sorry. I thought you were someone else. Anyway, thanks for the tip, but I think I'm gonna see what this shop's got to offer. I need the caffeine."

He shrugs, hunched shoulders rising, then slumping under the weight of his tattered rags and dirty coat. "Suit yourself. Don't say I didn't warn you."

Not gonna lie. At that very second, their coffee could be straight up piss and I'd still buy a cup just so I could use the excuse to get away from this weirdo. Mumbling a thanks I don't mean, I shake the ends of my hoodie so that they're covering my gloves. A quick swipe up top to make sure that my stupid pointy ears are tucked away and I'm set.

Purposely hurrying past him, I approach the cafe and immediately reach for the metal door handle—before going still.

I don't pull on it just yet. Instead, I wait.

Ever since I've escaped the asylum, the old paranoia is back. It's not just the fae I'm running from. Humans might not be as dangerous as the faerie races, but I've learned to trust my gut. It's one of the only things keeping me from getting caught, getting trapped, and getting carted back to Black Pine. I know better than to ignore it.

So when my stomach goes tight? I pause. The little hairs on the back of my neck stand up straight as a chill shivers down my spine.

Something's not right.

Bowing my head, I let my sunglasses slide down my nose so that I can get a better peek inside of the coffee shop. I don't know why, and it's entirely possible the bum put the worry in my head, but it seems as if I'm sensing... not *danger*, not really... something wrong coming from inside the cozy cafe.

A second later, I whip the sunglasses off. Using the edge of my sleeve to rub roughly at my eyes, I press my nose against the glass. I squint in disbelief.

You've gotta be kidding me.

It's the shock of red hair that hits me first, so bright that I'd put it down to a bad dye job if I didn't know better. Then there are the gold-rimmed glasses that shield his knowing gaze. The wispy goatee is gone, leaving behind a chin even weaker than I remember.

I recognize him in an instant. Dr. freaking Gillespie, my psychologist from Black Pine, is standing just inside the cafe, talking to the tall Asian kid manning the counter. The doctor's stocky body is angled so that I get a full-on peek at his profile.

It's enough. I know that it's him.

And I'm pretty sure he didn't come all the way to Acorn Falls for an espresso.

He's got a manila folder with him, tucked under his arm. I watch as he pulls it out, flipping it open, and removing a sheet of paper from inside. The ink bled through the page enough that I can tell it's a black and white photo.

How much do you want to bet it's a picture of me?

I knew it. I freaking knew it. So what if it's October now? My gut told me that the Black Pine staff wouldn't let me get away so easily—and that was before Nine explained how he and Rys arranged it so that I was put in that facility because it was full of fae-touched humans.

I don't know how Dr. Gillespie is involved. He only came to take over the psychologist job about a week before Nine broke me out of the asylum. He was so weird, though.

And now he's here.

I let my hand fall away from the door handle. No chance I'm going in this cafe now. I can't risk Dr. Gillespie seeing me.

Too late.

Before I can back away from the door, I watch as he nods at the associate, then turns.

I curse, then throw my body to the side. My back collides with the brick siding, scraping the crap out of my left arm and my hip as I try desperately to avoid being seen. My heart jumps to my throat and, without glancing behind me to check if he's coming, I kind of awkwardly half-hop, half-jog a few steps away from the door.

Anything to escape *now*.

Running off again, hiding from the Black Pine doctor... that's the only thought racing through my mind as I put distance between me and the cafe. Gotta get away, can't let him see me. Someone might have found Carolina by now. How long before they put two and two together and realize I might know something about that?

No. *No.* Running is the only option I've got.

Except I can't run. Tearing down the street would only make me more memorable, make it easier for someone else to track me. I've spent way too long figuring out how to stay under the radar. The glasses hide my eyes, Carolina's baseball cap covers my distinctive pale hair and the fae ears I can't disguise.

Why didn't I dye my hair?

I should've freaking dyed my hair.

I hear the door jingle open behind me and I make a split decision. Instead of going straight, I veer left, taking the corner with an awkward turn so that I don't run right over the man huddled just inside.

Within seconds, I realize two things.

One? He's gone. The homeless man who whispered his prophetic warning about the cafe is gone. I don't even see a single scrap of soiled fabric lying on the asphalt to mark where he'd been huddled a few minutes before.

His mysterious disappearance isn't even the worst of it, either.

This alley was an open one. I would've sworn it. Most of the breaks in this part of the downtown lead from the main street to the back doors; it's how I avoided the cop last time, taking an open path blocked off by a fence. When I passed by the bearded man earlier, I thought I saw straight through to the other side.

Not any longer.

It's a dead end. I'm boxed in, brick walls on three sides, a narrow opening on the fourth. A stack of boxes is piled up about halfway down the stretch, with a gloomy darkness at the far end. No open path, though. No fence.

No hope.

Crap. As I race toward the stack of boxes, crouching down so that I'm somewhat hidden, I have to wonder: did I go the wrong way? Or run further and faster than I thought? Maybe. It honestly doesn't matter since, with Dr. Gillespie's heavy footsteps chasing behind me, I'm about to be caught.

"Riley?" I don't see him yet, but I sure hear him. Excitement colors his nasally tone. "Riley! Don't run. I want to help you."

Shit.

Shit, shit, *shit*.

There goes any hope that he was just leaving the cafe at the same time and he didn't see me.

Damn it!

Okay. I've only got one shot at getting out of this without having to face off against my old psychologist. There's nothing left for me to do. If I don't want to walk out of the alleyway and slam right into the doctor, there's only one way for me to go.

Staying as low as possible to hide, I take off again, bolting down the dark depths of the alley, heading right for the shadows that seem to be calling out to me. I squeeze myself up against the wall, twisting my body until I've made it as small as possible.

Fighting back the panic, I risk closing my eyes for a few seconds. Then, hoping that this actually works, I try to pull the shadows toward me.

Nine was right. Sometimes I have to forget about what's possible and what's not, and when it comes to the power inside of me, I have to just let it happen.

The shadows greet me like an old friend. They lick at my cheek, causing the ends of my pale hair to flutter and sway before they rise up from the asphalt, wrapping around my legs, my middle, my throat. It's just about instant. By the time Dr. Gillespie strolls deep into the alley, checking behind the boxes, searching the closed-off space for me, I'm completely covered.

He pauses when he's about ten feet away from my hiding place. I have this irrational urge to back further away, moving deeper into the darkness until my back's up against the other wall. Since I don't want to risk catching his attention or making any noise, I stay put.

I might stop breathing a bit, too.

Go away, I plead inside my head, my teeth gritted to keep from blurting the words out loud. *It's just a shadow, you don't see me, and you should just go away.*

"Riley?" His voice softens. He doesn't have to shout because, for some reason, he knows I'm here. He just doesn't know *where*. "Come out. The whole facility has been worried sick about you. Black Pine needs you back. You're not in any trouble. Come on out."

That's gonna be a no.

Sorry, doc.

I shudder out a short breath, just enough so that I don't freaking pass out and land at his feet or something, and crack my eyes open again.

I don't know if he heard me. It's possible. With adrenaline rushing through me, every sound is amplified. I can hear the tiny bits of gravel shift under his feet as the doctor looks around, continuing to search.

Either way, as he lets the manila envelope fall to the ground, Dr. Gillespie suddenly yanks on his collar with one hand, the other reaching beneath his shirt to pull on... on *something*.

What the—

It almost looks like the necklace Carolina gave me. The same braided sinew strip that makes up the cord, tied securely around an iron nail that's gotta be at least twice the size as the one Carolina gave me. As if he knows about the fae—as if he *believes* in the faerie races—Dr. Gillespie has taken precautions to protect himself.

And that's not all.

Unlike mine, Dr. Gillespie's necklace has more than just the nail hanging off the cord. It's one of three things, even if it's the only one I recognize—or understand the importance of.

The nail is in the center. Closer to his left hand, there's some kind of crystalline stone that looks super heavy and kind of strange.

He ignores the crystal and the nail, using his right hand to lift up the third charm *thing*. I don't know what the hell it is. It's… it's a rock, just not like the rock Nine carries in his pocket. A little bit bigger than a quarter, the doctor's rock is shaped in an almost perfect circle, polished smooth, with another open circle in the center.

It reminds me of a stony donut. I've got no idea what it is.

With a flick of his wrist, he lifts his glasses, letting them rest on the top of his head. After squinting one of his bright blue eyes, Dr. Gillespie raises the donut-looking rock up to the other one. That close, the circle in the middle of the rock is some kind of peephole.

His head swivels, the tip of his tongue poking out as he peeks through it. Right when he's aiming the rock at me, he points.

A foxy grin tugs on his lips. "Gotcha," he whispers.

He can see me. I don't have a single clue how that's possible with a freaking rock, but my former psychologist is staring right in my direction, smiling like the cat that got the cream.

Plus, he said *gotcha*. No one ever says *gotcha* for a good reason.

He goes and proves me right a second later. Without lowering his rock or wiping that creepy grin off of his face, Dr. Gillespie calls out into the alley again.

"Riley, you must trust me. You don't have to hide, and you don't have to be afraid. I'm here to help you. That's all I've ever wanted to do. Remember? I'm your doctor. Let me help you."

Help me? Yeah. Right.

Help me get back to Black Pine and then, after they hear about what happened to me since Nine grabbed my hand and pulled me out of the asylum, make it so that I'm moved on to the adult facility for the rest of my life.

And that's if they don't blame me when they find Carolina's body and figure—rightly—that I had something to do with it.

I avoided manslaughter charges after Madelaine's murder when I was fifteen. I'm twenty-one now, and it's not like I can tell the police and the judges that Carolina wasted away because she didn't get enough Faerie food.

Oh, yeah. I'm gonna be locked up in the psych ward forever if I don't escape Dr. Gillespie now. The same Dr. Gillespie who has just proven that—like others in Black Pine—he's familiar enough with the fae to carry an iron nail and a weirdo seeing stone with him.

I back up. His head follows my every move.

Now that he can see me, I've lost any advantage I had. How much longer until he starts asking me about my parlor trick with the shadows? And then, after that, about Nine?

I can't do it. But can I get past him? Good question. On my best days, I could probably fight him off. Today... is not one of my best days. I haven't gotten any kind of restful sleep in more than two days. I'm tired. Weak. And, right now, I feel like a cornered animal. Part of me wants to lash out—even though I know it would be a bad idea to do that—while retreating seems like a good plan.

Without taking my gaze off of the doctor, I glance behind me out of the corner of one eye.

It's dark. Really dark. *Super* dark. At first, I wonder if maybe there's a way out behind the shadows—and then I realize something. Those aren't *just* shadows.

It's a patch of night in the middle of the afternoon.

No, it's a *portal*.

And I'm supposed to be able to shade-walk.

I haven't tried since the day Nine dragged me to Faerie and I had to let myself faint in order to travel back through the shadows. I spent most of my lonely nights at the Wilkes House playing with shadows, testing my control. I must have gotten pretty okay at it since I managed to hide my body inside of them before he used that rock to find me.

Can I jump through the portal and get out of here without Dr. Gillespie and his interesting necklace following behind me?

Well, only one way to find out.

Before the doctor can move any closer, I rise up from my partial crouch, sidle a few steps down the alley, then turn and run toward the portal.

"Riley, no!"

With Dr. Gillespie's furious shout a dying whisper behind me, I jump into the shadows, close my eyes, and hope like hell that I didn't just screw things up even worse.

CHAPTER 19

land on a fluffy bed of grass. It's soft and bouncy and, oh boy—

Blue

It's blue.

Damn it.

Faerie. Of course I've landed in Faerie.

It was my biggest fear. It's the reason why I kept from trying to shade-walk on my own, or while I was awake. I didn't know what I was doing and, after the way I must have fallen into a trap the first time I shade-walked, it seemed inevitable that I would end up crossing over instead of popping out of another portal in the human realm.

Which is exactly what just happened.

I immediately hop back up, leaving my sunglasses and my cap on the ground where they fell. No time to retrieve them. I can't protect myself if I'm flat on my belly or even on my hands and knees so it makes sense to get up first, worry about my disguise second.

Once I'm standing, my anxious hands flexing and twitching and trembling inside of my gloves, I spin around, hoping with everything I've got in me that I made it to the opposite side of Faerie.

Just not—

"Ah, crap," I mutter.

The Fae Queen's gardens. There's no denying that's where I am. The sky is the same dark magenta shade, mixed and swirled with clouds that are this deep golden color. Blue grass that's soft and springy, that looks like cotton candy. And the trees… sparkling silver, dripping with icicles that are more crystal than ice.

I take a deep breath and choke on the oppressive air. It's hot. Humid. A never-ending summer.

Now I'm pretty sure I know why. The Fae Queen rules all of Faerie, but she's got the power of the Seelie behind her. Nine told me once that she keeps her domain in the Summer Court.

It would explain the heat, at least.

I've got to get out of here.

My heart in my throat, I shield my gaze with my hand, looking for some way out. I turn. Nothing. No shadows. No portals, either. No pockets. All I see are the glittering trees, the weirdo grass, and the sky that looks like sunset no matter what time of day it is.

"Not leaving so soon, I hope."

At that sweet, soft female voice, I swivel back around.

And there she is.

She's… I don't want to say beautiful, because that doesn't do her justice. Gorgeous? An understatement. Stunning is close, since I'm totally stunned as I stare up at her.

Like the best of the fae, she's tall and slender, though she's also got a set of curves that make my stick figure want to cry out in envy. Her long, flowy gown is molded to every line of her perfect body, accentuating her trim waist. The skirt reaches just past her calves, revealing bare feet. Despite the way she's standing outdoors without any shoes on, her feet are as pristine and immaculate as every other inch of her.

Instinctively I hate her, and then feel guilty for it. I settle on being extremely jealous instead. And just a bit intimidated.

Her skin is the same shade as freshly fallen snow, with a rosy flush coloring her high cheekbones. Thick, glossy, golden blonde curls cascade down her back. Of all her features, though, it's her eyes that are the most striking. Big and wide and expressive, this fae has pale yellow eyes.

Not gold, like Rys's glowing peepers.

Yellow. Such a pale yellow, in fact, that it's almost like there's no pigment there at all. I've never seen a color like that before and, okay, it's kind of creepy.

And that's when she smiles down at me.

I stand my ground. Because she might be smiling with her lips, but those unblinking eyes are totally sizing me up. I'm betting she's trying to figure out who I am, what I'm doing here. I'm definitely doing the same thing to her. When the corners of her mouth lift a little higher, I figure she's doing a much better job than I am.

"Ah, Shadow," she says lightly. "It's about time you've finally arrived. I've been waiting for you."

I gulp.

Well, that answered my question. A lovely, unique fae wandering around the Fae Queen's garden who's been waiting for the Shadow?

It's Melisandre, isn't it?

Holy shit.

I should've taken my chances with Doctor Gillespie.

It takes me a second to realize that, even worse, she isn't alone. I was so distracted—first by her unearthly beauty, then by my realization that I'm face to face with my greatest threat—that I don't notice that, behind her, there are six guards.

They flank her, three on each side. On her left, she has three Dark Fae guards. On her right, three Light Fae guards.

The last one is Rys.

My breath catches in my throat when I recognize him. He's standing on the queen's farthest side. Now that, for the first time ever, I'm face to face with more of the fae, I can see that the coloring is pretty universal. The two other Seelie near Rys share the same tawny hair, the same golden eyes, the same bronze tan—just like the Unseelie are pale with dark hair that's a perfect contrast to their skin. They're not clones, though; each one has a different face, each one more beautiful than the last.

I could pick Rys out of a line-up of a hundred Seelie fae. Not only do I know him, so I can pick up on the small differences, but there's one big, honking one staring me in the face.

Or, rather, a mark on *his*.

He's got a scar, and not some small, tiny one, either. A slash that starts near the corner of his eye, crossing the height of his cheek down to the top of his lip. It's at least three inches long, bumpy, and, since it's kind of fresh, a nasty, violent purple.

That's from me. I know it is. *I* did that to him. There must've been iron in the shovel when I swung at him, because not only did it hurt him enough to let loose his fire, but it left its mark.

No wonder he's flanking the queen. After what happened at the cemetery, I'm probably at the top of his shit list. Melisandre is after my head? The sword hanging at his hip would probably do the job pretty easily.

Could this get any worse?

Shouldn't have let that thought cross my mind. As soon as it does, the queen gestures at me. It's obviously a signal because, the second her arm is lowered, her guards break formation. Instead of flanking her, they form a circle around me.

There goes any hope of escape.

I've got about four feet separating me from the fae. Far enough that I don't start freaking out about how they're all within touching distance, but still close. Too close.

I'm screwed, aren't I?

"Come now. We can't discuss matters out in the garden. Let's go into my palace. I know you've come all this way to force me from my throne, but I'll extend an invitation inside all the same. Follow me."

"I didn't mean—"

"Shadow, please." Her voice is still quiet, but soft it ain't. Melisandre puts steel in the way she calls me Shadow. "That can wait until we're inside. Now, you can follow me, or you can linger with my guards. Your choice."

"Don't touch me," I snap. I shoot warning glances at five of the six guards. I can't bring myself to even meet Rys's golden stare when, first, I'd have to look at the ugly scar. "I don't want any of you to touch me."

"No need for that if you come with me indoors. Agree now and you'll walk on your own."

At another royal wave, all six guards draw their swords. They're not metal because, well, *obviously*, but the blades look like they've been made of diamond, the way they glitter as they threaten.

She says I'll walk on my own? She's freaking right. When you're staring at six points coming at you from all directions, you move.

The queen leads the way. Because I need something to focus on that, you know, *isn't* the six sword-wielding guards surrounding me, I stare at the back of her dress. The gown fans out like a train, sliding over the weirdo grass, following her every sway. It doesn't get stuck on anything. Doesn't snag, even when we walk through the crystalline trees.

There's something about it that's familiar. If it wasn't for the pale blue color, I would think it's the same material as Nine's coat.

I would think it's shadows.

But that's impossible. Melisandre is the Fae Queen, and she lords over the Seelie Court. So she's a Light Fae, right? Blonde hair, pale eyes... all signs point to Seelie. What would a Light Fae be doing wearing a gown made of shadows?

That thought keeps me distracted through my march through the gardens. The second we pass under a marble arch and I'm facing a massive castle, it's got all my attention.

Sucker's *huge*.

I've never been to Disneyland. The Everetts tried to plan a trip once when they discovered I hadn't, but I was a broody teen and I turned their gracious offer down. Still, I watch TV. I've seen pictures.

This looks like Sleeping Beauty's castle. From the towers and the turrets, the stone facade, and the large glass windows, I feel like I've been thrown into a fairy tale. Faerie tale. Whatever.

This is the Fae Queen's palace?

And here comes Riley Thorne, fresh off of sleeping in the sewer and squatting in an abandoned, empty house.

Yeah. Magical, powerful ruler of the fae versus a half-human, half-fae whose claim to fame is that she can turn the shadows into a blanket and hop through them from one mess to another. What a fair fight.

Did I say I was screwed?

I'm totally fucked.

I RECOGNIZE THIS ROOM.

I've lost track of where she's brought me. After she's marched me under an arch, over a bridge, through an open doorway, then past room after room, I understand that she's doing this on purpose. Melisandre is being careful to keep me disoriented; even if I managed to slip away from her armed guards, I'd never find my way out. Plus, she's proving that she's the one in control. Like a puppy, I'll follow her wherever she leads, not because I *want* to, but because I prefer not to become a Riley-kebab.

But this room?

I recognize it right away.

The stairs that lead to nowhere. The ornately carved banister that looks like its made from glass. Blindingly white walls, and the door with its crystal knob.

This is the room I saw in my dream.

As she leads the way into the last room, taking her seat on a throne that looks like it's made of—what else?—crystal, I finally find the balls to say something.

This suspicion isn't new. A couple of times before now, I wondered if maybe... but I always found a reason to say no. That it couldn't be. That, despite the trouble I've been in, even my luck's not that shitty.

I can't deny it any longer, though. Moving through that familiar room, reliving the vision I had where I overheard Carolina plotting to betray me, I finally have to accept the truth.

"You... you're Carolina's mistress."

"I've answered to so many names over my life. Oberon's consort. Queen of the Seelie. The Fae Queen. Melisandre. Yet the mistress of a human... it's interesting that that's the one you chose to use."

Interesting nothing.

As soon as she confirms it, I can't help but think of how often Carolina bitterly cursed the fae in control of her life. And how she kept pushing me to follow the prophecy, to do whatever I had to to end the Fae Queen. She made it seem like her mistress would free her once the queen was dead.

No. If the Shadow ended the Fae Queen, *then* Carolina would've been freed from the bargain she made with Melisandre.

Only the queen's still standing. And Lina—

"She's dead," I tell her. "You let her die."

A heartless shrug shouldn't be so beautiful. "She did it to herself. I expect unwavering loyalty from my pets. Silly girl. She tried to save you, you know. She should've known better than to betray me."

"Betray you? She never betrayed you." No. Considering she died without admitting the identity of her mistress, even going so far as to convince me that she was a Dark Fae, Carolina *protected* Melisandre.

She doesn't see it that way.

"But she did, Shadow. She knew so few of our secrets, yet she couldn't keep them. Like iron. Like the charm she has you wearing." Waving at my chest, she orders, "Take off the necklace."

And throw away the only protection I have?

I gulp, suddenly fearful again, then shake my head. I don't even care that she knows I'm wearing it when it's tucked beneath my shirt. Doesn't matter. I'm not about to take it off.

Melisandre's lips curve.

"Rysdan," she calls out. "Remove the Shadow's necklace. If

you have to take her head to do so, so be it. I thought the halfling might want to bargain with me. It seems as if she'd rather throw her life away. Suits me just fine."

I don't know what hits me harder: her casual threat or the way she calls Rys by a different name. Rysdan... is that his fae name? Like how Nine's is Ninetroir? If the Fae Queen invokes it, will he be compelled to do what she says? I mean, she *is* the Fae Queen, the head of the Seelie Court, and he's one of her soldiers. Hell, if magic won't compel him, duty might.

Or, I realize as Rys takes a step out of formation, will the Light Fae come at me with his sword because I'm the one who destroyed his perfect, perfect face?

I've got no choice. Decapitation or capitulation? Yeah. No contest.

Holding out my hand, warding him off, I stammer out, "I... I'll take it off."

For the second time that I catch, Melisandre's gaze flickers over the leather stretched over my hand. I hate that she seems interested in my glove. What if she commands me to take that off next?

The iron nail is one thing. I won't take off my gloves. I *won't*.

"Toss it to the ground," Melisandre orders. "I'll have one of my pets retrieve it later. I wouldn't want to risk it harming any of my loyal guards."

Ouch. Nice way to remind me that I used iron against Rys—and that he's standing at her side, not mine.

Keeping my eyes on the queen, I dip my hand beneath my hoodie, pulling out the leather strap. I lift it up and over my head, then toss it to the ground like she told me to. For good measure, I nudge the iron nail away with the tip of my sneaker so that I'm not tempted to grab it again.

Melisandre purses her lips in open approval at how easily I

gave in, then folds her hands in front of her belly. Prim and proper, not the least bit murderous.

Yeah. Right.

"Tell me, Shadow. Is there anything else you shouldn't be carrying into my realm, you tricky girl?"

Since I don't want to risk her ordering Rys to come at me with his sword again, I think about it. Is there?

I have Carolina's baggie of money in one pocket, plus the scrap of paper I found near her cold hand. That's it. I'll need one if I manage to get out of this mess I'm in, and I refuse to part with Carolina's note before I get the chance to read it.

"No."

"Are you sure?"

Pretty sure. "Yes."

"Then what's in your pocket?"

"Nothing."

"Prove it." Her eyes seem to grow darker. They're... they're not so yellow anymore. More of a muddy gray, like storm clouds. Fitting, considering the way her expression looks thunderous all of a sudden. "Empty them."

I do.

I slip both hands into my hoodie pocket first since I doubt she's worried about the scrap of paper in my jeans. I pull out Carolina's extra cash in one hand. In the other, I have the piece of fabric that Nine was adamant that I keep with me.

Melisandre straightens in her throne, fingers gripping the edge of the arms. "You dare gather shadows in front of me when I'm being so generous?"

"I'm not doing anything," I protest. "It's not even a shadow. It's like a silk scarf or something."

"Is that what he told you?"

He? How does she know it's from Nine?

She points at me. She's so angry, she doesn't even name any particular guard. "Take it from her."

All six guards make a move toward me.

"You want it? Fine." I throw it far away from me, even further than my necklace. "There. It's yours."

As soon as it hits the floor, it sticks. That's... that's different. It doesn't crumple in a ball or slip away. Nope. It's like it soaks into the fancy tile that make up the floor in the queen's throne room.

It's the only spot of black in the whole room. It streaks across the floor, moving to the corner where two walls meet, growing larger and larger as it approaches. By the time it reaches the corner, the shadow darkens and stretches and twists until it's a patch of darkness about three feet high.

A figure comes striding in from the distance. Seconds later, he's stepping out of the portal, as beautiful and as untouchable as ever.

"Nine," I gasp.

I don't know whether to be happy or afraid that he's here. Happy because, if there's one soul in either realm that I can count on, it's Nine. And absolutely freaking terrified because I'm in Faerie, this is the queen, and now I've dragged my Shadow Man into this mess.

Don't know how, but there's no denying it.

"Ninetroir." The queen is visibly annoyed. "I should've remembered your parlor trick. You did so love to throw shadows around."

She's annoyed.

I'm *shocked*.

The queen knows his name, too. He told me once how he guarded it ruthlessly his whole life, that only a few had it, whether they earned it through a contract or a bargain or because it bettered him in some way.

He said I was the only one he gave it to without expecting anything in return. Well, the touch that saved my life from the charmed peach, but he would've eventually given it to me once I broke free of Rys's brand.

But Melisandre knows his true name. She knows Nine.

With a small smile, she turns to look at me. She doesn't have to keep her eyes on Nine. The second he popped into the room, every single Seelie fae turned their weapon in his direction.

The queen rises from her throne, stepping lightly down the stairs that lead from the throne's platform. She moves toward where I'm frozen in place, addressing only me, like we're sharing girl-talk or some crap like that.

"One of my favored guards," she confides. "I hand-picked him right out of the Unseelie Court myself, brought him to my academy. I had such hopes for him before he gave up his post. He was too young, I supposed. I never thought he'd betray me for a human."

What?

Nine was one of the Fae Queens guards?

What?

"It was such a surprise when he entered in the bargain that trapped him as your guardian. Especially since he's always hated humans. Isn't that right, Ninetroir?"

The words seem like they're pulled from him. Moving quickly, moving quietly, he steps between me and the queen. "Not Riley."

"Riley," she scoffs. She meets my gaze over Nine's shoulder and all I can see is how furious she is—and how she's going to keep pretending she's not. "A human name, too. If she's so proud of her fae side, she should at least use her true name."

Does she think she's being tricky? Maybe. Or maybe she just doesn't care about being subtle 'cause, well, she's not. Of course she wants my true name. She could command me to do anything, even command me to slit my own damn throat, if she had that name.

It takes everything I have not to flicker my gaze over in Rys's direction. He has it. He's used it countless times before. Wearing the mark from the shovel on his face, he could offer it to his queen and get revenge for the way I lashed out against him. And that's if he hasn't already—he's proven that he's not shy in calling me *Zella* when it suits him.

I brace myself, waiting for it.

Rys stays silent. I'm not sure why—I can't chance looking at him in case Melisandre picks up on it—and I'm irrationally grateful that the Light Fae who's made my life hell for so long is actually doing something to protect me for real.

I can't worry about that right now, though. Not when I have another fae standing in front of me, separating me from the Fae Queen, essentially doing the same exact thing.

"I won't let you face her yet. She's not ready."

"And you think you can stop me?"

Nine juts his chin out in an act of defiance. "If I have to."

I hope he's got a sword under his coat because, even now that there's the two of us, without a weapon, we're still super outnumbered.

To my surprise, Melisandre doesn't seem offended by his answer. "I was told your debt to the human mother was fulfilled. You don't have to protect her."

"I don't have to do anything," Nine counters. "I choose to."

"The Dark Fae," murmurs the queen. "I wondered which of my people would turn against me. You were always too close to the prophecy, Ninetroir. I should've known it would be you. That changes things."

It does? How?

And why does the way she say that have me just about to piss myself?

With one searching look past Nine, Melisandre actually moves away from us. That's a total surprise. I was expecting her to lash out at Nine, to command one of her guards to remove the new threat in the room.

She doesn't.

Instead, gliding to the side of the room where Nine's portal lingers, Melisandre moves like she could care less that me and Nine are still there. She keeps her back to us—which she can do without worry because of, you know, the six guards watching it—as she approaches a structure tucked near the furthest wall.

I don't know how I didn't notice it until now. Probably because the cloth covering it is white, just like the walls, and I've been a little preoccupied with the queen threatening to have her guard chop off my head.

Melisandre waves her hand. The cover slips away.

She turns, her stare immediately looking for me just as I realize what it is that she revealed to the rest of us.

It's two statues, just like the Jason one I found in her gardens.

One's fae. A male fae, definitely Seelie due to his coloring. He's a paler version of Rys, like he's been hidden in the darkness after a lifetime of living out in the sun. His eyes are closed, though I'm willing to bet they'd be the same golden shade, and his lips are pressed together.

He appears resigned, but at peace.

The other statue is his total opposite.

First off, it's a woman, and she seems to be cowering.

The poor chick looks to be a couple of years older than me.

Twenty-three, maybe twenty-four. She's a little shorter than I am, just as petite, with a sheet of white-blonde hair that falls past her shoulders. She's pretty—or she would be if she wasn't wearing a frightened expression, her mouth contorted in a silent scream, her big blue eyes wide and afraid.

She's not fae. The blue eyes are one clue, the perfect imperfections of her pretty face another. Laugh lines. Even as terrified as she was before she was frozen this way, I can make out laugh lines.

Humans have laugh lines. They have wrinkles and birthmarks and blemishes. Unlike a fae's airbrushed smooth features and eerily beautiful faces, a human's shows each year lived.

I feel a kinship to this poor woman. Almost like I should know her.

I don't, though. And when Melisandre asks in a mocking tone if I do—if I know either of them—I just shake my head.

She lets out a laugh. It's sweet and it's lovely, and it sends chills skittering down my spine.

And then she asks joyfully, "Truly? You don't recognize your parents?"

My... my *parents*?

I thought I was frozen in place before. Now? It's like my sneakers have been rooted to the floor. I can't talk, can't breathe, can't even freaking blink. I'm staring at the two of them in disbelief.

My *parents?*

CHAPTER 20

Over my shock of discovering that the two statues in front of me are my freaking *parents*, Melisandre continues talking.

Man, she must love the sound of her damn voice. Even if her explanation is actually helpful, I wish she'd just *shut up already*.

"In Faerie," purrs the queen, "my people can't use their charms on each other. It's why humans have their use. I couldn't compel Aislinn to do my bidding, and his human pet's ability to negate glamour meant she was useless to me. Still, they make lovely statues. I do so love to decorate my garden."

I shake my head roughly, forcing myself out of my shock-fueled daze. My fingers clench so tightly, my leather gloves groan.

Her eyes brighten. "Ah. That's right. You've been to my gardens before this afternoon. Did you enjoy your first welcome?"

Don't let her see how she affects you, Riley. Don't let her have an inch or she'll take a mile.

I gulp. "Can't say that I did."

"Oh. I thought you'd be pleased to see… now, what was that pet's name? Hmm. I should remember. He was so well-trained, keeping me informed on the goings-on of the Shadow for so long until I… hmm, well, I suppose I simply grew bored of him."

There's only one person she can mean.

"His name was Jason," I grit out.

"Ah. So it was. After a while, they all seem the same to me. Not these two, though. Aislinn and his human were different. Special. They created the Shadow." She waves her hand in my direction again. "They created you. And, instead of giving up their child, they sacrificed their lives to save yours. Now, it's your turn."

"My queen?" It's Rys speaking up. I'd know that voice anywhere. "I thought you were going to spare the Shadow."

Spare the Shadow? Yes, please.

Melisandre turns her head just enough so that while I'm still in her sight, she can make it clear that she's addressing Rys when she says, "Hold your tongue, or risk it. You've been warned."

Rys clamps his mouth shut. His golden gaze flashes murderously. Wisely, he shuts up.

Who was that look for? Me or the queen?

I'm not so sure. And, heeding his queen's warning, he stays quiet.

She nods royally, ending the motion with an almost unnoticeable shake that makes her blonde curls whisper enticingly over her slender shoulders.

"Pardon the interruption. Where were we? Ah, yes, the Shadow Prophecy… what a moldy, old thing. Why, who's to say that what's been handed down over the eons is the same as what was foretold? I had a pet once, I forget them now, who explained to me about this human game. Meanings can get twisted, the more folks who know a secret. And the Shadow Prophecy has always been.... mmm, shadowed in secrets."

No kidding. The piece of paper Carolina gave me with the prophecy scrawled on it was my be-all and end-all when it came to understanding all of this. Now that I know Carolina was serving the queen, can I even believe it?

Probably not.

"Still, in every version, it seems as if you've been fated to end my reign. Unfortunately, I'm quite fond of my position. I worked very hard to call the throne and the realm my own. I'm not about to allow some halfling to swan in and ruin it for me."

I really, really don't like the way she threatens to cut out tongues when someone speaks and she doesn't want them to. Like Rys, it's kept me quiet for a minute, but I have to defend myself.

"I'm not trying to do that," I argue. "I keep telling you people, I don't want anything to do with the fae. I just want to be left alone."

Her strange eyes glimmer. They're still not the same color they were out in the sunlight. The more I watch, the more it seems like they're closer to Nine's silver than Rys's gold.

"Yes, well, that's why I'd like to propose a trade. You for them," she says, waving in the direction of the fae and the woman frozen beside her. "Stay with me in Faerie, stay where I can keep my eye on you, and I'll set them free. No harm, no foul. I'll remove the spell and their imprisonment, let them go on their merry way. In my castle, you'll find it impossible to plot to steal my head. I won't have to destroy the halfling destined to end my reign, but I'll also have control of her. A perfect trade, in my opinion."

My heart just about stops at the same time as Melisandre does.

When I first saw the statues—when she first told me who those two people were—I was so stunned, I could barely understand the magnitude of her reveal. For twenty human years, my parents have been trapped in Faerie all because they wanted to save *me*.

It never occurred to me that I might be able to save them.

"You can... you can do that?"

"Certainly. And I'll do it if you agree to take their place."

"Two for one... that trade would be entirely in Riley's favor. That's not like you, Melisandre. Where is the sacrifice?" asks Nine. He shifts his weight, covering me as the Fae Queen glides back, coming to stand in front of us again instead of my freaking *parents*. "You said sacrifice. What are your intentions?"

"It's simple. I can't honestly be expected to leave the Shadow free. She's just beginning to come into her powers. None of us know what she'll eventually become. So, in exchange for Aislinn and his human, she'll stay in Faerie with me—just as they are."

A statue.

The Fae Queen wants me to willingly trade my freedom for that of my parents. It's not certain death, but I wouldn't be *alive*.

I also wouldn't have to worry about the queen coming after me, or her sending soldiers after me. A statue in her gardens... it's not the outcome I was hoping for, but I'm so freaking tired, it almost has a certain appeal.

When I don't immediately say no, Nine turns just enough so that he can look at my face. I don't know what it is that he sees in my expression—he sure doesn't like it, though.

"Riley, no. You can't do this."

"That's where you're wrong, Ninetroir. I think the Shadow has no choice *but* to agree to my terms."

Melisandre lifts her hand high. Another gesture. Another signal. Four of the six guards—two Dark Fae, two Light Fae, neither Rys—come forward, surrounding me and Nine at the corners.

"Show my guests to their quarters." Her pale pink lips curve, a dangerous smile tugging them upward. "I will see you again at the next moonrise. I trust you'll have time to think over my offer. I'll expect your answer then."

Quarters?

Try a cell.

After escorting us from the Fae Queen's throne room, the guards lead us through countless other rooms before marching me and Nine down one last narrow hall, glittering swords pointed at us from every angle.

We finally stop in front of a room with bars. Not six bars, like my window back at Black Pine, but at least fifty. They're not a dark metal, either—these bars are made of thick glass, but with a skinny bar of something that doesn't quite belong shoved in the middle.

It's iron. I don't know how I can be so sure, but I am. It's probably enough iron to weaken a fae—especially since it's probably some of the only iron in all of Faerie—and that, coupled with the bars and the empty room, make it clear to me what it's for.

Faerie jail. You've got to be kidding.

As we approach, the door swings outward.

"Inside," orders one of the Dark Fae guards.

Because I don't see what else we can do, both Nine and I step in. The door slams with an echo behind us.

As soon as we're alone in the cell, Nine whirls on me. He's so tall, so terrible, so utterly awe-inspiring, I tilt my head back as he looms in front of me. Though I'm close to shaking in my sneakers, I refuse to quail. I don't back down.

I've been expecting this.

The whole march through the palace, I could tell that Nine was just waiting for us to be alone so that he could tear into me. It's obvious that he's against me agreeing to the queen's terms, and he begins his argument by saying just that.

"I can't let you do this. Aislinn sacrificed himself so that you would survive. Your mother risked making a bargain with me—*me*, Riley—so that you'd be protected from the Fae Queen while you came of age. They would never want you to give up your life for them."

"I wouldn't know that," I retort. "I don't know anything about them at all because, for the last twenty years, they've been trapped in Faerie because of me."

"Not because of you. Understand me when I tell you this. They've been trapped in Faerie because of Melisandre. Not you."

Even though I'm looking up at Nine, all I see is the frightened look on my mom's face, the resigned air that surrounded my father. I let out a soft sigh. "I wish I could believe that."

"You can. Because I'm telling you it's so."

And he can't lie.

That's another way this Nine is so… so different than the Shadow Man I once knew. Back then, he spoke in riddles, using words that could mean anything and everything. Not Nine. Not now. As if he's trying to prove that I never have to wonder if he's manipulating me, he's begun to speak in absolutes.

Not *perhaps*. Not *maybe*. Not *it could be so*.

Too bad it's too late to change anything.

"It was easier when I thought they were dead," I confess, turning away from Nine. The weight of expectation in his gaze is too heavy. He's a Dark Fae—he doesn't understand how I feel. But he's also Nine, and I *need* him to. "It took so long for me to get past being abandoned as a baby. Honestly, I'm not sure I really did, but it became easier when I accepted they were gone. I mourned them, and I got over it. Fine. But they're alive, Nine. They're still around, just turned into statues. They don't deserve that."

"You don't deserve that, either."

Maybe. Maybe not.

I'm no saint. I'm not perfect. I've done some shitty things in my life, and I've had some fucking terrible things happen to me. People have been hurt because of me. They've *died*.

I couldn't save Madelaine.

I couldn't save Carolina.

I thought my mom was out of reach… but she's here. She's with my dad, a man who was nothing but a mystery—and I can save them.

Sure, it'll cost me my freedom, but maybe it's worth it.

One glance up at Nine and I know that, not only is he aware of where my thoughts—and my heart—are leading me, he so doesn't agree with me.

"You can't trust the queen."

Duh. "I know that."

"There's nothing to stop her from taking one of her guard's swords and lopping off your head once you've agreed to let her freeze you in place."

"I know that, too. I'm not a complete moron, Nine. If I do this, I'm pretty sure I'm not getting out of this in one piece. But isn't that what the prophecy said? It's either her or me, and it's not like I ever really believed I had a chance against the *queen* of the *fae*. At least, this way, I'm getting something out of it. I just hope that she lets you go, too. Maybe I can try to bargain with her some more, make sure you stay safe."

Nine's eyes gleam. "Don't worry about me. I've survived Melisandre before."

I'm beginning to realize that.

There's something there, and it's not only how easily he calls her by her name instead of her title, like Rys did. It's the way she coos his name, how she mentioned that she hand-picked him to join her guard, then lost him to, well, me.

I'm thinking that really pissed her off.

Great. So now she probably hates me for two reasons. I should probably count myself lucky that she didn't follow through with her threat and have Rys remove my head to get to my necklace then and there. At least, if I'm frozen as a statue first, I won't realize it when the fatal strike comes my way.

I just don't understand why she needs me to agree before she turns me into a statue. Is it because she wants to make me suffer first? The all-powerful Fae Queen should be able to snap her fingers or wave her hands and, *poof*, I'm frozen solid.

But she didn't. And I don't get it.

When I ask Nine, he doesn't act surprised that I've picked up on that. He does seem pleased, though.

"It's because you're the Shadow," he explains. "None of us know what the extent of your power is. When you were an infant, you were shade-walking better than fae who had existed for more than a hundred years. The shadows obey you. They protect you, too. Iron doesn't harm you. And when it comes to the touch..."

He trails off his sentence. I wait to see if he'll finish it and, when he doesn't, I prod him. "The touch?"

"It's different with you," Nine says. And he leaves it at that.

"So what's all that supposed to mean?"

"Honestly? I don't know. But I would've expected Melisandre to take out the threat the moment you landed in Faerie. It's why I insisted on you carrying part of my shadow wherever you went. As soon as you crossed into my world, I could get to you so long as you needed me."

"Your shadow?" I echo. "Is that what that scarf thing was?"

Nine nods. "I told you that you should've known what it was. I gave you part of my shadow to shield you while you learned how to conjure your own."

That's... okay, that's kind of cool. And now I feel a little stupid. For all the times I wrapped myself in blankets made of shadow, I never realized that Nine's scrap of fabric was the same thing.

Probably because it's thicker, stronger, and more real than any of the shadows I pull toward me. Makes sense, I guess. Nine's been around longer than me. Plus, as a Dark Fae, he must be a pro at manipulating shadows.

I have so much I could learn from him. Now that he's opening up to me, I'm probably going to have to leave him.

Because that's just my luck.

"I still don't get it, Nine. If you thought she'd gun for me, and I sure as hell did, why is she giving me the choice? Why am I still talking and moving instead of acting like I'm made of rock already?"

"I assume it's because you are the Shadow. Your magic is too different, too unpredictable. The only thing I can think is that Melisandre did attempt to immobilize you, then turned to the bargain when it failed."

I'm still getting a crash course in what it's like to be half-fae and the star of some ancient prophecy, but I've gotta agree with Nine. If she could've done it, she totally would have.

Which means that, if I want to make the best of this situation, I've only got one choice.

I can't escape. How could I? First off, I'm in *Faerie jail*. Second, it's not like there are a bunch of shadows or pockets lying around that I can use. Spoiler alert: in this bright, white palace, the only one I've seen is the one created when I threw Nine's shadow in the throne room.

And third?

I can't abandon my parents and Nine.

I *can't*.

I've spent my whole life being left behind by anyone and everyone I ever cared about it. Against my better judgment, I let my guard down around Nine again these last few weeks. And my parents... they didn't want to leave me. It wasn't their choice. I won't leave them like that if there's anything I can do to change it.

I can tell the second Nine understands that I've made up my mind. And it's not like I'm trying to be a martyr or anything, even if I, you know, am. What do I have to look forward to anyway? Being chased by the Fae Queen, forced to dodge the might of her Court, avoiding Faerie—which means I'll never be able to shadow travel again—and avoiding Dr. Gillespie at the same time. No way I've forgotten the weirdo stone he used to find me.

My old Black Pine psychologist is in this up to his fiery red eyebrows. If he was still looking for me months after my breakout, something tells me he's got his reasons.

Nine obviously doesn't return my feelings for him. Oh, he cares—in his own way, he definitely cares. But it's not the same.

It might be better to be a statue where panic attacks, burned hands, and a life of being chased are far behind me.

Nine steps toward me. He starts to reach for my hand, thinks better of it, then lays his arm at his side. Shame. I would've liked for him to touch me one last time before I tell the queen that I'll accept her bargain.

His voice drops. It's low and husky, and still one of the most alluring things I've ever heard. "Do you trust me?"

"Of course."

"You should never trust the fae, Shadow. Haven't I taught you anything?"

"You're not just any fae, Nine. You're the Shadow Man. And I trust you."

I love you.

I don't have to say the words. He knows. I know he does.

But he doesn't return them.

I didn't expect him to.

I also don't expect him to take one last, long look at my face before he turns, the long tail of his shadowy coat flaring out behind him. He strides over to the front of our cell, careful not to grasp the iron-filled bars with his bare hands.

"Guard!"

CHAPTER 21

It's one of the Light Fae guards who answers Nine's arrogant call.

Not Rys, and I can't even pretend to be surprised by that. After how publicly he sided with the queen, joining her guard again instead of continuing in his vain quest to convince me to mate him, there's no way he's gonna want anything to do with me now.

That bothers me. It shouldn't, but it does, and if I get out of this in one piece—and, preferably, *not* a frozen one—I'll have to unpack that later.

Way later.

For now, my plate's totally full.

The Light Fae approaches our cell cautiously, his careful step at odds with his bored yet haughty features. His hand rests on the hilt of his sword.

"Yes?" He looks down his perfectly sculpted nose at Nine. "What is it, Cursed One?"

"I want to meet with Melisandre. Immediately."

He *what*?

"Nine?" I hiss. "What are you doing?"

He has to have heard me. The tips of his pointed ears twitch, his head cocked slightly to the side as if he wants to turn. He doesn't, though.

The guard shows a little more interest. "I'll see if my queen is willing to meet with a traitor."

I flinch when the Light Fae calls Nine that. A traitor? That sounds bad. It's one thing to throw Nine in Faerie jail with me, but if she really believes that he's a traitor, what will happen to Nine when I'm gone?

I can't bring myself to ask him that, not even when the Light Fae leaves the vicinity of our cell. Besides, the guard isn't gone long and, by the time I try to figure out what I want to say to Nine—or how to say it—he's back again.

And he has a key.

Just like everything else I've seen in this castle, the key is made of some kind of crystal. The guard fits it into the keyhole, unlocking the cell door with an ominous *snick*. I wince, waiting for it to break.

It doesn't.

It's so freaking weird.

The Light Fae guard waves the door open, then stands back. After trading the key for his sword, he orders us both out of the cell.

"No," Nine immediately argues. "Leave her here."

I've already started to move toward the open door. "What? No! I'm going with you."

"Riley—"

"The Shadow comes, too. Queen's orders, I'm afraid."

I resist the urge to stick my tongue out at Nine. He doesn't honestly think that I'm about to let him out of my sight right now? Not when I'm absolutely convinced that, if anything happens to him while in the Fae Queen's palace, it's my damn fault?

Nine glowers the entire trek back to Melisandre's throne room. I don't know how much time has past since we were sent to the cell—it feels like we walked forever both there and back—yet barely anything seems to have changed since.

My parents are still frozen in the corner.

The queen is still perched regally in her glittering throne.

Four of the guard are flanking Melisandre, two on each side. I've got no clue if any of them are the same from before—except for Rys.

He's still here. And, when my glance flickers his way, there's a burning hunger that he can barely conceal behind his dutiful mask.

I turn away. I can't let myself be distracted by the Light Fae. Not when the queen is watching me like a cat ready to pounce.

Whether he means to or not, Nine moves so that, once again, he's shielding me. Protecting me. With nothing but his coat, his shadows, and his haughty determination, Nine is the only barrier standing between me and the Fae Queen.

And we both know it.

Her countenance is peaceful. Serene. Her eyes, though? They're hard. This is a fae who stole the throne from her husband, then held onto it with force and cruelty. I have to remember that. As gorgeous as she is, it's glamour. Such thick glamour, I keep getting glimpses of what her true appearance must be—but not enough.

She wants me to believe she's sweet. Innocent. But innocent monarchs don't have subjects who call their reign the Reign of the Damned.

I have to remember that, too.

With such a graceful maneuver, she'd make a prima ballerina look clumsy in comparison, Melisandre rises from her throne. She floats down the stairs of the platform, meeting me and Nine on the ground level.

Her guards are a silent shadow at her back.

They're not the only ones in the room any longer, I notice. There are at least twelve other fae—each one of them Seelie—milling around near the throne. They part like the Red Sea as Melisandre walks across the room, leaving her a wide path, each one showing respect by bowing their head as she passes.

I gulp.

Melisandre smiles.

"You've returned much sooner than I expected," she says, obviously addressing Nine. "What is it you want to ask of me?"

"I've come to ask you nothing. I will make an announcement, and I will offer you a bargain."

"You've intrigued me, Ninetroir. Go on. Make your announcement. After you've finished, we'll see to a bargain. I'm in a fair mood this eve. I might be willing to make two bargains."

Two. Because she's so sure that she's got me where she wants me.

She isn't wrong, either.

Nine looks around the room, meeting the gaze of the fae watching him interest.

"With the queen of all Faerie, her honored guards, and the Seelie Court as my witness, I'm here to claim what fate has given me. It was foretold that the Shadow would save Faerie by ending the Reign of the Damned, but that's the Shadow. I've known for a while that fate has her own plans for me. I've waited for countless years, hoping to find a *ffrindau* worthy of me. Riley was born to be mine. Now, in front of you all, I claim her. Until Oberon separates us, I belong to her as she belongs to me."

I— wait. What?

There's an angry buzz in my skull. The whispers might be from the shock of the others in the throne room—the high-pitched argument Melisandre telling Nine that he's making a mistake—but most of it comes from me.

What?

Did he just—

What?!

I told him once, right after his touch acted like a drug that made me lose all my damn sense, that if he asked me to be his *ffrindau*, I'd say yes. I never took it back.

He's not asking me, though.

In front of the Fae Queen and everyone else, Nine has just told them all that he's claiming me as his mate. That he's known all along that fate has chosen me for him and that, with his announcement, he's no longer fighting it.

That's okay. I stopped fighting it a long time ago, too.

While the crowd still reacts in open surprise, Nine reaches out and grabs my hand. There's no time for me to give him permission. I can hear the sizzle as his skin burns, smell the char of flesh in the air as he yanks me toward him.

His eyes are shining, glowing an unearthly silver color that has my breath tearing from my throat. I see everything in his eyes—every emotion, every thought, every hope—his love for me, the madness from a lifetime of waiting for his *ffrindau* only to have her be a half-human, half-fae reject who ran from the frying pan straight to the fire.

For the first time ever, he's completely vulnerable. He's dropped his guard, with the entire Seelie Court acting as a witness to it.

The least I can do is give him the same honor.

I shudder and blink. I can't find the words, don't even know how to say what it is I'm feeling inside—a terrible mixture of love, fear, and regret—but I drop the wall around my heart the second I meet his gaze again.

He has my permission. To hold me, to touch me, to love me.

This foolish fae claimed me in front of his queen, her court, and a roomful of soldiers.

He has my permission, and everything that goes with it.

Nine knows. My Shadow Man can see it written on every inch of my face.

The room falls away. Call me reckless, call me insane, but I allow myself to forget all about our audience and the threat they represent when I lose myself in the intensity of Nine's expression.

I tilt my head back, my lips parted in an open invitation. After only a moment's hesitation, he swoops down, slanting his mouth over mine, kissing me as if this might be his last act.

I go all in. Because, well, this might just be the last thing I do, too.

I'm half-fae. The blood of a Seelie mixed with a human woman runs through my veins. I might be vulnerable to the fae's touch magic, but I realize something in that instant: I can turn the touch around.

I can steal some of the power back from the fae touching me.

Does Nine know that? He has to—or he as to at least expect it. He looks so triumphant. So freaking proud of himself when he breaks the kiss and pulls away.

And, okay, that might have been one hell of a first kiss, but something just happened between us.

Something just happened to *me*.

I feel like I've been plugged into an outlet. I'm suddenly full of so much juice, it takes everything I have not to vibrate in place. I don't want to give any sign that his kiss did more than bring the butterflies in my belly flapping to life, but it's freaking hard.

The power is a heady rush. I'm wide awake, super alert, like I just downed three espressos straight.

Even better? My shadow senses are tingling.

I swear, I can sense the shadows from every corner of this room. There aren't many—it's just as bright as it was in my vision of Carolina with the queen—but each black spot is like a prickle against my consciousness. There's one in particular behind me that is tugging me toward it.

A pocket.

It's a pocket.

The last of Nine's shadow is calling me.

I'm distracted. I'll be the first one to admit it. Coming down from that electric first kiss, I'm so freaking distracted, I don't get that Nine has let go of me or moved toward Melisandre until I hear the harsh edge of his voice reverberate through the silent throne room.

"As her *ffrindau*, I invoke the right to accept your bargain in my mate's place. If it pleases you, my queen, I will join your garden if it means Riley doesn't. She stays alert, alive, and safe for as long as I'm under your spell."

Melisandre doesn't even hesitate. "I accept."

That's how easy it is. One second Nine is here with me, kissing me, standing up for me. The next? He's gone. Frozen in place, still hunched in a protective stance, his arm thrown out so that I'm shielded from behind him, Nine is gone.

And, to the queen, immediately forgotten.

She turns to me. "What about our trade, Shadow? Are you willing to give up your freedom for your parents?"

"But Nine… he just—"

"He just ensured that you would be kept as you are while he takes your place. However, nowhere in his bargain did he set the terms on future negotiations. Your parents are still under my spell. Should you choose to trade your freedom for theirs, I'll let them go. It's an entirely different bargain than the one Ninetroir so rashly made."

I never would have thought Nine was rash. However, even I can see the flaw in his bargain. So desperate to throw one last-ditch attempt to cover me from the Fae Queen, he neglected to think two steps ahead.

He didn't earn my parents' freedom. He just made it so that he threw his own away.

I won't let him do that.

"Perhaps you're willing to negotiate with me now. Things are going so wonderfully for me today, I'll even bargain for Ninetroir. What do you say?"

I'll do anything to bring him back. I can't even pretend that Nine doesn't mean something to me—I just kissed him in front of the whole Seelie Court, and there's no going back from that. She's got me right where she wants me.

Negotiate?

Ha.

"What do you want me to do?"

"Nothing now. For your parents' freedom, I insist on the earlier conditions. You in my garden where I can ensure you won't trouble me. But for your precious mate? Let's just say that I'd reserve a favor to call in at my leisure. So, do we have a deal?"

I don't even know how to answer that.

Nine taught me a lot of things when I was a kid and he was getting me ready for a lifetime of being the target of the Fae

Queen. I learned about touch magic and iron, how a fae can't lie, and the power of a bargain.

One of the most important lessons he drilled into my skull was about never letting yourself get in the debt of the fae. A contract needed to be just that—a contract with set terms and no wiggle room. If I accept Melisandre's conditions that she'll set Nine free from her spell for a favor she can call it in at any time, it'll be even worse than if she made me a statue right off.

She could make me do anything and *still* trap me in Faerie for the rest of my life.

But what can I do?

I open my mouth.

And that's when Rys does the same.

"Riley, the pocket!"

Without anyone noticing it, Rys moved away from his post right behind the queen, taking up a position closer to where the statues of my parents are. At his shout, he has the attention of the entire room.

He has his sword out. With his free hand, he gestures toward his chest.

It hits me in an instant what he means.

Rys is the one who taught me about the pockets. About how, as the Shadow, I'm drawn to them—and how I can make them work for me. With the last of Nine's shadow forming a weak portal at the point where the two walls meet, it's just enough of a pocket to trigger my shadow magic.

And now that I'm still buzzing with the power of Nine's touch, the shadows are so attuned to me, I could pull that toward me with barely any effort at all.

This... this just might work.

I bolt toward the corner. The whole room is so stunned at how openly Rys just betrayed his queen, no one even tries to stop me. I dash right by him, sparing only a single look as I aim right for the portal.

He nods, then lifts his sword even higher.

Rys was right, I realize as I tuck my body behind the towering statue of my father. When he told me that I can't rely on Nine to save me... he was right. Nine *can't* save me—but I sure as hell can save Nine.

Know what? Rys isn't the total monster I thought he is. Nine was right. Fae aren't only good and bad, but somewhere in between—just like humans.

But Rys is still fae, with the mythical race's power and weaknesses, and it's obvious he meant it when he said he would never harm me.

I should've known better than to doubt him when he told me.

The fae can't lie.

It all happens so fast after that. As soon as he shouts to me, Melisandre slashes her hand through the air. Her guards immediately surround him. As I frantically begin to pull the shadows toward me, weave them around me, the last glimpse I have of Rys is the scarred fae falling under the weight of the Fae Queen's devoted guards.

Despite our history, I wish I could save him, too.

Melisandre stands alone.

Her long blonde curls float behind her, as does the train to her gown, like there's wind in a room with no windows. She's as intimidating as she is lovely.

And it's all an act.

"Don't refuse me, Shadow. I won't make the same offer again."

Yeah. I didn't think she would.

I better hope that I make this count.

I clench my fists, close my eyes until they're mere slits in my face, then *pull*. It's amazing how quickly the shadows respond. The weak portal comes alive, tripling in size with my first attempt. It triples again with the second. As if I've been trained for this—as if this is what I was born to do—I call on the shadows a third time until there's enough power surrounding me, I can easily encompass half the throne room.

As quick as the surge came, it fizzles out just as fast. There were maybe a few seconds when I thought I could pull this off, then reality comes crashing in.

Good thing I manage to finish wrapping the shadows around all of us before I start to flag. Me, the statue of Nine in the center of the throne room, plus my parents. I feel the answering tug in my gut, know that I'm pushing myself to my absolute limits, and close my eyes all the way.

I don't need to see the fury on the Fae Queen's innocent-looking face to know that she's absolutely *livid*.

"Stop her," she commands her guards in a throaty roar. "Don't let the halfling escape!"

Too late, Queenie.

If it wasn't for the power Nine transferred over when he shared his touch magic with me, I don't think I could've done it. With my last bit of strength, I hold tight to my three passengers and push us through the shadows surrounding us.

I don't know where we're going to end up.

Doesn't matter.

Anywhere is better than here.

*fall in love
with the
shadow man...*

TOUCHED BY THE FAE   BOOK THREE

TOUCH

INTERNATIONAL BESTSELLING AUTHOR
JESSICA LYNCH

Copyright © 2020 by Jessica Lynch

All rights reserved.

No part of this book may be reproduced in any form or by any electronic or mechanical means, including information storage and retrieval systems, without written permission from the author, except for the use of brief quotations in a book review.

Cover by Jessica Lynch

CHAPTER 1

Before I even get the chance to meet my parents, I almost lose them.

The tug of the shadows is harder than I've ever experienced before. It takes everything I have to keep them wrapped around all four of us: me, my mom, my dad, and Nine. Once or twice, I panic that it's out of my control, that I'm going to shade-walk too far and I won't be able to keep us together.

Without the power that Nine gave to me when we shared our first kiss, I'm not sure I would've been able to.

Did he know what was going to happen? I think so. My Shadow Man has always had a tendency to keep everything locked up tight, bottled up inside, and I bet he'd been planning something like this since the minute I got snagged by the Seelie guards.

Was that why he kissed me?

He just claimed me in front of the whole Seelie Court, announcing that he was taking a half-human, half-fae woman as his *ffrindau*.

His soulmate.

Can he take it back? It was as a big a surprise to me as it was to everyone standing in the Fae Queen's throne room, and regardless of what happened after Nine did it, it's one of a hundred different thoughts beating at my brain as I struggle to move through the darkness.

Can he take it back?

I really, really hope not.

I push, telling myself that there's no time to think about that now. This is the first time I've ever purposely shade-walked without it being an accident, while I was asleep, or because I had no choice. Not like I had a choice this time around, either. I definitely didn't. Since it was between sticking around and waiting for Melisandre to turn me into a statue for her royal garden or getting the hell out of there, I went with option B.

One problem: *I don't have any clue what I'm doing.*

The last time I jumped into a portal to escape someone chasing me, I landed in Faerie, almost as if the shadows knew to bring me from the human world over in order to save me. What happens when I take a portal in Faerie instead?

As the shadows thin and the darkness lightens, the space spinning like I'm trapped in a midnight twister, I grit my teeth and close my eyes, using every drop of strength Nine passed to me to keep us all together.

My hair is whipping around me, slapping me in the face as the wind carries us through the portal. I push and I push, screaming through tight lips and a clenched jaw.

Don't puke, Riley. Don't puke.

The air is cold, the tips of my sensitive fae ears feeling like someone's shoved them in a freezer. I can't tell if it's been seconds or minutes that we've been trapped in this strange in-between place, probably because I'm not only clueless, but I'm lost, too.

Someone is slipping away. I can't tell who with my eyes screwed shut, but it doesn't matter. I'm not willing to sacrifice any of my passengers.

Somewhere safe, I think. I don't care where we end up, so long as it's safe.

Isn't that how Nine said it worked? When I shade-walked in my sleep, traveling through shadows as if I were a full-blooded Dark Fae instead of having a Light Fae father and a human mom, my body always knew to bring me home.

That used to be the asylum. Then it was my nightmare of an abandoned house where I squatted until it claimed a second life right in front of me.

First Madelaine, then Carolina. No way I can go back there.

But, then, *where*?

The wind dies down as quickly as it began. I can see light seeping in through the cracks of my eyelids as I drag us through the other side of the Unseelie portal.

We land in a heap. My mother, my father, me, and the statue that used to be Nine.

My eyes fly open, terror gripping me that I've left myself blind for too long. What if Melisandre sent some of her soldiers after me? I don't even know if that's possible—there's only one fae who's left his mark on my skin so that he can follow me anywhere and he's with me—but I have to be sure.

The first thing I see when I focus is that I'm inside… somewhere. It's not familiar, but I don't see anyone waiting with a sword—or a scared shitless expression that a bunch of people just popped up out of nowhere.

On the plus side, I didn't bring us back to the sewer or the death house.

That's something, at least.

Now that I've assured myself that there's no immediate threat waiting to toss me back at the Fae Queen, I start to move. I've only got one thing on my mind right now. It's not even something I realize as I'm doing it. I crawl out from under the others, then wheel around on my knees, reaching immediately for Nine. I touch his cheek.

I *touch* his cheek.

I can feel the chill through the leather glove that both shields and hides my reconstructed hands. His cheek is hard, too, and I don't mean his sculpted cheekbones. Even his flesh is hard as a rock.

No.

A *statue*.

It takes all of my energy—and I don't have much after that last bit of shadow travel—to heft Nine up by his arm. It's easier than I expect to pull him away from the rest of the pile of fallen bodies. He might be hard as stone to the touch. Surprisingly, he doesn't weigh as much as he should have if he really was a marble statue.

I get him up on his feet, making sure he's sturdy before I check him all over.

His body is frozen in the same position as it was a heartbeat before the Fae Queen turned him into a gorgeous Nine statue: his long dark hair raining down his back, his shoulders hunched forward, his arm thrown out protectively. He'd been trying to keep me behind him, sacrificing himself for me.

He made a mistake, though. A huge honking mistake. So desperate to protect me like he's done my entire life, Nine entered into a bargain before making sure that there wasn't a way that the Fae Queen could twist the terms. He didn't and she did and now Nine's frozen while Melisandre is probably losing her damn mind that I escaped her clutches before she could force me to suffer the same fate.

I would've, too. To save my parents.

That was the bargain—the deal—that Melisandre offered me. Give up my freedom, stand as a statue in her gardens where she could keep an eye on me, and she would let the parents I've never known go free.

For twenty years, they were frozen just like Nine, all because they'd had the bad luck to create a halfling that was the star of the Shadow Prophecy.

Just like Nine, they'd sacrificed themselves for me back when I was barely an infant. Trading my life for theirs… it had seemed like a good idea at the time. Besides, it wasn't like I thought I had any other way out of her palace in Faerie.

Until the golden fae who haunted my thoughts and my dreams for more than six years helped me escape…

No. Don't think about Rys, I tell myself. My last glimpse of the Light Fae was as he fell beneath the weight of Melisandre's personal guard.

I couldn't save him. I have to focus on the ones that I can.

Once I've proved to myself that Nine is completely still and unmoving but otherwise okay, I turn to my other two passengers and get a huge surprise.

My mother is awake.

My father… isn't.

He looks bad. Like, really bad. In the Fae Queen's Court, I compared my father to Rys. His skin wasn't as bronze as the other Light Fae. It was still a few shades darker than my pale tone.

Now, he's lost any color that he had.

What's going on?

When I stole them away from Melisandre's throne room,

they were statues just like Nine. The spell on them seems to have failed now that we're back in the human world. Though Ash looks like hell on the floor, his body is relaxed into a totally different position than it had been.

He's not frozen. Neither is Callie.

What's going on?

My mother has a dazed expression on her face as she slowly pulls herself into a sitting position. Her long white-blonde hair falls forward, a curtain that covers her shocky face. She shoves it over one shoulder, glancing around, her brow furrowing as she looks at our dingy surroundings. It's dark in here, the only light coming in through the shuttered windows, and she's obviously confused.

I know the second her gaze falls on the Light Fae lying on his side, his eyes closed, his chest still. Is he breathing? I... I can't tell and, hovering near the frozen Nine, I can't find the balls to check.

"Ash?"

She crawls over to him, reaching for him but not quite touching him. Her fingers are shaking, her eyes big and wild in her pretty face. Even as she rears back, her expression accusing, she's still so very lovely.

"He's... what did you do to him? Who *are* you?"

Isn't that a loaded question?

I can't bring myself to answer her. Not yet. A lump lodges in my throat as I gape like a fish. Finally, because I can't help but quail under the fierce yet frightened look on her face, I say, "I didn't have any choice. I had to bring him through the portal."

"Portal?" she echoes. "What kind? You don't look like one of his people."

No. I don't. Face to face with the mother I lost when I was one-year-old—looking at the woman I was convinced up until recently had abandoned me—there's no denying that I look like *her*.

Same delicate features. Same pale hair that falls in a straight sheet, though hers just about hits her elbows so it's longer than mine. Same blue eyes that are in abject disbelief of what we're seeing.

Shit, give or take a couple of years, we're the same age.

I gulp. "I'm half," I tell her, not ready to admit that I'm only half because of her. "But that's not the way we came here. I shade-walked with you guys to save you."

Her eyes are drawn back to her mate, to my dad, as she shudders out a breath.

"Why would you do that? Iron always made him sick, but Ash got used to it. Shadow travel, though? He's a Light Fae. Part of the Seelie. And no Seelie can survive walking through an Unseelie portal."

My stomach stinks.

Oh, no. Did I just kill my dad?

"I didn't know," I blurt out, dropping to my knees at her side. "I didn't have a choice. I don't know what she would've done to you guys if I left you behind."

"She?" My mother doesn't stop running her hands over him as if, some way, that'll help revive him. Except for the tiniest flutters of his eyelashes, he's as still as Nine. "The last thing I remember is being dragged in front of the Fae Queen. Who are you?" she asks again. "What's happening? What's going on?"

Somehow, telling this young-looking woman that I'm her twenty-one-year-old daughter doesn't seem like it would go over so well.

First, Ash.

First, we have to save my dad.

"Here. Let me. I did this to him… maybe I can help."

The shadows answer to me. If they're hurting him because he's a Light Fae like Rys, maybe I can do something to fix him. Mimicking the other woman, I place my hands over his middle, letting out a sharp curse when his body just... it *bucks*. A quick jerk, his body bowing as he rises a few inches off of the floor before slamming down on his back.

His eyelids flutter again, then he goes motionless.

Right over his belly, there's a ray of golden light that expands to a softball-sized circle.

My mother gasps. Reaching down, she grabs one of his limp hands in hers, squeezing it tight. "Ash! Ash, sweetheart! It's me, Callie!"

He doesn't answer.

"Do it again," she pleads. "Whatever you did, please do it again."

"I'll try."

When I lay my hands over him again, he doesn't react, though the golden glow seems to spread a little further. Frustrated, afraid, and panicking, it hits me that the leather might be holding me back. It's a cover, an added layer of protection, but could it be affecting me pulling on the shadows?

Only one way to find out.

I grip the glove by the tips of the fingers on my left hand, yanking on the thumb then the other four before quickly peeling the leather off. It's musty in this empty, quiet room, but it's chilly, too, and I feel it on the mottled, clammy skin.

Quickly, quickly, I pull off the second glove.

Out of the corner of my eyes, I notice that she recoils when she sees my bare hands.

If I wasn't so desperate to fix my mistake, that might have hurt. Me? I'm used to my ruined hands. And she might be my mother, but we're as much strangers as we are blood.

I'll deal with that later. Right now? I have to figure out a way to save my father.

Oh, this is so freaking weird. I have a *dad*.

I don't even have to touch him. I feel an answering tug in my gut as I reach for the shadows that I can sense burrowing deep inside of him. It's hard to explain how it feels. Almost like a prickle against my skin, an itch I can't scratch. I take a deep breath and grab it.

They come flying toward me, wrapping my hands, hiding them from sight as Ash starts to glow like he's on fire.

It only lasts for a moment. As the bright, golden light spreads across his long, lean body, it reaches a fever pitch before dimming just as suddenly. He gasps, though his eyes are still closed, and he shudders before his breath levels out. He's still not as dark of a bronze shade as… as Rys is—*was?*—but he's got *some* color back.

Thank God.

He's breathing. It's something. He's asleep now, and he probably needs it, but he's alive and I tell Callie as much as I sit back on my heels.

Even though the shadows are covering my hands, almost like they're make-shift gloves, I grab my discarded ones and hurriedly slip them back on.

Callie places her palm on the top of Ash's head, running her fingers through the tawny hair that's fanned out beneath him like a pillow. Her stricken look of fear has faded to one of pure relief as she finally tears her gaze away from him, glancing over at me.

"Thank you. For saving him."

"I had to." And not just because his near-death experience is totally my fault. "He's my… he's my father."

Her eyes widen and her mouth opens. Her head tilts just

enough to make it clear that she's taking all of me in. As if, for the first time since she came out from under the Fae Queen's spell, she's actually *seeing* me.

"Zella?" she whispers.

Oof.

"It's Riley, actually." And, okay, my quick answer is probably a bit cheeky. I can't help it. I've never been good with my emotions and, well, how am I supposed to react, coming face to face with the mother I thought was long gone? "The first foster home I went to, they changed my name."

Her voice breaks a little as she echoes, "Foster home?"

"No mom. No dad." I shrug. "I had to go somewhere, right?"

Her forehead furrows, faint wrinkles pulling on her brow as she asks me softly, "How old are you, Riley? How long has it been since the soldiers tried to take my baby from us?"

I'd been wondering how long it would take before she asked that question—and hoping against hope that I'd never have to answer it.

So, of course, it's the first thing she asks.

The lump in my throat seems to grow a little bigger. *My baby...* that's right. Because the last time we were together, I was a little butterball baby and she was running for her life, driving a stolen car that eventually ended up abandoned—along with me in the backseat—outside of a rundown gas station when the fae caught up with her.

That was twenty years ago.

"I turned twenty-one last summer," I tell her. "You were lost in Faerie for twenty years."

CHAPTER 2

My mother—*Callie*—is staring at me. I can feel it and, now that my heart has stopped racing and I'm sure that my father—*Ash*—is going to be okay, I purposely avoid her open attention.

This is too, too weird.

I mean, hell. I didn't know what to do when she was crying. Patting her on the back seemed a little awkward, and pretending that she shouldn't be upset was just *cold*. I had an urge to apologize, but since I didn't know why I should be apologizing or even how to say that I was sorry, I got up and acted as if I didn't notice her sobs.

I don't blame her. I'd be crying, too, if I woke up one morning and discovered I'd lost twenty years of my life in the blink of an eye.

Even now that she's sitting cross-legged at her mate's side, absently patting his hair as she silently watches me move around, I refuse to turn around.

Nine is standing where I put him a few feet away from us. I

glance at him, wondering why Melisandre's magic held through the portal when it came to him but not the other two. Could it be because the spell was fresh? I don't know, and I'd give every damn thing I have to know the answer to that so I could bring him back to me.

Not that I have much. I've got the clothes on my back, a pair of strangers that I suddenly feel like I'm responsible for, and that's about it. I don't even have the nail on a length of string that was my only protection against the fae. When the Fae Queen threatened my head for bringing the small piece of iron with me into Faerie, I had to remove it before she called on one of her Light Fae guards to do it for her.

I tiptoe around the disaster of a room.

I have no freaking clue where I am.

Traveling through a portal, crossing over from the human world to Faerie and back... I've often compared it to being in the middle of a tornado. Based on the level of destruction in this room? It's like I brought it in here with me.

Wherever *here* is.

Callie's soft, gentle voice cuts through the heavy, awkward silence.

"If I knew we were having guests, I would've straightened up. Then again, it didn't look like this the last time I was here." She exhales, a sound that could be a sigh or maybe a stifled chuckle. "Ash told me he would buy us time. I'm glad he's alive but, man, that couch was super expensive."

And now it's been ripped apart.

Wait—

I couldn't have heard her right. "What? You know that couch?"

It's so not about the couch.

Her voice is a little scratchy, rougher than before when she says, "This is our home."

The *our* hits me dead in the chest. I rub the spot beneath my tits with the heel of my hand. "Really?"

"Me and Ash. We live here. Or… lived here, I guess. Twenty years ago." She keeps saying it like that, disbelief mixed with sadness, and a touch of wistfulness thrown in for good measure as if thinking about all she's missed while she was trapped by the Fae Queen. It makes me squirm every time she mentions it. "It's still here. Ash was right."

I glance over my shoulder at her, daring a quick peek. "I don't get it."

A small smile tugs on her lips. "He brought as much magic to this place as he could. When he was sure that the queen would be coming after our family, he spent more than a year putting up the wards, concealing us as best he could. Her soldiers might hunt us down, but they wouldn't find it easy. Humans? Impossible. And now… look. It's still here."

It is. It also looks like someone—or a couple of someones—ransacked the place. Based on the slashes covering the poor couch, the pieces of hacked-at wood, the broken glass… they used a knife or something just as sharp to destroy it. Frustration that they came all that way only to find their prize missing?

Probably.

Slash marks…

My stomach tightens as I remember the diamond blades on the Fae Queen's soldier's swords.

How *lovely*.

"Why would they have come all the way here?"

She hesitates. I hear the hum as she searches for an answer and turn, giving her my profile. She's nibbling on her bottom lip. Her shadowed expression is locked on my face.

Duh.

"They were looking for me."

It's not a question.

Good thing, too, because I don't receive an answer for it. Not like I needed one but, right as Callie opens her mouth as if she had something to say, we hear the soft rustle of fabric against the floor as Ash finally rolls from his back to his side before tentatively pushing himself up.

She lets out a squeal of surprise coupled with joy as Ash slowly rises. He's weak, a little groggy, and the shadow travel didn't do him any favors, but as he straightens, I watch as a sliver of sunlight streams in through the window, landing on his outstretched arm.

He shudders, then pulls himself up to his considerable height. Straight-backed and proud, he turns in time to open his arms right as Callie throws herself into them.

For a few moments, it's as if I've disappeared. I'm gone. They only have eyes for each other.

And, though it's been only a couple of hours real time—not accounting for travel between the human world and Faerie—since I last spoke to Nine, I miss him so bad that I *hurt*.

My parents are murmuring to each other, speaking in hushed murmurs. They're not excluding me on purpose and, honestly, I'm glad. With Ash to distract Callie, it gives me a second to just breathe.

He's alive. I didn't kill him.

That's a plus.

Of course, I begin to think that might've been a bit of a mistake when my father slowly pulls away from my mother, throwing daggers across the room to where I placed Nine.

"Ninetroir."

His voice is low. Hard. I don't know if it's because he hasn't used it in twenty years or something else since every fae I've ever met has the most lovely, lyrical voice, but the rasp of it immediately has me on edge.

"What is he doing here?" he asks before jabbing a finger in my direction. "And who is this girl? She's touched..." He pauses, his lips curling back to reveal blindingly white canines as he bares his teeth. "She wears Ninetroir's brand. How can that be?"

The name is like a punch to my gut the second time he wields it, the reminder that I let Nine touch me—that I touched *him*—making me ache even harder. My heart twists and I take a deep breath.

Ninetroir. Nine's true name, one of the best gifts I've ever been given. And Ash is using it with an angry, rough edge cutting into his voice.

I wasn't expecting that. Nine never explained much about how he knew my dad, but I got the idea that they were... if not friends, then comrades.

Was I wrong?

Callie tilts her head back, looking up at Ash. "Don't you remember? You gave me the pebble, you told me to find him. It was our plan. You wanted to involve Ninetroir. I only did what you said."

I blink, stunned.

The pebble.

How does she know about the pebble?

For some reason, Nine has been carrying a pebble around with him lately. I remember thinking it was weird but not paying too much attention to it. As soon as I bring Nine back to life—and I will, I swear to myself—that's gonna change.

I need to know more about the pebble, especially now that Callie has mentioned it like that.

Ash, it seems, knows exactly what the meaning behind the pebble is. At least, he doesn't ask any follow-up questions. He just nods, accepting what Callie said. "That explains why Ninetroir is involved. But who is she?"

"Can't you tell?" Callie asks. "Ash, honey, isn't it obvious?"

I know what he's seeing. Honestly, the two of us could pass for sisters, if not twins, we look that similar. There's no denying that I'm related to Callie.

He scrutinizes me. I can see him putting two and two together and getting five. He doesn't want to admit the truth that's right in front of him.

And, shit, I can't do this right now.

I thought I could.

I *can't*.

"I'm, uh…" I gesture behind me, walking backward as I purposefully put space between us. This is just too weird for me right now. "I'm gonna go scout this place out, make sure nobody followed us here."

"What? No. Zel—"

Nope.

I cut Callie off before she can use that name again. I tap my chest, pointedly ignoring their curious expressions as they both lock in on my glove. Even if I thought this was the right time to explain my hands, I can't. I just… *can't*.

"My name is Riley," I remind Callie. "Riley Thorne." I meet Ash's strange golden gaze. "And, um, I guess I'm your daughter."

I'm so glad that I still have Carolina's money in my pocket. Without it, we'd be even more screwed than we already are.

As soon as I drop that bomb, I make my escape. I have every intention of returning—especially when Callie calls after me, asking me not to go—but I need a couple of minutes to myself, especially since Ash's response to my revelation is to gape at me like I've sprouted a second head or something.

So, before either one of them can try to stop me, I continue with my excuse, telling them that I'm scouting out the building, checking out the neighborhood, going for some food, and then I rush out of the room like I've got the devil chasing behind me.

Only it's not the devil. It's my past and, yeah, that's *worse*.

As I flee, I notice something. It turns out, the mess surrounding us is contained to the space we landed in.

That's the good news.

The bad news?

Our sanctuary is not in the best part of… wherever we are.

I probably should have asked Callie for more details about where we landed other than that it was their—*not my*—home. Once I slip out of the room, I realize that we're in an apartment building; there are at least four other doors on our floor, plus an elevator. The elevator is parked at the end of the hall. It smells even mustier out here, the weak lights barely enough to help guide me toward the elevator.

I tiptoe quietly since I don't want to disturb any neighbors. It makes matters worse when I climb inside and see that we're on the fourteenth floor. That leaves thirteen until the lobby and I keep my fingers crossed the whole time that no one joins me on the trip down.

Thinking ahead, I worry about how I'm going to sneak out of the lobby without anyone seeing me—only to discover that there's no one around. And I mean *no one*. I take a side-door just in case, and snort when I see that the glass door is shattered, yellow caution tape surrounding it.

Okay. That might explain it.

Wherever we are, it's nothing like Acorn Falls. It's an urban environment, a city with tall skyscrapers and countless businesses and storefronts everywhere. I don't go too far, since I'm not sure I'd be able to find my way back, and I settle on a fast food joint around the corner.

I'm anxious and worried and scared, but I'm also a little hungry so I jump at the chance for a snack. Who knows when I'll eat again next?

I retrace my steps, going back to the building I slipped out of earlier. On second inspection, it's a *dump*. I don't know how it's still standing. The front door has some more yellow caution tape binding it closed, and a big, red sign that reads **CONDEMNED** posted in the middle.

Condemned?

How *nice*.

Another big difference from Acorn Falls? There are homeless people on every corner. Normally, I don't think I would notice, but after my encounter with that man right before I saw Dr. Gillespie in the deli, I'm not taking any chances. I peek closely as I scurry pass, patting my loose hair around my weirdo fae ears so that they're hidden.

A man is slumped along the side of the building, right by the entrance that I used. I was rushing on my way out, recklessly trying to put distance between me and my parents at first, and I didn't notice him.

On my way back in, though?

There's something about him that makes me stop. I think back to just... shit, this morning? Technically, it was only this morning... I think back to this morning and I remember the old drunk with the watery blue eyes who tried to stop me from going into the deli.

His head is bowed, sleeping—at least, I *hope* he's sleeping. I wish I could see what his face looked like, or if his eyes are blue, before chiding myself for suspecting the worst.

That was Acorn Falls. This place... isn't.

And I'm being ridiculous.

I pull the wad of cash from my pocket, quickly pulling a bill from the stack before shoving it back in place.

He never stirs.

I fold the bill, sticking it inside the crumpled coffee cup set in front of him. There's a couple of quarters in there, maybe a penny or two, and I'm glad to see that I'm giving him a five. It's better than the single I thought I grabbed.

"Here you go. For whatever you need it for tonight."

My life's a mess. If I can make it a little easier for someone else, might as well.

ON MY WAY BACK IN, I'M TORN BETWEEN WANTING TO DIG INTO THE bag of food I picked up and getting a better look at our hideaway. The yellow tape was a big clue that something was off, not to mention the busted door and the funky, musty smell that permeates the whole place.

I peek my head into the stairwell I find off to the right side of the lobby. The lights flicker, the electric bulbs a high-pitched whine. With a loud *pop*, the one directly above me shorts out. I throw my hands over my head to protect it in case the glass shatters. Luckily, it doesn't, but that was too close a call.

Elevator, it is.

The ride back to the fourteenth floor goes a lot quicker now that I'm almost back. I try to come up with another excuse to run away again, realize that I can't avoid them forever—and, even if

I could, I couldn't leave Nine behind—then put on my big girl panties and go back inside the apartment.

I know I've got the right one when I see the furniture on the side, the scattered debris, my gorgeous Shadow Man still frozen in the corner, and my parents watching me carefully as if they expect me to bolt again.

They're not entirely wrong.

There's a small table set to the side of the front door. It somehow survived in one piece and I put the bag of take-out on top of it. Something tells me that the food's gonna have to wait a second.

I don't know what happened while I was gone, but the Light Fae seems a lot calmer now.

He's standing with Callie, his hands on her shoulders, his head dipped low as he looks directly at her face, almost like he keeps expecting her to disappear. Even when he backs away, glancing over at me as I shuffle into the room, he keeps one hand on her elbow.

With the other, he gestures for me to walk toward him.

"Come here. Give me your arm. Let me touch you."

I can't do it. I *can't*.

He doesn't know my history. He doesn't know my past. As a full-blooded fae, I should've expected him to want to do this.

I shake my head. "I'm not supposed to let anyone touch me."

Though Ash obviously doesn't understand how much meaning I throw behind such a simple sentence, he's quick enough to read between the lines.

"I'm your father, Zella. Even if I was at full-strength, my touch wouldn't affect you. My blood runs through your veins. I have no power over you."

Yeah. Maybe.

Except for my name, I'm thinking.

Despite me telling them both earlier that my name is Riley, this isn't the first time I've been called *Zella*. How much longer before he tacks on a command and I prove that, maybe his touch doesn't affect me, but his using my true name will?

I notice that he's careful not to do that. Ash might be giving me orders, but he doesn't use my true name when he does. He saves that to punctuate his statements, though, as if he wants to make sure I know he's talking to me.

When it comes to my parents, I'm not so sure how to address them, so I don't. I figure my best bet is to think of them as Ash and Callie, though the fact that they're my mom and dad is a constant refrain in the back of my flustered thoughts.

"Why do you have to touch me?" I ask suspiciously.

Not like I'm going to let him. Proving my point, I don't move any closer to him.

His lips purse. I don't think he likes me questioning him. Oh, well. He'll learn.

"It's another layer of protection."

Does he think I was born yesterday?

Okay. That's probably the worst way to look at it considering, but seriously? If he can't affect me with a touch, then there's only one reason he'd want to leave his mark—and it's so that he can try to erase Nine's.

That's gonna be a nope, especially since it's not like I can just snap my fingers and my haphephobia would disappear. When it comes to Nine, I can touch him. I'm beginning to think that it's only because it *is* Nine.

I shake my head and stay on the other side of the room. "No thanks."

"You're afraid," says Ash.

"I'm not—"

"Humans lie. So, it seems, do halflings. Zella, I can smell the fear coming from you."

"It's not you. I mean, I'm not afraid of you. It's just... I'm not so good with being touched."

"Oh, *sweetie*."

I can only imagine what kind of terrible thoughts are running through Callie's head. To make matters worse, not all of them are wrong—I didn't have the easiest time going from group home to group home, with a couple of fosters in between—but that's not what I meant.

"It's something I've dealt with for a long time," I say lightly, totally downplaying it while I offer an easy explanation. "When you're taught from an early age not to let the fae touch you, but that anyone could be a fae wearing glamour, it's understandable that you might develop a complex or two."

To my surprise—and obvious relief—he drops it. Letting his hand fall to his side, continuing to touch Callie as if that's the only thing keeping him grounded, Ash nods over at me. "Your mother tells me that you're the one who brought us out of Faerie and broke Melisandre's spell."

I definitely brought them through the portal—nearly killed Ash doing it, too—so there's no denying that. Breaking Melisandre's spell? I'm still trying to figure that part out.

"I had to." I'm wary. Defensive, too. It comes through in the careful edge to my voice. "I couldn't leave you there."

"What were you doing in Faerie? If Ninetroir was responsible for you, as I've been told, he should've kept you from the danger. His debt would demand it."

I don't like to think about Nine's debt. We got into a huge fight over it when I first discovered that he'd been commanded to watch over me all because he owed my parents a debt and my mother called it in the day the fae caught up with her. Now I know that the debt was only part of the reason he felt responsible for me. The fact that I was his fated mate was up there, too.

I've never been so good with authority figures. Add it to the undeniable truth that the Light Fae is a stranger to me and Ash has me crossing my arms over my chest as he stares across the room at me, expecting my answer.

Oh, he'll get it all right.

"It's not like I went there on purpose. It happened and I faced the Fae Queen and, sure, Nine's a statue now, but at least you two are okay. Right?"

"I know Melisandre. There's no way she would have let you escape from under her nose. Not with us, and not with someone she cursed." He shutters his eyes, a look of relief flashing across his features as he comes to the absolutely wrong conclusion. "You finished the prophecy. The false queen is gone."

I shake my head. "Um. No."

His eyes open. "No?"

"I didn't fight her. I kinda just stole you guys away from her. She's probably even more pissed off than before and, uh, she was pretty pissed to begin with."

"Then Melisandre will still be after you because you're the Shadow," Ash realizes. "This isn't over."

I shrug helplessly.

Callie gasps while Ash spits out a word, cursing in a language that isn't like anything in this world. And it totally is a curse. I don't need to understand what he's saying to know the meaning behind it.

Oops.

I guess they really thought I had ended the Fae Queen already.

Yeah, not quite.

CHAPTER 3

Before Ash says anything in response to that, I try to take control of the conversation.

I need *some* kind of control here.

"Now that you know she's still a threat, I have to ask. This place... do you think she'll follow us here?"

Because I'd been thinking about it while I did my quick tour around the building and the neighborhood. At first, I couldn't understand why this empty apartment was... I don't know... frozen in time or something. Callie tried to tell me it was magic and, okay, I got that.

Then I saw that the building has probably been condemned for a while. Unless the fae have a way to trace me here—and they don't, thanks to Nine's touch—I think this might be our safest option for a place to stay while we figure out our next step.

Which, whether Ash likes it or not, definitely involves fixing Nine.

It takes him a moment to answer me. Finally, he says, "It's

possible. She has a long memory and her loyal guard. She prefers to surround herself with Seelie, but she has just as many Unseelie who follow her despite her glamour. They won't be able to trace us here precisely, but if she sends out her full guard, she'll be able to search around the clock."

Not the answer I wanted to hear, but at least that answers another of my biggie questions.

"Because she's one of them, right? She's a Dark Fae."

He nods. "She hides it well. Even fooled Oberon in the beginning. But I used to be part of her guard. Only a few of us have ever seen her lose her glamour, but I can guarantee it. She's a Cursed One."

That doesn't change anything. At most, it just proves that Carolina was being honest when she told me that her mistress was a Dark Fae.

"I don't get why she hides it. Why the blonde hair? The yellow eyes? The act?"

"Melisandre always wanted to rule Faerie. The Shadow Court is second to the Summer Court, the Seelie Court. She could've easily taken the Unseelie throne but she'd still owe her allegiance to Oberon. So, instead, she passed herself off as one of his subjects before stealing his throne. She'll stop at nothing to keep it."

Don't I know it.

If it wasn't for Rys reminding me about the power of the pockets and distracting the Fae Queen's soldiers so I could escape, I might have learned that the hard way.

No.

Not *might*.

Considering I was seconds away from accepting her bargain, sacrificing my life and my freedom in exchange for my parents and Nine, if it wasn't for Rys's help and some quick thinking, I'd be a statue in the Fae Queen's garden somewhere.

And that's if she didn't follow through with her unsaid threat to lop off my head the first chance she got.

"Then it's a good thing that this place is warded." I turn to Callie. "That's what you said, right? They don't know that you guys are awake. How would they guess we'd come here?" I'm talking myself into believing that we're... if not safe, then at least *safer*. "The shadows leading us here has gotta be a huge break."

It bought us some time, I'm sure of it. Time that I can use to focus on what I'm going to do next: fix Nine.

I don't know what happened with my parents. They were statues when we were in Faerie. Now they're not. If I have to wrap Nine up in shadows and transport him there and back a hundred time, I will if only to have the chance to talk to him again and have him respond.

We have a *lot* to discuss.

I'm not even obsessing over the Fae Queen and her strange vendetta right now. Oh, I wasn't kidding when I said she's gonna be super pissed. In the back of my mind, I'm so freaking terrified about how she'll retaliate for my skin of the teeth escape. But Melisandre is in Faerie and I'm here in Newport—at least, that's what the address on the food receipt says—with my parents and my... mate?

So, yeah.

You can say that my priorities have shifted since this morning.

And then Ash goes on to tell me, as if he can read my mind, "Don't fret, Zella. You won't have to fear the queen much longer. Now that I'm here again, I will ensure that Melisandre pays for what she's done to our family."

Except to mumble, "It's Riley," I don't argue with him.

What can I say?

All I've ever wanted was someone to step in front of me, to protect me, to tell me that everything will be okay and that I have nothing to worry about.

I finally got that with Nine. My Shadow Man who spent my entire life teaching me, shielding me, making sure that I have enough information to protect myself. Then, when the Fae Queen used my parents as leverage against me, he made the ultimate sacrifice for me.

He gave up his life for mine. So desperate to save me, he didn't even think like a fae. Instead of looking two steps ahead, he fell right into Melisandre's trap.

Now he's a statue and it's all my fault. It's my turn to save him.

Not like I tell Ash that, either.

I don't have to.

One look. That's all it takes. A fleeting glance to where I propped Nine up in the corner of the destroyed apartment and my dad knows.

He knows—and he doesn't like it.

Maybe he *can* read minds...

If looks could kill, Nine would be going up in smoke. Ash's golden gaze glimmers as he bores holes into the Dark Fae.

"He shouldn't be here. He was charged with watching over you, keeping you safe. Callie told me she allowed him one touch. But the brand on your skin... it's far more recent than that."

Well, yeah. Because Nine touched me only hours ago when I gave him permission to kiss me—and then he claimed me.

Can Ash tell that about me, too?

His mouth goes tight and I'm thinking *yes*.

"Ninetroir owed me a debt," he says, glowering. "I didn't give him my daughter."

Only, if everything I've learned so far is true, he kinda did. At least, *Callie* did, didn't she? When she commanded him to save me right before the Light Fae captured her.

Was that first touch my undoing or the only thing that kept me alive for as long as it did?

It doesn't matter. Nine might have claimed me, but I have no problem claiming him back.

He's *my* Shadow Man.

Callie clears her throat, drawing my dad's attention over to her. I look, too, because it's better than watching him glare at Nine.

"What about the prophecy, Ash?" she says softly.

"The prophecy doesn't mean a thing," he replies. "How can it? There are so many different versions. The only thing they agree is that a halfling is fated to face Melisandre. That's all."

I'm not so sure what that has to do with Nine. Considering we only just managed to slip from the Fae Queen's grasp, I really don't want to be reminded how close I came to giving up my freedom when I finally did face Melisandre.

Or what she cost me when I didn't fall for her trap.

And now another Light Fae thinks they're going to keep me from the one person who was always there for me?

Dad or no dad, that's not gonna work for me.

The words burst out of me. Even if I wanted to swallow them back, it's impossible.

"It doesn't matter what the stupid prophecy says. Fated or not, I knew that I loved Nine long before I heard anything about the Shadow Prophecy. Now I know that I'm in love with him. You're fae. You've been frozen into some kind of statue, just like him. You know how terrible it is. I lost you guys for my whole life. I don't want to also lose my mate."

"No."

No?

He shakes his head, wincing slightly at the motion before stopping. His jaw tightens as he announces, "I forbid this mating. He can stay like he is. I won't let him have my daughter."

I almost don't believe what I'm hearing. I've known this guy for... what? Like half an hour? And he thinks he's going to separate me from Nine?

Callie tries to interject. "Ash—"

"I will not stand here and allow our daughter to bond herself to a Cursed One, fate or no fate. Ninetroir has always hated humans. He'd make her life miserable."

Is he fucking serious?

For too many years, Nine was the only person in my life who cared about me. So he had a disdain for other humans. He never hid that. But he liked *me*. He loves *me*.

I'm beginning to wonder if it was a mistake, taking this hardheaded fae male with me when I fled from Melisandre.

Callie eases toward her mate, trying to calm him as if she can sense that he's a walking timebomb and the fuse is already lit.

And then there's me. I'm seconds away from exploding myself.

"Ash, sweetheart. You have to admit that that's not the biggest problem we have at the moment. The queen's soldiers came after our baby once before. Now that we're home again, we have to focus on that."

"She's a shade-walker, and a good one. She has to be. Zella is right. Discounting our wards, the shadows would cover our trail. I have no idea how she knew to bring us here, but Melisandre won't be able to trace it unless she touched her."

Callie's hand flies to her face, her fingers running nervously over her bottom lip. "Do you think she did?"

Okay. I've had enough of this. "Hey! Can you not talk about me like I'm not here?"

He goes on as if he didn't hear me. "I can sense it on her skin. The possessive brand, the fae-touch... it belongs to Ninetroir. Zella is telling the truth. That's the mark of a *ffrindau*."

"soulmate," whispers my mom.

He jerks his head, an angry nod that has him wincing again a second later. He's hiding it pretty well, but the shadows and the iron are still affecting him.

But that doesn't stop him from reacting when Callie lowers her hand, hugging herself.

"So it's done. Our baby is mated to the Dark Fae I gave her to. This is all my fault."

Ash surges forward, wrapping Callie up in a comforting hug that sends a rush of mixed emotions through me.

"I swear to Oberon," he vows solemnly, "I will end Ninetroir before I let him claim our child."

Yup. This has gone way too far now.

Am I the only one who remembers that it's the Fae Queen we should all be worrying about? Not the frozen Nine statue?

"Oh my God. Really? I am *literally* right here. Nine, too. In case you haven't realized it by now, I chose to take him with us because he's *mine*. I love him. How would you like it if someone tried to separate you two? Ash? Callie? Huh?"

Know what? I think I've finally got my point across.

At my purposeful use of their names, my mother winces. Too bad. I'm still coming to grips that these two are my *parents* after believing for my entire life that I didn't have any. Between my abandonment issues and my panic disorder, they're lucky that I'm not running from this apartment, screaming at them to get away from me. In the heat of the moment, I've finally decided that I should just call them by their names because, shit, *mom* and *dad*... I can't.

Damn it.

Callie seems to understand, even if she doesn't like it. "Of course. We're sorry." She lays her hand on the side of Ash's throat. "Aren't we?"

Ash, who was visibly bristling following my heated question, relaxes under Callie's reassuring touch. He nods, then swallows roughly, his Adam's apple rising and falling with the motion. He unscrews his jaw just enough to say, "Yes."

The word seems like it's been dragged out of him. At least I know it's the truth.

I can't believe I'm having this argument. This morning, when I woke up in the Acorn Falls cemetery, my only thought was where I was going to go next now that returning to the Wilkes House—and Carolina's corpse—was abso-fucking-lutely impossible.

I've been running on empty ever since Rys found me sleeping next to Madelaine's grave. Between the way I attacked him with the shovel, then my flight into Acorn Falls' downtown for a stupid cup of coffee, to running from Dr. Gillespie and jumping into a portal that plopped me out in the Fae Queen's garden... and now this... I've been two steps ahead of actually processing everything that's happened to me in such a short time.

With Ash looming in front of me, Callie looking at me as if she still can't come to grips with the truth that I'm their daughter... well, shit. It suddenly catches up.

And I lose it.

The edge of my vision goes dark, blackness creeping in. The room is spinning. I start gulping in great big mouthfuls of air. It feels shallow, like someone is squeezing my chest and I can't fill my lungs up all the way. My ears are buzzing. My heart is thumping like mad.

The wave of panic crashes over my head. When it comes to the fight or flight reflex, I've always defaulted to one response.

I bolt.

Throwing the front door open, I run out of the apartment. I might've mumbled another excuse, something like I forgot ketchup packets or some shit like that, before I hoof it toward the elevator.

Anything to get out of there now.

I hear Callie call her mate's name, then say, "No, I've got this," before she bursts into the hall, closing the door behind her.

I'm not afraid of her. I'm not all that afraid of Ash, either—he's my father and I'd like to believe that means something—but he's fae. A Light Fae. A watered down version of the golden monster who haunted my dreams these last six years. When he starts making demands and decrees, his eyes lighting up like ember sparks in a dying fire, is it a surprise that he triggers my panic attacks?

But Callie… as she hurries after me, murmuring my name, I come to a halt. The urge to hide out in the elevator isn't so bad when it's just the two of us out here.

And then she says, "You have to forgive your father. I tried to explain to him everything you told me earlier. He's used to time going by and humans growing in a blink of an eye. He's Seelie… but you're his daughter. He… we can't believe that we missed *you* growing up."

The panic is terrible.

The guilt? Even *worse*.

"That's not my fault!" I'm shouting. I can't help it. "I didn't ask for this!"

"Sweetie, I know."

I throw my hand out, gesturing with my glove toward the closed door. "I didn't sign up to be the stupid Shadow. It's ruined my fucking life. I've spent twenty years with the threat of the fae hanging over my head. No parents. Everyone I ever cared about left me. The only one who seemed to was Nine and now he's gone."

Callie looks torn, like she doesn't know what to say to that. I don't blame her. Poor woman woke up from a twenty-year forced nap to find out that her precious baby is a wreck of an adult, that the world as she knows it is gone, and her mate is picking fights.

If I were in her shoes, I'd be praying for a trip back to the asylum. It's too much to ask of anyone. I'm seconds away from losing it and I *lived* through it. Callie got tossed from the frying pan into the fire—and she's looking over at me as if all she wants to do is make it all right.

It's that look. That maternal look that I've been missing my whole life that shatters me.

"Why did you leave me?" I ask. My voice breaks but I can't bring myself to care. No one else is around to hear it. "Why did you have to go?"

"Oh, sweetie." Callie's eyes glisten, the dark blue color—the same shade as mine—twinkling as she holds onto her tears. "That was the last thing I wanted to do. We knew that the Fae Queen would want to get to you sooner than later. We tried to be prepared. The iron in this building, keeping our home up high. The special wards. When they came, there was just enough time for two of us to get out. Me and my baby… me and you."

Just like it's only the two of us in the hallway now. Well, my dad, too, 'cause fae hearing is amazing. He's listening in on us. Bet.

I don't care. I need to hear this.

I need to *know*.

"And... Aislinn?"

Her head tilts a little, as if surprised that I know his true name. She lets it slip by, though, as she tells me, "My Ash stayed behind to give us the chance to get free. I'd say he's not an easy man to love, but we both know he's not a man. The fae are different. He doesn't mean to be so hard. He loves you."

He doesn't. He can't.

Ash doesn't know me. If he did, he'd know that I don't respond all that well to being told what to do among a whole host of other issues.

Callie nods assuringly. "Your father will do anything for his family. He sacrificed himself to buy us time. You've seen the apartment. They captured him, but he didn't go down easy."

"And then they captured you."

"That was my fault," she says again. "I know how to see through glamour. After I made my bargain with your... with Ninetroir, I was so relieved that I let down my guard." She frowns. "He was wearing a cap. I thought he was a harmless kid."

"Who?"

"The Light Fae who had the portal waiting inside of the damn Snack Shack. He let you go instead. You were just a child and he spared you. Your father and I... weren't."

No. They weren't, were they?

I'm speaking more to myself than my apologetic mother as I murmur, "So that's how I ended up an orphan in Black Pine."

It all makes sense now. Why she was driving a stolen car alone—since she was on the run without her mate—and why she was speeding like a bat out of hell as she pulled up to the abandoned gas station. The way the black and white, grainy security cam footage showed the pretty blonde woman talking to an empty shadow, and how she managed to disappear off the face of the planet after she followed the gas station "employee" into the rundown convenience store.

I'd often tortured myself with that footage, watching it over and over again as I tried to make sense of the reasons behind her inexplicable actions.

I wasn't abandoned. By making the deal with Nine, bartering my safety for a debt he owed my dad, Callie saved me from suffering the same fate that happened to her and Ash.

While I'm lost in my own thoughts, Callie looks confused, like she should know the name but can't quite place it.

She should.

"Black Pine?"

"It's where you left me," I explain. "The town with the gas station."

"Oh." She pales. "I guess I knew that."

"You do?"

"It seems like yesterday. To me, it really was." With a soft exhale, she says, "But twenty years…"

For me, Black Pine isn't just a place I knew from two decades ago when I was a baby. Fourteen years after the morning they discovered me in the backseat of a stolen Buick, I moved back to the small town in the middle of nowhere when my choice was between the asylum or jail.

"It's more than that."

"Zella?"

She let *Aislinn* pass. Just this one last time, I let her have *Zella*.

Instead, I tell her all about the asylum. It pours out of me.

Not the magic part—not about how it's a place where the fae stick troublesome humans to forget about them—but the sessions and the doctors and the therapy that, six years later, didn't do a damn thing to help me.

When I'm done, I cross my hands over my chest, building a barrier between us. It hadn't been my intention to show her just what a screw-up I am within hours of meeting me, but I couldn't help it.

I don't regret it, though. Especially since, once it's all out, I think that Callie is finally beginning to see *me*. Riley. Not the baby that she lost, but the woman that I've become.

Whether we like it or not, we're all in this together. From the moment Melisandre tried to use my long lost parents as a lure for her trap, I'm not just looking out for me.

Madelaine died because of me. Carolina... I still can't believe she's gone.

No matter what I have to do—no matter how strong I have to stand against my Light Fae father—I won't let there be any other casualties of this stupid war between me and the Fae Queen.

Once I come up with a way to save Nine, that is.

CHAPTER 4

The apartment has two bedrooms.

I've already seen the living room, since that's where we landed, and if you turn around, you see the hallway that cuts right into the kitchen. The foyer is on my left until I turn, and the hall leads to three doorways. The bathroom is behind one, Ash and Callie's bedroom is behind another, and then there's the last door.

It takes a while before I work up the nerve to go back inside instead of hiding out near the elevator. Ash is waiting for us just inside the foyer when I finally do, Callie guiding the way. The shadowed look on his pale bronze face tells me he heard every word, just like I thought. To my surprise, though, he doesn't say anything other than to offer me some of the cold food I brought back.

The power and the gas are on. Don't ask me how, since fae magic and electricity don't get along at the best of times, and it's not like someone's been paying the bills the last twenty years, but I've learned not to look a gift horse in the mouth. The microwave is old-fashioned and it takes Callie to operate it, but we nuke up the burgers and stand in the kitchen eating them together.

This has probably been one of the longest days of my life. Traumatic as hell, too. Aside from losing Nine and gaining my parents, it's barely been thirty-six hours since I returned to the Wilkes House and discovered Carolina the way I did.

I need *sleep*.

I wait until "dinner"'s done and the sun's gone down before I tell them that I'm about to crash. As soon as the light fades, I notice that Ash loses the little color he earned earlier when the sunlight hit his skin. The dark goes to work on him almost immediately. Callie sees it, too. When I mention I'm dying for some sleep, she agrees and the way she clasps Ash's hand to pull him toward their old bedroom is a major clue that she's pushing past her own apprehension and uncertainty by pouring all of her energy into looking out for him.

Good defense mechanism.

Me? I make sure the whole apartment is locked down.

Pointless, I know. If the place is condemned—and I didn't see any signs of a single squatter—it's not like anyone is going to try and break in. And if they do? I'm only worried about the fae, and they'll find a way in, locks or no locks. It makes me feel better, though, and as Callie and Ash retreat to the master, I take deep breath and head for the last room.

I open the door, but I can't bring myself to walk inside.

It's... it's a nursery.

I don't know why I'm so surprised. I am, though. It's so fucking creepy. This is their home—and it was mine once, too. Twenty years ago, I would've needed a nursery.

This is it.

I can't sleep in there. Except for the crib turned on its side, the tatters of a baby blanket that looks like it was hacked to pieces with a sword just like the couch in the living room, the nursery is in pristine condition. I almost expect a tired mama to come snuffling in, cooing a lullaby to their dozing infant.

Only the baby that lived here once upon a time is twenty-one, wary, and not about to step foot inside this room.

Nope.

Pulling the door closed with a gentle *snick*, I move softly down the hall, tiptoeing past my parents' master bedroom, and head back toward the living room.

Know what? I've slept in a cemetery. A sewer. An abandoned house.

Next to all that, even this place is like the Waldorf Astoria.

I shuffle some of the strewn debris away from the corner. I'm glad there isn't any glass, that on closer inspection the broken shards are hunks of plastic instead; it makes it easier to clear a spot for me. If we stay here—and, for the moment at least, I don't see what other choice we have—we're going to have to fix this place up to make it more livable.

Especially since the mess has gotta be a constant reminder to Callie and Ash what happened here—and what I'm desperate to avoid happening again.

Tomorrow, though. That's something to worry about tomorrow.

Tonight, I curl up in a ball, resting next to Nine's boot. I snagged a pillow from the destroyed couch. Once I'm settled, I call shadows toward me, sighing in relief when they come easily.

They're as warm as they are comforting, and they make one hell of a blanket.

For the first time in a long time, I close my eyes and don't worry about what's going to happen while I sleep.

It takes a couple of days before Ash is back at full-strength—or as much as he can hope to be, considering that, as one of his latest decrees, we're staying put in the human world.

The Light Fae, I'm learning, has a crapton of *decrees*. Just like *he's* learning that I'm not the best when it comes to being told what to do.

He's my dad. I get it. And it's obvious that he blames himself for everything that's happened. Then there's the whole me being claimed by Nine thing and I feel bad for Callie who is forced to act like a peacekeeper between the two of us.

I don't know how to be a daughter. That's the truth of it. I haven't had a family since before my stay in the asylum and, as much as I look back on my time with the Everetts with wistfulness and regret, I've always kept to myself.

It was safer that way.

Now I have these two and I don't know what to do with them. After Ash's announcement that he wants to take on Melisandre as soon as he's healed, I'm even more confused. To them, I'm their long lost child. To me, they're strangers.

I keep finding excuses to leave. It's bad enough that my stomach tightens every time I catch sight of the frozen Nine. Staying in the same room with a bonded couple who can't go more than a few seconds without touching each other, making sure they're still together... it's almost worse than the expectations in their expressions whenever they look at me.

They don't like me leaving but, short of ordering me to stay behind, they can't stop me—so they don't. Ash isn't ready to leave the sanctity of the apartment and Callie... she isn't ready to leave her mate. With warnings not to go too far and my promise that I'll keep my eye out for any threats, I slink outside if only to get away for a while.

This part of the slummy downtown Newport is the last place I'd expect to find any of the fae. I feel safe here—or as safe as possible, knowing the price on my head—and apart from being hours away from Acorn Falls and Black Pine, it's March now. I've been on the run from the asylum for nine months. They had to have given up on me.

Except, I'm willing to bet, for Dr. Gillespie.

Too bad I have no idea what he's all about. The way he chased me into the alley after tracking me down to Acorn Falls... seriously. What's the deal with him?

I'm not sure and, not gonna lie, when I walk around the downtown area, I'm not only watching out for a threat from Faerie. Any sign of my former psychologist... a flash of his fiery red hair, his nasal voice, anything... and I'm ready to book it.

I've been lucky so far. Going for groceries, stopping in at the Dunkin' on the corner for coffee and donuts, buying a newspaper from the convenience store and maybe a scratchie or two, and no one's even looked twice at me. Thank freaking God it's March because even my leather gloves don't stand out in the unseasonably chilly weather. Spring might suck in a couple of weeks but, since I don't even know if I'll still be around then, I'm not worried about it.

Like when I was squatting in the Wilkes House, I'm still careful when sneaking into the side entrance of the condemned building. I haven't seen a single cop patrolling this area. Doesn't mean they're not out there—and getting snagged heading into an abandoned building is the last thing I need.

My poor... my poor *parents* would freak, wouldn't they?

I'm not running on my own anymore. I... I guess I'm responsible for them. What will happen to Callie and Ash in this strange new world—strange and new to *them*—if I'm not here to help them?

Can't take any chances.

As I turn the corner, I see that the same homeless street sleeper that's always nearby is bunkered down with his blankets and his cardboard sign and the crumpled coffee cup set out in front of him. I noticed he was missing earlier on my way to the convenience store, but there he is.

I've got some change on me and a couple of dollars that I can spare. I'm going to eventually have to figure out a way to earn some money but, for now, Carolina's wad is enough to live on for a bit longer.

I can share.

However, before I can pull out any money to tuck into his cup, the man glances over at me. He must have heard my approach because he lifts his head, his weathered face twisted in a welcoming grimace.

I nod over at him, shuffling closer as I dig around in my pocket.

"It's you." He resettles himself in his makeshift nest. "You're back."

I guess I am. "Morning."

"I've been waiting for you. You dropped this." He pulls a grubby slip of paper from beneath his pile of blankets. It's folded in half and I have no clue what it's supposed to be. "Here."

When I don't take it from him, he sets it down, scooting it toward me with one filthy finger tipped with a dirty nail. "You don't want to touch me, girly. I get it. Still, this belongs to you."

He's not wrong. I don't want to touch him, just not for the reason he thinks.

"I think you've made a mistake—"

"You see me. You don't walk past me as if I'm not here. Just the other night, you placed a five in my cup. This fell out of your pocket. It's yours."

"Umm. Okay. If you say so."

"I made some corrections to it. It should help you."

"Thanks."

I think.

Bending down, I grab the folded up piece of paper, tucking it into my fist. Good thing I've still got my gloves on. I'm kind of iffy on taking something from anyone, no matter who they are. And I have no idea what it is he's giving me.

Or *why*.

I don't like how he says he's been waiting for me. I want to be like a ghost, as invisible as he thinks he is if only because I don't want to be on anybody's radar. I'm just a normal chick. A *nobody*.

Seems like I caught his attention, though.

Suspicion runs through me. It's not surprising. My Shadow Man taught me long ago to be wary and on my guard. With everything going on, I've been a little overwhelmed and, okay, a bit reckless.

Right now?

He's got *my* attention.

The other day, I wondered if maybe he could be the same street sleeper who warned me about Dr. Gillespie back in Acorn Falls. It didn't seem possible and I let it go.

Not this time. With all my alarm bells ringing, I pause along the curb, peering closely at him.

His vibrant green eyes aren't rimmed with red. They're not filmy or glazed, either. The man in Acorn Falls had blue eyes, too, I remember. And a full-on beard, not just the scruff. Plus, he reeked of old booze. This guy doesn't.

Still.

"Do I know you?"

"I don't know. Do I know *you*?"

I fucking hope not.

Just my luck. I throw a couple of dollars into a stranger's cup and, out of the whole neighborhood, he's the one who wonders if I'm familiar.

Good going, Riley.

I've gotta get away from him. This whole interaction is too strange and, believe me, I know what strange is. I offer him a half smile, shaking my head in answer to his question, then start to move away from him.

Two steps later I remember the empty coffee cup perched in front of him. Guy's a weirdo, sure, but I won't forget what it was like to sleep in the sewer and be so hungry that I thought it was a good idea to eat a cursed peach (even if I hadn't known it was cursed at the time). I might have the urge to run, but not quite yet.

"Um. Hang on." Still holding onto the scrap, I dig into my pocket, pulling out a couple of bills. I see a '1' printed on them in my haste. Could be a single, could be a ten. I don't care. I quickly shove them in his cup. "For you. Take care, buddy."

"You do the same."

He doesn't say 'thank you'. As I hurry away from him, it hits me that he didn't say 'thank you'. And it's not like I expect it. I'm not giving him money because I expect any gratitude or because I want to feel better about my shitty situation. Honestly, I couldn't care less that he accepted my money like it was his due. Hey, no strings attached, right?

Not when you've spent a lifetime running from the fae. The same fantastical creatures who abide by bargains and trickery but who refuse to offer any thanks.

I come to a sudden stop inside of the empty lobby of our building. His eyes were green. Not silver. Not gold. Green.

I should be fine.

Should be.

What did he give me, I wonder. I don't remember dropping anything.

As soon as I open it and see the two different handwritings cramped together on a page of crumpled paper, I suddenly remember.

I'm thrown back to that awful night when I discovered Carolina sprawled out on the floor of the Wilkes House. She was dead, a piece of paper a few inches from her outstretched hand. I grabbed that and her money, and while I've been blowing through her cash, I forgot all about the paper I had shoved in my jeans pocket.

This is it. It has to be.

I can't stop myself from reading it, then reading it again.

It says:

> between Faerie and
> ~~the~~ the Iron,
> she's destined to stay
> more than a lover,
> a consort, a friend ~~mates!~~
> when Dark ~~meets~~ Shadow,
> the Reign of the Damned
> shall end
> ~~come to an~~
>
> Born of both worlds
> welcome in none
> revels in the shadows
> preens in the sun
> a child with powers
> part human, part fae.

Holy shit. If this is what I think it is—and despite the highly questionable source, I'm betting it is—then I'm finally looking at what might be the complete Shadow Prophecy.

But... wait a second.

This isn't right. Even before the strange "corrections" and obvious additions, it isn't right.

Back in the abandoned house in Acorn Falls, Carolina and I dissected every line of the Shadow Prophecy after she insisted I memorize it. The whole part added to the bottom of the page, but meant for the top, wasn't in the prophecy Lina showed me. I mean, to be fair, she did tell me that her awful mistress—aka the horrible Fae Queen, Melisandre—only allowed her to have a snippet of it, but still.

What *is* this?

I recognize the original handwriting. It's definitely Lina's.

But it's *wrong*.

" '...more than an adviser, a confidante, a friend...'" I recite under my breath. That's what I remember. That's what she told me, made me memorize.

That's totally not what this says.

I glance back at the page, ignoring the added scribbles in script.

*...more than a lover,
a consort, a friend...*

That's, uh... that's a pretty big difference. Forget the rest of it. This one line changes everything. According to Lina's original version, the Dark Fae I was fated to partner up with was supposed to be a helper. An adviser.

If the prophecy said all along that I was fated to *mate* the Dark Fae, why didn't anyone tell me? It happened anyway, which only makes my stomach drop.

If that part of the prophecy came true without me knowing, what about the rest?

My fingers tighten around the edges of the crumpled paper, the sheet snug between my gloves. I've been carrying this paper around with me since I came back to the Wilkes House and found Lina. It was next to her body, almost as if she was holding it when she died. I never looked at it then—couldn't, not when I was running to save my own life—and forgot all about it until just now.

Hell, I never even noticed it when it fell from the pocket of my jeans.

Where did it come from? How did Lina get it? *Why*? Was she trying to warn me that the prophecy I knew was wrong? Or was it just one more lie?

I'll never know and, as I marvel at the page, I try not to obsess over it too much. It doesn't really matter, does it? How can it? My friend is gone and, based on the added scrawl near the top and bottom of the page, even her updated version is not even close to being complete.

That man…

How did *he* know this? Who is he?

How did he know to give me this?

Something's wrong. When I first thought he might be the same guy who warned me against Dr. Gillespie, I was worried that he was following me. It's not him. At least, I don't *think* it is—or didn't.

But how does he *know*?

A couple of minutes ago, I had to ask myself whether or not the homeless man hanging out outside of my parents' building could be part of Faerie all because he didn't say 'thank you'. I thought I was overreacting. Now I'm sure I'm onto something.

What the—

Who is he? Why did he give me this? How the hell does he know the rest of the Shadow Prophecy?

Can I even be sure that it's right? Ash admitted that there are way too many versions of it out there, despite it ruining my life, the only thing I can be sure of is that a halfling is prophesied to finish the Fae Queen's terrible reign as ruler over Faerie.

Except, in the few lines Carolina gave me, it never once mentioned a halfling.

> *...a child with powers,*
> *part human, part fae...*

This one does.

I mean, part human, part fae? Can't get any clearer than that.

And he added it to Lina's note.

The question echoes in my brain.

Why?

Only one way to find out.

Clenching the paper tightly, I spin on my heel and dash for the busted door. I quickly duck under the yellow caution tape, heading back toward where I left him before stopping short when I realize that the space is empty again.

He's *gone*.

I clench my fist.

Why am I not surprised?

CHAPTER 5

My parents are up in the apartment, waiting for me. As much as I wanted to spread out, go looking for the stranger and demand he explain this to me, I don't. I've already been gone for a bit and I don't want Callie and Ash to worry about me.

Not any more than they already have, I'm sure.

I swear, it's so weird, having people who are looking out for me. I haven't had that in a long, long time. Not since the Everetts, and considering I was a bratty and troublesome teen, I didn't really care about their feelings *or* their rules.

Back then, I kept expecting them to ship me off to the group home again anyway. Six years later, I know that my last set of foster parents were just trying their best and, while I might not be able to make it up to them, I'm trying my best not to disappoint my bio parents *too* much.

They don't know what to do with me just like I have no clue what to do with them. After our breakthrough the other day, I'm trying my best to keep our newfound relationship from getting too awkward. It's easy for me to treat them as long lost friends or something, but mom and dad? How? Especially when they're basically the same age as me.

Well, Callie is. Ash is... hey, he *looks* like he's my age and that's weird enough. Not to mention, he's got the same coloring as Rys; even more now that he's recovering. While their features are different—no way would I mistake one for the other—my dad is a reminder of the other Light Fae and I can't stop wondering about him.

It's been a couple of days since we escaped the Fae Queen's throne room and I haven't seen him at all. Not during the daylight or even in my dreams. It's like he's missing.

Missing or something even worse.

I hope he's okay. Despite all the crap he put me through, I almost wish he'd pop into the apartment, just so I could be sure that I didn't leave him to pay the price for helping me, my parents, and Nine get away.

I know it's unlikely. Even if he managed to escape Melisandre's soldiers, Rys wouldn't find it easy to track me down—and not just because I'm wearing Nine's brand instead of his.

The apartment I shade-walked to is on the second to last floor of a fifteen-story building. Apart from us, the whole place is eerily empty. It made me curious and leery at first, but now I'm just grateful for the privacy. It might be condemned, too dangerous for even the homeless to squat inside. Whatever. For now, it's the perfect hide-out for us fugitives.

Especially since it's warded up the wazoo. Between the iron frame and the magic protecting this place, Ash chose the building purposely to hide his family back when I was a baby. I'm still not so sure I understand how we got here, but until I can figure out how to break the spell on Nine, it works.

At least, it *did*. I think of the stranger with the green eyes as I press the elevator button with my thumb. As the doors *ding* open and I step inside, I decide to keep him and his paper to myself until I can figure out what to do about him.

Between getting to know my parents, saving Nine, and getting the Fae Queen off my back, worrying about a weirdo in the human world who knows all about the Shadow Prophecy is the last thing on my mind.

I press number fourteen and, as the elevator rises, I leave any thoughts of that guy and his "corrections" back on the ground floor. He'll be back. I'm sure of it. And when I see him again, I'll offer him the rest of Carolina's cash if he'll explain just how he's involved in all of this.

It didn't occur to me not to take the elevator until the doors closed behind me the first time I used it. I hadn't known the building was empty then and I was so frazzled, I wouldn't have cared if anyone saw me and wondered what was up with the chick in the gloves. As soon as I stepped outside and learned the truth about this place, I was shocked that the elevator worked. Since I'm way too out of shape to take fourteen flights every time I want some fresh air, I continue to chance the elevator.

A short ride later, the elevator *dings* again and I step out onto our floor. Within a couple of days, I can already pick out our door without even realizing it; it's that natural. The second on the left, marked by a stain of who-knows-what.

I let myself in.

"You're back." Callie lets out a sigh of relief. "Ash, she's back."

My dad was in the bedroom. The door swings inward as soon as Callie calls for him. He strides down the hall, meeting us in the living room. His golden eyes are bright, almost glowing as he looks from my mom to me and back, purposely avoiding Nine.

He waves for us to take a seat.

Callie does. I haven't quite shaken the last of my wariness from my encounter downstairs and I decline with a quick shake of my head.

It's obvious they've been waiting for me. Just like I thought.

Great.

"I trust you enjoyed your walk this morning."

"Yeah. I guess." I heft up my arm. There's a plastic bag hanging off the crook of my elbow. "I got you guys some bagels. I didn't know if you liked cream cheese or butter so I got both."

"Thanks, sweetie," murmurs Callie. "That was very thoughtful of you."

Thoughtful, nothing. So long as I have the money to get us food, I'm going to use it. We have to eat.

Ash doesn't say 'thanks'. I doubt I would've noticed normally, but it's just another reminder of that guy outside.

I shimmy the bag down my arm, setting it on the coffee table. It's right-side-up now. Glancing around, I see that the room is looking a lot neater than it has been. I guess, since Ash is doing better, my parents have started to straighten up the mess.

I would have, except the first morning I tried, I caught Callie sniffling again and I immediately stopped.

I made a conscious decision not to point that out then, just like I do now.

"You guys ready to eat?" I ask. "Or should we wait?"

"Let's wait a moment," Ash says. He cocks his head slightly. "Will it keep?"

I shrug. "Don't see why not."

"That's fine, then. My mate and I have something we would like to discuss with you."

The last time he wanted to have a serious conversation, Ash

tried to tell me that I wasn't allowed to be Nine's mate. I can't wait to see where this one goes.

"Sure. What's up?"

He looks over at Callie. She nods encouragingly back.

"I've accepted that you have some kind of bond with the Dark Fae. There's nothing I can do about that now, no way I can change what's happened. You say you love him. Do you love him enough to do whatever it takes to break Melisandre's spell?"

My heart nearly stops. I was halfway to arguing with Ash when he first mentioned reversing my claim to Nine—or his claim to me—and I'm glad I kept my mouth shut.

I swallow roughly and tell him honestly, "I would do anything."

"Then there's a way—"

That's all I need to hear.

"Okay. Let's do it. What do I have to do?"

"It won't be easy," hedges Ash. "And I wouldn't be able to help you."

And?

I didn't expect him to, anyway.

"That's fine. Whatever it is, I'll do it."

For Nine, I'll do anything.

"It's possible, but only if we have a stone from Brinkburn. *That* makes the quest nearly impossible, but it might be our only chance to reverse the curse without returning to Faerie and bargaining with Melisandre to do so."

Since going back to Faerie is out of the question, going with the nearly impossible plan is *my* only chance.

Not that I have any idea what Brinkburn is. It sounds… like something I've heard before. I could be making that up, I want to save Nine so bad, but it's such a strange word. I'm almost sure that I've heard of it.

"Okay. What's this Brinkburn thing? Is it a place? Here?"

In the human world?

I don't say it, but it's obvious what I mean.

"Yes," confirms Ash. "It's in the Iron. England?" He turns to look at Callie again. "Is that right?"

She nods.

Ugh. England. That's more than an ocean away from where we are. Shade-walking is a no-go, too. What if I aim for England and end up in Faerie? Considering my track record, it's more likely than I want to think about. A plane? Yeah, with what I.D.? And that's if we could even afford a plane ticket in the first place.

I huff. "You weren't kidding when you said impossible."

"Chin up, sweetie," says Callie. "We don't have to go there if we can find a stone. That's what's important."

"I wouldn't let you go there even if you could," adds Ash. "It's a place no fae can go and I would never send my daughter where I could not follow to keep her safe."

The way he says *my daughter* has me hunching in obvious discomfort. I can't help it. This is all so new.

If he notices, he pretends not to.

Callie pats the cushion of the couch next to her.

I pretend not to notice *that*.

"Okay. So we're not taking a trip to England. Works for me. But how do we find one of these stones?"

"And that's the tough part. There aren't too many of them in this world. Any Ironbound fae will destroy them since the relics of Brinkburn are nothing but dangerous in the wrong hands. Even if there were easily found, a regular human would never know. They look like regular, everyday pieces of glass. Some are white. Some are blue."

"Brown," adds Callie. "I saw one once that pretended to be a shattered beer bottle. Oh, and there was that pale pink crystal one I saw in a museum gift shop once."

Pride mixed with adoration flashes across Ash's face as he smiles over at Callie. "My mate has the sight. Without Callie, we would never stand a chance."

But we have Callie.

"You'll help me," I say, looking over at her.

If she looks a little crushed that I'd even have to ask her that, you'd never tell from the warmth in her voice. "Of course, I will."

"I can't handle it," cuts in Ash. "I can't touch it. I can tell you if it's strong enough to bring Nine back, but the rest is up to you and Callie."

"That's fine. And if Callie doesn't feel comfortable leaving the apartment yet, I'll go searching on my own, then bring it back for you guys to check it out. Whatever we have to do to find this crystal thing, I'll do it."

As soon as the words are out of my mouth, I freeze.

Crystal.

Wait a minute.

Wait a *minute*—

It couldn't be that easy, could it?

"Do you have a pen?" I ask. I think of the scrap of paper in my pocket, then decide against pulling it out in front of them. Until I can make some sense of it myself, I don't want to give them anything else to fret over. "And something to draw on?"

Callie nods. "We had a junk drawer. All odds and ends. If it's still in there, try the one next to the stove."

I head into the kitchen, pulling open the drawer she

mentioned. I rummage through it, trying not to let it bother me that everything inside of the drawer is as old as I am. Just like the rest of the apartment—well, the part that doesn't look like it's been through a tornado—it's all been frozen in time.

There's a notepad stowed near the back. At least five pens scattered among the old menus, the dried rubber bands, the containers of thumbtacks. I grab one at random, pray the ink's still good, and return to the living room.

I take a seat on the far edge of the couch, placing the open pad on top of my knee. I'm no Picasso or anything, but I guess I learned enough in art therapy to draw a passable picture of something that's just popped in my head.

Please, please, please.

My brow furrows. I can feel the lines forming as I struggle to remember the details. I only saw it once and, since I was kind of running for my life there when I did see it, there's no guarantee that it's perfect, but after a few minutes, I hold out the notepad to my parents.

Sketched in the center, I've drawn Dr. Gillespie's weird necklace, the one he kept tucked under his shirt. There's the string. The nail that's an exact duplicate to the one Carolina gave me and that I lost in Faerie. The rock with the hole in the center that he used to find me hidden in the shadows. And, as close as I can get, the strange crystal that stood out to me.

Ash draws in a sharp breath. "Where did you see this, Zella? Tell me."

"On my doctor," I immediately answer. A second later, I frown. "And don't do that, okay? Don't use my name to make me answer you. It's not fair."

He blinks, stunned. I know he's supposed to be my dad, but he's also a Light Fae. From the look on his face, I'm beginning to think no one's ever spoken to him like that.

Then my mother rises from her place on the couch, crossing over to Ash, then lays her hand on his clenched fist, and I'm sure of it.

"Ash—" she says softly.

He shakes his head. "No, my love. Our daughter... she's not wrong. I shouldn't have commanded her. My apologies," he says, turning to me with such earnestness in his gaze, I can't help but accept them. "When you were small, using your true name was habit to keep you safe. But you're not small anymore."

My lips quirk in a sad, almost smile. "Nope."

"In Faerie, we guard our true names ruthlessly. We take a second name that we answer to, but that holds no power over us. Like how I'm Ash, and your..." He shakes his head again. "How Ninetroir answers to Nine. Calling you by your true name might not be fair, but the fae don't care about fairness. We care about power. There's too much power in Zella. You need a second name."

This is so strange. Go back a couple of weeks and I didn't have any idea that I was part fae. Now I'm sitting in an abandoned apartment *with my parents* and the father I've never known is teaching me about my fae side as if we haven't just met.

He's right—well, about one thing, at least. Only a handful of people know my true name and, if it's possible, I want to keep it that way. Bad enough that Rys knows it and has shown he has no problem using it to suit him, but what if the Fae Queen convinces him to share it with her? He might not have when we were all in her throne room, but what about now? I grabbed my parents and Nine, leaving him to deal with Melisandre and her guards all by himself. If I was Rys, I'd sell me out the first chance I got.

So, yeah. Being controlled whenever someone calls me *Zella* isn't going to fly with me any longer. When it comes to me having a second name, though?

"I don't need a second name. I already have one. Remember?"

"Riley?" His perfect nose wrinkles. "The humans gave you that name."

I shrug. "So? I *am* half-human."

Ash's golden gaze slides over to his right. It softens when he looks at Callie.

On an exhale, he admits, "You are. And that might be the part that saves you."

Really? I toss the notepad onto the coffee table. "What's that mean?"

Leaning over, he gestures at my drawing. "Do you know what any of this does?"

"A little. I know about the iron nail, and I don't know exactly what's up with the rock that looks like a donut, but I saw the guy wearing this necklace lift it up to his eye like it was a microscope or something."

"A seeing stone," Ash says. "If it's a real one, it can be used to break any glamour."

I remember how Dr. Gillespie found me even while I was wrapped up in my shadows.

"Okay. Yeah. It's a real one." I tap the page with the tip of my glove. "I saw this on the other side of the necklace, too. A pale pink crystal, just like Callie said. I had no idea what it was. But now… what do you think?"

"I think you might've saved us the trouble of actually searching for a relic of Brinkburn. Where is it? Where can we find this? Who has it?"

"It was my doctor," I tell him again. "One of my psychologists—the last one I saw before Nine pulled me out of Black Pine. Dr. Gillespie. He yanked the necklace out from under his shirt right before he chased me into Faerie. If anyone has a Brinkburn thing, I'm betting it's him."

Ash thinks about it for a second.

"So this human…" he says, his raspy voice going soft. Thoughtful. "This Dr. Gillespie? You're sure he wears the trio of charms around his throat?"

I nod.

"And he knows who you are?"

He knows every damn thing about me. It's all in my folder—and that's not to mention everything I told him during the few sessions we had together.

I nod again.

"That won't stop me, though."

Callie gasps. "Riley, no—"

Ash places his hand on her shoulder. She turns into him, burying her face in his chest as my dad peers over her head at me, his jaw hard and his eyes blazing like golden fire.

"So you understand what you're going to have to do, don't you? To free Ninetroir?"

I nod one last time.

"I'm going to have to go back to the asylum."

CHAPTER 6

Black Pine.

When Nine first grabbed my hand and pulled me into the shadows, forcing me to leave my room in the asylum, I was furious. Not just at the touch—though that hadn't helped my anger—but because I didn't want to be a part of any of this.

I still don't. If I could throw the whole Shadow Prophecy over my shoulder and walk away from it, I'd gladly do so without ever glancing behind me a second time.

That's not possible, though. I know that—*now*. Back in June, when I was counting down the days until I turned twenty-one and could finally be free—*ha!*—I whole-heartedly believed that, once I was released from the asylum, it was done. Over. I could start my life again without Madelaine's death or Nine's warnings to haunt me.

Of course, that's when Nine found me. Then Rys.

One week passed. Then four months. Now it's been three-quarters of a year, I'm closing in on turning twenty-two, and going back to Black Pine is quite possibly the most stupid, reckless thing I could do.

It's a place where the fae put people to forget about them. Sure, it's a psych hospital—sorry, a "facility for wayward juveniles"—but it's also staffed by fae-touched humans, like Diana and Duncan. Shoot, if Jason and Carolina are any examples, I can't even trust the patients.

And now I'm going to willingly return.

It all comes down to stealing Dr. Gillespie's necklace to get my gloves on this Brinkburn thing. Ash is convinced that the crystal is all I need to reverse Melisandre's spell. Since he seems to know what he's talking about, I'm all aboard the 'save Nine by any means' train. A little petty theft? It's better than the alternative.

Callie hates the idea. Honestly, I'm pretty sure Ash does, too, but my dad is way better at hiding his thoughts and emotions. He's a fae. It figures.

Once I latch onto the idea, once I have even a speck of hope, I can't be stopped. As much as I'd rather never step foot inside the Black Pine facility ever again, it's all I want to do.

So I make plans. I make plans and I *practice*.

I know I'm gonna have to do this on my own. Ash won't be able to travel with me. As a Light Fae, he has his own magic. His own powers. Callie wasn't exaggerating when she told me that my shadows nearly killed him as we were escaping the Fae Queen. I saw it myself.

Taking a pocket to travel from the city to Black Pine? Even if he survived one of my shadows again, he'd be useless when we arrived at the asylum.

On the plus side, he's a pro when it comes to being a teacher. He might not be able to use the sunlight to move around like Rys did—he can't since he won't risk returning to Faerie during the night to recharge his strength—but he can explain how to do it.

The principles for shade-walking and Light Fae travel are basically the same. Within a couple of days, he actually manages to teach me how to make the shadows work for me without them dictating where I'm going to end up. It's touch, but I'm super fucking motivated.

Hey, anything to keep me from accidentally walking back into Faerie again.

It's not just about shade-walking. I spend every free moment that I can working on gathering shadows. Dr. Gillespie might have the seeing stone that looked straight through the shadowy disguise I used in the alleyway the last time we met. That's just one man. I still have the entire ward to worry about.

Now that I know fae-touched humans also are inside the Black Pine facility, I can't be too careful. My shadows are the only glamour that I have. I need to be able to call them easily, using them to conceal me and hide me while I sneak around my old floor.

And that's if I even manage to make it to the right floor in the first place.

When I'm not working with my shadows, I'm learning how to shade-walk while I'm conscious. With Ash's instruction, I start by creating my own pockets and turning them into portals. It's a struggle in the beginning. It leaves me so drained the first couple of times that I don't even have the energy to move through them.

The pull toward Faerie is too great. It would be so easy to slip into the shadows and land on the other side of the veil between worlds. I can't, though, and it takes everything I have to control where I end up.

I start with the inside of the apartment. Bedroom to bathroom. Living room to kitchen. It gets easier after a couple of tries. I keep on practicing. When I can shade-walk from our apartment to the abandoned lobby without a hitch in my breath, I begin to think that I can really do this.

I tell Nine every night that we're working on saving him. He can't hear me—my parents are proof since neither one remembers any of their imprisonment at all—but it makes me feel better.

Callie keeps track of the days. Every couple of mornings, I run down to the corner store and buy a newspaper so that we don't lose any; after my experience with Faerie, I keep expecting it to be like December or something. We don't, and as March turns to April, Ash and I agree that our best bet would be the second Sunday this month.

Easter.

It's a holiday. Back when I was still a "wayward juvenile" trapped in the asylum, I remember how hectic it was during any holiday season. Family visits and day-time passes were at a high then, and the staff was always short-handed. I'm hoping Dr. Gillespie will still be there—he's the one who has the Brinkburn around his throat, after all—and that any of the Fae Queen's *pets* won't be.

I don't necessarily want to confront my old psychologist at Black Pine. I don't know what he's doing there, or who he might be working with—or for. But since I don't have any other lead than that he worked for the facility as of October, it's my only chance to get a Brinkburn without sending Callie out to find one.

I can't do that. It's not fair to her. I know there's gonna come a time when she has to leave this apartment and realize that twenty years have gone by, that the world kept spinning while she was frozen in time under Melisandre's cruel curse. It's... it's just not yet.

Every time she looks at me, her dark blue eyes sad, I know she knows that twenty years have passed. I'm proof right here.

She doesn't want to push me to confront the queen. I don't want to admit that I'm still dealing with twenty years of feeling like I've been left to survive on my own.

We're all living in denial.

Well, except for Ash.

On Friday, two days before I'm supposed to put our plan into place, he calls for me. I walk into the living room to find Ash waiting.

And he's holding a *sword*.

One of those scary-ass swords that the fae guards carried with the silver hilt and the diamond blade.

Oh, boy.

My mom was in the kitchen, busying herself with reorganizing the drawers and making sense of the random groceries I keep bringing back to the apartment. When Ash called my name, she must have followed me because it's her incredulous voice that breaks the quiet.

"Ash, honey. What's this?"

"It's a sword."

No shit.

Callie frowns. "I thought you got rid of those."

"I did. I tucked them away for safe-keeping." His golden gaze dims to a simmering bronze. "Can't keep a sword around a baby."

Me. He's talking about me.

Only I'm not a baby anymore—and we all know it.

The room grows heavy with an awkward silence as Callie

purses her lips. She looks like she wants to say something more before she parts her lips and lets out a soft sigh.

"If you think it'll help…" She shakes her head, her long white-blonde hair—the same as mine—swaying with the motion. "You two do this. I'm going to take a shower."

Ash leans down, pressing his lips against her cheek. He murmurs something to her and the swaying stops. Callie nods and, pressing her hand to his chest, she rises up on the tips of her toes, shifting so that she could give him a quick kiss.

Feeling as if I'm intruding on something private, I turn away. My gaze searches out Nine. I lift my hands to my own lips, smoothing them with the worn leather, wishing it was Nine's breath warming them instead.

I only kissed Nine the one time. I would do just about anything to have the chance to do it again.

As if Ash can read my mind, he waits until Callie has closed the bedroom door behind her before he taps the point of his sword on the wooden floor, catching my attention.

I spin, whirling on him. "Huh?"

He lifts the sword, grabbing it by the tang so that he can offer me the hilt. "For you. You'll need this if you're going to fight Melisandre."

It's a good thing Callie found a reason to leave the room. Over the last few days, we've all made it a point not to discuss the inevitable outcome of the damn Shadow Prophecy. It's almost as if, if we don't talk about it, we can pretend that I'm not inching closer and closer to another confrontation with Melisandre.

Because I don't want to admit that, either, I do what I always do.

I scoff. And I definitely don't take the sword.

"Who says I'm going to fight her?"

"She may look innocent, but I assure you, she's not. She won't stand there and let you lop off her head. To get close to her, you'll need to get past her guards." Once he realizes that I'm not accepting it from him, Ash adjusts his hold on the sword, angling it so that weak lamp light glitters off the diamond edge. "I was one once, in a lifetime ago. I can train you. When the time comes to face her, I'll stand by your side. If the scheme to get the Brinkburn succeeds, we'll have Ninetroir's blade as well. Melisandre will regret targeting my daughter before her end."

I look at the sword.

I don't get it. First Rys. Then Carolina. Now Ash?

They don't get that I don't want to be a killer, do they?

It all goes back to Madelaine's murder. I spent more than six years feeling guilt for her death—to be honest, I still carry the blame for what happened to her—and it will forever weigh on me that everyone thinks I'm responsible for it.

And, well, I am. Without me and my connection to the fae, Madelaine would probably still be living happily with the Everetts. Maybe she'd be married. Maybe she'd be settled in a career. She always told me she wanted to be a vet because she loved animals.

Except she's dead now.

Rys killed her. The golden fae who saved my life, saved my parents and my mate, killed my sister.

I can't be like him. I *won't*. Even if it means I end up a headless statue in Melisandre's garden in Faerie, I won't be a killer.

End her reign has to mean something else. It just has to.

Now if only I can figure out how to tell Ash that...

Because it makes him happy, I decide to just take the sword from him after all. I know, deep down, that I'll never use it—he probably does, too—but I pay close attention as Ash teaches me how to open a pocket of my own to store the sword.

I try not to think about how I've seen this kind of parlor trick before. Except, as my dad shows me how to put the sword in, then take it out again, all I can remember is the coy and teasing look on Rys's face as he pulled a lantern full of faerie fire out of thin air.

Shake it off, Riley.
Don't think about Rys.
Focus on Nine.

I can do this.

The night before I'm going to shade-walk to the asylum, I decide that I should make a trial run to prove that I can cover the distance. I don't risk going to Black Pine, just in case, though Acorn Falls is as good a test as any.

And, okay. Maybe I wanted to stop by Madelaine's grave one last time

The trip to the cemetery is seamless. I land right beneath the overhang of the Richardsons' mausoleum, picking up for the first time that the dark patch isn't just dark—it's another Dark Fae portal masquerading as part of the human world.

Huh. No wonder I always traveled here while I was sleeping.

I don't stay long, crossing to the west side of the cemetery so that I can visit with Madelaine's stone angel for a little bit, before returning back to the apartment with a sense of relief and a thumb's up for my parents.

I'm as ready as I'll ever be.

BRIGHT AND EARLY THE NEXT MORNING, I WAKE UP WITH A PIT IN my stomach. It's Easter, but I'm not looking for any chocolate bunnies or hidden eggs.

I'm waiting to hopefully steal a necklace from my old psychologist.

Fun.

I choke down breakfast, my nerves making it difficult to eat. I repeat my silent promise to Nine that, if all goes according to plan, this might be his last day as a statue. After a quick shower, I change into a black hoodie and jeans I bought just for the occasion. I've practiced with my shadows enough that I'm confident they'll cover me. Nothing wrong with giving them a little help.

I braid my long hair in twin braids, purposely plaiting the strands so that they cover my pointed fae ears. I've got my sneakers and my gloves and a really bad feeling about this.

It's not gonna stop me.

Nothing can.

The three of us gather in the living room.

"Are you ready?" asks Ash.

Not even a little. But, since I'm pretty sure that I'll never be able to answer that question with a *yes* and mean it, I shrug and lie. "Of course."

"Good luck, sweetie," Callie tells me.

Ash nods his head. "You can do this."

I'm glad one of us thinks so.

Taking a deep breath, I lift my hand. Spreading my fingers as wide as they go before the leather glove groans, I twist my wrist and close my hand into a tight fist.

The portal pops into existence right in front of me as if it was only waiting for my signal.

Welp.

Here I go.

CHAPTER 7

My old room in Black Pine is empty.

I let out a huge sigh of relief when I appear in the portal and see that no one else is sleeping in my bed. It was mine for two full years, ever since I aged out of the last floor and got moved to the nineteen through twenty-one group, and while I'm not so naive to believe that they've kept it for me, waiting for me to return, I don't know what I would've done if I shade-walked here only to see someone else lying there.

I can sense something, though. Something... off. A prickle along the back of my neck, the tips of my freaky fae ears almost twitching.

Reaching up, I pat my fingers over my braids, making sure that the wind that accompanies my shadow travel didn't uncover my pointed ears. If everything goes to plan, no one will even see me, but knowing they're hidden makes me feel a little better.

Only a little. My stomach is tight, nerves and anxiety and the familiar motion sickness making me queasy as I step away from the corner, fully materializing in the room.

It's magic. That's the only way I can explain it. Maybe because I was never really gone from the asylum long enough to notice it—or because I was stubbornly ignoring any sign that the fae were real—but I can feel the magic reaching out toward me as I look around the room.

Someone touched by the fae has been in here.

It only takes me a second to realize that that person is *me*.

At least part of this strange magic and apprehensive feeling is because of me. The echoes of the touch I offered Rys while I was sedated, plus the grab Nine stole the last time I was standing in this room... I can *feel* it.

That's not all, either. With a jolt, I think of that first night outside of Black Pine, when Nine was warning me against returning. He said that the asylum was full of charmed and touched humans working with the fae.

Like Jason, who ended up as a statue in the Fae Queen's garden when she was done with him.

And, I remember with a sinking heart, Carolina.

Surrounded by them, I never would've known that they were touched by the fae. It was only if a Light Fae or one of the Dark tried to—what did he call it?—*enter my domain* that I would be able to sense it.

Except now, after being away so long, I guess I'm sensitive enough to pick up on any trace of Faerie magic. It's tough to explain. My skin feels itchy, like something is rubbing it the wrong way. I rub my forearm, the friction from my glove grounding me while it helps me get past the worst of it. It's still there, just not so bad once I get used to it.

That's one good thing. It could definitely come in handy if our plan *doesn't* go the way I want it to.

Tiptoeing toward the door, I dare a quick peek out in the hall. We chose Easter on purpose because it would be emptier than it usually is on the weekends. I figure, with the holiday and the fact that it's a Sunday, there's a good chance that Dr. Gillespie won't be around.

I'm okay with that. I like to think of this excursion as more of a recon mission. If I'm lucky, he'll have left the necklace with the Brinkburn on it in his drawer or something. If not there, then maybe I can find a clue to help me learn more about the doctor.

Like where to find him when he's not at Black Pine, for a start.

All I have right now is a name—Aidan Gillespie—and his place of employment. That's it. Not much to go on, and I didn't want to waste the little bit of data that comes with my pre-paid phone so my searches aren't that great, but even with a quick look, my old psychologist doesn't have any kind of presence online.

A phone number might have come in handy. An address, even better. Since I couldn't find either of those, I had no choice but to return to the asylum and hope for the best.

Fingers crossed.

I wait until the coast is clear, take a deep breath and slip out of my old room. Once out in the hall, I shield myself as best as I can before heading off toward Dr. Gillespie's office.

I cling to the shadows, my back against the wall, my fingers splayed at my side so that I can push off at any given second. No one sees me. As if they can tell that I'm hiding here, every nurse, orderly, and tech avoids this corner as they bustle by.

My heart thumps a little louder when Amy walks by, tucking a loose strand of dark hair out of her face and back into her neat ponytail. She's got her nose buried in a patient's chart, humming a cheery little tune as she goes, oblivious to the magic all around her.

She was good. Kind. Nice. I didn't appreciate her while I was committed to the asylum, and I wish I could tell her now that she was one bright spot in my otherwise dark days. I can't, though. I'm not an idiot. Appearing suddenly to say hi to my former tech will land me in straps faster than I can blink—and that's even if I don't scare the crap out of her by popping out of seemingly nowhere.

Seeing Amy tells me one thing, at least. It's still daytime. Unless her shift has changed in the time since I've been gone, she works during the morning until early evening. Good. I'm still getting the hang of shadow travel and I wasn't sure if I came straight to Black Pine from Newport or if I made a few unwanted stops along the way.

The only downside to arriving so early? Despite the holiday, the asylum is definitely hopping with activity. I stay in my hiding spot, watching as the staff go about their business. I'm purposely staking out Dr. Gillespie's office. It's the only choice I have. I don't know where else to find him and, since the last time I saw the crystal, he was wearing it around his throat, that's where I'm going to start my search for the Brinkburn thing.

It's my only hope.

For hours, he holds sessions with a variety of patients. I recognize a few—Whitney was the patient holed up in there with Dr. Gillespie when I first took up my position, and Tai comes slinking in sometime after lunch—and wait outside for the office to be empty.

It seems like it takes forever before he gives himself a break. After his latest patient leaves, the doctor follows behind him a few minutes later. I'm not sure if he's done for the day or if he's running to the staff cafeteria or something like that. Doesn't matter. As soon as he disappears into the stairwell that would take him to another floor, I make my move.

Slipping from the shadows, I hurry for the door, letting myself into his office.

It's exactly the same as it was the last time I had a session with Dr. Gillespie. The desk. The books piled up everywhere, though much neater than before. The stacks of manila folders.

I hurry toward the desk. When Dr. Gillespie walked by me on his way out of his office, I didn't notice if he was wearing the necklace beneath his dress shirt or not. Since it's not like I could grab him by the throat and check, I figure I should rifle through his drawers first, see what I can find.

If I'm lucky, the necklace will be in here. Since I'm pretty much convinced that—like Carolina—he's got that necklace on around the clock, I'm really just hoping to find out more about the man.

Like where he lives. It'll be way easier to lift the crystal without the threat of being caught by the facility's staff.

I grab the first drawer. It slides open easily.

Good. I was afraid he might have locked them.

A few seconds later, I see why he didn't bother. There's nothing of importance in here. Some post-it notes. Pens. A ton of paper clips. Nothing that helps me.

I'm looking for a phone. A wallet. Odds are that he's carrying both, but it's worth a shot. What about an address book? Do people still use those?

I tug open the next drawer.

This one is... weird.

There's a bunch of plants. Some of it looks like grass and leaves, while others are obviously flowers. I see pressed daisies, some red berries, and a yellow blossom. Tucked in the corner, he has a cloth pouch with *who-knows-what* inside.

When I go to grab it, my glove brushes against something much harder. I scoot the greenery away only to discover a pile of wooden rods lined up neatly near the bottom of the drawer.

I pick up one piece, rubbing my thumb along the worn edge.

I recognize this. When I was a kid, Nine brought me a length of wood similar to this and told me to always carry it. I kept it in my pocket or, more often, in my sock. It gave me blisters, but it was worth it—until my foster mother scolded me for playing with sticks inside.

It's rowan.

According to Nine, a good-sized length of rowan wood can help hide you from the fae. A type of protection that wasn't foolproof, but better than nothing.

Red flowers, too, I remember. Wearing your clothes inside out. Daisy chains—I used to weave them effortlessly when I was younger—and even four leaf clovers. They all offered a little bit of a shield.

And Dr. Gillespie has a whole drawer full of this kind of stuff.

Why?

Just as I'm putting the stick back into its place, I hear footsteps heading toward the door, followed by a nasal, whiny, male voice.

"—forgot something in my office."

Shit!

That's Dr. Gillespie out there. He's already coming back.

And I'm standing behind his desk.

I panic. Maybe it's because I'm back in the asylum again, or maybe it's because I thought I had a few more minutes to look around, but I lose all sense of reason. Instead of trying to hide in my shadows or even trying to create a portal then and there, I turn around wildly, looking for some way to escape.

Apart from the door that leads back to the hallway, there's one other one. I always thought it led to the doctor's private bathroom. Here's hoping that he doesn't need to take a piss.

Before Dr. Gillespie walks back into his office, I slam the drawer shut, dart around the desk and lunge for the other door.

I'm kind of right. It's... it's sort of a bathroom.

There's a small sink on one wall. A pot that could possibly be a toilet. And that's about it.

The room is about half the size of the nursery back in the apartment in Newport. Except for the sink and the maybe toilet, it's completely empty, unless you count the trio of ultra-bright lights screwed into the ceiling above my head. The bare walls are painted a glossy white that reflects the light, making it seem like I'm about to walk *inside* a lightbulb.

It stings my eyes at the same time as it makes my heart pound.

I've seen a room set up like this before. Way more ornate and with the entire Seelie Court milling about, Melisandre's throne room was purposely this bright so that the Dark Fae couldn't use their shadow magic anywhere near her.

The office door opens somewhere behind me, closing quickly with an ominous *snick*.

I spin around, blinking hurriedly to get my sight back.

Dr. Gillespie's expression goes from shocked to elated in between the shutters of my eyelids. "Riley," he drawls. "You're not supposed to be here."

No shit.

I'm caught. No doubt about that. So stunned by his weirdo room, I let Dr. Gillespie walk in and find me standing in the middle of his office.

What the hell am I supposed to do now?

I see his eyes flicker from me to the room behind me. "Look at that. I see you found my secret space."

Secret space... oh boy. I don't like the sound of *that*.

"I got the idea from Siúcra." At my blank look, he adds, "One of the main prisons in Faerie. Dark Fae and their shadows... it's not sun, but it's close enough. There isn't a speck of shadow in this whole room. You'll never escape."

I don't show him any surprise that he's talking about Faerie and the fae mainly because I'm *not* surprised. Surprise flew out the damn window that day in Acorn Falls when he was looking for me, then actually found me with that strange rock he wore on a string around his neck. The doctor knows about the fae.

Of course he does.

He's not wrong, either. This secret room of his is so bright, I'm still squinting because my eyes can't get used to it. Every corner is illuminated. If I somehow got locked inside of there, I'd be trapped since my shade-walking skill would be useless.

It's a good thing that I have no intention of getting locked inside.

I might not have wanted to announce my presence to the rest of the Black Pine staff earlier, but I will if I have to. At least, if they throw me back in my old room, I know there's a portal that's still functional. All I have to do is get past Dr. Gillespie and bolt from his office and I have a much better chance of finding another Brinkburn some other day.

As much as I hate giving in so easily, he can keep his.

I lean forward on my toes. That was my mistake. Before I can even decide how to get around him, Dr. Gillespie rushes me. There's no time for me to react as he raises his arms, grabs me by my shoulders, and shoves me hard.

I stumble backward, my arms wheeling as I try to stay on my

feet. Nope. I totally lose my balance, landing on my ass as I break some of the unexpected fall with my hands.

Staying down on the floor while my deranged doctor looms over me is probably not the smartest thing to do. I push myself up, climbing back to my feet before moving away from him.

He doesn't come any closer. His smile only widens, like he's pleased.

There isn't much space to wiggle around him. He's about my height. A little bit stocky. The idea of him putting his hands on me has my skin crawling, but I'm willing to risk it to get out of here.

Something stops me before I get within a few inches of the entrance. Self-preservation, maybe? My gut tells me to stop and, well, I'm so used to relying on myself, I listen.

That's when I notice the dirt on the floor.

Spinning around, I see that the trail continues around the entire room. It looks like the debris left behind from when you salt your sidewalks to protect it from ice: glittering white crystals scattered with black specks. Or, even more simply—

"What's this?" I ask suspiciously. "Salt and pepper? Really?"

"Looks like it, doesn't it? It took me a long time to find something that would work against a halfling. Coarse salt mixed with iron shavings. Once someone with fae blood gets inside of the circle, there's no getting out again without help, no matter how human they think they are."

I don't know what's worse: how casually he keeps discussing the fae as if it's a foregone conclusion that I would agree with him, or that he somehow is certain that I'm a halfling.

This just got a whole lot more complicated.

"Go on," he says. "Touch it. You'll see that I'm telling the truth."

He doesn't have to tell me twice. If he thinks I'm about to

just take his word for it, he's got another think coming. I was going to do it anyway, even though my special talent at being a human lie detector is telling me that he is actually being completely honest right now.

I step closer, lifting my hand to the space between the doorjamb. So. Yeah. There's definitely a resistance. A barrier.

Dropping to my knee, I reach for the edge of the circle. It's even more difficult. I push.

The instant my finger comes into contact with the mix, it begins to sizzle against the leather of my glove.

I yank my hand back.

"Told you, Riley. Perfect place to keep an errant halfling who just doesn't know how to stay put."

He keeps saying *halfling* like he freaking knows. That can't be possible. I didn't know until I was long gone from Black Pine. My hair is braided to cover the tips of my ears. No way he should know.

"What do you mean, halfling?" I say, bluffing.

"Part human. Part fae. In case you haven't figured it out yet, I know what you are and now? I've got you right where I want you."

Maybe I should've been expecting it. This room is obviously set up to be a prison just like the fairy jail he mentioned and, based on him having the necklace already, my old psychologist already knew more about the fae than even I did.

Then again, how the hell was I supposed to guess that Dr. Gillespie was going to trap me in a secret room if I ever dared to go back to the asylum?

This is crazy. It isn't lost on me that this is happening in a glorified psych hospital, either, but this is *nuts*. He can't do this.

"Let me out. You can't hold me like this."

"You've let the wrong people whisper in your ear for too

long, Riley. Not only did they trick you into believing that the fae aren't real, but you don't know the rules, do you?"

"Rules?" I burst out. "What rules? 'Cause I'm pretty sure there's a rule against shoving someone in a closet and trapping them with magic salt."

"In the human world, maybe. When it comes to someone from Faerie staking their—"

Their what?

Dr. Gillespie stops talking. At first, I don't know why, then I realize that two familiar voices are having a carefree conversation right outside of his office. It's muffled, due to the closed door, and I might not be able to understand exactly what they're saying, but I know who's out there.

Amy and Frankie.

I open my mouth to scream. I don't even care if I get in trouble over escaping the asylum all those months ago. The techs will help me get away from Dr. Gillespie. I'm almost positive.

I take a deep breath—

"I wouldn't do that if I were you. This is between you and me. They couldn't stop what I have planned even if they tried."

I don't want them to stop him. I just need a distraction.

"Worthless humans," sneers the doctor. "Not a drop of Faerie in either of them, not even a touch. You don't want to involve them."

Just because they're human, it doesn't make them worthless, I think to myself. However, before I can come up with a retort, I must've given away my opinion on my face because Dr. Gillespie's whole demeanor changes.

"Ah," he remarks, a gleam in his big, blue eyes. "Worthless to me, but maybe not so much to you."

I never see where he pulled it from. One second, his hands

are empty. The next? He's holding a switchblade that glimmers in the fluorescent bulbs. It's gotta be at least six inches long. Pristine steel. A real sticker.

I gulp.

This isn't going to end well at all, is it?

"Sit down, Riley."

I sit.

"Good girl."

Patronizing ass.

I bite my tongue. He's already proven that he's way more dangerous than I ever would have thought; if not dangerous, then definitely unpredictable. He has the knife.

I keep my mouth shut.

Once I'm down, Dr. Gillespie folds his knife, disappearing it into the pocket of his slacks. "See? I'm not an unreasonable man. I've told you all along that I'm here to help you. And I will. But first—"

A knock interrupts him.

With a warning look at me to keep quiet, he calls out, "I'm preparing for my next session. Is it important?"

A voice like a frog croaking comes through. Nurse Callahan. "Sorry to bother you, doctor, but we have a patient on the third floor insisting you come to him. There's a tech and an orderly sitting with him now, but he says he needs you. Can you fit him in?"

Dr. Gillespie scowls. I can tell that he doesn't want to leave me—even if I have no idea why—but that he's also hesitant to turn the head nurse away.

With a huff, he says, "I have a few minutes free. I'll be right there."

Then, lowering his voice, he tells me, "I won't be gone long. Get comfortable Riley. You're not going anywhere for a while."

CHAPTER 8

It doesn't take long for me to realize I'm fucked.

He locks the door after he closes it. It's pointless—after seeing him whip that knife out of nowhere, I'm not about to test him. I've got the blood of too many on my hands already. I love Nine. I really do. When I get out of here, I'm going to save him… but I won't sacrifice Amy or Frankie or anyone else just to shave off some time.

As soon as I'm pretty sure he's gone, I pull out the "pay as you go" phone I bought in case this went sideways fast. I picked a pair of them up from the convenience store in Newport, one for me and one for Callie. I wanted to be able to contact my parents and, after a crash course in what a smartphone was and how they worked, I promised I'd call her if necessary.

Of course, that was when I thought I was dealing with the regular staff of Black Pine, not a vindictive doctor who seems to know way more about Faerie than I do.

The phone was charged. I double-checked before I left the apartment, and I even tested to ensure that it would survive shadow travel. However, as soon as I discover a black screen, I realize that the magic of the salt and iron circle—or maybe the strange closet—must have done something to it.

It's dead.

Worthless.

Wonderful.

So my phone is out. Not like it would've been much help. I wouldn't have allowed Callie or Ash to come after me, though at least they would know there's a reason why I'm not returning just yet.

I hide it in my hoodie pocket just in case. Then, because there's nothing else I can do, I sit with my back against the wall and wait.

His cockiness is deserved. Between the barrier and the super bright lights, I'm not going anywhere. I try to pull some shadows out of thin air because I'd be a moron not to, but it's useless. All I do is make myself tired and frustrated and neither one of those emotions is going to help me right about now.

I feel like I should've been expecting something like this. The old Riley might have. The Riley who got a little complacent because she's been holed up with her parents... she forgot what life outside of the apartment was really like. Melisandre is my biggest threat—but she's not my only one.

With my phone dead, I don't have a watch or any way to tell time. It's a good thing that, despite all my other issues, I've never been claustrophobic. If I stretch out, there would be barely enough room for me, that's how narrow this room is. Six feet maybe? A couple of feet longer the other way, though that side is taken up by the "toilet" and the sink.

Anxiety prickles against my senses. It's not the space. I've been in worse. It's the lock. It's knowing that I all but walked into this mess and that, when I don't return home tonight, I'm going to put Callie and Ash through hell.

The minutes drag by. I blow the air out of my mouth, rubbing my forehead with my fingertips. The leather passing over my skin is reassuring. Another deep breath and I shake the growing panic off.

He won't leave me in here. I don't know much, but I'm absolutely sure of that. He was already boasting about how he had me where he wanted me. If Nurse Callahan didn't come along and interrupt his gloating, I might have a better idea of what he's after. I hate the idea that it's me. I'm hoping there's a misunderstanding but... yeah. I'm not about to hold my breath.

Damn it.

I HAVE NO IDEA HOW LONG IT TAKES BEFORE THE KNOB SQUEAKS, slowly turning.

There's nowhere for me to go. I back up anyway, putting as much distance between me and the door as it pulls open.

Dr. Gillespie is back. He's still wearing the same outfit as earlier with the added bonus of a sly smile as he meets my wary stare. He's carrying a plate.

He walks to the very edge of the circle, careful not to come into contact with the salt and iron mix. After setting it on the floor, he nudges the plate with the tip of his dress shoe so that it's on my side of the door.

"For you. Special delivery."

"What is it?"

"I thought it would be nice to treat you. You're my guest—"

"Captive," I mutter.

"Twelve of one, a dozen of the other," he says, his grin

turning impish. At that moment, I want nothing more than to slap it off his face. "I was sure you'd be tired of hospital food."

I look at the plate. It's fruit. Does he think I'm that much of a damn idiot?

He doesn't know about the peach. How could he? Carolina took that secret with her to her grave, and while I still don't know which one of Melisandre's guards left it for me to find, the only other person who knows that I almost got tricked into eating food from Faerie is Nine.

Fool me once, that's on you. I'm not about to let myself be fooled a second time.

"Thanks." My voice is flat. "I'll eat it later."

"You will."

He sounds so sure. I don't like that at all.

And then he adds, "It doesn't have to be this way. I tried to show you that I'm here to help you. You didn't have to run. You're hiding from the fae. I can help you do that."

It's not like I can pretend that I don't know what he's talking about. If my file, my history, and my own confession during session isn't enough to back him up, there's the way I'm trapped in the circle.

"I don't want your help. Let me out of here. I want to go home."

"I'm sorry, but that's not possible."

"Yes, it is. Listen—"

"Eat your dinner, Riley."

He's not listening to me. I need to make him listen to me. Sure, I came all the way back here because I have every intention of stealing his Brinkburn crystal if I can, but his halfling trap is a warning that *I* have to listen to.

"Dr. Gillespie, please—"

His face crinkles. Is that another smile? I think so. I think it's supposed to put me at ease.

Spoiler alert: it doesn't.

"I'm not your psychologist anymore," he says. "It's alright. You can call me Aidan now."

Yeah. That's not gonna happen.

Maybe if it was his true name and I could use it to compel him, but I've got no doubt in my mind that it isn't. Why would he give me any power over him? He wouldn't, and by dictating what I call him, he's just proving that he's the one holding all the cards.

I decide, then and there, that he'll be Gillespie to me from now until the day I die just because he told me otherwise. 'Cause he's right—he's not my doctor. He's just some insane man who went to the trouble of trapping me and thinks a plate of fruit is an acceptable peace offering.

Then again, I'm not about to cut off my nose to spite my face. Just in case he made a huge, honking mistake, I mutter under my breath, "Let me go, Aidan."

Like I expected, using that name does jackshit. His bushy, red eyebrows go up. "What was that? You say something, Riley?"

Gritting my teeth together, I shake my head.

A flash of disappointment is quickly replaced with steely determination. He starts to back away again, his hand on the edge of the door.

"In that case, good night. Get some rest. Perhaps you'll be in a more cooperative mood tomorrow."

Good night? So it's still the same day. That's good. But Gillespie telling me 'good night' and 'get some rest'? Oh, no. That's *not* good.

I scramble to my feet. I don't know why, except it bothers me the way that the red-haired creep is staring down his nose at me while I stay frozen on the floor.

"You can't leave me in here," I tell him.

"Why not? I made sure you have facilities. There's water in the tap, food waiting for you to eat it. You have everything you need for as long as I need to keep you here."

I goggle over at him. "And how long is that?"

"As long as it takes."

What the hell is *that* supposed to mean?

Before I can ask, he closes the door in my face.

I sputter and I stare at the back of the door as, once again, I find myself all alone.

Knock, knock.

I didn't mean to fall asleep. With the bright light, the pristine white wall, and my nerves ratcheted up past eleven, I thought I'd be up all night. Exhaustion and anxiety must have caught up with me sometime early this morning, though, because, at that sudden, sharp knock, I'm jolted out of a dreamless, restless sleep.

I'm slumped in the corner, my head nestled in my palm, my elbow propped up against my belly. I jerk awake, wincing as the searing light—and the truth of my predicament—hits me.

The knob turns. The door opens.

Gillespie stands there, peering at me from behind his glasses.

He frowns when he sees that the plate is on the other side of the room, still untouched. I'm hungry, but I'm not *that* hungry. Give me another day or so and I might start second-guessing the look of that fruit.

Not yet.

"Did you sleep well?"

"Like a baby," I lie.

His lips quiver, the frown quirking up to a noticeable smirk. "I'm glad."

I was lying. He's not.

Ugh.

I'm in way over my head right now. It gets even worse when the doctor disappears from the doorway. I hear a soft grunt, followed by the scraping of something heavy being dragged across the floor. A few seconds later, he reappears, tugging one of his chairs behind him.

Gillespie moves it so that he's facing me. He takes a seat, his wide blue eyes narrowed on me as I stay tucked in the corner.

When he does nothing but watch me closely, my nerves coupled with my frustration get the better of me.

"What do you want?" I snap.

Before I passed out, I spent long hours trying to understand why he was doing this since he hasn't told me yet. To go to the trouble of setting up the trap in the hope he could keep me here, even threatening to harm my old techs… he has a reason. I have no idea what it is, but I decided my best bet was to pretend to be the model prisoner so that he'll reveal his evil plan to me in time.

And… then I went ahead and let my frustration and fear get the better of me.

Whoops.

Good thing Gillespie doesn't seem to mind my snappish attitude. In fact, he seems to revel in it.

At least he answers me, though.

"What do I want? Honestly? Just to look at you," he tells me, his voice more nasal than usual.

Yeah. Because *that's* not creepy as hell.

"Well, don't. It's fucking weird."

"Sorry. I just... I can't believe you're here. Finally. It took me a very, very long time to find you, you know."

You, he says. Not someone who has a history of dealing with the fae. Not someone who's been to Faerie. Not a halfling. *You.*

In my recent experience, there's only one reason why someone is looking for me specifically.

I'm resigned as I scoff, "Let me guess. Because I'm the Shadow?"

"Because you're like me." Gillespie pushes his glasses up his nose, then says, "The fact that you're the Shadow is a bonus."

"Like you? You mean a whackjob shrink who thinks it's okay to lock his patients in a closet in his office?"

"Former patient. As far as the facility is concerned, Riley Thorne is no longer admitted here."

That's one good thing. If I can figure out how to escape, I won't have to worry about the asylum coming after me again.

"Besides," he says, leaning forward in his chair, elbows on his knees and a pleased grin stretching his lips, "that's not what I meant when I said that you're like me." He tilts his head, showing me his profile. "Notice anything different?"

I'm looking at his weak chin, the golden rim of his glasses as they curve around his ears—

His *pointed* ears.

Okay. I know damn sure that if his ears had always looked like that, I would've noticed before now.

"What? *How?*"

I'm gaping. Can't help it. And, from the way he preens as he shifts in his seat, he got exactly the reaction out of me that he was after.

Gillespie lifts his hand, stroking the tip of his ear. "Long hair on men isn't in fashion like it used to be. I had to learn how to hide them. Took some time, but even a halfling can use glamour."

Really?

I didn't know that, either.

"Can I ask you a question?"

Can I stop him?

I shrug.

"How old do you think I am?"

Weird question. And, shit, I don't know.

"Thirty-five?" I guess.

"Three hundred and six."

My jaw drops.

He goes on as if he hasn't just shocked the hell out of me.

"The fae are immortal. They can die, of course. Anything can die. It takes a lot to kill a creature from Faerie. So long as someone like us crosses the veil into Faerie from time to time, we can live just as long as a full-blooded fae."

Add that to something else I didn't know. Not only the earth-shattering revelation that, as a halfling, I could be immortal like Nine—but that he's telling me all of this for his own reasons.

I need to know what they are.

"Why are you doing this? Why me?"

"I don't know if you've noticed yet, but halflings aren't really welcomed in Faerie. The fae think of humans as disposable. Pets. Even if fate says something different, most fae would rather take a consort than mate with a human. Even then, they never have children and, if they do, they rarely survive. We're unique, you and me."

"There's gotta be more halflings floating around."

Gillespie shakes his head. "In my three centuries, you're the fourth one I met. And," he adds, "the only female."

Oh, no. No, no, no, no, *no*.

I huddle in the corner, slinking beneath my oversized black hoodie as the man lets his gaze roam openly over me, head to toe. I've seen that look before on men even older than Gillespie—well, not really, but they *looked* older than he appears. This time, it's so much worse.

"I've been waiting a long time for you," he says again, his nasal voice dropping in pitch. He's almost gargling on the words. "Make no mistake. You'll be my bride."

I almost throw up in my mouth.

"I won't let a human woman dilute my bloodline." His expression darkens suddenly, turning violent in a heartbeat as he spits out, "No fae female will have someone like me. My only choice is another halfling. It has to be you."

No it fucking doesn't.

"The fact that you're the Shadow makes it even better," he adds, the flash of darkness disappearing as he sits back in his seat, his unblinking blue eyes watching me closely from behind the thick lenses of his glasses. "I've heard some of the prophecy tied to your name. You're supposed to take care of the Fae Queen. When you become my bride and take her throne, I'll be the new king of Faerie. You will give me a son, start our legacy. The whole realm will have to bow down to me then."

Lord help me, my psychologist is *insane*.

First off, no way am I killing Melisandre. I told Nine that. Told Rys that. Made sure my mom and dad knew… shit, I even told the queen that herself. And even if, somehow, me being the Shadow leads to her being demoted or something, that doesn't mean I'm angling to be the new Fae Queen.

You've got to be kidding me.

I'm not about to marry Gillespie, either. Kids? Uh-uh. Not even counting the fact that I already have a mate, but this guy?

Ah, *hell* no.

If he notices that I'm shocked—and totally disgusted—into silence, he doesn't act like it. He keeps on talking, either oblivious or just plain not caring that I'm looking at him like he belongs in one of the asylum's rooms.

"The fae watching over you hid you away before I could track you down. You were a child. I bided my time, waiting for you to get older. Once I finally discovered you were here, I had no choice but to get to you any way that I could." He waves his hand up and down, gesturing to the fancy sweater, the pleated pants, the sensible shoes. "Aidan didn't have a prayer, but Dr. Gillespie did."

Wait a second. Is he saying—

I finally find my voice. "You came to work here... to get to me?"

"You were hidden very well," he says again. "It was my only choice. Once I got my doctorate, they finally let me in. Six years, I waited for my chance. To get to know you. To make you trust me. To show you the truth of what the world can be really like. You weren't supposed to run away. I ran out of time. And now look at us."

Right. I'm locked in his office and he's telling me that he wants me to marry him *and* be his broodmare.

Excuse me while I throw up for real this time.

I might've been an in-patient at the Black Pine facility for a long, long time, but I'm not the crazy one out of the two of us. Even when he was my doctor and I was biding my time before I'd be released, no way would I have ever turned to him for help.

Of course, then I remember how I basically begged for that med check when I was trying to medicate Nine and Rys away, and... okay. He has a point.

I'm different now. Changed. I've seen too much to go back to pretending the fae aren't real. They are. And, with Gillespie willing to spill the beans, I decide the only thing I can do is take advantage of that.

Plus, anything to get the idea of the two of us together out of my head…

"You're like me," I say, working hard not to give away how gross that makes me feel, just admitting that out loud. "You called Amy and Frankie humans. Is everyone else human here, too?"

Gillespie doesn't answer me right away. I can see the cogs working behind his eyes as if he's wondering what I can do with the information. He must figure it's harmless because, after a few tense moments, he shakes his head.

"Not everyone. A couple of the nurses, some techs, they're put here on purpose, straight out of Faerie. When you were younger, it seemed you were better at picking up on them so they were removed if you had a reaction. Once you stopped reacting, some of the fae-touched humans were allowed to become bolder."

Hmm. There *were* a lot of staff changes around the time I came to the asylum. Back then, I didn't know how Black Pine worked so I figured the turnover was normal. Then the therapy started, the sessions, the meds… and I guess I just didn't give a shit anymore.

"What about my doctors? Were they all in on it?"

"Not the doctors. Remember, Black Pine is a 'respectable' facility. There are real patients enrolled in its programs. Every doc that walks into this place is exactly who they say they are. They stay until they figure out something's not quite right."

I get that. If I thought staff turnover was bad, that was nothing compared to my doctors changing every couple of months.

But that doesn't make sense. If the doctors don't have anything to do with fae or Faerie, then what is he doing here? He has a degree—and I've seen the countless diplomas hanging on his wall myself which, in retrospect, should've been a tip-off that he wasn't as young as he appeared—so I know his credentials are legit.

"Do they know that you're part fae?" I ask him.

I don't even have to explain who I mean by 'they'.

"I'm over three hundred years old. I've spent a lot of time perfecting my glamour. I don't have a prophecy hanging over my head. My human side is my best disguise. They have no idea what I'm capable of."

He sounds proud, like he's happy to be fooling everyone else.

They have no idea what I'm capable of.

Considering I'm trapped in a closet, I think I'm beginning to have a good handle on that.

CHAPTER 9

Our strange game of twenty questions doesn't last much longer.

Regardless of my sudden appearance here—and his obvious pleasure at that fact—Gillespie still has a job to do. Just because he's trapped me behind the barrier of iron and salt, that doesn't mean that he's done seeing his patients.

At least, that's what he tells me as he gets up to put the chair away.

With an unnecessary warning to stay quiet, he promises that he'll check on me again in between patients. I'm not looking forward to it.

Even if I wanted to shout and draw attention to myself—risking the oblivious humans—I don't think I could. As soon as he closes the door, the room is silent. Kind of muffled. I can't hear a single thing through the wood, like it's been soundproofed or something.

Considering he's been prepping for this for longer than I want to think about, he probably did soundproof this space.

About an hour or so later, he pokes his head in, reminding me to eat my fruit if I'm hungry before asking if I'm ready to accept his proposal yet. I can't even bring myself to give him an answer. I keep hoping he's kidding.

Unfortunately, he's not.

Crazy bastard doesn't let up. After his last session, he decides to have another sit-down with me. I know it's bad when he pulls the chair back, a closed manila folder resting on his lap.

How much do I want to bet that that's my file?

He tries another approach. Now that we both know there's no hiding the truth about the fae, he asks me about my relationships with the two in my file. It's like I've been thrown back to the first day I met him, when Amy announced that the new psychologist wanted to meet with some of our group—before telling us all that I was chosen to be the first one to go down to his office.

In hindsight, I probably should've been more suspicious about that than I was.

Despite his poking and prying, I don't tell him about Nine. I already regret everything I told him back when I innocently thought he was trying to help me process my issues regarding the fae. With Gillespie putting it out there that he wants to knock me up—cue intense shuddering because *ew*, no—I keep Nine close to my chest.

Tough luck, doc. I've already got a soulmate.

And he's waiting for me to save him.

Now, if only I can find a way to save myself first...

"Rise and shine, Riley."

His smarmy voice grates on my nerves like fingernails down a chalkboard.

It's another morning. Unlike the night before, I barely slept a wink last night. My shitty situation has finally seemed to hit home. My anxiety kept me up while I obsessed over what I could do to get out of here.

The tips of my leather gloves are blackened. I pushed up against the barrier more times than I'm proud to admit because it was all I could do. Memories of Madelaine and Rys's Faerie fire beat at my brain the entire time I tried it, too, which made it a million times worse.

Still, I tried.

By the time he comes to visit me this morning, I'm torn between snapping and just rolling over and pretending that he's not there.

He wants attention. I don't want to give him any, especially when the bastard teases me with breakfast.

It's been almost two full days. My stomach aches from hunger, though I think I'm turning a corner on that. I drank a couple of handfuls of water from the tap when my mouth was too dry to take it any longer, but the fruit is still sitting on its plate, taunting me.

He brought me a sealed granola bar. I want it so bad, I'm willing to do almost anything for it… until he tells me I have to eat at least one grape from that other plate first. His eagerness as he waves the bar in front of me all but proves my suspicion.

He's done something to the fruit. I'd put money on it.

Come tomorrow, I might be desperate enough to try it. The hunger comes in waves, my anxiety pushing it aside. Right now I'm pissed off enough to refuse his offer.

He can take that bar and shove it up his ass for all I care. I only have one thing I'm worried about.

"How much longer are you going to keep me locked up in your office?"

Gillespie lowers the hand holding the bar out, his face pinching in annoyance. "Don't be like that. I know you don't like being stuck in here."

"Wow. Really? How did you guess?"

He ignores that. "I never meant for it to be forever. In fact, I was going to surprise you later, but we'll actually be leaving after my last patient this evening."

Huh?

We?

"Leaving? What do you mean? Leaving *where*?"

"It's simple. You're right. I can't keep you here forever. You're stubborn, but I already knew that from your file. If I let you, you'd starve to death and that can't happen. So I'm taking you with me. Maybe, once you stop entertaining these ideas that I'm going to let you go, you'll see how much better your life will be once we're sharing it."

He's absolutely right. I'd rather die. Of course, that's not something I tell the crazy bastard because, well, he is absolutely nuts.

Instead, I try to poke holes in his grand plan.

"How?" One of the techs will recognize me, or a nurse. It's bound to happen. "What if I see Amy or Penelope? One of the nurses? I'm not supposed to be here."

"Don't worry about that. I can glamour you enough that no one will know it's you." Gillespie disappears for a moment, returning with a bag in his hand. He drops it over the edge of the circle. "I can do faces, but not clothes. These scrubs will make it seem like you're just another tech."

He's thought this all through. He's... he's serious about this.

It's not just a cruel tease. I'm finally getting the hell out of here.

This is actually great news.

I have a *chance*.

Easy, Riley. Don't mess this up.

I try to hide my excitement, keeping my face as tired and aggravated as it's been for days as I remind him, "How am I supposed to leave? Don't know if you forgot, but your fancy salt over there won't let me anywhere near it."

"I'll let you free on the condition that you follow me home. Once you're there, I won't even have to lay the salt down. My wards will keep you inside."

If he says so.

"Okay," I lie.

He's a halfling. He has to know that, as a half-human, my word doesn't mean shit. I could promise him the stars and the moon and if he believes me, that's his own stupid fault.

Or maybe I'm the idiot for believing that I'm fooling anyone.

He wags his finger at me. "Don't get any funny ideas, either, Riley. There's nothing I won't do to take you with me. No one is indispensable. And even if you tried to hide..." Gillespie slips his hand beneath his shirt, yanking on a slender, leather twine that's hanging off his neck. Another tug and there it is: the necklace with the pale pink crystal, the rusty nail, and the donut-looking seeing stone. He taps that one with his finger. "You know I'll find you."

I almost stop breathing as he tucks it back into place.

He has it. Thank fucking God. He *has* it. I don't have to wonder about where he's kept the crystal, or if all of this was for nothing. If I can figure out a way to escape him after I get my hands on his necklace, then these last few days of hell would've been worth it.

I'll do anything I have to to get that necklace, even pretend like he's worn me down.

"I'll behave," I tell him. Then, to prove that I mean it, I crawl across the room, snatch an old, shriveled grape from the plate and pop it in my mouth. "See?"

All my years of practicing how to fake taking my nighttime meds come in handy. I squish the nasty grape into the gap between my molars and my cheek—and, jeez, it's super mushy once it's in there—before opening my mouth and showing him that it's gone.

He tosses the bar at me, the magnanimous lord throwing scraps to his dogs, before telling me to get some rest because I'm going to need it.

As soon as he locks the door again, I hop up from the floor and spit every last bit of the grape out of my mouth. I cup tap water in the well of my glove, rinsing my tongue, my teeth, my lips so that I don't swallow anything I shouldn't.

Once I've gotten the taste of the grape out of my mouth, I gobble the bar down. It's some kind of oatmeal, granola, chocolate chip mix and it's the best thing I've had in ages. I need the sugar. I need the energy. One way or another, I'm going to get myself out of this mess because being moved to a second location is the biggest no-no when it comes to being captured.

He'll do it, too. I have no doubt in my mind that Gillespie means every threat he so casually puts out there. He might've shown me his necklace, but I still remember the switchblade the outwardly prim and proper doctor keeps stowed in his pocket.

If I don't do what he wants, one of the asylum's patients or staff will pay for it. I can't let that happen.

I can't let him take me from this place, either.

When Nine first found me in the asylum, he tried to explain how—at that exact moment—Rys was a bigger threat than

Melisandre because he was sure that I was supposed to be his mate. His *ffrindau*. When it comes to a fae claiming their lifelong partner, nothing can stop them.

I learned that the hard way. Up until the second Nine claimed me in front of the Fae Queen's Court, Rys kept trying to convince me that I should choose him. He stopped short of grabbing me and dragging me to Faerie with him, but I suspect that that would've happened eventually once he realized that I was never going to go with him willingly.

Now it's been weeks since I've seen Rys. I thought my biggest problem was trying to figure out how to save Nine, then hide from Melisandre. Trying to steal Gillespie's crystal was supposed to be the easiest part of my plan.

I couldn't have been more wrong.

How was I supposed to know that my former psychologist was a halfling who has decided that he wants to shack up with me?

Living in his office inside of the asylum is one thing. Moving with him who knows where, leaving the last place that my parents know I was at... being forced into a place that he gleefully says is warded and protected so that I'll never be able to escape.

I believe him, too.

He has almost three hundred years on me. Countless lifetimes of experience. He knows how to glamour. He probably knows how to use the touch against me.

But I'm the damn Shadow—and I want it more.

I ONLY HAD A COUPLE OF HOURS TO FIGURE OUT WHAT TO DO. IT'S rough. Between not eating enough and definitely not getting enough sleep, my head feels hazy even though the sugar kind of helped. I have to force myself to think, knuckling my burning eyes when it seems useless.

Before I know it, I've run out of time.

"Are you ready?"

His blue eyes gleam in excitement, his bushy, red eyebrows rising sky-high as he looks me over. My skin crawls under his examination. He smiles as if he likes what he sees.

Probably because I've traded my hoodie and my pants for the pale blue nurses' scrubs he left for me earlier.

I have to play nice. So long as he keeps me behind the cursed circle, I'm stuck. So, pulling myself off of the ground, I get to my feet unsteadily, shuffling closer to him. I keep my arms crossed over my chest, a scowl on my face as I nod.

"The scrubs work perfectly. No one will stop us on our way to the car."

Here's hoping I don't get that far.

First things first. I'm still stuck in here. Jerking my chin at the line I just can't cross, I ask, "I changed like you wanted. Now how do you get me out of here?"

"It's simple enough." He holds out his hand. "You have to let me touch you."

I flinch. Can't help it, either.

Gillespie *laughs*.

"Oh, Riley. And I thought you said you weren't haphephobic."

I remember that. In our opening session, he accused me of having haphephobia. My immediate reaction back then had been to deny it.

I do the same thing now since he obviously expects me to.

"I'm not afraid."

"Oh? Then you won't mind taking my hand." He extends it a

little further. His fingers brush up against the invisible barrier that separates us.

"So I grab your hand—"

"And I pull you out. It's as simple as that."

For someone who's been conditioned her entire life not to willingly touch *anyone*, it isn't. Especially since I know that Gillespie is part fae. Touch magic... it could never be as simple as he's making it out to seem.

And that's when it hits me.

I know what I have to do.

I just hope it *works*.

"Okay." I nod. My tangled hair, the last of my knotted braids, falls forward as I slowly bob my head up and down. "Anything to get out of here."

I lift my hand, pressing the edge of my glove to the invisible barrier. Right as the tip of the leather begins to burn, Gillespie takes my fingers into his grip and pulls.

At that exact moment, I eagerly let him tug me toward him.

The second I step over the line, I make my move. Honestly, it was his own fault. He should've been expecting me to do *something*. And maybe he did. Maybe Gillespie had braced himself for me to push him away or something.

He probably didn't guess that I would want to touch him again.

His grip was too light. It's easy for me to slip my fingers out of his hold. But, instead of rising up to slap him or shove at his chest, I lash my hand out, wrapping my fingers around his wrist. I press the flat of my palm against his bare skin and let my fae side take over.

I did something just like this right after Nine claimed me in front of the Fae Queen's Court. Following his lead, totally unaware that it was even *possible*, I turned the touch around on Nine, taking his strength and his power into me.

Touch magic. Fae magic.

I'm part fae. It's about time I acted like it. Even more, I'm the Shadow.

Gillespie picked the wrong chick to mess with.

Who knows? Maybe he doesn't realize the extent of what I could do. Fair enough since I don't, either. Doesn't matter. As soon as I turn the touch around on him, my former doctor goes rigid as I suck out as much of his... I don't know, soul?... his soul as I can.

Something *pop*s over my head. The magic humming between us has blown out one of the lightbulbs. I can hear a high-pitched whine, then another *pop* as a second bulb goes kaput, then another.

Darkness falls around us, tendrils of shadows wisping their way around my legs as I use the touch to my advantage. Forget being weak. Forget being tired. I'm starving, but not for food.

I hunger for everything I can take from him.

I hunger for *revenge*.

I don't know how much more I can steal. Gillespie is bigger than me, stronger than me—or he *was*. His body bows as I tighten my grip on his arm. The leather doesn't stop me. Why would it? It's a part of me. I made it that way.

Time seems to stop. Riley doesn't exist.

Only the Shadow.

Shadow... my Shadow Man.

Nine.

I almost forgot. So wrapped up in making Gillespie pay, I almost forgot my whole reason for being here in the first place. Nine... I have to save Nine.

With my free hand, I slip my fingers under his shirt, grasping the leather twined around his neck. I yank it upward, lifting it over his head.

With the other one, I finally shove him away. I'm buzzing. I feel fucking *powerful*. One quick shove and Gillespie goes flying, his back slamming into his desk before he crumples in a heap.

I'm not touching him anymore. Good chance he busted the crap out of his back when he smashed into the hard wood, but he's a halfling like me. The touch is the only thing that matters—and I'm not touching him anymore.

The spell is broken. His paralysis? Gone. His immediate reaction is to let loose an angry, primal scream while he struggles to climb out of the wreckage of his desk.

I don't think he meant to do it. If he was thinking clearly—if he had realized that he's already let me out of the salt and iron circle—he wouldn't have done that. Because I learned something when he first trapped me in his hidden room.

When the door is closed, my prison is soundproofed. But when the door is open... the good doctor's office isn't.

Seconds. If I'm lucky, I only have seconds. Thanks to the power I stole from Gillespie, I reach out with my senses, pulling the shadows toward me easily. Avoiding the desk, I launch myself in the corner opposite the door. With my body crammed against the wall, my shadows melt into the ones that were already there.

I'm as good as invisible—at least, I *hope* so.

I can hear the slapping of non-slip shoes outside the office door. It's not just one person, either. His scream must have caught the attention of every staff member working on this floor.

It certainly seems that way when the door suddenly flies open.

"Dr. Gillespie, did that scream come from— oh, no!"

I recognize a couple of the curious faces in front. There's

Amy, the one who opened the door and who stopped talking when she saw Gillespie fighting against the rubble of his former desk. Kelsey is standing next to her. Frankie is at their back, his slicked-back, oily hair reflecting the few remaining overhead lights.

"We need a nurse, stat," calls out Amy, her voice going from apprehensive yet genial to business-like in an instant. "The doctor is down. Frankie, go find Nurse Pritchard. Someone has to check on him."

A familiar blonde female works her way through the small crowd. I gulp as it seems to part, letting her through.

I slink further away, hoping that the shadows do their job.

"Allow me," purrs Diana as she pushes past the final two techs ahead of her.

Her golden fae eyes flash as she spies Gillespie on the floor, and I'm the only one in the room who notices.

Welp. That's my cue to get the hell out of here.

Clutching my prized necklace tight in my fist, I slip even further into the shadows and let them finally guide me home.

CHAPTER 10

I stumble on the landing. I don't fall, though, reaching out to steady myself against the couch as I pop into existence.

I did it.

I fucking *did* it.

Gillespie's necklace is clutched in my other hand. As Callie jumps up from her place on the other end of the couch, her eyes widening as she squeaks out her mate's name, I hold it up.

The pink crystal shimmers in the weak lamplight, throwing sparkles across the floor.

"Riley, are you okay? We were so worried!" Callie is holding onto her phone, the twin to the one I left behind in the pocket of my hoodie. She tightens her grip on it. "You didn't call. We thought you were in trouble!"

Ash comes striding into the living room, his tawny hair streaming behind him as he glides in that eerily perfect way that the fae have. "Callie. She's here now. It's alright. Let her breathe."

"Two days," she squeaks. "Almost three. What happened?"

I'm stuck between the two of them, Callie on my right, Ash floating in on my left. All these weeks spent living with my parents and I'm still not used to being around them—or how much worry, concern, and affection is coming off them both.

I knew that my being missing would freak them out. Popping into the asylum was supposed to be an in-and-out mission. Of course, Gillespie changed all that.

I shove that all behind me. My whole life, I've been a pro at compartmentalizing. Don't want to deal with it? Shove it in the back of my mind and promise that I'll deal with it later.

If there's one thing I learned about having parents again for the first time since I was fifteen, it's that Callie and Ash are going to be after me to tell them where I went and what happened while I was gone.

Later.

I'll do that later.

Wrapping the twine around my glove, tucking the nail and the seeing stone out of sight, I turn to my right—to Callie—and hold out the crystal.

"Is this it? Please, tell me this is it."

We all know what my mission was about. Callie hesitates for a second, as if appraising the Brinkburn is the last of her worries, but she must have picked up on the urgency in my tone because she meets me halfway.

She extends her free hand, letting the crystal nestle on top of three fingers. Peering closely, she squints a little, seeing through any kind of glamour that's protecting this stupid thing.

Finally, she nods.

I take it back from Callie before thrusting it at Ash. "Here—"

My graceful, ethereal father actually stumbles back, throwing his hands up as if protecting himself.

"Ash? What are you doing?"

"You know I can't take that."

"Sorry, sorry!"

I cradle the necklace against my chest, moving it as far away from him as possible. What was I thinking? How could I forget?

During my training, when Ash was teaching me about portals, he also told me about the Brinkburn itself. When he first said that he couldn't touch the stone, he meant it. The point of the stone or the crystal or whatever the hell it is is that it has the power to neutralize fae magic. With another power, it can cancel out Melisandre's spell and bring Nine back to me. But if Ash touched it? It might just neutralize *him*.

I asked him what that meant. As far as I knew, the only thing that affected the fae was iron. Ash, unsurprisingly, changed the subject. The matter was closed after that.

There was one tiny upside to being locked away. Because I purposely didn't want to think about the mess I was in, I focused on things that I needed to understand.

Like the Brinkburn.

Gillespie is a halfling. No doubt about that since I saw the points of his ears. Like I'm supposed to be able to, he can wield this powerful crystal. I mean, hell, he wore it around his neck. That's some cockiness right there.

Makes sense to me, though. The more I thought about it, the more I had to accept that the crystal can do everything that Ash promised. And you know why? Because Gillespie *is* a halfling. He never should've been able to push past the iron and salt barrier that was strong enough to keep me trapped.

Unless he had a magical stone that neutralized fae magic.

Like I do now.

Here goes nothing.

I still don't know what it was that broke the paralysis spell on my parents. I have my suspicions about that, too, and I hope like hell I'm wrong. No time to worry about that right now, though.

Reaching up on my tip-toes, I widen the necklace as far as it goes before lowering it over Nine's head. I take a deep breath, say a fervent prayer, and let it fall so that the Brinkburn settles over his chest just like Ash explained ages ago.

For a heartbeat, nothing happens. Then, to my surprise— despite my dad warning me how it would work—the pale pink stone starts to glow. A shot of pure white light jumps out of the crystal before arcing and streaking outward like a contained firework.

It all happens so fast after that.

Nine's body goes boneless. As soon as he collapses, I drop to my knees and pull the necklace off of him. The nail gets tangled in his long, dark hair. I quickly unthread it from the thick strands. Once I have the whole necklace free, I pull it over my head, tucking the charms under the blue nurses' scrubs.

He's not a statue anymore.

Is he alive?

Yes.

His chest rises and falls. Even though his eyes are still clamped shut, I run my hand along his cheek. Cool, but not chilly. His skin is soft, too; no longer is he hard as stone.

I shudder out a breath.

Now all I have to do is wait for him to wake up again.

I DON'T WANT TO LEAVE HIM ALONE, BUT I'M ALSO EXTREMELY aware that it's been way too long since I've changed my panties, had a shower, or even brushed my teeth. My hair's a disaster and I had to trade my comfy jeans and my hoodie for shapeless scrubs to placate my bastard doctor.

Nine deserves better than that.

So, as soon as I've changed into my own clothes and my mouth is minty fresh and clean, I hurry back into the living room. One quick look reveals that Nine hasn't moved an inch while I was gone.

I meet Callie's gaze. She was the one who told me that my Shadow Man would be okay while I took a few minutes for myself. Now that I'm back, she nods and shares a smile before moving away from him, allowing me to take her place next to Nine.

He sleeps for more than an hour. I keep checking to see if his chest is moving, ready and willing to pull the Brinkburn back out if that'll do something. That's my last resort. Since Nine is no longer a statue—no longer under Melisndre's spell—I don't want to let the necklace get too close to him in case it hurts him instead.

Why won't he wake up?

I remind myself that the same thing happened with Ash. Because of the shadow travel, he was too weak to wake up as soon as Callie did. It's still light out. The clock reads that it's after six o'clock. Thanks to daylight saving time, I've got a couple of more hours before the sun goes down and, hopefully, the moonlight revives him.

Luckily, I don't have to wait that long.

A few minutes past seven, Nine's otherworldly silver eyes spring open. Like with Ash, he goes from entirely out of commission to running on all cylinders in seconds. It must be a fae thing. He'll never show any weakness so, even though he probably has no idea where he is or what's going on, he immediately adopts an expression of disdain mixed with utter lack of interest.

And then his gaze lands on me and everything changes.

He goes from lying on his back to crouching on his knees in front of me in a heartbeat. His actions are so fast, so fluid, that I totally wasn't expecting it. I shriek, suddenly falling, only to be saved by his hand

Nine lets go of me the instant that I'm steady again.

Resting on his heels, an unnamed emotion tugging at his lips, my Shadow Man only has eyes for me as he stares. His pointed ears twitch, his slender fingers digging into the hardwood floor as if he's itching to reach for me again, but won't let himself give in to the impulse.

"Riley…" His voice is just the same as I remember. Lyrical. Beautiful. But there's also that harsh edge that's undeniably Nine, and the barely constrained disappointment that I did something wrong. "What did you do to me?"

Not the greeting I expected. "What do you mean, what did I do? I saved you."

"I'm in the Iron." It's not a question. Throwing a searching look at me, Nine straightens, his signature duster barely wafting behind him as he rips his gaze away from my annoyed scowl before heading straight for the window at the other end of the living room.

The blinds are drawn. He jerks them open, cracking the two slats he yanked, letting the last of the daylight stream in.

He's not a vampire, but I've seen him get caught in a stray sunbeam before. It's like when he grabbed me without my permission. It burns him. Sure, he heals almost immediately, but as he shoves his pale hand in the sunlight, nothing seems to happen.

I gulp, my scowl fading into an openly worried expression.

Uh-oh.

Nine steps back. He marvels at his hand, twisting it back and forth, showing off his skin. There's a mild streak of red, almost like sunburn, but it's nothing compared to the fire that used to scorch his flesh.

"How long has it been?"

I... I don't know.

"Tell me."

"A while," I confess. "I lost track. But it's been a while."

"It's been too long. I have to go back. As soon as night falls, I have to take a portal back to Faerie. It's the only thing I can do."

From off to my left, I hear a *click* as a door closes. I search the room.

Ash and Callie are gone.

She probably dragged him out of the room so that I could have some privacy with Nine. I appreciate it at the same time as I wish they would've stayed behind me to offer me moral support.

Spinning back, I cringe when I see the dark look in Nine's normally silver eyes. His black eyebrows are a pair of slashes in his astonishingly beautiful face, a terrible expression that only highlights how incredible he is.

This is not what I was expecting out of our reunion. To Nine, he's only been gone for seconds. But to me? I've spent weeks worried about him, pushing myself farther than I ever had because I had one goal: to bring Nine back.

I spent *days* in a glorified closet. I remember every fucking second of what it was like to be trapped in that room, forced to talk to Gillespie, terrified that I'd never see Nine or my parents again.

I *touched* that creepy bastard.

And Nine has the balls to look at me like *I've* done something wrong.

Maybe I was too impatient. As a statue, it's not like he would've known if I waited a few more hours before I tried to bring him back with the Brinkburn. I haven't eaten enough. Lord knows I could use a shower and a nap.

I hadn't cared, though. The second I stumbled back into our apartment in Newport, I had to know if everything I went through was worth it. If the crystal shattered the spell on Nine, if I saved him, I could get past it all—I just needed my Shadow Man.

And all he wants to do is leave.

His explanations are worthless. I can barely hear them over the pulse of blood in my head, and the breaking of my heart.

"I'll never survive here. The sun… it's not made for my kind. And the iron… I can feel it around me already. Weakening me. Stealing my strength. I won't be able to protect you anymore. Don't you see?"

"What did you expect me to do?" I snap. "Leave you behind? Leave you with *her*?"

Nine reaches for me, his burned hand heading toward my cheek, pausing when a few inches still linger between us. He pulls back, and sighs. "Shadow—"

That name.

That *name*.

"Don't call me that."

He nods. "I understand."

Does he?

I want to launch myself at him. Throw myself into his arms, let him touch me while I'm pressing my skin against his, my lips against his. Was that kiss a fluke? Did I imagine his whole claiming me in front of the queen and her court?

I think I left that Nine behind in Faerie. Because this Nine? There's something in the set of his jaw, the dark look in his silver gaze that has me feeling like I'm a kid again and I've upset my Shadow Man.

The scoff escapes me. It's either that or a sob. "And I'm not asking you to protect me, Nine."

His lips thin. "That's my duty."

Right. His *duty* all because of a bargain he made with my mother more than twenty years ago.

"Callie told me all about it. About how the Fae Queen sent her soldiers after me, and how she used your debt to my father to trick you into agreeing to watch over me. Well, in case you haven't noticed it yet, my... my parents are back. You don't have to do your *duty* anymore, okay?"

"A human could never trick a fae."

Of course *that*'s what the Dark Fae took away from everything I just said.

"Whatever."

"Riley—"

This is the night in the cemetery all over again. When his honesty was too much for me and I couldn't take it.

I sent him away then.

This time, I don't. I can't.

Because I know—I *know*—that if I push Nine away this time, if I tell him to go away, there's a good chance he won't come back.

I can't do this. And when Nine reaches for me again, I pull back, dodging his fingers. I won't give him the satisfaction of sending him away.

I storm out of the apartment on my own instead.

CHAPTER 11

"Riley, wait up."

Ah, come on. Nine sent my mother down here after me? I can't believe this.

Pretending I don't hear her, I keep on walking, even picking up the pace. Sure, Callie is as human as I am—well, more, since I'm half—and the tech and the iron in the world around us doesn't affect her even a little. Whether it's day or night out, she can chase me all she wants and, as the pitter-patter of her light steps follow behind me, I'm willing to bet that that's her plan.

Back in March, back when Melisandre's spell on her was first broken, she wouldn't have been able to. She's gotten so much better lately. Once she realized that, as different as Newport is… as different as the world is… since she was captured and taken to Faerie, mostly everything around her was essentially the same at its core, she even started to take evening walks on her own.

She said it was because she wanted to see just how much

everything changed. I suspected it was because she had a hard time sitting around, fretting while Ash taught me maneuvers with his sword as he helped me plot how I was going to steal Gillespie's necklace.

Still, I know it's not fair. The world overwhelms her, and Callie doesn't like to be away from Ash for too long. There's only one thing that would actually compel her to willingly leave on her own.

Me.

I turn the corner, picking up the pace, longing for the days when I could just go, even run from a cop if I wanted to, and know that no one would be running after me.

I went from being on my own to having a mom, a dad, *and* a mate who wants to leave me the first chance he gets.

I scoff. Lucky me.

Nine's less than enthusiastic reaction is messing with me. Just because he's basically taken my heart and put it through a paper shredder, that doesn't mean that I should take it out on Callie. She's been nothing but kind and supportive to me since I rescued her from Faerie.

It's not her fault that Nine's being such a dick.

I stop short, waiting for Callie to catch up to me. When I hear her soft pants, her breathing a little heavy since she had to jog to reach me in time, I place my hands on my hips.

"What?"

"Where are you going?"

I grit my teeth to keep from snapping at her. Her question is almost innocent and, besides, if she wants to pretend that I'm not seconds away from losing it, so can I.

Exhaling roughly through my nose, I say, "For a walk."

"By yourself? You just got back. Aren't you hungry? Tired?"

She pauses for a second, then totally blows her spot by adding, "Don't you want to see your mate?"

"Yes to the first. Yes to the second. That's why I'm out here." *Lie*. "I saw Nine. He's fine. Now I want to get some food, get some sleep, and put this fucking day behind me."

Callie's face screws up, torn between curiosity and sympathy. She doesn't know what I've been through—that's on purpose—but she'd have to be way more optimistic than a fae-bonded human can be to think that I was missing for more than two days for a *good* reason.

She doesn't ask, probably because I already refused to talk about it before, and it's not like that's why she came running after me.

And we both know it.

She drops the pretenses just a little. Instead of bringing up my trip to Black Pine, she focuses right on my Shadow Man.

"Your father told me that Ninetroir—"

My stomach lurches. Nope. Can't handle his true name. Not right now.

"Nine," I correct.

That doesn't hurt so bad.

"Your father told me that Nine touched you. That he claimed you."

"I thought he did."

"Okay. Well... listen, 'touch' has a very different meaning to the fae. With permission, even the simplest contact, skin to skin, has power. Between mates... it can be magical and I'm fully human. I can see through glamour, but magic? It never affected me until I let Ash touch me the first time."

She sounds so wistful, like she's drawing on a treasured memory. Her lips quirk slightly.

That's not helping me, either.

"Callie. Is there a reason why you chased after me? Because, honestly, I'd rather be alone right now."

With a sideways look at the building, I know I'm right when I guessed that Nine sent her after me. It's daylight. Sun streaming everywhere. Even if he wanted to follow after me, he couldn't, and I'd be lying if I said that I hadn't thought of that when I sprinted for the elevator.

"Sweetie, you spent so long trying to bring him back to you, to break the nasty queen's spell on him... give him time. You remember what it was like for Ash. The fae don't like to let anyone see them weak. He'll get over it. You just need to be there for him."

She makes a ton of valid points. The Ash who came out of the stasis spell was argumentative and overcompensated by making all his crazy decrees. He calmed down after a couple of days had passed, so that within a week or so, he was the protective, kind, thoughtful fae male that I've come to know.

But Nine...

The part that kills me is that *his* reaction is spot-on. Maybe not for the Dark Fae I've known as an adult, but the Shadow Man who had begrudgingly watched me for years?

That wasn't my mate I walked out on. That was a relic from my past.

And maybe I'm the idiot for believing that he could ever want me the way I want him.

I want to cry. I hurt so bad, I want to *cry*. But I don't, because tears have never solved anything for me before and, when I feel this way, I've always just lashed out.

So I do.

"He wants to leave me," I snap. "Didn't he tell you that?"

Callie winces, but she doesn't back off.

"Bonded fae... soulmates. They can't leave their mates one

the bond is finalized. He's worried for you, Riley. Like your father, he wants to get rid of every single danger out there before he can be sure you're safe. He's just processing this badly. He needs to be with you more than ever."

I snort. "You don't know Nine. If he thinks it's for my own good, he'll go."

That falls in line with the new and improved Nine, too. Especially if he thinks he's helping me, I'd never be able to stop him.

"He won't be able to be separated from you for long. Even if he goes back, he'll return for you. He'll have to. He's your *ffrindau*."

"Tell that to him," I huff. "I wouldn't be surprised if he's already gone."

"You're serious." Callie looks confused. "When a fae fully bonds with his chosen soulmate, nothing can stop them from protecting them. Don't you have faith in him?"

I thought I did, but that's not the point. On a rough exhale, the truth slips out. "Honestly, I don't even know if he still wants to be mine."

"Well, it's not like he can take it back or anything."

I shrug.

Who the hell knows?

"But didn't you already..."

"Didn't we *what*?"

"You know." And then Callie does something that I would never have imagined her doing in a hundred years. Curling her fingers toward her thumb, she forms a circle with one hand. The other? She folds her fingers into a fist, save for the pointer finger. Then, with an impish expression, she pokes her pointer finger through the open hole a few times, raising her eyebrows at me as she does it.

I blink.

No. Way.

In my surprise, I blurt out, "What the hell are you doing?"

"Oh. Okay. Maybe you don't know. You see, when two people love each other very, very much, they will—"

White noise fills my head as a rush of embarrassment has my cheeks flaming up.

Is she...

Oh my God.

She *is*.

She's actually trying to give me a sex talk since she—very wrongly—assumes that I have no idea what her crude gesture was referring to.

A sex talk.

Really?

So, yeah. My mom's a teensy bit late for *that*.

I lost my virginity when I was twelve or thirteen. It made sense at the time; I don't regret it. My haphephobia and panic attacks were around then, but they were more manageable then since Madelaine's murder was the trigger that really put me in a bad place—and I don't just mean the asylum.

So long as I was the one initiating the contact, I liked to be touched. After a lifetime of feeling unloved, unwanted, and abandoned, in those few moments when I was connected to another person, I wasn't the reject orphan who was so awful, even her mother threw her away.

I was reckless and, I admit, very, very lucky. So many things could have gone wrong since I didn't even bother being careful. No STI's, no pregnancy scares, nothing that was forcibly taken from a hollow girl who was all but willing to give it away.

And then Madelaine died and, despite all of Nine's warnings, I nearly fell under Rys's sway. I almost let him touch me—

and that was one of the last times I *let* anyone touch me without a debilitating panic attack getting in the way.

Until Nine.

And, unless I'm really, really misunderstanding Callie, that's what she's expecting me to do.

Touch Nine.

Ah, hell. This is super, super awkward.

I clear my throat. "You don't have to give me the whole birds and the bees talk. I appreciate it, but you're a little late for that."

That familiar flash of sadness—the recognition that she missed my entire life while trapped in Faerie—twists her pretty face for a second before she nods. "I thought I would try."

"Appreciate it. Still, I'm good."

"So you and Nine already—"

Oof. And I thought my overwhelming embarrassment had started to recede a bit.

I shake my head.

"Oh. *Oh.* I thought..."

Yeah. We both know what she thought.

Callie winces. "Sorry. I shouldn't have pried. I just wanted to help."

The funny thing is, despite how super embarrassing this chat was, she actually did. Since Ash made it pretty clear that he was hoping that I would give up on Nine eventually, no matter how often I reminded him that my only goal was to save my Shadow Man, he didn't share too much about what it was like to be part of a mated pair.

An awkward discussion with my mom... this was one of those things I regretted not having while I was growing up. She might've been a bit late there, but this chat did what I probably wouldn't have been able to do on my own.

It evaporated my anger, making my frustration at Nine's reaction disappear like a puff of smoke.

I don't think I'll ever get her impish expression out of my mind, but that's okay. It's a memory I'll be able to treasure—once the red staining my cheeks finally fades away, that is.

"That's okay."

"Well, I know you said you were hungry. If you want to come back upstairs, I can make you a sandwich or something. There's still some food in the fridge. You can just tell me what you like."

That... actually sounds kinda nice. The granola bar from this morning is a distant memory, and my talk with her has made me realize that I *am* starving. I'll probably change my mind when I go back up and see that Nine is gone, but I still appreciate her offer.

"Alright."

"Really?"

I nod.

"Great. I think we have some salami or ham, a couple of types of cheeses. Cheddar? How does cheddar sound—"

As we turn the corner to head back toward the building, a male vice floats on the breeze.

"Evening, ladies."

Hang on. I know that voice.

Even though his head is bowed, his body covered by blankets he doesn't need since it's the middle of April and Newport is warming up, I'm absolutely positive that, if he looked up at me, his eyes would be vivid green.

Callie spares him a glance, mumbling a soft 'evening' though she doesn't even break her stride.

Me? I stop and stare.

He wasn't there. I know he wasn't. When I ran out the door,

this whole street was clear. I know, because I've spent weeks waiting to see the same street sleeper take up his spot outside of our condemned building.

And now, here he is.

On the plus side, no matter how easily he blends in with his surroundings, at least I know he's real. He's not a figment of my imagination if Callie can see him, too.

I have a sudden urge to walk over to him, to ask him about the paper he gave me with all of his "corrections" on it. Sometimes, that long ago morning seems like it had been a dream, though all I have to do is look at the scrap I keep hidden upstairs to know that I didn't make him up. I haven't seen him since that day, though, and I often wondered if that was on purpose.

I take a step toward him—

Callie is oblivious.

"Come on, Riley," she calls out to me when she senses that I've turned. "Let's go."

I throw one last curious look over my shoulder at the mysterious homeless man. Whether it's on purpose or not, with Callie's back turned to him, he lifts his head and meets my curious gaze.

I see the twinkle in his grass-colored, bright green eyes as he nods over at me, almost like he's daring me to come back to him.

I haven't forgotten about the note he passed me, or the "corrections" he made. And if Callie wasn't itching to return upstairs, desperate to go back to her own mate, I would have taken the time to grill this stranger with all the questions and concerns that I've kept bottled up inside these last few weeks.

I underestimated Gillespie. I'd be a fucking moron to let another quiet threat sneak up on me.

As far as I see it, anyone who knows anything about the Shadow Prophecy is definitely a threat.

Next time, I promise. Next time I see that man, I will make him tell me how he's involved—and what the hell he wants from me.

I learned a long time ago, no matter what, someone always wants something.

Even me.

I think of Nine and how he reached for my cheek before pulling back.

Especially me.

CHAPTER 12

When we walk into the apartment, my dad and Nine are squaring off in the living room.

I don't know how to react to that.

Honestly, part of me thought that Nine would already be gone, halfway back to Faerie to save his power and his strength. But he's not.

He's here.

The second thing I notice is that his fist is open. Sitting in the center of his palm, there's the same pebble Nine has shown me a few times now.

The same pebble that Callie mentioned when Ash asked what Nine was doing in the apartment when we all landed here together.

Okay. So it's obvious that we've walked into the middle of something. Some kind of argument between old friends, maybe, though that might be wishful thinking, believing Nine and my dad used to be friends. Who knows? It could be something else entirely.

I don't really care.

My attention goes straight to the pebble. I point.

"What is that? I finally have a chance to ask. I've got to know. What does that small rock have to do with anything?"

Ash shoots a nasty look at Nine. "You haven't told her?"

"She knows of my debt to her mother. I never had the opportunity to explain the meaning behind it."

Once upon a time I thought it was like his lucky charm or something. Then, when Callie brought it up, I convinced her to tell me more about it. It looked like a pebble, but it was *more*.

It was a symbol of the debt that Nine owed Ash.

So why is Nine holding it out to him now?

He made a point to tell me once that he didn't consider the debt closed. In a fit of anger, I told him that it was—that I didn't want to be treated like a responsibility he couldn't avoid—and that he could leave me the hell alone. He refused, then pocketed the pebble.

Is he trying to give it back?

My heart stops beating.

That's what he's doing, isn't it?

"If you're going to stay in our home, I expect you to be truthful with my daughter."

"I've never lied to Riley," argues Nine.

Yeah. Because he's fae. And the fae might not be able to tell a lie, but I know from experience that that doesn't mean they're always telling the truth.

"What's going on here?" I ask.

Ash coldly eyes Nine. "Tell her, Ninetroir. Or I will."

"Fine."

"Now."

Nine glares over at my dad. "I'm trying to decide where to begin."

"Try the beginning. The prophecy."

I groan. I'm so over the prophecy.

Nine's frown tells me he agrees. "Alright. There was a prophecy. About a mortal... who wasn't."

Sounds familiar. "Let me guess. Half-human. Half-fae."

He nods. "But it's not the Shadow Prophecy."

What?

"Nine, what are you saying?"

"When I was born, there was a prophecy. About a mortal who wasn't, and a fae who would be indebted to another before he could earn his fated mate." Nine reaches into the well of his palm, plucking the pebble out with two of his long, slender, pale fingers. He holds it up. "I've long owed Aislinn a debt. This pebble carries the weight of that debt."

"Not just a regular debt," cuts in Ash. "A life debt."

"A life debt?" I echo.

"Yes. Because he saved my life."

He did? No one's mentioned anything like that to me before.

"I didn't want to believe in the prophecy. As soon as I came of age, I had other things to do. I needed to begin my search. Melisandre was already on the throne and I wanted to do anything I could to change that. I was arrogant. Cocky. Sure of everything. Even more than now, if you can imagine. I thought I could beat fate. The fate of Faerie was more important than my happiness.

"My search took me right into the human world. This was years and years ago. It was easier to hide as a fae. A quick touch and I had the strength to make the shadows do my bidding. I'm a Dark Fae. It was my birthright. I could go anywhere, here or in Faerie. I was untouchable—or I thought I was. But no Unseelie can fight the sun without a little help."

Like being brought to the human world by a shadow-wielding halfling who kept him as a statue, acclimating him to the sun until he was more like me than the all-powerful Nine he's always been.

I gulp.

Nine keeps talking. Now that he's started, he finds it easier to continue.

"Aislinn was one of Melisandre's guards. She posted him along a Seelie portal, watching over the Iron. The human world. If it wasn't for a chance encounter when the shadows disappeared, the sun would have ended me. Only Aislinn was there as he pulled me back into Faerie. When I finally recovered, I owed him a debt."

"Because you can't beat fate," snaps Ash. "Foolish Dark Fae. You never should have tried."

I notice that there's less heat in Ash's tone now than before.

"It led me to Riley, so how can I regret it?" He folds his fist, tucking the pebble away into his pocket. "The prophecy was going to happen whether I wanted it to or not. I stopped searching the Iron because I finally realized that my fate was tied with Aislinn, one way or another."

"I couldn't get rid of him," muttered Ash.

Nine ignores him. "I went to the Shadow Academy, where the Unseelie guards are trained. Melisandre handpicked me to join her soldiers, but that was because Ash manipulated her to choose me. I needed to watch over him—and then he disappeared into the Iron, too."

Right. Because he met my mom and chose to stay with her.

Because it was possible. Nine just doesn't want to stay with *me*.

I don't want to hear about his past when I'm not too sure either one of us is going to have a future—especially not one together.

He wants to beat fate.

I'm supposed to be his fate.

"Half-human. Half-fae," I mutter again.

Suddenly, it clicks.

Nine's fate is tied to a mortal who wasn't, right? A halfling. And Gillespie told me that I'm the first female halfling he's met in his three hundred years…

I glare up at him. "Nine. I've got a question for you. How long did you know that I was going to be yours?"

The room quiets. I don't think anyone expected me to just put it out there like that.

They should've known better by now.

"I was sure the moment I found you in the asylum. You were on the cusp of turning twenty-one and… it was so obvious to me. Once you were twenty-one for sure, once the fae side of you came out, there was no denying it. The life debt to your sire, the Seelie blood in your veins… the way I was drawn to you. In trying to shield you from the Shadow Prophecy, I realized that mine had finally come to pass."

Ignoring the part about the Shadow Prophecy, I have to admit that that… actually explains a lot. I remember being a little weirded out—and, okay, a little flattered—at the way he seemed to gobble me up with his gaze that first night in my room in Black Pine. He couldn't stop watching me.

And then, after our trip to Faerie, right after my fae ears appeared… everything was different. Everything changed.

His touch was so much more powerful than it had been before. And I started to accept that the feelings toward Nine I always had were way more complicated than I thought.

Still.

"That's not what I asked, Nine," I tell him, steel in my voice.

I'm not going to let this go.

He knows it, too.

On a sigh, he admits, "I suspected it from the moment the gossips in Faerie whispered that Aislinn's human mate was with child."

Suspected it... What a fae way to put it. I learned that from Nine, too. The fae will never speak in absolutes unless there's no way around it.

But I *need* him to be absolute.

"Nine..." I say in warning, two seconds away from losing it.

"But I knew—some part of me just knew—from the very first touch."

Okay, then. I got my answer, didn't I?

"When I was an infant," I say flatly.

"Yes."

"Is... is that why you watched over me my whole life? Because of your prophecy?"

Nine can't lie. Once again, I bet he wishes he could.

He nods slowly. "The debt compelled me... but, yes, I would've done it anyway once I recognized who you were. You weren't my *ffrindau* then, but if you survived Melisandre long enough, one day you might be."

Might. Not is. Not was.

Might.

Welp. I guess that settles that.

So, yeah. I think I'm gonna need some time to deal with all of this. But since running out of the apartment again isn't an option, I struggle to find some way to change the subject.

He can tell. Sometimes it seems like Nine knows me better than anyone does. I don't know how I feel about that, either.

"I didn't want to bring this up. You have bigger concerns than me, but Aislinn insisted. And he's... he's right. This is his home. His family. I should respect that. He thought you needed to know the truth of my past. Now you know."

"It's fine. Forget it. It's not important right now."

"Riley—"

"Forget it," I say more firmly. "Tell me more about what you were doing in the human world before I was born. What was so important that you almost got trapped here in the sun? What exactly were you searching for?"

I can tell that he doesn't want to discuss it, but since I'm refusing to talk about *his* prophecy, he has no choice if he wants to keep the conversation going. And he does. Don't know why, but he does.

"Not what," Nine says at last. "Who."

"Sure," I agree. "Who were you searching for?"

"Oberon."

The name sounds familiar. "Who's that?"

"The rightful king of Faerie."

Okay. Back up.

"If he's the rightful king, then what's up with the Fae Queen?" You know, now that I think about it... "Hey, if everyone hates Melisandre, how did she become queen of Faerie in the first place?"

"Simple. She convinced the Seelie King that she was his *ffrindau*. I don't know if that's true or not. Only Oberon and Melisandre know if she was truly his fated soulmate, or just a consort. But, either way, he made her his queen and then..."

"Then what?"

"She overthrew him and had him banished him to Brinkburn."

Brinkburn. Wait a sec—

I slip Gillespie's necklace out from beneath my shirt,

showing Nine the crystal. I'm careful not to get too close, just in case, as I tap it with my finger. "Isn't that what this is?"

"It's only a piece," cuts in Ash. I give a start. I'd forgotten that my parents were still here. "It holds a sliver of that terrible place's power. It's why even a tiny stone or crystal from Brinkburn can break most spells."

When we were planning our heist at Black Pine, Ash made it clear that *a* Brinkburn was the crystal hanging off of Gillespie's necklace while Brinkburn itself was a location in England. Since going there was out of the question, I promptly forgot all about it.

Probably shouldn't have done that.

"So what is it? The place, I mean?"

"It's where fae get sent to die."

Wait—

"Aren't fae immortal? Well, except for cutting off their head because, okay, no one can survive that. But I didn't think there was any other way to kill them."

"There are three other ways."

For the first time since we walked into the apartment, my mom speaks up.

Nine glances over at Ash. "You told her of our weakness?"

Ash juts his chin out defiantly. "She's my *ffrindau*. I told her anything that might help her survive when Melisandre came for our child."

I try not to wince. I still can't get over the fact that I'm their child—and that, in their eyes, I'm supposed to be this chubby infant with rosy cheeks and a tuft of white-blonde hair sticking out of the top of my head.

No wonder my dad looked like he was ready to light Nine up. Not counting this crazy long and complicated history between them, Nine's still a grown male who laid a claim to his daughter and none of us know how we're supposed to deal with the overall weirdness of this strange situation.

Callie lifts her folded hand up. She extends one finger. "Iron." She extends a second. "Either the sun or shadows, depending on if they're an Unseelie or Seelie." She extends a third. "Brinkburn. You bury a fae on that land and there's no magic that'll save them."

"Exactly," Nine agrees. "And that's why it's so important for me to go back to Faerie. Especially now. We *need* Oberon."

That's a leap.

"Why do you think he's in Faerie?" I ask. "Maybe your instincts were right. Maybe he's here."

"I have to *hope* he isn't."

What?

"Why?"

"Because, when he broke free of Brinkburn, lore says that he escaped into the Iron more than two hundred years ago instead of returning to Faerie to take back his throne. He would've had to suffer through the industrial revolution when iron and steel ruled. It would've been too big a shock to one with that much Faerie blood. None of our kind could've survived that. Not even a king."

Oh, great. For a second there, I actually thought I might have a little bit of hope.

Damn it.

So, in the end, I win—if I can consider Nine begrudgingly sticking around because I begged him to a victory.

Since I'd do anything—even put up with his cold behavior—to keep him from going to Faerie when I can't risk it, I kinda do.

It's weird, though. I thought it was bad enough when I had to share the apartment with my newfound parents. Once we throw Nine into the mix, it's... I don't even know how to describe it. Weird is probably the best way to put it.

Callie keeps trying to come up with ways to leave me and Nine alone together. Ash, on the other hand, might begrudgingly co-exist with Nine, but there's still a ton of unresolved issues there. My dad still can't get past the idea that Nine is taking advantage of me, especially now that I know the truth of *his* prophecy, but it's not like that changes my feelings for him.

It... might change his feelings for me, though.

Ever since I broke the spell on him, Nine's been keeping his distance.

At first, I barely notice. The stress of everything that's been happening to me finally rears its ugly head. It breaks me. I mean it. The next morning, I wake up from my fitful sleep on the couch. I'm screaming. My brain throws me back to being trapped in Gillespie's white room and it takes until I can actually focus on my surroundings—the apartment—and see that I'm safe to stop.

I'm home.

The screaming catches everyone's attention, but I pointblank refuse to discuss what I went through to get the Brinkburn. I don't regret it, though I can't stop myself from thinking that *Nine* does. He stays, because I want him to, but I don't think anyone's happy about that.

Though my parents try to make up for my obvious distress by clearing out the nursery so that I have a proper place to sleep, I purposely choose to sleep on the couch. It's where I've spent most nights since we cleaned the place up, though that had more to do with being close to the frozen Nine than my deep-seated discomfort when it came to sleeping in the old nursery.

Now that he's back, I'm not sure what I'm supposed to do. Especially since Nine... he doesn't sleep. Not really.

When I suggest it has something to do with his being a statue for long, he doesn't deny it, though he tries to explain that, as a Dark Fae, he's more nocturnal than not. The small amount of magic he can draw toward him is only there at night. The sunlight makes him weak so, if he starts to falter, he drifts toward a patch of shadow and nods off during the day.

At night, he watches me sleep.

The first time I catch him—the second night when I purposely asked him to sit with me because I could hardly believe he was back and, uh, I didn't want to take up screaming alone again—he doesn't deny it. It seems like such a natural thing for him to be doing that I wonder if this isn't the first time he's done it.

How many times did he watch over me while I was a child? I thought I was awake for every one of his visits before I was put into the asylum. Was I wrong?

I don't ask.

It makes me feel a little better to think that maybe he still cares. Nine's always been better with actions than words, and as the days crawl pass, I see him watching me even when we're all awake.

A few days into our new reality, Ash tells me to check out the nursery. My dad is trying so hard not to take his obvious frustrations out on Nine, but I have to admit that he's gotten so much better at not making decrees or issuing commands—he even calls me Riley now—so, when he opens the door, I peek.

It's... not a nursery anymore.

I don't know where they got any of this stuff from. And it's not just Callie and Ash who'd been disappearing into that room the last few days. On my return trips from the outside—part looking for that homeless man who might have some answers, part finding an escape from my family upstairs—I see him slipping out of that room more than a couple of times.

I don't ask about that, either.

Between the three of them, they turned it into a sanctuary for me. A place I can be safe and on my own. There's a full-sized bed, brand new linens, and a dresser. Clothes—in a style just like I like—fill the drawers. A new pair of gloves, just waiting for me to break them in—are laid out on the top.

And when I try to tell Ash how much I appreciate the thought, he tells me almost begrudgingly that it's Nine who I owe my gratitude to. It was his idea.

A gift just for me.

I'm stubborn. Hurt. I don't say a word to Nine about it even as I do move into the room that night.

The bed is perfect. It feels like sleeping on a cloud.

I just wish I wasn't sleeping in it alone.

CHAPTER 13

I let myself into the apartment, carrying a few bags of groceries from the corner market.

We didn't really need much—with three of us feeling comfortable enough to walk around the neighborhood now, the fridge is always stocked. But, since I needed the excuse to get some fresh air earlier, I offered to take a run down to the store knowing that Nine couldn't come with me.

I'm beginning to think that I shouldn't have thrown such a stink about him going back to Faerie. He's obviously miserable here. The iron doesn't affect him as much, and his tolerance to the sun grows with every day. I watch him stand in front of the window for hours, as if he's forcing himself to get used to it. He wants to get stronger since he can't go back to Faerie.

For me. He's doing it for me.

The old familiar guilt settles in my gut as I find him standing there again. I force a smile to my face a second before he turns to welcome me back home.

"Where are my parents?" I ask as I set the groceries down.

"They... left."

Why am I not surprised?

I don't blame them. We've been forced into an incredibly close proximity these last few weeks. Of course, considering the talk I had with my mom the other day, all of their little day trip seems just a *little* too coincidental to me.

It isn't lost on either of them that Nine is still hanging out in the living room while I stay in my room. Despite their giving us as much privacy as Callie can by dragging my dad out with her, it's pointless.

Nine hasn't touched me yet. Not even an accidental brush in the hallway. Nothing at all.

I'm still grateful for her looking out for me like this. I'm also super glad that she feels confident enough to go out and leave me behind at all.

We've been hiding out long enough that the inherent need to actually *hide* isn't as bad as it was. Now that Callie is doing better with heading out, Ash has no problem joining her while it's bright. The two of them are rarely without the other.

Because they're mates and, according to Callie, that's how it's supposed to be with mates.

Then there's Nine.

I'm supposed to be his mate. I let him claim me in Faerie when he pulled me close and stole my kiss. I was totally down with being Nine's.

But what does that mean?

Even better, what does my Shadow Man think it means?

I still don't know.

I sigh. Weeks. It's been weeks. And maybe I'm too conditioned not to ask Nine anything from a lifetime of my Shadow Man always being the one to provide any answers for me, but I haven't been able to bring myself to ask him a single thing anymore.

Until now.

I'm so tired. I'm so unsure.

That familiar guarded expression he wears just about pushes me past my breaking point.

My shoulders slump. I throw my hands up in the air and sigh. "Oh, Nine. I— what the hell are we doing here?"

"Riley?"

"And I don't mean here," I say, just in case he gets the wrong impression. "This is the only place I have until the queen hunts me down."

His eyes flash. It's the most emotion I've seen from him in ages. "I won't let that happen."

He might not be able to stop it, either.

I can feel that my time is running out. Every morning, I wake up and I'm surprised to find that I'm still here. That I'm still with my parents, with Nine. I keep getting this feeling like she's getting closer and closer to finding out where I am, that as soon as she does, Melisandre will drag me kicking and screaming back to Faerie where we'll settle this once and for all.

I know I'll regret it forever if I leave things with Nine as they are. I've always been on my guard. Always careful to keep myself apart from everyone else because, well, in the end, they always leave.

Only, this time, I can't shake the feeling that I'm going to be the one who leaves everything behind.

Before I go, I have to settle this. I have to let him know that my feelings haven't changed.

"You might not have a choice. But, just in case, I want you to know that I love you. And you don't have to say anything—"

"I love you, Riley. More than anything else in either realm.

You must know that. I've always loved you, even if I love you... differently than before."

I latch onto that. "Differently? Differently how?"

He clenches his jaw, almost like he's said too much.

Oh, no. I'm not going to let him off that easy.

"Are you talking about how you claimed me?"

A muscle in his cheek jumps.

Gotcha.

Forgetting all about the groceries, I dare to cross the room, moving closer to Nine than I've gone since I used the Brinkburn on him.

"Are you talking about how you *touched* me? About how good it felt when I gave you permission and let you in?"

I want to let him all the way in.

"Riley. What are you..."

"Do it again."

He wants to. Holy shit. I can see it in his eyes... he definitely wants to. But then he shakes his head.

Damn it.

"I don't want to hurt you, Riley."

When he touches me without my permission, it doesn't hurt me. It hurts *him*. The last couple of times I let him touch me, I only felt pleasure.

I want him to feel that.

I move closer.

He steps back.

Come on, Nine.

I know exactly what this is, too. My poor Nine. It's like when he had to use touch magic to reverse the effects of eating the faerie fruit while erasing Rys's brand from my skin. It felt so good, I begged him to do it again, and he told me that it was simply the touch talking. That, in my right mind, I would never want to feel his skin on mine.

He's doubting himself. He doesn't think that I really want him.

And maybe that's my fault, too. I certainly haven't been giving him any "go" signs since he's been back.

That changes now.

"I've got a question." I inch closer to him. I smile, part seductive, part reassuring—and, won't you know, this time, Nine stays put. "That alright?"

He gulps, his voice gone unusually hoarse as he rasps out, "Ask it."

"Is there any way for you to touch me without you stealing part of my soul or you burning yourself? A way we can both feel good?"

He shudders out a breath. "You don't know what you're asking."

Yes. I do.

Because, thanks to Callie—my matchmaking mother—I kind of already know the answer.

"Answer me. Please."

"Once there's nothing left to take. Once I own every part of you. Once I claim you for my own, and you take me in return. Once I brand you as mine and you just say yes."

That's... what I thought.

It's like that fateful day in Faerie. When he stood up and told Melisandre's entire throne room full of fae that I was meant to be his. He took my hand, then took my kiss, and it was different than any other fae-touch I'd ever experienced.

He hasn't touched me since. Is it because he's waiting for that last touch?

Only one way to find out.

He might be good with waiting. Not me.

I've waited long enough.

I snag Nine by the hand. It feels… natural, almost. Like we fit.

Sure, there's that heartbeat where I ask myself *what the hell do you think you're doing*, but I'll probably always have that immediate reaction. If six years of therapy at Black Pine didn't help me when it came to my haphephobia, I'm probably a lost cause. That's okay, though. I don't want to touch anyone but my Shadow Man.

His fingers curve around mine. He strokes the side of my glove as if getting a feel for the leather.

And that's when I realize that he's probably never seen me without the protective layer since the fire.

Rys did. In the dream that wasn't a dream, the Light Fae used his charm and his magic to remove my gloves. It was one more reason why I'd believed that none of that strange dance was real—I'm *never* without my gloves. Of course, it was a trick. Just another way to steal a touch. Still, he saw them.

Suddenly, I have the urge to share them with Nine.

He claimed me. Verbally, at least. In front of the whole Seelie Court, he told the Fae Queen that we were meant to be. Well, if I'm going to give him everything—my heart, my soul, my touch —I want to make sure he knows exactly what he's getting.

Slowly, as if I'm performing the most seductive striptease (and, for me, it is), I loosen the leather that wraps my thumb before tugging on the other four fingers. Once it's free enough, I shimmy off the glove, then toss it to the floor. With Nine's attention firmly on what I'm doing, I do the same for the second hand.

They're not as bad as they were six years ago before all of the skin grafts, the autografts, the surgeries. Raw skin, new skin and molded into something that's uniquely mine, with scars and patches and ruined fingers that remind me just how dangerous the fae can be.

But not Nine. Never Nine.

I share with him the truth of all that I am because I want to *prove* to him that he's not the type of male that I'll ever be afraid of.

Back in the asylum, the night he finally admitted what I'd been willfully blind to all along—that he was, in fact, a Dark Fae—I acted like I was shocked. Deep down, though, I think I've always known. I just... I never thought of him as a danger to me. He wasn't one of *them*. He was my Shadow Man.

And I'll do anything to make his mine, even show him a part of me that I've rarely shared with anyone else.

He knows, too. He knows how important this is to me.

Slowly, gently, Nine takes my hand in his.

He brings my hand to his face, pressing his lips against it. My hands are clammy, the smell of leather and sweat, and they're the ugliest fucking things I've ever seen. And Nine kisses them, while murmuring, "You shouldn't hide them, Riley. They're *beautiful*."

His easy words hit me like an arrow to the heart. Because Nine *is* fae—and he can't lie.

That seals the deal for me. I was already on board with the final touch. Now? As long as my mate is down, there's no going back.

"Nine?"

"Mm?"

"*Yes*."

He freezes. For a second, he reminds me of the statue who risked everything to shield me from the Fae Queen, but then he lets out a small, involuntary shake, his silver eyes beginning to glow as he lets go of my hand.

"Riley… what are you saying?"

Isn't it obvious?

You just say yes. That's what he told me.

Well, here I am. Offering myself up to him on a silver platter, willing to give him everything he desires—while taking everything I've ever wanted.

My bare hands find their way to the middle of his slender body. I lift them slowly, rising them up his chest, feeling every heartbeat as his breath quickens.

"Touch me, Nine." Whoa. Is that throaty, husky voice mine? Okay, then. "Claim me."

His hands snap to my waist, fingers curling into the flesh peeking out above my hips.

Throwing my head back, I moan. His touch feels so *good*.

He dips his head, skimming his jaw along my exposed collarbone, the heat of his breath causing goosebumps to erupt all down my arms. I shiver. He tugs my lower body close, angling me up to press his pelvis against me.

There's a hitch in his usually controlled voice as he tells me, "I've been waiting close to a century… my whole Cursed life, Riley… to be this close to my mate."

I giggle. Actually *giggle*. "Only a hundred? Compared to Gillespie, you're almost a baby."

He pulls back, tilting his head as confusion blooms on his heavy-lidded face. "What?"

I drop it. Bringing up my old doctor again will totally kill the mood and I'm anxious to keep this going.

"Forget it." And, to give him a little encouragement, I swivel my lower half, coming into direct contact with the noticeable bulge of his erection.

He swallows his own gasp of pleasure. Like a magnet, his head is drawn back to the curve between my shoulder and my neck. He nuzzles my throat, small lightning-like shocks coursing through me with every point of contact.

Neither one of us is holding back.

Shadows fill the room. Through the slits in my eyes as I pull Nine closer, I see them. More than that, I *sense* them. I don't know if they're responding to me, or if it's Nine's Unseelie nature that draws them to us, like the long, shadowy duster he always wears. They surround us, offering us privacy, offering us safety, the wisps forming at our feet almost binding us together.

They want us to do this. I'm right there with them.

Nine's voice goes low. It's still soft, still beautiful, but it has an almost abrasive edge as he confesses, "I've waited a lifetime for my *ffrindau*. For you. You'll be my first."

"Your first what?"

"*Everything.*"

Oh.

When I'm silent too long, he begins to pull away.

Hang on. Does he think that'll change anything? Does he think I'll care?

I lean in, placing an open mouth kiss against his shoulder as I lower my hand to snag one of his off my hip. I squeeze his fingers, silently telling him that that's perfectly okay.

I want to be his first *everything*.

I can't say the same thing about him, though. He knows he can't. He was my Shadow Man, my nighttime visitor, and before he disappeared when I was fifteen, there were times as an angry, careless younger teen when I threw my conquests in his face.

I wanted to get a rise out of him then. I'm not proud of that, but I did. Nine was my only constant, the only one who *cared*, and maybe I wanted to make him jealous. I don't know. I've always loved him—even when I was way too young for it to be the kind of love that I have for him now—and maybe I was looking for some kind of sign, any sign that he cared for me, too.

The more Nine seemed nonplussed, the more guys I picked up.

Never at night, though. When I could avoid it, I never slept with anyone else at night.

Those hours of darkness were for my Shadow Man and me and that was it.

I don't have a number. Even if I did, I wouldn't tell him. As far as I'm concerned, anyone else I've ever touched simply disappeared once Nine claimed me in Faerie. That was just sex. Something I did because I was bored or lonely or because sometimes I ached for someone to touch me with kindness.

I'm standing here on the precipice of something so much bigger than that. I've given away my body before, but not my heart. Definitely not my soul.

I want Nine to have it all.

Pulling on his hand, smiling when I see the small flicker of surprise that I'm initiating contact, I lead him toward the bedroom. With his magic and his strength, I wouldn't be able to move him unless he wanted to go.

He knows what I want. He knows that I want him.

We're not going in there to sleep—at least not for a while, I'm hoping. And when he sends a pulse of pleasure to me through his touch, a tiny taste of what I have to look forward to, I spur Nine on a little faster.

If we're lucky, we'll make it in time to christen my new bed. Me? I'm not picky.

It's time for him to claim me entirely. And for me to claim *him*.

CHAPTER 14

Wow.

So that was just... *wow*.

Nine might not have ever done that before, but he was a natural. Seriously. Maybe the fact that I actually cared about him, too, had something to do with it, but that was the most amazing lay of my life.

And, until the prophecy catches up to me—or the Fae Queen does—I have that to look forward to.

Go, Riley.

Nine is sleeping next to me, sprawled out on the bed. A proud smile curves my lips. I really gave him a work-out, didn't I? My century-year-old fae... after everything we just did, he's earned his rest.

I prop myself up on my elbow, watching him sleep. There's something so vulnerable, so serene about his expression as he slumbers. I have the strongest desire to touch him again.

I move my other hand, about to stroke his long, raven-colored hair when my stomach jolts.

Oh. I forgot.

On the other side of my lust-fueled haze, I distinctly remember taking my gloves off and leaving them in the living room. I don't regret it, but seeing my hands now makes me uncomfortable.

I need my gloves. The Brinkburn, too. I took that off with my clothes, but it's too precious to leave lying around.

Gotta find it.

After checking once more that Nine is still slumbering, I quickly slip out of the bed before searching my side of the room for the necklace before I go for my gloves. Nine might have called my ruined hands beautiful, but it's gonna take a lot longer for me to believe that. I just don't feel right—just don't feel like *me*—without my gloves.

"Where are you going?"

At that familiar voice, I turn to see that my mate is suddenly wide awake.

His eyes glow vividly, the silver gleam so bright, his irises remind me of mirrors set into his beautiful face. His nostrils flare as he takes in a deep breath, a look of pure heat transforming his cool expression into something way more heated.

My lips quirk upward.

That's right. I'm still naked.

And though he's seen every inch of me, *touched* every inch of me, he looks like he's ready to do it all over again.

Know what? The gloves can wait.

It's Nine's turn to wear me out.

After he finishes, he pulls me close, tucking me under his

arm as if he's afraid that I'll try to sneak out of the bed again if he doesn't. He doesn't have anything to worry about there.

No chance of that happening since he just boned the last of my energy out of me.

Sleep. Sleep sounds pretty good right now.

As I begin to doze, Nine threads his fingers through my hair this time, reaching up to rest his fingers along the side of my throat. Since the actual claiming meant that he could touch me and it wouldn't affect me any more than any other sweet caress from my lover would, I notice that he can't keep his hands off of me. I... I like it. He's the only one who can do it, too, without me flipping out, and I'm so glad.

I *missed* being touched.

I preen at his gentle stroke, shimmying closer so that I'm wrapped up in the undeniable essence that is totally Nine. I breathe him in, feeling safe and secure and *loved*. For the first time in a long time, I can let my guard down around someone else.

I close my eyes and sigh.

"I'm beginning to think I finally understand why Oberon lost his crown to Melisandre."

I'm half asleep. My body feels limp with pleasure, my heart full of affection for my Shadow Man. Still, when his murmur finds its way to my ears, it's such a strange thing for him to say that I quirk one eye open.

"Really? Why's that?"

"Because if she made him feel anything like how you just made me feel, he would've been powerful to resist giving her anything she wanted."

Oh.

I snuggle closer to him. That might possibly be the sweetest thing I've ever heard anyone say to me, especially during pillow talk.

"You know, I was wondering something. Why did the crown belong to him in the first place? If he lost it so easily."

"It's because Oberon was born to be the Summer King."

I open my other eye, blinking up at him. "Huh?"

"The Summer King, the ruler of all Faerie, but especially the Light Fae. He ruled for centuries because no one else was strong enough to take the throne from him until Melisandre charmed the crown right from his head."

I can see that. As much as I hate her, with her glamour, there's no denying that the Fae Queen is the most beautiful woman I've ever seen. She's absolute perfection; with her innocent act, she must have been catnip to the king of Faerie.

There's only one thing I don't understand. Well, okay. That's an understatement. When it comes to the fae, there are so many things that I don't get. But, if there's one huge difference when it comes to Nine being my Shadow Man and my soulmate, it's that I can finally ask all my questions and he's actually feeling generous enough to answer them.

"Born to be the Summer King," I repeat. "How was Oberon *born* to be the king?"

And how can we find someone else to take on Melisandre? If Oberon is long gone, maybe there's another fae that can do exactly what she did and steal the crown so that I can finish the Shadow Prophecy once and for all without becoming a murderer.

Nine runs his fingers through my hair again, massaging my scalp with his fingertips. "He bore the mark of the Summer Court, the mark that makes him different from the rest of the Seelie. The Light Fae all have similar features. You know that.

Gold hair. Gold eyes. Gold skin. Oberon did, too, except for his eyes."

When it comes to the fae, the eyes are the biggest clue that they're not like humans. What kind did Oberon have if even he was set apart from the rest of the Light Fae?

"What was up with his eyes?"

"They were green."

I almost choke.

No way.

No fucking way.

I scramble away from him, climbing out of Nine's embrace before rising up on my knees, grabbing Nine's arm in excitement.

He gives it a tug, shifting my center of gravity as he rolls to his back. I tumble on top of him and, normally, I'd be perfectly okay with that. But not right now. This is *important*.

I push up, straddling him, bracing myself with my hands flush against his bare chest.

His eyes zero in on my tits. I smack him.

"Yes?"

"I know someone with green eyes." Nine's eyebrows rise and, okay, I get it. Lots of people have green eyes. "I mean, someone who knows about the fae."

And, with him watching my face now, I tell him all about the homeless man with the green eyes. Nine doesn't say anything as I explain. Once or twice, his shadowed gaze dips down to my boobs again.

Great. I've created a monster.

When I'm done, I ask him excitedly, "What if that's him? What if that's Oberon?"

"What if it isn't?" counters Nine.

I can't let myself think that. All along, I wondered what was up with that strange, mysterious man. The way he seemed to appear and disappear so suddenly, how he always seemed to be around when I was—unless I was looking for him, of course. And then there was how he knew about the Shadow Prophecy...

"We have to go find him. Now."

"No." Nine sets his jaw. "Later."

What? *No.*

I start to slide off of him.

His cool hand laying gently over mine stops me. I look back at him. "What?"

"I'll go with you. I'll help you find him if that's what you want. But, right now, I just want to lie here with you. Can I do that?"

My heart stutters in my chest.

Can he do that?

Shit.

I nod and, without another word, I shimmy back into the spot next to Nine. He lays out his arm while I snuggle up against him. He wraps it around me, rubbing my shoulder lightly as if he still can't get enough of me.

So what if I'm making up for too many years of missed caresses, lonely nights, and lost touches? I deserve it.

I deserve a little happiness.

And being with Nine? Nothing makes me happier.

OKAY. I TAKE THAT BACK.

Hunting down the mysterious street sleeper and seeing if my suspicions hold any water... that would make me fucking ecstatic.

Too bad it seems *impossible.*

Everything is against me. I swear it. Seriously. I mean, as soon as I throw myself into searching for him again, the weather goes to hell.

What's that saying? April flowers bring May flowers? The urban Newport's gonna have weeds sprouting from the cracks in its pavement at this rate because it *just doesn't stop raining.*

The homeless scatter. Of course they do. I would, too. Then I thought maybe they would be desperate enough to seek shelter inside of the abandoned building.

Nope.

We enlist my parents in the search, though I have no hope that Ash and Callie will be able to find him. If my suspicions are right, the only reason why the stranger keeps poking his nose around Newport is because of *me*.

So I spend countless days looking. I return to the apartment looking like a drowned rat half the time thanks to the constant storms, but I'm determined.

When I'm not trying to find the maybe-Oberon, it's back to training. Except now I don't have just one teacher. Ash and Nine take turns teaching me with their respective swords and techniques.

At least I finally learned how Nine was providing everything for the apartment. Though he can't go far, he still has enough magic left inside of him to use portals to zip around town. Not only that, but he's created his own pockets in the shadows, pulling all kinds of shit from out of there.

He has more clothes. Some money. And a *silver sword*.

Both fae males accept that me using a sword when I inevitably face Melisandre again is a last resort. I've gotten pretty good at it if I do say so myself, but that doesn't change my decision that I'd rather not be the one responsible for killing her, despite what the damn Shadow Prophecy says.

That's why I'm so desperate to see if that man really is the long deposed Summer King of Faerie in disguise. If that's Oberon and I can present him with the chance to take care of Melisandre for me… that would just be *perfect*.

He's my only hope.

Nine tours the neighborhood with me, too. Since the formal claiming, that final touch, the last of his sensitivity to the sunshine has finally disappeared. He doesn't like it, and he insists on wearing shades whenever we go out during the rare times it's not raining, but Nine can walk out into the sunlight without any side effects.

Not that he would stay behind, even if the sun still presented a threat to him. Callie hadn't been kidding when she said a bonded fae found it difficult to be separated from his mate for too long. It's like, every time I turn around, Nine's right there.

I wouldn't have it any other way.

About a week and a half into our search, the weather finally plays ball with us. The sun is bright, hanging high in a lovely blue sky. There's not a single cloud in sight. The puddles on the asphalt dry up and, slowly but surely, as it warms up, the homeless start to fill their corners again.

And there, propped up in his usual spot as if he's been waiting for us all along, is the man with the vivid green eyes.

I couldn't tell you if his face was the same or not. It's terrible to admit, but I never really paid all that much attention to him; his bright eyes were the only thing that stuck out at me and, now that I've heard all about the Summer King, I can't help but wonder if that was on purpose or not.

Know what I do notice? His props are missing.

The blankets are there, sure, but that's it. The crumpled coffee cup? Gone. The scattered newspapers, the cardboard sign? Nope.

Just him.

Just us.

As our shadows fall in front of him, his head picks up.

And he smiles.

"It's about time. I've been wondering when you wouldn't just see me, but see *me*."

Nine frowns. Not me. I know what he means. I know what he's saying. The day he gave me back Carolina's note, he said it was because I see him. And I did. I saw a grimy old man, begging with an almost empty coffee cup in front of him, and that was about it.

I can't see through glamour. There was one time that I thought I could and, thinking back, I wouldn't be surprised if that was just a glitch or my overactive imagination. Or maybe, like when Gillespie showed off his ears, Rys finally lost control over how he wanted me to see him.

Right now, I wish I could see what the homeless man really looks like because, well, he certainly isn't any kind of king. But those eyes…

As green as grass. Wide. *Knowing*.

This is Oberon. I don't know how I can tell, but I can.

"Please. I need your help."

"Why would I help you? I've done more than enough already. I gave you everything you needed. Helped you. In Acorn Falls with the rogue halfling. Here. That's much more than you should expect, and much kinder than I've ever been. I might have fallen from grace, child. I haven't forgotten who I was."

"Who are you?"

He smiles again.

"I could… I could pay you. I don't have much left, but whatever I have, it's yours. Just hear me out. It's not even a favor. It's a bargain. I have something you want."

He leans back, resting his head against the brick of the wall behind him. "I've been trapped in this world for close to two centuries. Adapt and survive. A king lives for revenge. A king requires wealth. Don't be fooled by my glamour, Shadow. I have more riches than I could ever need."

Nine goes eerily still. "You know who she is."

He nods. "As I know of you, Ninetroir."

His name. This guy knows Nine's true name.

"No human would dare use that name unless they were desperate. Only a fool would claim to be the missing Summer King when face to face with a Cursed One."

Oberon laughs. It's low, yet sweet, almost lyrical.

It's a laugh that belongs to a fae.

"A Cursed One with a weakness."

"My kind of fae has always drawn strength from the shadows. My Shadow just so happens to be Riley. A mate doesn't always have to be a weakness."

Oberon nods, conceding the point. "Agree to disagree. Just hope that your consort doesn't turn on you and send you to your death. Brinkburn isn't worth what any female offers."

Brinkburn. So he really did get sent there.

"Like you said. Agree to disagree." Nine gestures at Oberon. "You survived."

"I did."

"It's supposed to be impossible."

"Nothing's impossible," I mutter.

Oberon tilts his head in my direction. "You're learning."

I reach out and, hesitating for only a heartbeat, I lay my hand against the elbow of Nine's long jacket. "I had the best teacher."

"You're learning," the king says again, "but not enough."

"Hey—"

"Why you?" he asks suddenly. "What makes you so special? You're a halfling, born of a Blessed One and a human. But you wield the shadows like you're Unseelie. What are you?"

Is that a question? Or a test?

Feels like a test.

"I'm Riley. Just Riley."

"She's the Shadow," cuts in Nine, standing up for me. "Destined to end Melisandre's reign."

Oberon's face goes unreadable. Okay. I get the feeling like we just flunked his little test. Then, when he says, "Well, pity you'll never be able to do it on your own," I'm sure of it.

Does he think I don't know that? "That's why I thought you'd want to come with us. Come on. You've gotta want revenge. I can... I don't know... distract the queen and then you can—"

"Can *what*? Kill Melisandre for you?"

When he puts it like that, it sounds like a lot to ask. But I'm *desperate*.

"Why not?"

The fae have no problem with murder if it suits them. I lost my sister thanks to Rys's indifference toward humans and an inability to understand that her cruel murder would hurt me. Carolina? She starved to death because Melisandre wanted to make her pay. His old mate—wife—*whatever*... stole Faerie away from him for *two hundred years* and he doesn't want even a little bit of revenge?

One look at Oberon and I'm thinking: *guess not*.

"I gave you the prophecy. Did you read it?"

"I memorized it."

"Tell me. Does it say anything about the Summer King?"

"Well, no—"

"Oberon?"

"No."

"Any Seelie?"

I shake my head.

"'...*when Dark mates Shadow...*'" he begins.

I finish the quote for him. "'...*the Reign of the Damned shall come to an end...*'"

Oberon raises his eyebrows knowingly, then shrugs. "Prophecy's a prophecy. I can't jump in and finish, no matter what I owe her. It's between you and my former consort. Facing Melisandre... that's up to you, Shadow."

Yeah.

Of course it is.

CHAPTER 15

So, Oberon was a bust.

I'm not so surprised. It sucks, though. Not gonna lie. I was really hoping that the so-called Summer King would want to get revenge on Melisandre for stealing his crown. If it was me, I'd want to. Still, I get it. He was banished from his realm for more than two centuries because he picked the wrong chick to screw. He thought he was getting a mate and she tried to kill him.

Not what you call happily ever after, huh?

I guess it makes sense that he refused. If we're going based on the Shadow Prophecy, it doesn't say when the Dark and the Shadow pawn the whole thing off on the Summer King, does it?

Would've been amazing if it did, though.

I break the news to Callie and Ash. I know they tried not to get their hopes up that Oberon would be our Hail Mary play if only because they didn't want me to get *my* hopes up. It was a little late for that. I so wanted him to be my way out.

Ash's old sword is tucked in my bedroom where I've kept it

since he gave it to me. Nine has his hidden in the shadows. I might not have wanted to rely on their weapons to finish this but it seems more and more likely that my lessons are gonna have to come in handy.

I've known all along that it's her or me. Continuing to hide out... it's what I'm used to, but it can't last forever.

What to do now?

Hell if I know.

Since our only hope has proven to be a wash-out, the four of us sit in the living room, trying to figure out what our next step has to be. Ash and Callie are leaning into each other on the loveseat, I'm curled up in the corner of the couch while Nine sits on the edge of the armchair, boots to the floor, his shadowy duster flaring out behind him.

I nibble on my bottom lip. "I don't know," I say. "Oberon has a point. Sooner or later, Melisandre is gonna do something about me. I just—"

"*Sooner.*"

"What's that?"

He doesn't answer me. Instead, he gets to his feet, moving toward the front door. Tucking his hair behind his ears, I notice that the pointed tips twitch as if he's heard something that the rest of us haven't.

He turns back, looking straight at me. As our eyes meet, I notice that the golden gleam is almost orange all of a sudden.

"It'll be sooner," he says again.

I chuckle nervously. "Um. Ash. You sound kinda sure there."

"Oh, daughter. I'm sorry, but that's because I am."

Callie gasps. "Not again?"

When my dad nods, she hops off the sofa, flying into Ash's open arms.

Uh-oh.

I don't like this.

Neither, it seems, does Nine.

"Aislinn?" He unfolds his lithe body, rising up from the armchair. "What do you sense?"

Ash holds my mom close, rubbing her back soothingly as he keeps his ears cocked, obviously listening.

"Seelie. More than a few. I can sense them coming. The wards were holding"—Ash's golden gaze flares, his slender body bowing as if he's been hit but is still desperate to shield Callie— "but they're gone. They're on their way."

"It's just like last time," Callie whispers. "They're back. They want our baby."

"I won't let them have her. I vow it." He looks over her head, staring straight at me. "Riley, you have to get out of here before they make it to the top."

Get out of here? Already on it.

I immediately start to gather shadows, drawing them toward me. It's daylight. Barely afternoon. The fae surrounding the building would have to be Light Fae. If I shade-walk out of here, if I bring my family with me, we can escape Melisandre's soldiers before they can find us.

I'm not ready. I don't know if I ever will be, but I sure as hell know I'm not ready yet.

Callie turns away from Ash, her big blue eyes widening when she sees what I'm doing.

"No shadow travel. We can't. Ash… he's still a Light Fae. He's still Seelie."

Shit.

I let the shadows scatter. How could I have forgotten?

Callie could go. Nine, despite losing some of his luster while living in the human world, is a Dark Fae. The shadows are like a second skin for him. But Ash… the trip from Faerie over nearly killed an immortal fae. There's no way I can whisk him away with the rest of us.

"Okay. No shadow travel. But what can we do?"

Releasing Callie from his hold, he points toward the front door. "Go out in the hall," Ash says. "Get in the elevator. It's your only choice."

The elevator? That kind of makes sense. Callie told me how it was purposely reinforced with iron on all four sides, including the opening. It wasn't possible to line the entire building, but Ash is right. The elevator is our only hope if we want to get out of here without a confrontation.

Hey. It worked before, right?

Taking the elevator... that was the exact same escape plan my mother had when the Fae Queen's soldiers tracked down my parents more than twenty years ago. While Ash stayed back to confront the soldiers, he sent Callie—and baby Riley—into the elevator. None of the fae invaders would have dared to take the mechanical contraption. Not only would the iron drain them, but a fae fresh out of Faerie would be full of far too much magic. Even if they tried to weather the iron, their power would short the electricity and trap them in the metal box.

They would take the stairs. Ash seems sure of it, and I'm betting he's right.

Our apartment is so close to the top. They would have a long-ass climb ahead of them—but we still don't have much time to get out of here before the soldiers find us.

I've been in the elevator before. A bunch of times already, actually. It'll be a squeeze, but the four of us could fit.

"Okay. Come on. Let's go."

Ash looks over my head now, purposefully meeting Nine's gaze. "Who has the pebble? You or my daughter?"

Nine slips his hands into his pocket, pulling a fist out. Unfolding his fingers, he reveals the pebble nestled in his palm.

Relief passes over Ash's sculpted features.

"Protect her, Ninetroir."

"Melisandre will have to do more than turn me to stone to get her hands on my Shadow," vows Nine.

"What about you?" I ask Ash.

He sets his jaw. "They came after me before. I survived them once. I can do it again."

Callie turns in his arms, gripping him by the upper bicep. "And, this time, you'll have me."

"Callie—"

"Ash." She squeezes him, shaking her head frantically, the white-blonde mane swishing back and forth. "She has her mate. Don't send me away from mine."

Oh, she's *good*. Even before Ash nods, I know that my mom is going to get her way. Besides, there's no time left to argue. We have to go.

Now.

I'm not thinking clearly. My fight or flight reflex is already kicking in at just the thought that the Fae Queen's soldiers are somewhere nearby. They can't pop into our apartment, thanks to the wards and the crapton of iron built into this place, but Ash is right. They'll take the stairs if they have to, and they'll be fucking quick about it.

It doesn't even occur to me that, with Ash and Callie staying behind, I can create a portal and hop through it with Nine. I blame it on the adrenaline and the fear coursing through me.

Nine follows close behind me. I can sense him at my heels, the whisper of his hand against the small of my back as if he's pushing me toward the elevator. I jam my thumb into the *down* button. Because the elevator is still on our floor, the doors open right away and the two of us file in.

"Come on," I mutter under my breath, hitting the *doors close* button again and again until the ancient steel doors begin to inch their way closed.

It seems to take a hundred years. I let out a sigh of relief right as the doors finish sealing shut—and that's when I hear the female scream.

No.

I jab the *doors open* button with my thumb even though I know I'm too late. The car is already moving down.

That's okay. I start pushing the *14* key, hoping that the elevator will bring me back to our floor as soon as possible.

The scream settles it. I don't know what the hell compelled me to think it was a good idea to leave them behind. I can't abandon them up there if someone—or some*ones*—is making my mother scream.

Nine has been inspecting the elevator panel the entire time we've been inside. I know he's never been in here before—even now, trapped in the iron cell, he's looking a bit sickly and sallow—but you could've fooled me. He immediately shoots out his hand, one long, slender finger reaching right for the red knob that reads *pull emergency stop*.

He pulls it.

The elevator grinds to a sudden halt.

What?

"No," I yelp, slapping at his pale hand. "I'm going back up there."

"I can't let you do that."

Like *hell* he can't.

What is wrong with me? I'm being a complete moron. I'm the Shadow, right? Might as well prove it.

I don't need the elevator to move to get back to the apartment. Not when I can create a portal with my shadows.

Nine sucks in a breath, his cheekbones jutting out from his otherworldly face as his cheeks hollow. "What are you doing?"

"What does it look like?" I snap. "You won't let me take the elevator back up? I'll find another way."

"No, Riley. You shouldn't—"

He's right. I probably shouldn't—but I *have* to.

I continue to pull the shadows toward me. It's hard, and the iron lining the elevator's wall might not affect me, but it's also not doing my power any favors.

Frustration overwhelms me as my pocket slowly begins to form. Slow. So, so slow. If Callie is already screaming, that means the soldiers already got to her, right?

"Ninetroir, please." I clench my fists, pleading up at him as the wisps fill the corner of the small room. "You've got to help me. I have to go back!"

His eyes flash, darkening to a deep gun-metal grey for a moment before they're gleaming again.

"It doesn't work with mates," he tells me. "You can't compel me with my true name."

I wasn't trying to. "I don't want to force you. I'm asking you for your help. Please. Help me."

His expression softens. "Don't beg me. That's even worse."

Am I begging? I might be. "They lost twenty years trying to save me. I shouldn't have left them behind."

"You wouldn't have if Ash didn't compel you to."

Is that what happened? I thought I heard him say something to me as I hesitated in the front room. Did he use my true name and tell me to go? Maybe. Maybe not.

"It doesn't matter. You heard the scream, didn't you?"

"I fought alongside Ash. With his human with him, he'll be

unstoppable. A fae will go to any lengths to protect their mate. He won't let them get to her."

"But the scream," I insist. "That was hers. My mom's. Are you telling me that he'll still try to fight them if they managed to hurt her first?"

Nine's quiet for a moment. All I hear is the electrical whine in the elevator, the crackling of the lightbulb reacting to the magic inherent in my Shadow Man, and my quickened breath as I imagine a cadre of Light Fae turning their weapons on my parents because they were too stubborn to leave with me.

"You want this," he says at last. "This is important to you."

He finally gets it. "Yes."

"For you, Riley. *Anything*."

Before I can respond, Nine lashes his hand out, wrapping his fingers around my wrist. He tugs me toward him, pulling me into his arms. His embrace has the power to calm me, to set me at ease as I gasp, breathing him in.

"Nine, what—"

He breathes in deep, exhaling shakily as his long black hair flutters away from his face. His pale skin begins to glow. I... I've seen him do this before. Even though he's been weakened by staying in the human world, the vibrant silver glow is all I see as the lightbulb immediately shorts out, plunging us into darkness inside of the elevator.

Or maybe that's the pocket of my conjured shadows.

Nine bends his head, placing his mouth next to my jaw. "Hold on tight, Shadow. And, whatever you do, keep your eyes closed."

The next thing I know, we're standing in the corner of the apartment where Nine stood as a statue for those couple of weeks. Silver beams, shining fractals like shards of a shattered mirror shoot from Nine, announcing our sudden arrival.

I wasn't expecting it and, even though he warned me, I'm the dumbass who kept her eyes wide open as soon as reality shifted and we shade-walked from the stopped elevator back to the apartment.

On the plus side?

Melisandre's guards weren't expecting it, either.

I'll take what I can get.

CHAPTER 16

When the last of Nine's pulse of power clears, when I get my sight back and the guards regroup, I see that we're surrounded by five soldiers, all of them Light Fae. Same bronze-colored skin, tawny hair, the pristine white uniforms and the terrifyingly beautiful—yet undeniably dangerous—swords in their grip.

It strikes me that I don't see Rys among them.

I'm not even a little surprised at that.

Of the five, two are standing next to Callie while the other three surround Ash.

Tears make my mom's blue eyes glisten as she's been torn from her mate, though maybe that's the aftereffects of Nine's burst of silver light that stunned the guards enough to keep them from attacking us right off.

Ash, on the other hand, wears the same resigned yet defiant expression that was frozen on his handsome face when he was one of Melisandre's statues.

They both seem okay, though I have to tell myself that *okay* is definitely a relative term considering we're not only outnumbered, but the Light Fae soldiers are all visibly armed.

"Well. What do we have here?"

My heart leaps into my throat as I jolt in place.

So my survey was a little bit sloppy. Emerging from behind the open doorway that leads into the hall, there's a sixth soldier, the only one who is still wearing his sword at his hip. He keeps his hands folded primly behind his back as he surges forward.

He spares a quick glance at Nine before turning his gaze on me. His lips are pulled into a frown, head dipping up and down as he takes me in. He's gorgeous—because of course he is—but he also seems stern.

Or maybe that's the unimpressed expression twisting his features as he comes to a stop in the middle of the room.

Look at this guy. Big shot, right?

He has to be the leader. The one in charge.

I hate him already.

"You must be the Shadow," he says.

No shit, Sherlock.

"Who are you?"

He doesn't answer.

Why would he?

"You had to have been expecting us," he says instead. Gesturing with a long, slender finger, he waves me closer. "Come here. If you do as you're told, it's possible you might even survive meeting the queen."

That's not even a subtle threat. Either do what he wants and wait until Melisandre goes for my head or I could just lose it right here, right now.

Lovely.

Well, it's not as if I didn't know this was a possibility. My whole life, Nine warned me that the fae would be after me. Ever since he broke me out of the asylum, I've had one eye looking over my shoulder, waiting for the Fae Queen to get me.

Me.

"You're here for me?" I say, stepping toward him, moving quickly so that I can dodge Nine's grip when he tries to pull me back with him. He says my name. I keep walking. Holding out my arms, I shrug. "Fine. Let's make it easy. I'll go with you."

The lead soldier eyes me closely. There's still that look, like I'm a monkey that's surprised him by being smart enough to communicate or something, but he's cautious. I guess it still has everything to do with the Shadow Prophecy. Gillespie was right. A halfling isn't even worth a second look. The Shadow? Yeah. He's watching me super closely.

He's smart. I'll give him that.

"Like that?" he says coldly. "You'll give up your freedom and take the portal to Faerie without striking a bargain of your own. How… *human* of you."

"I didn't say all that," I admit. Hey. Maybe I'm finally getting in touch with my fae side because I'm definitely feeling a little tricksy. "I want a bargain first."

"Oh, Riley, sweetie, *no*—"

The lead soldier gestures with his hand. One of the other Light Fae lifts his diamond sword, putting the point to Callie's throat. She immediately goes still.

He raises his eyebrows, golden eyes locked on my face. "Go on."

I gulp. I can't afford to give anything away. Especially not to this Light Fae who, frankly, looks like he'd rather finish me off now and save himself the trouble.

"I'll go, but just me. I know my worth," I say, "and I want to bargain for my family's safety. There's six of you. Four of us. I'll go with you, but all you goons go with me. Leave them out of it." I tick them off on my fingers, careful not to give the Light Fae any way to twist the deal. "Ash. Callie. Nine. I'll trade my cooperation and my freedom for theirs."

The air shifts. Without me even having to see him, I know that Nine has glided forward, joining me at my back.

"Ash and his human can take their freedom," he tells the lead soldier. "Wherever Riley goes, I'll be at her side. I won't abandon her. Factor that into the bargain."

The soldier begins to disagree, shaking his head, stopping when my dad starts talking.

"He's her *ffrindau*," Ash says through clenched teeth. "If he doesn't want to be separated from her, you can't force it. He'd only follow behind her."

Really? That's news to me.

It must have something to do with the whole touch thing. After I gave him permission to touch me wherever he wanted to, to claim me fully as his soulmate while he offered himself back to me, he didn't need a brand on my skin to find me. He's imprinted on my heart.

My dad's not wrong. Nine could probably find me anywhere, in Faerie or in my world. Even when all he had was the trace of a finger against my cheek, he always knew where I was. After I gave him permission to touch every inch of me, there's no way I could escape him.

And I wouldn't have it any other way.

"Fully bonded?" asks the leader. "I was there when you made your claim. Was the ritual completed? The final touch?"

If I wasn't so scared out of my goddamn mind, worried about my parents and eager to save Nine's skin since I'm probably as good as a Riley statue, I might suffer a little humiliation that the Light Fae is basically asking for confirmation that Nine and I slept together.

Jesus Christ, my mom and dad are *right there.*

Thankfully, Nine doesn't go into any details. He simply nods.

The Light Fae looks surprised and a little amused. "The Shadow and the traitor. Well." He purses his lips. "The queen will be most pleased."

Of course she will. If I stood back and let Nine come along, the queen will definitely use him against me. That's like both of us signing our death warrant. After what happened last time, Nine will only try to stand in front of me again.

I can't let him do that.

I hold up my hand. "Hang on. I'm the one bargaining and I don't agree to that deal."

"Riley—"

"Not yet," I amend, cutting Nine off. "Just… give me a second. Alright? I want to talk to you first." I swivel, facing the soldier. "I want to talk to my mate."

The word feels strange on my tongue. Mate… it's such a simple word to explain everything Nine means to me. It's a word that the fae seem to understand, though, and the lead soldier waves me away.

"If you must, but make it quick."

Grabbing the edge of Nine's jacket, I drag him back to the corner. I notice that while each and every one of the soldiers is watching us closely, no one makes a move to follow us. Why would they? The one in charge gave us permission to talk to one another and, well, it's not like we're about to hop in the portal again and take off.

With Callie and Ash under guard, they've got me exactly where they want me. I gave away any hand I had when I came rushing back for them instead of escaping while I had the chance.

Once my back is up against the wall, my friendly shadows licking at my senses, I look imploringly at Nine. I try to keep my voice down, knowing full well that the entire room—except for my mom, maybe—has hearing excellent enough to pick up on every word.

"That was too easy," I murmur to him. "What did I miss? Did I miss anything?"

He takes my hand. Gives it a squeeze. "You don't really understand how valuable you are to the queen. She'll do anything to make sure you're not a threat to her or her reign."

Translation: *Melisandre still wants me dead, so she'll give me whatever I want so that I make it easier for her.*

"So I can trust him?"

Nine's silver eyes flash. "What's one of the first things I taught you?"

I know it's not the right time, but the sudden reappearance of my beloved mentor makes me feel better about this awful situation. "That I can never trust the fae."

"That's my Shadow."

I tilt my head back so that I can drink in every bit of him. "But I trust you."

"You were fated to be mine," Nine says, the harsh edge of his voice cutting me straight to my heart. "I only just got you for myself. I won't let anyone take you from me. You can always trust that."

He says it like we have a choice.

And know what? Maybe we *do*.

I'm not a killer. I'm *not*. But I'm also not about to roll over and let the Fae Queen get rid of me because she thinks I'm such a threat.

No matter what, it's time to face Melisandre. Nine's right. We only just began this life together. I finally have someone who wants me for me—who isn't going to get tired of me and walk away. He can't. Nine's stuck with me.

I'm not about to let my chance at my own happily ever after slip away

It'll work out. I tell myself that because, well, it's about fucking time something went right for me for once.

"Do you trust me?" I ask him.

If Nine were human, his brow would furrow at the heaviness of my question. It's a loaded one all right; we both know it. He's a Dark Fae, a creature of Faerie. He doesn't trust *anyone*.

Except, it seems, for me.

"Yes," he says.

It's the same exact exchange we had while the two of us were in the Faerie jail, waiting to be brought to see Melisandre again only, last time, Nine needed to know that I trusted him.

Okay, then.

I pat him on his chest, putting all of my love and affection into the touch, before turning to face the soldier again. I take a few steps away from Nine because, if I don't, there's a good chance that I'll run away with him after all.

"Promise me."

"Excuse me?"

"I'll feel better if you promise." I shrug, going for casual, desperately trying to hide how important this is to me. If it's just me and Nine, we could figure out another plan. Somehow. *Maybe*. But with my parents tagging along, heading back to Faerie where they were imprisoned for so, so long… I struggle to keep my expression neutral. "I know that the fae can't lie. So if you promise, if you swear to Oberon that you'll leave my parents alone, I'll go with you."

At the mention of the former ruler of Faerie, the heavy hush in the apartment is broken up by a gasp or two, followed by muted mutters from the soldiers.

"The Summer King is dead," says the leader. The mumbles quickly turn to echoes of his cold pronouncement. "I'll make no vow on his name, but swear on Faerie instead. If you come willingly to her castle, we'll leave the human and the fallen fae in peace. Do we have a bargain?"

He can't lie, so he obviously believes that Oberon is truly dead. Of course, I know better. Too bad Oberon didn't decide to side with me because wouldn't that be one hell of a surprise for these asshole soldiers?

I nod. "Yes."

"It's done. Des, call up a portal."

One of the soldiers immediately sheathes his sword; four more are still pointed at my parents. The Light Fae backs away from the circle of soldiers, lifting his bronze-colored arm high as he draws a rectangle in the air, a doorway with quick slashes of his hand.

Once he's done, he presses the flat of his palm against the space. Suddenly, a portal appears, a mixture of oranges, yellows, and white streaming in through the new rectangular shape.

The lead soldier gestures for me to step forward. "After you, Shadow."

I'm rooted to the wooden floor, blinded by the light at the same time as I'm terrified to move toward it.

I... I've never taken a Seelie portal before.

Nine leans into me, reminding me that he's here. He's with me.

I'm not doing this alone.

"I'll be with you, Riley." He takes my hand, rubbing his thumb against the leather stretched across my palm. "Every step of the way."

"Is it safe?" I whisper, unable to tear my gaze away from the searing light. I've lowered my lids, just a slit in my face, and it still burns something awful.

"As safe as iron," Nine says, sounding totally unconcerned. Yeah, right. I know better now. He's concealing how he truly feels because of the enemies in our audience, but he still reassures me with another gentle touch. "I'll be fine. It's you I'm worried about."

"I'm not."

Yeah... that's a straight up lie. If it was just a portal, I wouldn't care. It's just... it's a Seelie portal. It's so bright, so hot, my heart keeps thudding at the mere thought of getting any closer to the fiery wall.

It's not fire, I tell myself. It's just like traveling through the sun, the same way I slip through the shadows.

I should know.

I walked through fire to get to Madelaine. Rys's enchanted faerie fire, the blaze so consuming that it not only incinerated Nine's touch from my skin, but ruined my poor human hands. I was a kid. Apart from my shade-walking talent, my fae side hadn't kicked in yet and I couldn't heal it the same way that Nine could when a stolen touch burned his flesh.

"It's just like the night," calls out Ash. I hear a sound, a quick warning for him to stay in place, followed by my dad's voice ringing out again in open defiance of the soldier's orders. "You're one of us. You're my daughter. Seelie blood runs in your veins, Riley. It won't touch you. It won't touch you. And if it does, the shadows will protect you."

I wish I could believe that.

But that's the thing. Like Oberon reminded me, I'm a halfling. Rys's fire burned my hands because I'm not a full-blooded Seelie who can handle the day magic. My human half shields me from iron and being trapped by the truth, but what about this portal?

I take a breath, filtering any scents. *Nothing.* No charred flesh, scorched wood, burning hair... it's not fire. It's *not*.

Besides, I realize as my breathing slows, I once recklessly ran through the fire to try and save my sister. Would I do any less for my parents or my lover?

Okay.

Okay.

Let's do this.

Before I step closer to the portal, I glance over my shoulder, searching out Ash and Callie while trying not to make eye contact with the posturing guards watching over my parents.

"I'll be back," I tell them.

Callie's bright blue eyes dart to the point of the sword still at her throat, gauging the distance. She must decide that she's safe enough because she lets out a soft breath and nods.

But Ash... Ash knows what exactly I'm walking into—and I don't just mean the portal. He knows how dangerous Melisandre is. More importantly, he knows that, as a halfling, I *can* lie.

I might want to return.

Doesn't mean that that's likely to happen.

Considering the Shadow Prophecy is probably about to bite me in my ass, I doubt I'll ever see either one of them again.

CHAPTER 17

Just like I figured, it's warm in the portal. I find it difficult to breathe, though that probably as to do more with my anxiety than anything else.

Shadow travel is made up of a chilly, high-speed wind that's dark and triggers my motion sickness. The air in here is musty and steaming as we walk through the Seelie portal into Faerie. I can sense Nine right behind me and I can't help but think that, if this is terrible for me, it's gotta be torture for him.

Being dragged through a Dark Fae pocket nearly killed my Light Fae dad. How bad is the magic affecting Nine?

I need to do something for him. Help him… or—

I gasp, almost choking on the heat.

Ash's words pop into my head again. One of the last things he said to me before I left my parents behind.

It won't touch you. And if it does, the shadows will protect you.

Will they also protect Nine?

Only one way to find out.

I don't need any darkness to do this. Nine is made up of

shadows and, I guess I am, too. I pull them toward me, pouring as much strength and power into them as I can, creating some kind of buffer around Nine. Here's hoping it'll do something to keep the Light Fae magic from draining him.

I'm terrified that Nine will follow me right into an obvious trap only to be too weak to defend himself. I'll take care of him —I'll do whatever I have to in order to shield Nine this time— but hopefully the shadows will protect him for now.

We keep on pushing through the portal until, with a soft *pop*, it leads us right into a familiar space. I don't want them to know what I did so I purposely dissolve the shadows as soon as we cross over.

And then I swallow my groan.

Oh, come *on*.

Fairy jail. The Seelie portal brought us right back to the same cell that Melisandre put us in the last time we were here.

"Open," orders the lead soldier. The door opens and he says, "Inside."

We walk into the cell together because, well, we don't have any other choice.

The lead soldier gestures for two of his squad to stay put, watching over us, before heading off with the rest to tell the Fae Queen that we're here.

Once we're as alone as we're going to get, I squeeze Nine's hand. "You okay?"

A quick jerk of his head. A nod.

I exhale softly. Good.

Since the Fae Queen is the one who sent her soldiers to find us in Newport, I know she's eagerly waiting for news that they managed to bring me back to Faerie. I don't expect her to keep us locked in the cell for that long, and I'm not even a little surprised when, in no time, the lead soldier is back, ready to take us before her. In case he's worried we'll try something, every last one of his squad stands surrounding me and Nine, their swords at our back.

Whatever.

Let's get this over with.

Just like last time, the winding trip through the freaking huge palace takes forever. You think it would be over in a blink of an eye because I'm dreading it. Nope. It's just another layer of torture, the anticipating that each room we're led to will be the last—before discovering there's countless more we have to get through.

By the time he leads us into Melisandre's massive throne room—full of way too many fae, both Light and Dark—forcing us by swordpoint to stand before the actual throne, I'm so keyed up that I just want to throw out my arms and be like, *Fine, I'm here, what do you want now?*

It looks like half of Faerie has come out to see this confrontation. Because of course they did.

The Fae Queen is sitting primly on the throne, the skirt on her violet dress fanned out beneath her. She's wearing an opulent crown on the bed of her loose golden curls. Her lips are painted a soft pink. She smiles as her lead soldier bows, then retreats.

"Shadow. Ninetroir." Her pale yellow eyes sparkle. Some might think she's being sweet. Me? I know better. That's pure malice. "So glad you can join us."

From behind us, a loud, mocking voice calls out, "On your knees before the queen."

"Aven, please." Melisandre's perfect face goes from innocent to scandalized to amused in a few flashes. The prim little 'o' formed by her pouted lips turns into a small smile. "Then again, my subject has a point. I *am* the queen."

She lifts her hand, waving it, a gesture meant for the guards.

I can't turn since I'm surrounded, a threat at my back and in front of me. I don't know who called out—or what the guards are about to do—until Melisandre's lips curl just enough to have a shiver shooting down my spine.

"Down on your knees, Ninetroir."

Nine buckles.

No!

That's not right. The name isn't supposed to work. Not from her. She told me so herself. In Faerie, the fae can't use another's true name against them. It's why she couldn't just force Ash to hand me over when I was a baby, and Callie's gift of seeing through glamour saved her from being touched. It's why Melisandre turned them into statues—they were useless to her and, whatever her reasons, she didn't kill them outright.

I don't care about any of the threats around me. I only care about Nine. I turn to him—and that's when I realize something. It wasn't her command that had him moving, nearly falling forward.

Silver ichor pools beneath him.

Fae blood.

Oh, hell no.

The Fae Queen's soldier nearly cut him off at his knees. Hitting him with the edge of his sword, he tried to force Nine to kneel. It wasn't enough of a strike to cut entirely through the backs of his legs, but enough to make him stumble while leaving the evidence of the wound dripping onto the floor.

Rage. Pure incandescent rage. It slams into me and, as I whirl on Melisandre, I'm not sure what exactly I'm going to do.

Because that's the thing. When I get like this, even I don't know what I'm capable of.

I used to have a terrible problem controlling my anger. My

temper. When I lose my grip on it, nothing is impossible. It's why there was always that thought in the back of my mind: am I responsible? Did I kill Madelaine? Did I create the fae to cover up the darkness inside of me?

For too many years, it was safer to stay to myself. Getting close to someone else meant the risk of being abandoned, of being left behind, but it also meant that I gave myself my own weakness. When I lost it—like I'm about to lose it—nothing can stop me.

I ran through fire for Madelaine. As soon as I heard that fatal *snap* and saw her fall, not even the flames could have held me back. From going after my poor sister, from trying to save her, or from turning my rage on Rys.

When I finally calmed down, my rage turned to fear and I spent six years dreaming up the golden monster who stole my sister from me.

I refuse to be afraid. She wants to come after me. She can bring it.

Not Nine.

I won't let her touch Nine.

But what am I supposed to do?

Oberon's snide comment whispers in my head. Only it doesn't sound as snide as I remember, but almost prophetic. Like a hint or a clue.

Why you? What makes you so special? You're a halfling, born of a Blessed One and a human. But you wield the shadows like you're Unseelie. What are you?

I'm all three.

I'm the Shadow.

It isn't just about using the shadows to travel by myself. It's about using the shadows to break the rules that have always been in place. And what else can I use shadows for?

I… have an idea.

I start to build a pocket. I weave the shadows, gathering them toward me, rage paling in the face of my absolute concentration. The idea blossoms at the same time as the pocket does.

It's risky, but I don't have any other choice. Maybe she's expecting me to pull the same stunt as last time and, well, she'd be right. The pocket starts to widen, growing at a clip in the corner where I called for it the last time I was here. It's far enough out of her vision that I hope she doesn't pick up on it yet.

And if she does? That's fine. It's not only an escape portal that I'm working on.

It's Nine's pocket—the same pocket where he keeps his sword.

She pushed me to this. The one thing I never wanted to do. She left me no choice the second she sicced her guard on Nine.

I know how to get there, too. Pushing past Nine won't work, and I haven't forgotten about the pointed swords at my back or the crowd watching this as if it's all just entertainment for them. But, despite the blow to his knees, he's still standing. He's right at my side. I brush against him, pulling shadows from his coat, his clothes, his skin just like I did when we were in the Seelie portal.

They wrap around my glove, creeping up my wrist.

Just a little more…

That catches her attention. Before I can finish calling enough shadows so that I can slip through them and pop out on the other side of the throne room, Melisandre rises from her throne, a triumphant expression twisting her too-perfect features as she comes toward me.

"Enough of that. You're wasting your power. Now, tell me, are you ready to own up to your end of our bargain?"

Bargain? What bargain?

She's' doing it on purpose. Has to be. Drawing my attention away from my shadows by mentioning a bargain that doesn't exist.

Don't fall for it, Riley.

Her pale yellow eyes glow brightly in her golden face.

"We had an agreement, Shadow," she claims. "You as a statue for my garden in exchange for your parents' freedom. I gave them back to you. Now it's your turn to give me what I want." Her lips turn upward, a cruel smile that erases the whole innocent thing she's going for. "It's only fair."

I gave them back to you.

My concentration breaks. The shadows at my waist flutter and evaporate. I manage to hold onto the pocket in the corner because it's far enough developed to just disappear, but I forget all about my plans to chop off Melisandre's head myself when she says that.

Because she did, didn't she?

I always wondered why Nine was still a statue when we landed in the apartment in Newport, but Ash and Callie were alive and awake. The magic never made sense, but I was too grateful to question it any further. All my focus had been on bringing Nine back since I didn't have to worry about my parents.

But if Melisandre is telling the truth, then that would explain it. Before I finished pulling me, Nine, Callie, and Ash through the portal, she must have released the spell keeping my parents as statues.

She has to be telling the truth. Evil bitch or not, she's still a fae.

And fae can't lie.

Oh, no.

Oh, no, no, *no.*

I entered into a bargain with a fae. I gave my word that, if she let my parents go, I'd take their place.

She let them go.

I can't stop what's going to happen next if I tried.

Melisandre waves her hand. It's a graceful gesture, though the flinty look in her pale yellow eyes warns me what's coming a split second before I go absolutely still.

Nine finally reacts.

He'd been careful. Even after the guard slashed at him, he refused to react. This was my show, I guess; he was my back-up. He'd protect me and he'd cover me, but he wasn't going to get in my way.

Until I turned into a statue.

His hands go to my shoulders, shaking me as if that'll do something.

"Riley?" He shouts my name. "Riley!"

"Leave her, Ninetroir." Melisandre's coy laugh makes my poor ears want to bleed. "Perhaps, if you beg at my feet for my forgiveness, I'll let you visit the halfling in my garden. Until she has a little accident, of course. Statues don't just stay standing as long as they used to."

Nine's face is terrible. Lifting one hand high, showing the Fae Queen his palm, his pale skin starts to go even whiter as the entire hand glows.

He's going to shoot a blast of magic at her. Just like he did to distract the guards, only this time he's aiming for the Fae Queen —and he'll be next casualty. I know. And I can't do anything to stop him.

Wait—

My parents said they lost their years in captivity. One moment they were alive, then they were statues, and they don't remember a damn thing in between. Even Nine admitted that some of the most terrible few weeks of my life—when he was standing as a statue in the apartment—passed him by in seconds.

I can't move. I'm definitely frozen. But I... I can hear him.

Something's wrong with Melisandre's curse.

I struggle to lift my hand, desperate to catch Nine's attention before he gets himself killed.

My pinkie wiggles.

My lips part. "*N-n—*"

I want to say *Nine*. Or *no*. I get out the 'N' and that's about it. It's enough.

The silver glow building up in the center of Nine's palm dies. He spins, eyes wide as he plants both of his hands on my shoulders again.

This time, I feel it. By the time he shakes me again before pulling me into his embrace, the last of her spell slides off of me. I wrap my arms around Nine and give him a tight squeeze.

I'm okay.

For now, I'm okay.

Melisandre, on the other hand, is furious.

"That shouldn't be possible. What powers do you have?"

I regretfully pull away from Nine before reaching beneath my hoodie, revealing the necklace I stole from Gillespie. The Brinkburn. It neutralized her spell.

Ha!

Look at that.

Look at *that*.

Yes!

"No magic, just trickery. Still, the iron's bad enough," she sneers. "Now you bring a fae-killer into my Court? Do you have any idea what you've done?"

Hell, yeah, I do. I just saved my ass and I didn't even mean to.

"I'm done with these games. If I can't have you in my garden to remember my victory, I'll have to satisfy myself with your head instead. Guards. Kill the Shadow."

Uh-oh.

What am I supposed to do now?

Nine lurches toward me, wrapping his arms around me as if he's all the protection I need against the Fae Queen's soldiers and their diamond-edged swords. Only the killing strike doesn't come. It's like the guards, despite Melisandre's command, are frozen in place.

The air changes, the room gone quiet, as a voice rings out, "I'd reconsider that if I were you."

I... I know that voice.

Oberon—the same Oberon who told me that he didn't want to get involved—has just emerged from the portal I was working on in the corner of the throne room. He hasn't come alone, either. As he pulls himself out of the pitch-black shadows, he's carrying Nine's silver sword with him.

Melisandre sneers at his unkempt appearance at first, but I can tell the exact moment when she sees through his glamour and recognizes who he really is. And even if she wasn't able to, I'm thinking that the green eyes are all she needs to see before she knows exactly who has just used my portal to burst into her throne room.

"*You.*"

"Me," Oberon agrees. "Miss me, wife?"

"What are you doing here? You're supposed to be dead."

"Thanks for reminding me." There isn't a single sound as Oberon moves across the room, to the center in front of the queen's throne—or his throne. I'm not so sure. "I'm so glad I decided to take the Shadow up on her invitation to visit my former bride. Just as she reveals the Brinkburn. Plot twist, eh? Sorry. Human term. I've lived alongside them for long enough. But you, Melisandre, you'd know all about a fae-killer, wouldn't you?"

Ash told me before that Melisandre was a pro when it came to holding onto her glamour. He mentioned that, as one of her favored guards before he defected to be with my mom, he saw her lose it a couple of times. He just never explained what made her drop it.

I'm, uh, thinking it's fear.

Makes sense. As the all-powerful ruler of Faerie, there couldn't be much that frightened Melisandre. Having her long, lost husband return from the dead after more than two centuries? Yeah. That'll do it.

I've accepted that, when it comes to seeing through glamour, I wasn't born with my mom's talent. It took me way too long to recognize that Oberon was more than some homeless bum haunting my street corner, and only after years could I see that Rys wasn't as perfect as he appeared to be.

In front of us all, she seems to change. Her skin pales, though that might be from the surprise of seeing Oberon again. But then her eyes go from yellow to grey, her long curls from blonde to black, and her perfect, perfect face to something just not quite.

She's not the only one who changes. One second, the homeless man I thought I knew is standing there. Grimy jeans, a dirty flannel, matted hair. In between one blink and the next, someone else has taken his place.

This man is tall. Limber. Lean. His back is straight; no bowing down, tucking his head into his chin, arching his body to hide his true shape. His skin is a beautiful deep bronze, tanner than any other Light Fae I've ever seen. His hair is shorter than most, but the color is so rich, so gold, that I almost wonder if it's from a box. It's too gorgeous to be natural.

Like the other Light Fae in the room, he's dressed in pristine white. He looks immaculate, yet powerful, and I'm so fucking glad he showed up.

I also find it nearly impossible to believe this is the homeless man I used to give singles and fives to. One peek at his brilliant green eyes, though, and I know it's him.

Plus, he's still holding tightly to Nine's sword. So there's that, too.

His eyes find mine. "Afternoon, Riley."

What is he playing at? "Um. Hi."

"Your mom's that sweet lady named Callie, right? Human."

"Uh, yeah."

"And your father? One of mine. Aislinn."

"That's right."

"A halfling. Born in the Iron, but the shadows consider you one of theirs. So does Faerie. That's interesting."

If he says so.

"Ninetroir," Oberon says, greeting Nine. "A Cursed One."

"I am."

The imposing Light Fae turns toward me again. "He's your mate. You've chosen a Dark Fae to be your mate. Yes?"

...when Dark mates Shadow, the Reign of the Damned must come to an end...

Oh my God.

Oh my *God*.

A smile teases at the corner of my lip. He's fae. The *king* of the Fae.

And I think I finally figured out what he's doing.

"That's absolutely right."

Oberon strides forward, putting his body between me and

Melisandre. I notice there's still enough space for him to swing, though, and I can see the fear rushing across the former Fae Queen's face when she realizes it.

"Seems to me that the Shadow Prophecy has been foretold and come to pass. Halfling. Shadows. Dark mate. Now it's time to end the impostor's reign." He hefts up the sword. "I've been waiting two hundred years for this."

There's only one thing left for Melisandre to do. Folding her fingers together, she pleads, "Oberon, please. I *loved* you."

"Yes. Well, I thought I loved you once, too." The bright light of the pristine room glances off the edge of the silver sword as Oberon swings it effortlessly. The cut is quick. It's clean. One strike and Melisandre's head goes one way, her body the other.

My stomach curls in on itself as I fight the urge to throw up.

He... he did it. I've always known that there was no way in hell I could've ever actually killed Melisandre, but he did it as easily as breathing.

Oberon shrugs, lowering the point of his sword back to the tile. "I was wrong."

No one says a damn word as he wipes his hands on his white pants before stepping over Melisandre's remains, purposely striding toward the throne. With the attention of the entire court on him, he eases himself onto the seat.

His hands grip the throne's arms.

His green eyes gleam.

Nine drops to a knee. It's gotta hurt like hell, considering his injury is still bleeding freely, but he does it anyway. Following his lead, I hurriedly get to the floor.

"Long reign Oberon," he calls out, "the one and only Summer King."

As the echoes from the court surrounding us fill the throne

room, I close my eyes. Mostly because I really don't want to see Melisandre, but also because I can't believe it.

It's over.

Done.

Finally.

CHAPTER 18

Did I think that everything was over just because Oberon showed up out of nowhere and killed Melisandre for me?

Yeah. Super wrong on *that* one.

I wait for Nine to do something. Say something. He's the Dark Fae. He's the one who is familiar with Faerie and its ways. So long as he stays on the ground, head bowed, I'm going to do the same.

Even if my neck starts to ache after a minute or two.

From beneath the fringe of hair falling into my face, I sneak a peek at the room around me. Every single person in the Court has followed Nine's lead, genuflecting in front of the king who, I notice, is absolutely glowing.

It's not just the clothes. The homeless man I knew is absolutely gone. Oberon has shaken off the last of his earthly glamour, a subtle golden aura surrounding him as he casts an appraising gaze over the assembled fae.

His voice booms, echoing through the quiet. "Rise."

I scramble to my feet, moving before I give my body the command to go. I'm not the only one, either. There's something in his tone, something none of us can ignore. It's power and it's awe and it's a hint of a threat all wrapped in one. It's like he's saying, *the king is back, get used to it.*

Holy crap. I'm so glad he's on my side.

With Oberon still sitting on his throne, hands curved around the edge of the throne's arms, his immaculate boots pressed hard to the tile floor, he calls out a name.

"Helix."

One of the guards moves forward. I realize with a start that it's the Light Fae that led the cadre of soldiers who brought me back to Faerie.

He doesn't look surprised that he's being summoned by the newly returned king. In fact, that unamused, almost constipated expression is missing as he bows his head. "Welcome back, your highness."

"It's been too long. Tell me," Oberon says, almost conversationally, "are you still loyal to the Court or just the crown?"

His meaning couldn't be any clearer. The former queen still has the crystalline crown nestled securely on top of her detached head.

I try not to peek back over there again.

Too late.

Don't hurl, Riley. Don't hurl...

I swallow roughly, just managing to keep my bile back as Helix answers, "To the Seelie Court and its rightful king, of course."

Smart fae. Or, at least, one who's attached to his head.

"Oh." Oberon's lips curve. "Prove it."

A shiver runs down my spine at the cold way Oberon says that. Prove it? What does he mean, prove it?

Helix gives one decisive nod before unsheathing the sword at his hip. It's a little different than the swords the other fae threatened my mom with. It's long, slender, *sharp*, but it's also got this eerie yellow glow edging it. He weighs it in his hand, the air crackling like logs in a fire as the blade slices through it.

Obviously satisfied, Helix's fingers tighten on the hilt as he strides toward the crowd. A murmur breaks out, tension filling the air as the Light Fae moves like spilled sunlight cutting through the room.

I don't know what he's doing. Don't know what he's looking for, either. I hold my breath because I can *feel* the promise of death that follows in his wake.

It might have been daylight when the Seelie guard came after us, but the iron in the building had definitely weakened Helix. Here, in Faerie, his glow is nearly a match to Oberon's. When I thought that he'd kill me so much as look at me if I wasn't any worth to him, I was right.

Thank fucking God I am the Shadow.

Helix stops, his focus on a mixed group of obvious nobles: two females and three males, all of them Seelie except for a dark-haired beauty with skin so pale, I can nearly see through it. For a second, I think that she's the one that Helix has picked out for some reason. She's one of only a few females in the Court—probably because Melisandre didn't want any competition—and obviously Unseelie, as rare as Nine in the Fae Queen's palace.

It's not her, though. When Helix draws his arm back, slashing upward with his sharp as hell sword, it's one of the Light Fae males who loses his head. Like Melisandre, as soon as it's separated, the body buckles as the head lands with a *thud*.

His immediate circle scatters, each moving away as if Helix would aim for their head next.

I gasp, my own hand rising to shield my throat.

As I gape at the fallen fae, Nine reaches for my other hand, intertwining our fingers together, his pale fingers a stark contrast to my black leather gloves. He gives my fingers a gentle squeeze, a reminder that we're in this together.

His touch is reassuring. Calming, even. I feel grounded and alive, and super grateful that Helix kept his sword sheathed the entire time he was inside the apartment.

While the hushed Court stares at the lead soldier and his victim, Oberon looks over at us—more specifically, *at me*. It's like I can feel his gaze. I peer over my shoulder only to find myself gazing straight into his vivid green eyes.

I'd like to pretend that he's zeroed in on anyone else in the throne room but I know better. My luck's always been shit, and even when I fooled myself for a few short seconds that this was over, that I'd be halfway back to the human world once Melisandre was taken out, deep down I knew that I wouldn't be getting off that easy.

He doesn't say anything, just looks at me. I try to hide how much that casual display of violence got to me since it only makes it that much more noticeable I'm different. That I'm other.

That I'm a halfling.

Sure, Oberon took some kind of interest in me. Because of the Shadow Prophecy, I was his best—if not his *only*—hope of getting revenge on Melisandre. Now that we've accomplished it, what does that mean for me?

I'm... not looking forward to finding out.

After watching me closely for a beat longer, Oberon turns his attention back to Helix.

"Why did he deserve your blade?"

"Aven took your place in Melisandre's bed," he explains. "His loyalty was to her alone. He would've already been plotting his vengeance for you destroying his lover and taking her head."

"Fair enough. I've only just regained my throne. I'd hate to let the seat grow cold so quickly." He leans back in his throne, that sly smile widening just enough to show he totally doesn't mean any humor by his glib response. "Are there others that I should be concerned with?"

Helix shakes his head, pointing his sword to the tile as he steps away from the noble he just so easily executed. Thick rivulets of gold-colored blood drip down the blade, pooling on the floor as he turns toward the throne. "None that warrant an immediate reaction."

"Good. Clear the room, then return."

The lead soldier nods just the once, then sheathes his bloody sword. After talking to two other Light Fae—two members of the squad that Melisandre sent to my parents' apartment—he starts herding the rest of the Court out of the throne room. The two other guards gather up the fallen corpses and the separated heads before following Helix through the door.

I started to move, too, because I figured *clear the room* was as good a sign as any that it was time to get the hell out. Another squeeze from Nine has me pausing.

Glancing up at him, he murmurs, "Wait."

Ugh. I was hoping he wouldn't say that.

"I'm sorry you had to witness that, Riley," Oberon says, purposely using my name instead of my... I guess, *title* now that we're on our own. "Melisandre might've taken it too far during her Reign of the Damned, but a little cruelty is expected among the fae. A weak king doesn't keep his crown. I lost it once." His voice lowers, a promise in each word as he adds, "I won't make that mistake again."

"Um. Okay." What else am I supposed to say? I go with the

truth. "I'm glad, but now that you've proven that you're still a badass, can we go?"

I glance over at Nine, realizing that I just made a pretty big assumption there. We're mates, fully bonded *ffrindau*, but I never had a plan for after defeating Melisandre since, honestly, I never thought I *could*. So talks of the future? Those had all been put on hold until I was sure I'd have one.

With a shrug, trying to conceal how fast my heart is racing at the fear that our plans for *what comes next* won't match, I say, "I mean, if that's what you want to do. Either way, I've got to go back."

Nine slowly untangles his hand from mine, reaching into the depths of his pants. He pulls out the pebble that he's been carrying my entire life. "So long as you trust me with this, I'll go wherever you go, my Shadow."

So long as I trust him with *me*...

I lay my hand on his elbow, forming an unbreakable tether with my Dark Fae. It's so easy, so natural, and I know that if anyone else even comes close, the panic will come back with a vengeance, but not Nine.

Fate put us together. Not even a nasty, vicious Fae Queen could tear us apart.

Oberon doesn't even try.

A hint of amusement crosses his face. "Leaving so soon?"

Crap. I didn't offend him, did I?

"When the soldiers found us in my parents' apartment, I got the leader... that Helix guy... to agree to leave them alone. Melisandre isn't a threat anymore. I want to go back and tell Callie and Ash that we did it."

"And you can. But, first, I'd like to reward you."

"That's not necessary," cuts in Nine.

Oberon's eyes turn dark, a quick flash before they're back to their glassy green color. "I've eliminated one Unseelie this eve, Ninetroir. It would be no trouble to dispatch another."

Translation: *Don't try me, or you're next.*

Nine bristles, his shoulders tensing under his shadowy duster, but he smartly keeps quiet.

I know what this is about. Despite everything we've been through—despite his promise that we'd be partners instead of him acting as my protector—Nine is still trying to guard me against the rest of Faerie. I appreciate it, but it's a little late for that now. Ever since he broke me out of Black Pine last summer, I've had to be a quick study when it came to surviving the fae.

One thing I learned?

"A Light Fae told me once that it's considered a slight to refuse a generous gift," I say. "Whatever the reward is, if I take it, then can we go?"

"What can I offer you that's fair enough?" muses Oberon. "If it weren't for you performing your role as the Shadow as only you could, I'd still be trapped in the Iron, living on spite and the promise of revenge on my former consort. Ask for anything. It's yours."

"Well," I begin, because, hey, if he's offering… "a little money wouldn't hurt."

Nine angles his head toward me. He keeps his voice low, though we both know that Oberon is listening to every word when he begins by saying, "No offense meant, but you don't need to ask for that. I have more than enough to spoil you for the rest of your life."

"Yeah, in Faerie," I remind him. In the human world, he has the clothes on his back and that's about it—which is precisely why I brought it up. "And we can come back if you want to, but right now I'm just looking forward to a normal, no-prophecy, no-asylum life where I don't have to look over my shoulder every two seconds. Honestly, that's all I want."

Money would go a long way in helping with that. I'll have to get a job eventually, maybe something under the table since I don't know how a background check will work in my favor considering my history, but I have my parents to help out and my Shadow Man who deserves the best that I can give him in return.

He looks down at me, his gorgeous expression made all the more irresistible in the way he smolders. "I understand. It's a good thing that gems hold value in your world, too." His eyes gleam. "In our world."

There goes my heart thumping away like crazy again. To hear Nine correct himself and refer to the human world as *our* world? I want to throw myself into his arms and show him just how much that means to me.

How much *he* means to me.

Can't, though. Still having an audience with Oberon who, with a knowing expression on his timeless face, has a pretty good idea of the lusty thoughts running through my mind.

I clear my throat. "Know what? Forget the money. If you can vow that the fae won't come chasing after me ever again, I'll consider us square."

"Done," he announces. "And because I won't require it, I'll still arrange for the wealth I accumulated to be brought to your home."

"That's—"

Too much. Way, way too much.

Another thing I learned?

Fae don't do favors and, honestly, they don't do gifts, either. Everything they do is with the aim of one-upping someone else, of having the power and the scales tipping toward them. I don't ever want to be in a fae's debt—especially not this fae.

Oberon holds up his hand. "Consider it repayment for the money you slipped my way when you thought I was nothing but a humble beggar."

I might've thrown a couple of bucks his way when his glamour presented him as a homeless guy. If his boasting from the other day can be believed, it's like tossing him a penny and getting back a hundred dollar bill.

Then again, it's not like he's going to use it...

Besides, it might have taken me a second to figure out what Oberon is really doing, but now that I'm paying attention, it's super obvious. Whether it's true or not, the Summer King believes that he's in my debt for regaining his throne. It doesn't matter that I'm the prophesied halfling in the Shadow Prophecy and that I was supposed to end Melisandre's reign. He *owes* me.

No wonder he refused to help us when we confronted him in the human world. In his eyes, the balance would be lopsided in *my* favor. Of course he has to balance it out before he can let me leave.

I don't say *thank you*, because that's definitely an insult to the fae; that's something else I learned a long time ago. So, instead, I tell him, "I'll expect it as soon as possible."

"Of course. Anything else?"

Nine flexes his fingers. Not so noticeably, and I probably picked up on it because I'm in tune with every flutter, every sneer, every shift of weight as he stands by my side, but enough that I know he's dying to tell me that that's enough.

Not because he's trying to control me. I think my mate has finally figured out that the time for telling me what I can and can not do is way behind us. However, just because Oberon sided with me against the former queen, it doesn't mean I can trust him.

He's not only a Light Fae. He's the freakin' Summer King.

One small step and I go from balancing what he thinks he owes me to being in his debt—and that's one place I never want to be. Too bad that I have to push it.

And I have to. Whenever I wasn't obsessing over the conflicting Shadow Prophecies, Nine being a statue, or Melisandre hunting us down, I wondered over Rys's fate.

No doubt in my mind that, if he could get to me, Rys would've popped up by now. He promised he'd always come for me. So what if I didn't *want* him to? That hadn't stopped him before, and it's bothered me for a while now that he just... disappeared.

I don't know how Nine is going to react, but I have to ask.

I have to know.

EPILOGUE

"Actually, yes. You probably don't know... I mean, you just got here yourself... but do you think you could find out what happened to Rys?"

Oberon blinks slowly, puzzled. "Rys. I'm not familiar with that name. Seelie? One of mine?"

To be more accurate, he was probably one of Melisandre's before he betrayed the Fae Queen and helped me to escape. Since I don't want to tell Oberon that, I shrug. "I think so."

"Is that the Light Fae whose brand you once wore?"

Nine's long coat flares behind him, the shadows responding to his bad mood. Any relief he felt when Oberon appeared and fought Melisandre is long gone, and I'm even more anxious to get the hell out of here before Oberon makes good on his threat to eliminate another Dark Fae.

It's not like I like the reminder of Rys's touch, either. But... hey. I'm still struggling with guilt. Maybe I could have saved him. Maybe I could have stretched the shadow a little further to include Rys. Sure, shadow travel nearly killed Ash, and I remember how the portal left black streaks on his bronzed complexion that morning in the mausoleum, but still.

Maybe—

I nod. "Yeah. That's him."

Before Oberon can say anything else, the door opens and Helix walks back into the throne room on his own.

Oberon gestures at him. "Helix." Then, as if I've never met him before, he tells me, "A member of my old guard. I'm glad to see you've survived Melisandre's reign, Captain."

Helix nods. "Thank you, your highness. I've done what you've ordered. The castle is clear, with my best soldiers going through Melisandre's staff now, searching for any whose loyalty might not be to the true and proper king."

"Well done. As efficient as ever, and as ambitious, I'm sure. I can work with that. Now, what can you tell me of the Seelie known as—"

He looks at me again.

"Rys," I supply.

"Rys."

Helix stops dead in his tracks. His back goes ramrod straight, his features entirely expressionless. He hesitates for way longer than I can take before he says, "Melisandre punished him."

"Punished him," I squeak out. Oh, man. I *knew* it. "How did she punish him?"

Helix stays quiet.

Oberon leans forward in his throne. "Answer the Shadow," he commands. "What did my treasonous consort do with one of my fae?"

"Rysdan was charged with being a traitor. Rather than call for his head or his soul, Melisandre chose leniency for a former favored soldier."

"Leniency," repeats Oberon. "That doesn't sound like her."

Helix hesitates before admitting, "He was put into Siúcra."

"As I thought. A fate worse than death then, disguised as kindness. Just like Melisandre."

"Why?" I wonder. "What's..." I try to repeat what Helix said. I butcher it and it comes out like, "sucker?"

"Siúcra," Oberon corrects, his voice going almost gentle as he addresses me. "The inescapable prison of Faerie. Once you're locked inside, there's no getting out."

"What? *Ever*?"

"I'm afraid not."

Whoa.

I... I don't know what to say about that. All this time, I let myself believe that Rys was okay. That even though the last time I saw him he was being bombarded by Melisandre's soldiers, he was fine. I convinced myself that he'd finally stopped chasing me because he respected Nine's claim, and that without his brand on my skin, Rys couldn't find me.

But he's in prison. Faerie prison.

The Fae Queen ordered me and Nine into a cell once. I remember making a joke about it, calling it fairy jail, almost amazed that something like that existed. There were only a handful of cells built inside of her elaborate castle, far away from her throne room, and it never occurred to me to wonder if the cells were permanent—or only a holding area for those Melisandre wanted to punish.

Like Rys.

Oberon can't lie to me. When he says that there's no escape from this Siúcra place, he means it. And *that* means that Rys is—

He's—

Gone.

I should be happy. I should be relieved. The golden fae, the monster with an angel's face who haunted my nightmares and stole my sister from me... he can't come after me again. I'm finally free of him, except there's part of me that can't forget his earnest declarations of affection and how careful he was to keep me from harm, even when I pushed him way further than I ever should have.

He tricked my mom—but he didn't hurt her. He killed Madelaine—but he's fae and he didn't understand the importance of human friendships. He turned Nine into his rival—but then he held his own against his comrades so that I could escape with my soulmate after Melisandre turned Nine into a statue.

Overall, I should hate Rys.

I don't.

I always thought he was the villain in my story. Of course, that ended up being Melisandre. Gillespie, too, if I'm being honest. Rys was just Rys, and I might not have wanted to be his *ffrindau*, but I never wanted to see him punished because of me, either.

This sucks.

Nine told me something like that once when I called Rys a monster. There's no good and bad. Despite being called the Cursed Ones and the Blessed Ones, it comes down to light and dark—and it's pretty literal at that. The Light Fae rule during the sun, the Dark Fae belong to the shadows, but good and bad? Human concepts. Just like people, the fae are complicated.

Maybe I'm more fae than I thought. I *hate* the idea of owing Rys anything. Him being stuck in that Su-crah place... yeah, that's on me.

And I hate that, too.

"But... you're the king. Can't you do something? He wouldn't be in there if it wasn't for me."

"I can't. Believe me, there's no escape."

"No one walks out of Siúcra," murmurs Nine. "It's not so

easy as that. It requires a sacrifice, and that's if you even found a way out. The prison never lets anyone leave."

I look from Nine to the king and back. "So Rys…"

"He's alive," offers Oberon.

"But he's in jail."

He looks to Helix.

Helix nods.

"Yes."

"So I'm betting he'd rather not be."

"If the prison has its hooks in your Seelie, then he wouldn't be," agrees Oberon. "I can't give you the Seelie's freedom. Siúcra claims its own and, even as the Summer King, my power only goes so far and that's with the whole Court behind me. I've only just reclaimed my crown. Money and permission to shade-walk as you please, that I can do."

And that's still giving me a lot, since I already asked him to kill the Fae Queen so that I didn't have to.

"I understand."

I don't like it, but I understand.

"Then we have an agreement."

I slump under the weight of his announcement. Whoa. Did I make a mistake? Probably. It wouldn't be the first time, and I'm eager to get away from Faerie while Oberon is still pleased with me.

He waves Helix forward, lowering his voice so that he can have a private conversation with the lead soldier. I'm sure Nine is listening but I take his action as what it is: a dismissal.

Yup. Time to go.

I reach out with my senses. There aren't as many shadows in this room without Melisandre's power—her glamour hid her Unseelie nature, but the shadows gave her away—but I'm a pro at wrangling them now. I gather up enough to create a portal that would lead us back to the human world.

Nine immediately knows what I've done. He glances over at the patch of darkness blooming in the far corner of the emptied throne room, then looks at me.

"You ready?" he asks.

As he does, he holds his hand out. Without even a second's thought, I slip my glove into the nestle of his palm.

His touch is everything that I need.

"Always."

I fell in love with the shadow man...

TOUCHED BY THE FAE · BOOK FOUR

ZELLA

INTERNATIONAL BESTSELLING AUTHOR
JESSICA LYNCH

Copyright © 2020 by Jessica Lynch

All rights reserved.

No part of this book may be reproduced in any form or by any electronic or mechanical means, including information storage and retrieval systems, without written permission from the author, except for the use of brief quotations in a book review.

Cover by Jessica Lynch

CHAPTER 1

Oh, great.

Nine's gone again.

I rub the back of my neck, take a deep breath, and blow out a puff of air.

At this point, I don't know if I'm frustrated or disappointed. Probably both.

Ugh.

Walking out into an empty living room... that's nothing new. Not lately. Ever since he surprised me with an apartment of our own a floor below my parents, my mate has spent most days *out* of it. I guess I don't really blame him. He has this need to provide, to go out and turn his never-ending supply of priceless gems into whatever he thinks *I* need. I've given up on trying to figure out how he does it, since I know he has this thing about dealing with humans, and I just decided to go along with it and make room for everything he brings back.

I blame Ash. Though it's been weeks since I worried that Nine and my dad were going to get into it over me, I almost long for those days. I liked them better when they didn't get along. Nowadays—now that the mating is final and Ash can't change it—the two of them seem to have their heads together way more than they should.

Ash was the one who put the idea in Nine's head that, as my *ffrindau*—my soulmate—it was up to Nine to provide for me the way that he does for my mom. I lost my shit the first time I found out that Ash was badgering Nine because, for nearly my whole damn life, Nine's been taking care of me. I'm not a material girl. I don't need him to buy me things to prove that he loves me. He does that by just being him.

I thought I got that through his hard head, but he still keeps bringing me... weird stuff. I kinda get it. Nine's fae, he's spent his long, *long* life in Faerie, and this is the most amount of time he's spent in the human world. I can forgive him for thinking that an antique, wooden wine rack is way more essential than, I don't know, a toaster or something. He doesn't know, but he's trying and he's trying because he wants me to be happy.

And I am. For the first time in my life, I'm so stinking happy. Melisandre is dead. My parents are alive. Oberon kept his part of the bargain, sending me more money than I'll ever be able to spend in this lifetime. I've got stacks and stacks of cash in a spare bedroom since Nine stubbornly insists on paying for everything himself. If it makes him happy, cool, but I'm comforted by the stash. It's nice to know it's there.

And, okay. As pushy as Ash is, it was a great idea for the two of us—me and Nine—to pick an empty apartment in the condemned building and turn it into our dream home. With the threat of the Fae Queen and her soldiers finally over and done with, I can just be with my Shadow Man.

Except quiet time with my mate didn't last as long as I liked. Mainly because, apart from the bed that Ash and Nine moved down for us, the apartment literally *was* empty. We didn't have anything. I didn't care. Honestly, I was good with the bed so long as I got a fridge to go along with it.

Hey. What can I say? I'm easy to please.

Not my mate. The next morning, he went out and came back with a couch. I was super impressed. Then he brought home the wooden wine rack and, yeah. That was a bit odd.

It got odder. Figuring it wasn't worth trying to explain why I didn't necessarily need a potted tree or a golden candelabra, I went along with it because Nine obviously had this desire to provide for me.

But that's not all he's doing, either. Now that we've decided that we're going to make our main home here in the human world instead of in Faerie, Nine is working to prove that he can make it work. He can be a Dark Fae who walks in the sunshine, who clings to his shadows (and his shadowy duster) no matter how he struggles, who can push past the iron sickness.

He doesn't have to go outside when the sun's up. He chooses to because it's his way of showing me that he can live in the human world *with* me.

It's the only upside to Melisandre's curse, the cruel spell that had Nine standing as a statue for so long, I thought I had lost him forever. Though he didn't remember any of his imprisonment, the weeks he spent in the apartment helped him acclimate to the human world. It doesn't affect him as bad as it should've.

At least, that's what he tells me. And the fae can't lie.

Still, I gotta admit that Nine's insistence to step out during the day is so different than anything I'm used to. My whole life, whenever Nine came to visit me, he was careful to leave before dawn. If he wanted to hang onto his fae magic, he needed to return to Faerie before the sun had the chance to weaken him. Now he purposely goes out into it, as if he's building up a resistance to it. And if it bothers me that he's gone more than he's home during the day? I keep quiet.

So long as he comes home to me, I guess I'm okay with whatever he does.

I've asked so damn much of him already. Just leaving Faerie is one hell of a sacrifice. I can't tell him to stay in because I want him to. It's not fair, especially when I know that he's spending a lot of time with my dad, using whatever tricks and magic they have to glamour and ward our building.

Ash did a lot of the work more than twenty years ago when he first mated my mom. It's the only reason why the building survived being condemned in the shady part of Newport where we live now. The wards shielded it, too. It's safe and it's quiet and the four of us are the only ones inside.

After spending six years in the asylum, it's fucking paradise.

Nine wants to keep it that way. As devoted to Callie as Ash is, my dad has made it clear that he will stop at nothing to make sure we're safe. It bothers him that Melisandre's guards broke through his wards *twice* now. So what if we don't have to worry about her anymore? The two guys insist on reinforcing them so that they're protected around the clock.

Not that Nine tells me that that's what he's doing. Nope. As if he can't shake the habit of watching out for me, he changes the subject whenever I ask. He's a tricky, evasive bastard, but what did I expect? I mated a fae.

And it's not like he's the only one who's being careful. I try to convince myself over and over again that I'm safe. Now that the Shadow Prophecy has been fulfilled and Melisandre is dead, my role as the Shadow is done. Oberon, the Summer King, is back on his throne. Considering I all but handed it to him when I opened a portal to let him sneak into Faerie, he owes me.

Not like I'm stupid enough to point that out to him.

We all have to find our place in this new life. Ash and Callie lost twenty years thanks to the Fae Queen's curse. Nine has never spent more than a few hours at a time in the human world.

And me?

Between hopping from foster home to foster home, watching my sister be murdered by a Light Fae, then being admitted to the Black Pine Facility for Wayward Juveniles for six years, I'm just as lost and confused as they are.

So I cling to what I know. On what I can do.

When Nine and Ash are out doing whatever it is they're doing, I check in on Callie. Make sure my mom's still adjusting well, maybe take a walk with her, get to know her more without the threat of my death looming over my head.

But that's not all.

I'm the Shadow. Hey, I've finally accepted it. It is what it is, right?

And, even after everything that happened, I still have my powers. I can create shadows out of almost nothing, pulling them toward me, twisting them, making them do whatever I want. Whenever I have the time, I play with them. I've gotten really good at shade-walking, and I travel to all the places I wished I could see while I was locked up at Black Pine.

I bring Callie with me sometimes. At night, when Nine is in his element, I open a portal and we explore the human world, always returning to our bedroom before the sun is up again. At least… we *did*. The last few times I asked, he came up with an excuse why we should stay in. And since staying in means staying in bed together, I can't say that I was against the plan at all.

I still fiddle with portals whenever Nine goes out, though. Because that's the only downside when it comes to being the

Shadow now that the Shadow Prophecy is over and done with. There's no one else like me—at least, that's what Gillespie said when he told me that I'm the first female halfling he's met in *three hundred years*—and I'm kind of still making things up as I go.

The portals are the biggest clue when it comes to that.

I finally figured that there's a difference between a Dark Fae portal created from a pocket and something that I make out of my shadows. I never would've caught onto that if it wasn't for what happened with Oberon.

The second-to-last time I was in Faerie, I was so desperate to escape the Fae Queen that I turned an Unseelie pocket into a way out. Seemed like a good idea at the time, except I nearly killed poor Ash. Light Fae, the Seelie… they can't take a Dark Fae portal or shade-walk. Just like how I was fucking terrified when it came to Nine choosing to follow me into the fire of a Light Fae portal. I was sure it would be torture for him and, desperate to shield him, I wrapped him in shadows so that he'd survive.

But Oberon…

My plan was to create a portal from my shadows and use it to escape or, I don't know, pop out on the other side of the room and maybe distract Melisandre. Of course, that hadn't happened. She managed to curse me, but since I was still wearing the Brinkburn crystal then, it didn't take.

And that's when Oberon strode into the throne room, the badass wielding Nine's sword up until the moment he lopped his former consort's head right off.

My stomach still goes queasy at that memory. But there's no denying that the Summer King did it. Powerful and strong, he used my Unseelie portal to confront Melisandre—and it didn't seem to affect him at all.

I asked Nine about it when things settled down again. Oberon's the *Summer King*; you can't get any more Seelie than that. The Dark Fae portal should've brought him to his knees at the very least.

My Shadow Man is my mate now, but I've known him nearly my whole life. When I was a child, he was the one I looked up to. Part guardian, part mentor. While our relationship is decades old, the romantic element is so precious but, yeah, still new. Sometimes Nine slips right back into the role of my teacher and I let him because it's one more reminder for me that he's always been there.

His answer shocked me.

Turns out that it's all because I'm the Shadow. Part-human, part-Light Fae, and with a touch of Dark Fae magic since I've been able to shade-walk since I was an infant, I was the only person—person, fae, whatever—who could've pulled off what I did.

Without me weaving that portal and leaving it open, Oberon never would've popped in to confront Melisandre and take his throne back.

Oberon spent two centuries here. In the human world. No one knows how he held on for so long, but I'm betting it had something to do with not being able to cross back into Faerie. He made it seem like it was his choice. The more I think of it, the more I realized that that was bullshit.

He needed me. Why else had he followed me, watching me, helping me along the way? When Gillespie tracked me down in Acorn Falls, Oberon warned me. In Newport, he gave me the real Shadow Prophecy.

And then, when I wove an escape portal from the shadows while I was in Faerie, Oberon waltzed right through it as if he guessed I would.

No. Not guess.

Know.

The Shadow Prophecy unfolded just like it was supposed to, didn't it? *When Dark mates Shadow, the Reign of the Damned must come to an end...* I mated Nine, and Oberon ended Melisandre's reign as Fae Queen of Faerie.

So maybe it *was* fate. Still, weeks later, I can't help but wonder if fate had a little push. Doesn't matter. With Oberon's help or not, Melisandre is dead.

I'm safe. I'm *free*.

Oberon allowed us to come back to the human world. Feeling like he owed me something, he rewarded me with all that money. Oberon even gave his word that none of the fae would ever chase after me. They have no reason to ever come after any of us ever again.

But that's the thing. Nine's not so sure. My parents? You could tell from their elation and their relief when we made it back in one piece that they'd thought they lost me forever.

My overprotective father and possessive mate are convinced that there might be someone who wants me to pay for bringing about the Fae Queen's death.

I like to think they're wrong.

Honestly, after everything that's happened to me, I *have* to.

CHAPTER 2

Today's haul includes a leather recliner chair, a pretty-smelling candle, a bag of books that I'm actually interested in checking out, and a three-foot-long gothic-style mirror that kinda scares me.

I don't even want to know how many gems he used to get this stuff. I tried once to remind Nine that it might be easier to use Oberon's money, that he could hold onto his wealth from Faerie, and the look he gave me had me shrugging it off.

Whatever makes him happy.

I'm pulling the Suzie Homemaker routine in the kitchen. Cooking has been a shit ton of trial and error considering I've never really learned how to do it before, but I'm nothing if not determined. I'm sick of fast food and, well, I'm sort of married now. With everything he's doing for me, I like the idea of doing something for Nine.

And if my tricky fae goes out of his way to find things to tell me he likes in my creations, I only love him more for it.

Thank God Callie knows what she's doing. She's got a

hundred recipes up in that head of hers and, with her help, the food's always edible at least. Plus, it gives me another way to bond with her.

I grabbed Callie earlier and the two of us went shopping for groceries at the big supermarket across Newport. I always get a little antsy after I finish practicing with my portals. You'd think I'd be drained, but the shadows seem to invigorate me. It's weird, but I'm getting used to it, and I zipped us behind the shop where no one would notice two blonde chicks stepping out of the shadows.

When we come back, Nine's still gone. I try not to let it bug me that it's been... what? Eight hours since he's been out? I have to remind myself that, just because we're mated now, it doesn't mean that I own him.

Nine is more than a century old. When he was my age, before he infiltrated the Fae Queen's guard, he used to cross over from Faerie all the time. Of course, that was when the sun still meant almost certain death. If there's one plus side to his stubborn insistence of going out during the day, it's that he's built up a tolerance to both daylight *and* iron.

And he's doing it all for me.

When the door to my apartment opens, I'm hoping it's Nine, only to be disappointed when it's Ash looking for Callie. Not like my dad even has to look too hard for her. He always knows where to find his mate.

I've gotta give him credit. Though he continues to struggle when it comes to me being grown and mated to his old friend, he finally realized that me and Nine were a package deal. The dirty looks and snide comments stopped, even if I'm still trying to get him to call me *Riley* instead of *Zella*.

There's only two people who have his loyalty: Callie and me. In Ash's eyes, we're his family. He tolerates Nine because I ask him to, but, despite Ash and Nine's complicated history (including a life debt that Nine owed my dad), Ash is definitely on my side.

And, alright. Maybe I use it against him a little bit.

I can't help it. Just because the fae ended up being real, that doesn't change a lot of the issues that landed me in Black Pine. Unable to form personal relationships, abandonment issues, a deep-seated fear that everyone I've ever known or loved will eventually leave me... those didn't just go away. I'm not a light switch that can be flicked *off*.

Nine loves me. I know it. He's been the only constant in my life, except for the six years when I was in the asylum. We're mated now. He can't leave me.

At least, that's what I tell myself. And then I remember how Oberon and Melisandre's story ended and sue me for being insecure, okay?

That's how I know what Nine's up to when he goes out during the day. My mate isn't really hiding it from me or anything, but he seems to tense up when I ask him too many questions. That's Nine, for you, though. He's never liked to have anyone ask him anything, even me.

When he was my mentor, he used to tell me that I'd learn any answer in time.

I don't want to wait, so I asked Ash instead. I didn't think I was being sneaky, either. The two former fae guards were just doing what they were trained long ago to do: protect. Only they're not responsible for the Fae Queen anymore.

Nine is using his limited magic to glamour the building so that I'm safe. Ash is devoted to taking care of his mate and his child.

I accept it. Don't like how Nine thinks it's something I need to be shielded *from*, but I get it.

As Nine figures out where he's going to put his funky gothic mirror, I call out to him, "You ready to eat?"

He still has that easy glide as he suddenly appears in the kitchen. "Whenever you are."

I turn—and I stare.

It happens sometimes. When I'm not expecting him, coming face to face with his beauty can make me a little screwy. He's just so fucking gorgeous, I'm stunned as I ask myself: how did I end up with him?

He's looking different these days. Due to his newfound relationship with the sun, his pale skin has picked up some color. Not much, but his unearthly glow isn't as noticeable unless we're surrounded by the dark. His hair? He cut it short, the raven-colored length snipped so that it mimics a human hairstyle.

When he asked me if I thought he should cut it or not, I told him honestly that I didn't care. It's his hair. I'd love him no matter what.

He insisted on it. Since he didn't want to waste any magic on glamouring himself so that he fit in, he decided to chop it off. My mom told me that he'd worn his hair that short when she first met him, and I had to admit I dug the way the soft strands seemed to curl around his pointed ear.

And if I wondered why Oberon could still glamour himself after two hundred years in the human world and Nine was sure he couldn't, I kept my trap shut.

Because, you know what? I don't think Oberon was funneling any of his spare magic into glamouring a fourteen-story, condemned building in the middle of Newport.

He smiles, his silver eyes gleaming in male satisfaction as he recognizes the effect he has on me. "Dinner smells great, Riley."

"Thanks. It's Callie's recipe. I made extras. Ash said you got through the fifth floor today." The words slip out without me even thinking about what I'm saying. "You must be starving. Want to grab plates?"

"Aislinn said what?"

Oops.

Ah, well. It was probably time the cat was out of the bag anyway. I've been watching him leave every day for a while now, acting as if the time alone isn't bothering me while he purposely hides the fact that he's worried about my safety.

Doesn't he think I'm worried about *him*?

Playing it off, I tell Nine, "My dad stopped by earlier. He told me all about it. You guys are working hard. I appreciate it."

I might.

He doesn't.

Nine's eyes flash. Instead of going to grab the plates like I asked, he stays where he is as he shakes his head slowly. "I warned him."

I don't like the way that sounds.

"Warned him about what?"

His lips thin. "I need his help with the wards, but I won't let him interfere."

Interfere? What?

I'm so lost. Sometimes, when Nine lets down his guard and shows me just how jealous he can get... not gonna lie. It's *super* hot. But right now?

I roll my eyes. "Nine... he's my dad."

"And you're my mate," he counters. "I'll be the one to protect you, Riley. He can take care of Callie. You're mine."

"You mean your responsibility," I scoff, turning so that I'm looking at the pot on the stove instead of the angry look on his face.

I don't even sense him moving. Suddenly, he's right

behind me.

Spinning me around, his hands gentle on my elbow, his dark expression locked on my face as he promises, "My *everything*."

Okay. That does it. My heart simply melts. Everything he's done—everything he *does*—is for me. It's obvious. But damn if he isn't trying too hard.

At the end of the day, there's only one thing I need from Nine.

"I don't need you to protect me anymore," I tell him, leaning into him. Dinner can wait. Right now, my attention is solely on Nine. "I just need you to love me."

My message hits home.

His glower fades a bit, the jagged edge of his fury smoothing out as he loops an arm around my waist before tugging me close. Nine presses his lips to the top of my head before pressing his chilled cheek against my overheated one. As a Dark Fae, he's always a little cold, but that's okay. I usually have a lot of fun trying to warm him up.

Nine's breath fans the tip of my pointed ear, sending a rush of shivers down my spine. I'm hyper aware of his slender fingers resting on my hip. He's touching me—and I wouldn't have it any other way.

"Love you, Shadow?" he murmurs. "That's all I do."

Good. Because loving him is all *I* do.

I think of my shadows. Of my portals. Of my secret worry that this is just too good to last. That something's going to come along and screw this up because that's what has always happened to me.

Well, for the most part loving him is all I do.

I turn my face toward him, angling my chin so that my lips are next to his. Nine takes the invitation and, as he holds me in his arms, I let his kiss push all my thoughts and worries away.

THEY'RE BACK THE NEXT MORNING, MOST LIKELY BECAUSE NINE isn't.

We had a long talk last night. I told him how I felt, and he seemed to understand that I wasn't trying to be clingy on purpose or anything. Of the two of us, Nine might've been the virgin, but I've never had a real relationship, either. Just because we're fated soulmates, that didn't mean we had it easy.

Communication is key. Nine wants me to be honest with how much Ash told me about their work on the building, and I want him to just include me.

By the time we fell into bed together, I thought we worked things out. And if I got the sinking feeling that there was still something he wasn't telling me, I purposely ignored it.

I remember him leaving the bed this morning. He caressed my cheek, chuckling when I swatted his hand before leaning down to kiss my forehead. He brought me breakfast—I mumbled I wasn't hungry—and then I fell back asleep.

I thought he did, too.

Nope.

A peek at the clock tells me that it's way past the normal time that I would get up. No surprise, considering he kept me up way late. Normally, I wouldn't have cared.

Normally, he would still be in bed with me.

Only he's not.

Ugh.

It bothers me that it seems like I opened up and poured my heart out to him last night only for Nine to yes me to death before slipping out early this morning. I have half a mind to use our bond to track him down before deciding against it.

It's the power of the touch. So long as I had his trace on my skin, Nine was always able to find me. When Rys replaced Nine's touch with his, Nine couldn't track me down until I gave him permission to touch me again.

Now that we're mated, he doesn't need permission. He's had it completely from the minute he claimed me and I accepted his claim. But that's the thing about the final touch between fae mates. I'm under his skin as much as he's on mine.

And I'm half-fae. If I try, I can find him wherever he is.

I've never done it before. It didn't seem right. I trust him more than I've ever trusted anyone. Even if I don't like his strange disappearances, I know he's not doing anything bad.

So, instead of giving in to my anxieties, I push up off of the bed, shuffle into the bathroom, and take a shower. After I'm dressed, I skip the breakfast that Nine left out for me—my queasy stomach can't handle that right now—and decide to go upstairs and talk to Callie.

She might not be a halfling, but she's got a couple of years under her belt when it comes to being a fae's mate. This won't be the first time I've gone to her for advice—probably won't be the last, either—and I'm hoping that she can give me some insight on what's going on with Nine.

There's no reason to keep the doors locked in our building. Since we've lived in it, no one else has stepped foot inside thanks to Ash's twenty-year-old wards. With the added glamour from Nine and Ash these last few weeks, it's almost impenetrable to anyone but another fae.

And if the fae try breaking in? Melisandre's Light Fae guards have already proven that they can. So what's the point of locks?

I still knock, though, since it's the polite thing to do. And because I'm trying to prove to Ash that he should do the same when he comes down to our apartment.

After he almost caught me and Nine going at it one evening,

I'm afraid he might walk in and see something that he definitely wouldn't want to. Then again, if that's what it takes for him to give us some privacy...

"Riley. Come on in."

I don't even ask Callie how she knows it's me as I pull open the front door. Who else would it be?

After shutting the door behind me, I take a couple of steps inside the apartment, freezing when I notice that she's not alone. Sitting next to her on the couch, his arm stretched behind her as the happy couple cuddles, is Ash.

"What are you doing here?"

He doesn't seem too offended as he remarks, "This *is* my home."

"Obviously. It's just... Nine's out. I thought you would be, too."

Ash and Callie exchange a look. Slowly, Ash removes his hand from around his mate. He leans forward, his elbows on his knees as if he's about to stand up.

I back away.

Oh, I don't like *that* at all. Especially when Callie nods her head encouragingly at her mate. "Tell her, sweetheart. She needs to know."

"Is it about Nine?"

Ash nods. He stays seated for now. "I've been talking to him."

That doesn't bode well. "When you're whipping up glamours and wards, right?"

"Yes. And... other times."

"Spit it out, Ash. I'm listening."

"Very well. He came to me shortly after you moved to your own space. Not as Ninetroir seeking Aislinn, but as a *ffrindau* meeting his mate's father."

You've got to be kidding me.

"Come *on*. Don't tell me that Nine actually asked you for your blessing when it came to us being together."

Ash shakes his head. "No. But he asked me to tell him all about Gillespie."

My heart just about stops at that name. "He did *what*?"

"And I told him."

"You didn't," I breathe out.

One look at the arrogant expression on my dad's face and I know the truth.

He did. He totally did.

"Why?"

Ash juts out his chin. "Because, if it was your mother, I wouldn't stop until I eliminated the threat to my mate."

"Oh, Ash—"

"You didn't want me to retaliate for what that halfling monster did to our girl," he says, turning to look at Callie. "You thought it would only push her away. But Ninetroir has a right to know. And, as her *ffrindau*, he has the authority to avenge her. So I told him."

Is he kidding? I wish, but I've gotten to know him well enough that my Light Fae father is dead serious.

"When?"

He raises his eyebrows.

I scowl. "When, Ash? How long has Nine known?"

I know it's not a good idea to have secrets in a committed relationship, but when I used the Brinkburn to bring Nine back, my time as a captive in Gillespie's office was too raw. Too fresh. For God's sake, I'd just escaped the asylum seconds before I tossed the necklace over Nine's head and prayed that it would save him.

After that, it just never seemed right. Since the last thing I saw before I escaped his office was the glamoured tech Diana reaching for him, I figured he wouldn't be bothering me anymore. So, well, Nine didn't need to know, right?

I guess I was wrong when Ash admits, "I told him the morning after your return from Faerie."

Time flows funny in Faerie. I learned that one the hard way. The first time I crossed over, I lost a week. I've lost months. I was so scared that, when Oberon let us go, years would've past. Luckily, it had only been about three days.

And on the fourth Ash told Nine all about Gillespie.

That was *weeks* ago.

Suspicion mingled with sudden worry makes my hands go slick inside of my leather gloves. Gulping, I ask nervously, "Why are you telling me this now?"

I think I know. I hope I'm wrong.

"Because, this morning, he told me that he's finally gotten a lead on where he can find the halfling."

My knees go shaky. As I stumble, I reach out for the small table in the hallway, using it to keep me on my feet.

Callie gasps. "Riley—"

"I'm okay."

I'm so not okay.

"He's your mate, Zella," Ash reminds me. "Gillespie tried to keep you locked away with him. Ninetroir can't let that slide. Don't you understand?"

Maybe?

I don't know.

I do know one thing, though. Gillespie is fucking nuts. Dude is *crazy*. I never even wanted to think about him again. I sure as hell didn't want Nine having anything to do with him.

Too late.

CHAPTER 3

Half an hour ago, I decided against using Nine's touch to follow his trace.

But that was half an hour ago.

Closing my eyes, I can... I can *sense* him. It's as instinctive as gathering my shadows—which I also start to do. Instead of locking in on a place, like Faerie, Black Pine, or the Acorn Falls cemetery, I focus on my mate.

Peering through the slits in my eyes, I make sure that the portal is big enough for the three of us to move through before I step forward.

I don't even bother arguing again. I wasted too many minutes trying to tell Ash and Callie that I didn't need them to follow me after Nine. It's bad enough that he's going after Gillespie. I hate the idea of my old doctor getting anywhere near him or my parents.

There's no changing their minds, though. And I get it. I do. After the way I left them behind when me and Nine went back to Faerie to face Melisandre, even I don't think it's fair to take this portal alone.

Because it's one I made from my own shadows instead of an Unseelie pocket, it's safe for my dad to take. He tucks Callie in close, then lays his hand on my shoulder and, together, the three of us jump through my portal.

I'm so focused on finding Nine that, when I come through the shadows on the other side, it takes me a second to recognize the institution in front of me. When I do? I shrink back into the shadows and try to control the panic that slams into me like a damn truck.

Callie picks up on it immediately. Ducking out from under Ash's arm, she moves in front of me, her big blue eyes wide in concern. "Riley, honey. You okay?"

She doesn't know what this place is. How can she? She's heard some of my stories about the asylum, but she's never been here.

And I never wanted to return.

Why is Nine here? I mean, after the way I left things with Gillespie on Easter, my doctor can't really still be working here, right?

"Yeah. I'm fine."

Though Callie obviously doesn't believe me, I work hard to shake the panic off. Maybe this is a glitch. Just because I thought I followed my Shadow Man here, maybe I'm wrong.

Please let me be wrong.

Where are you, Nine?

It's that same feeling, that same sense that I know where he is. Only, this time, I'm not looking for him. I've *found* him.

We're tucked beneath an overhang in the parking lot across from the Black Pine facility's facade. Luckily for us, the shadows were strong enough to carry us here *and* provide us with enough cover to watch the front of the building without being seen.

It's not a very busy street. This part of Black Pine is the far end of the Mulberry Bend that's shielded by trees, dotted with empty buildings. It's not too far from where I was abandoned, actually—or where Callie was captured by Rys.

A shiver runs down my spine.

Shake that off, too, Riley, I tell myself. Don't think about the past.

Think about Nine.

And there he is. I'd know that backside everywhere.

Callie follows my gaze. Thanks to the wide windows that make up the front of the asylum—trying to make it more open, and not like the stereotypical psych hospital—I can see right inside. There's the receptionist's desk, expensive chairs that fill the open room, the row of locked doors and gleaming elevators, and a lean, limber male with dark hair standing in front of the desk.

As if he can sense me, Nine peers behind his shoulder out through the open door. After a second, he turns to the receptionist again but he doesn't give us his back. He swivels on his heel, presenting his profile as he leans in to say something to her.

"You see him?" whispers Callie.

"Of course I see him! He's right there." And he's way too close to the woman sat behind the desk. My hands flex, itching to grab Nine by the back of his leather duster and drag him out of there.

Hmm. I guess I can get a little jealous, too.

I force myself to push that emotion aside. The blondie at the desk might be pretty, but she's not his mate. I am. There's only one reason that he's even talking to her and it's because he has bigger fish to fry.

He wants Gillespie. I want him out of there.

Anywhere but the asylum, I swear. I could've supported him through this anywhere but the asylum. Just because Oberon is ruling over all of Faerie now, that doesn't change the fact that the asylum has long been infiltrated by Melisandre's people. It's too much of a risk to get some payback.

"Nine," I mutter, shielding my gaze with the edge of my glove. "What are you *doing*?"

"Do you want me to go in there?" murmurs my mom.

That's not that great of an idea, either. Callie… she looks too much like me. There's no way around that. We share the same oval-shaped face, wide blue eyes, delicate features, and white-blonde hair that hangs past our shoulders.

I escaped that place almost a year ago. I don't think that that's long enough that they forgot about me.

"That's… that's okay."

Ash lets out a haughty sound. "What's wrong, Zella? Ninetroir knows what he's doing. Don't you trust your mate?"

"I trust him. I don't trust that one of the fae-touched humans in there won't see a fae and his good intentions will go to hell."

"They won't know he's fae," says Callie. "He's wearing a glamour."

He is?

"What do you mean? He looks just like himself."

"No. He's not."

"You sure?"

"The man at the desk has light brown hair that's cut really short," Callie explains. "He's wearing jeans and a baseball jersey with a pair of sneakers. I can see through it to know that it's really Nine in there, but he's definitely glamoured."

I let out a small sigh of relief.

Nine's glamour doesn't work on me. It never has. I didn't know that until right after he first broke me out of the asylum. That probably should've been another clue that we were meant to be something more, but I was just shocked that anyone could actually *look* like Nine does.

But if no one else can tell that he's my Shadow Man... well, I guess it's not so bad now.

Don't get me wrong. It's still fucking awful. But it's not *so* bad.

And that's when I see Nine hold up his hand, extending one slender finger as if telling her to wait, before he starts toward the door.

I've got no doubt in my mind that he's coming for me.

Before he reaches the door, I turn to look at the overhang. I gesture to the patch of black that wavers behind Ash.

"Go back."

"Excuse me?"

"Please, Ash. You, too, Callie. I have to talk to Nine and that's gonna be hard if you two are still here. I promise that I'll come get you if I need to. Just... let me talk to my mate."

"Zella—"

Callie lays her hand on my dad's arm, cutting him off before he can tack an order at the end of that. He's gotten so much better at calling me Riley lately, but sometimes he slips.

"We'll see you back at the apartment. Won't we, Ash?"

Ash's golden gaze flares, his irises turning a brilliant, molten gold as he glares over my head at Nine's approach.

My body prickles in awareness. In the few seconds that I've had my back turned, he left the asylum, crossed the street, and he's *there*.

"I told you before, Ninetroir. You tell my daughter the truth or I will."

On that note, Ash pulls Callie close and, with a small wave courtesy of my mom, the two of them melt into the shadows.

Taking a deep breath, I turn around. My smile is shaky as I take in Nine's closed-off expression. "Hey."

"I never lie to you," he immediately says. "Even if I could, I wouldn't."

He doesn't have to lie. All he has to do is forget to mention the truth and I'd never know.

"Don't blame my dad. I don't."

"No. You blame me." His silver eyes seem almost too pale in the sunlight. He stopped wearing his sunglasses when he got used to the brightness, and I guess his glamour means that no one else will notice his otherworldly eyes. No one else but me, that is. "Aislinn told you what I'm doing here."

I shrug. "He's a gossip. What can I say?"

I don't know what it is about my flippant comment, but the tension surrounding Nine suddenly breaks.

I'll take it.

Until Nine takes my glove in his hand and with a certainty that has my stomach tightening says, "I have to do this, Shadow. You won't stop me, will you?"

"Can I?" This one is the furthest thing from flippant. I mean it when I add, "Can I really?"

Nine exhales roughly through his nose. "You can," he admits. "If you ask me to leave, I'll go with you right now."

"Is that because you got the answer you wanted already?"

He doesn't answer me.

"Tricky fae."

"For you there is nothing that I won't do."

I know that.

I jerk my chin over at the asylum. It looks too... shiny for what it represents in my memories. I only walked through those doors once—six years ago—and maybe I was still lost in the fog of grief, but I don't remember it looking like that.

"Is he in there?"

I don't have to say who. We both know.

Nine shakes his head. "No."

That's a relief. Not a big one, but a relief all the same.

"You're going to go after him, though, aren't you?"

Nine sets his jaw. "I don't know how much Aislinn explained this to you, but I have to do this. I can do whatever I can to make our house a home... I can ward it and add iron and glamour it so that it's our sanctuary... but I can't rest knowing that there's another man out there who's hurt you. Rys is in Siúcra," he reminds me, "and he'd never go after you again now that you've accepted me as your *ffrindau*. But this half-human doctor... he's too dangerous to be left on his own. How long before he comes after you again?"

"He... he won't."

"You're right. Once I've finished what I've set out to do, he won't."

He sounds so sure. And I know that, despite his assurances, there's not a damn thing I can do to stop him from going after Gillespie.

"How do you even know where he is?"

"The girl at the desk told me his address. It's not in Black Pine or Newport, but I'll find him."

I'm sure he will.

But wait—

"She just... she just gave up his address like that?"

A shadow covers Nine's expression, there and gone again. "I might've had to compel her for the information."

Because of course he did.

The fae have a whole arsenal of tricks when it comes to dealing with humans. Charm and compulsion, glamour and, most importantly, the touch.

I *hate* the idea that he might've touched her to get answers about where to find Gillespie. Jealousy twists me up so badly that I can't stop from demanding, "Did you touch her?"

Nine wraps me up in his arms. Holding me close, in a throaty voice that echoes all the way through me, he promises, "I would never."

"Okay. Okay... sorry about that. I should've known better."

"You're the last one I've ever touched. From the day I gave my word that I'd watch over you, there's been no one else. I need you to know that."

I press my lips against his chest, feeling the chill of his skin through his thin shirt. "I do. And I know that you're doing this for me. So... I guess I should let you."

Nine pulls back, his expression guarded. "I can't let you come with me."

Tricky fae who knows me very, very well. I was two seconds away from insisting on tagging along when he says that. My shade-walking ability will make it easy for him to get to Gillespie and... do what he feels like he has to. And the only way I'll offer him a portal is if he lets me go, too.

Only he sees right through me.

"Then how are you getting there?"

His eyes flicker behind me.

At first, I don't get it. We're in a parking lot. There's about six cars scattered among the lines.

"That one," Nine says.

I turn again and, this time, I'm gaping at this one fancy car parked a few feet away from me. It's a gleaming silver two-door, with black rims and tinted windows. It looks like it would be perfect for a Dark Fae.

Shit, it looks like it cost a *fortune*.

"You're kidding me," I breathe out. "Tell me you're joking."

"I told you, Shadow." His lyrical voice is soft, but there's no mistaking the pride that underlines it. "My gems work just as well in the Iron as they do in Faerie."

"You bought a car? Wait a second—you can *drive* a car?"

"The last time I lingered so long in this world, these vehicles were just becoming popular. I remembered that. I can't rely on shade-walking anymore, but I was determined to get around. It took a few days to get used to it... I have to keep the windows down no matter what to fight the iron... but it does the job."

"So you don't need me?"

He grabs me again. "Oh, Riley, I'll always need you," he murmurs before he dips his head, his lips landing softly on mine.

I know what he's doing. I let him do it anyway. Sinking into his embrace, I lose myself in his kiss because I know—I *know*—that as soon as he breaks his kiss, he's going to climb inside of that car and he's going to go after Gillespie and I'm not going to stop him.

And I don't.

CHAPTER 4

Waiting for Nine to come back to me is pure hell.

I wish there was a way I could've offered him a shadow or a portal or something and that he would've taken it. I'd feel so much better if I knew that he could use the shadows to escape if necessary.

But, ugh, he *can't*.

For the first few days he was living in the human world after the Brinkburn canceled Melisandre's spell, Nine still had a little of his Dark Fae powers left. He could still shade-walk, but he lost that ability weeks ago. Unless I take him with me, like I did with my parents, he has to walk.

No wonder he spent so long working on his plan to get at Gillespie. Without involving me and asking me to give him a hand—or a portal—he has to think like a human.

I still can't get over Nine *driving* a *car*.

He's adapting to living in the human world way better than I expected. Hell, it's even better than *I* have.

I don't know if I'm jealous or impressed. And then I think

about why he felt like he needed to get a car and I'm scared out of my mind.

Can Nine still operate his pockets? He told me once that it's just an extension of his magic, that he can always access what he keeps stored there. Can he reach for his sword? I remember the knife that Gillespie carried on him. Nine is quick. Is he quicker than a knife?

Oh, man. Oh, man, oh, man, *ohman*.

I'm pacing. Up and down, up and down. I nibble on the tip of my glove, not quite biting down on the worn leather. Shit, I haven't even thought of biting my nails since way before the faerie fire that ruined my hands, and here I am.

It's been hours. And, okay, I have to account for him traveling to wherever Gillespie is. That takes time. What if my old doctor isn't home? That could take even longer if Nine has to wait for him. Then there's whatever happens once Nine gets his hands on him...

I shouldn't be worried. For more years than I've been alive, Nine was a member of the Fae Queen's elite guard. He was trained in the Shadow Academy and I've seen first-hand that he knows how to use his sword. Between my mate and my dad, the two of them tried their best to train me just in case I needed to protect myself against Melisandre. He's good. I know he is.

And hell if Gillespie doesn't deserve it. If I hadn't tricked him into letting me out of the shadowless room before I turned the touch around on him, he would've taken me somewhere else and Nine would probably still be a statue. Who knows what would have happened to me?

My wacko doctor wanted to *breed* with me.

I shudder, wrapping my arms around my middle, and wait.

I wish I thought to give him one of the pay-as-you-go phones that I have. When I went after him earlier, the phone was an afterthought. All along, I never figured that my Dark Fae mate would want anything to do with human tech.

Yeah. Definitely wrong on *that* one.

I can't call him. I can't risk trying to transport to him again. For one thing, I'm not exactly sure what Nine's got in mind when it comes to taking care of Gillespie—though it doesn't take a genius to guess. Last thing I need is to pop in on them in the middle of that and, I don't know, distract Nine or something. For another, I want to prove to my mate that I trust him.

Even if it drives me bonkers to wait.

It seems like forever before I finally hear the door to our apartment opening. I hold my breath, since it's equally likely that my parents are coming down to check on me again, and my heart skips a couple of beats when I see Nine striding into the room.

"Nine, what—"

He shakes his head. His expression is shadowed, his silver eyes a dark, gun-metal grey. Something's not right.

I close my mouth.

On a sigh, he tells me, "Don't ask me. Not yet. Later, okay?"

"Okay. I won't ask."

Nine relaxes a fraction. His shoulders dip and I realize that he walked in all stiff, like he expected me to jump right at him the second he entered the apartment. Which I totally did.

He really knows me, doesn't he?

My pulse is racing. Now that I can see for myself that he's in one piece, all I want to do is touch him. Hold him. Prove that he's here with me. It doesn't even seem strange to me, given how I'll probably be haphephobic my whole life, but this is Nine.

There are only three people who can touch me without me losing it. It took some time for me to get used to my mom's gentle touches, my father's firm hand. But Nine... once upon a time he convinced me never to let a fae touch me. Now? I know why.

It's the power of the touch, and I'm addicted.

"I'm going to take a shower," Nine says. "I'd like to talk to you when I'm done, if that's alright. Once I'm clean."

"Do you want me to come with?"

"More than anything, but not right now. I'll be quick. Wait for me?"

I nod.

He disappears into the bedroom. A few seconds later, I hear the water turn on.

I stay in the living room, not so sure what to do with myself. Because it seems like a good idea, I keep on pacing while I wait for Nine to come back out.

He doesn't take long. In less than ten minutes, he's back. His pitch-black hair is damp, a couple stray curls falling in front of his forehead, making him appear softer than usual. His clothes are fresh—still all black—and he's pulled his shadowy duster back on, though he's cuffed the sleeves so that a stretch of his pale forearms are peeking out from beneath the wide hems.

Nine is barefoot. His steps are careful and noiseless as he glides toward me.

"It's so good to see you," he murmurs.

Weird, since he saw me ten minutes ago. And a couple of hours ago. This morning. Last night.

"Ditto," I tell him. "I missed you."

He nods. "Things will be different starting now. I promise you, Riley."

What's that supposed to mean?

"Okay. Well, um, what did you want to talk about?" From the solemn look on his gorgeous face, I'm thinking that his encounter with Gillespie is still way off the table. My heart starts pounding a little when an awful idea pops in my head. "Hey. We're okay, right?"

Halflings can lie. I used to do it all the time. My human blood cancels out my fae side when it comes to telling untruths. I try not to lie to Nine—what kind of relationship will work if it's built on deception?—but all I can remember is that Gillespie was like me.

What did he tell Nine?

"Sit with me."

That's not a yes, is it?

I take a deep breath. It's shallow, like I'm having a hard time getting enough air into my lungs, and I feel my pulse thudding as Nine leads me into the living room. He gestures for me to sit on the couch and I do, plopping down on the edge while leaving enough room for him to sit next to me.

But he doesn't. Instead, Nine sinks down gracefully so that he's on his knees in front of me. It puts us at eye-level, his silver gaze locked on my face. He places one hand on my thigh almost reverentially.

I don't like this. It's almost as if he's genuflecting to me or something.

Uh-uh.

"What are you doing? Get up. Don't do that."

I grip him by his other arm, trying to pull him off the floor. It's not right, seeing him on his knees in front me like that. I'm not strong enough, though, and he doesn't budge.

"First let me ask you for something. If you honor me with it, I have something to give you in return. Do we have a bargain?"

He's being too serious. It's, uh, starting to freak me out.

And I was pretty freaked to begin with.

"I'll give you whatever you want, Nine. You know that. Besides, you give me too much already. We're mates."

"Please, Shadow. Do this for me."

Shadow, I notice. Not Riley.

It strikes me at that moment that Nine is a Dark Fae. No matter how bonded we are, there are parts of him that I can't change. That I wouldn't even if I could. He might be busying himself buying human knick-knacks and driving a car, but he's still a century-old fae male.

If he feels like we have to keep a balance, I can deal. It's way better than feeling like one of us is in debt to the other. He wants a bargain? He can have whatever he wants from me and I'll always consider it fair.

"Okay."

"Give me your name."

That's... not what I was expecting. "My what?"

"Your name. May I have it?"

He knows my name. He was there when my first foster family called me Riley Thorne. He gave me the name *Shadow* when I was a kid. And as for *Zella*... there's no way he doesn't know that that is my true name.

But I've never actually *given* it to him. I tried once. When I was hiding out in the sewer, lost in a haze of confusion and lust after Nine touched me to save me from the cursed peach, he gave me his—Ninetroir—and all the power that goes with owning a creature's true name. But he wouldn't let me give him mine.

Until now.

I don't know why he's asking me for it. I gave him my heart too many years ago to count, and I gave him my entire body when I accepted him as my mate. If he wants my name, too, he can have it.

"Zella," I tell him. "My name is Zella."

Nine closes his eyes. His dark lashes settle on the heights of his cheeks, his pale skin taking on a soft glow as he absorbs the weight of my name. We might be in the human world, surrounded by iron and tech, but there's definitely magic in our exchange. I can feel it teasing against my senses, tickling the tips of my fae ears, strengthening the bond between me and Nine.

The moment doesn't last. By the time Nine opens his eyes again, the feeling's gone. But so is the serious look twisting his stunning features. The hard edge of his jaw softens as his bright silver eyes shine.

Nine smiles.

It's a good thing I'm perched on the edge of the couch. I go weak at the open emotion splayed across his face. He wasn't kidding when he said I'd honor him with my name. I can tell. Just those two-syllables had the power of bringing my Shadow Man back to me.

God, I fucking love him.

"Thank you."

I blink. Did he just say—

The fae don't do thanks, just like they don't do favors. Nine taught me that. He used to hate it when I tried to thank him for, well, *anything*, telling me that I'd never want to be put in his debt. So what does it mean when he says that to me?

Before I can ask, he reaches into his pocket. He pulls out a fist. As I watch curiously, Nine unfolds his hand, revealing a rock with a small hole drilled in the center.

"This is for you," he says. "For your necklace. I thought you could wear it."

I pat the small lump beneath my shirt. Ever since I stole the necklace from Gillespie, yanking it over his head while I had him frozen by my touch, I've kept it on. I *earned* it, and I'm so damn grateful that it saved Nine.

Not that I'm still walking around with the same three charms that Gillespie had. The Brinkburn is locked away, just in case. The iron nail, too. I don't want to accidentally hurt either Nine or my dad by wearing a fae-killer around my throat. It's there in case we need it, but I don't have to actually keep it on me.

The seeing stone, though? That's the one charm I left hanging on the twine. Now that I know that Faerie creatures are crossing the veil all the time, I keep the seeing stone on me since Callie's gift didn't get passed on to me. Using my old doctor's stone, I can be sure that a glamour-wearing fae won't be able to trick me the way that Oberon did.

But if I already have a seeing stone, why is Nine giving me this... this pebble? The hole isn't big enough anyway. I could just about thread it on the twine and that's about it...

Wait a second—

Pebble?

"Nine... is this what I think it is?"

"It's just a pebble."

"But isn't it..."

It is. I'm sure it is.

That pebble represents the life debt he owed to Ash. When Callie wanted to call it in, she gave the pebble to Nine and he vowed to watch over me. Every time I saw the thing, it was just another reminder that Nine was only sticking around because he *owed* someone.

In my anger, I told him a couple of times that his debt was clear. That he owed me shit. No matter what, he stubbornly clung to the pebble as if he didn't want to sever our growing bond. And I get it. At least, I get it *now*.

Still—

"Why are you giving me this?"

"It's important to me that you have this. Once, it meant something else. Now? It's a pebble, nothing more. I need you to know this. I love you. Not because of a debt. Not because of a prophecy. Not because of fate. I love you because of who you are and how strong you are. You're my mate. You owe me nothing while I… I owe you everything."

He offers the pebble out to me.

I don't take it. Not yet. And not because I don't understand the meaning behind his seemingly simple gesture, either.

Something else catches my attention instead and, as I recognize it suddenly, I go motionless. On the edge of his shadowy duster, something sparkles. I narrow my eyes, my stomach twisting when I notice the silver-colored blood dotting the side of his sleeve.

Fae blood. *His* blood.

No wonder he ran right to the bedroom to get clean and change. He must have missed a spot, though, because there's no way that isn't his blood splattered on his coat. And if Nine was bleeding, then that meant that he hadn't gone to Gillespie to have a rational conversation with my crazy old doctor.

Not that I thought so, but still. A girl could hope.

I have to ask. I have to *know*. "Do you owe me an answer?"

"Riley—"

"I'm serious. Are you going to tell me what happened with… you know? It's later."

His expression closes off again. "Not late enough."

"Nine," I say, using the same tone of voice that he did when he said my name.

"I did what I had to. I hope you understand."

I wish I did.

"Yeah? And what was that?"

Nine hesitates. "He's no longer a threat. Be satisfied with that."

I... I don't know if I can be. I mean, I appreciate that Nine's trying to shield me from the gory details but, hell, I was there when Oberon cut off Melisandre's head. I don't think anything can shock me like that did.

I open my mouth to tell him so.

"Riley." He holds up the pebble again, effectively silencing me.

He doesn't use my true name, I notice. And that's because he wanted it as a gift, not a way to order me around. He couldn't anyway, since bonded mates can't use their mate's name against them, but still.

If I wanted to push it, I would. Nine knows that. I'm not the type of woman who is going to sit back and be told what to do. But... well, I don't really want to know. And if he wants to shield me from whatever he had to do to protect me, I'll let him.

So, staying quiet, I remove my necklace and offer it to him.

Nine unknots the twine, slipping the pebble over it until it's nestled beside the seeing stone. Once he's satisfied, he ties it again before slipping it back over my head.

I pat the necklace, reassured by the added weight of the pebble.

Because he's right. It's just a pebble now, isn't it?

A small smile curving his lips, Nine takes my hand, intertwining his pale fingers with the worn leather that covers mine. It never occurs to him to ask me to remove it so that he can press his flesh to mine. He doesn't mind my gloves or my insistence that I wear them always. As far as he's concerned, they're just part of who I am, and he loves me.

He loves all of me.

Every broken, bruised, burned inch of Riley Thorne. And I love my Shadow Man even more for it.

And that's the thing.

Life isn't easy. It isn't *nice*. It's rough, it's raw, and it's *real*. With the blood of a Seelie mingled with that of a human running through my veins—as the mate of an Unseelie who is absolutely devoted to me—I guess this is some kind of fairy tale. When I look at Nine, before I get lost in his otherworldly silver gaze and the heat of his touch, I know I'm peering up at my happily-ever-after.

And, when I'm with him, I'm super fucking happy.

But I'm not whole. I'm not fixed. I'll always be twitchy, and if I live on the edge of an all-consuming panic attack, that's the price I'll pay to have gotten where I am. My life might not have been easy, but, really, whose is? As long as I can tolerate Nine's touch, I'm good.

Melisandre is dead. Gillespie... well, Nine won't tell me exactly what went down, but he's not a threat to me anymore. I don't have to worry about them.

Doesn't mean I don't have to worry, though.

And, a few months into our happy ending, when a bright light nearly blinds us before Helix, the Summer King's favored guard, comes striding into our apartment, I'm reminded of that all over again...

TRAPPED

SNEAK PEEK AT THE FIRST BOOK IN ELLE AND RYS'S STORY

These cuffs are super heavy.

They're made of iron. Of course they are. I'm at the mercy of the fae, a prisoner of the Seelie Court, and iron is one of the only things that can hold any of the magical races here. From goblins to redcaps, sprites to the Seelie themselves, the iron saps their strength and makes them easy to contain.

I'm not magic. I don't have a drop of power in me. I'm just an idiot human who made a wrong turn while walking through her local park and stupidly stepped right through a fairy circle. Trapping me in these cuffs is overkill, but tell that to the fae guard marching me down the open hallway that leads right inside of Siúcra, the infamous Faerie prison—and my new home.

That's not all. If I think the cuffs are bad, the glowing, diamond-edged sword pointed at my back is ten times worse.

The guard can't touch me; not with his bare skin at least. I learned *that* one the hard way. As a Seelie, one of the high fae races that rule over Faerie, he literally can't touch me unless I give him permission to. One stolen caress and his perfect bronze skin will look like someone's dipped it into a fryer.

As a human, it's the only power that I have. I can't compel anyone, I can't create portals on a whim, I can't fly. I don't have any super strength, like the trolls do, and while I can lie, I can't see how that's a plus. But I'm a rare unclaimed human in a world where that means something to the race in charge, and while my skin is a lure and a temptation to the fae, they can't touch me without causing themselves terrible pain if I don't actually *let* them.

Then again, considering he can run me through with his sword if I so much as blink funny, it's not like my "power" counts for squat. When I'm a Helen-kabob, it doesn't matter if I gave him permission or not. He can touch me because I'll be dead.

So, yeah. I'd like to avoid both of those happening if I can.

I made it this long, right? Through being poisoned, then captured, then sold to a Seelie noble who didn't like being told *no*, I'm still standing. They haven't broken me yet.

Unfortunately, something tells me that they're just getting started.

They… in this case, I mean the fae guards who are responsible for bringing me here. Though, after all I've been through lately, the guards are just the last link in a super shitty chain that began when I *brilliantly* thought it might be a good idea to play around with a fairy circle.

There were three of the guards when I was arrested, one called 'Captain' and his two sidekicks. Then the one in charge realized that it didn't take that many of them to transport little ol' me and he stuck me with Bram, he of the pointy sword behind me.

I didn't mind Bram too much. I work in retail so I get the

whole 'he's just doing his job' thing. He fed me, gave my privacy when I had to use the little girl's bush, and if it sucks that he kept me locked in the back of the caravan wearing these cuffs for three days while we traveled from Veron's palace to Siúcra, well, I get it.

Technically, I *am* a prisoner. If I could figure out how to get out of here, I'd definitely be a flight risk. All I've done since I found myself in Faerie is try to escape it. Keeping me in irons, locked behind bars... smart.

It's been ten days already. Ten days since I stormed out on my boyfriend, took a walk in the park by my apartment to cool off, and kind of, sort of waltzed right through a fairy circle.

Ten looooong days since I crossed the veil into Faerie.

It feels like a lifetime. Now that I've been sentenced to a stay inside of Siúcra, it might just turn *into* a lifetime.

I don't know about you, but when I think of "fairy jail", I think of something totally different than what I'm looking at right now. In a world where there are enchanted gardens with trees made of crystal, a magenta sky, and grass that looks like light blue cotton candy, I was expecting a little... more.

Faerie is... it's hard to explain. When I was a little girl, my mother used to tell me all kinds of fantastical stories about a magical world in another realm. She called it Faerie, said it was across the veil, and it was the home to every creature in every myth and legend ever written or told. Elves, fairies, trolls, gnomes, redcaps, water sprites... the list goes on and on.

I had an idea of it in my head. I grew up on a bunch of fantasy films, including some that were popular when my mom was a teen. *Labyrinth* was one. *Willow* was another. *The Neverending Story*. *Princess Bride*. To me, Faerie was some kind of amalgamation of those movies, plus classics like *The Wizard of Oz* and *Alice in Wonderland* thrown in for a little extra flavor.

And it's kind of like that. Between the magic everywhere and the traps, plus the foliage that just convinces you you're in another world, it's definitely nothing like the city where I was born and raised.

Of course, then I actually ended up in this crazy place and, since then, I've gotten a crash course in just how different Faerie is from all of my expectations.

The jail, though? Earlier, Bram led me through the back gates and an intimidating entrance. I put my brave face on—my *this is just another day in the life of Helen Andrews* face—just in time to step into the first row of completely packed cells. And, okay. I've never been in jail before. But I watch a crapton of TV with my boyfriend and Jim has always gotten a kick out of prison shows. I know what to expect.

At least, I *thought* I did. And, for the most part, the layout is just like the layout of every other prison I've ever seen.

What's so unexpected and different?

The prison guard.

I swallow and, instead of looking at him for long, I drop my gaze. I don't want to be dazzled and—ah, hell—the fae male striding purposely toward me is definitely a sight to behold.

The newcomer is the opposite of the golden, bright, gorgeous Seelie males I've grown used to. While still breathtaking in his way, there's no denying the edge of darkness... of *danger*... that shadows him. He has skin so pale, it nearly glows, and a head of thick, glossy, black hair that's shockingly even with his chin instead of falling down his slender back. And his eyes...

The pupils are as black as his hair. The irises are a shiny, gleaming silver that are as lovely as they are off-putting. As I dare another peek at him, trapped by those mirror-like eyes, I notice that he hardly blinks. My eyes water just thinking about it.

I swallow nervously. Ah, crap. I might've spent the last few days surrounded by Seelie males, but I've been warned that there were two type of fae who rule over Faerie. The Seelie—and the Unseelie.

The Dark Fae.

The Cursed Ones.

And it looks like I've just met my first one.

He stops when there's barely a foot separating us, the two of us so close I can feel the chill coming off his skin. The guard's gaze travels the length of my body, head to toe, up and down. I want to think he's assessing me for possible danger—as if the cuffed human can be a threat to anyone in Faerie—but I know better.

Okay. This guy is amazing to look at. He's still a creep.

Just my luck.

"That's enough, soldier." He nods over my shoulder to Bram. "I'll take over from here."

I'm almost annoyed at how easily Bram clicks his heels and disappears back down the hall, abandoning me to the guard. Because Veron refused to arrange for a portal to the prison, I spent the last few days traveling with the Seelie soldier. Sure, I was locked up tight, and he barely spoke except to occasionally check on me and respond to some of my determined babbling, but still. A goodbye wouldn't have killed him.

It's weird. I used to think that every fae had the ability to conjure portals. Nope. Only the strongest of the Light Fae, the Seelie, can create portals made of fire that allow them to zip all over Faerie. Just like the Dark Fae, the Unseelie, can supposedly travel through shadows. Without a portal, I had to walk—or, in the case of Bram's prison transport, ride in the back of a horse-drawn caravan.

I'm dirty. Dusty. I've been wearing the same clothes for a

week and a half. My hair is braided out of my face to hide the fact that it desperately needs a wash. I probably smell like horse shit.

And the darkly handsome Unseelie guard is looking at me like I've just stepped off the cover of Sports Illustrated.

"What's your name?" he asks me.

"Elle."

His silver eyes gleam. "Is that your true name?"

It's the only name he's going to get.

I learned that the even harder way. Names have power in Faerie, even for a human like me.

Though I didn't think it was possible, he inches even closer. "Call me Dusk."

I press my lips together. I'm not calling him a damn thing.

He grins. It's almost wolfish, and definitely a threat.

I gulp.

The door behind me eases open again. When I see a flash of bronze out of the corner of my eye, I swivel, thinking that it's Bram returning.

Is he coming for me? Did Veron finally realize I called his bluff and he's backing down?

After three days of hell in the back of the caravan, is that dickhead calling this whole thing off before I'm taken to a cell?

It only takes about five seconds before I realize that the Seelie striding toward me isn't Bram. He has the same coloring, the same sword hanging at his hip, but it's the clothes that tip me off. Bram, like the other fae soldiers who Veron sicced on me, wore a different uniform.

This is another guard. Just a Seelie one this time.

He does a double-take when he sees me, his golden gaze lingering on my face as if he can't believe what he's seeing.

I bite back a sigh.

I'm used to it. Even back home my style choices often earned me a second look. I guess most people don't expect a petite blonde chick to rock a leather jacket. Or maybe it's my hair.

It's usually my hair.

You'd think, in a place like Faerie where brownies are two-foot-high creatures covered in thick, brown fur and trolls seem like they've been carved from stone, seeing someone with teal streaks in their hair wouldn't be a big deal. The nix I met when I was being auctioned off at the Faerie market had green hair for goodness' sake!

Nope. Just like the Unseelie guard, this one also stares, though there's an element of surprise written across his flawless features that I much prefer to the other guard's open leer.

He recovers quickly, though. By the time he reaches us, his expression is flat. Unimpressed.

"Dusk. I've just been told of our newest arrival. This is her? The human?"

Oh. That's right. He's probably staring because of *what* I am, not what I look like.

I'm not really sure how, but some of the creatures in Faerie can tell right off the bat that I'm different rather than just glamouring myself with magic I don't have. With the nix, she knew because I immediately grabbed for the iron bars in the cage I was thrown in before the cruel redcap had me put up for bidding at the auction block. The fae? It's obvious to them because, one glimpse of my bare skin, and they know I've never been touched by one of their kind.

Lucky me.

"Yes. The lord's soldier placed her into my charge." Dusk's lyrical fae voice develops an undeniably possessive edge when he says that. *My* charge. I don't like that. I don't like that one bit.

"I'm bringing her to her cell before starting the next round of patrols."

"Where are you putting her?"

The Unseelie shrugs. It's an eerily graceful gesture. "I thought I would give her a cell near Posey. Keep the females together."

"Are you sure that's a good idea? It's in the furthest recesses of the prison."

"I know that." Something sparks in Dusk's mirror-like eyes. "Even more of a reason to tuck the human out of sight."

"If it won't offend, I think I have a better idea."

Better idea? Better than being hidden away like some dirty secret?

Yes, please.

"I'm listening."

"There's an open cell across from the traitor," the Seelie guard says. "No one else shares the wing with him. We can place her there."

"With the human lover? Oh, Saxon... and to think your kind calls me cruel because I'm a Cursed One."

"You don't think it's a good idea?"

"He's rarely in his cell. I think it's a *fantastic* idea." Dusk pauses for a second, then grins at the other guard. "Have you heard? This human has never been touched."

My stomach drops. No wonder he likes the idea of an empty cell. For the same reason he thought it would be a good idea to stick me out in the boonies.

No witnesses, right?

Freaking lovely.

You think I would've expected this by now. Being "untouched" is what landed me here in the first place. A Seelie noble thought I'd fall prey to his looks and his charms and his money.

I told him to get bent.

He had me arrested.

All because of the magic in a fae's touch. It just takes a human like me giving them permission and a fae can steal part of our soul with a brush of their hand. It makes them strong. It makes them *powerful*. They would do anything for the rush—but they have to have our permission first.

They'll cajole you. Glamour you. *Trick* you. Compel you if they can. They'll do anything to convince you to give them all you have. And when you do—*if* you do—you're left as nothing but a slave to the whims of a fantastical creature who will crush you as easily as kiss you.

No, thanks.

The Unseelie guard reaches for me. I don't know if he's testing me or if, like Veron, he's willing to risk a burn in order to grab me, but I'm not about to stand here and take it.

I jerk away from him, the chains on my cuffs rattling as I avoid his outstretched hand. "Don't touch me."

"I'll do it," offers the Seelie guard—Saxon—as he reaches to grab the elbow of my leather jacket. "I'll escort the human prisoner to her cell."

"No." As I twist my body again, avoiding his outstretched fingers, my heart pounds wildly in my chest. I *hate* confrontations, have never been good at fighting back unless provoked, but this is important. I could've avoided the whole being imprisoned thing if I just gave permission to Veron and still I refused, just like I'm refusing now. "I don't want you to touch me, either."

Though I shouldn't be surprised—I saw what a stolen touch

did to Veron when he tried—I kind of am when Saxon immediately pulls his hand back, not willing to risk it.

He turns to Dusk instead. "Are there any diamaint gloves in the guards' room? With a human prisoner, we'll need one."

Dusk's silver eyes darken to a deep grey as he keeps his stare on me. That wolfish grin is gone, but I can tell that my refusal has only captured more of his attention.

Good going, Hel. Just what I wanted.

He purses his lips. "It's possible. It isn't often Siúcra accepts a human, and I've never met one who wasn't a slave to the touch, but yes, it's possible. Go look. Check in with the captain if you must."

"Should I meet you here after?"

"I won't need the diamaint just yet. If she knows what's good for her, she'll give me her touch before long. 'Til then, the iron and the blade will do."

He pulls his sword from its sheath, angling it toward me so that I can't miss the sharp edge. "Are you certain, Elle? You'd like it so much better if I led you there by hand."

No. *He* would like it better if he did.

I nod.

"You'll change your mind," he murmurs. "I'll enjoy ensuring that you do. Now move."

He doesn't really need the sword. The iron handcuffs, either. I've had days to resign myself to this and the time riding in the back of the caravan didn't do much to change my mind.

Sleep with a Seelie noble who "bought" me or go to prison? I could only make one choice. There's not going to be any last-minute reprieve for me, and until I can figure out how to escape, I have to play nice.

Alright then.

Let's go.

So I guess men are men wherever you are. Faerie or the human world, magic or mortal... they're all the same.

Wonderful.

Catcalls follow as Dusk forces me to continue my march through the prison. As we go, I hear a few of the prisoners try to convince the guard to leave me with them, and I try not to pay attention to the things they tell me they want to do to me.

Dusk eventually orders them all to be quiet. They listen, too, which I didn't expect considering one of the wings is full of trolls. They're three times as big as Dusk, but they seem to quail when the Unseelie guard turns his silver stare on them. When another of the prisoners—I don't know what this guy is except he's furry and hunched over a bit—tries to test him, Dusk's pale skin takes on an otherworldly glow that has the next few rows' worth of prisoners shutting up at his approach.

I try not to stare. I thought I had seen everything Faerie had to offer, between the pixie and the dwarves, the nix, the redcap, and the trolls... I was super wrong about that. There are creatures locked up in this prison that I can't even begin to figure out what they are. Some of them kind of look human—like the fae—but when I pass this childlike creature with triangle ears and a fox tail, I actually stop to get a better look.

It's so cute—until it snaps its teeth at me and I jump so high, I nearly impale myself on Dusk's sword when I land again.

He doesn't reach to steady me. Since it would burn the crap out of his hand if he did, Dusk glides away, lowering his sword while I try to calm my racing heart.

"Be grateful that I'm assigning you to another wing," he says, his voice pitched low, for my ears only. "I could easily leave you among the lower races should I choose to. Remember my generosity, human. You won't be getting much of it from anyone else."

A chill runs up and down my spine. He means it, too. No one from Faerie can lie, which is the single advantage that I have as a human.

"Where am I going?" I ask. It just slips out, but I have to know. "Is it much further?"

The prison is huge. I only saw a glimpse of it as Bram led me out of the caravan, but, from the outside, it looks like it could pass for a stadium if it wasn't for the high gate that surrounds it. There must be room for hundreds of cells in here and, as I drag my feet, chained hands bumping into my stiff thighs, I feel like I've passed most of them already.

With a royal shake of his head, gesturing with his perfectly sculpted chin, Dusk indicates that I should start walking again. I can hear a high-pitched chittering sound coming from the cell behind me.

I pick up the pace.

"It isn't much farther now," Dusk tells me. "Three more wings 'til we reach yours. I've the perfect one in mind. The queen prefers to turn her traitors and betrayers into decorations for her gardens. There aren't many who are imprisoned here, but those who are have their own wing. That's where I'll be keeping you."

Since I don't even want to know what that means—decorations for her gardens?—I duck my head and keep on marching.

Three wings. Okay. I can do this.

Each section of the prison is separated by some kind of glass partition that only disappears when Dusk murmurs a foreign world. It kind of sounds like he's saying *pad*-something, but even in my head I can't mimic his accent right. The clear doors dissipate in a shower of silver sparkles, reforming the instant we step through.

More magic.

Of course.

Now that I have some idea of what to expect, I count the doors from that point on. Not because I have any hope of escaping, but because I just want this part of the nightmare to be over with at last. I'm going to jail. No way around that fact right now. And while I thought I could maybe get away from Bram during the days we traveled here, I obviously didn't and now I'm stuck.

Once we pass through one, two, three more sections, we arrive in an empty wing. And I mean *empty*. Unlike every other wing I've been paraded past, none of the cells are occupied.

Hey, wait. Wasn't there supposed to be another prisoner here? At least one more?

I didn't want to be stuck with the catcalling inmates, but I don't want to be all on my own, either. Not with the guard's threat—*You'll change your mind. I'll enjoy ensuring that you do...*—still bouncing around my brain.

"This one will be yours." Dusk moves toward the first cell on the left. He waves his hand in front of the closed door with its narrow bars. It springs open. "Get in."

I don't have a choice. Before he can tell me again, I step inside the cell—and gasp when the heavy cuffs just fall away from my wrists, landing on the floor with a *clank* an instant before my cell door slams shut behind me.

AVAILABLE NOW
TRAPPED (IMPRISONED BY THE FAE #1)

I didn't mean to cross over into Faerie. It was an accident. And now... now I'm in jail.

Fairy jail. It's a thing.

When I refused the attentions of a Seelie noble, I earned myself a one-way ticket to Siúcra, the most infamous prison in the Fae Queen's Court.

I'm still reeling over the fact that the fae are real. That Faerie is a real place, and that there are real consequences to being a human surrounded by the amazingly gorgeous—if also amazingly heartless—creatures in this world.

Their cruelty doesn't stop after I'm captured. Turns out, I'm the only human in my wing of the prison. And, I find out pretty quickly, the only female.

Ah, *crap*.

Thank goodness for Rys. He might not be the friendliest cellmate, but so long as I don't ask him questions about why he's locked up, he's willing to watch my back. Know what? That totally works for me, especially since I can't seem to keep my eyes off of *his*.

I'm in jail. Falling for another prisoner should be the last thing on my mind. Then again, Rys is a Light Fae. A Seelie. He's one of *them*. Sure, he might be stuck here with me now, but he used to guard this place. He knows the way out—he just doesn't *want* to leave.

He's got a past. One look at the ragged scar ruining his otherwise perfect fae features and even I can tell that he's not as innocent as he claims. But no matter how hard I try to get him to see things my way, he refuses to get involved.

Just like he refuses to admit that he can sense the crazy attraction brewing between us.

It started out as protection before it blossomed into something... *more*, whether he wants to pretend or not. And when he finally decides it's time for him to break free, I know I'll do whatever I have to to make sure that he takes me with him.

****Trapped** is the first book in an exciting new fae series by the author of **Touched by the Fae**. Featuring a directionally-challenged, mouthy human heroine, the scarred Light Fae who'd rather stay in jail, and their quest to save Faerie together—well, once they break out of Siúcra, that is.

It's also a steamy supernatural prison romance, with a bunch of profanity, an attempted sexual assault (don't worry, the guy gets what's coming to him!), and is fully intended for adult readers only.

Out now!
Or you can get the complete series in a box set!

AVAILABLE NOW
GLAMOUR EYES (REJECTED BY THE FAE #1)

She doesn't want anything to do with the fae... too bad that won't stop *him*.

Callie Brooks has a gift, though that's not exactly what she calls it. She *sees* things—has been able to since she was a little girl—and it's more of a nuisance than anything else. But so long as she pretends that she can't, she's safe. The strange creatures won't bother her if she keeps herself from staring. After more than twenty years, she's gotten pretty good at it, too. Nothing surprises her any more.

Until she sees *him*.

Aislinn is a Light Fae. One of the Seelie, and a member of the Fae Queen's guard.

After a foolish mistake inadvertently offends Melisandre, the queen punishes Ash by moving his guard post to the human world. It's an insult, but he accepts the post in the Iron because it's better to be bored than to be another statue in Melisandre's garden—or worse. What's a decade or two of human watching so long as he gets to keep his head?

Cloaked in glamour, no one is supposed to know he's crossed over. Which is why he's so… so *interested* by the curious human who seems to watch him back—and whose pretty blue eyes can see right through his glamour.

The fae trick humans. They use them. They touch them, then discard them. Ash always thought he was like the rest of his kind.

Now? He's a fae who *wants* a human, and will stop at nothing to figure out what it is about Callie that makes him—and her—different than the rest… especially when he decides to seduce her and she rejects him outright.

That only makes him want him more. And hopefully he can convince Callie to agree to accept his touch before the Fae Queen realizes that his attention has wavered, otherwise it won't be Ash who gets punished this time.

It'll be *Callie*.

**Glamour Eyes *is part one of a duet featuring the very human Callie and the Light Fae male who will give up everything to have her…*

Out now!
Or you can get it in a duet collection.

STAY IN TOUCH

Stay tuned for what's coming up next!

Follow me at any of these places—or sign up for my newsletter—for news, promotions, upcoming releases, and more:

jessica@jessicalynchwrites.com

JessicaLynchWrites.com
Jessica's Newsletter
Jessica's Store

ALSO BY JESSICA LYNCH

Welcome to Hamlet

You Were Made For Me*

Don't Trust Me

Ophelia

Let Nothing You Dismay

I'll Never Stop

Wherever You Go

Here Comes the Bride

Tesoro

That Girl Will Never Be Mine

Welcome to Hamlet: I-III**

No Outsiders Allowed: IV-VI**

Holidays in Hamlet

Gloria

Holly

Mirrorside

Tame the Spark*

Stalk the Moon

Hunt the Stars

The Witch in the Woods

Hide from the Heart

Chase the Beauty

Flee the Sun

Curse the Flame

The Other Duet**

The Claws Clause

Mates*

Hungry Like a Wolf

Of Mistletoe and Mating

No Way

Season of the Witch

Rogue

Sunglasses at Night

Ghost of Jealousy

Broken Wings

Of Santa and Slaying

Born to Run

Uptown Girl

A Pack of Lies

Here Kitty, Kitty

Ordinance 7304: the Bond Laws**

Living on a Prayer**

Diamonds Are a Witch's Best Friend**

The Curse of the Othersiders

Ain't No Angel*

True Angel

Night Angel

Lost Angel

Claws and Wings**

The Shadow Pack

Total Eclipse

A Shot in the Dark

Purple Moon

Touched by the Fae

Favor*

Asylum

Shadow

Touch

Zella

The Shadow Prophecy**

Imprisoned by the Fae

Tricked*

Trapped

Escaped

Freed

Gifted

The Shadow Realm**

Rejected by the Fae

Glamour Eyes

Glamour Lies

Through the Veil**

Forged in Twilight

House of Cards

Ace of Spades

Royal Flush

Claws and Fangs

(written under Sarah Spade)

Leave Janelle*

Never His Mate

Always Her Mate

Forever Mates

Hint of Her Blood

Taste of His Skin

Stay With Me

Never Say Never: Gem & Ryker

Sombra Demons

Drawn to the Demon Duke*

Mated to the Monster

Santa Claws

Stolen by the Shadows

Bonded to the Beast

Fated to the Phantom

* prequel story

** boxed set collection

Printed in Great Britain
by Amazon